DATE DUE

JE 14'72			

✶ *FROM THE OCEAN, FROM THE STARS*

BY THE SAME AUTHOR

Fiction

ISLANDS IN THE SKY
PRELUDE TO SPACE
AGAINST THE FALL OF NIGHT
THE SANDS OF MARS
CHILDHOOD'S END
EXPEDITION TO EARTH
EARTHLIGHT
REACH FOR TOMORROW
THE CITY AND THE STARS
TALES FROM THE *White Hart*
THE DEEP RANGE
THE OTHER SIDE OF THE SKY
ACROSS THE SEA OF STARS
A FALL OF MOONDUST

Nonfiction

INTERPLANETARY FLIGHT
THE EXPLORATION OF SPACE
GOING INTO SPACE
THE COAST OF CORAL
THE MAKING OF A MOON
THE REEFS OF TAPROBANE
VOICE ACROSS THE SEA
THE CHALLENGE OF THE SPACESHIP
THE CHALLENGE OF THE SEA

With Mike Wilson

THE FIRST FIVE FATHOMS
BOY BENEATH THE SEA

With R. A. Smith

THE EXPLORATION OF THE MOON

FROM THE OCEAN, FROM THE STARS

An omnibus containing the complete novels

THE DEEP RANGE *and* THE CITY AND THE STARS

and twenty-four short stories

by ARTHUR C. CLARKE

Harcourt, Brace & World, Inc., New York

D E

Library of Congress Catalog Card Number: 62–8058
Printed in the United States of America

TO FRANCES AND DENVER

CONTENTS

Introduction ix

I THE DEEP RANGE 1

II THE OTHER SIDE OF THE SKY 167

THE NINE BILLION NAMES OF GOD 169

REFUGEE 176

THE OTHER SIDE OF THE SKY:

Special Delivery 187

Feathered Friend 190

Take a Deep Breath 193

Freedom of Space 195

Passer-by 198

The Call of the Stars 201

THE WALL OF DARKNESS 205

SECURITY CHECK 221

NO MORNING AFTER 226

VENTURE TO THE MOON:

The Starting Line 232

Robin Hood, F.R.S. 235

Green Fingers 239

All That Glitters 243

Watch This Space 247

A Question of Residence 250

PUBLICITY CAMPAIGN 255

ALL THE TIME IN THE WORLD 259

COSMIC CASANOVA 270

THE STAR 276

OUT OF THE SUN 282
TRANSIENCE 289
THE SONGS OF DISTANT EARTH 295

III THE CITY AND THE STARS 321

INTRODUCTION

Although their themes and settings differ so widely, the two novels in this volume owe their existence to the same somewhat improbable episode in my life—an expedition to the Great Barrier Reef of Australia which occupied my partner, Mike Wilson, and myself during most of 1955. For an account of Heron Island as it is today, seventy years before the opening of *The Deep Range,* I therefore refer any interested reader to *The Coast of Coral.* Perhaps I had better warn hopeful marine biologists that the University of Queensland's existing facilities on the island still have a long way to go before they match those in the novel.

The City and the Stars was written while I was on the way to the Great Barrier Reef—much of it, indeed, aboard S.S. *Himalaya.* The knowledge that I was about to spend some months diving amid sharks of doubtful docility was the chief spur to action, for the novel represented unfinished business that had bothered me for some years. It may or may not be true, as Dr. Johnson stated, that nothing settles a man's mind so much as the knowledge that he will be hanged in the morning, but for my part I can testify that the thought of not returning from the Reef was the main reason why *The City and the Stars* was completed at this particular time.

The first draft, however, was begun some eighteen years earlier, in 1937. After numerous revisions during and after the war, it was published in 1948 under the title *Against the Fall of Night.* Although this work was well received, it had most of the defects of a first novel, and my dissatisfaction with it increased steadily through the years. Moreover, the progress of science during the two decades since the story was first conceived made many of the original ideas naïve, and opened up vistas and possibilities quite unimagined when the book was originally planned. In particular, certain developments in information theory suggested profound changes in the human way of life, and I wished to incorporate these into the book I had attempted, but so far failed, to write.

About a quarter of the present work appears in *Against the Fall of Night;* I believe that even those who have read the earlier book (which stubbornly refuses to go out of print) will find that this is virtually a new novel.

And thereby hangs a tale. Not long ago a certain psychiatrist and one of her patients discovered a mutual interest in my work (no conclusions, please, should be drawn from this). They thought they were talking about the same novel, but in fact the psychiatrist had read *The City and the Stars* and the patient *Against the Fall of Night*—and neither knew that the other book existed. By the time the two readers had compared their memories, finding obvious similarities of name and incident yet total differences of plot, each was convinced that the other was suffering from hallucinations. I dread to think what might have happened, to doctor and patient, had the psychiatrist not made contact with me (ex officio), before the situation got too complicated. Perhaps I had better make one categorical promise here and now: *The City and the Stars* is the final, definitive version.

The stories in *The Other Side of the Sky* were written during 1947–57, and with the three earlier collections, *Expedition to Earth, Reach for Tomorrow,* and *Tales from the "White Hart,"* all my shorter works of fiction that I think worth preserving are now in volume form.

I have thrice—to my knowledge, that is—written stories based on ideas provided by someone else. My friends will testify that I am too sober a person to have imagined "No Morning After," which is due to A. H. Smith, while "All the Time in the World" springs from the dubious talents of Mike Wilson. In 1953, I turned the latter tale into a television play, which went out over the American Broadcasting Company network. Since then I have successfully avoided any entanglements with TV, though a purely social contact with "Captain Video" was undoubtedly responsible for "Security Check."

"The Nine Billion Names of God" was the product of a rainy afternoon in New York; the screen rights were bought by a Hollywood movie company in a moment of mental aberration, and I am still awaiting the result with mixed feelings.

"Refugee," to the utter confusion of indexers, was first published by Anthony Boucher in *The Magazine of Fantasy and Science Fiction* as "?" since he found my original title unsatisfactory and promptly started a competition to find a better one, finally settling upon "This Earth of Majesty." To add to the chaos, Ted Carnell, in the British magazine *New Worlds,* called it "Royal Prerogative."

"The Star" has a very unusual history. In 1954, Carl Biemiller of

Holiday magazine asked me to write an astronomical article, which I tackled with some reluctance because it involved a considerable amount of research (*i.e.*, work). It proved well worth it, however, because after publication in *Holiday* the piece concerned—whose title I won't mention because it would give away the plot—was picked by *Reader's Digest.* Then the London *Observer* announced a short-story competition on the subject "2500 AD," and I realized that I had a theme already to hand. The story was written in a state of unusually intense emotion; needless to say, it wasn't even placed among the "also rans." (The winners were later published in book form under the title *2,500 AD,* and readers may amuse themselves by making their own judgments.) As some compensation, however, on its eventual magazine appearance "The Star" was voted the best science-fiction story of 1956.

"Venture to the Moon" also has an unusual genesis. It was written as a series of six independent but linked stories for the London *Evening Standard,* and when the commission was first proposed I turned it down. It appeared impossible to write stories in only 1,500 words which would be understandable to a mass readership despite being set in a totally alien environment, but on second thought this seemed such an interesting challenge that I decided to tackle it. The resulting series was successful enough to demand a second, "The Other Side of the Sky," which by good luck appeared on the London newsstands just when Sputnik I appeared in the sky.

ARTHUR C. CLARKE

Colombo
1961

THE DEEP RANGE

Part I · The Apprentice

CHAPTER ONE

There was a killer loose on the range. The South Pacific air patrol had seen the great corpse staining the sea crimson as it wallowed in the waves. Within seconds, the intricate warning system had been alerted; from San Francisco to Brisbane, men were moving counters and drawing range circles on the charts. And Don Burley, still rubbing the sleep from his eyes, was hunched over the control board of Scoutsub 5 as it dropped down to the twenty-fathom line.

He was glad that the alert was in his area; it was the first real excitement for months. Even as he watched the instruments on which his life depended, his mind was ranging far ahead. What could have happened? The brief message had given no details; it had merely reported a freshly killed right whale lying on the surface about ten miles behind the main herd, which was still proceeding north in panic-stricken flight. The obvious assumption was that, somehow, a pack of killer whales had managed to penetrate the barriers protecting the range. If that was so, Don and all his fellow wardens were in for a busy time.

The pattern of green lights on the telltale board was a glowing symbol of security. As long as that pattern was unchanged, as long as none of those emerald stars winked to red, all was well with Don and his tiny craft. Air—fuel—power—this was the triumvirate that ruled his life. If any one of these failed, he would be sinking in a steel coffin down toward the pelagic ooze, as Johnnie Tyndall had done the season before last. But there was no reason why they should fail, and the accidents one foresaw, Don told himself reassuringly, were never those that happened.

He leaned across the tiny control board and spoke into the mike. Sub 5 was still close enough to the mother ship for radio to work, but before long he'd have to switch to the ultrasonics.

"Setting course 255, speed 50 knots, depth 20 fathoms, full sonar coverage. Estimated time to target area 40 minutes. Will report at ten-minute intervals until contact is made. That is all. Out."

The acknowledgment from the *Rorqual* was barely audible, and Don switched off the set. It was time to look around.

He dimmed the cabin lights so that he could see the scanner screen more clearly, pulled the Polaroid glasses down over his eyes, and peered into the depths. It took a few seconds for the two images to fuse together in his mind; then the 3-D display sprang into stereoscopic life.

This was the moment when Don felt like a god, able to hold within his hands a circle of the Pacific twenty miles across, and to see clear down to the still largely unexplored depths two thousand fathoms below. The slowly rotating beam of inaudible sound was searching the world in which he floated, seeking out friend and foe in the eternal darkness where light could never penetrate. The pattern of soundless shrieks, too shrill even for the hearing of the bats who had invented sonar millions of years before man, pulsed out into the watery night; the faint echoes came tingling back, were captured and amplified, and became floating, blue-green flecks on the screen.

Through long practice, Don could read their message with effortless ease. Five hundred feet below, stretching out to the limits of his submerged horizon, was the Scattering Layer—the blanket of life that covered half the world. The sunken meadow of the sea, it rose and fell with the passage of the sun, hovering always at the edge of darkness. During the night it had floated nearly to the surface, but the dawn was now driving it back into the depths.

It was no obstacle to his sonar. Don could see clear through its tenuous substance to the ooze of the Pacific floor, over which he was driving high as a cloud above the land. But the ultimate depths were no concern of his; the flocks he guarded, and the enemies who ravaged them, belonged to the upper levels of the sea.

Don flicked the switch of the depth selector, and his sonar beam concentrated itself into the horizontal plane. The glimmering echoes from the abyss vanished, and he could see more clearly what lay around him here in the ocean's stratospheric heights. That glowing cloud two miles ahead was an unusually large school of fish; he wondered if Base knew about it, and made an entry in his log. There were some larger blips at the edge of the school—the carnivores pursuing the cattle, ensuring that the endlessly turning wheel of life and death would never lose momentum. But this conflict was no affair of Don's; he was after bigger game.

Sub 5 drove on toward the west, a steel needle swifter and more deadly than any other creature that roamed the seas. The tiny cabin, now lit only by the flicker of lights from the instrument board, pulsed with power as the spinning turbines thrust the water aside. Don glanced at the chart and noted that he was already halfway to the target area. He wondered if he should surface to have a look at the dead whale; from its injuries he might be able to learn something about its assailants. But that would mean further delay, and in a case like this time was vital.

The long-range receiver bleeped plaintively, and Don switched over to Transcribe. He had never learned to read code by ear, as some people could do, but the ribbon of paper emerging from the message slot saved him the trouble.

AIR PATROL REPORTS SCHOOL 50–100 WHALES HEADING 95 DEGREES GRID REF X186593 Y432011 STOP MOVING AT SPEED AFTER CHANGE OF COURSE STOP NO SIGN OF ORCAS BUT PRESUME THEY ARE IN VICINITY STOP RORQUAL

Don considered this last piece of deduction highly unlikely. If the orcas—the dreaded killer whales—had indeed been responsible, they would surely have been spotted by now as they surfaced to breathe. Moreover, they would never have let the patrolling plane scare them away from their victim, but would have remained feasting on it until they had gorged themselves.

One thing was in his favor; the frightened herd was now heading almost directly toward him. Don started to set the co-ordinates on the plotting grid, then saw that it was no longer necessary. At the extreme edge of his screen, a flotilla of faint stars had appeared. He altered course slightly, and drove head on to the approaching school.

Part of the message was certainly correct; the whales were moving at unusually high speed. At the rate they were traveling, he would be among them in five minutes. He cut the motors and felt the backward tug of the water bringing him swiftly to rest.

Don Burley, a knight in armor, sat in his tiny, dim-lit room a hundred feet below the bright Pacific waves, testing his weapons for the conflict that lay ahead. In these moments of poised suspense, before action began, he often pictured himself thus, though he would have admitted it to no one in the world. He felt, too, a kinship with all shepherds who had guarded their flocks back to the dawn of time. Not only was he Sir Lancelot, he was also David, among ancient Palestinian hills, alert for the mountain lions that would prey upon his father's sheep.

Yet far nearer in time, and far closer in spirit, were the men who had marshaled the great herds of cattle on the American plains, scarcely three lifetimes ago. They would have understood his work, though his implements would have been magic to them. The pattern was the same; only the scale of things had altered. It made no fundamental difference that the beasts Don herded weighed a hundred tons and browsed on the endless savannas of the sea.

The school was now less than two miles away, and Don checked his scanner's steady circling to concentrate on the sector ahead. The picture on the screen altered to a fan-shaped wedge as the sonar beam started to flick from side to side; now he could count every whale in the school, and could even make a good estimate of its size. With a practiced eye, he began to look for stragglers.

Don could never have explained what drew him at once toward those four echoes at the southern fringe of the school. It was true that they were a little apart from the rest, but others had fallen as far behind. There is some sixth sense that a man acquires when he has stared long enough into a sonar screen—some hunch which enables him to extract more from the moving flecks than he has any right to do. Without conscious thought, Don reached for the controls and started the turbines whirling once more.

The main body of the whale pack was now sweeping past him to the east. He had no fear of a collision; the great animals, even in their panic, could sense his presence as easily as he could detect theirs, and by similar means. He wondered if he should switch on his beacon. They might recognize its sound pattern, and it would reassure them. But the still unknown enemy might recognize it too, and would be warned.

The four echoes that had attracted his attention were almost at the center of the screen. He closed for an interception, and hunched low over the sonar display as if to drag from it by sheer will power every scrap of information the scanner could give. There were two large echoes, some distance apart, and one was accompanied by a pair of smaller satellites. Don wondered if he was already too late; in his mind's eye he could picture the death struggle taking place in the water less than a mile ahead. Those two fainter blips would be the enemy, worrying a whale while its mate stood by in helpless terror, with no weapons of defense except its mighty flukes.

Now he was almost close enough for vision. The TV camera in Sub 5's prow strained through the gloom, but at first could show nothing but the fog of plankton. Then a vast, shadowy shape appeared in the center of the screen, with two smaller companions below it. Don was seeing, with the greater precision but hopelessly limited range of light, what the sonar scanners had already told him.

Almost at once he saw his incredible mistake: the two satellites were calves. It was the first time he had ever met a whale with twins, although multiple births were not uncommon. In normal circumstances, the sight would have fascinated him, but now it meant that he had jumped to the wrong conclusion and had lost precious minutes. He must begin the search again.

As a routine check, he swung the camera toward the fourth blip on the sonar screen—the echo he had assumed, from its size, to be another adult whale. It is strange how a preconceived idea can affect a man's understanding of what he sees; seconds passed before Don could interpret the picture before his eyes—before he knew that, after all, he had come to the right place.

"Jesus!" he said softly. "I didn't know they grew that big." It was a shark, the largest he had ever seen. Its details were still obscured, but there was only one genus it could belong to. The whale shark and the basking shark might be of comparable size, but they were harmless herbivores. This was the king of all selachians—*Carcharodon*—the Great White Shark. Don tried to recall the figures for the largest known specimen. In 1990, or thereabouts, a fifty-footer had been killed off New Zealand, but this one was half as big again.

These thoughts flashed through his mind in an instant, and in that same moment he saw that the great beast was already maneuvering for the kill. It was heading for one of the calves, and ignoring the frantic mother. Whether this was cowardice or common sense there was no way of telling; perhaps such distinctions were meaningless to the shark's tiny and utterly alien mind.

There was only one thing to do. It might spoil his chance of a quick kill, but the calf's life was more important. He punched the button of the siren, and a brief, mechanical scream erupted into the water around him.

Shark and whales were equally terrified by the deafening shriek. The shark jerked round in an impossibly tight curve, and Don was nearly jolted out of his seat as the autopilot snapped the sub onto a new course. Twisting and turning with an agility equal to that of any other sea creature of its size, Sub 5 began to close in upon the shark, its electronic brain automatically following the sonar echo and thus leaving Don free to concentrate on his armament. He needed that freedom; the next operation was going to be difficult unless he could hold a steady course for at least fifteen seconds. At a pinch he could use his tiny rocket torps to make a kill; had he been alone and faced with a pack of orcas, he would certainly have done so. But that was messy and brutal, and there was a neater way. He had always preferred the technique of the rapier to that of the hand grenade.

Now he was only fifty feet away, and closing rapidly. There might never be a better chance. He punched the launching stud.

From beneath the belly of the sub, something that looked like a sting ray hurtled forward. Don had checked the speed of his own craft; there was no need to come any closer now. The tiny, arrow-shaped hydrofoil, only a couple of feet across, could move far faster than his vessel and would close the gap in seconds. As it raced forward, it spun out the thin line of the control wire, like some underwater spider laying its thread. Along that wire passed the energy that powered the sting, and the signals that steered the missile to its goal. It responded so instantly to his orders that Don felt he was controlling some sensitive, high-spirited steed.

The shark saw the danger less than a second before impact. The resemblance of the sting to an ordinary ray confused it, as the designers had intended. Before the tiny brain could realize that no ray behaved like this, the missile had struck. The steel hypodermic, rammed forward by an exploding cartridge, drove through the shark's horny skin, and the great fish erupted in a frenzy of terror. Don backed rapidly away, for a blow from that tail would rattle him around like a pea in a can and might even damage the sub. There was nothing more for him to do, except to wait while the poison did its work.

The doomed killer was trying to arch its body so that it could snap at the poisoned dart. Don had now reeled the sting back into its slot amidships, pleased that he had been able to retrieve the missile undamaged. He watched with awe and a dispassionate pity as the great beast succumbed to its paralysis.

Its struggles were weakening. It was now swimming aimlessly back and forth, and once Don had to sidestep smartly to avoid a collision. As it lost control of buoyancy, the dying shark drifted up to the surface. Don did not bother to follow; that could wait until he had attended to more important business.

He found the cow and her two calves less than a mile away, and inspected them carefully. They were uninjured, so there was no need to call the vet in his highly specialized two-man sub which could handle any cetological crisis from a stomach-ache to a Caesarean.

The whales were no longer in the least alarmed, and a check on the sonar had shown that the entire school had ceased its panicky flight. He wondered if they already knew what had happened; much had been learned about their methods of communication, but much more was still a mystery.

"I hope you appreciate what I've done for you, old lady," he muttered. Then, reflecting that fifty tons of mother love was a slightly awe-inspiring sight, he blew his tanks and surfaced.

It was calm, so he opened the hatch and popped his head out of the tiny conning tower. The water was only inches below his chin, and from time to time a wave made a determined effort to swamp him. There was little danger of this happening, for he fitted the hatch so closely that he was quite an effective plug.

Fifty feet away, a long gray mound, like an overturned boat, was rolling on the surface. Don looked at it thoughtfully, wondering how much compressed air he'd better squirt into the corpse to prevent it sinking before one of the tenders could reach the spot. In a few minutes he would radio his report, but for the moment it was pleasant to drink the fresh Pacific breeze, to feel the open sky above his head, and to watch the sun begin its long climb toward noon.

Don Burley was the happy warrior, resting after the one battle that man would always have to fight. He was holding at bay the specter of famine which had confronted all earlier ages, but which would never threaten the world again while the great plankton farms harvested their millions of tons of protein, and the whale herds obeyed their new masters. Man had come back to the sea, his ancient home, after aeons of exile; until the oceans froze, he would never be hungry again. . . .

Yet that, Don knew, was the least of his satisfactions. Even if what he was doing had been of no practical value, he would still have wished to do it. Nothing else that life could offer matched the contentment and the calm sense of power that filled him when he set out on a mission such as this. Power? Yes, that was the right word. But it was not a power that would ever be abused; he felt too great a kinship with all the creatures who shared the seas with him—even those it was his duty to destroy.

To all appearances, Don was completely relaxed, yet had any one of the many dials and lights filling his field of view called for attention he would have been instantly alert. His mind was already back on the *Rorqual,* and he found it increasingly hard to keep his thoughts away from his overdue breakfast. In order to make the time pass more swiftly, he started mentally composing his report. Quite a few people, he knew, were going to be surprised by it. The engineers who maintained the invisible fences of sound and electricity which now divided the mighty Pacific into manageable portions would have to start looking for the break; the marine biologists who were so confident that sharks never attacked whales would have to think up excuses. Both enterprises, Don was quite sure, would be successfully carried out, and then everything would be under control again, until the sea contrived its next crisis.

But the crisis to which Don was now unwittingly returning was a man-made one, organized without any malice toward him at the highest official levels. It had begun with a suggestion in the Space Department, duly referred up to the World Secretariat. It had risen still higher until it reached the World Assembly itself, where it had come to the approving ears of the senators directly interested. Thus converted from a suggestion to an order, it had filtered down through the Secretariat to the World Food Organization, thence to the Marine Division, and finally to the Bureau of Whales. The whole process had taken the incredibly short time of four weeks.

Don, of course, knew nothing of this. As far as he was concerned, the complicated workings of global bureaucracy resolved themselves into the greeting his skipper gave him when he walked into the *Rorqual's* mess for his belated breakfast.

"Morning, Don. Headquarters wants you to run over to Brisbane—they've got some job for you. Hope it doesn't take too long; you know how shorthanded we are."

"What kind of a job?" asked Don suspiciously. He remembered an unfortunate occasion when he had acted as a guide to a permanent under-secretary who had seemed to be a bit of a fool, and whom he had treated accordingly. It had later turned out that the P.U.—as might have been guessed from his position—was a very shrewd character indeed and knew exactly what Don was doing.

"They didn't tell me," said the skipper. "I'm not quite sure they know themselves. Give my love to Queensland, and keep away from the casinos on the Gold Coast."

"Much choice I have, on *my* pay," snorted Don. "Last time I went to Surfer's Paradise, I was lucky to get away with my shirt."

"But you brought back a couple of thousand on your first visit."

"Beginner's luck—it never happened again. I've lost it all since then, so I'll stop while I still break even. No more gambling for me."

"Is that a bet? Would you put five bucks on it?"

"Sure."

"Then pay over—you've already lost by accepting."

A spoonful of processed plankton hovered momentarily in mid-air while Don sought for a way out of the trap.

"Just try and get me to pay," he retorted. "You've got no witnesses, and I'm no gentleman." He hastily swallowed the last of his coffee, then pushed aside his chair and rose to go.

"Better start packing, I suppose. So long, Skipper—see you later."

The captain of the *Rorqual* watched his first warden sweep out of the room like a small hurricane. For a moment the sound of Don's passage echoed back along the ship's corridors; then comparative silence descended again.

The skipper started to head back to the bridge. "Look out, Brisbane," he muttered to himself; then he began to rearrange the watches and to compose a masterly memorandum to HQ asking how he was expected to run a ship when thirty per cent of her crew were permanently absent on leave or special duty. By the time he reached the bridge, the only thing that had stopped him from resigning was the fact that, try as he might, he couldn't think of a better job.

CHAPTER TWO

Though he had been kept waiting only a few minutes, Walter Franklin was already prowling impatiently around the reception room. Swiftly he examined and dismissed the deep-sea photographs hanging on the walls; then he sat for a moment on the edge of the table, leafing through the pile of magazines, reviews, and reports which always accumulated in such places. The popular magazines he had already seen—for the last few weeks he had had little else to do but read—and few of the others looked interesting. Somebody, he supposed, had to go through these lavishly electroprinted food-production reports as part of their job; he wondered how they avoided being hypnotized by the endless columns of statistics. *Neptune,* the house organ of the Marine Division, seemed a little more promising, but as most of the personalities discussed in its columns were unknown to him he soon became bored with it. Even its fairly lowbrow articles were largely over his head, assuming a knowledge of technical terms he did not possess.

The receptionist was watching him—certainly noticing his impatience, perhaps analyzing the nervousness and insecurity that lay behind it. With a distinct effort, Franklin forced himself to sit down and to concentrate on yesterday's issue of the Brisbane *Courier*. He had almost become interested in an editorial requiem on Australian cricket, inspired by the recent Test results, when the young lady who guarded the director's office smiled sweetly at him and said: "Would you please go in now, Mr. Franklin?"

He had expected to find the director alone, or perhaps accompanied by a secretary. The husky young man sitting in the other visitor's chair seemed out of place in this orderly office, and was staring at him with more curiosity than friendliness. Franklin stiffened at once; they had been discussing him, he knew, and automatically he went on the defensive.

Director Cary, who knew almost as much about human beings as he did about marine mammals, sensed the strain immediately and did his best to dispel it.

"Ah, there you are, Franklin," he said with slightly excessive heartiness. "I hope you've been enjoying your stay here. Have my people been taking care of you?"

Franklin was spared the trouble of answering this question, for the director gave him no time to reply.

"I want you to meet Don Burley," he continued. "Don's First Warden on the *Rorqual,* and one of the best we've got. He's been assigned to look after you. Don, meet Walter Franklin."

They shook hands warily, weighing each other. Then Don's face broke into a reluctant smile. It was the smile of a man who had been given a job he didn't care for but who had decided to make the best of it.

"Pleased to meet you, Franklin," he said. "Welcome to the Mermaid Patrol."

Franklin tried to smile at the hoary joke, but his effort was not very successful. He knew that he should be friendly, and that these people were doing their best to help him. Yet the knowledge was that of the mind, not the heart; he could not relax and let himself meet them halfway. The fear of being pitied and the nagging suspicion that they had been talking about him behind his back, despite all the assurances he had been given, paralyzed his will for friendliness.

Don Burley sensed nothing of this. He only knew that the director's office was not the right place to get acquainted with a new colleague, and before Franklin was fully aware of what had happened he was out of the building, buffeting his way through the shirt-sleeved crowds in George Street, and being steered into a minute bar opposite the new post office.

The noise of the city subsided, though through the tinted glass walls Franklin could see the shadowy shapes of the pedestrians moving to and fro. It was pleasantly cool here after the torrid streets; whether or not Brisbane should be air-conditioned—and if so, who should have the resulting multimillion-dollar contract—was still being argued by the local politicians, and meanwhile the citizens sweltered every summer.

Don Burley waited until Franklin had drunk his first beer and called for replacements. There was a mystery about his new pupil, and as soon as possible he intended to solve it. Someone very high up in the division —perhaps even in the World Secretariat itself—must have organized this. A first warden was not called away from his duties to wet-nurse someone who was obviously too old to go through the normal training channels. At a guess he would say that Franklin was the wrong side of thirty; he had never heard of anyone that age getting this sort of special treatment before.

One thing was obvious about Franklin at once, and that only added to the mystery. He was a spaceman; you could tell them a mile away. That should make a good opening gambit. Then he remembered that the director had warned him, "Don't ask Franklin too many questions. I don't know what his background is, but we've been specifically told not to talk about it with him."

That might make sense, mused Don. Perhaps he was a space pilot who had been grounded after some inexcusable lapse, such as absent-mindedly arriving at Venus when he should have gone to Mars.

"Is this the first time," Don began cautiously, "that you've been to Australia?" It was not a very fortunate opening, and the conversation might have died there and then when Franklin replied: "I was born here."

Don, however, was not the sort of person who was easily abashed. He merely laughed and said, half-apologetically, "Nobody ever tells me anything, so I usually find out the hard way. I was born on the other side of the world—over in Ireland—but since I've been attached to the Pacific branch of the bureau I've more or less adopted Australia as a second home. Not that I spend much time ashore! On this job you're at sea eighty per cent of the time. A lot of people don't like that, you know."

"It would suit me," said Franklin, but left the remark hanging in the air. Burley began to feel exasperated—it was such hard work getting anything out of this fellow. The prospect of working with him for the next few weeks began to look very uninviting, and Don wondered what he had done to deserve such a fate. However, he struggled on manfully.

"The superintendent tells me that you've a good scientific and engineering background, so I can assume that you'll know most of the things that our people spend the first year learning. Have they filled you in on the administrative background?"

"They've given me a lot of facts and figures under hypnosis, so I could lecture you for a couple of hours on the Marine Division—its history, organization, and current projects, with particular reference to the Bureau of Whales. But it doesn't *mean* anything to me at present."

Now we seem to be getting somewhere, Don told himself. The fellow can talk after all. A couple more beers, and he might even be human.

"That's the trouble with hypnotic training," agreed Don. "They can pump the information into you until it comes out of your ears, but you're never quite sure how much you really know. And they can't teach you manual skills, or train you to have the right reactions in emergencies. There's only one way of learning anything properly—and that's by actually doing the job."

He paused, momentarily distracted by a shapely silhouette parading on the other side of the translucent wall. Franklin noticed the direction of his gaze, and his features relaxed into a slight smile. For the first time the tension lifted, and Don began to feel that there was some hope of establishing contact with the enigma who was now his responsibility.

With a beery forefinger, Don started to trace maps on the plastic table top.

"This is the setup," he began. "Our main training center for shallow-water operations is here in the Capricorn Group, about four hundred miles north of Brisbane and forty miles out from the coast. The South Pacific fence starts here, and runs on east to New Caledonia and Fiji. When the whales migrate north from the polar feeding grounds to have their calves in the tropics, they're compelled to pass through the gaps we've left here. The most important of these gates, from our point of view, is the one right here off the Queensland coast, at the southern entrance to the Great Barrier Reef. The reef provides a kind of natural channel, averaging about fifty miles wide, almost up to the equator. Once we've herded the whales into it, we can keep them pretty well under control. It didn't take much doing; many of them used to come this way long before we appeared on the scene. By now the rest have been so well conditioned that even if we switched off the fence it would probably make no difference to their migratory pattern."

"By the way," interjected Franklin, "is the fence purely electrical?"

"Oh no. Electric fields control fish pretty well but don't work satisfactorily on mammals like whales. The fence is largely ultrasonic—a curtain of sound from a chain of generators half a mile below the surface. We can get fine control at the gates by broadcasting specific orders; you can set a whole herd stampeding in any direction you wish by playing back a recording of a whale in distress. But it's not very often we have to do anything drastic like that; as I said, nowadays they're too well trained."

"I can appreciate that," said Franklin. "In fact, I heard somewhere that the fence was more for keeping other animals out than for keeping the whales in."

"That's partly true, though we'd still need some kind of control for rounding up our herds at census or slaughtering. Even so, the fence isn't perfect. There are weak spots where generator fields overlap, and sometimes we have to switch off sections to allow normal fish migration. Then, the really big sharks, or the killer whales, can get through and play hell. The killers are our worst problem; they attack the whales when they are feeding in the Antarctic, and often the herds suffer ten per cent losses. No one will be happy until the killers are wiped out, but no one can think of an economical way of doing it. We can't patrol the entire ice pack with subs, though when I've seen what a killer can do to a whale I've often wished we could."

There was real feeling—almost passion—in Burley's voice, and Franklin looked at the warden with surprise. The "whaleboys," as they had been inevitably christened by a nostalgically minded public in search of heroes, were not supposed to be much inclined either to thought or emotions. Though Franklin knew perfectly well that the tough, uncomplicated characters who stalked tight lipped through the pages of contemporary submarine sagas had very little connection with reality, it was hard to escape from the popular clichés. Don Burley, it was true, was far from tight lipped, but in most other respects he seemed to fit the standard specification very well.

Franklin wondered how he was going to get on with his new mentor—indeed, with his new job. He still felt no enthusiasm for it; whether that would come, only time would show. It was obviously full of interesting and even fascinating problems and possibilities, and if it would occupy his mind and give him scope for his talents, that was as much as he could hope for. The long nightmare of the last year had destroyed, with so much else, his zest for life—the capacity he had once possessed for throwing himself heart and soul into some project.

It was difficult to believe that he could ever recapture the enthusiasm that had once taken him so far along paths he could never tread again. As he glanced at Don, who was still talking with the fluent lucidity of a man who knows and loves his job, Franklin felt a sudden and disturbing sense of guilt. Was it fair to Burley to take him away from his work and to turn him, whether he knew it or not, into a cross between a nursemaid and kindergarten teacher? Had Franklin realized that very similar thoughts had already crossed Burley's mind, his sympathy would have been quenched at once.

"Time we caught the shuttle to the airport," said Don, looking at his watch and hastily draining his beer. "The morning flight leaves in thirty minutes. I hope all your stuff's already been sent on."

"The hotel said they'd take care of it."

"Well, we can check at the airport. Let's go."

Half an hour later Franklin had a chance to relax again. It was typical of Burley, he soon discovered, to take things easily until the last possible moment and then to explode in a burst of activity. This burst carried them from the quiet bar to the even more efficiently silenced plane. As they took their seats, there was a brief incident that was to puzzle Don a good deal in the weeks that lay ahead.

"You take the window seat," he said. "I've flown this way dozens of times."

He took Franklin's refusal as ordinary politeness, and started to insist. Not until Franklin had turned down the offer several times, with increasing determination and even signs of annoyance, did Burley realize that his companion's behavior had nothing to do with common courtesy. It seemed incredible, but Don could have sworn that the other was scared stiff. What sort of man, he wondered blankly, would be terrified of taking a window seat in an ordinary aircraft? All his gloomy premonitions about his new assignment, which had been partly dispelled during their earlier conversation, came crowding back with renewed vigor.

The city and the sunburned coast dropped below as the lifting jets carried them effortlessly up into the sky. Franklin was reading the paper with a fierce concentration that did not deceive Burley for a moment. He decided to wait for a while, and apply some more tests later in the flight.

The Glasshouse Mountains—those strangely shaped fangs jutting from the eroded plain—swept swiftly beneath. Then came the little coastal towns, through which the wealth of the immense farm lands of the interior had once passed to the world in the days before agriculture went to sea. And then—only minutes, it seemed, after take-off—the first islands of the Great Barrier Reef appeared like deeper shadows in the blue horizon mists.

The sun was shining almost straight into his eyes, but Don's memory could fill in the details which were lost in the glare from the burning waters. He could see the low, green islands surrounded by their narrow borders of sand and their immensely greater fringes of barely submerged coral. Against each island's private reef the waves of the Pacific would be marching forever, so that for a thousand miles into the north snowy crescents of foam would break the surface of the sea.

A century ago—fifty years, even—scarcely a dozen of these hundreds of islands had been inhabited. Now, with the aid of universal air transport, together with cheap power and water-purification plants, both the state and the private citizen had invaded the ancient solitude of the reef. A few fortunate individuals, by means that had never been perfectly clear, had managed to acquire some of the smaller islands as their personal property. The entertainment and vacation industry had taken over others, and had not always improved on Nature's handiwork. But the greatest landowner in the reef was undoubtedly the World Food Organization, with its complicated hierarchy of fisheries, marine farms, and research departments, the full extent of which, it was widely believed, no merely human brain could ever comprehend.

"We're nearly there," said Burley. "That's Lady Musgrave Island we've just passed—main generators for the western end of the fence. Capricorn Group under us now—Masthead, One Tree, North-West, Wilson—and Heron in the middle, with all those buildings on it. The big tower is Administration—the aquarium's by that pool—and look, you can see a couple of subs tied up at that long jetty leading out to the edge of the reef."

As he spoke, Don watched Franklin out of the corner of his eye. The other had leaned toward the window as if following his companion's running commentary, yet Burley could swear that he was not looking at the panorama of reefs and islands spread out below. His face was tense and strained; there was an indrawn, hooded expression in his eyes as if he was forcing himself to see nothing.

With a mingling of pity and contempt, Don understood the symptoms if not their cause. Franklin was terrified of heights; so much, then, for the theory that he was a spaceman. Then what was he? Whatever the answer, he hardly seemed the sort of person with whom one would wish to share the cramped quarters of a two-man training sub. . . .

The plane's shock absorbers touched down on the rectangle of scorched and flattened coral that was the Heron Island landing platform. As he stepped out into the sunlight, blinking in the sudden glare, Franklin seemed to make an abrupt recovery. Don had seen seasick passengers undergo equally swift transformations on their return to dry land. If Franklin is no better as a sailor than an airman, he thought, this crazy assignment won't last more than a couple of days and I'll be able to get back to work. Not that Don was in a great rush to return immediately; Heron Island was a pleasant place where you could enjoy yourself if you knew how to deal with the red tape that always entangled headquarters establishments.

A light truck whisked them and their belongings along a road beneath an avenue of Pisonia trees whose heavily leafed branches blocked all direct sunlight. The road was less than a quarter of a mile long, but it spanned the little island from the jetties and maintenance plants on the west to the administration buildings on the east. The two halves of the island were partly insulated from each other by a narrow belt of jungle which had been carefully preserved in its virgin state and which, Don remembered sentimentally, was full of interesting tracks and secluded clearings.

Administration was expecting Mr. Franklin, and had made all the necessary arrangements for him. He had been placed in a kind of privileged limbo, one stage below the permanent staff like Burley, but several stages above the ordinary trainees under instruction. Surprisingly, he had a room of his own—something that even senior members of the bureau could not always expect when they visited the island. This was a great relief to Don, who had been afraid he might have to share quarters with his mysterious charge. Quite apart from any other factors, that would have interfered badly with certain romantic plans of his own.

He saw Franklin to his small but attractive room on the second floor of the training wing, looking out across the miles of coral which stretched eastward all the way to the horizon. In the courtyard below, a group of trainees, relaxing between classes, was chatting with a second warden instructor whom Don recognized from earlier visits but could not name. It was a pleasant feeling, he mused, going back to school when you already knew all the answers.

"You should be comfortable here," he said to Franklin, who was busy unpacking his baggage. "Quite a view, isn't it?"

Such poetic ecstasies were normally foreign to Don's nature, but he could not resist the temptation of seeing how Franklin would react to the leagues of coral-dappled ocean that lay before him. Rather to his disappointment, the reaction was quite conventional; presumably Franklin was not worried by a mere thirty feet of height. He looked out of the window, taking his time and obviously admiring the vista of blues and greens which led the eye out into the endless waters of the Pacific.

Serve you right, Don told himself—it's not fair to tease the poor devil. Whatever he's got, it can't be fun to live with.

"I'll leave you to get settled in," said Don, backing out through the door. "Lunch will be coming up in half an hour over at the mess—that building we passed on the way in. See you there."

Franklin nodded absently as he sorted through his belongings and piled shirts and underclothes on the bed. He wanted to be left alone while he adjusted himself to the new life which, with no particular enthusiasm, he had now accepted as his own.

Burley had been gone for less than ten minutes when there was a knock on the door and a quiet voice said, "Can I come in?"

"Who's there?" asked Franklin, as he tidied up the debris and made his room look presentable.

"Dr. Myers."

The name meant nothing to Franklin, but his face twisted into a wry smile as he thought how appropriate it was that his very first visitor should be a doctor. What kind of a doctor, he thought he could guess.

Myers was a stocky, pleasantly ugly man in his early forties, with a disconcertingly direct gaze which seemed somewhat at variance with his friendly, affable manner.

"Sorry to butt in on you when you've only just arrived," he said apologetically. "I had to do it now because I'm flying out to New Caledonia this afternoon and won't be back for a week. Professor Stevens asked me to look you up and give you his best wishes. If there's anything you want, just ring my office and we'll try to fix it for you."

Franklin admired the skillful way in which Myers had avoided all the obvious dangers. He did *not* say—true though it undoubtedly was—"I've discussed your case with Professor Stevens." Nor did he offer direct help; he managed to convey the assumption that Franklin wouldn't need it and was now quite capable of looking after himself.

"I appreciate that," said Franklin sincerely. He felt he was going to like Dr. Myers, and made up his mind not to resent the surveillance he would undoubtedly be getting. "Tell me," he added, "just what do the people here know about me?"

"Nothing at all, except that you are to be helped to qualify as a warden as quickly as possible. This isn't the first time this sort of thing has happened, you know—there have been high-pressure conversion courses before. Still, it's inevitable that there will be a good deal of curiosity about you; that may be your biggest problem."

"Burley is dying of curiosity already."

"Mind if I give you some advice?"

"Of course not—go ahead."

"You'll be working with Don continually. It's only fair to him, as well as to yourself, to confide in him when you feel you can do so. I'm sure you'll find him quite understanding. Or if you prefer, I'll do the explaining."

Franklin shook his head, not trusting himself to speak. It was not a matter of logic, for he knew that Myers was talking sense. Sooner or later it would all have to come out, and he might be making matters worse by postponing the inevitable. Yet his hold upon sanity and self-respect was still so precarious that he could not face the prospect of working with men who knew his secret, however sympathetic they might be.

"Very well. The choice is yours and we'll respect it. Good luck—and let's hope all our contacts will be purely social."

Long after Myers had gone, Franklin sat on the edge of the bed, staring out across the sea which would be his new domain. He would need the luck that the other had wished him, yet he was beginning to feel a renewed interest in life. It was not merely that people were anxious to help him; he had received more than enough help in the last few months. At last he was beginning to see how he could help himself, and so discover a purpose for his existence.

Presently he jolted himself out of his daydream and looked at his watch. He was already ten minutes late for lunch, and that was a bad start for his new life. He thought of Don Burley waiting impatiently in the mess and wondering what had happened to him.

"Coming, teacher," he said, as he put on his jacket and started out of the room. It was the first time he had made a joke with himself for longer than he could remember.

CHAPTER THREE

When Franklin first saw Indra Langenburg she was covered with blood up to her elbows and was busily hacking away at the entrails of a ten-foot tiger shark she had just disemboweled. The huge beast was lying, its pale belly upturned to the sun, on the sandy beach where Franklin took his morning promenade. A thick chain still led to the hook in its mouth; it had obviously been caught during the night and then left behind by the falling tide.

Franklin stood for a moment looking at the unusual combination of attractive girl and dead monster, then said thoughtfully: "You know, this is not the sort of thing I like to see before breakfast. Exactly what are you doing?"

A brown, oval face with very serious eyes looked up at him. The foot-long, razor-sharp knife that was creating such havoc continued to slice expertly through gristle and guts.

"I'm writing a thesis," said a voice as serious as the eyes, "on the vitamin content of shark liver. It means catching a lot of sharks; this is my third this week. Would you like some teeth? I've got plenty, and they make nice souvenirs."

She walked to the head of the beast and inserted her knife in its gaping jaws, which had been propped apart by a block of wood. A quick jerk of her wrist, and an endless necklace of deadly ivory triangles, like a band saw made of bone, started to emerge from the shark's mouth.

"No thanks," said Franklin hastily, hoping she would not be offended. "Please don't let me interrupt your work."

He guessed that she was barely twenty, and was not surprised at meeting an unfamiliar girl on the little island, because the scientists at the Research Station did not have much contact with the administrative and training staff.

"You're new here, aren't you?" said the bloodstained biologist, sloshing a huge lump of liver into a bucket with every sign of satisfaction. "I didn't see you at the last HQ dance."

Franklin felt quite cheered by the inquiry. It was so pleasant to meet someone who knew nothing about him, and had not been speculating about his presence here. He felt he could talk freely and without restraint for the first time since landing on Heron Island.

"Yes—I've just come for a special training course. How long have you been here?"

He was making pointless conversation just for the pleasure of the company, and doubtless she knew it.

"Oh, about a month," she said carelessly. There was another slimy, squelching noise from the bucket, which was now nearly full. "I'm on leave here from the University of Miami."

"You're American, then?" Franklin asked. The girl answered solemnly: "No; my ancestors were Dutch, Burmese, and Scottish in about equal proportions. Just to make things a little more complicated, I was born in Japan."

Franklin wondered if she was making fun of him, but there was no trace of guile in her expression. She seemed a really nice kid, he thought, but he couldn't stay here talking all day. He had only forty minutes for breakfast, and his morning class in submarine navigation started at nine.

He thought no more of the encounter, for he was continually meeting new faces as his circle of acquaintances steadily expanded. The high-pressure course he was taking gave him no time for much social life, and for that he was grateful. His mind was fully occupied once more; it had taken up the load with a smoothness that both surprised and gratified him. Perhaps those who had sent him here knew what they were doing better than he sometimes supposed.

All the empirical knowledge—the statistics, the factual data, the ins and outs of administration—had been more or less painlessly pumped into Franklin while he was under mild hypnosis. Prolonged question periods, where he was quizzed by a tape recorder that later filled in the right answers, then confirmed that the information had really taken and had not, as sometimes happened, shot straight through the mind leaving no permanent impression.

Don Burley had nothing to do with this side of Franklin's training, but, rather to his disgust, had no chance of relaxing when Franklin was being looked after elsewhere. The chief instructor had gleefully seized this opportunity of getting Don back into his clutches, and had "suggested," with great tact and charm, that when his other duties permitted Don might like to lecture to the three courses now under training on the island. Outranked and outmaneuvered, Don had no alternative but to acquiesce with as good grace as possible. This assignment, it seemed, was not going to be the holiday he had hoped.

In one respect, however, his worst fears had not materialized. Franklin was not at all hard to get on with, as long as one kept completely away from personalities. He was very intelligent and had clearly had a technical training that in some ways was much better than Don's own. It was seldom necessary to explain anything to him more than once, and long before they had reached the stage of trying him out on the synthetic trainers, Don could see that his pupil had the makings of a good pilot. He was skillful with his hands, reacted quickly and accurately, and had that indefinable poise which distinguishes the first-rate pilot from the merely competent one.

Yet Don knew that knowledge and skill were not in themselves sufficient. Something else was also needed, and there was no way yet of telling if Franklin possessed it. Not until Don had watched his reactions as he sank down into the depths of the sea would he know whether all this effort was to be of any use.

There was so much that Franklin had to learn that it seemed impossible that anyone could absorb it all in two months, as the program insisted. Don himself had taken the normal six months, and he somewhat resented the assumption that anyone else could do it in a third of the time, even with the special coaching he was giving. Why, the mechanical side of the job alone—the layout and design of the various classes of subs—took at least two months to learn, even with the best of instructional aids. Yet at the same time he had to teach Franklin the principles of seamanship and underwater navigation, basic oceanography, submarine signaling and communication, and a substantial amount of ichthyology, marine psychology, and, of course, cetology. So far Franklin had never even seen a whale, dead or alive, and that first encounter was something that Don looked forward to witnessing. At such a moment one could learn all that one needed to know about a man's fitness for this job.

They had done two weeks' hard work together before Don first took Franklin under water. By this time they had established a curious relationship which was at once friendly and remote. Though they had long since ceased to call each other by their surnames, "Don" and "Walt" was as far as their intimacy went. Burley still knew absolutely nothing about Franklin's past, though he had evolved a good many theories. The one which he most favored was that his pupil was an extremely talented criminal being rehabilitated after total therapy. He wondered if Franklin was a murderer, which was a stimulating thought, and half hoped that this exciting hypothesis was true.

Franklin no longer showed any of the obvious peculiarities he had revealed on their first meeting, though he was undoubtedly more nervous and highly strung than the average. Since this was the case with many of the best wardens, it did not worry Don. Even his curiosity about Franklin's past had somewhat lessened, for he was far too busy to bother about it. He had learned to be patient when there was no alternative, and he did not doubt that sooner or later he would discover the whole story. Once or twice, he was almost certain, Franklin had been on the verge of some revelation, but then had drawn back. Each time Don had pretended that nothing had happened, and they had resumed their old, impersonal relationship.

It was a clear morning, with only a slow swell moving across the face of the sea, as they walked along the narrow jetty that stretched from the western end of the island out to the edge of the reef. The tide was in, but though the reef flat was completely submerged the great plateau of coral was nowhere more than five or six feet below the surface, and its every detail was clearly visible through the crystal water. Neither Franklin nor Burley spared more than a few glances for the natural aquarium above which they were walking. It was too familiar to them both, and they knew that the real beauty and wonder of the reef lay in the deeper waters farther out to sea.

Two hundred yards out from the island, the coral landscape suddenly dropped off into the depths, but the jetty continued upon taller stilts until it ended in a small group of sheds and offices. A valiant, and fairly successful, attempt had been made to avoid the grime and chaos usually inseparable from dockyards and piers; even the cranes had been designed so that they would not offend the eye. One of the terms under which the Queensland government had reluctantly leased the Capricorn Group to the World Food Organization was that the beauty of the islands would not be jeopardized. On the whole, this part of the agreement had been well kept.

"I've ordered two torpedoes from the garage," said Burley as they walked down the flight of stairs at the end of the jetty and passed through the double doors of a large air lock. Franklin's ears gave the disconcerting internal "click" as they adjusted themselves to the increased pressure; he guessed that he was now about twenty feet below the water line. Around him was a brightly lighted chamber crammed with various types of underwater equipment, from simple lungs to elaborate propulsion devices. The two torpedoes that Don had requisitioned were lying in their cradles on a sloping ramp leading down into the still water at the far end of the chamber. They were painted the bright yellow reserved for training equipment, and Don looked at them with some distaste.

"It's a couple of years since I used one of these things," he said to Franklin. "You'll probably be better at it than I am. When I get myself wet, I like to be under my own power."

They stripped to swim trunks and pull-overs, then fastened on the harness of their breathing equipment. Don picked up one of the small but surprisingly heavy plastic cylinders and handed it to Franklin.

"These are the high-pressure jobs that I told you about," he said. "They're pumped to a thousand atmospheres, so the air in them is denser than water. Hence these buoyancy tanks at either end to keep them in neutral. The automatic adjustment is pretty good; as you use up your air the tanks slowly flood so that the cylinder stays just about weightless. Otherwise you'd come up to the surface like a cork whether you wanted to or not."

He looked at the pressure gauges on the tanks and gave a satisfied nod.

"They're nearly half charged," he said. "That's far more than we need. You can stay down for a day on one of these tanks when it's really pumped up, and we won't be gone more than an hour."

They adjusted the new, full-face masks that had already been checked for leaks and comfortable fitting. These would be as much their personal property as their toothbrushes while they were on the station, for no two people's faces were exactly the same shape, and even the slightest leak could be disastrous.

When they had checked the air supply and the short-range underwater radio sets, they lay almost flat along the slim torpedoes, heads down behind the low, transparent shields which would protect them from the rush of water sweeping past at speeds of up to thirty knots. Franklin settled his feet comfortably in the stirrups, feeling for the throttle and jet reversal controls with his toes. The little joy stick which allowed him to "fly" the torpedo like a plane was just in front of his face, in the center of the instrument board. Apart from a few switches, the compass, and the meters giving speed, depth, and battery charge, there were no other controls.

Don gave Franklin his final instructions, ending with the words: "Keep about twenty feet away on my right, so that I can see you all the time. *If* anything goes wrong and you do have to dump the torp, for heaven's sake remember to cut the motor. We don't want it charging all over the reef. All set?"

"Yes—I'm ready," Franklin answered into his little microphone.

"Right—here we go."

The torpedoes slid easily down the ramps, and the water rose above their heads. This was no new experience to Franklin; like most other people in the world, he had occasionally tried his hand at underwater swimming and had sometimes used a lung just to see what it was like. He felt nothing but a pleasant sense of anticipation as the little turbine started to whir beneath him and the walls of the submerged chamber slid slowly past.

The light strengthened around them as they emerged into the open and pulled away from the piles of the jetty. Visibility was not very good—thirty feet at the most—but it would improve as they came to deeper water. Don swung his torpedo at right angles to the edge of the reef and headed out to sea at a leisurely five knots.

"The biggest danger with these toys," said Don's voice from the tiny loudspeaker by Franklin's ear, "is going too fast and running into something. It takes a lot of experience to judge underwater visibility. See what I mean?"

He banked steeply to avoid a towering mass of coral which had suddenly appeared ahead of them. If the demonstration had been planned, thought Franklin, Don had timed it beautifully. As the living mountain swept past, not more than ten feet away, he caught a glimpse of a myriad brilliantly colored fish staring at him with apparent unconcern. By this time, he assumed, they must be so used to torpedoes and subs that they were quite unexcited by them. And since this entire area was rigidly protected, they had no reason to fear man.

A few minutes at cruising speed brought them out into the open water of the channel between the island and the adjacent reefs. Now they had room to maneuver, and Franklin followed his mentor in a series of rolls and loops and great submarine switchbacks that soon had him hopelessly lost. Sometimes they shot down to the sea bed, a hundred feet below, then broke surface like flying fish to check their position. All the time Don kept up a running commentary, interspersed with questions designed to see how Franklin was reacting to the ride.

It was one of the most exhilarating experiences he had ever known. The water was much clearer out here in the channel, and one could see for almost a hundred feet. Once they ran into a great school of bonitos, which formed an inquisitive escort until Don put on speed and left them behind. They saw no sharks, as Franklin had half expected, and he commented to Don on their absence.

"You won't see many while you're riding a torp," the other replied. "The noise of the jet scares them. If you want to meet the local sharks, you'll have to go swimming in the old-fashioned way—or cut your motor and wait until they come to look at you."

A dark mass was looming indistinctly from the sea bed, and they reduced speed to a gentle drift as they approached a little range of coral hills, twenty or thirty feet high.

"An old friend of mine lives around here," said Don. "I wonder if he's home? It's been about four years since I saw him last, but that won't seem much to him. He's been around for a couple of centuries."

They were now skirting the edge of a huge green-clad mushroom of coral, and Franklin peered into the shadows beneath it. There were a few large boulders there, and a pair of elegant angelfish which almost disappeared when they turned edge on to him. But he could see nothing else to justify Burley's interest.

It was very unsettling when one of the boulders began to move, fortunately not in his direction. The biggest fish he had ever seen—it was almost as long as the torpedo, and very much fatter—was staring at him with great bulbous eyes. Suddenly it opened its mouth in a menacing yawn, and Franklin felt like Jonah at the big moment of his career. He had a glimpse of huge, blubbery lips enclosing surprisingly tiny teeth; then the great jaws snapped shut again and he could almost feel the rush of displaced water.

Don seemed delighted at the encounter, which had obviously brought back memories of his own days as a trainee here.

"Well, it's nice to see old Slobberchops again! Isn't he a beauty? Seven hundred and fifty pounds if he's an ounce. We've been able to identify him on photos taken as far back as eighty years ago, and he wasn't much smaller then. It's a wonder he escaped the spear fishers before this area was made a reservation."

"I should think," said Franklin, "that it was a wonder the spear fishers escaped him."

"Oh, he's not really dangerous. Groupers only swallow things they can get down whole—those silly little teeth aren't much good for biting. And a full-sized man would be a trifle too much for him. Give him another century for that."

They left the giant grouper still patrolling the entrance to its cave, and continued on along the edge of the reef. For the next ten minutes they saw nothing of interest except a large ray, which was lying on the bottom and took off with an agitated flapping of its wings as soon as they approached. As it flew away into the distance, it seemed an uncannily accurate replica of the big delta-winged aircraft which had ruled the air for a short while, sixty or seventy years ago. It was strange, thought Franklin, how Nature had anticipated so many of man's inventions—for example, the precise shape of the vehicle on which he was riding, and even the jet principle by which it was propelled.

"I'm going to circle right around the reef," said Don. "It will take us about forty minutes to get home. Are you feeling O.K.?"

"I'm fine."

"No ear trouble?"

"My left ear bothered me a bit at first, but it seems to have popped now."

"Right—let's go. Follow just above and behind me, so I can see you in my rearview mirror. I was always afraid of running into you when you were on my right."

In the new formation, they sped on toward the east at a steady ten knots, following the irregular line of the reef. Don was well satisfied with the trip; Franklin had seemed perfectly at home under water—though one could never be sure of this until one had seen how he faced an emergency. That would be part of the next lesson; Franklin did not know it yet, but an emergency had been arranged.

CHAPTER FOUR

It was hard to distinguish one day from another on the island. The weather had settled in for a period of prolonged calm, and the sun rose and set in a cloudless sky. But there was no danger of monotony, for there was far too much to learn and do.

Slowly, as his mind absorbed new knowledge and skills, Franklin was escaping from whatever nightmare must have engulfed him in the past. He was, Don sometimes thought, like an overtightened spring that was now unwinding. It was true that he still showed occasional signs of nervousness and impatience when there was no obvious cause for them, and once or twice there had been flare-ups that had caused brief interruptions in the training program. One of these had been partly Don's fault, and the memory of it still left him annoyed with himself.

He had not been too bright that morning, owing to a late night with the boys who had just completed their course and were now full-fledged third wardens (probationary), very proud of the silver dolphins on their tunics. It would not be true to say that he had a hangover, but all his mental processes were extremely sluggish, and as bad luck would have it they were dealing with a subtle point in underwater acoustics. Even at the best of times, Don would have passed it by somewhat hastily, with a lame: "I've never been into the math, but it seems that if you take the compressibility and temperature curves this is what happens. . . ."

This worked on most pupils, but it failed to work on Franklin, who had an annoying fondness for going into unnecessary details. He began to draw curves and to differentiate equations while Don, anxious to conceal his ignorance, fumed in the background. It was soon obvious that Franklin had bitten off more than he could chew, and he appealed to his tutor for assistance. Don, both stupid and stubborn that morning, would not admit frankly that he didn't know, with the result that he gave the impression of refusing to co-operate. In no time at all, Franklin lost his temper and walked out in a huff, leaving Don to wander to the dispensary. He was not pleased to find that the entire stock of "morning-after" pills had already been consumed by the departing class.

Fortunately, such incidents were rare, for the two men had grown to respect each other's abilities and to make those allowances that are essential in every partnership. With the rest of the staff, and with the trainees, however, Franklin was not popular. This was partly because he avoided close contacts, which in the little world of the island gave him a reputation for being standoffish. The trainees also resented his special privileges—particularly the fact that he had a room of his own. And the staff, while grumbling mildly at the extra work he involved, were also annoyed because they could discover so little about him. Don had several times found himself, rather to his surprise, defending Franklin against the criticisms of his colleagues.

"He's not a bad chap when you get to know him," he had said. "If he doesn't want to talk about his past, that's his affair. The fact that a lot of people way up in the administration must be backing him is good enough for me. Besides, when I've finished with him he'll be a better warden than half the people in this room."

There were snorts of disbelief at this statement, and someone asked: "Have you tried any tricks on him yet?"

"No, but I'm going to soon. I've thought up a nice one. Will let you know how he makes out."

"Five to one he panics."

"I'll take that. Start saving up your money."

Franklin knew nothing of his financial responsibilities when he and Don left the garage on their second torpedo ride, nor had he reason to suspect the entertainment that had been planned for him. This time they headed south as soon as they had cleared the jetty, cruising about thirty feet below the surface. In a few minutes they had passed the narrow channel blasted through the reef so that small ships could get in to the Research Station, and they circled once round the observation chamber from which the scientists could watch the inhabitants of the sea bed in comfort. There was no one inside at the moment to look out at them through the thick plate-glass windows; quite unexpectedly, Franklin found himself wondering what the little shark fancier was doing today.

"We'll head over to the Wistari Reef," said Don. "I want to give you some practice in navigation."

Don's torpedo swung round to the west as he set a new course, out into the deeper water. Visibility was not good today—less than thirty feet—and it was difficult to keep him in sight. Presently he halted and began to orbit slowly as he gave Franklin his instructions.

"I want you to hold course 250 for one minute at twenty knots, then 010 for the same time and speed. I'll meet you there. Got it?"

Franklin repeated the instructions and they checked the synchronization of their watches. It was rather obvious what Don was doing; he had given his pupil two sides of an equilateral triangle to follow, and would doubtless proceed slowly along the third to make the appointment.

Carefully setting his course, Franklin pressed down the throttle and felt the surge of power as the torpedo leaped forward into the blue haze. The steady rush of water against his partly exposed legs was almost the only sensation of speed; without the shield, he would have been swept away in a moment. From time to time he caught a glimpse of the sea bed—drab and featureless here in the channel between the great reefs—and once he overtook a school of surprised batfish which scattered in dismay at his approach.

For the first time, Franklin suddenly realized, he was alone beneath the sea, totally surrounded by the element which would be his new domain. It supported and protected him—yet it would kill him in two or three minutes at the most if he made a mistake or if his equipment failed. That knowledge did not disturb him; it had little weight against the increasing confidence and sense of mastery he was acquiring day by day. He now knew and understood the challenge of the sea, and it was a challenge he wished to meet. With a lifting of the heart, he realized that he once more had a goal in life.

The first minute was up, and he reduced speed to four knots with the reverse jet. He had now covered a third of a mile and it was time to start on the second leg of the triangle, to make his rendezvous with Don.

The moment he swung the little joy stick to starboard, he knew that something was wrong. The torpedo was wallowing like a pig, completely out of control. He cut speed to zero, and with all dynamic forces gone the vessel began to sink very slowly to the bottom.

Franklin lay motionless along the back of his recalcitrant steed, trying to analyze the situation. He was not so much alarmed as annoyed that his navigational exercise had been spoiled. It was no good calling Don, who would now be out of range—these little radio sets could not establish contact through more than a couple of hundred yards of water. What was the best thing to do?

Swiftly, his mind outlined alternative plans of action, and dismissed most of them at once. There was nothing he could do to repair the torp, for all the controls were sealed and, in any event, he had no tools. Since both rudder and elevator were out of action, the trouble was quite fundamental, and Franklin was unable to see how such a simultaneous breakdown could have happened.

He was now about fifty feet down, and gaining speed as he dropped to the bottom. The flat, sandy sea bed was just coming into sight, and for a moment Franklin had to fight the automatic impulse to press the button which would blow the torpedo's tanks and take him up to the surface. That would be the worst thing to do, natural though it was to seek air and sun when anything went wrong under water. Once on the bottom, he could take his time to think matters out, whereas if he surfaced the current might sweep him miles away. It was true that the station would soon pick up his radio calls once he was above water—but he wanted to extricate himself from this predicament without any outside help.

The torp grounded, throwing up a cloud of sand which soon drifted away in the slight current. A small grouper appeared from nowhere, staring at the intruder with its characteristic popeyed expression. Franklin had no time to bother with spectators, but climbed carefully off his vehicle and pulled himself to the stern. Without flippers, he had little mobility under water, but fortunately there were sufficient handholds for him to move along the torpedo without difficulty.

As Franklin had feared—but was still unable to explain—the rudder and elevator were flopping around uselessly. There was no resistance when he moved the little vanes by hand, and he wondered if there was any way in which he could fix external control lines and steer the torpedo manually. He had some nylon line, and a knife, in the pouch on his harness, but there seemed no practical way in which he could fasten the line to the smooth, streamlined vanes.

It looked as if he would have to walk home. That should not be too difficult—he could set the motor running at low speed and let the torp pull him along the bottom while he aimed it in the right direction by brute force. It would be clumsy, but seemed possible in theory, and he could think of nothing better.

He glanced at his watch; it had been only a couple of minutes since he had tried to turn at the leg of the triangle, so he was no more than a minute late at his destination. Don would not be anxious yet, but before long he would start searching for his lost pupil. Perhaps the best thing to do would be to stay right here until Don turned up, as he would be bound to do sooner or later. . . .

It was at this moment that suspicion dawned in Franklin's mind, and almost instantly became a full-fledged conviction. He recalled certain rumors he had heard, and remembered that Don's behavior before they set out had been—well, slightly skittish was the only expression for it, as if he had been cherishing some secret joke.

So that was it. The torpedo had been sabotaged. Probably at this very moment Don was hovering out there at the limits of visibility, waiting to see what he would do and ready to step in if he ran into real trouble. Franklin glanced quickly round his hemisphere of vision, to see if the other torp was lurking in the mist, but was not surprised that there was no sign of it. Burley would be too clever to be caught so easily. This, thought Franklin, changed the situation completely. He not only had to extricate himself from his dilemma, but, if possible, he had to get his own back on Don as well.

He walked back to the control position, and switched on the motor. A slight pressure on the throttle, and the torp began to stir restlessly while a flurry of sand was gouged out of the sea bed by the jet. A little experimenting showed that it was possible to "walk" the machine, though it required continual adjustments of trim to stop it from climbing up to the surface or burying itself in the sand. It was, thought Franklin, going to take him a long time to get home this way, but he could do it if there was no alternative.

He had walked no more than a dozen paces, and had acquired quite a retinue of astonished fish, when another idea struck him. It seemed too good to be true, but it would do no harm to try. Climbing onto the torpedo and lying in the normal prone position, he adjusted the trim as carefully as he could by moving his weight back and forth. Then he tilted the nose toward the surface, pushed his hands out into the slip stream on either side, and started the motor at quarter speed.

It was hard on his wrists, and his responses had to be almost instantaneous to check the weaving and bucking of the torpedo. But with a little experimenting, he found he could use his hands for steering, though it was as difficult as riding a bicycle with one's arms crossed. At five knots, the area of his flattened palms was just sufficient to give control over the vehicle.

He wondered if anyone had ever ridden a torp this way before, and felt rather pleased with himself. Experimentally, he pushed the speed up to eight knots, but the pressure on his wrists and forearms was too great and he had to throttle back before he lost control.

There was no reason, Franklin told himself, why he should not now make his original rendezvous, just in case Don was waiting there for him. He would be about five minutes late, but at least it would prove that he could carry out his assignment in the face of obstacles which he was now quite sure were entirely man-made.

Don was nowhere in sight when he arrived, and Franklin guessed what had happened. His unexpected mobility had taken Burley by surprise, and the warden had lost him in the submarine haze. Well, he could keep on looking. Franklin made one radio call as a matter of principle, but there was no reply from his tutor. "I'm going home!" he shouted to the watery world around him; still there was silence. Don was probably a good quarter of a mile away, conducting an increasingly more anxious search for his lost pupil.

There was no point in remaining below the surface and adding to the difficulties of navigation and control. Franklin took his vehicle up to the top and found that he was less than a thousand yards from the Maintenance Section jetty. By keeping the torp tail heavy and nose up he was able to scorch along on the surface like a speedboat without the slightest trouble, and he was home in five minutes.

As soon as the torpedo had come out of the anticorrosion sprays which were used on all equipment after salt-water dives, Franklin got to work on it. When he pulled off the panel of the control compartment, he discovered that his was a very special model indeed. Without a circuit diagram, it was not possible to tell exactly what the radio-operated relay unit he had located could do, but he did not doubt that it had an interesting repertory. It could certainly cut off the motor, blow or flood the buoyancy tanks, and reverse the rudder and elevator controls. Franklin suspected that compass and depth gauge could also be sabotaged if required. Someone had obviously spent a great deal of loving care making this torpedo a suitable steed for overconfident pupils. . . .

He replaced the panel and reported his safe return to the officer on duty. "Visibility's very poor," he said, truthfully enough. "Don and I lost each other out there, so I thought I'd better come in. I guess he'll be along later."

There was considerable surprise in the mess when Franklin turned up without his instructor and settled quietly down in a corner to read a magazine. Forty minutes later, a great slamming of doors announced Don's arrival. The warden's face was a study in relief and perplexity as he looked around the room and located his missing pupil, who stared back at him with his most innocent expression and said: "What kept you?"

Burley turned to his colleagues and held out his hand.

"Pay up, boys," he ordered.

It had taken him long enough to make up his mind, but he realized that he was beginning to like Franklin.

CHAPTER FIVE

The two men leaning on the rails around the main pool of the aquarium did not, thought Indra as she walked up the road to the lab, look like the usual run of visiting scientists. It was not until she had come closer and was able to get a good look at them that she realized who they were. The big fellow was First Warden Burley, so the other must be the famous mystery man he was taking through a high-pressure course. She had heard his name but couldn't remember it, not being particularly interested in the activities of the training school. As a pure scientist, she tended to look down on the highly practical work of the Bureau of Whales—though had anyone accused her outright of such intellectual snobbery she would have denied it with indignation.

She had almost reached them before she realized that she had already met the smaller man. For his part, Franklin was looking at her with a slightly baffled, "Haven't we seen each other before?" expression.

"Hello," she said, coming to a standstill beside them. "Remember me? I'm the girl who collects sharks."

Franklin smiled and answered: "Of course I remember: it still turns my stomach sometimes. I hope you found plenty of vitamins."

Yet strangely enough, the puzzled expression—so typical of a man straining after memories that will not come—still lingered in his eyes. It made him look lost and more than a little worried, and Indra found herself reacting with a sympathy, which was disconcerting. She had already had several narrow escapes from emotional entanglements on the island, and she reminded herself firmly of her resolution: "Not until *after* I've got my master's degree . . ."

"So you know each other," said Don plaintively. "You might introduce me." Don, Indra decided, was perfectly safe. He would start to flirt with her at once, like any warden worthy of his calling. She did not mind that in the least; though big leonine blonds were not precisely her type, it was always flattering to feel that one was causing a stir, and she knew that there was no risk of any serious attachment here. With Franklin, however, she felt much less sure of herself.

They chattered pleasantly enough, with a few bantering undertones, while they stood watching the big fish and porpoises circling slowly in the oval pool. The lab's main tank was really an artificial lagoon, filled and emptied twice a day by the tides, with a little assistance from a pumping plant. Wire-mesh barriers divided it into various sections through which mutually incompatible exhibits stared hungrily at each other; a small tiger shark, with the inevitable sucker fish glued to its back, kept patrolling its underwater cage, unable to take its eyes off the succulent pompano parading just outside. In some enclosures, however, surprising partnerships had developed. Brilliantly colored crayfish, looking like overgrown shrimps that had been sprayed with paint guns, crawled a few inches away from the incessantly gaping jaws of a huge and hideous moray eel. A school of fingerlings, like sardines that had escaped from their tin, cruised past the nose of a quarter-ton grouper that could have swallowed them all at one gulp.

It was a peaceful little world, so different from the battlefield of the reef. But if the lab staff ever failed to make the normal feeding arrangements, this harmony would quickly vanish and in a few hours the population of the pool would start a catastrophic decline.

Don did most of the talking; he appeared to have quite forgotten that he had brought Franklin here to see some of the whale-recognition films in the lab's extensive library. He was clearly trying to impress Indra, and quite unaware of the fact that she saw through him completely. Franklin, on the other hand, obviously saw both sides of the game and was mildly entertained by it. Once, Indra caught his eye, when Don was holding forth about the life and hard times of the average warden, and they exchanged the smiles of two people who share the same amusing secret. And at that moment Indra decided that, after all, her degree might not be the most important thing in the world. She was still determined not to get herself involved—but she had to learn more about Franklin. What was his first name? Walter. It was not one of her favorites, but it would do.

In his calm confidence that he was laying waste another susceptible female heart, Don was completely unaware of the undercurrents of emotion that were sweeping around him yet leaving him utterly untouched. When he suddenly realized that they were twenty minutes late for their appointment in the projection room, he pretended to blame Franklin, who accepted the reproof in a good-natured but slightly absent-minded manner. For the rest of the morning, indeed, Franklin was rather far away from his studies; but Don noticed nothing at all.

The first part of the course was now virtually completed; Franklin had learned the basic mechanics of the warden's profession and now needed the experience that only time would give. In almost every respect, he had exceeded Burley's hopes, partly because of his original scientific training, partly because of his innate intelligence. Yet there was more to it even than this; Franklin had a drive and determination that was sometimes frightening. It was as if success in this course was a matter of life and death to him. True, he had been slow in starting; for the first few days he had been listless and seemingly almost uninterested in his new career. Then he had come to life, as he awoke to the wonder and challenge—the endless opportunity—of the element he was attempting to master. Though Don was not much given to such fancies, it seemed to him that Franklin was like a man awakening from a long and troubled sleep.

The real test had been when they had first gone under water with the torpedoes. Franklin might never use a torp again—except for amusement—during his entire career; they were purely shallow-water units designed for very short-range work, and as a warden, Franklin would spend all his operational time snug and dry behind the protective walls of a sub. But unless a man was at ease and confident—though not overconfident—when he was actually immersed in water, the service had no use for him, however qualified he might be in other respects.

Franklin had also passed, with a satisfactory safety margin, the decompression, CO_2, and nitrogen narcosis tests. Burley had put him in the station's "torture chamber," where the doctors slowly increased the air pressure and took him down on a simulated dive. He had been perfectly normal down to 150 feet; thereafter his mental reactions became sluggish and he failed to do simple sums correctly when they were given to him over the intercom. At 300 feet he appeared to be mildly drunk and started cracking jokes which reduced him to tears of helpless laughter but which were quite unfunny to those outside—and embarrassingly so to Franklin himself when they played them back to him later. Three hundred and fifty feet down he still appeared to be conscious but refused to react to Don's voice, even when it started shouting outrageous insults. And at 400 feet he passed out completely, and they brought him slowly back to normal.

Though he would never have occasion to use them, he was also tested with the special breathing mixtures which enable a man to remain conscious and active at far greater depths. When he did any deep dives, he would not be wearing underwater breathing gear but would be sitting comfortably inside a sub breathing normal air at normal pressure. But a warden had to be a Jack of all underwater trades, and never knew what equipment he might have to use in an emergency.

Burley was no longer scared—as he had once been—at the thought of sharing a two-man training sub with Franklin. Despite the other's underlying reticence and the mystery which still surrounded him, they were partners now and knew how to work together. They had not yet become friends, but had reached a state which might be defined as one of tolerant respect.

On their first sub run, they kept to the shallow waters between the Great Barrier Reef and the mainland, while Franklin familiarized himself with the control, and above all with the navigational instruments. If you could run a sub here, said Don, in this labyrinth of reefs and islands, you could run it anywhere. Apart from trying to charge Masthead Island at sixty knots, Franklin performed quite creditably. His fingers began to move over the complex control board with a careful precision which, Don knew, would soon develop into automatic skill. His scanning of the many meters and display screens would soon be unconscious, so that he would not even be aware that he saw them—until something called for his attention.

Don gave Franklin increasingly more complicated tasks to perform, such as tracing out improbable courses by dead reckoning and then checking his position on the sonar grid to see where he had actually arrived. It was not until he was quite sure that Franklin was proficient in handling a sub that they finally went out into deep water over the edge of the continental shelf.

Navigating a Scoutsub was merely the beginning; one had to learn to see and feel with its senses, to interpret all the patterns of information displayed on the control board by the many instruments which were continually probing the underwater world. The sonic senses were perhaps, the most important. In utter darkness, or in completely turbid water, they could detect all obstacles out to a range of ten miles, with great accuracy and in considerable detail. They could show the contours of the ocean bed, or with equal ease could detect any fish more than two or three feet long that came within half a mile. Whales and the larger marine animals they could spot right out to the extreme limit of range, fixing them with pinpoint accuracy.

Visible light had a more limited role. Sometimes, in deep ocean waters far from the eternal rain of silt which sloughs down from the edges of the continents, it was possible to see as much as two hundred feet—but that was rare. In shallow coastal waters, the television eye could seldom peer more than fifty feet, but within its range it gave a definition unmatched by the sub's other senses.

Yet the subs had not only to see and feel; they also had to act. Franklin must learn to use a whole armory of tools and weapons: borers to collect specimens of the sea bed, meters to check the efficiency of the fences, sampling devices, branders for painlessly marking un-co-operative whales, electric probes to discourage marine beasts that became too inquisitive—and, most seldom used of all, the tiny torpedoes and poisoned darts that could slay in seconds the mightiest creatures of the seas.

In daily cruises far out into the Pacific, Franklin learned to use these tools of his new trade. Sometimes they went through the fence, and it seemed to Franklin that he could feel its eternal high-pitched shrieking in his very bones. Halfway around the world it now extended, its narrow fans of radiation reaching up to the surface from the deeply submerged generators.

What, wondered Franklin, would earlier ages have thought of this? In some ways it seemed the greatest and most daring of all man's presumptions. The sea, which had worked its will with man since the beginning of time, had been humbled at last. Not even the conquest of space had been a greater victory than this.

And yet—it was a victory that could never be final. The sea would always be waiting, and every year it would claim its victims. There was a roll of honor that Franklin had glimpsed briefly during his visit to the head office. Already it bore many names, and there was room for many more.

Slowly, Franklin was coming to terms with the sea, as must all men who have dealings with it. Though he had had little time for nonessential reading, he had dipped into *Moby Dick,* which had been half-jokingly, half-seriously called the bible of the Bureau of Whales. Much of it had seemed to him tedious, and so far removed from the world in which he was living that it had no relevance. Yet occasionally Melville's archaic, sonorous prose touched some chord in his own mind, and gave him a closer understanding of the ocean which he, too, must learn to hate and love.

Don Burley, however, had no use at all for *Moby Dick* and frequently made fun of those who were always quoting it.

"We could show Melville a thing or two!" he had once remarked to Franklin, in a very condescending tone.

"Of course we could," Franklin had answered. "But would you have the guts to stick a spear into a sperm whale from an open boat?"

Don did not reply. He was honest enough to admit that he did not know the answer.

Yet there was one question he was now close to answering. As he watched Franklin learn his new skills, with a swiftness which could undoubtedly make him a first warden in no more than four or five years, he knew with complete certainty what his pupil's last profession had been. If he chose to keep it a secret, that was his own affair. Don felt a little aggrieved by such lack of trust; but sooner or later, he told himself, Franklin would confide in him.

Yet it was not Don who was the first to learn the truth. By the sheerest of accidents, it was Indra.

CHAPTER SIX

They now met at least once a day in the mess, though Franklin had not yet made the irrevocable, almost unprecedented, step of moving from his table to the one at which the research staff dined. That would be a flamboyant declaration which would set every tongue on the island wagging happily, and in any case it would not be justified by the circumstances. As far as Indra and Franklin were concerned, the much-abused phrase "we're just friends" was still perfectly true.

Yet it was also true that they had grown very fond of each other, and that almost everyone except Don was aware of it. Several of Indra's colleagues had said to her approvingly, "You're thawing out the iceberg," and the compliment had flattered her. The few people who knew

Franklin well enough to banter with him had made warning references to Don, pointing out that first wardens had reputations to maintain. Franklin's reaction had been a somewhat forced grin, concealing feelings which he could not fully analyze himself.

Loneliness, the need to escape from memories, a safety valve to guard him against the pressure under which he was working—these factors were at least as important as the normal feelings of any man for a girl as attractive as Indra. Whether this companionship would develop into anything more serious, he did not know. He was not even sure if he wished it to do so.

Nor, for her part, was Indra, though her old resolve was weakening. Sometimes she indulged in reveries wherein her career took very much of a second place. One day, of course, she was going to marry, and the man she would choose would be very much like Franklin. But that it might *be* Franklin was a thought from which she still shied away.

One of the problems of romance on Heron Island was that there were far too many people in too small a space. Even the fragment that was left of the original forest did not provide enough seclusion. At night, if one wandered through its paths and byways, carrying a flashlight to avoid the low-hanging branches, one had to be very tactful with the beam. One was liable to find that favorite spots had already been requisitioned, which would be extremely frustrating if there was nowhere else to go.

The fortunate scientists at the Research Station, however, had an invaluable escape route. All the large surface craft and all the underwater vessels belonged to Administration, though they were made available to the lab for official business. But by some historical accident, the lab had a tiny private fleet consisting of one launch and two catamarans. No one was quite sure who owned the latter, and it was noticeable that they were always at sea when the auditors arrived for the annual inventory.

The little cats did a great deal of work for the lab, since they drew only six inches of water and could operate safely over the reef except at low tide. With a stiff wind behind them, they could do twenty knots with ease, and races between the two craft were frequently arranged. When they were not being used for other business, the scientists would sail them to the neighboring reefs and islands to impress their friends—usually of the opposite sex—with their prowess as seamen.

It was a little surprising that ships and occupants had always come back safely from these expeditions. The only casualties had been to morale; one first warden of many years seniority had had to be carried off the boat after a pleasure trip, and had sworn that nothing would ever induce him to travel on the *surface* of the sea again.

When Indra suggested to Franklin that he might like to sail to Masthead Island, he accepted at once. Then he said cautiously: "Who'll run the boat?"

Indra looked hurt.

"I will, of course," she answered. "I've done it dozens of times." She seemed to be half-expecting him to doubt her competence, but Franklin knew better than to do so. Indra, he had already discovered, was a very levelheaded girl—perhaps too levelheaded. If she said she could do a job, that was that.

There was still, however, one other point to be settled. The cats could take four people; who would the other two be?

Neither Indra nor Franklin actually voiced the final decision. It hovered in the air while they discussed various possible companions, starting with Don and working down the list of Indra's friends at the lab. Presently the conversation died out into one of those portentous pauses which can sometimes occur even in a roomful of chattering people.

In the sudden silence, each realized that the other was thinking the same thought, and that a new phase had begun in their relationship. They would take no one with them to Masthead; for the first time, they would have the solitude that had never been possible here. That this could lead only to one logical conclusion they refused to admit, even to themselves, the human mind having a remarkable capacity for self-deceit.

It was well into the afternoon before they were able to make all their arrangements and escape. Franklin felt very guilty about Don, and wondered what his reactions would be when he found out what had happened. He would probably be mortified, but he was not the sort to hold a grudge and he would take it like a man.

Indra had thought of everything. Food, drinks, sunburn lotion, towels—she had overlooked nothing that such an expedition might need. Franklin was impressed by her thoroughness, and was amused to find himself thinking that so competent a woman would be very useful to have around the house. Then he reminded himself hastily that women who were too efficient were seldom happy unless they ran their husbands' lives as well as their own.

There was a steady wind blowing from the mainland, and the cat bounded across the waves like a living creature. Franklin had never before been in a sailing boat, and he found the experience an exhilarating one. He lay back on the worn but comfortable padding of the open cockpit, while Heron Island receded into the distance at an astonishing speed. It was restful to watch the twin, creamy wakes trace their passage across the sea, and to caress with the eye the straining, power-filled curves of the sails. With a mild and fleeting regret, Franklin wished that all man's machines could be as simple and efficient as this one. What a contrast there was between this vessel and the crowded complexities of the subs he was now learning to handle! The thought passed swiftly; there were some tasks which could not be achieved by simple means, and one must accept the fact without complaint.

On their left, they were now skirting the long line of rounded coral boulders which centuries of storms had cast up upon the edge of the Wistari Reef. The waves were breaking against the submerged ramparts with a relentless and persistent fury which had never impressed Franklin so much as now. He had seen them often enough before—but never from so close at hand, in so frail a craft.

The boiling margin of the reef fell astern; now they had merely to wait while the winds brought them to their goal. Even if the wind failed—which was most unlikely—they could still make the trip on the little auxiliary hydrojet engine, though that would only be used as a last resort. It was a matter of principle to return with a full fuel tank.

Although they were now together and alone for almost the first time since they had met, neither Franklin nor Indra felt any need to talk. There seemed a silent communion between them which they did not wish to break with words, being content to share the peace and wonder of the open sea and the open sky. They were enclosed between two hemispheres of flawless blue, clamped together at the misty rim of the horizon, and nothing else of the world remained. Even time seemed to have faltered to a stop; Franklin felt he could lie here forever, relaxing in the gentle motion of the boat as it skimmed effortlessly over the waves.

Presently a low, dark cloud began to solidify, then to reveal itself as a tree-clad island with its narrow sandy shore and inevitable fringing reef. Indra bestirred herself and began to take an active interest in navigation once more, while Franklin looked rather anxiously at the breakers which seemed to surround the island in one continuous band.

"How are we going to get in?" he asked.

"Round the lee side; it won't be rough there, and the tide should be high enough for us to go in across the reef. If it isn't, we can always anchor and wade ashore."

Franklin was not altogether happy about so casual an approach to what seemed a serious problem, and he could only hope that Indra really did know what she was doing. If she made a mistake, they might have an uncomfortable though not particularly dangerous swim ahead, followed after a long wait by an ignominious rescue when someone came from the lab to look for them.

Either it was easier than it appeared to an anxious novice, or else Indra's seamanship was of a high order. They circled halfway around the island, until they came to a spot where the breakers subsided into a few choppy waves. Then Indra turned the prow of the cat toward the land, and headed straight for shore.

There were no sounds of grinding coral or splintering plastic. Like a bird, the catamaran flew in across the narrow edge of the reef, now clearly visible just below the broken and unsettled water. It skimmed past this danger zone, and then was over the peaceful surface of the lagoon, seeming to gain speed as it approached the beach. Seconds before impact, Indra furled the mainsail. With a soft thud, the vessel hit the sand and coasted up the gentle slope, coming to rest with more than half its length above the water line.

"Here we are," said Indra. "One uninhabited coral island, in full working order." She seemed more relaxed and lighthearted than Franklin had ever before seen her; he realized that she, too, had been working under pressure and was glad to escape from the daily routine for a few hours. Or was it the stimulating effect of his company that was turning her from a serious student into a vivacious girl? Whatever the explanation, he liked the change.

They climbed out of the boat and carried their gear up the beach into the shade of the coconut palms, which had been imported into these islands only during the last century to challenge the predominance of the Pisonia and the stilt-rooted pandanus. It seemed that someone else had also been here recently, for curious tracks apparently made by narrow-gauge caterpillar treads marched up out of the water and vanished inland. They would have been quite baffling to anyone who did not know that the big turtles had been coming ashore to lay their eggs.

As soon as the cat had been made secure, Franklin and Indra began a tour of exploration. It was true that one coral island was almost exactly the same as another; the same pattern was repeated endlessly over and over again, with few variations. Yet even when one was aware of that, and had landed on dozens of islands, every new one presented a fresh challenge which had to be accepted.

They began the circumnavigation of their little world, walking along the narrow belt of sand between the forest and the sea. Sometimes, when they came to a clearing, they made short forays inland, deliberately trying to lose themselves in the tangle of trees so that they could pretend that they were in the heart of Africa and not, at the very most, a hundred yards from the sea.

Once they stopped to dig with their hands at the spot where one of the turtle tracks terminated on a flat-ended sand dune. They gave up when they were two feet down and there was still no sign of the leathery, flexible eggs. The mother turtle, they solemnly decided, must have been making false trails to deceive her enemies. For the next ten minutes, they elaborated this fantasy into a startling thesis on reptile intelligence, which, far from gaining Indra new qualifications, would undoubtedly have cost her the degree she already possessed.

Inevitably the time came when, having helped each other over a patch of rough coral, their hands failed to separate even though the path was smooth once more. Neither speaking, yet each more conscious of the other's presence than they had ever been before, they walked on in the silence of shared contentment.

At a leisurely stroll, pausing whenever they felt like it to examine some curiosity of the plant or animal world, it took them almost two hours to circumnavigate the little island. By the time they had reached the cat they were very hungry, and Franklin began to unpack the food hamper with unconcealed eagerness while Indra started working on the stove.

"Now I'm going to brew you a billy of genuine Australian tea," she said.

Franklin gave her that twisted, whimsical smile which she found so attractive.

"It will hardly be a novelty to me," he said. "After all, I was born here."

She stared at him in astonishment which gradually turned to exasperation. "Well, you might have told me!" she said. "In fact, I really think—" Then she stopped, as if by a deliberate effort of will, leaving the uncompleted sentence hanging in mid-air. Franklin had no difficulty in finishing it. She had intended to say, "It's high time you told me something about yourself, and abandoned all this silly reticence."

The truth of the unspoken accusation made him flush, and for a moment some of his carefree happiness—the first he had known for so many months—drained away. Then a thought struck him which he had never faced before, since to do so might have jeopardized his friendship with Indra. She was a scientist and a woman, and therefore doubly inquisitive. Why was it that she had never asked him any questions about his past life? There could be only one explanation. Dr. Myers, who was unobtrusively watching over him despite the jovial pretense that he was doing nothing of the sort, must have spoken to her.

A little more of his contentment ebbed as he realized that Indra must feel sorry for him and must wonder, like everyone else, exactly what had happened to him. He would not, he told himself bitterly, accept a love that was founded on pity.

Indra seemed unaware of his sudden brooding silence and the conflict that now disturbed his mind. She was busy filling the little stove by a somewhat primitive method that involved siphoning fuel out of the hydrojet's tank, and Franklin was so amused by her repeated failures that he forgot his momentary annoyance. When at last she had managed to light the stove, they lay back under the palms, munching sandwiches and waiting for the water to boil. The sun was already far down the sky, and Franklin realized that they would probably not get back to Heron Island until well after nightfall. However, it would not be dark, for the moon was nearing full, so even without the aid of the local beacons the homeward journey would present no difficulties.

The billy-brewed tea was excellent, though doubtless far too anemic for any old-time swagman. It washed down the remainder of their food very efficiently, and as they relaxed with sighs of satisfaction their hands once again found each other. Now, thought Franklin, I should be perfectly content. But he knew that he was not; something that he could not define was worrying him.

His unease had grown steadily stronger during the last few minutes, but he had tried to ignore it and force it down into his mind. He knew that it was utterly ridiculous and irrational to expect any danger here, on this empty and peaceful island. Yet little warning bells were ringing far down in the labyrinths of his brain, and he could not understand their signals.

Indra's casual question came as a welcome distraction. She was staring intently up into the western sky, obviously searching for something.

"Is it really true, Walter," she asked, "that if you know where to look for her you can see Venus in the daytime? She was so bright after sunset last night that I could almost believe it."

"It's perfectly true," Franklin answered. "In fact, it isn't even difficult. The big problem is to locate her in the first place; once you've done that, she's quite easy to see."

He propped himself up against a palm trunk, shaded his eyes from the glare of the descending sun, and began to search the western sky with little hope of discovering the elusive silver speck he knew to be shining there. He had noticed Venus dominating the evening sky during the last few weeks, but it was hard to judge how far she was from the sun when both were above the horizon at the same time.

Suddenly—unexpectedly—his eyes caught and held a solitary silver star hanging against the milky blue of the sky. "I've found her!" he exclaimed, raising his arm as a pointer. Indra squinted along it, but at first could see nothing.

"You've got spots before the eyes," she taunted.

"No—I'm not imagining things. Just keep on looking," Franklin answered, his eyes still focused on the dimensionless star which he knew he would lose if he turned away from it even for a second.

"But Venus *can't* be there," protested Indra. "That's much too far north."

In a single, sickening instant Franklin knew that she was right. If he had any doubt, he could see now that the star he was watching was moving swiftly across the sky, rising out of the west and so defying the laws which controlled all other heavenly bodies.

He was staring at the Space Station, the largest of all the satellites now circling Earth, as it raced along its thousand-mile-high orbit. He tried to turn his eyes away, to break the hypnotic spell of that man-made, unscintillating star. It was as if he was teetering on the edge of an abyss; the terror of those endless, trackless wastes between the worlds began to invade and dominate his mind, to threaten the very foundations of his sanity.

He would have won the struggle, no more than a little shaken, had it not been for a second accident of fate. With the explosive suddenness with which memory sometimes yields to persistent questioning, he knew what it was that had been worrying him for the last few minutes. It was the smell of the fuel that Indra had siphoned from the hydrojet—the unmistakable, slightly aromatic tang of synthene. And crowding hard upon that recognition was the memory of where he had last met that all-too-familiar odor.

Synthene—first developed as a rocket propellant—now obsolete like all other chemical fuels, except for low-powered applications like the propulsion of space suits.

Space suits.

It was too much; the double assault defeated him. Both sight and smell had turned traitor in the same instant. Within seconds, the patiently built dikes which now protected his mind went down before the rising tide of terror.

He could feel the Earth beneath him spinning dizzily through space. It seemed to be whirling faster and faster on its axis, trying to hurl him off like a stone from a sling by the sheer speed of its rotation. With a choking cry, he rolled over on his stomach, buried his face in the sand, and clung desperately to the rough trunk of the palm. It gave him no security; the endless fall began again. . . . Chief Engineer Franklin, second in command of the *Arcturus,* was in space once more, at the beginning of the nightmare he had hoped and prayed he need never retrace.

CHAPTER SEVEN

In the first shock of stunned surprise, Indra sat staring foolishly at Franklin as he groveled in the sand and wept like a heartbroken child. Then compassion and common sense told her what to do; she moved swiftly to his side and threw her arms around his heaving shoulders.

"Walter!" she cried. "You're all right—there's nothing to be afraid of!"

The words seemed flat and foolish even as she uttered them, but they were the best she had to offer. Franklin did not seem to hear; he was still trembling uncontrollably, still clinging to the tree with desperate determination. It was pitiful to see a man reduced to such a state of abject fear, so robbed of all dignity and pride. As Indra crouched over him, she realized that between his sobs he was calling a name—and even at such a moment as this she could not depress a stab of jealousy. For it was the name of a woman; over and over again, in a voice so low as to be barely audible, Franklin would whisper "Irene!" and then be convulsed by a fresh paroxysm of weeping.

There was something here beyond Indra's slight knowledge of medicine. She hesitated for a moment, then hurried to the catamaran and broke open its little first-aid kit. It contained a vial of potent pain-killing capsules, prominently labeled ONLY ONE TO BE TAKEN AT ANY TIME, and with some difficulty she managed to force one of these into Franklin's mouth. Then she held him in her arms while his tremors slowly subsided and the violence of the attack ebbed away.

It is hard to draw any line between compassion and love. If such a division exists, Indra crossed it during this silent vigil. Franklin's loss of manhood had not disgusted her; she knew that something terrible indeed must have happened in his past to bring him to this state. Whatever it was, her own future would not be complete unless she could help him fight it.

Presently Franklin was quiet, though apparently still conscious. He did not resist when she rolled him over so that his face was no longer half-buried in the sand, and he relaxed his frenzied grip upon the tree. But his eyes were empty, and his mouth still moved silently though no words came from it.

"We're going home," whispered Indra, as if soothing a frightened child. "Come along—it's all right now."

She helped him to his feet, and he rose unresistingly. He even assisted her, in a mechanical way, to pack their equipment and to push the catamaran off the beach. He seemed nearly normal again, except that he would not speak and there was a sadness in his eyes that tore at Indra's heart.

They left the island under both sail and power, for Indra was determined to waste no time. Even now it had not occurred to her that she might be in any personal danger, so many miles from any help, with a man who might be mad. Her only concern was to get Franklin back to medical care as quickly as she could.

The light was failing fast; the sun had already touched the horizon and darkness was massing in the east. Beacons on the mainland and the surrounding islands began, one by one, to spring to life. And, more brilliant than any of them, there in the west was Venus, which had somehow caused all this trouble. . . .

Presently Franklin spoke, his words forced but perfectly rational. "I'm very sorry about this, Indra," he said. "I'm afraid I spoiled your trip."

"Don't be silly," she answered. "It wasn't your fault. Just take it easy—don't talk unless you want to." He relapsed into silence, and spoke no more for the rest of the voyage. When Indra reached out to hold his hand again, he stiffened defensively in a way which said, without actually rejecting her, that he would prefer no such contact. She felt hurt, but obeyed his unspoken request. In any event, she was busy enough picking out the beacons as she made the tricky passage between the reefs.

She had not intended to be out as late as this, even though the rising moon was now flooding the sea with light. The wind had freshened, and all too close at hand the breakers along the Wistari Reef were appearing and vanishing in deadly lines of luminous, ghostly white. She kept one eye on them, and the other on the winking beacon that marked the end of the Heron jetty. Not until she could see the jetty itself and make out the details of the island was she able to relax and give her attention once more to Franklin.

He appeared almost normal again when they had berthed the catamaran and walked back to the lab. Indra could not see his expression, for there were no lights here on this part of the beach, and the palms shaded them from the moon. As far as she could tell, his voice was under full control when he bade her good night.

"Thank you for everything, Indra. No one could have done more."

"Let me take you to Dr. Myers right away. You've got to see him."

"No—there's nothing he can do. I'm quite all right now—it won't happen again."

"I still think you should see him. I'll take you to your room and then go and call him."

Franklin shook his head violently.

"That's one thing I don't want you to do. Promise me you won't call him."

Sorely troubled, Indra debated with her conscience. The wisest thing to do, she was sure, was to make the promise—and then to break it. Yet if she did so, Franklin might never forgive her. In the end, she compromised.

"Will you go and see him yourself, if you won't let me take you?"

Franklin hesitated before answering. It seemed a shame that his parting words with this girl, whom he might have loved, should be a lie. But in the drugged calm that had come upon him now he knew what he must do.

"I'll call him in the morning—and thanks again." Then he broke away, with a fierce finality, before Indra could question him further.

She watched him disappear into the darkness, along the path that led to the training and administration section. Happiness and anxiety were contending for her soul—happiness because she had found love, anxiety because it was threatened by forces she did not understand. The anxiety resolved itself into a single nagging fear: Should she have insisted, even against his will, that Franklin see Dr. Myers at once?

She would have had no doubt of the answer could she have watched Franklin double back through the moonlit forest and make his way, like a man in a waking dream, to the dock from which had begun all his journeys down into the sea.

The rational part of his mind was now merely the passive tool of his emotions, and they were set upon a single goal. He had been hurt too badly for reason to control him now; like an injured animal, he could think of nothing but the abating of his pain. He was seeking the only place where for a little while he had found peace and contentment.

The jetty was deserted as he made the long, lonely walk out to the edge of the reef. Down in the submarine hangar, twenty feet below the water line, he made his final preparations with as much care as he had ever done on his many earlier trips. He felt a fleeting sense of guilt at robbing the bureau of some fairly valuable equipment and still more valuable training time; but it was not his fault that he had no other choice.

Very quietly, the torp slipped out beneath the submerged archway and set course for the open sea. It was the first time that Franklin had ever been out at night; only the fully enclosed subs operated after darkness, for night navigation involved dangers which it was foolhardy for unprotected men to face. That was the least of Franklin's worries as he set the course he remembered so well and headed out into the channel that would lead him to the sea.

Part of the pain, but none of the determination, lifted from his mind. This was where he belonged; this was where he had found happiness. This was where he would find oblivion.

He was in a world of midnight blue which the pale rays of the moon could do little to illumine. Around him strange shapes moved like phosphorescent ghosts, as the creatures of the reef were attracted or scattered by the sound of his passing. Below him, no more than shadows in a deeper darkness, he could see the coral hills and valleys he had grown to know so well. With a resignation beyond sadness, he bade them all adieu.

There was no point in lingering, now that his destiny was clear before him. He pushed the throttle full down, and the torpedo leaped forward like a horse that had been given the spur. The islands of the Great Barrier Reef were falling swiftly behind him, and he was heading out into the Pacific at a speed which no other creature of the sea could match.

Only once did he glance up at the world he had abandoned. The water was fantastically clear, and a hundred feet above his head he could see the silver track of the moon upon the sea, as few men could ever have witnessed it before. He could even see the hazy, dancing patch of light that was the moon itself, refracted through the water surface yet occasionally freezing, when the moving waves brought a moment of stability, into a perfect, flawless image.

And once a very large shark—the largest he had ever seen—tried to pursue him. The great streamlined shadow, leaving its phosphorescent wake, appeared suddenly almost dead ahead of him, and he made no effort to avoid it. As it swept past he caught a glimpse of the inhuman, staring eye, the slatted gills, and the inevitable retinue of pilot fish and remora. When he glanced back the shark was following him—whether motivated by curiosity, sex, or hunger he neither knew nor cared. It remained in sight for almost a minute before his superior speed left it behind. He had never met a shark that had reacted in this way before; usually they were terrified of the turbine's warning scream. But the laws that ruled the reef during the day were not those that prevailed in the hours of darkness.

He raced on through the luminous night that covered half the world, crouching behind his curved shield for protection against the turbulent waters he was sundering in his haste to reach the open sea. Even now he was navigating with all his old skill and precision; he knew exactly where he was, exactly when he would reach his objective—and exactly how deep were the waters he was now entering. In a few minutes, the sea bed would start slanting sharply down and he must say his last farewell to the reef.

He tilted the nose of the torp imperceptibly toward the depths and at the same time cut his speed to a quarter. The mad, roaring rush of waters ceased; he was sliding gently down a long, invisible slope whose end he would never see.

Slowly the pale and filtered moonlight began to fade as the water thickened above him. Deliberately, he avoided looking at the illuminated depth gauge, avoided all thought of the fathoms that now lay overhead. He could feel the pressure on his body increasing minute by minute, but it was not in the least unpleasant. Indeed, he welcomed it; he gave himself, a willing sacrifice, gladly into the grasp of the great mother of life.

The darkness was now complete. He was alone, driving through a night stranger and more palpable than any to be found upon the land. From time to time he could see, at an unguessable distance below him, tiny explosions of light as the unknown creatures of the open sea went about their mysterious business. Sometimes an entire, ephemeral galaxy would thrust forth and within seconds die; perhaps that other galaxy, he told himself, was of no longer duration, of no greater importance, when seen against the background of eternity.

The dreamy sleep of nitrogen narcosis was now almost upon him; no other human being, using a compressed-air lung alone, could ever have been so deep and returned to tell the tale. He was breathing air at more than ten times normal pressure, and still the torpedo was boring down into the lightless depths. All responsibility, all regrets, all fears had been washed away from his mind by the blissful euphoria that had invaded every level of consciousness.

And yet, at the very end, there was one regret. He felt a mild and wistful sadness that Indra must now begin again her search for the happiness he might have given her.

Thereafter there was only the sea, and a mindless machine creeping ever more slowly down to the hundred-fathom line and the far Pacific wastes.

CHAPTER EIGHT

There were four people in the room, and not one of them was talking now. The chief instructor was biting his lip nervously, Don Burley sat looking stunned, and Indra was trying not to cry. Only Dr. Myers seemed fairly well under control, and was silently cursing the fantastic, the still inexplicable bad luck that had brought this situation upon them. He would have sworn that Franklin was well on the road to recovery, well past any serious crisis. And now this!

"There's only one thing to do," said the chief instructor suddenly. "And that's to send out all our underwater craft on a general search."

Don Burley stirred himself, slowly and as if carrying a great weight upon his shoulders.

"It's twelve hours now. In that time he could have covered five hundred miles. And there are only six qualified pilots on the station."

"I know—it would be like looking for a needle in a haystack. But it's the only thing we can do."

"Sometimes a few minutes of thought can save a good many hours of random searching," said Myers. "After half a day, a little extra time will make no difference. With your permission, I'd like to have a private talk with Miss Langenburg."

"Of course—if she agrees."

Indra nodded dumbly. She was still blaming herself bitterly for what had happened—for not going to the doctor immediately when they had returned to the island. Her intuition had failed her then; now it told her that there was no possibility of any hope, and she could only pray that it was wrong again.

"Now, Indra," said Myers kindly when the others had left the room, "if we want to help Franklin we've got to keep our heads, and try to guess what he's done. So stop blaming yourself—this isn't your fault. I'm not sure if it's anyone's fault."

It might be mine, he added grimly to himself. But who could have guessed? We understand so little about astrophobia, even now . . . and heaven knows it's not in my line.

Indra managed a brave smile. Until yesterday, she had thought she was very grown-up and able to take care of herself in any situation. But yesterday was a very, very long time ago.

"Please tell me," she said, "what is the matter with Walter. I think it would help me to understand."

It was a sensible and reasonable request; even before Indra had made it, Myers had come to the same conclusion.

"Very well—but remember, this is confidential, for Walter's own sake. I'm only telling it to you because this is an emergency and you may be able to help him if you know the facts.

"Until a year ago, Walter was a highly qualified spaceman. In fact, he was chief engineer of a liner on the Martian run, which as you know is a very responsible position indeed, and that was certainly merely the beginning of his career.

"Well, there was some kind of emergency in mid-orbit, and the ion drive had to be shut off. Walter went outside in a space suit to fix it—nothing unusual about that, of course. Before he had finished the job, however, his suit failed. No—I don't mean it leaked. What happened was that the propulsion system jammed *on,* and he couldn't shut off the rockets that allowed him to move around in space.

"So there he was, millions of miles from anywhere, building up speed away from his ship. To make matters worse, he'd crashed against some part of the liner when he started, and that had snapped off his radio antenna. So he couldn't talk or receive messages—couldn't call for help or find out what his friends were doing for him. He was completely alone, and in a few minutes he couldn't even see the liner.

"Now, no one who has not been in a situation like that can possibly imagine what it's like. We can try, but we can't really picture being absolutely isolated, with stars all around us, not knowing if we'll ever be rescued. No vertigo that can ever be experienced on Earth can match it—not even seasickness at its worst, and that's bad enough.

"It was four hours before Walter was rescued. He was actually quite safe, and probably knew it—but that didn't make any difference. The ship's radar had tracked him, but until the drive was repaired it couldn't go after him. When they did get him aboard he was—well, let's say he was in a pretty bad way.

"It took the best psychologists on Earth almost a year to straighten him out, and as we've seen, the job wasn't finished properly. And there was one factor that the psychologists could do nothing about."

Myers paused, wondering how Indra was taking all this, how it would affect her feelings toward Franklin. She seemed to have got over her initial shock; she was not, thank God, the hysterical type it was so difficult to do anything with.

"You see, Walter was married. He had a wife and family on Mars, and was very fond of them. His wife was a second-generation colonist, the children, of course, third-generation ones. They had spent all their lives under Martian gravity—had been conceived and born in it. And so they could never come to Earth, where they would be crushed under three times their normal weight.

"At the same time, Walter could never go back into space. We could patch up his mind so that he could function efficiently here on Earth, but that was the best we could do. He could never again face free fall, the knowledge that there was space all around him, all the way out to the stars. And so he was an exile on his own world, unable ever to see his family again.

"We did our best for him, and I still think it was a good best. This work here could use his skills, but there were also profound psychological reasons why we thought it might suit him, and would enable him to rebuild his life. I think you probably know those reasons as well as I do, Indra—if not better. You are a marine biologist and know the links we have with the sea. We have no such links with space, and so we shall never feel at home there—at least as long as we are men.

"I studied Franklin while he was here; he knew I was doing it, and didn't mind. All the while he was improving, getting to love the work. Don was very pleased with his progress—he was the best pupil he'd ever met. And when I heard—don't ask me how!—that he was going around with you, I was delighted. For he has to rebuild his life all along the line, you know. I hope you don't mind me putting it this way, but when I found he was spending his spare time with you, and even making time to do it, I knew he had stopped looking back.

"And now—this breakdown. I don't mind admitting that I'm completely in the dark. You say that you were looking up at the Space Station, but that doesn't seem enough cause. Walter had a rather bad fear of heights when he came here, but he'd largely got over that. Besides, he must have seen the station dozens of times in the morning or evening. There must have been some other factor we don't know."

Dr. Myers stopped his rapid delivery, then said gently, as if the thought had only just struck him: "Tell me, Indra—had you been making love?"

"No," she said without hesitation or embarrassment. "There was nothing like that."

It was a little hard to believe, but he knew it was the truth. He could detect—so clear and unmistakable!—the note of regret in her voice.

"I was wondering if he had any guilt feelings about his wife. Whether he knows it or not, you probably remind him of her, which is why he was attracted to you in the first place. Anyway, *that* line of reasoning isn't enough to explain what happened, so let's forget it.

"All we know is that there was an attack, and a very bad one. Giving him that sedative was the best thing you could have done in the circumstances. You're *quite* sure that he never gave any indication of what he intended to do when you got him back to Heron?"

"Quite sure. All he said was, 'Don't tell Dr. Myers.' He said there was nothing you could do."

That, thought Myers grimly, might well be true, and he did not like the sound of it. There was only one reason why a man might hide from the only person who could help him. That was because he had decided he was now beyond help.

"But he promised," Indra continued, "to see you in the morning."

Myers did not reply. By this time they both knew that that promise had been nothing more than a ruse.

Indra still clung desperately to one last hope.

"Surely," she said, her voice quavering as if she did not really believe her own words, "if he'd intended to do—something drastic—he'd have left a message for somebody."

Myers looked at her sadly, his mind now completely made up.

"His parents are dead," he replied. "He said good-by to his wife long ago. What message was there for him to leave?"

Indra knew, with a sickening certainty, that he spoke the truth. She might well be the only person on Earth for whom Franklin felt any affection. And he had made his farewell with her. . . .

Reluctantly, Myers rose to his feet.

"There's nothing we can do," he said, "except to start a general search. There may be a chance that he's just blowing off steam at full throttle, and will creep in shame-faced some time this morning. It's happened before."

He patted Indra's bowed shoulders, then helped her out of the chair. "Don't be too upset, my dear. Everyone will do his best." But in his heart he knew it was too late. It had been too late hours before, and they were going through the motions of search and rescue because there were times when no one expected logic to be obeyed.

They walked together to the assistant chief instructor's office, where the C.I. and Burley were waiting for them. Dr. Myers threw open the door—and stood paralyzed on the threshold. For a moment he thought that he had two more patients—or that he had gone insane himself. Don and the chief instructor, all distinctions of rank forgotten, had their arms around each other's shoulders and were shaking with hysterical laughter. There was no doubt of the hysteria; it was that of relief. And there was equally no doubt about the laughter.

Dr. Myers stared at this improbable scene for perhaps five seconds, then glanced swiftly around the room. At once he saw the message form lying on the floor where one of his temporarily disordered colleagues had dropped it. Without asking their permission, he rushed forward and picked it up.

He had to read it several times before it made any sense; then he, too, began to laugh as he had not done for years.

✶ *CHAPTER NINE*

Captain Bert Darryl was looking forward to a quiet trip; if there was any justice in this world, he was certainly due for one. Last time there had been that awkward affair with the cops at Mackay; the time before there had been that uncharted rock off Lizard Island; and before *that,* by crikey, there'd been that trigger-happy young fool who had used a nondetachable harpoon on a fifteen-foot tiger and had been towed all over the sea bed.

As far as one could tell by appearances, his customers seemed a reasonable lot this time. Of course, the Sports Agency always guaranteed their reliability as well as their credit—but all the same it was surprising what he sometimes got saddled with. Still, a man had to earn a living, and it cost a lot to keep this old bucket waterproof.

By an odd coincidence, his customers always had the same names—Mr. Jones, Mr. Robinson, Mr. Brown, Mr. Smith. Captain Bert thought it was a crazy idea, but that was just another of the agency's little ways. It certainly made life interesting, trying to figure out who they really were. Some of them were so cautious that they wore rubber face masks the whole trip—yes, even under their diving masks. They would be the important boys who were scared of being recognized. Think of the scandal, for instance, if a supreme court judge or chief secretary of the Space

Department was found poaching on a World Food reservation! Captain Bert thought of it, and chuckled.

The little five-berth sports cruiser was still forty miles off the outer edge of the reef, feeling her way in from the Pacific. Of course, it was risky operating so near the Capricorns, right in enemy territory as it were. But the biggest fish were here, just because they were the best protected. You had to take a chance if you wanted to keep your clients satisfied. . . .

Captain Bert had worked out his tactics carefully, as he always did. There were never any patrols out at night, and even if there were, his long-range sonar would spot them and he could run for it. So it would be perfectly safe creeping up during darkness, getting into position just before dawn, and pushing his eager beavers out of the air lock as soon as the sun came up. He would lie doggo on the bottom, keeping in touch through the radios. If they got out of range, they'd still have his low-powered sonar beacon to home on. And if they got too far away to pick up *that,* serve 'em jolly well right. He patted his jacket where the four blood chits reposed safely, absolving him of all responsibility if anything happened to Messrs. Smith, Jones, Robinson, or Brown. There were times when he wondered if it was really any use, considering these weren't their real names, but the agency told him not to worry. Captain Bert was not the worrying type, or he would have given up this job long ago.

At the moment, Messrs. S., J., R., and B. were lying on their respective couches, putting the final touches to the equipment they would not need until morning. Smith and Jones had brand-new guns that had obviously never been fired before, and their webbing was fitted with every conceivable underwater gadget. Captain Bert looked at them sardonically; they represented a type he knew very well. They were the boys who were so keen on their equipment that they never did any shooting, either with the guns or their cameras. They would wander happily around the reef, making such a noise that every fish within miles would know exactly what they were up to. Their beautiful guns, which could drill a thousand-pound shark at fifty feet, would probably never be fired. But they wouldn't really mind; they would enjoy themselves.

Now Robinson was a very different matter. His gun was slightly dented, and about five years old. It had seen service, and he obviously knew how to handle it. He was not one of those catalogue-obsessed sportsmen who had to buy the current year's model as soon as it came out, like a woman who couldn't bear to be behind the fashion. Mr. Robinson, Captain Bert decided, would be the one who would bring back the biggest catch.

As for Brown—Robinson's partner—he was the only one that Captain Bert hadn't been able to classify. A well-built, strong-featured man in the forties, he was the oldest of the hunters and his face was vaguely familiar. He was probably some official in the upper echelons of the state, who had felt the need to sow a few wild oats. Captain Bert, who was constitutionally unable to work for the World State or any other employer, could understand just how he felt.

There were more than a thousand feet of water below them, and the reef was still miles ahead. But one never took anything for granted in this business, and Captain Bert's eyes were seldom far from the dials and screens of the control board, even while he watched his little crew preparing for their morning's fun. The clear and tiny echo had barely appeared on the sonar scanner before he had fastened on to it.

"Big shark coming, boys," he announced jovially. There was a general rush to the screen.

"How do you know it's a shark?" someone asked.

"Pretty sure to be. Couldn't be a whale—they can't leave the channel inside the reef."

"Sure it's not a sub?" said one anxious voice.

"Naow. Look at the size of it. A sub would be ten times as bright on the screen. Don't be a nervous Nelly."

The questioner subsided, duly abashed. No one said anything for the next five minutes, as the distant echo closed in toward the center of the screen.

"It'll pass within a quarter of a mile of us," said Mr. Smith. "What about changing course and seeing if we can make contact?"

"Not a hope. He'll run for it as soon as he picks up our motors. If we stopped still he might come and sniff us over. Anyway, what would be the use? You couldn't get at him. It's night and he's well below the depth where you could operate."

Their attention was momentarily distracted by a large school of fish—probably tuna, the captain said—which appeared on the southern sector of the screen. When that had gone past, the distinguished-looking Mr. Brown said thoughtfully: "Surely a shark would have changed course by now."

Captain Bert thought so too, and was beginning to be puzzled. "Think we'll have a look at it," he said. "Won't do any harm."

He altered course imperceptibly; the strange echo continued on its unvarying way. It was moving quite slowly, and there would be no difficulty in getting within visual distance without risk of collision. At the point of nearest approach, Captain Bert switched on the camera and the U.V. searchlight—and gulped.

"We're rumbled, boys. It's a cop."

There were four simultaneous gasps of dismay, then a chorus of "But you told us . . ." which the captain silenced with a few well-chosen words while he continued to study the screen.

"Something funny here," he said. "I was right first time. That's no sub—it's only a torp. So it can't detect us, anyway—they don't carry that kind of gear. But what the hell's it doing out here at night?"

"Let's run for it!" pleaded several anxious voices.

"Shurrup!" shouted Captain Bert. "Let me think." He glanced at the depth indicator. "Crikey," he muttered, this time in a much more subdued voice. "We're a hundred fathoms down. Unless that lad's breathing some fancy mixture, he's had it."

He peered closely at the image on the TV screen; it was hard to be certain, but the figure strapped to the slowly moving torp seemed abnormally still. Yes—there was no doubt of it; he could tell from the attitude of the head. The pilot was certainly unconscious, probably dead.

"This is a bloody nuisance," announced the skipper, "but there's nothing else to do. We've got to fetch that guy in."

Someone started to protest, then thought better of it. Captain Bert was right, of course. The later consequences would have to be dealt with as they arose.

"But how are you going to do it?" asked Smith. "We can't go outside at this depth."

"It won't be easy," admitted the captain. "It's lucky he's moving so slowly. I think I can flip him over."

He nosed in toward the torp, making infinitely delicate adjustments with the controls. Suddenly there was a clang that made everybody jump except the skipper, who knew when it was coming and exactly how loud it would be.

He backed away, and breathed a sigh of relief.

"Made it first time!" he said smugly. The torp had rolled over on its back, with the helpless figure of its rider now dangling beneath it in his harness. But instead of heading down into the depths, it was now climbing toward the distant surface.

They followed it up to the two-hundred-foot mark while Captain Bert gave his detailed instructions. There was still a chance, he told his passengers, that the pilot might be alive. But if he reached the surface he'd certainly be dead—compression sickness would get him as he dropped from ten atmospheres to one.

"So we've got to haul him in around the hundred-and-fifty-foot level —no higher—and then start staging him in the air lock. Well, who's going to do it? *I* can't leave the controls."

No one doubted that the captain was giving the single and sufficient reason, and that he would have gone outside without hesitation had there been anyone else aboard who could operate the sub. After a short pause, Smith said: "I've been three hundred feet down on normal air."

"So have I," interjected Jones. "Not at night, of course," he added thoughtfully.

They weren't exactly volunteering, but it would do. They listened to the skipper's instructions like men about to go over the top, then put on their equipment and went reluctantly into the air lock.

Fortunately, they were in good training and he was able to bring them up to the full pressure in a couple of minutes. "O.K., boys," he said. "I'm opening the door—here you go!"

It would have helped them could they have seen his searchlight, but it had been carefully filtered to remove all visible light. Their hand torches were feeble glowworms by comparison, as he watched them moving across to the still-ascending torp. Jones went first, while Smith played out the line from the air lock. Both vessels were moving faster than a man could swim, and it was necessary to play Jones like a fish on a line so that as he trailed behind the sub he could work his way across to the torpedo. He was probably not enjoying it, thought the skipper, but he managed to reach the torp on the second try.

After that, the rest was straightforward. Jones cut out the torp's motor, and when the two vessels had come to a halt Smith went to help him. They unstrapped the pilot and carried him back to the sub; his face mask was unflooded, so there was still hope for him. It was not easy to manhandle his helpless body into the tiny air lock, and Smith had to stay outside, feeling horribly lonely, while his partner went ahead.

And thus it was that, thirty minutes later, Walter Franklin woke in a surprising but not totally unfamiliar environment. He was lying in a bunk aboard a small cruiser-class sub, and five men were standing around him. Oddest of all, four of the men had handkerchiefs tied over their faces so that he could only see their eyes. . . .

He looked at the fifth man—at his scarred and grizzled countenance and his rakish goatee. The dirty nautical cap was really quite superfluous; no one would have doubted that this was the skipper.

A raging headache made it hard for Franklin to think straight. He had to make several attempts before he could get out the words: "Where am I?"

"Never you mind, mate," replied the bearded character. "What *we* want to know is what the hell were you doing at a hundred fathoms with a standard compressed-air set. Crikey, he's fainted again!"

The second time Franklin revived, he felt a good deal better, and sufficiently interested in life to want to know what was going on around him. He supposed he should be grateful to these people, whoever they were, but at the moment he felt neither relief nor disappointment at having been rescued.

"What's all this for?" he said, pointing to the conspiratorial handkerchiefs. The skipper, who was now sitting at the controls, turned his head and answered laconically: "Haven't you worked out where you are yet?"

"No."

"Mean ter say you don't know who *I* am?"

"Sorry—I don't."

There was a grunt that might have signified disbelief or disappointment.

"Guess you must be one of the new boys. I'm Bert Darryl, and you're on board the *Sea Lion*. Those two gentlemen behind you risked their necks getting you in."

Franklin turned in the direction indicated, and looked at the blank triangles of linen.

"Thanks," he said, and then stopped, unable to think of any further comment. Now he knew where he was, and could guess what had happened.

So this was the famous—or notorious, depending on the point of view—Captain Darryl, whose advertisements you saw in all the sporting and marine journals. Captain Darryl, the organizer of thrilling underwater safaris; the intrepid and skillful hunter—and the equally intrepid and skillful poacher, whose immunity from prosecution had long been a source of cynical comment among the wardens. Captain Darryl—one of the few genuine adventurers of this regimented age, according to some. Captain Darryl, the big phony, according to others. . . .

Franklin now understood why the rest of the crew was masked. This was one of the captain's less legitimate enterprises, and Franklin had heard that on these occasions his customers were often from the very highest ranks of society. No one else could afford to pay his fees; it must cost a lot to run the *Sea Lion,* even though Captain Darryl was reputed never to pay cash for anything and to owe money at every port between Sydney and Darwin.

Franklin glanced at the anonymous figures around him, wondering who they might be and whether he knew any of them. Only a halfhearted effort had been made to hide the powerful big-game guns piled on the other bunk. Just where was the captain taking his customers, and what were they after? In the circumstances, he had better keep his eyes shut and learn as little as possible.

Captain Darryl had already come to the same conclusion.

"You realize, mate," he said over his shoulder as he carefully blocked Franklin's view of the course settings, "that your presence aboard is just a little bit embarrassing. Still, we couldn't let you drown, even though you deserved it for a silly stunt like that. The point is—what are we going to do with you now?"

"You could put me ashore on Heron. We can't be very far away." Franklin smiled as he spoke, to show how seriously he intended the suggestion to be taken. It was strange how cheerful and lighthearted he now felt; perhaps it was a merely physical reaction—and perhaps he was really glad at having been given a second chance, a new lease on life.

"What a hope!" snorted the captain. "These gentlemen have paid for their day's sport, and they don't want you boy scouts spoiling it."

"They can take off those handkerchiefs, anyway. They don't look very comfortable—and if I recognize someone, I won't give him away."

Rather reluctantly, the disguises were removed. As he had expected—and hoped—there was no one here whom he knew, either from photographs or direct contact.

"Only one thing for it," said the captain. "We'll have to dump you somewhere before we go into action." He scratched his head as he reviewed his marvelously detailed mental image of the Capricorn Group, then came to a decision. "Anyway, we're stuck with you for tonight, and I guess we'll have to sleep in shifts. If you'd like to make yourself useful, you can get to work in the galley."

"Aye, aye, sir," said Franklin.

The dawn was just breaking when he hit the sandy beach, staggered to his feet, and removed his flippers. ("They're my second-best pair, so mind you post them back to me," Captain Bert had said as he pushed him through the air lock.) Out there beyond the reef, the *Sea Lion* was departing on her dubious business, and the hunters were getting ready for their sortie. Though it was against his principles and his duties, Franklin could not help wishing them luck.

Captain Bert had promised to radio Brisbane in four hours' time, and the message would be passed on to Heron Island immediately. Presumably that four hours would give the captain and his clients the time they needed to make their assault and to get clear of W.F.O. waters.

Franklin walked up the beach, stripped off his wet equipment and clothes, and lay down to watch the sunrise he had never dreamed he would see. He had four hours to wait, to wrestle with his thoughts and face life once more. But he did not need the time, for he had made the decision hours ago.

His life was no longer his to throw away if he chose; not when it had been given back to him, at the risk of their own, by men he had never met before and would never see again.

CHAPTER TEN

"You realize, of course," said Myers, "that I'm only the station doctor, not a high-powered psychiatrist. So I'll have to send you back to Professor Stevens and his merry men."

"Is that really necessary?" asked Franklin.

"I don't think it is, but I can't accept the responsibility. If I was a gambler like Don, I'd take very long odds that you'll never play this trick again. But doctors can't afford to gamble, and anyway I think it would be a good idea to get you off Heron for a few days."

"I'll finish the course in a couple of weeks. Can't it wait until then?"

"Don't argue with doctors, Walt—you can't win. And if my arithmetic is correct, a month and a half is *not* a couple of weeks. The course can wait for a few days; I don't think Prof Stevens will keep you very long. He'll probably give you a good dressing-down and will send you straight back. Meanwhile, if you're interested in my views, I'd like to get 'em off my chest."

"Go ahead."

"First of all, we know *why* you had that attack when you did. Smell is the most evocative of all the senses, and now that you've told me that a spaceship air lock always smells of synthene the whole business makes sense. It was hard luck that you got a whiff of the stuff just when you were looking at the Space Station: the damn thing's nearly hypnotized me sometimes when I've watched it scuttling across the sky like some mad meteor.

"But that isn't the whole explanation, Walter. You had to be, let's say, emotionally sensitized to make you susceptible. Tell me—have you got a photograph of your wife here?"

Franklin seemed more puzzled than disturbed by the unexpected, indeed apparently incongruous, question.

"Yes," he said. "Why do you ask?"

"Never mind. May I have a look at it?"

After a good deal of searching, which Myers was quite sure was unnecessary, Franklin produced a leather wallet and handed it over. He did not look at Myers as the doctor studied the woman who was now parted from her husband by laws more inviolable than any that man could make.

She was small and dark, with lustrous brown eyes. A single glance told Myers all that he wanted to know, yet he continued to gaze at the photograph with an unanalyzable mixture of compassion and curiosity. How, he wondered, was Franklin's wife meeting her problem? Was she, too, rebuilding her life on that far world to which she was forever bound by genetics and gravity? No, forever was not quite accurate. She could safely journey to the Moon, which had only half the gravity of her native world. But there would be no purpose in doing so, for Franklin could never face even the trifling voyage from Earth to Moon.

With a sigh, Dr. Myers closed the wallet. Even in the most perfect of social systems, the most peaceful and contented of worlds, there would still be heartbreak and tragedy. And as man extended his powers over the universe, he would inevitably create new evils and new problems to plague him. Yet, apart from its details, there was nothing really novel about this case. All down the ages, men had been separated—often forever—from those they loved by the accident of geography or the malice of their fellows.

"Listen, Walt," said Myers as he handed back the wallet. "I know a few things about you that even Prof Stevens doesn't, so here's my contribution.

"Whether you realize it consciously or not, Indra is like your wife. That, of course, is why you were attracted to her in the first place. At the same time, that attraction has set up a conflict in your mind. You don't want to be unfaithful even to someone—please excuse me for speaking so bluntly—who might as well be dead as far as you are concerned. Well—do you agree with my analysis?"

Franklin took a long time to answer. Then he said at last: "I think there may be something in that. But what am I to do?"

"This may sound cynical, but there is an old saying which applies in this case. 'Co-operate with the inevitable.' Once you admit that certain aspects of your life are fixed and have to be accepted, you will stop fighting against them. It won't be a surrender; it will give you the energy you need for the battles that still have to be won."

"What does Indra really think about me?"

"The silly girl's in love with you, if that's what you want to know. So the least you can do is to make it up to her for all the trouble you've caused."

"Then do you think I should marry again?"

"The fact that you can ask that question is a good sign, but I can't answer it with a simple 'yes' or 'no.' We've done our best to rebuild your professional life; we can't give you so much help with your emotional one. Obviously, it's highly desirable for you to establish a firm and stable relationship to replace the one you have lost. As for Indra—well, she's a charming and intelligent girl, but no one can say how much of her present feelings are due to sympathy. So don't rush matters; let them take their time. You can't afford to make any mistakes.

"Well, that finishes the sermon—except for one item. Part of the trouble with you, Walter Franklin, is that you've always been too independent and self-reliant. You refused to admit that you had limitations, that you needed help from anyone else. So when you came up against something that was too big for you, you really went to pieces, and you've been hating yourself for it ever since.

"Now that's all over and done with; even if the old Walt Franklin was a bit of a stinker, we can make a better job of the Mark II. Don't you agree?"

Franklin gave a wry smile; he felt emotionally exhausted, yet at the same time most of the remaining shadows had lifted from his mind. Hard though it had been for him to accept help, he had surrendered at last and he felt better for it.

"Thanks for the treatment, Doc," he said. "I don't believe the specialists could do any better, and I'm quite sure now that this trip back to Prof Stevens isn't necessary."

"So am I—but you're going just the same. Now clear out and let me get on with my proper work of putting sticking plaster on coral cuts."

Franklin was halfway through the door when he paused with a sudden, anxious query.

"I almost forgot—Don particularly wants to take me out tomorrow in the sub. Will that be O.K.?"

"Oh, sure—Don's big enough to look after you. Just get back in time for the noon plane, that's all I ask."

As Franklin walked away from the office and two rooms grandly called "Medical Center" he felt no resentment at having been ordered off the island. He had received far more tolerance and consideration than he had expected—perhaps more than he deserved. All the mild hostility that had been focused upon him by the less-privileged trainees had vanished at a stroke, but it would be best for him to escape for a few days from an atmosphere that had become embarrassingly sympathetic. In particular, he found it hard to talk without a sense of strain with Don and Indra.

He thought again of Dr. Myers' advice, and remembered the jolting leap his heart had given at the words "the silly girl's in love with you." Yet it would be unfair, he knew, to take advantage of the present emotional situation; they could only know what they meant to each other when they had both had time for careful and mature thought. Put that way, it seemed a little cold-blooded and calculating. If one was really in love, did one stop to weigh the pros and cons?

He knew the answer to that. As Myers had said, he could not afford any more mistakes. It was far better to take his time and be certain than to risk the happiness of two lives.

The sun had barely lifted above the miles of reef extending to the east when Don Burley hauled Franklin out of bed. Don's attitude toward him had undergone a change which it was not easy to define. He had been shocked and distressed by what had occurred and had tried, in his somewhat boisterous manner, to express sympathy and understanding. At the same time, his *amour-propre* had been hurt; he could not quite believe, even now, that Indra had never been seriously interested in him but only in Franklin, whom he had never thought of as a rival. It was not that he was jealous of Franklin; jealousy was an emotion beyond him. He was worried—as most men are occasionally throughout their lives—by his discovery that he did not understand women as well as he had believed.

Franklin had already packed, and his room looked bleak and bare. Even though he might be gone for only a few days, the accommodation was needed too badly for it to be left vacant just to suit his convenience. It served him right, he told himself philosophically.

Don was in a hurry, which was not unusual, but there was also a conspiratorial air about him, as if he had planned some big surprise for Franklin and was almost childishly anxious that everything should come off as intended. In any other circumstances, Franklin would have suspected some practical joke, but that could hardly be the explanation now.

By this time, the little training sub had become practically an extension of his own body, and he followed the courses Don gave him until he knew, by mental dead reckoning, that they were somewhere out in the thirty-mile-wide channel between Wistari Reef and the mainland. For some reason of his own, which he refused to explain, Don had switched off the pilot's main sonar screen, so that Franklin was navigating blind. Don himself could see everything that was in the vicinity by looking at the repeater set at the rear of the cabin, and though Franklin was occasionally tempted to glance back at it he managed to resist the impulse. This was, after all, a legitimate part of his training; one day he might have to navigate a sub that had been blinded by a breakdown of its underwater senses.

"You can surface now," said Don at last. He was trying to be casual, but the undercurrent of excitement in his voice could not be concealed. Franklin blew the tanks, and even without looking at the depth gauge knew when he broke surface by the unmistakable rolling of the sub. It was not a comfortable sensation, and he hoped that they would not stay here for long.

Don gave one more glance at his private sonar screen, then gestured to the hatch overhead.

"Open up," he said. "Let's have a look at the scenery."

"We may ship some water," protested Franklin. "It feels pretty rough."

"With the two of us in that hatch, not much is going to leak past. Here—put on this cape. That'll keep the spray out of the works."

It seemed a crazy idea, but Don must have a good reason. Overhead, a tiny elliptical patch of sky appeared as the outer seal of the conning tower opened. Don scrambled up the ladder first; then Franklin followed, blinking his eyes against the wind-swept spray.

Yes, Don had known what he was doing. There was little wonder that he had been so anxious to make this trip before Franklin left the island. In his own way, Don was a good psychologist, and Franklin felt an inexpressible gratitude toward him. For this was one of the great moments of his life; he could think of only one other to match it: the moment when he had first seen Earth, in all its heart-stopping beauty, floating against the infinitely distant background of the stars. This scene, also, filled his soul with the same awe, the same sense of being in the presence of cosmic forces.

The whales were moving north, and he was among them. During the night, the leaders must have passed through the Queensland Gate, on the way to the warm seas in which their young could be safely born. A living armada was all around him, plowing steadfastly through the waves with effortless power. The great dark bodies emerged streaming from the water, then sank with scarcely a ripple back into the sea. As Franklin watched, too fascinated to feel any sense of danger, one of the enormous beasts surfaced less than forty feet away. There was a roaring whistle of air as it emptied its lungs, and he caught a mercifully weakened breath of the fetid air. A ridiculously tiny eye stared at him—an eye that seemed lost in the monstrous, misshapen head. For a moment the two mammals—the biped who had abandoned the sea, the quadruped who had returned to it—regarded each other across the evolutionary gulf that separated them. What did a man look like to a whale? Franklin asked himself, and wondered if there was any way of finding the answer. Then the titanic bulk tilted down into the sea, the great flukes lifted themselves into the air, and the waters flowed back to fill the sudden void.

A distant clap of thunder made him look toward the mainland. Half a mile away, the giants were playing. As he watched, a shape so strange that it was hard to relate it to any of the films and pictures he had seen emerged from the waves with breath-taking slowness, and hung poised for a moment completely out of the water. As a ballet dancer seems at the climax of his leap to defy gravity, so for an instant the whale appeared to hang upon the horizon. Then, with that same unhurried grace, it tumbled back into the sea, and seconds later the crash of the impact came echoing over the waves.

The sheer slowness of that huge leap gave it a dreamlike quality, as if the sense of time had been distorted. Nothing else conveyed so clearly to Franklin the immense size of the beasts that now surrounded him like moving islands. Rather belatedly, he wondered what would happen if one of the whales surfaced beneath the sub, or decided to take too close an interest in it. . . .

"No need to worry," Don reassured him. "They know who we are. Sometimes they'll come and rub against us to remove parasites, and then it gets a bit uncomfortable. As for bumping into us accidentally—they can see where they're going a good deal better than we can."

As if to refute this statement, a streamlined mountain emerged dripping from the sea and showered water down upon them. The sub rocked crazily, and for a moment Franklin feared it was going to overturn; then it righted itself, and he realized that he could, quite literally, reach out and touch the barnacle-encrusted head now lying on the waves. The weirdly shaped mouth opened in a prodigious yawn, the hundreds of strips of whalebone fluttering like a Venetian blind in a breeze.

Had he been alone, Franklin would have been scared stiff, but Don seemed the complete master of the situation. He leaned out of the hatch and yelled in the direction of the whale's invisible ear: "Move over momma! We're not your baby!"

The great mouth with its hanging draperies of bone snapped shut, the beady little eye—strangely like a cow's and seemingly not much larger—looked at them with what might have been a hurt expression. Then the sub rocked once more, and the whale was gone.

"It's quite safe, you see," Don explained. "They're peaceful, good-natured beasts, except when they have their calves with them. Just like any other cattle."

"But would you get this close to any of the toothed whales—the sperm whale, for instance?"

"That depends. If it was an old rogue male—a real Moby Dick—I wouldn't care to try it. Same with killer whales; they might think I was good eating, though I could scare them off easily enough by turning on the hooter. I once got into a harem of about a dozen sperm whales, and the ladies didn't seem to mind, even though some of them had calves with them. Nor did the old man, oddly enough. I suppose he knew I wasn't a rival." He paused thoughtfully, then continued. "That was the only time I've actually seen whales mating. It was pretty awe-inspiring—gave me such an inferiority complex it put me off my stroke for a week."

"How many would you say there are in this school?" asked Franklin.

"Oh, about a hundred. The recorders at the gate will give the exact figure. So you can say there are at least five thousand tons of the best meal and oil swimming around us—a couple of million dollars, if it's worth a penny. Doesn't all that cash make you feel good?"

"No," said Franklin. "And I'm damn sure it doesn't make any difference to you. Now I know why you like this job, and there's no need to put on an act about it."

Don made no attempt to answer. They stood together in the cramped hatchway, not feeling the spray upon their faces, sharing the same thoughts and emotions, as the mightiest animals the world had ever seen drove purposefully past them to the north. It was then that Franklin knew, with a final certainty, that his life was firmly set upon its new course. Though much had been taken from him which he would never cease to regret, he had passed the stage of futile grief and solitary brooding. He had lost the freedom of space, but he had won the freedom of the seas.

That was enough for any man.

CHAPTER ELEVEN

CONFIDENTIAL—TO BE KEPT IN SEALED ENEVELOPE

Attached is the medical report on Walter Franklin, who has now successfully completed his training and has qualified as third warden with the highest rating ever recorded. In view of certain complaints from senior members of Establishment and Personnel Branch that earlier reports were too technical for comprehension, I am giving this summary in language understandable even to administrative officers.

Despite a number of personality defects, W.F.'s capability rating places him in that small group from which future heads of technical departments must be drawn—a group so desperately small that, as I have frequently pointed out, the very existence of the state is threatened unless we can enlarge it. The accident which eliminated W.F. from the Space Service, in which he would have undoubtedly had a distinguished career, left him in full possession of all his talents and presented us with an opportunity which it would have been criminal to waste. Not only did it give us a chance of studying what has since become the classic textbook case of astrophobia, but it offered us a striking challenge in rehabilitation. The analogies between sea and space have often been pointed out, and a man used to one can readily adapt to the other. In this case, however, the differences between the two media were equally important; at the simplest level, the fact that the sea is a continuous and sustaining fluid, in which vision is always limited to no more than a few yards, gave W.F. the sense of security he had lost in space.

The fact that, toward the end of his training, he attempted suicide may at first appear to argue against the correctness of our treatment. This is not the case; the attempt was due to a combination of quite unforeseeable factors (Paragraphs 57–86 of attached report), and its outcome, as often happens, was an improvement in the stability of the subject. The method chosen for the attempt is also highly significant in itself and proves that we had made a correct choice of W.F.'s new vocation. The seriousness of the attempt may also be questioned; had W.F. been really determined to kill himself, he would have chosen a simpler and less fallible method of doing so.

Now that the subject has re-established—apparently successfully—his emotional life and has shown only trivial symptoms of disturbance, I am confident that we need expect no more trouble. Above all, it is important that we interfere with him as little as possible. His independence and originality of mind, though no longer as exaggerated as they were, are a fundamental part of his personality and will largely determine his future progress.

Only time will show whether all the skill and effort lavished on this case will be repaid in cents and dollars. Even if it is not, those engaged upon it have already received their reward in the rebuilding of a life, which will certainly be useful and may be invaluable.

Ian K. Stevens
Director, Division of Applied Psychiatry,
World Health Organization

Part II · The Warden

CHAPTER TWELVE

Second Warden Walter Franklin was having his monthly shave when the emergency call came through. It had always seemed a little surprising to him that, after so many years of research, the biochemists had not yet found an inhibitor that would put one's bristles permanently out of action. Still, one should not be ungrateful; only a couple of generations ago, incredible though it seemed, men had been forced to shave themselves every day, using a variety of complicated, expensive, and sometimes lethal instruments.

Franklin did not stop to wipe the layer of cream from his face when he heard the shrill whining of the communicator alarm. He was out of the bathroom, through the kitchen, and into the hall before the sound had died away and the instrument had been able to get its second breath. As he punched the Receive button, the screen lighted up and he was looking into the familiar but now harassed face of the Headquarters operator.

"You're to report for duty at once, Mr. Franklin," she said breathlessly.

"What's the trouble?"

"It's Farms, sir. The fence is down somewhere and one of the herds has broken through. It's eating the spring crop, and we've got to get it out as quickly as we can."

"Oh, is that all?" said Franklin. "I'll be over at the dock in ten minutes."

It was an emergency all right, but not one about which he could feel very excited. Of course, Farms would be yelling its head off as its production quota was being whittled down by thousands of half-ton nibbles. But he was secretly on the side of the whales; if they'd managed to break into the great plankton prairies, then good luck to them.

"What's all the fuss about?" said Indra as she came out of the bedroom, her long, dark hair looking attractive even at this time of the morning as it hung in lustrous tresses over her shoulders. When Franklin told her, she appeared worried.

"It's a bigger emergency than you seem to think," she said. "Unless you act quickly, you may have some very sick whales on your hands. The spring overturn was only two weeks ago, and it's the biggest one we've ever had. So your greedy pets will be gorging themselves silly."

Franklin realized that she was perfectly right. The plankton farms were no affair of his, and formed a completely independent section of the Marine Division. But he knew a great deal about them, since they were an alternative and to some extent rival method of getting food from the sea. The plankton enthusiasts claimed, with a good deal of justice, that crop growing was more efficient than herding, since the whales themselves fed on the plankton and were therefore farther down the food chain. Why waste ten pounds of plankton, they argued, to produce one pound of whale, when you could harvest it directly?

The debate had been in progress for at least twenty years, and so far neither side could claim to have won. Sometimes the argument had been quite acrimonious and had echoed, on an infinitely larger and more sophisticated scale, the rivalry between homesteaders and cattle barons in the days when the American Midwest was being settled. But unfortunately for latter-day mythmakers, competing departments of the Marine Division of the World Food Organization fought each other purely with official minutes and the efficient but unspectacular weapons of bureaucracy. There were no gun fighters prowling the range, and if the fence had gone down it would be due to purely technical troubles, not midnight sabotage. . . .

In the sea as on the land, all life depends upon vegetation. And the amount of vegetation in turn depends upon the mineral content of the medium in which it grows—the nitrates, phosphates, and scores of other basic chemicals. In the ocean, there is always a tendency for these vital substances to accumulate in the depths, far below the regions where light penetrates and therefore plants can exist and grow. The upper few hundred feet of the sea is the primary source of its life; everything below that level preys, at second or third hand, on the food formed above.

Every spring, as the warmth of the new year seeps down into the ocean, the waters far below respond to the invisible sun. They expand and rise, lifting to the surface, in untold billions of tons, the salts and minerals they bear. Thus fertilized by food from below and sun from above, the floating plants multiply with explosive violence, and the creatures which browse upon them flourish accordingly. And so spring comes to the meadows of the sea.

This was the cycle that had repeated itself at least a billion times before man appeared on the scene. And now he had changed it. Not content with the upwelling of minerals produced by Nature, he had sunk his atomic generators at strategic spots far down into the sea, where the raw heat they produced would start immense, submerged fountains lifting their chemical treasure toward the fruitful sun. This artificial enhancement of the natural overturn had been one of the most unexpected, as well as the most rewarding, of all the many applications of nuclear energy. By this means alone, the output of food from the sea had been increased by almost ten per cent.

And now the whales were busily doing their best to restore the balance.

The roundup would have to be a combined sea and air operation. There were too few of the subs, and they were far too slow, to do the job unassisted. Three of them—including Franklin's one-man scout—were being flown to the scene of the breakthrough by a cargo plane which would drop them and then co-operate by spotting the movements of the whales from the air, if they had scattered over too large an area for the subs' sonar to pick them up. Two other planes would also try to scare the whales by dropping noise generators near them, but this technique had never worked well in the past and no one really expected much success from it now.

Within twenty minutes of the alarm, Franklin was watching the enormous food-processing plants of Pearl Harbor falling below as the jets of the freighter hauled him up into the sky. Even now, he was still not fond of flying and tried to avoid it when he could. But it no longer worried him, and he could look down on the world beneath without qualms.

A hundred miles east of Hawaii, the sea turned suddenly from blue to gold. The moving fields, rich with the year's first crop, covered the Pacific clear out to the horizon, and showed no sign of ending as the plane raced on toward the rising sun. Here and there the mile-long skimmers of the floating harvesters lay upon the surface like the enigmatic toys of some giant children, while beside them, smaller and more compact, were the pontoons and rafts of the concentration equipment. It was an impressive sight, even in these days of mammoth engineering achievements, but it did not move Franklin. He could not become excited over a billion tons of assorted diatoms and shrimps—not even though he knew that they fed a quarter of the human race.

"Just passing over the Hawaiian Corridor," said the pilot's voice from the speaker. "We should see the break in a minute."

"I can see it now," said one of the other wardens, leaning past Franklin and pointing out to sea. "There they are—having the time of their lives."

It was a spectacle which must be making the poor farmers tear their hair. Franklin suddenly remembered an old nursery rhyme he had not thought of for at least thirty years:

Little Boy Blue, come blow your horn,
The sheep's in the meadow, the cow's in the corn.

There was no doubt that the cows were in the corn, and Little Boy Blue was going to have a busy time getting them out. Far below, myriads of narrow swathes were being carved in the endless yellow sea, as the ravenous, slowly moving mountains ate their way into the rich plankton meadows. A blue line of exposed water marked the track of each whale as it meandered through what must be a cetacean heaven—a heaven from which it was Franklin's job to expel it as promptly as possible.

The three wardens, after a final radio briefing, left the cabin and went down to the hold, where the little subs were already hanging from the davits which would lower them into the sea. There would be no difficulty about this operation; what might not be so easy would be getting them back again, and if the sea became rough they might have to go home under their own power.

It seemed strange to be inside a submarine inside an airplane, but Franklin had little time for such thoughts as he went through the routine cockpit drill. Then the speaker on his control panel remarked: "Hovering at thirty feet; now opening cargo hatches. Stand by, Number One Sub." Franklin was number two; the great cargo craft was poised so steadily, and the hoists moved down so smoothly, that he never felt any impact as the sub dropped into its natural element. Then the three scouts were fanning out along the tracks that had been assigned to them, like mechanized sheep dogs rounding up a flock.

Almost at once, Franklin realized that this operation was not going to be as simple as it looked. The sub was driving through a thick soup that completely eliminated vision and even interfered seriously with sonar. What was still more serious, the hydrojet motors were laboring unhappily as their impellers chewed through the mush. He could not afford to get his propulsion system clogged; the best thing to do would be to dive below the plankton layer and not to surface until it was absolutely necessary.

Three hundred feet down, the water was merely murky and though vision was still impossible he could make good speed. He wondered if the greedily feasting whales above his head knew of his approach and realized that their idyl was coming to an end. On the sonar screen he could see their luminous echoes moving slowly across the ghostly mirror of the air-water surface which his sound beams could not penetrate. It was odd how similar the surface of the sea looked from below both to the naked eye and to the acoustical senses of the sonar.

The characteristically compact little echoes of the two other subs were moving out to the flanks of the scattered herd. Franklin glanced at the chronometer; in less than a minute, the drive was due to begin. He switched on the external microphones and listened to the voices of the sea.

How could anyone have ever thought that the sea was silent! Even man's limited hearing could detect many of its sounds—the clashing of chitinous claws, the moan of great boulders made restive by the ocean swell, the high-pitched squeak of porpoises, the unmistakable "flick" of a shark's tail as it suddenly accelerates on a new course. But these were merely the sounds in the audible spectrum; to listen to the full music of the sea one must go both below and above the range of human hearing. This was a simple enough task for the sub's frequency converters; if he wished, Franklin could tune in to any sounds from almost a million cycles a second down to vibrations as sluggish as the slow opening of an ancient, rusty door.

He set the receiver to the broadest band, and at once his mind began to interpret the multitudinous messages that came pouring into the little cabin from the watery world outside. The man-made noises he dismissed at once; the sounds of his own sub and the more distant whines of his companion vessels were largely eliminated by the special filters designed for that purpose. But he could just detect the distinctive whistles of the three sonar sets—his own almost blanketing the others—and beyond those the faint and far-off BEEP-BEEP-BEEP of the Hawaiian Corridor. The double fence which was supposed to channel the whales safely through the rich sea farms sent out its pulses at five-second intervals, and though the nearest portion of the fence was out of action the more distant parts of the sonic barrier could be clearly heard. The pulses were curiously distorted and drawn-out into a faint continuous echo as each new burst of sound was followed at once by the delayed waves from more and more remote regions of the fence. Franklin could hear each pulse running away into the distance, as sometimes a clap of thunder may be heard racing across the sky.

Against this background, the sounds of the natural world stood out sharp and clear. From all directions, with never a moment's silence, came the shrill shrieks and squealings of the whales as they talked to one another or merely gave vent to their high spirits and enjoyment. Franklin could distinguish between the voices of the males and the females, but he was not one of those experts who could identify individuals and even interpret what they were trying to express.

There is no more eerie sound in all the world than the screaming of a herd of whales, when one moves among it in the depths of the sea. Franklin had only to close his eyes and he could imagine that he was lost in some demon-haunted forest, while ghosts and goblins closed in upon him. Could Hector Berlioz have heard this banshee chorus, he would have known that Nature had already anticipated his "Dream of the Witches' Sabbath."

But weirdness lies only in unfamiliarity, and this sound was now part of Franklin's life. It no longer gave him nightmares, as it had sometimes done in his early days. Indeed, the main emotion that it now inspired in him was an affectionate amusement, together with a slight surprise that such enormous animals produced such falsetto screams.

Yet there was a memory that the sound of the sea sometimes evoked. It no longer had power to hurt him, though it could still fill his heart with a wistful sadness. He remembered all the times he had spent in the signals rooms of spaceships or space stations, listening to the radio waves coming in as the monitors combed the spectrum in their automatic search. Sometimes there had been, like these same ghostly voices calling in the night, the sound of distant ships or beacons, or the torrents of high-speed code as the colonies talked with Mother Earth. And always one could hear a perpetual murmuring background to man's feeble transmitters, the endless susurration of the stars and galaxies themselves as they drenched the whole universe with radiation.

The chronometer hand came around to zero. It had not scythed away the first second before the sea erupted in a hellish cacophony of sound—a rising and falling ululation that made Franklin reach swiftly for the volume control. The sonic mines had been dropped, and he felt sorry for any whales who were unlucky enough to be near them. Almost at once the pattern of echoes on the screen began to change, as the terrified beasts started to flee in panic toward the west. Franklin watched closely, preparing to head off any part of the herd that looked like it would miss the gap in the fence and turn back into the farms.

The noise generators must have been improved, he decided, since the last time this trick had been tried—or else these whales were more amenable. Only a few stragglers tried to break away, and it was no more than ten minutes' work to round them up on the right path and scare them back with the subs' own sirens. Half an hour after the mines had been dropped, the entire herd had been funneled back through the invisible gap in the fence, and was milling around inside the narrow corridor. There was nothing for the subs to do but to stand by until the engineers had carried out their repairs and the curtain of sound was once more complete.

No one could claim that it was a famous victory. It was just another day's work, a minor battle in an endless campaign. Already the excitement of the chase had died away, and Franklin was wondering how long it would be before the freighter could hoist them out of the ocean and fly them back to Hawaii. This was, after all, supposed to be his day off, and he had promised to take Peter down to Waikiki and start teaching him how to swim.

Even when he is merely standing by, a good warden never lets his attention stray for long from his sonar screen. Every three minutes, without any conscious thought, Franklin switched to the long-range scan and tilted the transmitter down toward the sea bed, just to keep track of what was going on around him. He did not doubt that his colleagues were doing exactly the same, between wondering how long it would be before they were relieved. . . .

At the very limit of his range, ten miles away and almost two miles down, a faint echo had crawled onto the edge of the screen. Franklin looked at it with mild interest; then his brows knit in perplexity. It must be an unusually large object to be visible at such a distance—something quite as large as a whale. But no whale could be swimming at such a depth; though sperm whales had been encountered almost a mile down, this was beyond the limits at which they could operate, fabulous divers though they were. A deep-sea shark? Possibly, thought Franklin; it would do no harm to have a closer look at it.

He locked the scanner onto the distant echo and expanded the image as far as the screen magnification would allow. It was too far away to make out any detail, but he could see now that he was looking at a long, thin object—and that it was moving quite rapidly. He stared at it for a moment, then called his colleagues. Unnecessary chatter was discouraged on operations, but here was a minor mystery that intrigued him.

"Sub Two calling," he said. "I've a large echo bearing 185 degrees, range 9.7 miles, depth 1.8 miles. Looks like another sub. You know if anyone else is operating around here?"

"Sub One calling Sub Two," came the first reply. "That's outside my range. Could be a Research Department sub down there. How big would you say your echo is?"

"About a hundred feet long. Maybe more. It's doing over ten knots."

"Sub Three calling. There's no research vessel around here. The *Nautilus IV* is laid up for repairs, and the *Cousteau's* in the Atlantic. Must be a fish you've got hold of."

"There aren't any fish this size. Have I permission to go after it? I think we ought to check up."

"Permission granted," answered Sub One. "We'll hold the gap here. Keep in touch."

Franklin swung the sub around to the south, and brought the little vessel up to maximum speed with a smooth rush of power. The echo he was chasing was already too deep for him to reach, but there was always the chance that it might come back to the surface. Even if it did not, he would be able to get a much clearer image when he had shortened his range.

He had traveled only two miles when he saw that the chase was hopeless. There could be no doubt; his quarry had detected either the vibrations of his motor or his sonar and was plunging at full speed straight down to the bottom. He managed to get within four miles, and then the signal was lost in the confused maze of echoes from the ocean bed. His last glimpse of it confirmed his earlier impression of great length and relative thinness, but he was still unable to make out any details of its structure.

"So it got away from you," said Sub One. "I thought it would."

"Then you know what it was?"

"No—nor does anyone else. And if you'll take my advice, you won't talk to any reporters about it. If you do, you'll never live it down."

Momentarily frozen with astonishment, Franklin stared at the little loudspeaker from which the words had just come. So they had not been pulling his leg, as he had always assumed. He remembered some of the tales he had heard in the bar at Heron Island and wherever wardens gathered together after duty. He had laughed at them then, but now he knew that the tales were true.

That nervous echo skittering hastily out of range had been nothing less than the Great Sea Serpent.

Indra, who was still doing part-time work at the Hawaii Aquarium when her household duties permitted, was not as impressed as her husband had expected. In fact, her first comment was somewhat deflating.

"Yes, but *which* sea serpent? You know there are at least three totally different types."

"I certainly didn't."

"Well, first of all there's a giant eel which has been seen on three or four occasions but never properly identified, though its larvae were caught back in the 1940s. It's known to grow up to sixty feet long, and that's enough of a sea serpent for most people. But the really spectacular one is the oarfish—*Regalecus glesne*. That's got a face like a horse, a crest of brilliant red quills like an Indian brave's headdress—and a snakelike body which may be seventy feet long. Since we know that these things exist, how do you expect us to be surprised at anything the sea can produce?"

"What about the third type you mentioned?"

"That's the one we haven't identified or even described. We just call it 'X' because people still laugh when you talk about sea serpents. The only thing that we know about it is that it undoubtedly exists, that it's extremely sly, and that it lives in deep water. One day we'll catch it, but when we do it will probably be through pure luck."

Franklin was very thoughtful for the rest of the evening. He did not like to admit that, despite all the instruments that man now used to probe the sea, despite his own continual patrolling of the depths, the ocean still held many secrets and would retain them for ages yet to come. And he knew that, though he might never see it again, he would be haunted all his life by the memory of that distant, tantalizing echo as it descended swiftly into the abyss that was its home.

CHAPTER THIRTEEN

There are many misconceptions about the glamour of a warden's life. Franklin had never shared them, so he was neither surprised nor disappointed that so much of his time was spent on long, uneventful patrols far out at sea. Indeed, he welcomed them. They gave him time to think, yet not time to brood—and it was on these lonely missions in the living heart of the sea that his last fears were shed and his mental scars finally healed.

The warden's year was dominated by the pattern of whale migration, but that pattern was itself continually changing as new areas of the sea were fenced and fertilized. He might spend summer moving cautiously through the polar ice, and winter beating back and forth across the equator. Sometimes he would operate from shore stations, sometimes from mobile bases like the *Rorqual,* the *Pequod,* or the *Cachelot.* One season he might be wholly concerned with the great whalebone or baleen whales, who literally strained their food from the sea as they swam, mouth open, through the rich plankton soup. And another season he would have to deal with their very different cousins, the fierce, toothed cetaceans of whom the sperm whales were the most important representatives. These were no gentle herbivores, but pursued and fought their monstrous prey in the lightless deep half a mile from the last rays of the sun.

There would be weeks or even months when a warden would never see a whale. The bureau had many calls on its equipment and personnel, and whales were not its only business. Everyone who had dealings with the sea appeared to come, sooner or later, to the Bureau of Whales with an appeal for help. Sometimes the requests were tragic; several times a year subs were sent on usually fruitless searches for drowned sportsmen or explorers.

At the other extreme, there was a standing joke that a senator had once asked the Sydney office to locate his false teeth, lost when the Bondi surf worked its will upon him. It was said that he had received, with great promptness, the foot-wide jaws of a tiger shark, with an apologetic note saying that these were the only unwanted teeth that an extensive search had been able to find off Bondi Beach.

Some tasks that came the warden's way had a certain glamour, and were eagerly sought after when they arose. A very small and understaffed section of the Bureau of Fisheries was concerned with pearls, and during the slack season wardens were sometimes detached from their normal work and allowed to assist on the pearl beds.

Franklin had one such tour of duty in the Persian Gulf. It was straightforward work, not unlike gardening, and since it involved diving to depths never greater than two hundred feet simple compressed-air equipment was used and the diver employed a torpedo for moving around. The best areas for pearl cultivation had been carefully populated with selected stock, and the main problem was protecting the oysters from their natural enemies—particularly starfish and rays. When they had time to mature, they were collected and carried back to the surface for inspection—one of the few jobs that no one had ever been able to mechanize.

Any pearls discovered belonged, of course, to the Bureau of Fisheries. But it was noticeable that the wives of all the wardens posted to this duty very soon afterward sported pearl necklaces or earrings—and Indra was no exception to this rule.

She had received her necklace the day she gave birth to Peter, and with the arrival of his son it seemed to Franklin that the old chapter of his life had finally closed. It was not true, of course; he could never forget—nor did he wish to—that Irene had given him Roy and Rupert, on a world which was now as remote to him as a planet of the farthest star. But the ache of that irrevocable parting had subsided at last, for no grief can endure forever.

He was glad—though he had once bitterly resented it—that it was impossible to talk to anyone on Mars, or indeed anywhere in space beyond the orbit of the Moon. The six-minute time lag for the round trip, even when the planet was at its nearest, made conversation out of the question, so he could never torture himself by feeling in the presence of Irene and the boys by calling them up on the visiphone. Every Christmas they exchanged recordings and talked over the events of the year; apart from occasional letters, that was the only personal contact they now had, and the only one that Franklin needed.

There was no way of telling how well Irene had adjusted to her virtual widowhood. The boys must have helped, but there were times when Franklin wished that she had married again, for their sakes as well as hers. Yet somehow he had never been able to suggest it, and she had never raised the subject, even when he had made this step himself.

Did she resent Indra? That again was hard to tell. Perhaps some jealousy was inevitable; Indra herself, during the occasional quarrels that punctuated their marriage, made it clear that she sometimes disliked the thought of being only the second woman in Franklin's life.

Such quarrels were rare, and after the birth of Peter they were rarer. A married couple forms a dynamically unstable system until the arrival of the first child converts it from a double to a triple group.

Franklin was as happy now as he had ever hoped to be. His family gave him the emotional security he needed; his work provided the interest and adventure which he had sought in space, only to lose again. There was more life and wonder in the sea than in all the endless empty leagues between the planets, and it was seldom now that his heart ached for the blue beauty of the crescent Earth, the swirling silver mist of the Milky Way, or the tense excitement of landfall on the moons of Mars at the end of a long voyage.

The sea had begun to shape his life and thought, as it must that of all men who try to master it and learn its secrets. He felt a kinship with all the creatures that moved throughout its length and depth, even when they were enemies which it was his duty to destroy. But above all, he felt a sympathy and an almost mystical reverence, of which he was half ashamed, toward the great beasts whose destinies he ruled.

He believed that most wardens knew that feeling, though they were careful to avoid admitting it in their shoptalk. The nearest they came to it was when they accused each other of being "whale happy," a somewhat indefinable term which might be summed up as acting more like a whale than a man in a given situation. It was a form of identification without which no warden could be really good at his job, but there were times when it could become too extreme. The classic case—which everyone swore was perfectly true—was that of the senior warden who felt he was suffocating unless he brought his sub up to blow every ten minutes.

Being regarded—and regarding themselves—as the elite of the world's army of underwater experts, the wardens were always called upon when there was some unusual job that no one else cared to perform. Sometimes these jobs were so suicidal that it was necessary to explain to the would-be client that he must find another way out of his difficulties.

But occasionally there was no other way, and risks had to be taken. The bureau still remembered how Chief Warden Kircher, back in '22, had gone up the giant intake pipes through which the cooling water flowed into the fusion power plant supplying half the South American continent. One of the filter grilles had started to come loose, and could be fixed only by a man on the spot. With strong ropes tied around his body to prevent him from being sucked through the wire meshing, Kircher had descended into the roaring darkness. He had done the job and returned safely; but that was the last time he ever went under water.

So far, all Franklin's missions had been fairly conventional ones; he had had to face nothing as hair-raising as Kircher's exploit, and was not sure how he would react if such an occasion arose. Of course, he could always turn down any assignment that involved abnormal risks; his contract was quite specific on that point. But the "suicide clause," as it was sardonically called, was very much a dead letter. Any warden who invoked it, except under the most extreme circumstances, would incur no displeasure from his superiors, but he would thereafter find it very hard to live with his colleagues.

Franklin's first operation beyond the call of duty did not come his way for almost five years—five busy, crowded, yet in retrospect curiously uneventful, years. But when it came, it more than made up for the delay.

✶ *CHAPTER FOURTEEN*

The chief accountant dropped his tables and charts on the desk, and peered triumphantly at his little audience over the rims of his antiquated spectacles.

"So you see, gentlemen," he said, "there's no doubt about it. In this area here"—he stabbed at the map again—"sperm whale casualties have been abnormally high. It's no longer a question of the usual random variations in the census numbers. During the migrations of the last five years, no less than nine plus or minus two whales have disappeared in this rather small area.

"Now, as you are all aware, the sperm whale has no natural enemies, except for the orcas that occasionally attack small females with calves. But we are quite sure that no killer packs have broken into this area for several years, and at least three adult males have disappeared. In our opinion, that left only one possibility.

"The sea bed here is slightly less than four thousand feet down, which means that a sperm whale can just reach it with a few minutes' time for hunting on the bottom before it has to return for air. Now, ever since it was discovered that Physeter feeds almost exclusively on squids, naturalists have wondered whether a squid can ever win when a whale attacks it. The general opinion was that it couldn't, because the whale is much larger and more powerful.

"But we must remember that even today no one knows how big the giant squid does grow; the Biology Section tells me that tentacles of *Bathyteutis Maximus* have been found up to eighty feet long. Moreover, a squid would only have to keep a whale held down for a matter of a few minutes at this depth, and the animal would drown before it could get back to the surface. So a couple of years ago we formulated the theory that in this area there lives at least one abnormally large squid. We—ahem—christened him Percy.

"Until last week, Percy was only a theory. Then, as you know, Whale S.87693 was found dead on the surface, badly mauled and with its body covered with the typical scars caused by squid claws and suckers. I would like you to look at this photograph."

He pulled a set of large glossy prints out of his brief case and passed them around. Each showed a small portion of a whale's body which was mottled with white streaks and perfectly circular rings. A foot ruler lay incongruously in the middle of the picture to give an idea of the scale.

"Those, gentlemen, are sucker marks. They go up to six inches in diameter. I think we can say that Percy is no longer a theory. The question is: What do we do about him? He is costing us at least twenty thousand dollars a year. I should welcome any suggestions."

There was a brief silence while the little group of officials looked thoughtfully at the photographs. Then the director said: "I've asked Mr. Franklin to come along and give his opinion. What do you say, Walter? Can you deal with Percy?"

"If I can find him, yes. But the bottom's pretty rugged down there, and it might be a long search. I couldn't use a normal sub, of course—there'd be no safety margin at that depth, especially if Percy started putting on the squeeze. Incidentally, what size do you think he is?"

The chief accountant, usually so glib with figures, hesitated for an appreciable instant before replying.

"This isn't *my* estimate," he said apologetically, "but the biologists say he may be a hundred and fifty feet long."

There were some subdued whistles, but the director seemed unimpressed. Long ago he had learned the truth of the old cliché that there were bigger fish in the sea than ever came out of it. He knew also that, in a medium where gravity set no limit to size, a creature could continue to grow almost indefinitely as long as it could avoid death. And of all the inhabitants of the sea, the giant squid was perhaps the safest from attack. Even its one enemy, the sperm whale, could not reach it if it remained below the four-thousand-foot level.

"There are dozens of ways we can kill Percy if we can locate him," put in the chief biologist. "Explosives, poison, electrocution—any of them would do. But unless there's no alternative, I think we should avoid killing. He must be one of the biggest animals alive on this planet, and it would be a crime to murder him."

"Please, Dr. Roberts!" protested the director. "May I remind you that this bureau is only concerned with food production—not with research or the conservation of any animals except whales. And I do think that murder is rather a strong term to apply to an overgrown mollusk."

Dr. Roberts seemed quite unabashed by the mild reprimand.

"I agree, sir," he said cheerfully, "that production is our main job, and that we must always keep economic factors in mind. At the same time, we're continually co-operating with the Department of Scientific Research and this seems another case where we can work together to our mutual advantage. In fact, we might even make a profit in the long run."

"Go on," said the director, a slight twinkle in his eye. He wondered what ingenious plan the scientists who were supposed to be working for him had cooked up with their opposite numbers in Research.

"No giant squid has ever been captured alive, simply because we've never had the tools for the job. It would be an expensive operation, but if we are going to chase Percy anyway, the additional cost should not be very great. So I suggest that we try to bring him back alive."

No one bothered to ask how. If Dr. Roberts said it could be done, that meant he had already worked out a plan of campaign. The director, as usual, bypassed the minor technical details involved in hauling up several tons of fighting squid from a depth of a mile, and went straight to the important point.

"Will Research pay for any of this? And what will you do with Percy when you've caught him?"

"Unofficially, Research will provide the additional equipment if we make the subs and pilots available. We'll also need that floating dock we borrowed from Maintenance last year; it's big enough to hold two whales, so it can certainly hold one squid. There'll be some additional expenditure here—extra aeration plant for the water, electrified mesh to stop Percy climbing out, and so on. In fact, I suggest that we use the dock as a lab while we're studying him."

"And after that?"

"Why, we sell him."

"The demand for hundred-and-fifty-foot squids as household pets would seem to be rather small."

Like an actor throwing away his best line, Dr. Roberts casually produced his trump card.

"If we can deliver Percy alive and in good condition, Marineland will pay fifty thousand dollars for him. That was Professor Milton's first informal offer when I spoke to him this morning. I've no doubt that we can get more than that; I've even been wondering if we could arrange things on a royalty basis. After all, a giant squid would be the biggest attraction Marineland ever had."

"Research was bad enough," grumbled the director. "Now it looks as if you're trying to get us involved in the entertainment business. Still, as far as I'm concerned it sounds fairly plausible. If Accounts can convince me that the project is not too expensive, and if no other snags turn up, we'll go ahead with it. That is, of course, if Mr. Franklin and his colleagues think it can be done. They're the people who'll have to do the work."

"If Dr. Roberts has any practical plan, I'll be glad to discuss it with him. It's certainly a very interesting project."

That, thought Franklin, was the understatement of the year. But he was not the sort of man who ever waxed too enthusiastic over any enterprise, having long ago decided that this always resulted in eventual disappointment. If "Operation Percy" came off, it would be the most exciting job he had ever had in his five years as a warden. But it was too good to be true; something would turn up to cancel the whole project.

It did not. Less than a month later, he was dropping down to the sea bed in a specially modified deep-water scout. Two hundred feet behind him, Don Burley was following in a second machine. It was the first time they had worked together since those far-off days on Heron Island, but when Franklin had been asked to choose his partner he had automatically thought of Don. This was the chance of a lifetime, and Don would never forgive him if he selected anyone else.

Franklin sometimes wondered if Don resented his own rapid rise in the service. Five years ago, Don had been a first warden; Franklin, a completely inexperienced trainee. Now they were both first wardens, and before long Franklin would probably be promoted again. He did not altogether welcome this, for, though he was ambitious enough, he knew that the higher he rose in the bureau the less time he would spend at sea. Perhaps Don knew what he was doing; it was very hard to picture him settling down in an office. . . .

"Better try your lights," said Don's voice from the speaker. "Doc Roberts wants me to get a photograph of you."

"Right," Franklin replied. "Here goes."

"My—you *do* look pretty! If I was another squid, I'm sure I'd find you irresistible. Swing broadside a minute. Thanks. Talk about a Christmas tree! It's the first time I've ever seen one making ten knots at six hundred fathoms."

Franklin grinned and switched off the illuminations. This idea of Dr. Roberts' was simple enough, but it remained to be seen if it would work. In the lightless abyss, many creatures carry constellations of luminous organs which they can switch on or off at will, and the giant squid, with its enormous eyes, is particularly sensitive to such lights. It uses them not only to lure its prey into its clutches, but also to attract its mates. If squids were as intelligent as they were supposed to be, thought Franklin, Percy would soon see through his disguise. It would be ironic, however, if a deep-diving sperm whale was deceived and he had an unwanted fight on his hands.

The rocky bottom was now only five hundred feet below, every detail of it clearly traced on the short-range sonar scanner. It looked like an unpromising place for a search; there might be countless caves here in which Percy could hide beyond all hope of detection. On the other hand, the whales had detected him—to their cost. And anything that Physeter can do, Franklin told himself, my sub can do just as well.

"We're in luck," said Don. "The water's as clear as I've ever seen it down here. As long as we don't stir up any mud, we'll be able to see a couple of hundred feet."

That was important; Franklin's luminous lures would be useless if the water was too turbid for them to be visible. He switched on the external TV camera, and quickly located the faint glow of Don's starboard light, two hundred feet away. Yes, this was extremely good luck; it should simplify their task enormously.

Franklin tuned in to the nearest beacon and fixed his position with the utmost accuracy. To make doubly sure, he got Don to do the same, and they split the difference between them. Then, cruising slowly on parallel courses, they began their careful search of the sea bed.

It was unusual to find bare rock at such a depth, for the ocean bed is normally covered with a layer of mud and sediment hundreds or even thousands of feet thick. There must, Franklin decided, be powerful currents scouring this area clear—but there was certainly no current now, as his drift meter assured him. It was probably seasonal, and associated with the ten-thousand-foot-deeper cleft of the Miller Canyon, only five miles away.

Every few seconds, Franklin switched on his pattern of colored lights, then watched the screen eagerly to see if there was any response. Before long he had half a dozen fantastic deep-sea fish following him—nightmare creatures, two or three feet long, with enormous jaws and ridiculously attenuated feelers and tendrils trailing from their bodies. The lure of his lights apparently overcame their fear of his engine vibration, which was an encouraging sign. Though his speed quickly left them behind, they were continually replaced by new monsters, no two of which appeared to be exactly the same.

Franklin paid relatively little attention to the TV screen; the longer-range senses of the sonar, warning him of what lay in the thousand feet ahead of him, were more important. Not only had he to keep a lookout for his quarry, but he had to avoid rocks and hillocks which might suddenly rear up in the track of the sub. He was doing only ten knots, which was slow enough, but it required all his concentration. Sometimes he felt as if he was flying at treetop height over hilly country in a thick fog.

They traveled five uneventful miles, then made a hairpin turn and came back on a parallel course. If they were doing nothing else, thought Franklin, at least they were producing a survey of this area in more detail than it had ever been mapped before. Both he and Don were operating with their recorders on, so that the profile of the sea bed beneath them was being automatically mapped.

"Whoever said this was an exciting life?" said Don when they made their fourth turn. "I've not even seen a baby octopus. Maybe we're scaring the squids away."

"Roberts said they're not very sensitive to vibrations, so I don't think that's likely. And somehow I feel that Percy isn't the sort who's easily scared."

"*If* he exists," said Don skeptically.

"Don't forget those six-inch sucker marks. What do you think made them—mice?"

"Hey!" said Don. "Have a look at that echo on bearing 250, range 750 feet. Looks like a rock, but I thought it moved then."

Another false alarm, Franklin told himself. No—the echo did seem a bit fuzzy. By God, it *was* moving!

"Cut speed to half a knot," he ordered. "Drop back behind me—I'll creep up slowly and switch on my lights."

"It's a weird-looking echo. Keeps changing size all the time."

"That sounds like our boy. Here we go."

The sub was now moving across an endless, slightly tilted plain, still accompanied by its inquisitive retinue of finned dragons. On the TV screen all objects were lost in the haze at a distance of about a hundred and fifty feet; the full power of the ultraviolet projectors could probe the water no farther than this. Franklin switched off his headlights and all external illumination, and continued his cautious approach using the sonar screen alone.

At five hundred feet the echo began to show its unmistakable structure; at four hundred feet there was no longer any doubt; at three hundred feet Franklin's escort of fish suddenly fled at high speed as if aware that this was no healthy spot. At two hundred feet he turned on his visual lures, but he waited a few seconds before switching on the searchlights and TV.

A forest was walking across the sea bed—a forest of writhing, serpentine trunks. The great squid froze for a moment as if impaled by the searchlights; probably it could see them, though they were invisible to human eyes. Then it gathered up its tentacles with incredible swiftness, folding itself into a compact, streamlined mass—and shot straight toward the sub under the full power of its own jet propulsion.

It swerved at the last minute, and Franklin caught a glimpse of a huge and lidless eye that must have been at least a foot in diameter. A second later there was a violent blow on the hull, followed by a scraping sound as of great claws being dragged across metal. Franklin remembered the scars he had so often seen on the blubbery hides of sperm whales, and was glad of the thickness of steel that protected him. He could hear the wiring of his external illumination being ripped away; no matter—it had served its purpose.

It was impossible to tell what the squid was doing; from time to time the sub rocked violently, but Franklin made no effort to escape. Unless things got a little too rough, he proposed to stay here and take it.

"Can you see what he's doing?" he asked Don, rather plaintively.

"Yes—he's got his eight arms wrapped around you, and the two big tentacles are waving hopefully at me. And he's going through the most beautiful color changes you can imagine—I can't begin to describe them. I wish I knew whether he's really trying to eat you—or whether he's just being affectionate."

"Whichever it is, it's not very comfortable. Hurry up and take your photos so that I can get out of here."

"Right—give me another couple of minutes so I can get a movie sequence as well. Then I'll try to plant my harpoon."

It seemed a long two minutes, but at last Don had finished. Percy still showed none of the shyness which Dr. Roberts had rather confidently predicted, though by this time he could hardly have imagined that Franklin's sub was another squid.

Don planted his dart with neatness and precision in the thickest part of Percy's mantle, where it would lodge securely but would do no damage. At the sudden sting, the great mollusk abruptly released its grip, and Franklin took the opportunity for going full speed ahead. He felt the horny palps grating over the stern of the sub; then he was free and rising swiftly up toward the distant sky. He felt rather pleased that he had managed to escape without using any of the battery of weapons that had been provided for this very purpose.

Don followed him at once, and they circled five hundred feet above the sea bed—far beyond visual range. On the sonar screen the rocky bottom was a sharply defined plane, but now at its center pulsed a tiny, brilliant star. The little beacon—less than six inches long and barely an inch wide—that had been anchored in Percy was already doing its job.

It would continue to operate for more than a week before its batteries failed.

"We've tagged him!" cried Don gleefully. "Now he can't hide."

"As long as he doesn't get rid of that dart," said Franklin cautiously. "If he works it out, we'll have to start looking for him all over again."

"*I* aimed it," pointed out Don severely. "Bet you ten to one it stays put."

"If I've learned one thing in this game," said Franklin, "it's not to accept your bets." He brought the drive up to maximum cruising power, and pointed the sub's nose to the surface, still more than half a mile away. "Let's not keep Doc Roberts waiting—the poor man will be crazy with impatience. Besides, I want to see those pictures myself. It's the first time I've ever played a starring role with a giant squid."

And this, he reminded himself, was only the curtain raiser. The main feature had still to begin.

CHAPTER FIFTEEN

"How nice it is," said Franklin, as he relaxed lazily in the contour-form chair on the porch, "to have a wife who's not scared stiff of the job I'm doing."

"There are times when I am," admitted Indra. "I don't like these deep-water operations. If anything goes wrong down there, you don't have a chance."

"You can drown just as easily in ten feet of water as ten thousand."

"That's silly, and you know it. Besides, no warden has ever been killed by drowning, as far as I've ever heard. The things that happen to them are never as nice and simple as that."

"I'm sorry I started this conversation," said Franklin ruefully, glancing around to see if Peter was safely out of earshot. "Anyway, you're not worried about Operation Percy, are you?"

"No, I don't think so. I'm as anxious as everybody else to see you catch him—and I'm still more interested to see if Dr. Roberts can keep him alive." She rose to her feet and walked over to the bookshelf recess into the wall. Plowing through the usual pile of papers and magazines that had accumulated there, she finally unearthed the volume for which she was looking.

"Listen to this," she continued, "and remember that it was written almost two hundred years ago." She began to read in her best lecture-room voice, while Franklin listened at first with mild reluctance, and then with complete absorption.

"In the distance, a great white mass lazily rose, and rising higher and higher, and disentangling itself from the azure, at last gleamed before our prow like a snow-slide, new slid from the hills. Thus glistening for a moment, as slowly it subsided, and sank. Then once more arose, and silently gleamed. It seemed not a whale; and yet is this Moby Dick? thought Daggoo. Again the phantom went down, but on reappearing once more, like a stiletto-like cry that startled every man from his nod, the negro yelled out—'There! there again! there she breaches! Right ahead! The White Whale! The White Whale!'

"The four boats were soon on the water; Ahab's in advance, and all swiftly pulling towards their prey. Soon it went down, and while, with oars suspended, we were awaiting its appearance, lo! in the same spot where it sank, once more it slowly rose. Almost forgetting for the moment all thoughts of Moby Dick, we now gazed at the most wondrous phenomenon which the secret seas have hitherto revealed to mankind. A vast pulpy mass, furlongs in length and breadth, of a glancing cream-colour, lay floating on the water, innumerable long arms radiating from its centre, and curling and twisting like a nest of anacondas, as if blindly to catch at any hapless object within reach. No perceptible face or front did it have; no conceivable token of either sensation or instinct; but undulated there on the billows, an unearthly, formless, chance-like apparition of life.

"As with a low sucking sound it slowly disappeared again, Starbuck still gazing at the agitated waters where it had sunk, with a wild voice exclaimed—'Almost rather had I seen Moby Dick and fought him, then to have seen thee, thou white ghost!'

" 'What was it, Sir?' said Flask.

" 'The great live squid, which, they say, few whale-ships ever beheld, and returned to their ports to tell of it.'

"But Ahab said nothing; turning his boat, he sailed back to the vessel; the rest as silently following."

Indra paused, closed the book, and waited for her husband's response. Franklin stirred himself in the too-comfortable couch and said thoughtfully: "I'd forgotten that bit—if I ever read as far. It rings true to life, but what was a squid doing on the surface?"

"It was probably dying. They sometimes surface at night, but never in the daytime, and Melville says this was on 'one transparent blue morning.' "

"Anyway, what's a furlong? I'd like to know if Melville's squid was as big as Percy. The photos make him a hundred and thirty feet from his flukes to the tips of his feelers."

"So he beats the largest blue whale ever recorded."

"Yes, by a couple of feet. But of course he doesn't weigh a tenth as much."

Franklin heaved himself from his couch and went in search of a dictionary. Presently Indra heard indignant noises coming from the living room, and called out: "What's the matter?"

"It says here that a furlong is an obsolete measure of length equal to an eighth of a mile. Melville was talking through his hat."

"He's usually very accurate, at least as far as whales are concerned. But 'furlong' is obviously ridiculous—I'm surprised no one's spotted it before. He must have meant fathoms, or else the printer got it wrong."

Slightly mollified, Franklin put down the dictionary and came back to the porch. He was just in time to see Don Burley arrive, sweep Indra off her feet, plant a large but brotherly kiss on her forehead, and dump her back in her chair.

"Come along, Walt!" he said. "Got your things packed? I'll give you a lift to the airport."

"Where's Peter hiding?" said Franklin. "Peter! Come and say good-by—Daddy's off to work."

A four-year-old bundle of uncontrollable energy came flying into the room, almost capsizing his father as he jumped into his arms.

"Daddy's going to bring me back a 'quid?" he asked.

"Hey—how did you know about all this?"

"It was on the news this morning, while you were still asleep," explained Indra. "They showed a few seconds of Don's film, too."

"I was afraid of that. Now we'll have to work with a crowd of cameramen and reporters looking over our shoulders. That means that something's sure to go wrong."

"They can't follow us down to the bottom, anyway," said Burley.

"I hope you're right—but don't forget we're not the only people with deep-sea subs."

"I don't know how you put up with him," Don protested to Indra. "Does he *always* look on the black side of things?"

"Not always," smiled Indra, as she unraveled Peter from his father. "He's cheerful at least twice a week."

Her smile faded as she watched the sleek sportster go whispering down the hill. She was very fond of Don, who was practically a member of the family, and there were times when she worried about him. It seemed a pity that he had never married and settled down; the nomadic, promiscuous life he led could hardly be very satisfying. Since they had known him, he had spent almost all his time on or under the sea, apart from hectic leaves when he had used their home as a base—at their invitation but often to their embarrassment when there were unexpected lady guests to entertain at breakfast.

Their own life, by many standards, had been nomadic enough, but at least they had always had a place they could call home. That apartment in Brisbane, where her brief but happy career as a lecturer at the University of Queensland had ended with the birth of Peter; that bungalow in Fiji, with the roof that had a mobile leak which the builders could never find; the married quarters at the South Georgia whaling station (she could still smell the mountains of offal, and see the gulls wheeling over the flensing yards); and, finally, this house looking out across the sea to the other islands of Hawaii. Four homes in five years might seem excessive to many people, but for a warden's wife Indra knew she had done well.

She had few regrets for the career that had been temporarily interrupted. When Peter was old enough, she told herself, she would go back to her research; even now she read all the literature and kept in touch with current work. Only a few months ago the *Journal of Selachians* had published her letter "On the possible evolution of the Goblin Shark (*Scapanorhynchus owstoni*)," and she had since been involved in an enjoyable controversy with all five of the scientists qualified to discuss the subject.

Even if nothing came of these dreams, it was pleasant to have them and to know you might make the best of both worlds. So Indra Franklin, housewife and ichthyologist, told herself as she went back into the kitchen to prepare lunch for her ever-hungry son.

The floating dock had been modified in many ways that would have baffled its original designers. A thick steel mesh, supported on sturdy insulators, extended its entire length, and above this mesh was a canvas awning to cut out the sunlight which would injure Percy's sensitive eyes and skin. The only illumination inside the dock came from a battery of amber-tinted bulbs; at the moment, however, the great doors at either end of the huge concrete box were open, letting in both sunlight and water.

The two subs, barely awash, lay tied up beside the crowded catwalk as Dr. Roberts gave his final instructions.

"I'll try not to bother you too much when you're down there," he said, "but for heaven's sake tell me what's going on."

"We'll be too busy to give a running commentary," answered Don with a grin, "but we'll do our best. And if anything goes wrong, trust us to yell right away. All set, Walt?"

"O.K.," said Franklin, climbing down into the hatch. "See you in five hours, with Percy—I hope."

They wasted no time in diving to the sea bed; less than ten minutes later there was four thousand feet of water overhead, and the familiar rocky terrain was imaged on TV and sonar screen. But there was no sign of the pulsing star that should have indicated the presence of Percy.

"Hope the beacon hasn't packed up," said Franklin as he reported this news to the hopefully waiting scientists. "If it has, it may take us days to locate him again."

"Do you suppose he's left the area? I wouldn't blame him," added Don.

Dr. Roberts' voice, still confident and assured, came down to them from the distant world of sun and light almost a mile above.

"He's probably hiding in a cleft, or shielded by rock. I suggest you rise five hundred feet so that you're well clear of all the sea-bed irregularities, and start a high-speed search. That beacon has a range of more than a mile, so you'll pick him up pretty quickly."

An hour later even the doctor sounded less confident, and from the comments that leaked down to them over the sonar communicator it appeared that the reporters and TV networks were getting impatient.

"There's only one place he can be," said Roberts at last. "If he's there at all, and the beacon's still working, he must have gone down into the Miller Canyon."

"That's fifteen thousand feet deep," protested Don. "These subs are only cleared for twelve."

"I know—I know. But he won't have gone to the bottom. He's probably hunting somewhere down the slope. You'll see him easily if he's there."

"Right," replied Franklin, not very optimistically. "We'll go and have a look. But if he's more than twelve thousand feet down, he'll have to stay there."

On the sonar screen, the canyon was clearly visible as a sudden gap in the luminous image of the sea bed. It came rapidly closer as the two subs raced toward it at forty knots—the fastest creatures, Franklin mused, anywhere beneath the surface of the sea. He had once flown low toward the Grand Canyon, and seen the land below suddenly whipped away as the enormous cavity gaped beneath him. And now, though he must rely for vision solely on the pattern of echoes brought back by his probing sound waves, he felt exactly that same sensation as he swept across the edge of this still mightier chasm in the ocean floor.

He had scarcely finished the thought when Don's voice, high-pitched with excitement, came yelling from the speaker.

"There he is! A thousand feet down!"

"No need to break my eardrums," grumbled Franklin. "I can see him."

The precipitous slope of the canyon wall was etched like an almost vertical line down the center of the sonar screen. Creeping along the face of that wall was the tiny, twinkling star for which they had been searching. The patient beacon had betrayed Percy to his hunters.

They reported the situation to Dr. Roberts; Franklin could picture the jubilation and excitement up above, some hints of which trickled down through the open microphone. Presently Dr. Roberts, a little breathless, asked: "Do you think you can still carry out our plan?"

"I'll try," he answered. "It won't be easy with this cliff face right beside us, and I hope there aren't any caves Percy can crawl into. You ready, Don?"

"All set to follow you down."

"I think I can reach him without using the motors. Here we go."

Franklin flooded the nose tanks, and went down in a long, steep glide—a silent glide, he hoped. By this time, Percy would have learned caution and would probably run for it as soon as he knew that they were around.

The squid was cruising along the face of the canyon, and Franklin marveled that it could find any food in such a forbidding and apparently lifeless spot. Every time it expelled a jet of water from the tube of its siphon it moved forward in a distinct jerk; it seemed unaware that it was no longer alone, since it had not changed course since Franklin had first observed it.

"Two hundred feet—I'm going to switch on my lights again," he told Don.

"He won't see you—visibility's only about eighty today."

"Yes, but I'm still closing in—he's spotted me! Here he comes!"

Franklin had not really expected that the trick would work a second time on an animal as intelligent as Percy. But almost at once he felt the sudden thud, followed by the rasping of horny claws as the great tentacles closed around the sub. Though he knew that he was perfectly safe, and that no animal could harm walls that had been built to withstand pressures of a thousand tons on every square foot, that grating, slithering sound was one calculated to give him nightmares.

Then, quite suddenly, there was silence. He heard Don exclaim, "Christ, that stuff acts quickly! He's out cold." Almost at once Dr. Roberts interjected anxiously: "Don't give him too much! And keep him moving so that he'll still breathe!"

Don was too busy to answer. Having carried out his role as decoy, Franklin could do nothing but watch as his partner maneuvered dexterously around the the great mollusk. The anesthetic bomb had paralyzed it completely; it was slowly sinking, its tentacles stretched limply upward. Pieces of fish, some of them over a foot across, were floating away from the cruel beak as the monster disgorged its last meal.

"Can you get underneath?" Don asked hurriedly. "He's sinking too fast for me."

Franklin threw on the drive and went around in a tight curve. There was a soft thump, as of a snowdrift falling from a roof, and he knew that five or ten tons of gelatinous body were now draped over the sub.

"Fine—hold him there—I'm getting into position."

Franklin was now blind, but the occasional clanks and whirs coming from the water outside told him what was happening. Presently Don said triumphantly: "All set! We're ready to go."

The weight lifted from the sub, and Franklin could see again. Percy had been neatly gaffed. A band of thick, elastic webbing had been fastened around his body at the narrowest part, just behind the flukes. From this harness a cable extended to Don's sub, invisible in the haze a hundred feet away. Percy was being towed through the water in his normal direction of motion—backward. Had he been conscious and actively resisting, he could have escaped easily enough, but in his present state the collar he was wearing enabled Don to handle him without difficulty. The fun would begin when he started to revive. . . .

Franklin gave a brief eyewitness description of the scene for the benefit of his patiently waiting colleagues a mile above. It was probably being broadcast, and he hoped that Indra and Peter were listening. Then he settled down to keep an eye on Percy as the long haul back to the surface began.

They could not move at more than two knots, lest the collar lose its none-too-secure grip on the great mass of jelly it was towing. In any event, the trip back to the surface had to take at least three hours, to give Percy a fair chance of adjusting to the pressure difference. Since an air-breathing—and therefore more vulnerable—animal like a sperm whale could endure almost the same pressure change in ten or twenty minutes, this caution was probably excessive. But Dr. Roberts was taking no chances with his unprecedented catch.

They had been climbing slowly for nearly an hour, and had reached the three-thousand-foot level, when Percy showed signs of life. The two long arms, terminating in their great sucker-covered palps, began to writhe purposefully; the monstrous eyes, into which Franklin had been staring half hypnotized from a distance of no more than five feet, began to light once more with intelligence. Quite unaware that he was speaking in a breathless whisper, he swiftly reported these symptoms to Dr. Roberts.

The doctor's first reaction was a hearty sigh of relief: "Good!" he said. "I was afraid we might have killed him. Can you see if he's breathing properly? Is the siphon contracting?"

Franklin dropped a few feet so that he could get a better view of the fleshy tube projecting from the squid's mantle. It was opening and closing in an unsteady rhythm which seemed to be getting stronger and more regular at every beat.

"Splendid!" said Dr. Roberts. "He's in fine shape. As soon as he starts to wriggle too hard, give him one of the small bombs. But leave it until the last possible moment."

Franklin wondered how that moment was to be decided. Percy was now beginning to glow a beautiful blue; even with the searchlights switched off he was clearly visible. Blue, he remembered Dr. Roberts saying, was a sign of excitement in squids. In that case, it was high time he did something.

"Better let go that bomb. I think he's getting lively," he told Don.

"Right—here it is."

A glass bubble floated across Franklin's screen and swiftly vanished from sight.

"The damn thing never broke!" he cried. "Let go another one!"

"O.K.—here's number two. I hope this works; I've only got five left."

But once again the narcotic bomb failed. This time Franklin never saw the sphere; he only knew that instead of relaxing into slumber once more Percy was becoming more active second by second. The eight short tentacles—short, that is, compared with the almost hundred-foot reach of the pair carrying the grasping palps—were now beginning to twine briskly together. He recalled Melville's phrase: "Like a nest of anacondas." No; somehow that did not seem to fit. It was more like a miser—a submarine Shylock—twisting his fingers together as he gloated over his wealth. In any event, it was a disconcerting sight when those fingers were a foot in diameter and were operating only two yards away. . . .

"You'll just have to keep on trying," he told Don. "Unless we stop him soon, he'll get away."

An instant later he breathed a sigh of relief as he saw broken shards of glass drifting by. They would have been quite invisible, surrounded as they were by water, had they not been fluorescing brilliantly under the light of his ultraviolet searchlight. But for the moment he was too relieved to wonder why he had been able to see something as proverbially elusive as a piece of broken glass in water; he only knew that Percy had suddenly relaxed again and no longer appeared to be working himself into a rage.

"What happened?" said Dr. Roberts plaintively from above.

"These confounded knockout drops of yours. Two of them didn't work. That leaves me with just four—and at the present rate of failure I'll be lucky if even one goes off."

"I don't understand it. The mechanism worked perfectly every time we tested it in the lab."

"Did you test it at a hundred atmospheres pressure?"

"Er—no. It didn't seem necessary."

Don's "Huh!" seemed to say all that was needful about biologists who tried to dabble with engineering, and there was silence on all channels for the next few minutes of slow ascent. Then Dr. Roberts, sounding a little diffident, came back to the subject.

"Since we can't rely on the bombs," he said, "you'd better come up more quickly. He'll revive again in about thirty minutes."

"Right—I'll double speed. I only hope this collar doesn't slip off."

The next twenty minutes were perfectly uneventful; then everything started to happen at once.

"He's coming around again," said Franklin. "I think the higher speed has waked him up."

"I was afraid of that," Dr. Roberts answered. "Hold on as long as you can, and then let go a bomb. We can only pray that *one* of them will work."

A new voice suddenly cut into the circuit.

"Captain here. Lookout has just spotted some sperm whales about two miles away. They seem to be heading toward us; I suggest you have a look at them—we've got no horizontal search sonar on this ship."

Franklin switched quickly over to the long-range scanner and picked up the echoes at once.

"Nothing to worry about," he said. "If they come too close, we can scare them away." He glanced back at the TV screen and saw that Percy was now getting very restive.

"Let go your bomb," he told Don, "and keep your fingers crossed."

"I'm not betting on *this,*" Don answered. "Anything happen?"

"No; another dud. Try again."

"That leaves three. Here goes."

"Sorry—I can see that one. It isn't cracked."

"Two left. Now there's only one."

"That's a dud too. What had we better do, Doc? Risk the last one? I'm afraid Percy will slip off in a minute."

"There's nothing else we can do," replied Dr. Roberts, his voice now clearly showing the strain. "Go ahead, Don."

Almost at once Franklin gave a cry of satisfaction.

"We've made it!" he shouted. "He's knocked cold again! How long do you think it will keep him under this time?"

"We can't rely on more than twenty minutes, so plan your ascent accordingly. We're right above you—and remember what I said about taking at least ten minutes over that last two hundred feet. I don't want any pressure damage after all the trouble we've been to."

"Just a minute," put in Don. "I've been looking at those whales. They've put on speed and they're coming straight toward us. I think they've detected Percy—or the beacon we put in him."

"So what?" said Franklin. "We can frighten them with—oh."

"Yes—I thought you'd forgotten that. These aren't patrol subs, Walt. No sirens on them. And you can't scare sperm whales just by revving your engines."

That was true enough, though it would not have been fifty years ago, when the great beasts had been hunted almost to extinction. But a dozen generations had lived and died since then; now they recognized the subs as harmless, and certainly no obstacle to the meal they were anticipating. There was a real danger that the helpless Percy might be eaten before he could be safely caged.

"I think we'll make it," said Franklin, as he anxiously calculated the speed of the approaching whales. This was a hazard that no one could have anticipated; it was typical of the way in which underwater operations developed unexpected snags and complications.

"I'm going straight up to the two-hundred-foot level," Don told him. "We'll wait there just as long as it's safe, and then run for the ship. What do you think of that, Doc?"

"It's the only thing to do. But remember that those whales can make fifteen knots if they have to."

"Yes, but they can't keep it up for long, even if they see their dinner slipping away. Here we go."

The subs increased their rate of ascent, while the water brightened around them and the enormous pressure slowly relaxed. At last they were back in the narrow zone where an unprotected man could safely dive. The mother ship was less than a hundred yards away, but this final stage in the climb back to the surface was the most critical of all. In this last two hundred feet, the pressure would drop swiftly from eight atmospheres to only one—as great a change in ratio as had occurred in the previous quarter of a mile. There were no enclosed air spaces in Percy which might cause him to explode if the ascent was too swift, but no one could be certain what other internal damage might occur.

"Whales only half a mile away," reported Franklin. "Who said they couldn't keep up that speed? They'll be here in two minutes."

"You'll have to hold them off somehow," said Dr. Roberts, a note of desperation in his voice.

"Any suggestions?" asked Franklin, a little sarcastically.

"Suppose you pretend to attack; that might make them break off."

This, Franklin told himself, was not his idea of fun. But there seemed no alternative; with a last glance at Percy, who was now beginning to stir again, he started off at half-speed to meet the advancing whales.

There were three echoes dead ahead of him—not very large ones, but he did not let that encourage him. Even if those were the relatively diminutive females, each one was as big as ten elephants and they were coming toward him at a combined speed of forty miles an hour. He was making all the noise he could, but so far it seemed to be having no effect.

Then he heard Don shouting: "Percy's waking up fast! I can feel him starting to move."

"Come straight in," ordered Dr. Roberts. "We've got the doors open."

"And get ready to close the back door as soon as I've slipped the cable. I'm going straight through—I don't want to share your swimming pool with Percy when he finds what's happened to him."

Franklin heard all this chattering with only half an ear. Those three approaching echoes were ominously close. Were they going to call his bluff? Sperm whales were among the most pugnacious animals in the sea, as different from their vegetarian cousins as wild buffaloes from a herd of prize Guernseys. It was a sperm whale that had rammed and sunk the *Essex* and thus inspired the closing chapter of *Moby Dick;* he had no desire to figure in a submarine sequel.

Yet he held stubbornly to his course, though now the racing echoes were less than fifteen seconds away. Then he saw that they were beginning to separate; even if they were not scared, the whales had become confused. Probably the noise of his motors had made them lose contact with their target. He cut his speed to zero, and the three whales began to circle him inquisitively, at a range of about a hundred feet. Sometimes he caught a shadowy glimpse of them on the TV screen. As he had thought, they were young females, and he felt a little sorry to have robbed them of what should have been their rightful food.

He had broken the momentum of their charge; now it was up to Don to finish his side of the mission. From the brief and occasionally lurid comments from the loudspeaker, it was obvious that this was no easy task. Percy was not yet fully conscious, but he knew that something was wrong and he was beginning to object.

The men on the floating dock had the best view of the final stages. Don surfaced about fifty yards away—and the sea behind him became covered with an undulating mass of jelly, twisting and rolling on the waves. At the greatest speed he dared to risk, Don headed for the open end of the dock. One of Percy's tentacles made a halfhearted grab at the entrance, as if in a somnambulistic effort to avoid captivity, but the speed at which he was being hurried through the water broke his grip. As soon as he was safely inside, the massive steel gates began to close like horizontally operating jaws, and Don jettisoned the towrope fastened around the squid's flukes. He wasted no time in leaving from the other exit, and the second set of lock gates started to close even before he was through. The caging of Percy had taken less than a quarter of a minute.

When Franklin surfaced, in company with three disappointed but not hostile sperm whales, it was some time before he could attract any attention. The entire personnel of the dock were busy staring, with awe, triumph, scientific curiosity, and even downright disbelief, at the monstrous captive now swiftly reviving in his great concrete tank. The water was being thoroughly aerated by the streams of bubbles from a score of pipes, and the last traces of the drugs that had paralyzed him were being flushed out of Percy's system. Beneath the dim amber light that was now the sole illumination inside the dock, the giant squid began to investigate its prison.

First it swam slowly from end to end of the rectangular concrete box, exploring the sides with its tentacles. Then the two immense palps started to climb into the air, waving toward the breathless watchers gathered round the edge of the dock. They touched the electrified netting—and flicked away with a speed that almost eluded the eye. Twice again Percy repeated the experiment before he had convinced himself that there was no way out in this direction, all the while staring up at the puny spectators with a gaze that seemed to betoken an intelligence every wit as great as theirs.

By the time Don and Franklin came aboard, the squid appeared to have settled down in captivity, and was showing a mild interest in a number of fish that had been dropped into its tank. As the two wardens joined

Dr. Roberts behind the wire meshing, they had their first clear and complete view of the monster they had hauled up from the ocean depths.

Their eyes ran along the hundred and more feet of flexible, sinewy strength, the countless claw-ringed suckers, the slowly pulsing jet, and the huge staring eyes of the most superbly equipped beast of prey the world had ever seen. Then Don summed up the thoughts that they were both feeling.

"He's all yours, Doc. I hope you know how to handle him."

Dr. Roberts smiled confidently enough. He was a very happy man, though a small worry was beginning to invade his mind. He had no doubt at all that he could handle Percy, and he was perfectly right. But he was not so sure that he could handle the director when the bills came in for the research equipment he was going to order—and for the mountains of fish that Percy was going to eat.

CHAPTER SIXTEEN

The secretary of the Department of Scientific Research had listened to him attentively enough—and not merely with attention, Franklin told himself, but with a flattering interest. When he had finished the sales talk which had taken such long and careful preparation, he felt a sudden and unexpected emotional letdown. He knew that he had done his best; what happened now was largely out of his hands.

"There are a few points I would like to clear up," said the secretary. "The first is a rather obvious one. Why didn't you go to the Marine Division's own research department instead of coming all the way up to World Secretariat level and contacting D.S.R.?"

It was, Franklin admitted, a rather obvious point—and a somewhat delicate one. But he knew that it would be raised, and he had come prepared.

"Naturally, Mr. Farlan," he answered, "I did my best to get support in the division. There was a good deal of interest, especially after we'd captured that squid. But Operation Percy turned out to be much more expensive than anyone had calculated, and there were a lot of awkward questions about it. The whole affair ended with several of our scientists transferring to other divisions."

"I know," interjected the secretary with a smile. "We've got some of them."

"So any research that isn't of direct practical importance is now frowned on in the division, which is one reason why I came to you. And, frankly, it hasn't the authority to do the sort of thing I propose. The cost of running even two deep-sea subs is considerable, and would have to be approved at higher than divisional level."

"But if it was approved, you are confident that the staff could be made available?"

"Yes, at the right time of the year. Now that the fence is practically one hundred per cent reliable—there's been no major breakdown for three years—we wardens have a fairly slack time except at the annual roundups and slaughterings. That's why it seemed a good idea—"

"To utilize the wasted talents of the wardens?"

"Well, that's putting it a little bluntly. I don't want to give the idea that there is any inefficiency in the bureau."

"I wouldn't dream of suggesting such a thing," smiled the secretary. "The other point is a more personal one. Why are you so keen on this project? You have obviously spent a lot of time and trouble on it—and, if I may say so, risked the disapproval of your superiors by coming directly to me."

That question was not so easy to answer, even to someone you knew well, still less to a stranger. Would this man, who had risen so high in the service of the state, understand the fascination of a mysterious echo on a sonar screen, glimpsed only once, and that years ago? Yes, he would, for he was at least partly a scientist.

"As a chief warden," explained Franklin, "I probably won't be on sea duty much longer. I'm thirty-eight, and getting old for this kind of work. And I've an inquisitive type of mind; perhaps I should have been a scientist myself. This is a problem I'd like to see settled, though I know the odds against it are pretty high."

"I can appreciate that. This chart of confirmed sightings covers about half the world's oceans."

"Yes, I know it looks hopeless, but with the new sonar sets we can scan a volume three times as great as we used to, and an echo that size is easy to pick up. It's only a matter of time before somebody detects it."

"And you want to be that somebody. Well, that's reasonable enough. When I got your original letter I had a talk with my marine biology people, and got about three different opinions—none of them very encouraging. Some of those who admit that these echoes have been seen say that they are probably ghosts due to faults in the sonar sets or returns from discontinuities of some kind in the water."

Franklin snorted. "Anyone who's seen them would know better than that. After all, we're familiar with all the ordinary sonar ghosts and false returns. We have to be."

"Yes, that's what I feel. Some more of my people think that the—let us say—conventional sea serpents have already been accounted for by squids, oarfish, and eels, and that what your patrols have been seeing is either one of these or else a large deep-sea shark."

Franklin shook his head. "I know what all those echoes look like. This is quite different."

"The third objection is a theoretical one. There simply isn't enough food in the extreme ocean depths to support any very large and active forms of life."

"No one can be sure of that. Only in the last century scientists were saying that there could be no life at all on the ocean bed. We know what nonsense *that* turned out to be."

"Well, you've made a good case. I'll see what can be done."

"Thank you very much, Mr. Farlan. Perhaps it would be best if no one in the bureau knew that I'd come to see you."

"We won't tell them, but they'll guess." The secretary rose to his feet, and Franklin assumed that the interview was over. He was wrong.

"Before you go, Mr. Franklin," said the secretary, "you might be able to clear up one little matter that's been worrying me for a good many years."

"What's that, sir?"

"I've never understood what a presumably well-trained warden would be doing in the middle of the night off the Great Barrier Reef, breathing compressed air five hundred feet down."

There was a long silence while the two men, their relationship suddenly altered, stared at each other across the room. Franklin searched his memory, but the other's face evoked no echoes; that was so long ago, and he had met so many people during the intervening years.

"Were you one of the men who pulled me in?" he asked. "If so, I've a lot to thank you for." He paused for a moment, then added, "You see, that wasn't an accident."

"I rather thought so; that explains everything. But before we change the subject, just what happened to Bert Darryl? I've never been able to find the true story."

"Oh, eventually he ran out of credit; he could never make the *Sea Lion* pay its way. The last time I ever saw him was in Melbourne; he was heartbroken because customs duties had been abolished and there was no way an honest smuggler could make a living. Finally he tried to collect the insurance on the *Sea Lion;* he had a convincing fire and had to abandon ship off Cairns. She went to the bottom, but the appraisers went after her, and started asking some very awkward questions when they found that all the valuable fittings had been removed before the fire. I don't know how the captain got out of that mess.

"That was about the end of the old rascal. He took to the bottle in earnest, and one night up in Darwin he decided to go for a swim off the jetty. But he'd forgotten that it was low tide—and in Darwin the tide drops thirty feet. So he broke his neck, and a lot of people besides his creditors were genuinely sorry."

"Poor old Bert. The world will be a dull place when there aren't any more people like him."

That was rather a heretical remark, thought Franklin, coming from the lips of so senior a member of the World Secretariat. But it pleased him greatly, and not merely because he agreed with it. He knew now that he had unexpectedly acquired an influential friend, and that the chances of his project going forward had been immeasurably improved.

He did not expect anything to happen in a hurry, so was not disappointed as the weeks passed in silence. In any event, he was kept busy; the slack season was still three months away, and meanwhile a whole series of minor but annoying crises crowded upon him.

And there was one that was neither minor nor annoying, if indeed it could be called a crisis at all. Anne Franklin arrived wide-eyed and wide-mouthed into the world, and Indra began to have her first serious doubts of continuing her academic career.

Franklin, to his great disappointment, was not home when his daughter was born. He had been in charge of a small task force of six subs, carrying out an offensive sweep off the Pribilof Islands in an attempt to cut down the number of killer whales. It was not the first mission of its kind, but it was the most successful, thanks to the use of improved techniques. The characteristic calls of seals and the smaller whales had been recorded and played back into the sea, while the subs had waited silently for the killers to appear.

They had done so in hundreds, and the slaughter had been immense. By the time the little fleet returned to Base, more than a thousand orcas had been killed. It had been hard and sometimes dangerous work, and despite its importance Franklin had found this scientific butchery extremely depressing. He could not help admiring the beauty, speed, and ferocity of the hunters he was himself hunting, and toward the end of the mission he was almost glad when the rate of kill began to fall off. It seemed that the orcas were learning by bitter experience, and the bureau's statisticians would have to decide whether or not it would be economically worthwhile repeating the operation next season.

Franklin had barely had time to thaw out from this mission and to fondle Anne gingerly, without extracting any signs of recognition from her, when he was shot off to South Georgia. His problem there was to discover why the whales, who had previously swum into the slaughtering pens without any qualms, had suddenly become suspicious and shown a great reluctance to enter the electrified sluices. As it turned out, he did nothing at all to solve the mystery; while he was still looking for psychological factors, a bright young plant inspector discovered that some of the bloody waste from the processing plants was accidentally leaking back into the sea. It was not surprising that the whales, though their sense of smell was not as strongly developed as in other marine animals, had become alarmed as the moving barriers tried to guide them to the place where so many of their relatives had met their doom.

As a chief warden, already being groomed for higher things, Franklin was now a kind of mobile trouble shooter who might be sent anywhere in the world on the bureau's business. Apart from the effect on his home life he welcomed this state of affairs. Once a man had learned the mechanics of a warden's trade, straightforward patrolling and herding had little future in it. People like Don Burley got all the excitement and pleasure they needed from it, but then Don was neither ambitious nor much of an intellectual heavyweight. Franklin told himself this without any sense of superiority; it was a simple statement of fact which Don would be the first to admit.

He was in England, giving evidence as an expert witness before the Whaling Commission—the bureau's state-appointed watchdog—when he received a plaintive call from Dr. Lundquist, who had taken over when Dr. Roberts had left the Bureau of Whales to accept a much more lucrative appointment at the Marineland aquarium.

"I've just had three crates of gear delivered from the Department of Scientific Research. It's nothing we ever ordered, but your name is on it. What's it all about?"

Franklin thought quickly. It *would* arrive when he was away, and if the director came across it before he could prepare the ground there would be fireworks.

"It's too long a story to give now," Franklin answered. "I've got to go before the committee in ten minutes. Just push it out of the way somewhere until I get back—I'll explain everything then."

"I hope it's all right—it's most unusual."

"Nothing to worry about—see you the day after tomorrow. If Don

Burley comes to Base, let him have a look at the stuff. But I'll fix all the paper work when I get back."

That, he told himself, would be the worst part of the whole job. Getting equipment that had never been officially requisitioned onto the bureau's inventory without too many questions was going to be at least as difficult as locating the Great Sea Serpent. . . .

He need not have worried. His new and influential ally, the secretary of the Department of Scientific Research, had already anticipated most of his problems. The equipment was to be on loan to the bureau, and was to be returned as soon as it had done its job. What was more, the director had been given the impression that the whole thing was a D.S.R. project; he might have his doubts, but Franklin was officially covered.

"Since you seem to know all about it, Walter," he said in the lab when the gear was finally unpacked, "you'd better explain what it's supposed to do."

"It's an automatic recorder, much more sophisticated than the ones we have at the gates for counting the whales as they go through. Essentially, it's a long-range sonar scanner that explores a volume of space fifteen miles in radius, clear down to the bottom of the sea. It rejects all fixed echoes, and will only record moving objects. And it can also be set to ignore all objects of less than any desired size. In other words, we can use it to count the number of whales more than, say, fifty feet long, and take no notice of the others. It does this once every six minutes—two hundred and forty times a day—so it will give a virtually continuous census of any desired region."

"Quite ingenious. I suppose D.S.R. wants us to moor the thing somewhere and service it?"

"Yes—and to collect the recordings every week. They should be very useful to us as well. Er—there are three of the things, by the way."

"Trust D.S.R. to do it in style! I wish we had as much money to throw around. Let me know how the things work—if they do."

It was as simple as that, and there had been no mention at all of sea serpents.

Nor was there any sign of them for more than two months. Every week, whatever patrol sub happened to be in the neighborhood would bring back the records from the three instruments, moored half a mile below sea level at the spots Franklin had chosen after a careful study of all the known sightings. With an eagerness which slowly subsided to a stubborn determination, he examined the hundreds of feet of old-fashioned sixteen-millimeter film—still unsurpassed in its own field as a recording medium. He looked at thousands of echoes as he projected the film, condensing into minutes the comings and goings of giant sea creatures through many days and nights.

Usually the pictures were blank, for he had set the discriminator to reject all echoes from objects less than seventy feet in length. That, he calculated, should eliminate all but the very largest whales—and the quarry he was seeking. When the herds were on the move, however, the film would be dotted with echoes which would jump across the screen at fantastically exaggerated speeds as he projected the images. He was watching the life of the sea accelerated almost ten thousand times.

After two months of fruitless watching, he began to wonder if he had chosen the wrong places for all three recorders, and was making plans to move them. When the next rolls of film came back, he told himself, he would do just that, and he had already decided on the new locations.

But this time he found what he had been looking for. It was on the edge of the screen, and had been caught by only four sweeps of the scanner. Two days ago that unforgotten, curiously linear echo had appeared on the recorder; now he had evidence, but he still lacked proof.

He moved the other two recorders into the area, arranging the three instruments in a great triangle fifteen miles on a side, so that their fields overlapped. Then it was a question of waiting with what patience he could until another week had passed.

The wait was worth it; at the end of that time he had all the ammunition he needed for his campaign. The proof was there, clear and undeniable.

A very large animal, too long and thin to be any of the known creatures of the sea, lived at the astonishing depth of twenty thousand feet and came halfway to the surface twice a day, presumably to feed. From its intermittent appearance on the screens of the recorders, Franklin was able to get a fairly good idea of its habits and movements. Unless it suddenly left the area and he lost track of it, there should be no great difficulty in repeating the success of Operation Percy.

He should have remembered that in the sea nothing is ever twice the same.

CHAPTER SEVENTEEN

"You know, dear," said Indra, "I'm rather glad this is going to be one of your last missions."

"If you think I'm getting too old—"

"Oh, it's not only that. When you're on headquarters duty we'll be able to start leading a normal social life. I'll be able to invite people to dinner without having to apologize because you've suddenly been called out to round up a sick whale. And it will be better for the children; I won't have to keep explaining to them who the strange man is they sometimes meet around the house."

"Well, it's not *that* bad, is it, Pete?" laughed Franklin, tousling his son's dark, unruly hair.

"When are you going to take me down in a sub, Daddy?" asked Peter, for approximately the hundredth time.

"One of these days, when you're big enough not to get in the way."

"But if you wait until I am big, I *will* get in the way."

"There's logic for you!" said Indra. "I told you my child was a genius."

"He may have got his hair from you," said Franklin, "but it doesn't follow that you're responsible for what lies beneath it." He turned to Don, who was making ridiculous noises for Anne's benefit. She seemed unable to decide whether to laugh or to burst into tears, but was obviously giving the problem her urgent attention. "When are you going to settle down to the joys of domesticity? You can't be an honorary uncle all your life."

For once, Don looked a little embarrassed.

"As a matter of fact," he said slowly, "I am thinking about it. I've met someone at last who looks as if she might be willing."

"Congratulations! I thought you and Marie were seeing a lot of each other."

Don looked still more embarrassed.

"Well—ah—it isn't Marie. I was just trying to say good-by to *her*."

"Oh," said Franklin, considerably deflated. "Who is it?"

"I don't think you know her. She's named June—June Curtis. She isn't in the bureau at all, which is an advantage in some ways. I've not quite made up my mind yet, but I'll probably ask her next week."

"There's only one thing to do," said Indra firmly. "As soon as you come back from this hunt, bring her around to dinner and I'll tell you what we think of her."

"And I'll tell her what we think of *you,*" put in Franklin. "We can't be fairer than that, can we?"

He remembered Indra's words—"this is going to be one of your last missions"—as the little depth ship slanted swiftly down into the eternal night. It was not strictly true, of course; even though he had now been promoted to a permanent shore position, he would still occasionally go to sea. But the opportunities would become fewer and fewer; this was his swan song as a warden, and he did not know whether to be sorry or glad.

For seven years he had roamed the oceans—one year of his life to each of the seas—and in that time he had grown to know the creatures of the deep as no man could ever have done in any earlier age. He had watched the sea in all its moods; he had coasted over mirror-flat waters, and had felt the surge of mighty waves lifting his vessel when it was a hundred feet below the storm-tossed surface. He had looked upon beauty and horror and birth and death in all their multitudinous forms, as he moved through a liquid world so teeming with life that by comparison the land was an empty desert.

No man could ever exhaust the wonder of the sea, but Franklin knew that the time had come for him to take up new tasks. He looked at the sonar screen for the accompanying cigar of light which was Don's ship, and thought affectionately of their common characteristics and of the differences which now must take them further and further apart. Who would have imagined, he told himself, that they would become such good friends, that far-off day when they had met warily as instructor and pupil?

That had been only seven years ago, but already it was hard for him to remember the sort of person he had been in those days. He felt an abiding gratitude for the psychologists who had not only rebuilt his mind but had found him the work that could rebuild his life.

His thoughts completed the next, inevitable step. Memory tried to re-create Irene and the boys—good heavens, Rupert would be twelve years old now!—around whom his whole existence had once revolved, but who now were strangers drifting further and further apart year by year. The last photograph he had of them was already more than a year old; the last letter from Irene had been posted on Mars six months ago, and he reminded himself guiltily that he had not yet answered it.

All the grief had gone long ago; he felt no pain at being an exile in his own world, no ache to see once more the faces of friends he had known in the days when he counted all space his empire. There was only a wistful sadness, not even wholly unpleasant, and a mild regret for the inconstancy of sorrow.

Don's voice broke into his reverie, which had never taken his attention away from his crowded instrument panel.

"We're just passing my record, Walt. Ten thousand's the deepest I've ever been."

"And we're only halfway there. Still, what difference does it make if you've got the right ship? It just takes a bit longer to go down, and a bit longer to come up. These subs would still have a safety factor of five at the bottom of the Philippine Trench."

"That's true enough, but you can't convince me there's no psychological difference. Don't *you* feel two miles of water on your shoulders?"

It was most unlike Don to be so imaginative; usually it was Franklin who made such remarks and was promptly laughed at. If Don was getting moody, it would be best to give him some of his own medicine.

"Tell me when you've got to start bailing," said Franklin. "If the water gets up to your chin, we'll turn back."

He had to admit that the feeble joke helped his own morale. The knowledge that the pressure around him was rising steadily to five tons per square inch did have a definite effect on his mind—an effect he had never experienced in shallow-water operations where disaster could be just as instantaneous, just as total. He had complete confidence in his equipment and knew that the sub would do all that he asked it to; but he still felt that curious feeling of depression which seemed to have taken most of the zest out of the project into which he had put so much effort.

Five thousand feet lower down, that zest returned with all its old vigor. They both saw the echo simultaneously, and for a moment were shouting at cross purposes until they remembered their signals discipline. When silence had been restored, Franklin gave his orders.

"Cut your motor to quarter speed," he said. "We know the beast's very sensitive and we don't want to scare it until the last minute."

"Can't we flood the bow tanks and glide down?"

"Take too long—he's still three thousand feet below. And cut your sonar to minimum power; I don't want him picking up our pulses."

The animal was moving in a curiously erratic path at a constant depth, sometimes making little darts to right or left as if in search of food. It was following the slopes of an unusually steep submarine mountain, which rose abruptly some four thousand feet from the sea bed. Not for the first time, Franklin thought what a pity it was that the world's most stupendous scenery was all sunk beyond sight in the ocean depths. Nothing on the land could compare with the hundred-mile-wide canyons of the North Atlantic, or the monstrous potholes that gave the Pacific the deepest soundings on earth.

They sank slowly below the summit of the submerged mountain—a mountain whose topmost peak was three miles below sea level. Only a little way beneath them now that mysteriously elongated echo seemed to be undulating through the water with a sinuous motion which reminded Franklin irresistibly of a snake. It would, he thought, be ironic if the Great Sea Serpent turned out to be exactly that. But that was impossible, for there were no water-breathing snakes.

Neither man spoke during the slow and cautious approach to their goal. They both realized that this was one of the great moments of their lives, and wished to savor it to the full. Until now, Don had been mildly skeptical, believing that whatever they found would be no more than some already-known species of animal. But as the echo on the screen expanded, so its strangeness grew. This was something wholly new.

The mountain was now looming above them; they were skirting the foot of a cliff more than two thousand feet high, and their quarry was less than half a mile ahead. Franklin felt his hand itching to throw on the ultraviolet searchlights which in an instant might solve the oldest mystery of the sea, and bring him enduring fame. How important to him was that? he asked himself, as the seconds ticked slowly by. That it was important, he did not attempt to hide from himself. In all his career, he might never have another opportunity like this. . . .

Suddenly, without the slightest warning, the sub trembled as if struck by a hammer. At the same moment Don cried out: "My God—what was that?"

"Some damn fool is letting off explosives," Franklin replied, rage and frustration completely banishing fear. "Wasn't everyone notified of our dive?"

"That's no explosion. I've felt it before—it's an earthquake."

No other word could so swiftly have conjured up once more all that terror of the ultimate depths which Franklin had felt brushing briefly against his mind during their descent. At once the immeasurable weight of the waters crushed down upon him like a physical burden; his sturdy craft seemed the frailest of cockleshells, already doomed by forces which all man's science could no longer hold at bay.

He knew that earthquakes were common in the deep Pacific, where the weights of rock and water were forever poised in precarious equilibrium. Once or twice on patrols he had felt distant shocks—but this time, he felt certain, he was near the epicenter.

"Make full speed for the surface," he ordered. "That may be just the beginning."

"But we only need another five minutes," Don protested. "Let's chance it, Walt."

Franklin was sorely tempted. That single shock might be the only one; the strain on the tortured strata miles below might have been relieved. He glanced at the echo they had been chasing; it was moving much faster now, as if it, too, had been frightened by this display of Nature's slumbering power.

"We'll risk it," Franklin decided. "But if there's another one we'll go straight up."

"Fair enough," answered Don. "I'll bet you ten to one—"

He never completed the sentence. This time the hammer blow was no more violent, but it was sustained. The entire ocean seemed to be in travail as the shock waves, traveling at almost a mile a second, were reflected back and forth between surface and sea bed. Franklin shouted the one word "Up!" and tilted the sub as steeply as he dared toward the distant sky.

But the sky was gone. The sharply defined plane which marked the water-air interface on the sonar screen had vanished, replaced by a meaningless jumble of hazy echoes. For a moment Franklin assumed that the set had been put out of action by the shocks; then his mind interpreted the incredible, the terrifying picture that was taking shape upon the screen.

"Don," he yelled, "run for the open sea—the mountain's falling!"

The billions of tons of rock that had been towering above them were sliding down into the deep. The whole face of the mountain had split away and was descending in a waterfall of stone, moving with a deceptive slowness and an utterly irresistible power. It was an avalanche in slow motion, but Franklin knew that within seconds the waters through which his sub was driving would be torn with falling debris.

He was moving at full speed, yet he seemed motionless. Even without the amplifiers, he could hear through the hull the rumble and roar of grinding rock. More than half the sonar image was now obliterated, either by solid fragments or by the immense clouds of mud and silt that were now beginning to fill the sea. He was becoming blind; there was nothing he could do but hold his course and pray.

With a muffled thud, something crashed against the hull and the sub groaned from end to end. For a moment Franklin thought he had lost control; then he managed to fight the vessel back to an even keel. No sooner had he done this than he realized he was in the grip of a powerful current, presumably due to water displaced by the collapsing mountain.

He welcomed it, for it was sweeping him to the safety of the open sea, and for the first time he dared to hope.

Where was Don? It was impossible to see his echo in the shifting chaos of the sonar screen. Franklin switched his communication set to high power and started calling through the moving darkness. There was no reply; probably Don was too busy to answer, even if he had received the signal.

The pounding shock waves had ceased; with them had gone the worst of Franklin's fears. There was no danger now of the hull being cracked by pressure, and by this time, surely, he was clear of the slowly toppling mountain. The current that had been aiding his engines had now lost its strength, proving that he was far away from its source. On the sonar screen, the luminous haze that had blocked all vision was fading minute by minute as the silt and debris subsided.

Slowly the wrecked face of the mountain emerged from the mist of conflicting echoes. The pattern on the screen began to stabilize itself, and presently Franklin could see the great scar left by the avalanche. The sea bed itself was still hidden in a vast fog of mud; it might be hours before it would be visible again and the damage wrought by Nature's paroxysm could be ascertained.

Franklin watched and waited as the screen cleared. With each sweep of the scanner, the sparkle of interference faded; the water was still turbid, but no longer full of suspended matter. He could see for a mile—then two—then three.

And in all that space there was no sign of the sharp and brilliant echo that would mark Don's ship. Hope faded as his radius of vision grew and the screen remained empty. Again and again he called into the lonely silence, while grief and helplessness strove for the mastery of his soul.

He exploded the signal grenades that would alert all the hydrophones in the Pacific and send help racing to him by sea and air. But even as he began his slowly descending spiral search, he knew that it was in vain.

Don Burley had lost his last bet.

Part III · The Bureaucrat

✶ CHAPTER EIGHTEEN

The great Mercator chart that covered the whole of one wall was a most unusual one. All the land areas were completely blank; as far as this map maker was concerned, the continents had never been explored. But the sea was crammed with detail, and scattered over its face were countless spots of colored light, projected by some mechanism inside the wall. Those spots moved slowly from hour to hour, recording as they did so, for skilled eyes to read, the migration of all the main schools of whales that roamed the seas.

Franklin had seen the master chart scores of times during the last fourteen years—but never from this vantage point. For he was looking at it now from the director's chair.

"There's no need for me to warn you, Walter," said his ex-chief, "that you are taking over the bureau at a very tricky time. Sometime in the next five years we're going to have a showdown with the farms. Unless we can improve our efficiency, plankton-derived proteins will soon be substantially cheaper than any we can deliver.

"And that's only one of our problems. The staff position is getting more difficult every year—and this sort of thing isn't going to help."

He pushed a folder across to Franklin, who smiled wryly when he saw what it contained. The advertisement was familiar enough; it had appeared in all the major magazines during the past week, and must have cost the Space Department a small fortune.

An underwater scene of improbable clarity and color was spread across two pages. Vast scaly monsters, more huge and hideous than any that had lived on Earth since the Jurassic period, were battling each other in the crystalline depths. Franklin knew, from the photographs he had seen, that they were very accurately painted, and he did not grudge the illustrator his artistic license in the matter of underwater clarity.

The text was dignified and avoided sensationalism; the painting was sensational enough and needed no embellishment. The Space Department, he read, urgently needed young men as wardens and food production experts for the exploitation of the seas of Venus. The work, it was added, was probably the most exciting and rewarding to be found anywhere in the solar system; pay was good and the qualifications were not as high as those needed for space pilot or astrogator. After the short list of physical and educational requirements, the advertisement ended with the words which the Venus Commission had been plugging for the last six months, and which Franklin had grown heartily tired of seeing: HELP TO BUILD A SECOND EARTH.

"Meanwhile," said the ex-director, "our problem is to keep the first one going, when the bright youngsters who might be joining us are running away to Venus. And between you and me, I shouldn't be surprised if the Space Department has been after some of our men."

"They wouldn't do a thing like that!"

"Wouldn't they now? Anyway, there's a transfer application in from First Warden McRae; if you can't talk him out of it, try to find what made him want to leave."

Life was certainly going to be difficult, Franklin thought. Joe McRae was an old friend; could he impose on that friendship now that he was Joe's boss?

"Another of your little problems is going to be keeping the scientists under control. Lundquist is worse than Roberts ever was; he's got about six crazy schemes going, and at least Roberts only had one brainstorm at a time. He spends half his time over on Heron Island. It might be a good idea to fly over and have a look at him. That was something I never had a chance to get around to."

Franklin was still listening politely as his predecessor continued, with obvious relish, to point out the many disadvantages of his new post. Most of them he already knew, and his mind was now far away. He was thinking how pleasant it would be to begin his directorate with an official visit to Heron Island, which he had not seen for nearly five years, and which had so many memories of his first days in the bureau.

Dr. Lundquist was flattered by the new director's visit, being innocent enough to hope that it might lead to increased support for his activities. He would not have been so enthusiastic had he guessed that the opposite was more likely to be the case. No one could have been more sympathetic than Franklin to scientific research, but now that he had to approve the bills himself he found that his point of view was subtly altered. Whatever Lundquist was doing would have to be of direct value to the bureau. Otherwise it was out—unless the Department of Scientific Research could be talked into taking it over.

Lundquist was a small, intense little man whose rapid and somewhat jerky movements reminded Franklin of a sparrow. He was an enthusiast of a type seldom met these days, and he combined a sound scientific background with an unfettered imagination. How unfettered, Franklin was soon to discover.

Yet at first sight it seemed that most of the work going on at the lab was of a fairly routine nature. Franklin spent a dull half-hour while two young scientists explained the methods they were developing to keep whales free of the many parasites that plagued them, and then escaped by the skin of his teeth from a lecture on cetacean obstetrics. He listened with more interest to the latest work on artificial insemination, having in the past helped with some of the early—and often hilariously unsuccessful—experiments along this line. He sniffed cautiously at some synthetic ambergris, and agreed that it seemed just like the real thing. And he listened to the recorded heartbeat of a whale before and after the cardiac operation that had saved its life, and pretended that he could hear the difference.

Everything here was perfectly in order, and just as he had expected. Then Lundquist steered him out of the lab and down to the big pool, saying as he did so: "I think you'll find this more interesting. It's only in the experimental stage, of course, but it has possibilities."

The scientist looked at his watch and muttered to himself, "Two minutes to go; she's usually in sight by now." He glanced out beyond the reef, then said with satisfaction, "Ah—there she is!"

A long black mound was moving in toward the island, and a moment later Franklin saw the typical stubby spout of vapor which identified the humpback whale. Almost at once he saw a second, much smaller spout, and realized that he was watching a female and her calf. Without hesitation, both animals came in through the narrow channel that had been blasted through the coral years ago so that small boats could come up to the lab. They turned left into a large tidal pool that had not been here on Franklin's last visit, and remained there waiting patiently like well-trained dogs.

Two lab technicians, wearing oilskins, were trundling something that looked like a fire extinguisher to the edge of the pool. Lundquist and Franklin hurried to join them, and it was soon obvious why the oilskins were necessary on this bright and cloudless day. Every time the whales spouted there was a miniature rainstorm, and Franklin was glad to borrow protection from the descending and nauseous spray.

Even a warden seldom saw a live whale at such close quarters, and under such ideal conditions. The mother was about fifty feet long, and, like all humpbacks, very massively built. She was no beauty, Franklin decided, and the large, irregular warts along the leading edges of her flippers did nothing to add to her appearance. The little calf was about twenty feet in length, and did not appear to be too happy in its confined quarters, for it was anxiously circling its stolid mother.

One of the scientists gave a curious, high-pitched shout, and at once the whale rolled over on her side, bringing half of her pleated belly out of the water. She did not seem to mind when a large rubber cup was placed over the now-exposed teat; indeed, she was obviously co-operating, for the meter on the collecting tank was recording an astonishing rate of flow.

"You know, of course," explained Lundquist, "that the cows eject their milk under pressure, so that the calves can feed when the teats are submerged without getting water in their mouths. But when the calves are *very* young, the mother rolls over like this so that the baby can feed above water. It makes things a lot simpler for us."

The obedient whale, without any instructions that Franklin could detect, had now circled round in her pen and was rolling over on the other side, so that her second teat could be milked. He looked at the meter; it now registered just under fifty gallons, and was still rising. The calf was obviously getting worried, or perhaps it had become excited by the milk that had accidentally spilled into the water. It made several attempts to bunt its mechanical rival out of the way, and had to be discouraged by a few sharp smacks.

Franklin was impressed, but not surprised. He knew that this was not the first time that whales had been milked, though he did not know that it could now be done with such neatness and dispatch. But where was it leading? Knowing Dr. Lundquist, he could guess.

"Now," said the scientist, obviously hoping that the demonstration had made its desired impact, "we can get at least five hundred pounds of milk a day from a cow without interfering with the calf's growth. And if we start breeding for milk as the farmers have done on land, we should be able to get a ton a day without any trouble. You think that's a lot? I regard it as quite a modest target. After all, prize cattle have given over a hundred pounds of milk a day—and a whale weighs a good deal more than twenty times as much as a cow!"

Franklin did his best to interrupt the statistics.

"That's all very well," he said. "I don't doubt your figures. And equally I don't doubt that you can process the milk to remove that oily taste—yes, I've tried it, thanks. But how the devil are you going to round up all the cows in a herd—especially a herd that migrates ten thousand miles a year?"

"Oh, we've worked all that out. It's partly a matter of training, and we've learned a lot getting Susan here to obey our underwater recordings. Have you ever been to a dairy farm and watched how the cows walk into the autolactor at milking time and walk out again—without a human being coming within miles of the place? And believe me, whales are a lot smarter and more easily trained than cows! I've sketched out the rough designs for a milk tanker that can deal with four whales at once, and could follow the herd as it migrates. In any case, now that we can control the plankton yield we can stop migration if we want to, and keep the whales in the tropics without them getting hungry. The whole thing's quite practical, I assure you."

Despite himself, Franklin was fascinated by the idea. It had been suggested, in some form or other, for many years, but Dr. Lundquist seemed to have been the first to do anything about it.

The mother whale and her still somewhat indignant calf had now set out to sea, and were soon spouting and diving noisily beyond the edge of the reef. As Franklin watched them go, he wondered if in a few years' time he would see hundreds of the great beasts lined up obediently as they swam to the mobile milking plants, each delivering a ton of what was known to be one of the richest foods on earth. But it might remain only a dream; there would be countless practical problems to be faced, and what had been achieved on the laboratory scale with a single animal might prove out of the question in the sea.

"What I'd like you to do," he said to Lundquist, "is to let me have a report showing what an—er—whale dairy would require in terms of equipment and personnel. Try to give costs wherever you can. And then estimate how much milk it could deliver, and what the processing plants would pay for that. Then we'll have something definite to work on. At the moment it's an interesting experiment, but no one can say if it has any practical application."

Lundquist seemed slightly disappointed at Franklin's lack of enthusiasm, but rapidly warmed up again as they walked away from the pool. If Franklin had thought that a little project like setting up a whale dairy had exhausted Lundquist's powers of extrapolation, he was going to learn better.

"The next proposal I want to talk about," began the scientist, "is still entirely in the planning stage. I know that one of our most serious problems is staff shortage, and I've been trying to think of ways in which we can improve efficiency by releasing men from routine jobs."

"Surely that process has gone about as far as it can, short of making everything completely automatic? Anyway, it's less than a year since the last team of efficiency experts went over us." (And, added Franklin to himself, the bureau isn't quite back to normal yet.)

"My approach to the problem," explained Lundquist, "is a little unconventional, and as an ex-warden yourself I think you'll be particularly interested in it. As you know, it normally takes two or even three subs to round up a large school of whales; if a single sub tries it, they'll scatter in all directions. Now this has often seemed to me a shocking waste of man power and equipment, since all the thinking could be done by a single warden. He only needs his partners to make the right noises in the right places—something a machine could do just as well."

"If you're thinking of automatic slave subs," said Franklin, "it's been tried—and it didn't work. A warden can't handle two ships at once, let alone three."

"I know all about *that* experiment," answered Lundquist. "It could have been a success if they'd tackled it properly. But my idea is much more revolutionary. Tell me—does the name 'sheep dog' mean anything to you?"

Franklin wrinkled his brow. "I think so," he replied. "Weren't they dogs that the old-time shepherds used to protect their flocks, a few hundred years ago?"

"It happened until less than a hundred years ago. And 'protect' is an understatement with a vengeance. I've been looking at film records of sheep dogs in action, and no one who hadn't seen them would believe some of the things they could do. Those dogs were so intelligent and so well-trained that they could make a flock of sheep do anything the shepherd wanted, merely at a word of command from him. They could split a flock into sections, single out one solitary sheep from its fellows, or keep a flock motionless in one spot as long as their master ordered.

"Do you see what I am driving at? We've been training dogs for centuries, so such a performance doesn't seem miraculous to us. What I am suggesting is that we repeat the pattern in the sea. We know that a good many marine mammals—seals and porpoises, for instance—are at least as intelligent as dogs, but except in circuses and places like Marineland there's been no attempt to train them. You've seen the tricks our porpoises here can do, and you know how affectionate and friendly they are. When you've watched these old films of sheep-dog trials, you'll agree that anything a dog could do a hundred years ago we can teach a porpoise to do today."

"Just a minute," said Franklin, a little overwhelmed. "Let me get this straight. Are you proposing that every warden should have a couple of—er—hounds working with him when he rounds up a school of whales?"

"For certain operations, yes. Of course, the technique would have limitations; no marine animal has the speed and range of a sub, and the hounds, as you've called them, couldn't always get to the places where they were needed. But I've done some studies and I think it would be possible to double the effectiveness of our wardens in this way, by eliminating the times when they had to work in pairs or trios."

"But," protested Franklin, "what notice would whales take of porpoises? They'd ignore them completely."

"Oh, I wasn't suggesting that we should use porpoises; that was merely an example. You're quite right—the whales wouldn't even notice them. We'll have to use an animal that's fairly large, at least as intelligent as the porpoise, and which whales will pay a great deal of attention to indeed. There's only one animal that fills the bill, and I'd like your authority to catch one and train it."

"Go on," said Franklin, with such a note of resignation in his voice that even Lundquist, who had little sense of humor, was forced to smile.

"What I want to do," he continued, "is to catch a couple of killer whales and train them to work with one of our wardens."

Franklin thought of the thirty-foot torpedoes of ravening power he had so often chased and slaughtered in the frozen polar seas. It was hard to picture one of these ferocious beasts tamed to man's bidding; then he remembered the chasm between the sheep dog and the wolf, and how that had long ago been bridged. Yes, it could be done again—if it was worthwhile.

When in doubt, ask for a report, one of his superiors had once told him. Well, he was going to bring back at least two from Heron Island, and they would both make very thought-provoking reading. But Lundquist's schemes, exciting though they were, belonged to the future; Franklin had to run the bureau as it was here and now. He would prefer to avoid drastic changes for a few years, until he had learned his way about. Besides, even if Lundquist's ideas could be proved practical, it would be a long, stiff battle selling them to the people who approved the funds. "I want to buy fifty milking machines for whales, please." Yes, Franklin could picture the reaction in certain conservative quarters. And as for training killer whales—why, they would think he had gone completely crazy.

He watched the island fall away as the plane lifted him toward home (strange, after all his travels, that he should be living again in the country of his birth). It was almost fifteen years since he had first made this journey with poor old Don; how glad Don would have been, could he have seen this final fruit of his careful training! And Professor Stevens, too—Franklin had always been a little scared of him, but now he could have looked him in the face, had he still been alive. With a twinge of remorse, he realized that he had never properly thanked the psychologist for all that he had done.

Fifteen years from a neurotic trainee to director of the bureau; that wasn't bad going. And what now, Walter? Franklin asked himself. He felt no need of any further achievement; perhaps his ambition was now satisfied. He would be quite content to guide the bureau into a placid and uneventful future.

It was lucky for his peace of mind that he had no idea how futile that hope was going to be.

CHAPTER NINETEEN

The photographer had finished, but the young man who had been Franklin's shadow for the last two days still seemed to have an unlimited supply of notebooks and questions. Was it worth all this trouble to have your undistinguished features—probably superimposed on a montage of whales—displayed upon every bookstand in the world? Franklin doubted it, but he had no choice in the matter. He remembered the saying: "Public servants have no private lives." Like all aphorisms, it was only half true. No one had ever heard of the last director of the bureau, and he might have led an equally inconspicuous existence if the Marine Division's Public Relations Department had not decreed otherwise.

"Quite a number of your people, Mr. Franklin," said the young man from *Earth Magazine*, "have told me about your interest in the so-called Great Sea Serpent, and the mission in which First Warden Burley was killed. Have there been any further developments in this field?"

Franklin sighed; he had been afraid that this would come up sooner or later, and he hoped that it wouldn't be overplayed in the resulting article. He walked over to his private file cabinet, and pulled out a thick folder of notes and photographs.

"Here are all the sightings, Bob," he said. "You might like to have a glance through them—I've kept the record up to date. One day I hope we'll have the answer; you can say it's still a hobby of mine, but it's one I've had no chance of doing anything about for the last eight years. It's up to the Department of Scientific Research now—not the Bureau of Whales. We've other jobs to do."

He could have added a good deal more, but decided against it. If Secretary Farlan had not been transferred from D.S.R. soon after the tragic failure of their mission, they might have had a second chance. But in the inquiries and recriminations that had followed the disaster, the opportunity had been lost, possibly for years. Perhaps in every man's life there must be some cherished failure, some unfinished business which outweighed many successes.

"Then there's only one other question I want to ask," continued the reporter. "What about the future of the bureau? Have you any interesting long-term plans you'd care to talk about?"

This was another tricky one. Franklin had learned long ago that men in his position must co-operate with the press, and in the last two days his busy interrogator had practically become one of the family. But there were some things that sounded a little too farfetched, and he had contrived to keep Dr. Lundquist out of the way when Bob had flown over to Heron Island. True, he had seen the prototype milking machine and been duly impressed by it, but he had been told nothing about the two young killer whales being maintained, at great trouble and expense, in the enclosure off the eastern edge of the reef.

"Well, Bob," he began slowly, "by this time you probably know the statistics better than I do. We hope to increase the size of our herds by ten per cent over the next five years. If this milking scheme comes off—and it's still purely experimental—we'll start cutting back on the sperm whales and will build up the humpbacks. At the moment we are providing twelve and a half per cent of the total food requirements of the human race, and that's quite a responsibility. I hope to see it fifteen per cent while I'm still in office."

"So that everyone in the world will have whale steak at least once a week, eh?"

"Put it that way if you like. But people are eating whale all day without knowing it—every time they use cooking fat or spread margarine on a piece of bread. We could double our output and we'd get no credit for it, since our products are almost always disguised in something else."

"The Art Department is going to put that right; when the story appears, we'll have a picture of the average household's groceries for a week, with a clock face on each item showing what percentage of it comes from whales."

"That'll be fine. Er—by the way—have you decided what you're going to call me?"

The reporter grinned.

"That's up to my editor," he answered. "But I'll tell him to avoid the word 'whaleboy' like the plague. It's too hackneyed, anyway."

"Well, I'll believe you when we see the article. Every journalist promises he won't call us that, but it seems they can never resist the temptation. Incidentally, when do you expect the story to appear?"

"Unless some news story crowds it off, in about four weeks. You'll get the proofs, of course, before that—probably by the end of next week."

Franklin saw him off through the outer office, half sorry to lose an entertaining companion who, even if he asked awkward questions, more than made up for it by the stories he could tell about most of the famous men on the planet. Now, he supposed, he belonged to that group himself, for at least a hundred million people would read the current "Men of *Earth*" series.

The story appeared, as promised, four weeks later. It was accurate, well-written, and contained one mistake so trivial that Franklin himself had failed to notice it when he checked the proofs. The photographic coverage was excellent and contained an astonishing study of a baby whale suckling its mother—a shot obviously obtained at enormous risk and after months of patient stalking. The fact that it was actually taken in the pool at Heron Island without the photographer even getting his feet wet was an irrelevance not allowed to distract the reader.

Apart from the shocking pun beneath the cover picture ("Prince of Whales," indeed!), Franklin was delighted with it; so was everyone else in the bureau, the Marine Division, and even the World Food Organization itself. No one could have guessed that within a few weeks it was to involve the Bureau of Whales in the greatest crisis of its entire history.

It was not lack of foresight; sometimes the future can be charted in advance, and plans made to meet it. But there are also times in human affairs when events that seem to have no possible connection—to be as remote as if they occurred on different planets—may react upon each other with shattering violence.

The Bureau of Whales was an organization which had taken half a century to build up, and which now employed twenty thousand men and possessed equipment valued at over two billion dollars. It was a typical unit of the scientific world state, with all the power and prestige which that implied.

And now it was to be shaken to its foundations by the gentle words of a man who had lived half a thousand years before the birth of Christ.

Franklin was in London when the first hint of trouble came. It was not unusual for officers of the World Food Organization to bypass his immediate superiors in the Marine Division and to contact him directly. What was unusual, however, was for the secretary of the W.F.O. himself to interfere with the everyday working of the bureau, causing Franklin to cancel all his engagements and to find himself, still a little dazed, flying halfway around the world to a small town in Ceylon of which he had never heard before and whose name he could not even pronounce.

Fortunately, it had been a hot summer in London and the extra ten degrees at Colombo was not unduly oppressive. Franklin was met at the airport by the local W.F.O. representative, looking very cool and comfortable in the sarong which had now been adopted by even the most conservative of westerners. He shook hands with the usual array of minor officials, was relieved to see that there were no reporters around who might tell him more about this mission than he knew himself, and swiftly transferred to the cross-country plane which would take him on the last hundred miles of his journey.

"Now," he said, when he had recovered his breath and the miles of neatly laid-out automatic tea plantations were flashing past beneath him, "you'd better start briefing me. Why is it so important to rush me to Anna—whatever you call the place?"

"Anuradhapura. Hasn't the secretary told you?"

"We had just five minutes at London Airport. So you might as well start from scratch."

"Well, this is something that has been building up for several years. We've warned Headquarters, but they've never taken us seriously. Now your interview in *Earth* has brought matters to a head; the Mahanayake Thero of Anuradhapura—he's the most influential man in the East, and you're going to hear a lot more about him—read it and promptly asked us to grant him facilities for a tour of the bureau. We can't refuse, of course, but we know perfectly well what he intends to do. He'll take a team of cameramen with him and will collect enough material to launch an all-out propaganda campaign against the bureau. Then, when it's had time to sink in, he'll demand a referendum. And if that goes against us, we *will* be in trouble."

The pieces of the jigsaw fell into place; the pattern was at last clear. For a moment Franklin felt annoyed that he had been diverted across the world to deal with so absurd a challenge. Then he realized that the men who had sent him here did not consider it absurd; they must know, better than he did, the strength of the forces that were being marshaled. It was never wise to underestimate the power of religion, even a religion as pacific and tolerant as Buddhism.

The position was one which, even a hundred years ago, would have seemed unthinkable, but the catastrophic political and social changes of the last century had all combined to give it a certain inevitability. With the failure or weakening of its three great rivals, Buddhism was now the only religion that still possessed any real power over the minds of men.

Christianity, which had never fully recovered from the shattering blow given it by Darwin and Freud, had finally and unexpectedly succumbed before the archaeological discoveries of the late twentieth century. The Hindu religion, with its fantastic pantheon of gods and goddesses, had failed to survive in an age of scientific rationalism. And the Mohammedan faith, weakened by the same forces, had suffered additional loss of prestige when the rising Star of David had outshone the pale crescent of the Prophet.

These beliefs still survived, and would linger on for generations yet, but all their power was gone. Only the teachings of the Buddha had maintained and even increased their influence, as they filled the vacuum left by the other faiths. Being a philosophy and not a religion, and relying on no revelations vulnerable to the archaeologist's hammer, Buddhism had been largely unaffected by the shocks that had destroyed the other giants. It had been purged and purified by internal reformations, but its basic structure was unchanged.

One of the fundamentals of Buddhism, as Franklin knew well enough, was respect for all other living creatures. It was a law that few Buddhists had ever obeyed to the letter, excusing themselves with the sophistry that it was quite in order to eat the flesh of an animal that someone else had killed. In recent years, however, attempts had been made to enforce this rule more rigorously, and there had been endless debates between vegetarians and meat eaters covering the whole spectrum of crankiness. That these arguments could have any practical effect on the work of the World Food Organization was something that Franklin had never seriously considered.

"Tell me," he asked, as the fertile hills rolled swiftly past beneath him, "what sort of man is this Thero you're taking me to see?"

"Thero is his title; you can translate it by archbishop if you like. His real name is Alexander Boyce, and he was born in Scotland sixty years ago."

"Scotland?"

"Yes—he was the first westerner ever to reach the top of the Buddhist hierarchy, and he had to overcome a lot of opposition to do it. A bhikku—er, monk—friend of mine once complained that the Maha Thero was a typical elder of the kirk, born a few hundred years too late—so he'd reformed Buddhism instead of the church of Scotland."

"How did he get to Ceylon in the first place?"

"Believe it or not, he came out as a junior technician in a film company. He was about twenty then. The story is that he went to film the statue of the Dying Buddha at the cave temple of Dambulla, and became converted. After that it took him twenty years to rise to the top, and he's been responsible for most of the reforms that have taken place since then. Religions get corrupt after a couple of thousand years and need a spring-cleaning. The Maha Thero did that job for Buddhism in Ceylon by getting rid of the Hindu gods that had crept into the temples."

"And now he's looking around for fresh worlds to conquer?"

"It rather seems like it. He pretends to have nothing to do with politics, but he's thrown out a couple of governments just by raising his finger, and he's got a huge following in the East. His 'Voice of Buddha' programs are listened to by several hundred million people, and it's estimated that at least a billion are sympathetic toward him even if they won't go all the way with his views. So you'll understand why we are taking this seriously."

Now that he had penetrated the disguise of an unfamiliar name, Franklin remembered that the Venerable Alexander Boyce had been the subject of a cover story in *Earth Magazine* two or three years ago. So they had something in common; he wished now that he had read that article, but at the time it had been of no interest to him and he could not even recall the Thero's appearance.

"He's a deceptively quiet little man, very easy to get on with," was the reply to his question. "You'll find him reasonable and friendly, but once he's made up his mind he grinds through all opposition like a glacier. He's not a fanatic, if that's what you are thinking. If you can prove to him that any course of action is essential, he won't stand in the way even though he may not like what you're doing. He's not happy about our local drive for increased meat production, but he realizes that everybody can't be a vegetarian. We compromised with him by not building our new slaughterhouse in either of the sacred cities, as we'd intended to do originally."

"Then why should he suddenly have taken an interest in the Bureau of Whales?"

"He's probably decided to make a stand somewhere. And besides—don't you think whales are in a different class from other animals?" The remark was made half apologetically, as if in the expectation of denial or even ridicule.

Franklin did not answer; it was a question he had been trying to decide for twenty years, and the scene now passing below absolved him from the necessity.

He was flying over what had once been the greatest city in the world—a city against which Rome and Athens in their prime had been no more than villages—a city unchallenged in size or population until the heydays of London and New York, two thousand years later. A ring of huge artificial lakes, some of them miles across, surrounded the ancient home of the Singhalese kings. Even from the air, the modern town of Anuradhapura showed startling contrasts of old and new. Dotted here and there among the colorful, gossamer buildings of the twenty-first century were the immense, bell-shaped domes of the great dagobas. The mightiest of all—the Abhayagiri Dagoba—was pointed out to Franklin as the plane flew low over it. The brickwork of the dome had long ago been overgrown with grass and even small trees, so that the great temple now appeared no more than a curiously symmetrical hill surmounted by a broken spire. It was a hill exceeded in size by one only of the pyramids that the Pharaohs had built beside the Nile.

By the time that Franklin had reached the local Food Production office, conferred with the superintendent, donated a few platitudes to a reporter who had somehow discovered his presence, and eaten a leisurely meal, he felt that he knew how to handle the situation. It was, after all, merely another public-relations problem; there had been a very similar one about three weeks ago, when a sensational and quite inaccurate newspaper story about methods of whale slaughtering had brought a dozen Societies for the Prevention of Cruelty down upon his head. A fact-finding commission had disposed of the charges very quickly, and no permanent damage had been done to anybody except the reporter concerned.

He did not feel quite so confident, a few hours later, as he stood looking up at the soaring, gilded spire of the Ruanveliseya Dagoba. The immense white dome had been so skillfully restored that it seemed inconceivable that almost twenty-two centuries had passed since its foundations were laid. Completely surrounding the paved courtyard of the temple was a line of life-sized elephants, forming a wall more than a quarter of a mile long. Art and faith had united here to produce one of the world's masterpieces of architecture, and the sense of antiquity was overwhelming. How many of the creations of modern man, wondered Franklin, would be so perfectly preserved in the year 4000?

The great flagstones in the courtyard were burning hot, and he was glad that he had retained his stockings when he left his shoes at the gate. At the base of the dome, which rose like a shining mountain toward the cloudless blue sky, was a single-storied modern building whose clean lines and white plastic walls harmonized well with the work of architects who had died a hundred years before the beginning of the Christian era.

A saffron-robed bhikku led Franklin into the Thero's neat and comfortably air-conditioned office. It might have been that of any busy administrator, anywhere in the world, and the sense of strangeness, which had made him ill at ease ever since he had entered the courtyard of the temple, began to fade.

The Maha Thero rose to greet him; he was a small man, his head barely reaching the level of Franklin's shoulders. His gleaming, shaven scalp somehow depersonalized him, making it hard to judge what he was thinking and harder still to fit him into any familiar categories. At first sight, Franklin was not impressed; then he remembered how many small men had been movers and shakers of the world.

Even after forty years, the Mahanayake Thero had not lost the accent of his birth. At first it seemed incongruous, if not slightly comic, in these surroundings, but within a few minutes Franklin was completely unaware of it.

"It's very good of you to come all this way to see me, Mr. Franklin," said the Thero affably as he shook hands. "I must admit that I hardly expected my request to be dealt with quite so promptly. It hasn't inconvenienced you, I trust?"

"No," replied Franklin manfully. "In fact," he added with rather more truth, "this visit is a novel experience, and I'm grateful for the opportunity of making it."

"Excellent!" said the Thero, apparently with genuine pleasure. "I feel just the same way about my trip down to your South Georgia base, though I don't suppose I'll enjoy the weather there."

Franklin remembered his instructions—"Head him off if you possibly can, but don't try to put any fast ones across on him." Well, he had been given an opening here.

"That's one point I wanted to raise with you, Your Reverence," he answered, hoping he had chosen the correct honorific. "It's midwinter in

South Georgia, and the base is virtually closed down until the late spring. It won't be operating again for about five months."

"How foolish of me—I should have remembered. But I've never been to the Antarctic and I've always wanted to; I suppose I was trying to give myself an excuse. Well—it will have to be one of the northern bases. Which do you suggest—Greenland or Iceland? Just tell me which is more convenient. We don't want to cause any trouble."

It was that last phrase which defeated Franklin before the battle had fairly begun. He knew now that he was dealing with an adversary who could be neither fooled nor deflected from his course. He would simply have to go along with the Thero, dragging his heels as hard as he could, and hoping for the best.

CHAPTER TWENTY

The wide bay was dotted with feathery plumes of mist as the great herd milled around in uncertain circles, not alarmed by the voices that had called it to this spot between the mountains, but merely undecided as to their meaning. All their lives the whales had obeyed the orders that came, sometimes in the form of water-borne vibrations, sometimes in electric shocks, from the small creatures whom they recognized as masters. Those orders, they had come to learn, had never harmed them; often, indeed, they had led them to fertile pastures which they would never have found unaided, for they were in regions of the sea which all their experience and the memories of a million years told them should be barren. And sometimes the small masters had protected them from the killers, turning aside the ravening packs before they could tear their living victims into fragments.

They had no enemies and no fears. For generations now they had roamed the peaceful oceans of the world, growing fatter and sleeker and more contented than all their ancestors back to the beginning of time. In fifty years they had grown, on an average, ten per cent longer and thirty per cent heavier, thanks to the careful stewardship of the masters. Even now the lord of all their race, the hundred-and-fifty-one-foot blue whale B.69322, universally known as Leviathan, was sporting in the Gulf Stream with his mate and newborn calf. Leviathan could never have reached his present size in any earlier age; though such matters were beyond proof, he was probably the largest animal that had ever existed in the entire history of Earth.

Order was emerging out of chaos as the directing fields started to guide the herd along invisible channels. Presently the electric barriers gave way to concrete ones; the whales were swimming along four parallel canals, too narrow for more than one to pass at a time. Automatic senses weighed and measured them, rejecting all those below a certain size and diverting them back into the sea—doubtless a little puzzled, and quite unaware how seriously their numbers had been depleted.

The whales that had passed the test swam on trustfully along the two remaining channels until presently they came to a large lagoon. Some tasks could not be left entirely to machines; there were human inspectors here to see that no mistakes had been made, to check the condition of the animals, and to log the numbers of the doomed beasts as they left the lagoon on their last, short swim into the killing pens.

"B.52111 coming up," said Franklin to the Thero as they stood together in the observation chamber. "Seventy-foot female, known to have had five calves—past the best age for breeding." Behind him, he knew the cameras were silently recording the scene as their ivory-skulled, saffron-robed operators handled them with a professional skill which had surprised him until he learned that they had all been trained in Hollywood.

The whale never had any warning; it probably never even felt the gentle touch of the flexible copper fingers as they brushed its body. One moment it was swimming quietly along the pen; a second later it was a lifeless hulk, continuing to move forward under its own momentum. The fifty-thousand-ampere current, passing through the heart like a stroke of lightning, had not even allowed time for a final convulsion.

At the end of the killing pen, the wide conveyer belt took the weight of the immense body and carried it up a short slope until it was completely clear of the water. Then it began to move slowly forward along an endless series of spinning rollers which seemed to stretch halfway to the horizon.

"This is the longest conveyor of its kind in the world," Franklin explained with justifiable pride. "It may have as many as ten whales—say a thousand tons—on it at one time. Although it involves us in considerable expense, and greatly restricts our choice of site, we always have the processing plant at least half a mile from the pens, so there is no danger of the whales being frightened by the smell of blood. I think you'll agree that not only is the slaughtering instantaneous but the animals show no alarm whatsoever right up to the end."

"Perfectly true," said the Thero. "It all seems very humane. Still, if the whales did get frightened it would be very difficult to handle them, wouldn't it? I wonder if you would go to all this trouble merely to spare their feelings?"

It was a shrewd question, and like a good many he had been asked in the last few days Franklin was not quite sure how to answer it.

"I suppose," he said slowly, "that would depend on whether we could get the money. It would be up to the World Assembly, in the final analysis. The finance committees would have to decide how kind we could afford to be. It's a theoretical question, anyway."

"Of course—but other questions aren't so theoretical," answered the Venerable Boyce, looking thoughtfully at the eighty tons of flesh and bone moving away into the distance. "Shall we get back to the car? I want to see what happens at the other end."

And I, thought Franklin grimly, will be very interested to see how you and your colleagues take it. Most visitors who went through the processing yards emerged rather pale and shaken, and quite a few had been known to faint. It was a standard joke in the bureau that this lesson in food production removed the appetites of all who watched it for several hours after the experience.

The stench hit them while they were still a hundred yards away. Out of the corner of his eye, Franklin could see that the young bhikku carrying the sound recorder was already showing signs of distress, but the Maha Thero seemed completely unaffected. He was still calm and dispassionate five minutes later as he stared down into the reeking inferno where the great carcasses were torn asunder into mountains of meat and bone and guts.

"Just think of it," said Franklin, "for almost two hundred years this job was done by men, often working on board a pitching deck in filthy weather. It's not pretty to watch even now, but can you imagine being down there hacking away with a knife nearly as big as yourself?"

"I think I could," answered the Thero, "but I'd prefer not to." He turned to his cameramen and gave some brief instructions, then watched intently as the next whale arrived on the conveyer belt.

The great body had already been scanned by photoelectric eyes and its dimensions fed into the computer controlling the operations. Even when one knew how it was done, it was uncanny to watch the precision with which the knives and saws moved out on their extensible arms, made their carefully planned pattern of cuts, and then retreated again. Huge grabs seized the foot-thick blanket of blubber and stripped it off as a man peels a banana, leaving the naked, bleeding carcass to move on along the conveyer to the first stage of its dismemberment.

The whale traveled as fast as a man could comfortably walk, and disintegrated before the eyes of the watchers as they kept pace with it. Slabs of meat as large as elephants were torn away and went sliding down side chutes; circular saws whirred through the scaffolding of ribs in a cloud of bone dust; the interlinked plastic bags of the intestines, stuffed with perhaps a ton of shrimps and plankton from the whale's last meal, were dragged away in noisome heaps.

It had taken less than two minutes to reduce a lord of the sea to a bloody shambles which no one but an expert could have recognized. Not even the bones were wasted; at the end of the conveyer belt, the disarticulated skeleton fell into a pit where it would be ground into fertilizer.

"This is the end of the line," said Franklin, "but as far as the processing side is concerned it's only the beginning. The oil has to be extracted from the blubber you saw peeled off in stage one; the meat has to be cut down into more manageable portions and sterilized—we use a high-intensity neutron source for that—and about ten other basic products have to be sorted out and packed for shipment. I'll be glad to show you around any part of the factory you'd like to see. It won't be quite so gruesome as the operations we've just been watching."

The Thero stood for a moment in thoughtful silence, studying the notes he had been making in his incredibly tiny handwriting. Then he looked back along the bloodstained quarter-mile of moving belt, toward the next whale arriving from the killing pen.

"There's one sequence I'm not sure we managed to film properly," he said, coming to a sudden decision. "If you don't mind, I'd like to go back to the beginning and start again."

Franklin caught the recorder as the young monk dropped it. "Never mind, son," he said reassuringly, "the first time is always the worst. When you've been here a few days, you'll be quite puzzled when newcomers complain of the stink."

That was hard to believe, but the permanent staff had assured him that it was perfectly true. He only hoped that the Venerable Boyce was not so thoroughgoing that he would have a chance of putting it to the proof.

"And now, Your Reverence," said Franklin, as the plane lifted above the snow-covered mountains and began the homeward flight to London and Ceylon, "do you mind if I ask how you intend to use all the material you've gathered?"

During the two days they had been together, priest and administrator had established a degree of friendship and mutual respect that Franklin, for his part, still found as surprising as it was pleasant. He considered—as who does not?—that he was good at summing men up, but there were depths in the Mahanayake Thero beyond his powers of analysis. It did not matter; he now knew instinctively that he was in the presence not only of power but also of—there was no escaping from that trite and jejune word—goodness. He had even begun to wonder, with a mounting awe that at any moment might deepen into certainty, if the man who was now his companion would go down into history as a saint.

"I have nothing to hide," said the Thero gently, "and, as you know, deceit is contrary to the teachings of the Buddha. Our position is quite simple. We believe that all creatures have a right to life, and it therefore follows that what you are doing is wrong. Accordingly, we would like to see it stopped."

That was what Franklin had expected, but it was the first time he had obtained a definite statement. He felt a slight sense of disappointment; surely someone as intelligent as the Thero must realize that such a move was totally impracticable, since it would involve cutting off one eighth of the total food supply of the world. And for that matter, why stop at whales? What about cows, sheep, pigs—all the animals that man kept in luxury and then slaughtered at his convenience?

"I know what you are thinking," said the Thero, before he could voice his objections. "We are fully aware of the problems involved, and realize that it will be necessary to move slowly. But a start must be made somewhere, and the Bureau of Whales gives us the most dramatic presentation of our case."

"Thank you," answered Franklin dryly. "But is that altogether fair? What you've seen here happens in every slaughterhouse on the planet. The fact that the scale of operations is different hardly alters the case."

"I quite agree. But we are practical men, not fanatics. We know perfectly well that alternative food sources will have to be found before the world's meat supplies can be cut off."

Franklin shook his head in vigorous disagreement.

"I'm sorry," he said, "but even if you could solve the supply problem, you're not going to turn the entire population of the planet into vegetarians—unless you are anxious to encourage emigration to Mars and Venus. I'd shoot myself if I thought I could never eat a lamb chop or a well-done steak again. So your plans are bound to fail on two counts: human psychology and the sheer facts of food production."

The Maha Thero looked a little hurt.

"My dear Director," he said, "surely you don't think we would overlook something as obvious as that? But let me finish putting our point of view before I explain how we propose to implement it. I'll be interested in studying your reactions, because you represent the maximum—ah—consumer resistance we are likely to meet."

"Very well," smiled Franklin. "See if you can convert me out of my job."

"Since the beginning of history," said the Thero, "man has assumed that the other animals exist only for his benefit. He has wiped out whole species, sometimes through sheer greed, sometimes because they destroyed his crops or interfered with his other activities. I won't deny that he often had justification, and frequently no alternative. But down the ages man has blackened his soul with his crimes against the animal kingdom—some of the very worst, incidentally, being in your particular profession, only sixty or seventy years ago. I've read of cases where harpooned whales died after hours of such frightful torment that not a scrap of their meat could be used—it was poisoned with the toxins produced by the animal's death agonies."

"Very exceptional," interjected Franklin. "And anyway we've put a stop to that."

"True, but it's all part of the debt we have to discharge."

"Svend Foyn wouldn't have agreed with you. When he invented the explosive harpoon, back in the 1870s, he made an entry in his diary thanking God for having done all the work."

"An interesting point of view," answered the Thero dryly. "I wish I'd had a chance of arguing it with him. You know, there is a simple test which divides the human race into two classes. If a man is walking along the street and sees a beetle crawling just where he is going to place his foot—well, he can break his stride and miss it or he can crush it into pulp. Which would *you* do, Mr. Franklin?"

"It would depend on the beetle. If I knew it was poisonous, or a pest, I'd kill it. Otherwise I'd let it go. That, surely, is what any reasonable man would do."

"Then we are not reasonable. We believe that killing is only justified to save the life of a higher creature—and it is surprising how seldom that situation arises. But let me get back to my argument; we seem to have lost our way.

"About a hundred years ago an Irish poet named Lord Dunsany wrote a play called *The Use of Man,* which you'll be seeing on one of our TV programs before long. In it a man dreams that he's magically transported out of the solar system to appear before a tribunal of animals—and if he cannot find two to speak on his behalf, the human race is doomed. Only the dog will come forward to fawn over his master; all the others remember their old grievances and maintain that they would have been better off if man had never existed. The sentence of annihilation is about to be pronounced when another sponsor arrives in the nick of time, and humanity is saved. The only other creature who has any use for man is —the mosquito.

"Now you may think that is merely an amusing jest; so, I am sure, did Dunsany—who happened to be a keen hunter. But poets often speak hidden truths of which they themselves are unaware, and I believe that this almost forgotten play contains an allegory of profound importance to the human race.

"Within a century or so, Franklin, we will literally be going outside the solar system. Sooner or later we will meet types of intelligent life much higher than our own, yet in forms completely alien. And when that time comes, the treatment man receives from his superiors may well depend upon the way he has behaved toward the other creatures of his own world."

The words were spoken so quietly, yet with such conviction, that they struck a sudden chill into Franklin's soul. For the first time he felt that there might be something in the other's point of view—something, that is, besides mere humanitarianism. (But could humanitarianism ever be "mere"?) He had never liked the final climax of his work, for he had long ago developed a great affection for his monstrous charges, but he had always regarded it as a regrettable necessity.

"I grant that your points are well made," he admitted, "but whether we like them or not, we have to accept the realities of life. I don't know who coined the phrase 'Nature red in tooth and claw,' but that's the way she is. And if the world has to choose between food and ethics, I know which will win."

The Thero gave that secret, gentle smile which, consciously or otherwise, seemed to echo the benign gaze that so many generations of artists had made the hallmark of the Buddha.

"But that is just the point, my dear Franklin," he answered. "There is no longer any need for a choice. Ours is the first generation in the world's history that can break the ancient cycle, and eat what it pleases without spilling the blood of innocent creatures. I am sincerely grateful to you for helping to show me how."

"Me!" exploded Franklin.

"Exactly," said the Thero, the extent of his smile now far exceeding the canons of Buddhist art. "And now, if you will excuse me, I think I'll go to sleep."

CHAPTER TWENTY-ONE

"So this," grumbled Franklin, "is my reward for twenty years of devoted public service—to be regarded even by my own family as a bloodstained butcher."

"But all that was true, wasn't it?" said Anne, pointing to the TV screen, which a few seconds ago had been dripping with gore.

"Of course it was. But it was also very cleverly edited propaganda. I could make out just as good a case for our side."

"Are you sure of that?" asked Indra. "The division will certainly want you to, but it may not be easy."

Franklin snorted indignantly.

"Why, those statistics are all nonsense! The very idea of switching our entire herds to milking instead of slaughtering is just crazy. If we converted all our resources to whale-milk production we couldn't make up a quarter of the loss of fats and protein involved in closing down the processing plants."

"Now, Walter," said Indra placidly, "there's no need to break a blood vessel trying to keep calm. What's really upset you is the suggestion that the plankton farms should be extended to make up the deficit."

"Well, you're the biologist. Is it practical to turn that pea soup into prime ribs of beef or T-bone steaks?"

"It's obviously *possible*. It was a very clever move, having the chef of the Waldorf tasting both the genuine and the synthetic product, and being unable to tell the difference. There's no doubt you're going to have a lovely fight on your hands—the farm people will jump right in on the Thero's side of the fence, and the whole Marine Division will be split wide open."

"He probably planned that," said Franklin with reluctant admiration. "He's diabolically well-informed. I wish now I hadn't said so much about the possibilities of milk production during that interview—and they did overplay it a bit in the final article. I'm sure that's what started the whole business."

"That's another thing I was going to mention. Where did he get the figures on which he based his statistics? As far as I know, they have never been published anywhere outside the bureau."

"You're right," conceded Franklin. "I should have thought of that before. First thing tomorrow morning I'm going out to Heron Island to have a little talk with Dr. Lundquist."

"Will you take me, Daddy," pleaded Anne.

"Not this time, young lady. I wouldn't like an innocent daughter of mine to hear some of the things I may have to say."

"Dr. Lundquist is out in the lagoon, sir," said the chief lab assistant. "There's no way of contacting him until he decides to come up."

"Oh, isn't there? I could go down and tap him on the shoulder."

"I don't think that would be at all wise, sir. Attila and Genghis Khan aren't very fond of strangers."

"Good God—is he swimming with *them!*"

"Oh yes—they're quite fond of him, and they've got very friendly with the wardens who work with them. But anyone else might be eaten rather quickly."

Quite a lot seemed to be going on, thought Franklin, that he knew very little about. He decided to walk to the lagoon; unless it was extremely hot, or one had something to carry, it was never worthwhile to take a car for such short distances.

He had changed his mind by the time he reached the new eastern jetty. Either Heron Island was getting bigger or he was beginning to feel his years. He sat down on the keel of an upturned dinghy, and looked out to sea. The tide was in, but the sharp dividing line marking the edge of the reef was clearly visible, and in the fenced-off enclosure the spouts of the two killer whales appeared as intermittent plumes of mist. There was a small boat out there, with somebody in it, but it was too far away for him to tell whether it was Dr. Lundquist or one of his assistants.

He waited for a few minutes, then telephoned for a boat to carry him out to the reef. In slightly more time than it would have taken him to swim there, he arrived at the enclosure and had his first look at Attila and Genghis Khan.

The two killer whales were a little under thirty feet long, and as his boat approached them they simultaneously reared out of the water and stared at him with their huge, intelligent eyes. The unusual attitude, and the pure white of the bodies now presented to him, gave Franklin the uncanny impression that he was face to face not with animals but with beings who might be higher in the order of creation than himself. He knew that the truth was far otherwise, and reminded himself that he was looking at the most ruthless killer in the sea.

No, that was not quite correct. The *second* most ruthless killer in the sea. . . .

The whales dropped back into the water, apparently satisfied with their scrutiny. It was then that Franklin made out Lundquist, working about thirty feet down with a small torpedo loaded with instruments. Probably the commotion had disturbed him, because he came quickly to the surface and lay treading water, with his face mask pushed back, as he recognized his visitor.

"Good morning, Mr. Franklin. I wasn't expecting you today. What do you think of my pupils?"

"Very impressive. How well are they learning their lessons?"

"There's no doubt about it—they're brilliant. Even cleverer than porpoises, and surprisingly affectionate when they get to know you. I can teach them to do anything now. If I wanted to commit the perfect murder, I could tell them that you were a seal on an ice floe, and they'd have the boat over in two seconds."

"In that case, I'd prefer to continue our conversation back on land. Have you finished whatever you're doing?"

"It's never finished, but that doesn't matter. I'll ride the torp back—no need to lift all this gear into the boat."

The scientist swung his tiny metal fish around toward the island, and promptly set off at a speed which the dinghy could not hope to match. At once the two killers streaked after him, their huge dorsal fins leaving a creamy wake in the water. It seemed a dangerous game of tag to play, but before Franklin could discover what would happen when the killers caught the torpedo, Lundquist had crossed the shallow but clearly marked mesh around the enclosure, and the two whales broke their rush in a flurry of spray.

Franklin was very thoughtful on the way back to land. He had known Lundquist for years, but now he felt that this was the first time he had ever really seen him. There had never been any doubt concerning his originality—indeed, his brilliance—but he also appeared to possess unsuspected courage and initiative. None of which, Franklin determined grimly, would help him unless he had a satisfactory answer to certain questions.

Dressed in his everyday clothes, and back in the familiar laboratory surroundings, Lundquist was the man Franklin had always known. "Now, John," he began, "I suppose you've seen this television propaganda against the bureau?"

"Of course. But is it *against* us?"

"It's certainly against our main activity, but we won't argue that point. What I want to know is this: Have you been in touch with the Maha Thero?"

"Oh yes. He contacted me immediately after that article appeared in *Earth Magazine.*"

"And you passed on confidential information to him?"

Lundquist looked sincerely hurt.

"I resent that, Mr. Franklin. The only information I gave him was an advance proof of my paper on whale-milk production, which comes out in the *Cetological Review* next month. You approved it for publication yourself."

The accusations that Franklin was going to make collapsed around his ears, and he felt suddenly rather ashamed of himself.

"I'm sorry, John," he said. "I take that back. All this has made me a bit jumpy, and I just want to sort out the facts before HQ starts chasing me. But don't you think you should have told me about this inquiry?"

"Frankly, I don't see why. We get all sorts of queries every day, and I saw no reason to suppose that this was not just another routine one. Of course, I was pleased that somebody was taking a particular interest in my special project, and I gave them all the help I could."

"Very well," said Franklin resignedly. "Let's forget the post-mortem. But answer for me this question: As a scientist, do you really believe that we can afford to stop whale slaughtering and switch over to milk and synthetics?"

"Given ten years, we can do it if we have to. There's no technical objection that I can see. Of course I can't guarantee the figures on the plankton-farming side, but you can bet your life that the Thero had accurate sources of information there as well."

"But you realize what this will mean! If it starts with whales, sooner or later it will go right down the line through all the domestic animals."

"And why not? The prospect rather appeals to me. If science and religion can combine to take some of the cruelty out of Nature, isn't that a good thing?"

"You sound like a crypto-Buddhist—and I'm tired of pointing out that there's no cruelty in what we are doing. Meanwhile, if the Thero asks any more questions, kindly refer him to me."

"Very good, Mr. Franklin," Lundquist replied rather stiffly. There was an awkward pause, providentially broken by the arrival of a messenger.

"Headquarters wants to speak to you, Mr. Franklin. It's urgent."

"I bet it is," muttered Franklin. Then he caught sight of Lundquist's still somewhat hostile expression, and could not suppress a smile.

"If you can train orcas to be wardens, John," he said, "you'd better start looking around for a suitable mammal—preferably amphibious—to be the next director."

On a planet of instantaneous and universal communications, ideas spread from pole to pole more rapidly than they could once have done by word of mouth in a single village. The skillfully edited and presented program which had spoiled the appetites of a mere twenty million people on its first appearance had a far larger audience on its second. Soon there were few other topics of conversation; one of the disadvantages of life in a peaceful and well-organized world state was that with the disappearance of wars and crises very little was left of what was once called "news." Indeed, the complaint had often been made that since the ending of national sovereignty, history had also been abolished. So the argument raged in club and kitchen, in World Assembly and lonely space freighter, with no competition from any other quarter.

The World Food Organization maintained a dignified silence, but behind the scenes there was furious activity. Matters were not helped by the brisk lobbying of the farm group, which it had taken no great foresight on Indra's part to predict. Franklin was particularly annoyed by the efforts of the rival department to profit from his difficulties, and made several protests to the Director of Plankton Farms when the infighting became a little too rough. "Damn it all, Ted," he had snarled over the viewphone on one occasion, "you're just as big a butcher as I am. Every ton of raw plankton you process contains half a billion shrimps with as much right to life, liberty, and the pursuit of happiness as my whales. So don't try to stand in a white sheet. Sooner or later the Thero will work down to you—this is only the thin edge of the wedge."

"Maybe you're right, Walter," the culprit had admitted cheerfully enough, "but I think the farms will last out my time. It's not easy to make people sentimental over shrimps—they don't have cute little ten-ton babies to nurse."

That was perfectly true; it was very hard to draw the line between maudlin sentimentality and rational humanitarianism. Franklin remembered a recent cartoon showing the Thero raising his arms in protest while a shrieking cabbage was brutally dragged from the ground. The artist had taken no sides; he had merely summed up the viewpoint of those who considered that a great deal of fuss was being made about nothing. Perhaps this whole affair would blow over in a few weeks when people became bored and started arguing about something else—but he doubted it. That first television program had shown that the Thero was an expert in molding public opinion; he could be relied upon not to let his campaign lose momentum.

It took less than a month for the Thero to obtain the ten per cent vote needed under the constitution to set up a commission of inquiry. The fact that one tenth of the human race was sufficiently interested in the matter to request that all the facts be laid before it did not mean that they agreed with the Thero; mere curiosity and the pleasure of seeing a department of the state fighting a defensive rear-guard action was quite enough to account for the vote. In itself, a commission of inquiry meant very little. What would matter would be the final referendum on the commission's report, and it would be months before that could be arranged.

One of the unexpected results of the twentieth century's electronic revolution was that for the first time in history it was possible to have a truly democratic government—in the sense that every citizen could express his views on matters of policy. What the Athenians, with indifferent success, had tried to do with a few thousand score of free men could now be achieved in a global society of five billions. Automatic sampling devices originally devised for the rating of television programs had turned out to have a far wider significance, by making it a relatively simple and inexpensive matter to discover exactly what the public really thought on any subject.

Naturally, there had to be safeguards, and such a system would have been disastrous before the days of universal education—before, in fact, the beginning of the twenty-first century. Even now, it was possible for some emotionally laden issue to force a vote that was really against the best interests of the community, and no government could function unless it held the final right to decide matters of policy during its term of office. Even if the world demanded some course of action by a ninety-nine per cent vote, the state could ignore the expressed will of the people —but it would have to account for its behavior at the next election.

Franklin did not relish the privilege of being a key witness at the commission's hearings, but he knew that there was no way in which he could escape this ordeal. Much of his time was now spent in collecting data to refute the arguments of those who wished to put an end to whale slaughtering, and it proved to be a more difficult task than he had imagined. One could not present a neat, clear-cut case by saying that processed whale meat cost so much per pound by the time it reached the consumer's table whereas synthetic meats derived from plankton or algae would cost more. Nobody knew—there were far too many variables. The biggest unknown of all was the cost of running the proposed sea dairies, if it was decided to breed whales purely for milk and not for slaughter.

The data were insufficient. It would be honest to say so, but there was pressure on him to state outright that the suspension of whale slaughtering would never be a practical or economic possibility. His own loyalty to the bureau, not to mention the security of his present position, prompted him in the same direction.

But it was not merely a matter of economics; there were emotional factors which disturbed Franklin's judgment and made it impossible for him to make up his mind. The days he had spent with the Maha Thero, and his brief glimpse of a civilization and a way of thought far older than his own, had affected him more deeply than he had realized. Like most men of his highly materialistic era, he was intoxicated with the scientific and sociological triumphs which had irradiated the opening decades of the twenty-first century. He prided himself on his skeptical rationalism, and his total freedom from superstition. The fundamental questions of philosophy had never bothered him greatly; he knew that they existed, but they had seemed the concern of other people.

And now, whether he liked it or not, he had been challenged from a quarter so unexpected that he was almost defenseless. He had always considered himself a humane man, but now he had been reminded that humanity might not be enough. As he struggled with his thoughts, he became progressively more and more irritable with the world around him, and matters finally became so bad that Indra had to take action.

"Walter," she said firmly, when Anne had gone tearfully to bed after a row in which there was a good deal of blame on both sides, "it will save a lot of trouble if you face the facts and stop trying to fool yourself."

"What the devil do you mean?"

"You've been angry with everybody this last week—with just one exception. You've lost your temper with Lundquist—though that was partly my fault—with the press, with just about every other bureau in the division, with the children, and any moment you're going to lose it with me. But there's one person you're not angry with—and that's the Maha Thero, who's the cause of all the trouble."

"Why should I be? He's crazy, of course, but he's a saint—or as near it as I ever care to meet."

"I'm not arguing about that. I'm merely saying that you really agree with him, but you won't admit it."

Franklin started to explode. "That's utterly ridiculous!" he began. Then his indignation petered out. It *was* ridiculous; but it was also perfectly true.

He felt a great calm come upon him; he was no longer angry with the world and with himself. His childish resentment of the fact that *he* should be the man involved in a dilemma not of his making suddenly evaporated.

There was no reason why he should be ashamed of the fact that he had grown to love the great beasts he guarded; if their slaughter could be avoided, he should welcome it, whatever the consequences to the bureau.

The parting smile of the Thero suddenly floated up into his memory. Had that extraordinary man foreseen that he would win him around to his point of view? If his gentle persuasiveness—which he had not hesitated to combine with the shock tactics of that bloodstained television program—could work with Franklin himself, then the battle was already half over.

CHAPTER TWENTY-TWO

Life was a good deal simpler in the old days, thought Indra with a sigh. It was true that Peter and Anne were both at school or college most of the time, but somehow that had given her none of the additional leisure she had expected. There was so much entertaining and visiting to do, now that Walter had moved into the upper echelons of the state. Though perhaps that was exaggerating a little; the director of the Bureau of Whales was still a long way—at least six steps—down from the rarefied heights in which the president and his advisers dwelt.

But there were some things that cut right across official rank. No one could deny that there was a glamour about Walt's job and an interest in his activities that had made him known to a far wider circle than the other directors of the Marine Division, even before the *Earth Magazine* article or the present controversy over whale slaughtering. How many people could name the director of Plankton Farms or of Fresh-Water Food Production? Not one to every hundred that had heard of Walter. It was a fact that made her proud, even though at the same time it exposed Walter to a good deal of interdepartmental jealousy.

Now, however, it seemed likely to expose him to worse than that. So far, no one in the bureau, still less any of the higher officials of the Marine Division or the World Food Organization imagined for one moment that Walter had any private doubts or that he was not wholeheartedly in support of the *status quo*.

Her attempts to read the current *Nature* were interrupted by the private-line viewphone. It had been installed, despite her bitter protests, the day that Walter had become director. The public service, it seemed, was not good enough; now the office could get hold of Walter whenever it liked, unless he took precautions to frustrate it.

"Oh, good morning, Mrs. Franklin," said the operator, who was now practically a friend of the family. "Is the director in?"

"I'm afraid not," said Indra with satisfaction. "He hasn't had a day off for about a month, and he's out sailing in the bay with Peter. If you want to catch him, you'll have to send a plane out; J.94's radio has broken down again."

"*Both* sets? That's odd. Still, it's not urgent. When he comes in, will you give him this memo?"

There was a barely audible click, and a sheet of paper drifted down into the extra large-sized memorandum basket. Indra read it, gave the operator an absent-minded farewell, and at once called Franklin on his perfectly serviceable radio.

The creak of the rigging, the soft rush of water past the smooth hull—even the occasional cry of a sea bird—these sounds came clearly from the speaker and transported her at once out into Moreton Bay.

"I thought you'd like to know, Walter," she said, "the Policy Board is having its special meeting next Wednesday, here in Brisbane. That gives you three days to decide what you're going to tell them."

There was a slight pause during which she could hear her husband moving about the boat; then Franklin answered: "Thanks, dear. I know what I've got to say—I just don't know how to say it. But there's something I've thought of that you can do to help. You know all the wardens' wives—suppose you call up as many as you can, and try to find what their husbands feel about this business. Can you do that without making it look too obvious? It's not so easy for me, nowadays, to find what the men in the field are thinking. They're too liable to tell me what they imagine I want to know."

There was a wistful note in Franklin's voice which Indra had been hearing more and more frequently these days, though she knew her husband well enough to be quite sure that he had no real regrets for having taken on his present responsibilities.

"That's a good idea," she said. "There are at least a dozen people I should have called up weeks ago, and this will give me an excuse. It probably means that we'll have to have another party though."

"I don't mind that, as long as I'm still director and can afford to pay for it. But if I revert to a warden's pay in a month or so, we'll have to cut out the entertaining."

"You don't really think—"

"Oh, it won't be as bad as that. But they may shift me to some nice safe job, though I can't imagine what use I am now outside the bureau. GET OUT OF THE WAY, YOU BLASTED FOOL—CAN'T YOU SEE WHERE

YOU'RE GOING? Sorry, dear—too many week-end sailors around. We'll be back in ninety minutes, unless some idiot rams us. Pete says he wants honey for tea. Bye now."

Indra looked thoughtfully at the radio as the sounds of the distant boat ceased abruptly. She half wished that she had accompanied Walter and Pete on their cruise out into the bay, but she had faced the fact that her son now needed his father's company rather than hers. There were times when she grudged this, realizing that in a few months they would both lose the boy whose mind and body they had formed, but who was now slipping from their grasp.

It was inevitable, of course; the ties that bound father and son together must now drive them apart. She doubted if Peter realized why he was so determined to get into space; after all, it was a common enough ambition among boys of his age. But he was one of the youngest ever to obtain a triplanetary scholarship, and it was easy to understand why. He was determined to conquer the element that had defeated his father.

But enough of this daydreaming, she told herself. She got out her file of visiphone numbers, and began to tick off the names of all the wardens' wives who would be at home.

The Policy Board normally met twice a year, and very seldom had much policy to discuss, since most of the bureau's work was satisfactorily taken care of by the committees dealing with finance, production, staff, and technical development. Franklin served on all of these, though only as an ordinary member, since the chairman was always someone from the Marine Division or the World Secretariat. He sometimes came back from the meetings depressed and discouraged; what was very unusual was for him to come back in a bad temper as well.

Indra knew that something had gone wrong the moment he entered the house. "Let me know the worst," she said resignedly as her exhausted husband flopped into the most comfortable chair in sight. "Do you have to find a new job?"

She was only half joking, and Franklin managed a wan smile. "It's not as bad as that," he answered, "but there's more in this business than I thought. Old Burrows had got it all worked out before he took the chair; someone in the Secretariat had briefed him pretty thoroughly. What it comes to is this: Unless it can be proved that food production from whale milk and synthetics will be *drastically* cheaper than the present method, whale slaughtering will continue. Even a ten per cent saving isn't regarded as good enough to justify a switch-over. As Burrows put it, we're concerned with cost accounting, not abstruse philosophical principles like justice to animals.

"That's reasonable enough, I suppose, and certainly I wouldn't try to fight it. The trouble started during the break for coffee, when Burrows got me into a corner and asked me what the wardens thought about the whole business. So I told him that eighty per cent of them would like to see slaughtering stopped, even if it meant a rise in food costs. I don't know why he asked me this particular question, unless news of our little survey has leaked out.

"Anyway, it upset him a bit and I could see him trying to get around to something. Then he put it bluntly that I'd be a key witness when the inquiry started, and that the Marine Division wouldn't like me to plead the Thero's case in open court with a few million people watching. 'Suppose I'm asked for my personal opinion?' I said. 'No one's worked harder than me to increase whale-meat and oil production, but as soon as it's possible I'd like to see the bureau become a purely conservation service.' He asked if this was my considered viewpoint and I told him that it was.

"Then things got a bit personal, though still in a friendly sort of way, and we agreed that there was a distinct cleavage of opinion between the people who handled whales as whales and those who saw them only as statistics on food-production charts. After that Burrows went off and made some phone calls, and kept us all waiting around for half an hour while he talked to a few people up in the Secretariat. He finally came back with what were virtually my orders, though he was careful not to put it that way. It comes to this: I've got to be an obedient little ventriloquist's dummy at the inquiry."

"But suppose the other side asks you outright for your personal views?"

"Our counsel will try to head them off, and if he fails I'm not supposed to have any personal views."

"And what's the point of all this?"

"That's what I asked Burrows, and I finally managed to get it out of him. There are political issues involved. The Secretariat is afraid that the Maha Thero will get too powerful if he wins this case, so it's going to be fought whatever its merits."

"Now I understand," said Indra slowly. "Do you think that the Thero is after political power?"

"For its own sake—no. But he may be trying to gain influence to put across his religious ideas, and that's what the Secretariat's afraid of."

"And what are you going to do about it?"

"I don't know," Franklin answered. "I really don't know."

He was still undecided when the hearings began and the Maha Thero made his first personal appearance before a world-wide audience. He was not, Franklin could not help thinking as he looked at the small, yellow-robed figure with its gleaming skull, very impressive at first sight. Indeed, there was something almost comic about him—until he began to speak, and one knew without any doubt that one was in the presence both of power and conviction.

"I would like to make one thing perfectly clear," said the Maha Thero, addressing not only the chairman of the commission but also the unseen millions who were watching this first hearing. "It is not true that we are trying to enforce vegetarianism on the world, as some of our opponents have tried to maintain. The Buddha himself did not abstain from eating meat, when it was given to him; nor do we, for a guest should accept gratefully whatever his host offers.

"Our attitude is based on something deeper and more fundamental than food prejudices, which are usually only a matter of conditioning. What is more, we believe that most reasonable men, whether their religious beliefs are the same as ours or not, will eventually accept our point of view.

"It can be summed up very simply, though it is the result of twenty-six centuries of thought. We consider that it is wrong to inflict injury or death on any living creature, but we are not so foolish as to imagine that it can be avoided altogether. Thus we recognize, for example, the need to kill microbes and insect pests, much though we may regret the necessity.

"But as soon as such killing is no longer essential, it should cease. We believe that this point has now arrived as far as many of the higher animals are concerned. The production of all types of synthetic protein from purely vegetable sources is now an economic possibility—or it will be if the effort is made to achieve it. Within a generation, we can shed the burden of guilt which, however lightly or heavily it has weighed on individual consciences, must at some time or other have haunted all thinking men as they look at the world of life which shares their planet.

"Yet this is not an attitude which we seek to enforce on anyone against his will. Good actions lose any merit if they are imposed by force. We will be content to let the facts we will present speak for themselves, so that the world may make its own choice."

It was, thought Franklin, a simple, straightforward speech, quite devoid of any of the fanaticism which would have fatally prejudiced the case in this rational age. And yet the whole matter was one that went beyond reason; in a purely logical world, this controversy could never have arisen, for no one would have doubted man's right to use the animal kingdom as he felt fit. Logic, however, could be easily discredited here; it could be used too readily to make out a convincing case for cannibalism.

The Thero had not mentioned, anywhere in his argument, one point which had made a considerable impact on Franklin. He had not raised the possibility that man might someday come into contact with alien life forms that might judge him by his conduct toward the rest of the animal kingdom. Did he think that this was so far-fetched an idea that the general public would be unable to take it seriously, and would thus grow to regard his whole campaign as a joke? Or had he realized that it was an argument that might particularly appeal to an ex-astronaut? There was no way of guessing; in either event it proved that the Thero was a shrewd judge both of private and public reactions.

Franklin switched off the receiver; the scenes it was showing now were quite familiar to him, since he had helped the Thero to film them. The Marine Division, he thought wryly, would now be regretting the facilities it had offered His Reverence, but there was nothing else it could have done in the circumstances.

In two days he would be appearing to give his evidence; already he felt more like a criminal on trial than a witness. And in truth he was on trial—or, to be more accurate, his conscience was. It was strange to think that having once tried to kill himself, he now objected to killing other creatures. There was some connection here, but it was too complicated for him to unravel—and even if he did, it would not help him to solve his dilemma.

Yet the solution was on the way, and from a totally unexpected direction.

CHAPTER TWENTY-THREE

Franklin was boarding the plane that would take him to the hearings when the "Sub-Smash" signal came through. He stood in the doorway, reading the scarlet-tabbed message that had been rushed out to him, and at that moment all his other problems ceased to exist.

The SOS was from the Bureau of Mines, the largest of all the sections of the Marine Division. Its title was a slightly misleading one, for it did not run a single mine in the strict sense of the word. Twenty or thirty years ago there had indeed been mines on the ocean beds, but now the sea itself was an inexhaustible treasure chest. Almost every one of the natural elements could be extracted directly and economically from the millions of tons of dissolved matter in each cubic mile of sea water. With the perfection of selective ion-exchange filters, the nightmare of metal shortages had been banished forever.

The Bureau of Mines was also responsible for the hundreds of oil wells that now dotted the sea beds, pumping up the precious fluid that was the basic material for half the chemical plants on earth—and which earlier generations, with criminal shortsightedness, had actually burned for fuel. There were plenty of accidents that could befall the bureau's world-wide empire; only last year Franklin had lent it a whaling sub in an unsuccessful attempt to salvage a tank of gold concentrate. But this was far more serious, as he discovered after he had put through a few priority calls.

Thirty minutes later he was airborne, though not in the direction he had expected to be going. And it was almost an hour after he had taken off before all the orders had been given and he at last had a chance of calling Indra.

She was surprised at the unexpected call, but her surprise quickly turned to alarm. "Listen, dear," Franklin began, "I'm not going to Berne after all. Mines has had a serious accident and has appealed for our help. One of their big subs is trapped on the bottom—it was drilling a well and hit a high-pressure gas pocket. The derrick was blown over and toppled on the sub so that it can't get away. There's a load of VIPs aboard, including a senator and the director of Mines. I don't know how we're going to pull them out, but we'll do our best. I'll call you again when I've got time."

"Will you have to go down yourself?" asked Indra anxiously.

"Probably. Now don't look so upset! I've been doing it for years!"

"I'm *not* upset," retorted Indra, and Franklin knew better than to contradict her. "Good-by, darling," he continued, "give my love to Anne, and don't worry."

Indra watched the image fade. It had already vanished when she realized that Walter had not looked so happy for weeks. Perhaps that was not the right word to use when men's lives were at stake; it would be truer to say that he looked full of life and enthusiasm. She smiled, knowing full well the reason why.

Now Walter could get away from the problems of his office, and could lose himself again, if only for a while, in the clear-cut and elemental simplicities of the sea.

"There she is," said the pilot of the sub, pointing to the image forming at the edge of the sonar screen. "On hard rock eleven hundred feet down. In a couple of minutes we'll be able to make out the details."

"How's the water clarity—can we use TV?"

"I doubt it. That gas geyser is still spouting—there it is—that fuzzy echo. It's stirred up all the mud for miles around."

Franklin stared at the screen, comparing the image forming there with the plans and sketches on the desk. The smooth ovoid of the big shallow-water sub was partly obscured by the wreckage of the drills and derrick—a thousand or more tons of steel pinning it to the ocean bed. It was not surprising that, though it had blown its buoyancy tanks and turned its jets on to full power, the vessel had been unable to move more than a foot or two.

"It's a nice mess," said Franklin thoughtfully. "How long will it take for the big tugs to get here?"

"At least four days. *Hercules* can lift five thousand tons, but she's down at Singapore. And she's too big to be flown here; she'll have to come under her own steam. You're the only people with subs small enough to be airlifted."

That was true enough, thought Franklin, but it also meant that they were not big enough to do any heavy work. The only hope was that they could operate cutting torches and carve up the derrick until the trapped sub was able to escape.

Another of the bureau's scouts was already at work; someone, Franklin told himself, had earned a citation for the speed with which the torches had been fitted to a vessel not designed to carry them. He doubted if even the Space Department, for all its fabled efficiency, could have acted any more swiftly than this.

"Captain Jacobsen calling," said the loud-speaker. "Glad to have you with us, Mr. Franklin. Your boys are doing a good job, but it looks as if it will take time."

"How are things inside?"

"Not so bad. The only thing that worries me is the hull between bulkheads three and four. It took the impact there, and there's some distortion."

"Can you close off the section if a leak develops?"

"Not very well," said Jacobsen dryly. "It happens to be the middle of the control room. If we have to evacuate that, we'll be completely helpless."

"What about your passengers?"

"Er—they're fine," replied the captain, in a tone suggesting that he was giving some of them the benefit of a good deal of doubt. "Senator Chamberlain would like a word with you."

"Hello, Franklin," began the senator. "Didn't expect to meet you again under these circumstances. How long do you think it will take to get us out?"

The senator had a good memory, or else he had been well briefed. Franklin had met him on not more than three occasions—the last time in Canberra, at a session of the Committee for the Conservation of Natural Resources. As a witness, Franklin had been before the C.C.N.R. for about ten minutes, and he would not have expected its busy chairman to remember the fact.

"I can't make any promises, Senator," he answered cautiously. "It may take some time to clear away all this rubbish. But we'll manage all right—no need to worry about that."

As the sub drew closer, he was not so sure. The derrick was over two hundred feet long, and it would be a slow business nibbling it away in sections that the little scoutsubs could handle.

For the next ten minutes there was a three-cornered conference between Franklin, Captain Jacobsen, and Chief Warden Barlow, skipper of the second scoutsub. At the end of that time they had agreed that the best plan was to continue to cut away the derrick; even taking the most pessimistic view, they should be able to finish the job at least two days before the *Hercules* could arrive. Unless, of course, there were any unexpected snags; the only possible danger seemed to be the one that Captain Jacobsen had mentioned. Like all large undersea vessels, his ship carried an air-purifying plant which would keep the atmosphere breathable for weeks, but if the hull failed in the region of the control room all the sub's essential services would be disrupted. The occupants might retreat behind the pressure bulkheads, but that would give them only a temporary reprieve, because the air would start to become foul immediately. Moreover, with part of the sub flooded, it would be extremely difficult even for the *Hercules* to lift her.

Before he joined Barlow in the attack on the derrick, Franklin called Base on the long-range transmitter and ordered all the additional equipment that might conceivably be needed. He asked for two more subs to be flown out at once, and started the workshops mass producing buoyancy tanks by the simple process of screwing air couplings onto old oil drums. If enough of these could be hitched to the derrick, it might be lifted without any help from the submarine salvage vessel.

There was one other piece of equipment which he hesitated for some time before ordering. Then he muttered to himself: "Better get too much than too little," and sent off the requisition, even though he knew that the Stores Department would probably think him crazy.

The work of cutting through the girders of the smashed derrick was tedious, but not difficult. The two subs worked together, one burning through the steel while the other pulled away the detached section as soon as it came loose. Soon Franklin became completely unconscious of time; all that existed was the short length of metal which he was dealing with at that particular moment. Messages and instructions continually came and went, but another part of his mind dealt with them. Hands and brain were functioning as two separate entities.

The water, which had been completely turbid when they arrived, was now clearing rapidly. The roaring geyser of gas that was bursting from the sea bed barely a hundred yards away must have sucked in fresh water to sweep away the mud it had originally disturbed. Whatever the explanation, it made the task of salvage very much simpler, since the subs' external eyes could function again.

Franklin was almost taken aback when the reinforcements arrived. It seemed impossible that he had been here for more than six hours; he felt neither tired nor hungry. The two subs brought with them, like a long procession of tin cans, the first batch of the buoyancy tanks he had ordered.

Now the plan of campaign was altered. One by one the oil drums were clipped to the derrick, air hoses were coupled to them, and the water inside them was blown out until they strained upward like captive balloons. Each had a lifting power of two or three tons; by the time a hundred had been attached, Franklin calculated, the trapped sub might be able to escape without any further help.

The remote handling equipment on the outside of the scoutsub, so seldom used in normal operations, now seemed an extension of his own arms. It had been at least four years since he had manipulated the ingenious metal fingers that enabled a man to work in places where his unprotected body could never go—and he remembered, from ten years earlier still, the first time he had attempted to tie a knot and the hopeless tangle he had made of it. That was one of the skills he had hardly ever used; who would have imagined that it would be vital now that he had left the sea and was no longer a warden?

They were starting to pump out the second batch of oil drums when Captain Jacobsen called.

"I'm afraid I've got bad news, Franklin," he said, his voice heavy with apprehension. "There's water coming in, and the leak's increasing.

At the present rate, we'll have to abandon the control room in a couple of hours."

This was the news that Franklin had feared. It transformed a straightforward salvage job into a race against time—a race hopelessly handicapped, since it would take at least a day to cut away the rest of the derrick.

"What's your internal air pressure?" he asked Captain Jacobsen.

"I've already pushed it up to five atmospheres. It's not safe to put it up any farther."

"Take it up to eight if you can. Even if half of you pass out, that won't matter as long as someone remains in control. And it may help to keep the leak from spreading, which is the important thing."

"I'll do that—but if most of us are unconscious, it won't be easy to evacuate the control room."

There were too many people listening for Franklin to make the obvious reply—that if the control room had to be abandoned it wouldn't matter anyway. Captain Jacobsen knew that as well as he did, but some of his passengers might not realize that such a move would end any chance of rescue.

The decision he had hoped he would not have to make was now upon him. This slow whittling away of the wreckage was not good enough; they would have to use explosives, cutting the fallen derrick at the center, so that the lower, unsupported portion would drop back to the sea bed and its weight would no longer pin down the sub.

It had been the obvious thing to do, even from the beginning, but there were two objections: one was the risk of using explosives so near the sub's already weakened hull; the other was the problem of placing the charges in the correct spot. Of the derrick's four main girders, the two upper ones were easily accessible, but the lower pair could not be reached by the remote handling mechanisms of the scoutsubs. It was the sort of job that only an unencumbered diver could do, and in shallow water it would not have taken more than a few minutes.

Unfortunately, this was not shallow water; they were eleven hundred feet down—and at a pressure of over thirty atmospheres.

✶ *CHAPTER TWENTY-FOUR*

"It's too great a risk, Franklin. I won't allow it."

It was not often, thought Franklin, that one had a chance of arguing with a senator. And if necessary he would not merely argue; he would defy.

"I know there's a danger, sir," he admitted, "but there's no alternative. It's a calculated risk—one life against twenty-three."

"But I thought it was suicide for an unprotected man to dive below a few hundred feet."

"It is if he's breathing compressed air. The nitrogen knocks him out first, and then oxygen poisoning gets him. But with the right mixture it's quite possible. With the gear I'm using, men have been down fifteen hundred feet."

"I don't want to contradict you, Mr. Franklin," said Captain Jacobsen quietly, "but I believe that only one man has reached fifteen hundred—and then under carefully controlled conditions. *And* he wasn't attempting to do any work."

"Nor am I; I just have to place those two charges."

"But the pressure!"

"Pressure never makes any difference, Senator, as long as it's balanced. There may be a hundred tons squeezing on my lungs—but I'll have a hundred tons inside and won't feel it."

"Forgive me mentioning this—but wouldn't it be better to send a younger man?"

"I won't delegate this job, and age makes no difference to diving ability. I'm in good health, and that's all that matters." Franklin turned to his pilot and cut the microphone switch.

"Take her up," he said. "They'll argue all day if we stay here. I want to get into that rig before I change my mind."

He was wrestling with his thoughts all the way to the surface. Was he being a fool, taking risks which a man in his position, with a wife and family, ought never to face? Or was he still, after all these years, trying to prove that he was no coward, by deliberately meeting a danger from which he had once been rescued by a miracle?

Presently he was aware of other and perhaps less flattering motives. In a sense, he was trying to escape from responsibility. Whether his mission failed or succeeded, he would be a hero—and as such it would not be quite so easy for the Secretariat to push him around. It was an interesting problem; could one make up for lack of moral courage by proving physical bravery?

When the sub broke surface, he had not so much resolved these questions as dismissed them. There might be truth in every one of the charges he was making against himself; it did not matter. He knew in his heart that what he was doing was the right thing, the only thing. There was no other way in which the men almost a quarter of a mile below him could be saved, and against that fact all other considerations were meaningless.

The escaping oil from the well had made the sea so flat that the pilot of the cargo plane had made a landing, though his machine was not intended for amphibious operations. One of the scoutsubs was floating on the surface while her crew wrestled with the next batch of buoyancy tanks to be sunk. Men from the plane were helping them, working in collapsible boats that had been tossed into the water and automatically inflated.

Commander Henson, the Marine Division's master diver, was waiting in the plane with the equipment. There was another brief argument before the commander capitulated with good grace and, Franklin thought, a certain amount of relief. If anyone else was to attempt this mission, there was no doubt that Henson, with his unparalleled experience, was the obvious choice. Franklin even hesitated for a moment, wondering if by stubbornly insisting on going himself, he might not be reducing the chances of success. But he had been on the bottom and knew exactly what conditions were down there; it would waste precious time if Henson went down in the sub to make a reconnaissance.

Franklin swallowed his pH pills, took his injections, and climbed into the flexible rubber suit which would protect him from the near-zero temperature on the sea bed. He hated suits—they interfered with movement and upset one's buoyancy—but this was a case where he had no choice. The complex breathing unit, with its three cylinders—one the ominous red of compressed hydrogen—was strapped to his back, and he was lowered into the sea.

Commander Henson swam around him for five minutes while all the fittings were checked, the weight belt was adjusted, and the sonar transmitter tested. He was breathing easily enough on normal air, and would not switch over to the oxyhydrogen mixture until he had reached a depth of three hundred feet. The change-over was automatic, and the demand regulator also adjusted the oxygen flow so that the mixture ratio was correct at any depth. As correct as it could be, that is, for a region in which man was never intended to live. . . .

At last everything was ready. The explosive charges were securely attached to his belt, and he gripped the handrail around the tiny conning tower of the sub. "Take her down," he said to the pilot. "Fifty feet a minute, and keep your forward speed below two knots."

"Fifty feet a minute it is. If we pick up speed, I'll kill it with the reverse jets."

Almost at once, daylight faded to a gloomy and depressing green. The water here on the surface was almost opaque, owing to the debris thrown up by the oil well. Franklin could not even see the width of the conning tower; less than two feet from his eyes the metal rail blurred and faded into nothingness. He was worried; if necessary, he could work by touch alone, but he knew that the water was much clearer on the bottom.

Only thirty feet down, he had to stop the descent for almost a minute while he cleared his ears. He blew and swallowed frantically before the comforting "click" inside his head told him that all was well; how humiliating it would have been, he thought, had he been forced back to the surface because of a blocked Eustachian tube! No one would have blamed him, of course; even a mild cold could completely incapacitate the best diver—but the anticlimax would have been hard to live down.

The light was fading swiftly as the sun's rays lost their battle with the turbid water. A hundred feet down, he seemed to be in a world of misty moonlight, a world completely lacking color or warmth. His ears were giving him no trouble now, and he was breathing without effort, but he felt a subtle depression creeping over him. It was, he was sure, only an effect of the failing light—not a premonition of the thousand feet of descent that still lay ahead of him.

To occupy his mind, he called the pilot and asked for a progress report. Fifty drums had now been attached to the derrick, giving a total lift of well over a hundred tons. Six of the passengers in the trapped sub had become unconscious but appeared to be in no danger; the remaining seventeen were uncomfortable, but had adapted themselves to the increased pressure. The leak was getting no worse, but there were now three inches of water in the control room, and before long there would be danger of short circuits.

"Three hundred feet down," said Commander Henson's voice. "Check your hydrogen-flow meter—you should be starting the switch-over now."

Franklin glanced down at the compact little instrument panel. Yes, the automatic change-over was taking place. He could detect no difference in the air he was breathing, but in the next few hundred feet of descent most of the dangerous nitrogen would be flushed out. It seemed strange to replace it with hydrogen, a far more reactive—and even explosive—gas, but hydrogen produced no narcotic effects and was not trapped in the body tissues as readily as nitrogen.

It seemed to have grown no darker in the last hundred feet; his eyes had accustomed themselves to the low level of illumination, and the water was slightly clearer. He could now see for two or three yards along the smooth hull he was riding down into the depths where only a handful of unprotected men had ever ventured—and fewer still returned to tell the story.

Commander Henson called him again. "You should be on fifty per cent hydrogen now. Can you taste it?"

"Yes—a metallic sort of flavor. Not unpleasant, though."

"Talk as slowly as you can," said the commander. "It's hard to understand you—your voice sounds so high-pitched now. Are you feeling quite O.K.?"

"Yes," replied Franklin, glancing at his depth gauge. "Will you increase my rate of descent to a hundred feet a minute? We've no time to waste."

At once he felt the vessel sinking more swiftly beneath him as the ballast tanks were flooded, and for the first time he began to feel the pressure around him as something palpable. He was going down so quickly that there was a slight lag as the insulating layer of air in his suit adjusted to the pressure change; his arms and legs seemed to be gripped as if by a huge but gentle vice, which slowed his movements without actually restricting them.

The light had now nearly gone, and as if in anticipation of his order the pilot of the sub switched on his twin searchlights. There was nothing for them to illumine, here in this empty void midway between sea bed and sky, but it was reassuring to see the double nimbus of scattered radiance floating in the water ahead of him. The violet filters had been removed, for his benefit, and now that his eyes had something distant to focus upon he no longer felt so oppressively shut in and confined.

Eight hundred feet down—more than three quarters of the way to the bottom. "Better level off here for three minutes," advised Commander Henson. "I'd like to keep you here for half an hour, but we'll have to make it up on the way back."

Franklin submitted to the delay with what grace he could. It seemed incredibly long; perhaps his time sense had been distorted, so that what was really a minute appeared like ten. He was going to ask Commander Henson if his watch had stopped when he suddenly remembered that he had a perfectly good one of his own. The fact that he had forgotten something so obvious was, he realized, rather a bad sign; it suggested that he was becoming stupid. However, if he was intelligent enough to know that he was becoming stupid things could not be too bad. . . . Luckily the descent started again before he could get too involved in this line of argument.

And now he could hear, growing louder and louder each minute, the incessant roar of the great geyser of gas belching from the shaft which inquisitive and interfering man had drilled in the ocean bed. It shook the sea around him, already making it hard to hear the advice and comments of his helpers. There was a danger here as great as that of pressure itself if the gas jet caught him, he might be tossed hundreds of feet upward in a matter of seconds and would explode like a deep-sea fish dragged suddenly to the surface.

"We're nearly there," said the pilot, after they had been sinking for what seemed an age. "You should be able to see the derrick in a minute; I'll switch on the lower lights."

Franklin swung himself over the edge of the now slowly moving sub and peered down the misty columns of light. At first he could see nothing; then, at an indeterminate distance, he made out mysterious rectangles and circles. They baffled him for a moment before he realized that he was seeing the air-filled drums which were now straining to lift the shattered derrick.

Almost at once he was able to make out the framework of twisted girders below them, and presently a brilliant star—fantastically out of place in this dreary underworld—burst into life just outside the cone of his searchlights. He was watching one of the cutting torches at work, manipulated by the mechanical hands of a sub just beyond visual range.

With great care, his own vessel positioned him beside the derrick, and for the first time he realized how hopeless his task would have been had he been compelled to rely on touch to find his way around. He could see the two girders to which he had to attach his charge; they were hemmed in by a maze of smaller rods, beams, and cables through which he must somehow make his way.

Franklin released his hold of the sub which had towed him so effortlessly into the depths, and with slow, easy strokes swam toward the derrick. As he approached, he saw for the first time the looming mass of the trapped sub, and his heart sank as he thought of all the problems that must still be solved before it could be extricated. On a sudden impulse, he swam toward the helpless vessel and banged sharply on the hull with a pair of wire cutters from his little tool kit. The men inside knew that he was here, of course, but the signal would have an altogether disproportionate effect on their morale.

Then he started work. Trying to ignore the throbbing vibration which filled all the water around him and made it difficult to think, he began a careful survey of the metal maze into which he must swim.

It would not be difficult to reach the nearest girder and place the charge. There was an open space between three I beams, blocked only by a loop of cable which could be easily pushed out of the way (but he'd have to watch that it didn't tangle in his equipment when he swam past it). Then the girder would be dead ahead of him; what was more, there was room to turn around, so that he could avoid the unpleasant necessity of creeping out backward.

He checked again, and could see no snags. To make doubly sure, he talked it over with Commander Henson, who could see the situation almost as well on the TV screen of the sub. Then he swam slowly into the derrick, working his way along the metal framework with his gloved hands. He was quite surprised to find that, even at this depth, there was no shortage of the barnacles and other marine growths which always make it dangerous to touch any object which had been underwater for more than a few months.

The steel structure was vibrating like a giant tuning fork; he could feel the roaring power of the uncapped well both through the sea surrounding him and through the metal beneath his hands. He seemed to be imprisoned in an enormous, throbbing cage; the sheer noise, as well as the awful pressure, was beginning to make him dull and lethargic. It now needed a positive effort of will to take any action; he had to keep reminding himself that many lives besides his own depended upon what he was doing.

He reached the girder and slowly taped the flat package against the metal. It took a long time to do it to his satisfaction, but at last the explosive was in place and he felt sure that the vibration would not dislodge it. Then he looked around for his second objective—the girder forming the other edge of the derrick.

He had stirred up a good deal of dirt and could no longer see so clearly, but it seemed to Franklin that there was nothing to stop him crossing the interior of the derrick and completing the job. The alternative was to go back the way he had come, and then swim right around to the other side of the wreckage. In normal circumstances that would have been easy enough—but now every movement had to be considered with care, every expenditure of effort made grudgingly only after its need had been established beyond all doubt.

With infinite caution, he began to move through the throbbing mist. The glare of the searchlights, pouring down upon him, was so dazzling that it pained his eyes. It never occurred to him that he had only to speak into his microphone and the illumination would be reduced instantly to whatever level he wished. Instead, he tried to keep in whatever shadow he could find among the confused pile of wreckage through which he was moving.

He reached the girder, and crouched over it for a long time while he tried to remember what he was supposed to be doing here. It took Commander Henson's voice, shouting in his ears like some far-off echo, to call him back to reality. Very carefully and slowly he taped the precious slab into position; then he floated beside it, admiring his meaningless handiwork, while the annoying voice in his ear grew ever more insistent. He could stop it, he realized, by throwing away his face mask and the irritating little speaker it contained. For a moment he toyed with this idea, but discovered that he was not strong enough to undo the straps holding the mask in place. It was too bad; perhaps the voice would shut up if he did what it told him to.

Unfortunately, he had no idea which was the right way out of the maze in which he was now comfortably ensconced. The light and noise were very confusing; when he moved in any direction, he sooner or later banged into something and had to turn back. This annoyed but did not alarm him, for he was quite happy where he was.

But the voice would not give him any peace. It was no longer at all friendly and helpful; he dimly realized that it was being downright rude, and was ordering him about in a manner in which—though he could not remember why—people did not usually speak to him. He was being given careful and detailed instructions which were repeated over and over again, with increasing emphasis, until he sluggishly obeyed them. He was too tired to answer back, but he wept a little at the indignity to which he was being subjected. He had never been called such things in his life, and it was very seldom indeed that he had heard such shocking language as was now coming through his speaker. Who on earth would yell at him this way? "Not that way, you goddammed fool, sir! To the left—LEFT! That's fine—now forward a bit more—don't stop there! Christ, he's gone to sleep again. WAKE UP—SNAP OUT OF IT OR I'LL KNOCK YOUR BLOODY BLOCK OFF!! That's a good boy—you're nearly there—just another couple of feet . . ." and so on endlessly, and some of it with very much worse language than that.

Then, quite to his surprise, there was no longer twisted metal around him. He was swimming slowly in the open, but he was not swimming for long. Metal fingers closed upon him, none too gently, and he was lifted into the roaring night.

From far away he heard four short, muffled explosions, and something deep down in his mind told him that for two of these he was responsible. But he saw nothing of the swift drama a hundred feet below as the radio fuses detonated and the great derrick snapped in two. The section lying across the trapped submarine was still too heavy to be lifted clear by the buoyancy tanks, but now that it was free to move it teetered for a moment like a giant seesaw, then slipped aside and crashed onto the sea bed.

The big sub, all restraint removed, began to move upward with increasing speed; Franklin felt the wash of its close passage, but was too bemused to realize what it meant. He was still struggling back into hazy consciousness; around eight hundred feet, quite abruptly, he started to react to Henson's bullying ministrations, and, to the commander's vast relief, began to answer him back in kind. He cursed wildly for about a hundred feet, then became fully aware of his surroundings and ground to an embarrassed halt. Only then did he realize that his mission had been successful and that the men he had set out to rescue were already far above him on their way back to the surface.

Franklin could make no such speed. A decompression chamber was waiting for him at the three-hundred-foot level, and in its cramped confines he was to fly back to Brisbane and spend eighteen tedious hours before all the absorbed gas had escaped from his body. And by the time the doctors let him out of their clutches, it was far too late to suppress the tape recording that had circulated throughout the entire bureau. He was a hero to the whole world, but if he ever grew conceited he need only remind himself that all his staff had listened gleefully to every word of Commander Henson's fluently profane cajoling of their director.

CHAPTER TWENTY-FIVE

Peter never looked back as he walked up the gangplank into the projectile from which, in little more than half an hour, he would have his first view of the receding Earth. Franklin could understand why his son kept his head averted; young men of eighteen do not cry in public. Nor, for that matter, he told himself fiercely, do middle-aged directors of important bureaus.

Anne had no such inhibitions; she was weeping steadily despite all that Indra could do to comfort her. Not until the doors of the spaceship had finally sealed and the thirty-minute warning siren had drowned all other noises did she subside into an intermittent sniffling.

The tide of spectators, of friends and relatives, of cameramen and Space Department officials, began to retreat before the moving barriers. Clasping hands with his wife and daughter, Franklin let himself be swept along with the flood of humanity. What hopes and fears, sorrows and joys surrounded him now! He tried to remember his emotions at his first take-off; it must have been one of the great moments of his life—yet all recollection of it had gone, obliterated by thirty years of later experience.

And now Peter was setting out on the road his father had traveled half a lifetime before. May you have better luck among the stars than I did, Franklin prayed. He wished he could be there at Port Lowell when

Irene greeted the boy who might have been her son, and wondered how Roy and Rupert would receive their half-brother. He was sure that they would be glad to meet him; Peter would not be as lonely on Mars as Ensign Walter Franklin had once been.

They waited in silence while the long minutes wore away. By this time, Peter would be so interested in the strange and exciting world that was to be his home for the next week that he would already have forgotten the pain of parting. He could not be blamed if his eyes were fixed on the new life which lay before him in all its unknown promise.

And what of his own life? Franklin asked himself. Now that he had launched his son into the future, could he say that he had been a success? It was a question he found very hard to answer honestly. So many things that he had attempted had ended in failure or even in disaster. He knew now that he was unlikely to rise any farther in the service of the state; he might be a hero, but he had upset too many people when he became the surprised and somewhat reluctant ally of the Maha Thero. Certainly he had no hope of promotion—nor did he desire it—during the five or ten years which would be needed to complete the reorganization of the Bureau of Whales. He had been told in as many words that since he was partly responsible for the situation—the mess, it was generally called—he could sort it out himself.

One thing he would never know. If fate had not brought him public admiration and the even more valuable—because less fickle—friendship of Senator Chamberlain, would he have had the courage of his newfound convictions? It had been easy, as the latest hero that the world had taken to its heart but would forget tomorrow, to stand up in the witness box and state his beliefs. His superiors could fume and fret, but there was nothing they could do but accept his defection with the best grace they could muster. There were times when he almost wished that the accident of fame had not come to his rescue. And had his evidence, after all, been decisive? He suspected that it had. The result of the referendum had been close, and the Maha Thero might not have carried the day without his help.

The three sharp blasts of the siren broke into his reverie. In that awe-inspiring silence which still seemed so uncanny to those who remembered the age of rockets, the great ship sloughed away its hundred thousand tons of weight and began the climb back to its natural element. Half a mile above the plain, its own gravity field took over completely, so that it was no longer concerned with terrestrial ideas of "up" or "down." It lifted its prow toward the zenith, and hung poised for a moment like a metal obelisk miraculously supported among the clouds. Then, in that same awful silence, it blurred itself into a line—and the sky was empty.

The tension broke. There were a few stifled sobs, but many more laughs and jokes, perhaps a little too high-pitched to be altogether convincing. Franklin put his arms around Anne and Indra, and began to shepherd them toward the exit.

To his son, he willingly bequeathed the shoreless seas of space. For himself, the oceans of this world were sufficient. Therein dwelt all his subjects, from the moving mountain of Leviathan to the newborn dolphin that had not yet learned to suckle under water.

He would guard them to the best of his knowledge and ability. Already he could see clearly the future role of the bureau, when its wardens would be in truth the protectors of all the creatures moving in the sea. All? No—that, of course, was absurd; nothing could change or even greatly alleviate the incessant cruelty and slaughter that raged through all the oceans of the world. But with the great mammals who were his kindred, man could make a start, imposing his truce upon the battlefield of Nature.

What might come of that in the ages ahead, no one could guess. Even Lundquist's daring and still unproved plan for taming the killer whales might no more than hint of what the next few decades would bring. They might even bring the answer to the mystery which haunted him still, and which he had so nearly solved when that submarine earthquake robbed him of his best friend.

A chapter—perhaps the best chapter—of his life was closing. The future would have many problems, but he did not believe that ever again would he have to face such challenges as he had met in the past. In a sense, his work was done, even though the details were merely beginning.

He looked once more at the empty sky, and the words that the Mahanayake Thero had spoken to him as they flew back from the Greenland station rose up out of memory like a ground swell on the sea. He would never forget that chilling thought: *"When that time comes, the treatment man receives from his superiors may well depend upon the way he has behaved toward the other creatures of his own world."*

Perhaps he was a fool to let such phantasms of a remote and unknowable future have any influence upon his thoughts and acts, but he had no regrets for what he had done. As he stared into the blue infinity that had swallowed his son, the stars seemed suddenly very close. "Give us another hundred years," he whispered, "and we'll face you with clean hands and hearts—whatever shape you be."

"Come along, dear," said Indra, her voice still a little unsteady. "You haven't much time. The office asked me to remind you—the Committee on Interdepartmental Standardization meets in half an hour."

"I know," said Franklin, blowing his nose firmly and finally. "I wouldn't dream of keeping it waiting."

THE OTHER SIDE OF THE SKY

✕ THE NINE BILLION NAMES OF GOD

This is a slightly unusual request," said Dr. Wagner, with what he hoped was commendable restraint. "As far as I know, it's the first time anyone's been asked to supply a Tibetan monastery with an Automatic Sequence Computer. I don't wish to be inquisitive, but I should hardly have thought that your—ah—establishment had much use for such a machine. Could you explain just what you intend to do with it?"

"Gladly," replied the lama, readjusting his silk robes and carefully putting away the slide rule he had been using for currency conversions. "Your Mark V Computer can carry out any routine mathematical operation involving up to ten digits. However, for our work we are interested in *letters,* not numbers. As we wish you to modify the output circuits, the machine will be printing words, not columns of figures."

"I don't quite understand. . . ."

"This is a project on which we have been working for the last three centuries—since the lamasery was founded, in fact. It is somewhat alien to your way of thought, so I hope you will listen with an open mind while I explain it."

"Naturally."

"It is really quite simple. We have been compiling a list which shall contain all the possible names of God."

"I beg your pardon?"

"We have reason to believe," continued the lama imperturbably, "that all such names can be written with not more than nine letters in an alphabet we have devised."

"And you have been doing this for three centuries?"

"Yes: we expected it would take us about fifteen thousand years to complete the task."

"Oh," Dr. Wagner looked a little dazed. "Now I see why you

wanted to hire one of our machines. But exactly what is the *purpose* of this project?"

The lama hesitated for a fraction of a second, and Wagner wondered if he had offended him. If so, there was no trace of annoyance in the reply.

"Call it ritual, if you like, but it's a fundamental part of our belief. All the many names of the Supreme Being—God, Jehovah, Allah, and so on—they are only man-made labels. There is a philosophical problem of some difficulty here, which I do not propose to discuss, but somewhere among all the possible combinations of letters that can occur are what one may call the *real* names of God. By systematic permutation of letters, we have been trying to list them all."

"I see. You've been starting at AAAAAAA . . . and working up to ZZZZZZZ. . . ."

"Exactly—though we use a special alphabet of our own. Modifying the electromatic typewriters to deal with this is, of course, trivial. A rather more interesting problem is that of devising suitable circuits to eliminate ridiculous combinations. For example, no letter must occur more than three times in succession."

"Three? Surely you mean two."

"Three is correct: I am afraid it would take too long to explain why, even if you understood our language."

"I'm sure it would," said Wagner hastily. "Go on."

"Luckily, it will be a simple matter to adapt your Automatic Sequence Computer for this work, since once it has been programed properly it will permute each letter in turn and print the result. What would have taken us fifteen thousand years it will be able to do in a hundred days."

Dr. Wagner was scarcely conscious of the faint sounds from the Manhattan streets far below. He was in a different world, a world of natural, not man-made, mountains. High up in their remote aeries these monks had been patiently at work, generation after generation, compiling their lists of meaningless words. Was there any limit to the follies of mankind? Still, he must give no hint of his inner thoughts. The customer was always right. . . .

"There's no doubt," replied the doctor, "that we can modify the Mark V to print lists of this nature. I'm much more worried about the problem of installation and maintenance. Getting out to Tibet, in these days, is not going to be easy."

"We can arrange that. The components are small enough to travel by air—that is one reason why we chose your machine. If you can get them to India, we will provide transport from there."

"And you want to hire two of our engineers?"

"Yes, for the three months that the project should occupy."

"I've no doubt that Personnel can manage that." Dr. Wagner scribbled a note on his desk pad. "There are just two other points—"

Before he could finish the sentence the lama had produced a small slip of paper.

"This is my certified credit balance at the Asiatic Bank."

"Thank you. It appears to be—ah—adequate. The second matter is so trivial that I hesitate to mention it—but it's surprising how often the obvious gets overlooked. What source of electrical energy have you?"

"A diesel generator providing fifty kilowatts at a hundred and ten volts. It was installed about five years ago and is quite reliable. It's made life at the lamasery much more comfortable, but of course it was really installed to provide power for the motors driving the prayer wheels."

"Of course," echoed Dr. Wagner. "I should have thought of that."

The view from the parapet was vertiginous, but in time one gets used to anything. After three months, George Hanley was not impressed by the two-thousand-foot swoop into the abyss or the remote checkerboard of fields in the valley below. He was leaning against the wind-smoothed stones and staring morosely at the distant mountains whose names he had never bothered to discover.

This, thought George, was the craziest thing that had ever happened to him. "Project Shangri-La," some wit back at the labs had christened it. For weeks now the Mark V had been churning out acres of sheets covered with gibberish. Patiently, inexorably, the computer had been rearranging letters in all their possible combinations, exhausting each class before going on to the next. As the sheets had emerged from the electromatic typewriters, the monks had carefully cut them up and pasted them into enormous books. In another week, heaven be praised, they would have finished. Just what obscure calculations had convinced the monks that they needn't bother to go on to words of ten, twenty, or a hundred letters, George didn't know. One of his recurring nightmares was that there would be some change of plan, and that the high lama (whom they'd naturally called Sam Jaffe, though he didn't look a bit like him) would suddenly announce that the project would be extended to approximately A.D. 2060. They were quite capable of it.

George heard the heavy wooden door slam in the wind as Chuck came out onto the parapet beside him. As usual, Chuck was smoking one of the cigars that made him so popular with the monks—who, it seemed, were quite willing to embrace all the minor and most of the major pleasures of life. That was one thing in their favor: they might be crazy, but they weren't bluenoses. Those frequent trips they took down to the village, for instance . . .

"Listen, George," said Chuck urgently. "I've learned something that means trouble."

"What's wrong? Isn't the machine behaving?" That was the worst contingency George could imagine. It might delay his return, and nothing could be more horrible. The way he felt now, even the sight of a TV commercial would seem like manna from heaven. At least it would be some link with home.

"No—it's nothing like that." Chuck settled himself on the parapet, which was unusual because normally he was scared of the drop. "I've just found what all this is about."

"What d'ya mean? I thought we knew."

"Sure—we know what the monks are trying to do. But we didn't know *why*. It's the craziest thing—"

"Tell me something new," growled George.

"—but old Sam's just come clean with me. You know the way he drops in every afternoon to watch the sheets roll out. Well, this time he seemed rather excited, or at least as near as he'll ever get to it. When I told him that we were on the last cycle he asked me, in that cute English accent of his, if I'd ever wondered what they were trying to do. I said, 'Sure'—and he told me."

"Go on: I'll buy it."

"Well, they believe that when they have listed all His names—and they reckon that there are about nine billion of them—God's purpose will be achieved. The human race will have finished what it was created to do, and there won't be any point in carry on. Indeed, the very idea is something like blasphemy."

"Then what do they expect us to do? Commit suicide?"

"There's no need for that. When the list's completed, God steps in and simply winds things up . . . bingo!"

"Oh, I get it. When we finish our job, it will be the end of the world."

Chuck gave a nervous little laugh.

"That's just what I said to Sam. And do you know what happened? He looked at me in a very queer way, like I'd been stupid in class, and said, 'It's nothing as trivial as *that*.'"

George thought this over for a moment.

"That's what I call taking the Wide View," he said presently. "But what d'you suppose we should do about it? I don't see that it makes the slightest difference to us. After all, we already knew that they were crazy."

"Yes—but don't you see what may happen? When the list's complete and the Last Trump doesn't blow—or whatever it is they expect—*we* may get the blame. It's our machine they've been using. I don't like the situation one little bit."

"I see," said George slowly. "You've got a point there. But this sort of thing's happened before, you know. When I was a kid down in Louisiana we had a crackpot preacher who once said the world was going to end next Sunday. Hundreds of people believed him—even sold their homes. Yet when nothing happened, they didn't turn nasty, as you'd expect. They just decided that he'd made a mistake in his calculations and went right on believing. I guess some of them still do."

"Well, this isn't Louisiana, in case you hadn't noticed. There are just two of us and hundreds of these monks. I like them, and I'll be sorry for old Sam when his lifework backfires on him. But all the same, I wish I was somewhere else."

"I've been wishing that for weeks. But there's nothing we can do until the contract's finished and the transport arrives to fly us out."

"Of course," said Chuck thoughtfully, "we could always try a bit of sabotage."

"Like hell we could! That would make things worse."

"Not the way I meant. Look at it like this. The machine will finish its run four days from now, on the present twenty-hours-a-day basis. The transport calls in a week. O.K.—then all we need to do is to find something that needs replacing during one of the overhaul periods—something that will hold up the works for a couple of days. We'll fix it, of course, but not too quickly. If we time matters properly, we can be down at the airfield when the last name pops out of the register. They won't be able to catch us then."

"I don't like it," said George. "It will be the first time I ever walked out on a job. Besides, it would make them suspicious. No, I'll sit tight and take what comes."

"I *still* don't like it," he said, seven days later, as the tough little mountain ponies carried them down the winding road. "And don't you think I'm running away because I'm afraid. I'm just sorry for those poor old guys up there, and I don't want to be around when they find what suckers they've been. Wonder how Sam will take it?"

"It's funny," replied Chuck, "but when I said good-by I got the idea he knew we were walking out on him—and that he didn't care because he knew the machine was running smoothly and that the job would soon be finished. After that—well, of course, for him there just isn't any After That. . . ."

George turned in his saddle and stared back up the mountain road. This was the last place from which one could get a clear view of the lamasery. The squat, angular buildings were silhouetted against the afterglow of the sunset: here and there, lights gleamed like portholes in the side of an ocean liner. Electric lights, of course, sharing the same circuit as the Mark V. How much longer would they share it? wondered George. Would the monks smash up the computer in their rage and disappointment? Or would they just sit down quietly and begin their calculations all over again?

He knew exactly what was happening up on the mountain at this very moment. The high lama and his assistants would be sitting in their silk robes, inspecting the sheets as the junior monks carried them away from the typewriters and pasted them into the great volumes. No one would be saying anything. The only sound would be the incessant patter, the never-ending rainstorm of the keys hitting the paper, for the Mark V itself was utterly silent as it flashed through its thousands of calculations a second. Three months of this, thought George, was enough to start anyone climbing up the wall.

"There she is!" called Chuck, pointing down into the valley. "Ain't she beautiful!"

She certainly was, thought George. The battered old DC3 lay at the end of the runway like a tiny silver cross. In two hours she would be bearing them away to freedom and sanity. It was a thought worth savoring like a fine liqueur. George let it roll round his mind as the pony trudged patiently down the slope.

The swift night of the high Himalayas was now almost upon them. Fortunately, the road was very good, as roads went in that region, and they were both carrying torches. There was not the slightest danger, only a certain discomfort from the bitter cold. The sky overhead was perfectly clear, and ablaze with the familiar, friendly stars. At least there would be no risk, thought George, of the pilot being unable to take off because of weather conditions. That had been his only remaining worry.

He began to sing, but gave it up after a while. This vast arena of mountains, gleaming like whitely hooded ghosts on every side, did not encourage such ebullience. Presently George glanced at his watch.

"Should be there in an hour," he called back over his shoulder to Chuck. Then he added, in an afterthought: "Wonder if the computer's finished its run. It was due about now."

Chuck didn't reply, so George swung round in his saddle. He could just see Chuck's face, a white oval turned toward the sky.

"Look," whispered Chuck, and George lifted his eyes to heaven. (There is always a last time for everything.)

Overhead, without any fuss, the stars were going out.

✶ REFUGEE

When he comes aboard," said Captain Saunders, as he waited for the landing ramp to extrude itself, "what the devil shall I call him?"

There was a thoughtful silence while the navigation officer and the assistant pilot considered this problem in etiquette. Then Mitchell locked the main control panel, and the ship's multitudinous mechanisms lapsed into unconsciousness as power was withdrawn from them.

"The correct address," he drawled slowly, "is 'Your Royal Highness.' "

"Huh!" snorted the captain. "I'll be damned if I'll call anyone *that!"*

"In these progressive days," put in Chambers helpfully, "I believe that 'Sir' is quite sufficient. But there's no need to worry if you forget: it's been a long time since anyone went to the Tower. Besides, this Henry isn't as tough a proposition as the one who had all the wives."

"From all accounts," added Mitchell, "he's a very pleasant young man. Quite intelligent, too. He's often been known to ask people technical questions that they couldn't answer."

Captain Saunders ignored the implications of this remark, beyond resolving that if Prince Henry wanted to know how a Field Compensation Drive Generator worked, then Mitchell could do the explaining. He got gingerly to his feet—they'd been operating on half a gravity during flight, and now they were on Earth, he felt like a ton of bricks—and started to make his way along the corridors that led to the lower air lock. With an oily purring, the great curving door side-stepped out of his way. Adjusting his smile, he walked out to meet the television cameras and the heir to the British throne.

The man who would, presumably, one day be Henry IX of England was still in his early twenties. He was slightly below average height, and had fine-drawn, regular features that really lived up to all the genealogical clichés. Captain Saunders, who came from Dallas and had no intention of being impressed by any prince, found himself unexpectedly moved by the wide, sad eyes. They were eyes that had seen too many receptions and parades, that had had to watch countless totally uninteresting things, that had never been allowed to stray far from the carefully planned official routes. Looking at that proud but weary face, Captain Saunders glimpsed for the first time the ultimate loneliness of royalty. All his dislike of that institution became suddenly trivial against its real defect: what was wrong with the Crown was the unfairness of inflicting such a burden on any human being. . . .

The passageways of the *Centaurus* were too narrow to allow for general sight-seeing, and it was soon clear that it suited Prince Henry very well to leave his entourage behind. Once they had begun moving through the ship, Saunders lost all his stiffness and reserve, and within a few minutes was treating the prince exactly like any other visitor. He did not realize that one of the earliest lessons royalty has to learn is that of putting people at their ease.

"You know, Captain," said the prince wistfully, "this is a big day for us. I've always hoped that one day it would be possible for spaceships to operate from England. But it still seems strange to have a port of our own here, after all these years. Tell me—did you ever have much to do with rockets?"

"Well, I had some training on them, but they were already on the way out before I graduated. I was lucky: some older men had to go back to school and start all over again—or else abandon space completely if they couldn't convert to the new ships."

"It made as much difference as that?"

"Oh yes—when the rocket went, it was as big as the change from sail to steam. That's an analogy you'll often hear, by the way. There was a glamour about the old rockets, just as there was about the old windjammers, which these modern ships haven't got. When the *Centaurus* takes off, she goes up as quietly as a balloon—and as slowly, if she wants to. But a rocket blast-off shook the ground for miles, and you'd be deaf for days if you were too near the launching apron. Still, you'll know all that from the old news recordings."

The prince smiled.

"Yes," he said. "I've often run through them at the Palace. I think I've watched every incident in all the pioneering expeditions. I was sorry to see the end of the rockets, too. But we could never have had a spaceport here on Salisbury Plain—the vibration would have shaken down Stonehenge!"

"Stonehenge?" queried Saunders as he held open a hatch and let the prince through into Hold Number 3.

"Ancient monument—one of the most famous stone circles in the world. It's really impressive, and about three thousand years old. See it if you can—it's only ten miles from here."

Captain Saunders had some difficulty in suppressing a smile. What an odd country this was: where else, he wondered, would you find contrasts like this? It made him feel very young and raw when he remembered that back home Billy the Kid was ancient history, and there was hardly anything in the whole of Texas as much as five hundred years old. For the first time he began to realize what tradition meant: it gave Prince Henry something that he could never possess. Poise—self-confidence, yes, that was it. And a pride that was somehow free from arrogance because it took itself so much for granted that it never had to be asserted.

It was surprising how many questions Prince Henry managed to ask in the thirty minutes that had been allotted for his tour of the freighter. They were not the routine questions that people asked out of politeness, quite uninterested in the answers. H.R.H. Prince Henry knew a lot about spaceships, and Captain Saunders felt completely exhausted when he handed his distinguished guest back to the reception committee, which had been waiting outside the *Centaurus* with well-simulated patience.

"Thank you very much, Captain," said the prince as they shook hands in the air lock. "I've not enjoyed myself so much for ages. I hope you have a pleasant stay in England, and a successful voyage." Then his retinue whisked him away, and the port officials, frustrated until now, came aboard to check the ship's papers.

"Well," said Mitchell when it was all over, "what did you think of our Prince of Wales?"

"He surprised me," answered Saunders frankly. "I'd never have guessed he was a prince. I always thought they were rather dumb. But heck, he *knew* the principles of the Field Drive! Has he ever been up in space?"

"Once, I think. Just a hop above the atmosphere in a Space Force ship. It didn't even reach orbit before it came back again—but the Prime Minister nearly had a fit. There were questions in the House and editorials in the *Times*. Everyone decided that the heir to the throne was too valuable to risk in these newfangled inventions. So, though he has the rank of commodore in the Royal Space Force, he's never even been to the moon."

"The poor guy," said Captain Saunders.

He had three days to burn, since it was not the captain's job to supervise the loading of the ship or the preflight maintenance. Saunders knew skippers who hung around breathing heavily on the necks of the servicing engineers, but he wasn't that type. Besides, he wanted to see London. He had been to Mars and Venus and the moon, but this was his first visit to England. Mitchell and Chambers filled him with useful information and put him on the monorail to London before dashing off to see their own families. They would be returning to the spaceport a day before he did, to see that everything was in order. It was a great relief having officers one could rely on so implicitly: they were unimaginative and cautious, but thoroughgoing almost to a fault. If *they* said that everything was shipshape, Saunders knew he could take off without qualms.

The sleek, streamlined cylinder whistled across the carefully tailored landscape. It was so close to the ground, and traveling so swiftly, that one could only gather fleeting impressions of the towns and fields that flashed by. Everything, thought Saunders, was so incredibly compact, and on such a Lilliputian scale. There were no open spaces, no fields more than a mile long in any direction. It was enough to give a Texan claustrophobia—particularly a Texan who also happened to be a space pilot.

The sharply defined edge of London appeared like the bulwark of some walled city on the horizon. With few exceptions, the buildings were quite low—perhaps fifteen or twenty stories in height. The monorail shot through a narrow canyon, over a very attractive park, across a river that was presumably the Thames, and then came to rest with a steady, powerful surge of deceleration. A loud-speaker announced, in a modest voice that seemed afraid of being overheard: "This is Paddington. Passengers for the North please remain seated." Saunders pulled his baggage down from the rack and headed out into the station.

As he made for the entrance to the Underground, he passed a bookstall and glanced at the magazines on display. About half of them, it seemed, carried photographs of Prince Henry or other members of the royal family. This, thought Saunders, was altogether too much of a good thing. He also noticed that all the evening papers showed the prince entering or leaving the *Centaurus,* and bought copies to read in the subway—he begged its pardon, the "Tube."

The editorial comments had a monotonous similarity. At last, they rejoiced, England need no longer take a back seat among the spacegoing nations. Now it was possible to operate a space fleet without having a million square miles of desert: the silent, gravity-defying ships of today could land, if need be, in Hyde Park, without even disturbing the ducks on the Serpentine. Saunders found it odd that this sort of patriotism had managed to survive into the age of space, but he guessed that the British had felt it pretty badly when they'd had to borrow launching sites from the Australians, the Americans, and the Russians.

The London Underground was still, after a century and a half, the best transport system in the world, and it deposited Saunders safely at his destination less than ten minutes after he had left Paddington. In ten minutes the *Centaurus* could have covered fifty thousand miles; but space, after all, was not quite so crowded as this. Nor were the orbits of space craft so tortuous as the streets Saunders had to negotiate to reach his hotel. All attempts to straighten out London had failed dismally, and it was fifteen minutes before he completed the last hundred yards of his journey.

He stripped off his jacket and collapsed thankfully on his bed. Three quiet, carefree days all to himself: it seemed too good to be true.

It was. He had barely taken a deep breath when the phone rang.

"Captain Saunders? I'm so glad we found you. This is the B.B.C. We have a program called 'In Town Tonight' and we were wondering . . ."

The thud of the air-lock door was the sweetest sound Saunders had heard for days. Now he was safe: nobody could get at him here in his armored fortress, which would soon be far out in the freedom of space. It was not that he had been treated badly: on the contrary, he had been treated altogether too well. He had made four (or was it five?) appearances on various TV programs; he had been to more parties than he could remember; he had acquired several hundred new friends and (the way his head felt now) forgotten all his old ones.

"Who started the rumor," he said to Mitchell as they met at the port, "that the British were reserved and standoffish? Heaven help me if I ever meet a *demonstrative* Englishman."

"I take it," replied Mitchell, "that you had a good time."

"Ask me tomorrow," Saunders replied. "I may have reintegrated my psyche by then."

"I saw you on that quiz program last night," remarked Chambers. "You looked pretty ghastly."

"Thank you: that's just the sort of sympathetic encouragement I need at the moment. I'd like to see you think of a synonym for 'jejune' after you'd been up until three in the morning."

"Vapid," replied Chambers promptly.

"Insipid," said Mitchell, not to be outdone.

"You win. Let's have those overhaul schedules and see what the engineers have been up to."

Once seated at the control desk, Captain Saunders quickly became his usual efficient self. He was home again, and his training took over. He knew exactly what to do, and would do it with automatic precision. To right and left of him, Mitchell and Chambers were checking their instruments and calling the control tower.

It took them an hour to carry out the elaborate preflight routine. When the last signature had been attached to the last sheet of instructions, and the last red light on the monitor panel had turned to green, Saunders flopped back in his seat and lit a cigarette. They had ten minutes to spare before take-off.

"One day," he said, "I'm going to come to England incognito to find what makes the place tick. I don't understand how you can crowd so many people onto one little island without it sinking."

"Huh," snorted Chambers. "You should see Holland. That makes England look as wide open as Texas."

"And then there's this royal family business. Do you know, wherever I went everybody kept asking me how I got on with Prince Henry—what we'd talked about—didn't I think he was a fine guy, and so on. Frankly, I got fed up with it. I can't imagine how you've managed to stand it for a thousand years."

"Don't think that the royal family's been popular all the time," replied Mitchell. "Remember what happened to Charles the First? And some of the things we said about the early Georges were quite as rude as the remarks your people made later."

"We just happen to like tradition," said Chambers. "We're not afraid to change when the time comes, but as far as the royal family is concerned —well, it's unique and we're rather fond of it. Just the way you feel about the Statue of Liberty."

"Not a fair example. I don't think it's right to put human beings up on a pedestal and treat them as if they're—well, minor deities. Look at Prince Henry, for instance. Do you think he'll ever have a chance of doing the things he really wants to do? I saw him three times on TV when I was in London. The first time he was opening a new school somewhere; then he was giving a speech to the Worshipful Company of Fishmongers at the Guildhall (I swear I'm not making *that* up), and finally he was receiving an address of welcome from the mayor of Podunk, or whatever your equivalent is." ("Wigan," interjected Mitchell.) "I think I'd rather be in jail than live that sort of life. Why can't you leave the poor guy alone?"

For once, neither Mitchell nor Chambers rose to the challenge. Indeed, they maintained a somewhat frigid silence. That's torn it, thought Saunders. I should have kept my big mouth shut; now I've hurt their feelings. I should have remembered that advice I read somewhere: "The British have two religions—cricket and the royal family. Never attempt to criticize either."

The awkward pause was broken by the radio and the voice of the spaceport controller.

"Control to *Centaurus*. Your flight lane clear. O.K. to lift."

"Take-off program starting—*now!*" replied Saunders, throwing the master switch. Then he leaned back, his eyes taking in the entire control panel, his hands clear of the board but ready for instant action.

He was tense but completely confident. Better brains than his—brains of metal and crystal and flashing electron streams—were in charge of the *Centaurus* now. If necessary, he could take command, but he had never yet lifted a ship manually and never expected to do so. If the automatics failed, he would cancel the take-off and sit here on Earth until the fault had been cleared up.

The main field went on, and weight ebbed from the *Centaurus*. There were protesting groans from the ship's hull and structure as the strains redistributed themselves. The curved arms of the landing cradle were carrying no load now; the slightest breath of wind would carry the freighter away into the sky.

Control called from the tower: "Your weight now zero: check calibration."

Saunders looked at his meters. The upthrust of the field would now exactly equal the weight of the ship, and the meter readings should agree with the totals on the loading schedules. In at least one instance this check had revealed the presence of a stowaway on board a spaceship—the gauges were as sensitive as that.

"One million, five hundred and sixty thousand, four hundred and twenty kilograms," Saunders read off from the thrust indicators. "Pretty good—it checks to within fifteen kilos. The first time I've been underweight, though. You could have taken on some more candy for that plump girl friend of yours in Port Lowell, Mitch."

The assistant pilot gave a rather sickly grin. He had never quite lived down a blind date on Mars which had given him a completely unwarranted reputation for preferring statuesque blondes.

There was no sense of motion, but the *Centaurus* was now falling up into the summer sky as her weight was not only neutralized but reversed. To the watchers below, she would be a swiftly mounting star, a silver globule climbing through and beyond the clouds. Around her, the blue of the atmosphere was deepening into the eternal darkness of space. Like a bead moving along an invisible wire, the freighter was following the pattern of radio waves that would lead her from world to world.

This, thought Captain Saunders, was his twenty-sixth take-off from Earth. But the wonder would never die, nor would he ever outgrow the feeling of power it gave him to sit here at the control panel, the master of forces beyond even the dreams of mankind's ancient gods. No two departures were ever the same: some were into the dawn, some toward the sunset, some above a cloud-veiled Earth, some through clear and sparkling skies. Space itself might be unchanging, but on Earth the same pattern never recurred, and no man ever looked twice at the same landscape or the same sky. Down there the Atlantic waves were marching eternally toward Europe, and high above them—but so far below the *Centaurus!*—the glittering bands of cloud were advancing before the same winds. England began to merge into the continent, and the European coast line became foreshortened and misty as it sank hull down beyond the curve of the world. At the frontier of the west, a fugitive stain on the horizon was the first hint of America. With a single glance, Captain Saunders could span all the leagues across which Columbus had labored half a thousand years ago.

With the silence of limitless power, the ship shook itself free from the last bonds of Earth. To an outside observer, the only sign of the energies it was expending would have been the dull red glow from the radiation fins around the vessel's equator, as the heat loss from the mass-converters was dissipated into space.

"14:03:45," wrote Captain Saunders neatly in the log. "Escape velocity attained. Course deviation negligible."

There was little point in making the entry. The modest 25,000 miles an hour that had been the almost unattainable goal of the first astronauts had no practical significance now, since the *Centaurus* was still accelerating and would continue to gain speed for hours. But it had a profound psychological meaning. Until this moment, if power had failed, they would have fallen back to Earth. But now gravity could never recapture them: they had achieved the freedom of space, and could take their pick of the planets. In practice, of course, there would be several kinds of hell to pay if they did not pick Mars and deliver their cargo according to plan. But Captain Saunders, like all spacemen, was fundamentally a romantic. Even on a milk run like this he would sometimes dream of the ringed glory of Saturn or the somber Neptunian wastes, lit by the distant fires of the shrunken sun.

An hour after take-off, according to the hallowed ritual, Chambers left the course computer to its own devices and produced the three glasses that lived beneath the chart table. As he drank the traditional toast to Newton, Oberth, and Einstein, Saunders wondered how this little ceremony had originated. Space crews had certainly been doing it for at least sixty years: perhaps it could be traced back to the legendary rocket engineer who made the remark, "I've burned more alcohol in sixty seconds than you've ever sold across this lousy bar."

Two hours later, the last course correction that the tracking stations on Earth could give them had been fed into the computer. From now on, until Mars came sweeping up ahead, they were on their own. It was a lonely thought, yet a curiously exhilarating one. Saunders savored it in his mind. There were just the three of them here—and no one else within a million miles.

In the circumstances, the detonation of an atomic bomb could hardly have been more shattering than the modest knock on the cabin door. . . .

Captain Saunders had never been so startled in his life. With a yelp that had already left him before he had a chance to suppress it, he shot out of his seat and rose a full yard before the ship's residual gravity field dragged him back. Chambers and Mitchell, on the other hand, behaved with traditional British phlegm. They swiveled in their bucket seats, stared at the door, and then waited for their captain to take action.

It took Saunders several seconds to recover. Had he been confronted with what might be called a normal emergency, he would already have been halfway into a space suit. But a diffident knock on the door of the control cabin, when everybody else in the ship was sitting beside him, was not a fair test.

A stowaway was simply impossible. The danger had been so obvious, right from the beginning of commercial space flight, that the most stringent precautions had been taken against it. One of his officers, Saunders knew, would always have been on duty during loading; no one could possibly have crept in unobserved. Then there had been the detailed preflight inspection, carried out by both Mitchell and Chambers. Finally, there was the weight check at the moment before take-off; *that* was conclusive. No, a stowaway was totally . . .

The knock on the door sounded again. Captain Saunders clenched his fists and squared his jaw. In a few minutes, he thought, some romantic idiot was going to be very, very sorry.

"Open the door, Mr. Mitchell," Saunders growled. In a single long stride, the assistant pilot crossed the cabin and jerked open the hatch.

For an age, it seemed, no one spoke. Then the stowaway, wavering slightly in the low gravity, came into the cabin. He was completely self-possessed, and looked very pleased with himself.

"Good afternoon, Captain Saunders," he said, "I must apologize for this sudden intrusion."

Saunders swallowed hard. Then, as the pieces of the jigsaw fell into place, he looked first at Mitchell, then at Chambers. Both of his officers stared guilelessly back at him with expressions of ineffable innocence. "So *that's* it," he said bitterly. There was no need for any explanations: everything was perfectly clear. It was easy to picture the complicated negotiations, the midnight meetings, the falsification of records, the off-loading of nonessential cargoes that his trusted colleagues had been conducting behind his back. He was sure it was a most interesting story, but he didn't want to hear about it now. He was too busy wondering what the *Manual of Space Law* would have to say about a situation like this, though he was already gloomily certain that it would be of no use to him at all.

It was too late to turn back, of course: the conspirators wouldn't have made an elementary miscalculation like that. He would just have to make the best of what looked to be the trickiest voyage in his career.

He was still trying to think of something to say when the PRIORITY signal started flashing on the radio board. The stowaway looked at his watch.

"I was expecting that," he said. "It's probably the Prime Minister. I think I'd better speak to the poor man."

Saunders thought so too.

"Very well, Your Royal Highness," he said sulkily, and with such emphasis that the title sounded almost like an insult. Then, feeling much put upon, he retired into a corner.

It was the Prime Minister all right, and he sounded very upset. Several times he used the phrase "your duty to your people" and once there was a distinct catch in his throat as he said something about "devotion of your subjects to the Crown." Saunders realized, with some surprise, that he really meant it.

While this emotional harangue was in progress, Mitchell leaned over to Saunders and whispered in his ear:

"The old boy's on a sticky wicket, and he knows it. The people will be behind the prince when they hear what's happened. Everybody knows he's been trying to get into space for years."

"I wish he hadn't chosen *my* ship," said Saunders. "And I'm not sure that this doesn't count as mutiny."

"The heck it does. Mark my words—when this is all over you'll be the only Texan to have the Order of the Garter. Won't that be nice for you?"

"Shush!" said Chambers. The prince was speaking, his words winging back across the abyss that now sundered him from the island he would one day rule.

"I am sorry, Mr. Prime Minister," he said, "if I've caused you any alarm. I will return as soon as it is convenient. Someone has to do everything for the first time, and I felt the moment had come for a member of my family to leave Earth. It will be a valuable part of my education, and will make me more fitted to carry out my duty. Good-by."

He dropped the microphone and walked over to the observation window—the only spaceward-looking port on the entire ship. Saunders watched him standing there, proud and lonely—but contented now. And as he saw the prince staring out at the stars which he had at last attained, all his annoyance and indignation slowly evaporated.

No one spoke for a long time. Then Prince Henry tore his gaze away from the blinding splendor beyond the port, looked at Captain Saunders, and smiled.

"Where's the galley, Captain?" he asked. "I may be out of practice, but when I used to go scouting I was the best cook in my patrol."

Saunders slowly relaxed, then smiled back. The tension seemed to lift from the control room. Mars was still a long way off, but he knew now that this wasn't going to be such a bad trip after all. . . .

✶ THE OTHER SIDE OF THE SKY

SPECIAL DELIVERY

I can still remember the excitement, back in 1957, when Russia launched the first artificial satellites and managed to hang a few pounds of instruments up here above the atmosphere. Of course, I was only a kid at the time, but I went out in the evening like everyone else, trying to spot those little magnesium spheres as they zipped through the twilight sky hundreds of miles above my head. It's strange to think that some of them are still there—but that now they're *below* me, and I'd have to look down toward Earth if I wanted to see them. . . .

Yes, a lot has happened in the last forty years, and sometimes I'm afraid that you people down on Earth take the space stations for granted, forgetting the skill and science and courage that went to make them. How often do you stop to think that all your long-distance phone calls, and most of your TV programs, are routed through one or the other of the satellites? And how often do you give any credit to the meteorologists up here for the fact that weather forecasts are no longer the joke they were to our grandfathers, but are dead accurate ninety-nine per cent of the time?

It was a rugged life, back in the seventies, when I went up to work on the outer stations. They were being rushed into operation to open up the millions of new TV and radio circuits which would be available as soon as we had transmitters out in space that could beam programs to anywhere on the globe.

The first artificial satellites had been very close to Earth, but the three stations forming the great triangle of the Relay Chain had to be twenty-two thousand miles up, spaced equally around the equator. At this altitude—and at no other—they would take exactly a day to go around their orbit, and so would stay poised forever over the same spot on the turning Earth.

In my time I've worked on all three of the stations, but my first tour of duty was aboard Relay Two. That's almost exactly over Entebbe, Uganda, and provides service for Europe, Africa, and most of Asia. Today it's a huge structure hundreds of yards across, beaming thousands of simultaneous programs down to the hemisphere beneath it as it carries the radio traffic of half the world. But when I saw it for the first time from the port of the ferry rocket that carried me up to orbit, it looked like a junk pile adrift in space. Prefabricated parts were floating around in hopeless confusion, and it seemed impossible that any order could ever emerge from this chaos.

Accommodation for the technical staff and assembling crews was primitive, consisting of a few unserviceable ferry rockets that had been stripped of everything except air purifiers. "The Hulks," we christened them; each man had just enough room for himself and a couple of cubic feet of personal belongings. There was a fine irony in the fact that we were living in the midst of infinite space—and hadn't room to swing a cat.

It was a great day when we heard that the first pressurized living quarters were on their way up to us—complete with needle-jet shower baths that would operate even here, where water—like everything else—had no weight. Unless you've lived aboard an overcrowded spaceship, you won't appreciate what that meant. We could throw away our damp sponges and feel really clean at last. . . .

Nor were the showers the only luxury promised us. On the way up from Earth was an inflatable lounge spacious enough to hold no fewer than eight people, a microfilm library, a magnetic billiard table, lightweight chess sets, and similar novelties for bored spacemen. The very thought of all these comforts made our cramped life in the Hulks seem quite unendurable, even though we were being paid about a thousand dollars a week to endure it.

Starting from the Second Refueling Zone, two thousand miles above Earth, the eagerly awaited ferry rocket would take about six hours to climb up to us with its precious cargo. I was off duty at the time, and stationed myself at the telescope where I'd spent most of my scanty leisure. It was impossible to grow tired of exploring the great world hanging there in space beside us; with the highest power of the telescope, one seemed to be only a few miles above the surface. When there were no clouds and the seeing was good, objects the size of a small house were easily visible. I had never been to Africa, but I grew to know it well while I was off duty in Station Two. You may not believe this, but I've often spotted elephants moving across the plains, and the immense herds of zebras and antelopes were easy to see as they flowed back and forth like living tides on the great reservations.

But my favorite spectacle was the dawn coming up over the mountains in the heart of the continent. The line of sunlight would come sweeping across the Indian Ocean, and the new day would extinguish the tiny, twinkling galaxies of the cities shining in the darkness below me. Long before the sun had reached the lowlands around them, the peaks of Kilimanjaro and Mount Kenya would be blazing in the dawn, brilliant stars still surrounded by the night. As the sun rose higher, the day would march swiftly down their slopes and the valleys would fill with light. Earth would then be at its first quarter, waxing toward full.

Twelve hours later, I would see the reverse process as the same mountains caught the last rays of the setting sun. They would blaze for a little while in the narrow belt of twilight; then Earth would spin into darkness, and night would fall upon Africa.

It was not the beauty of the terrestrial globe I was concerned with now. Indeed, I was not even looking at Earth, but at the fierce blue-white star high above the western edge of the planet's disk. The automatic freighter was eclipsed in Earth's shadow; what I was seeing was the incandescent flare of its rockets as they drove it up on its twenty-thousand-mile climb.

I had watched ships ascending to us so often that I knew every stage of their maneuver by heart. So when the rockets didn't wink out, but continued to burn steadily, I knew within seconds that something was wrong. In sick, helpless fury I watched all our longed-for comforts—and, worse still, our mail!—moving faster and faster along the unintended orbit. The freighter's autopilot had jammed; had there been a human pilot aboard, he could have overridden the controls and cut the motor, but now all the fuel that should have driven the ferry on its two-way trip was being burned in one continuous blast of power.

By the time the fuel tanks had emptied, and that distant star had flickered and died in the field of my telescope, the tracking stations had confirmed what I already knew. The freighter was moving far too fast for Earth's gravity to recapture it—indeed, it was heading into the cosmic wilderness beyond Pluto. . . .

It took a long time for morale to recover, and it only made matters worse when someone in the computing section worked out the future history of our errant freighter. You see, nothing is ever really lost in space. Once you've calculated its orbit, you know where it is until the end of eternity. As we watched our lounge, our library, our games, our mail receding to the far horizons of the solar system, we knew that it would all come back one day, in perfect condition. If we have a ship standing by it will be easy to intercept it the second time it comes around the sun—quite early in the spring of the year A.D. 15,862.

FEATHERED FRIEND

To the best of my knowledge, there's never been a regulation that forbids one to keep pets in a space station. No one ever thought it was necessary—and even had such a rule existed, I am quite certain that Sven Olsen would have ignored it.

With a name like that, you will picture Sven at once as a six-foot-six Nordic giant, built like a bull and with a voice to match. Had this been so, his chances of getting a job in space would have been very slim; actually he was a wiry little fellow, like most of the early spacers, and managed to qualify easily for the 150-pound bonus that kept so many of us on a reducing diet.

Sven was one of our best construction men, and excelled at the tricky and specialized work of collecting assorted girders as they floated around in free fall, making them do the slow-motion, three-dimensional ballet that would get them into their right positions, and fusing the pieces together when they were precisely dovetailed into the intended pattern. I never tired of watching him and his gang as the station grew under their hands like a giant jigsaw puzzle; it was a skilled and difficult job, for a space suit is not the most convenient of garbs in which to work. However, Sven's team had one great advantage over the construction gangs you see putting up skyscrapers down on Earth. They could step back and admire their handiwork without being abruptly parted from it by gravity. . . .

Don't ask me why Sven wanted a pet, or why he chose the one he did. I'm not a psychologist, but I must admit that his selection was very sensible. Claribel weighed practically nothing, her food requirements were infinitesimal—and she was not worried, as most animals would have been, by the absence of gravity.

I first became aware that Claribel was aboard when I was sitting in the little cubbyhole laughingly called my office, checking through my lists of technical stores to decide what items we'd be running out of next. When I heard the musical whistle beside my ear, I assumed that it had come over the station intercom, and waited for an announcement to follow. It didn't; instead, there was a long and involved pattern of melody that made me look up with such a start that I forgot all about the angle beam just behind my head. When the stars had ceased to explode before my eyes, I had my first view of Claribel.

She was a small yellow canary, hanging in the air as motionless as a hummingbird—and with much less effort, for her wings were quietly folded along her sides. We stared at each other for a minute; then, before I had quite recovered my wits, she did a curious kind of backward loop I'm sure no earthbound canary had ever managed, and departed with a few leisurely flicks. It was quite obvious that she'd already learned how to operate in the absence of gravity, and did not believe in doing unnecessary work.

Sven didn't confess to her ownership for several days, and by that time it no longer mattered, because Claribel was a general pet. He had smuggled her up on the last ferry from Earth, when he came back from leave—partly, he claimed, out of sheer scientific curiosity. He wanted to see just how a bird would operate when it had no weight but could still use its wings.

Claribel thrived and grew fat. On the whole, we had little trouble concealing our unauthorized guest when VIPs from Earth came visiting. A space station has more hiding places than you can count; the only problem was that Claribel got rather noisy when she was upset, and we sometimes had to think fast to explain the curious peeps and whistles that came from ventilating shafts and storage bulkheads. There were a couple of narrow escapes—but then who would dream of looking for a canary in a space station?

We were now on twelve-hour watches, which was not as bad as it sounds, since you need little sleep in space. Though of course there is no "day" and "night" when you are floating in permanent sunlight, it was still convenient to stick to the terms. Certainly when I woke up that "morning" it felt like 6:00 A.M. on Earth. I had a nagging headache, and vague memories of fitful, disturbed dreams. It took me ages to undo my bunk straps, and I was still only half awake when I joined the remainder of the duty crew in the mess. Breakfast was unusually quiet, and there was one seat vacant.

"Where's Sven?" I asked, not very much caring.

"He's looking for Claribel," someone answered. "Says he can't find her anywhere. She usually wakes him up."

Before I could retort that she usually woke me up, too, Sven came in through the doorway, and we could see at once that something was wrong.

He slowly opened his hand, and there lay a tiny bundle of yellow feathers, with two clenched claws sticking pathetically up into the air.

"What happened?" we asked, all equally distressed.

"I don't know," said Sven mournfully. "I just found her like this."

"Let's have a look at her," said Jock Duncan, our cook-doctor-dietitian. We all waited in hushed silence while he held Claribel against his ear in an attempt to detect any heartbeat.

Presently he shook his head. "I can't hear anything, but that doesn't prove she's dead. I've never listened to a canary's heart," he added rather apologetically.

"Give her a shot of oxygen," suggested somebody, pointing to the green-banded emergency cylinder in its recess beside the door. Everyone agreed that this was an excellent idea, and Claribel was tucked snugly into a face mask that was large enough to serve as a complete oxygen tent for her.

To our delighted surprise, she revived at once. Beaming broadly, Sven removed the mask, and she hopped onto his finger. She gave her series of "Come to the cookhouse, boys" trills—then promptly keeled over again.

"I don't get it," lamented Sven. "What's wrong with her? She's never done this before."

For the last few minutes, something had been tugging at my memory. My mind seemed to be very sluggish that morning, as if I was still unable to cast off the burden of sleep. I felt that I could do with some of that oxygen—but before I could reach the mask, understanding exploded in my brain. I whirled on the duty engineer and said urgently:

"Jim! There's something wrong with the air! That's why Claribel's passed out. I've just remembered that miners used to carry canaries down to warn them of gas."

"Nonsense!" said Jim. "The alarms would have gone off. We've got duplicate circuits, operating independently."

"Er—the second alarm circuit isn't connected up yet," his assistant reminded him. That shook Jim; he left without a word, while we stood arguing and passing the oxygen bottle around like a pipe of peace.

He came back ten minutes later with a sheepish expression. It was one of those accidents that couldn't possibly happen; we'd had one of our rare eclipses by Earth's shadow that night; part of the air purifier had frozen up, and the single alarm in the circuit had failed to go off. Half a million dollars' worth of chemical and electronic engineering had let us down completely. Without Claribel, we should soon have been slightly dead.

So now, if you visit any space station, don't be surprised if you hear an inexplicable snatch of bird song. There's no need to be alarmed: on the contrary, in fact. It will mean that you're being doubly safeguarded, at practically no extra expense.

TAKE A DEEP BREATH

A long time ago I discovered that people who've never left Earth have certain fixed ideas about conditions in space. Everyone "knows," for example, that a man dies instantly and horribly when exposed to the vacuum that exists beyond the atmosphere. You'll find numerous gory descriptions of exploded space travelers in the popular literature, and I won't spoil your appetite by repeating them here. Many of those tales, indeed, are basically true. I've pulled men back through the air lock who were very poor advertisements for space flight.

Yet, at the same time, there are exceptions to every rule—even this one. I should know, for I learned the hard way.

We were on the last stages of building Communications Satellite Two; all the main units had been joined together, the living quarters had been pressurized, and the station had been given the slow spin around its axis that had restored the unfamiliar sensation of weight. I say "slow," but at its rim our two-hundred-foot-diameter wheel was turning at thirty miles an hour. We had, of course, no sense of motion, but the centrifugal force caused by this spin gave us about half the weight we would have possessed on Earth. That was enough to stop things from drifting around, yet not enough to make us feel uncomfortably sluggish after our weeks with no weight at all.

Four of us were sleeping in the small cylindrical cabin known as Bunkhouse Number 6 on the night that it happened. The bunkhouse was at the very rim of the station; if you imagine a bicycle wheel, with a string of sausages replacing the tire, you have a good idea of the layout. Bunkhouse Number 6 was one of these sausages, and we were slumbering peacefully inside it.

I was awakened by a sudden jolt that was not violent enough to cause me alarm, but which did make me sit up and wonder what had happened. Anything unusual in a space station demands instant attention, so I reached for the intercom switch by my bed. "Hello, Central," I called. "What was that?"

There was no reply; the line was dead.

Now thoroughly alarmed, I jumped out of bed—and had an even bigger shock. *There was no gravity.* I shot up to the ceiling before I was able to grab a stanchion and bring myself to a halt, at the cost of a sprained wrist.

It was impossible for the entire station to have suddenly stopped rotating. There was only one answer; the failure of the intercom and, as I quickly discovered, of the lighting circuit as well forced us to face the appalling truth. We were no longer part of the station; our little cabin had somehow come adrift, and had been slung off into space like a raindrop falling on a spinning flywheel.

There were no windows through which we could look out, but we were not in complete darkness, for the battery-powered emergency lights had come on. All the main air vents had closed automatically when the pressure dropped. For the time being, we could live in our own private atmosphere, even though it was not being renewed. Unfortunately, a steady whistling told us that the air we did have was escaping through a leak somewhere in the cabin.

There was no way of telling what had happened to the rest of the station. For all we knew, the whole structure might have come to pieces, and all our colleagues might be dead or in the same predicament as we—drifting through space in leaking cans of air. Our one slim hope was the possibility that we were the only castaways, that the rest of the station was intact and had been able to send a rescue team to find us. After all, we were receding at no more than thirty miles an hour, and one of the rocket scooters could catch up to us in minutes.

It actually took an hour, though without the evidence of my watch I should never have believed that it was so short a time. We were now gasping for breath, and the gauge on our single emergency oxygen tank had dropped to one division above zero.

The banging on the wall seemed like a signal from another world. We banged back vigorously, and a moment later a muffled voice called to us through the wall. Someone outside was lying with his space-suit helmet pressed against the metal, and his shouted words were reaching us by direct conduction. Not as clear as radio—but it worked.

The oxygen gauge crept slowly down to zero while we had our council of war. We would be dead before we could be towed back to the station; yet the rescue ship was only a few feet away from us, with its air lock already open. Our little problem was to cross that few feet—*without* space suits.

We made our plans carefully, rehearsing our actions in the full knowledge that there could be no repeat performance. Then we each took a deep, final swig of oxygen, flushing out our lungs. When we were all ready, I banged on the wall to give the signal to our friends waiting outside.

There was a series of short, staccato raps as the power tools got to work on the thin hull. We clung tightly to the stanchions, as far away as possible from the point of entry, knowing just what would happen. When it came, it was so sudden that the mind couldn't record the sequence of events. The cabin seemed to explode, and a great wind tugged at me. The last trace of air gushed from my lungs, through my already-opened mouth. And then—utter silence, and the stars shining through the gaping hole that led to life.

Believe me, I didn't stop to analyze my sensations. I think—though I can never be sure that it wasn't imagination—that my eyes were smarting and there was a tingling feeling all over my body. And I felt very cold, perhaps because evaporation was already starting from my skin.

The only thing I can be certain of is that uncanny silence. It is never completely quiet in a space station, for there is always the sound of machinery or air pumps. But this was the absolute silence of the empty void, where there is no trace of air to carry sound.

Almost at once we launched ourselves out through the shattered wall, into the full blast of the sun. I was instantly blinded—but that didn't matter, because the men waiting in space suits grabbed me as soon as I emerged and hustled me into the air lock. And there, sound slowly returned as the air rushed in, and we remembered we could breathe again. The entire rescue, they told us later, had lasted just twenty seconds. . . .

Well, we were the founding members of the Vacuum-Breathers' Club. Since then, at least a dozen other men have done the same thing, in similar emergencies. The record time in space is now two minutes; after that, the blood begins to form bubbles as it boils at body temperature, and those bubbles soon get to the heart.

In my case, there was only one aftereffect. For maybe a quarter of a minute I had been exposed to *real* sunlight, not the feeble stuff that filters down through the atmosphere of Earth. Breathing space didn't hurt me at all—but I got the worst dose of sunburn I've ever had in my life.

FREEDOM OF SPACE

Not many of you, I suppose, can imagine the time before the satellite relays gave us our present world communications system. When I was a boy, it was impossible to send TV programs across the oceans, or even to establish reliable radio contact around the curve of the Earth without picking up a fine assortment of crackles and bangs on the way. Yet now we take interference-free circuits for granted, and think nothing of seeing our friends on the other side of the globe as clearly as if we were standing face to face. Indeed, it's a simple fact that without the satellite relays, the whole structure of world commerce and industry would collapse. Unless we were up here on the space stations to bounce their messages around the globe, how do you think any of the world's big business organizations could keep their widely scattered electronic brains in touch with each other?

But all this was still in the future, back in the late seventies, when we were finishing work on the Relay Chain. I've already told you about some of our problems and near disasters; they were serious enough at the time, but in the end we overcame them all. The three stations spaced around Earth were no longer piles of girders, air cylinders, and plastic pressure chambers. Their assembly had been completed, we had moved aboard, and could now work in comfort, unhampered by space suits. And we had gravity again, now that the stations had been set slowly spinning. Not real gravity, of course; but centrifugal force feels exactly the same when you're out in space. It was pleasant being able to pour drinks and to sit down without drifting away on the first air current.

Once the three stations had been built, there was still a year's solid work to be done installing all the radio and TV equipment that would lift the world's communications networks into space. It was a great day when we established the first TV link between England and Australia. The signal was beamed up to us in Relay Two, as we sat above the center of Africa, we flashed it across to Three—poised over New Guinea—and they shot it down to Earth again, clear and clean after its ninety-thousand-mile journey.

These, however, were the engineers' private tests. The official opening of the system would be the biggest event in the history of world communication—an elaborate global telecast, in which every nation would take part. It would be a three-hour show, as for the first time the live TV camera roamed around the world, proclaiming to mankind that the last barrier of distance was down.

The program planning, it was cynically believed, had taken as much effort as the building of the space stations in the first place, and of all the problems the planners had to solve, the most difficult was that of choosing a *compère* or master of ceremonies to introduce the items in the elaborate global show that would be watched by half the human race.

Heaven knows how much conniving, blackmail, and downright character assassination went on behind the scenes. All we knew was that a week before the great day, a nonscheduled rocket came up to orbit with Gregory Wendell aboard. This was quite a surprise, since Gregory wasn't as big a TV personality as, say, Jeffers Jackson in the U.S. or Vince Clifford in Britain. However, it seemed that the big boys had canceled each other out, and Gregg had got the coveted job through one of those compromises so well known to politicians.

Gregg had started his career as a disc jockey on a university radio station in the American Midwest, and had worked his way up through the Hollywood and Manhattan night-club circuits until he had a daily, nation-wide program of his own. Apart from his cynical yet relaxed personality, his biggest asset was his deep velvet voice, for which he could probably thank his Negro blood. Even when you flatly disagreed with what he was saying—even, indeed, when he was tearing you to pieces in an interview—it was still a pleasure to listen to him.

We gave him the grand tour of the space station, and even (strictly against regulations) took him out through the air lock in a space suit. He loved it all, but there were two things he liked in particular. "This air you make," he said, "it beats the stuff we have to breathe down in New York. This is the first time my sinus trouble has gone since I went into TV." He also relished the low gravity; at the station's rim, a man had half his normal, Earth weight—and at the axis he had no weight at all.

However, the novelty of his surroundings didn't distract Gregg from his job. He spent hours at Communications Central, polishing his script and getting his cues right, and studying the dozens of monitor screens that would be his windows on the world. I came across him once while he was running through his introduction of Queen Elizabeth, who would be speaking from Buckingham Palace at the very end of the program. He was so intent on his rehearsal that he never even noticed I was standing beside him.

Well, that telecast is now part of history. For the first time a billion human beings watched a single program that came "live" from every corner of the Earth, and was a roll call of the world's greatest citizens. Hundreds of cameras on land and sea and air looked inquiringly at the turning globe; and at the end there was that wonderful shot of the Earth through a zoom lens on the space station, making the whole planet recede until it was lost among the stars. . . .

There were a few hitches, of course. One camera on the bed of the Atlantic wasn't ready on cue, and we had to spend some extra time looking at the Taj Mahal. And owing to a switching error Russian subtitles were superimposed on the South American transmission, while half the

U.S.S.R. found itself trying to read Spanish. But this was nothing to what *might* have happened.

Through the entire three hours, introducing the famous and the unknown with equal ease, came the mellow yet never orotund flow of Gregg's voice. He did a magnificent job; the congratulations came pouring up the beam the moment the broadcast finished. But he didn't hear them; he made one short, private call to his agent, and then went to bed.

Next morning, the Earth-bound ferry was waiting to take him back to any job he cared to accept. But it left without Gregg Wendell, now junior station announcer of Relay Two.

"They'll think I'm crazy," he said, beaming happily, "but why should I go back to that rat race down there? I've all the universe to look at, I can breathe smog-free air, the low gravity makes me feel a Hercules, and my three darling ex-wives can't get at me." He kissed his hand to the departing rocket. "So long, Earth," he called. "I'll be back when I start pining for Broadway traffic jams and bleary penthouse dawns. And if I get homesick, I can look at anywhere on the planet just by turning a switch. Why, I'm more in the middle of things here than I could ever be on Earth, yet I can cut myself off from the human race whenever I want to."

He was still smiling as he watched the ferry begin the long fall back to Earth, toward the fame and fortune that could have been his. And then, whistling cheerfully, he left the observation lounge in eight-foot strides to read the weather forecast for Lower Patagonia.

PASSER-BY

It's only fair to warn you, right at the start, that this is a story with no ending. But it has a definite beginning, for it was while we were both students at Astrotech that I met Julie. She was in her final year of solar physics when I was graduating, and during our last year at college we saw a good deal of each other. I've still got the woolen tam-o'shanter she knitted so that I wouldn't bump my head against my space helmet. (No, I never had the nerve to wear it.)

Unfortunately, when I was assigned to Satellite Two, Julie went to the Solar Observatory—at the same distance from Earth, but a couple of degrees eastward along the orbit. So there we were, sitting twenty-two thousand miles above the middle of Africa—but with nine hundred miles of empty, hostile space between us.

At first we were both so busy that the pang of separation was somewhat lessened. But when the novelty of life in space had worn off, our thoughts began to bridge the gulf that divided us. And not only our thoughts, for I'd made friends with the communications people, and we used to have little chats over the interstation TV circuit. In some ways it made matters worse seeing each other face to face and never knowing just how many other people were looking in at the same time. There's not much privacy in a space station. . . .

Sometimes I'd focus one of our telescopes onto the distant, brilliant star of the observatory. In the crystal clarity of space, I could use enormous magnifications, and could see every detail of our neighbors' equipment—the solar telescopes, the pressurized spheres of the living quarters that housed the staff, the slim pencils of visiting ferry rockets that had climbed up from Earth. Very often there would be space-suited figures moving among the maze of apparatus, and I would strain my eyes in a hopeless attempt at identification. It's hard enough to recognize anyone in a space suit when you're only a few feet apart—but that didn't stop me from trying.

We'd resigned ourselves to waiting, with what patience we could muster, until our Earth leave was due in six months' time, when we had an unexpected stroke of luck. Less than half our tour of duty had passed when the head of the transport section suddenly announced that he was going outside with a butterfly net to catch meteors. He didn't become violent, but had to be shipped hastily back to Earth. I took over his job on a temporary basis and now had—in theory at least—the freedom of space.

There were ten of the little low-powered rocket scooters under my proud command, as well as four of the larger interstation shuttles used to ferry stores and personnel from orbit to orbit. I couldn't hope to borrow one of *those,* but after several weeks of careful organizing I was able to carry out the plan I'd conceived some two micro-seconds after being told I was now head of transport.

There's no need to tell how I juggled duty lists, cooked logs and fuel registers, and persuaded my colleagues to cover up for me. All that matters is that, about once a week, I would climb into my personal space suit, strap myself to the spidery framework of a Mark III Scooter, and drift away from the station at minimum power. When I was well clear, I'd go over to full throttle, and the tiny rocket motor would hustle me across the nine-hundred-mile gap to the observatory.

The trip took about thirty minutes, and the navigational requirements were elementary. I could see where I was going and where I'd come from, yet I don't mind admitting that I often felt—well, a trifle lonely—

around the mid-point of the journey. There was no other solid matter within almost five hundred miles—and it looked an awfully long way down to Earth. It was a great help, at such moments, to tune the suit radio to the general service band, and to listen to all the back-chat between ships and stations.

At mid-flight I'd have to spin the scooter around and start braking, and ten minutes later the observatory would be close enough for its details to be visible to the unaided eye. Very shortly after that I'd drift up to a small, plastic pressure bubble that was in the process of being fitted out as a spectroscopic laboratory—and there would be Julie, waiting on the other side of the air lock. . . .

I won't pretend that we confined our discussions to the latest results in astrophysics, or the progress of the satellite construction schedule. Few things, indeed, were further from our thoughts; and the journey home always seemed to flash by at a quite astonishing speed.

It was around mid-orbit on one of those homeward trips that the radar started to flash on my little control panel. There was something large at extreme range, and it was coming in fast. A meteor, I told myself—maybe even a small asteroid. Anything giving such a signal should be visible to the eye: I read off the bearings and searched the star fields in the indicated direction. The thought of a collision never even crossed my mind; space is so inconceivably vast that I was thousands of times safer than a man crossing a busy street on Earth.

There it was—a bright and steadily growing star near the foot of Orion. It already outshone Rigel, and seconds later it was not merely a star, but had begun to show a visible disk. Now it was moving as fast as I could turn my head; it grew to a tiny, misshaped moon, then dwindled and shrank with that same silent, inexorable speed.

I suppose I had a clear view of it for perhaps half a second, and that half-second has haunted me all my life. The—object—had already vanished by the time I thought of checking the radar again, so I had no way of gauging how close it came, and hence how large it really was. It could have been a small object a hundred feet away—or a very large one, ten miles off. There is no sense of perspective in space, and unless you know what you are looking at, you cannot judge its distance.

Of course, it *could* have been a very large and oddly shaped meteor; I can never be sure that my eyes, straining to grasp the details of so swiftly moving an object, were not hopelessly deceived. I may have imagined that I saw that broken, crumpled prow, and the cluster of dark ports like the sightless sockets of a skull. Of one thing only was I certain, even in that brief and fragmentary vision. If it *was* a ship, it was not one of ours. Its shape was utterly alien, and it was very, very old.

It may be that the greatest discovery of all time slipped from my grasp as I struggled with my thoughts midway between the two space stations. But I had no measurements of speed or direction; whatever it was that I had glimpsed was now lost beyond recapture in the wastes of the solar system.

What should I have done? No one would ever have believed me, for I would have had no proof. Had I made a report, there would have been endless trouble. I should have become the laughingstock of the Space Service, would have been reprimanded for misuse of equipment—and would certainly not have been able to see Julie again. And to me, at that age, nothing else was as important. If you've been in love yourself, you'll understand; if not, then no explanation is any use.

So I said nothing. To some other man (how many centuries hence?) will go the fame for proving that we were not the first-born of the children of the sun. Whatever it may be that is circling out there on its eternal orbit can wait, as it has waited ages already.

Yet I sometimes wonder. Would I have made a report, after all—had I known that Julie was going to marry someone else?

THE CALL OF THE STARS

Down there on Earth the twentieth century is dying. As I look across at the shadowed globe blocking the stars, I can see the lights of a hundred sleepless cities, and there are moments when I wish that I could be among the crowds now surging and singing in the streets of London, Capetown, Rome, Paris, Berlin, Madrid. . . . Yes, I can see them all at a single glance, burning like fireflies against the darkened planet. The line of midnight is now bisecting Europe: in the eastern Mediterranean a tiny, brilliant star is pulsing as some exuberant pleasure ship waves her searchlights to the sky. I think she is deliberately aiming at us; for the past few minutes the flashes have been quite regular and startlingly bright. Presently I'll call the communications center and find out who she is, so that I can radio back our own greetings.

Passing into history now, receding forever down the stream of time, is the most incredible hundred years the world has ever seen. It opened with the conquest of the air, saw at its mid-point the unlocking of the atom—and now ends with the bridging of space.

(For the past five minutes I've been wondering what's happening to Nairobi; now I realize that they are putting on a mammoth fireworks display. Chemically fueled rockets may be obsolete out here—but they're still using lots of them down on Earth tonight.)

The end of a century—and the end of a millennium. What will the hundred years that begin with two and zero bring? The planets, of course; floating there in space, only a mile away, are the ships of the first Martian expedition. For two years I have watched them grow, assembled piece by piece, as the space station itself was built by the men I worked with a generation ago.

Those ten ships are ready now, with all their crews aboard, waiting for the final instrument check and the signal for departure. Before the first day of the new century has passed its noon, they will be tearing free from the reins of Earth, to head out toward the strange world that may one day be man's second home.

As I look at the brave little fleet that is now preparing to challenge infinity, my mind goes back forty years, to the days when the first satellites were launched and the moon still seemed very far away. And I remember—indeed, I have never forgotten—my father's fight to keep me down on Earth.

There were not many weapons he had failed to use. Ridicule had been the first: "Of course they can do it," he had sneered, "but what's the point? Who wants to go out into space while there's so much to be done here on Earth? There's not a single planet in the solar system where men can live. The moon's a burnt-out slag heap, and everywhere else is even worse. *This* is where we were meant to live."

Even then (I must have been eighteen or so at the time) I could tangle him up in points of logic. I can remember answering, "How do you know where we were meant to live, Dad? After all, we were in the sea for about a billion years before we decided to tackle the land. Now we're making the next big jump: I don't know where it will lead—nor did that first fish when it crawled up on the beach, and started to sniff the air."

So when he couldn't outargue me, he had tried subtler pressures. He was always talking about the dangers of space travel, and the short working life of anyone foolish enough to get involved in rocketry. At that time, people were still scared of meteors and cosmic rays; like the "Here Be Dragons" of the old map makers, they were the mythical monsters on the still-blank celestial charts. But they didn't worry me; if anything they added the spice of danger to my dreams.

While I was going through college, Father was comparatively quiet

My training would be valuable whatever profession I took up in later life, so he could not complain—though he occasionally grumbled about the money I wasted buying all the books and magazines on astronautics that I could find. My college record was good, which naturally pleased him; perhaps he did not realize that it would also help me to get my way.

All through my final year I had avoided talking of my plans. I had even given the impression (though I am sorry for that now) that I had abandoned my dream of going into space. Without saying anything to him, I put in my application to Astrotech, and was accepted as soon as I had graduated.

The storm broke when that long blue envelope with the embossed heading "Institute of Astronautical Technology" dropped into the mailbox. I was accused of deceit and ingratitude, and I do not think I ever forgave my father for destroying the pleasure I should have felt at being chosen for the most exclusive—and most glamorous—apprenticeship the world has ever known.

The vacations were an ordeal; had it not been for Mother's sake, I do not think I would have gone home more than once a year, and I always left again as quickly as I could. I had hoped that Father would mellow as my training progressed and as he accepted the inevitable, but he never did.

Then had come that stiff and awkward parting at the spaceport, with the rain streaming down from leaden skies and beating against the smooth walls of the ship that seemed so eagerly waiting to climb into the eternal sunlight beyond the reach of storms. I know now what it cost my father to watch the machine he hated swallow up his only son: for I understand many things today that were hidden from me then.

He knew, even as we parted at the ship, that he would never see me again. Yet his old, stubborn pride kept him from saying the only words that might have held me back. I knew that he was ill, but how ill, he had told no one. That was the only weapon he had not used against me, and I respect him for it.

Would I have stayed had I known? It is even more futile to speculate about the unchangeable past than the unforeseeable future; all I can say now is that I am glad I never had to make the choice. At the end he let me go; he gave up his fight against my ambition, and a little while later his fight with Death.

So I said good-by to Earth, and to the father who loved me but knew no way to say it. He lies down there on the planet I can cover with my hand; how strange it is to think that of the countless billion human beings whose blood runs in my veins, I was the very first to leave his native world. . . .

The new day is breaking over Asia; a hairline of fire is rimming the eastern edge of Earth. Soon it will grow into a burning crescent as the sun comes up out of the Pacific—yet Europe is preparing for sleep, except for those revelers who will stay up to greet the dawn.

And now, over there by the flagship, the ferry rocket is coming back for the last visitors from the station. Here comes the message I have been waiting for: CAPTAIN STEVENS PRESENTS HIS COMPLIMENTS TO THE STATION COMMANDER. BLAST-OFF WILL BE IN NINETY MINUTES; HE WILL BE GLAD TO SEE YOU ABOARD NOW.

Well, Father, now I know how you felt: time has gone full circle. Yet I hope that I have learned from the mistakes we both made, long ago. I shall remember you when I go over there to the flagship *Starfire* and say good-by to the grandson you never knew.

✶ THE WALL OF DARKNESS

Many and strange are the universes that drift like bubbles in the foam upon the River of Time. Some—a very few—move against or athwart its current; and fewer still are those that lie forever beyond its reach, knowing nothing of the future or the past. Shervane's tiny cosmos was not one of these: its strangeness was of a different order. It held one world only—the planet of Shervane's race—and a single star, the great sun Trilorne that brought it life and light.

Shervane knew nothing of night, for Trilorne was always high above the horizon, dipping near it only in the long months of winter. Beyond the borders of the Shadow Land, it was true, there came a season when Trilorne disappeared below the edge of the world, and a darkness fell in which nothing could live. But even then the darkness was not absolute, though there were no stars to relieve it.

Alone in its little cosmos, turning the same face always toward its solitary sun, Shervane's world was the last and the strangest jest of the Maker of the Stars.

Yet as he looked across his father's lands, the thoughts that filled Shervane's mind were those that any human child might have known. He felt awe, and curiosity, and a little fear, and above all a longing to go out into the great world before him. These things he was still too young to do, but the ancient house was on the highest ground for many miles and he could look far out over the land that would one day be his. When he turned to the north, with Trilorne shining full upon his face, he could see many miles away the long line of mountains that curved around to the right, rising higher and higher, until they disappeared behind him in the direction of the Shadow Land. One day, when he was older, he would go through those mountains along the pass that led to the great lands of the east.

On his left was the ocean, only a few miles away, and sometimes

Shervane could hear the thunder of the waves as they fought and tumbled on the gently sloping sands. No one knew how far the ocean reached. Ships had set out across it, sailing northward while Trilorne rose higher and higher in the sky and the heat of its rays grew ever more intense. Long before the great sun had reached the zenith, they had been forced to return. If the mythical Fire Lands did indeed exist, no man could ever hope to reach their burning shores—unless the legends were really true. Once, it was said, there had been swift metal ships that could cross the ocean despite the heat of Trilorne, and so come to the lands on the other side of the world. Now these countries could be reached only by a tedious journey over land and sea, which could be shortened no more than a little by traveling as far north as one dared.

All the inhabited countries of Shervane's world lay in the narrow belt between burning heat and insufferable cold. In every land, the far north was an unapproachable region smitten by the fury of Trilorne. And to the south of all countries lay the vast and gloomy Shadow Land, where Trilorne was never more than a pale disk on the horizon, and often was not visible at all.

These things Shervane learned in the years of his childhood, and in those years he had no wish to leave the wide lands between the mountains and the sea. Since the dawn of time his ancestors and the races before them had toiled to make these lands the fairest in the world; if they had failed, it was by a narrow margin. There were gardens bright with strange flowers, there were streams that trickled gently between moss-grown rocks to be lost in the pure waters of the tideless sea. There were fields of grain that rustled continually in the wind, as if the generations of seeds yet unborn were talking one to the other. In the wide meadows and beneath the trees the friendly cattle wandered aimlessly with foolish cries. And there was the great house, with its enormous rooms and its endless corridors, vast enough in reality but huger still to the mind of a child. This was the world in which Shervane had passed his years, the world he knew and loved. As yet, what lay beyond its borders had not concerned his mind.

But Shervane's universe was not one of those free from the domination of time. The harvest ripened and was gathered into the granaries; Trilorne rocked slowly through its little arc of sky, and with the passing seasons Shervane's mind and body grew. His land seemed smaller now: the mountains were nearer and the sea was only a brief walk from the great house. He began to learn of the world in which he lived, and to be made ready for the part he must play in its shaping.

Some of these things he learned from his father, Sherval, but most he was taught by Grayle, who had come across the mountains in the days o his father's father, and had now been tutor to three generations of Shervane's family He was fond of Grayle, though the old man taught him many things he had no wish to learn, and the years of his boyhood passed pleasantly enough until the time came for him to go through the mountains into the lands beyond. Ages ago his family had come from the great countries of the east, and in every generation since, the eldest son had made that pilgrimage again to spend a year of his youth among his cousins. It was a wise custom, for beyond the mountains much of the knowledge of the past still lingered, and there one could meet men from other lands and study their ways.

In the last spring before his son's departure, Sherval collected three of his servants and certain animals it is convenient to call horses, and took Shervane to see those parts of the land he had never visited before. They rode west to the sea, and followed it for many days, until Trilorne was noticeably nearer the horizon. Still they went south, their shadows lengthening before them, turning again to the east only when the rays of the sun seemed to have lost all their power. They were now well within the limits of the Shadow Land, and it would not be wise to go farther south until the summer was at its height.

Shervane was riding beside his father, watching the changing landscape with all the eager curiosity of a boy seeing a new country for the first time. His father was talking about the soil, describing the crops that could be grown here and those that would fail if the attempt were made. But Shervane's attention was elsewhere: he was staring out across the desolate Shadow Land, wondering how far it stretched and what mysteries it held.

"Father," he said presently, "if you went south in a straight line, right across the Shadow Land, would you reach the other side of the world?"

His father smiled.

"Men have asked that question for centuries," he said, "but there are two reasons why they will never know the answer."

"What are they?"

"The first, of course, is the darkness and the cold. Even here, nothing can live during the winter months. But there is a better reason, though I see that Grayle has not spoken of it."

"I don't think he has: at least, I do not remember."

For a moment Sherval did not reply. He stood up in his stirrups and surveyed the land to the south.

"Once I knew this place well," he said to Shervane. "Come—I have something to show you."

They turned away from the path they had been following, and for several hours rode once more with their backs to the sun. The land was rising slowly now, and Shervane saw that they were climbing a great ridge of rock that pointed like a dagger into the heart of the Shadow Land. They came presently to a hill too steep for the horses to ascend, and here they dismounted and left the animals in the servants' charge.

"There is a way around," said Sherval, "but it is quicker for us to climb than to take the horses to the other side."

The hill, though steep, was only a small one, and they reached its summit in a few minutes. At first Shervane could see nothing he had not met before; there was only the same undulating wilderness, which seemed to become darker and more forbidding with every yard that its distance from Trilorne increased.

He turned to his father with some bewilderment, but Sherval pointed to the far south and drew a careful line along the horizon.

"It is not easy to see," he said quietly. "My father showed it to me from this same spot, many years before you were born."

Shervane stared into the dusk. The southern sky was so dark as to be almost black, and it came down to meet the edge of the world. But not quite, for along the horizon, in a great curve dividing land from sky yet seeming to belong to neither, was a band of deeper darkness, black as the night which Shervane had never known.

He looked at it steadfastly for a long time, and perhaps some hint of the future may have crept into his soul, for the darkling land seemed suddenly alive and waiting. When at last he tore his eyes away, he knew that nothing would ever be the same again, though he was still too young to recognize the challenge for what it was.

And so, for the first time in his life, Shervane saw the Wall.

In the early spring he said farewell to his people, and went with one servant over the mountains into the great lands of the eastern world. Here he met the men who shared his ancestry, and here he studied the history of his race, the arts that had grown from ancient times, and the sciences that ruled the lives of men. In the places of learning he made friends with boys who had come from lands even farther to the east: few of these was he likely to see again, but one was to play a greater part in his life than either could have imagined. Brayldon's father was a famous architect, but his son intended to eclipse him. He was traveling from land to land, always learning, watching, asking questions. Though he was only a few years older than Shervane, his knowledge of the world was infinitely greater—or so it seemed to the younger boy.

Between them they took the world to pieces and rebuilt it according to their desires. Brayldon dreamed of cities whose great avenues and stately towers would shame even the wonders of the past, but Shervane's interests lay more with the people who would dwell in those cities, and the way they ordered their lives.

They often spoke of the Wall, which Brayldon knew from the stories of his own people, though he himself had never seen it. Far to the south of every country, as Shervane had learned, it lay like a great barrier athwart the Shadow Land. In high summer it could be reached, though only with difficulty, but nowhere was there any way of passing it, and none knew what lay beyond. A hundred times the height of a man, it encircled the entire world, never pausing even when it reached the wintry sea that washed the shores of the Shadow Land. Travelers had stood upon those lonely beaches, scarcely warmed by the last thin rays of Trilorne, and had seen how the dark shadow of the Wall marched out to sea contemptuous of the waves beneath its feet. And on the far shores, other travelers had watched it come striding in across the ocean, to sweep past them on its journey round the world.

"One of my uncles," said Brayldon, "once reached the Wall when he was a young man. He did it for a wager, and he rode for ten days before he came beneath it. I think it frightened him—it was so huge and cold. He could not tell whether it was made of metal or of stone, and when he shouted, there was no echo at all, but his voice died away quickly as if the Wall were swallowing the sound. My people believe it is the end of the world, and there is nothing beyond."

"If that were true," Shervane replied, with irrefutable logic, "the ocean would have poured over the edge before the Wall was built."

"Not if Kyrone built it when He made the world."

Shervane did not agree.

"*My* people believe it is the work of man—perhaps the engineers of the First Dynasty, who made so many wonderful things. If they really had ships that could reach the Fire Lands—and even ships that could fly—they might have possessed enough wisdom to build the Wall."

Brayldon shrugged.

"They must have had a very good reason," he said. "We can never know the answer, so why worry about it?"

This eminently practical advice, as Shervane had discovered, was all that the ordinary man ever gave him. Only philosophers were interested in unanswerable questions: to most people, the enigma of the Wall, like the problem of existence itself, was something that scarcely concerned their minds. And all the philosophers he had met had given him different answers.

First there had been Grayle, whom he had questioned on his return from the Shadow Land. The old man had looked at him quietly and said:

"There is only one thing behind the Wall, so I have heard. And that is madness."

Then there had been Artex, who was so old that he could scarcely hear Shervane's nervous questioning. He gazed at the boy through eyelids that seemed too tired to open fully, and had replied after a long time:

"Kyrone built the Wall in the third day of the making of the world. What is beyond, we shall discover when we die—for there go the souls of all the dead."

Yet Irgan, who lived in the same city, had flatly contradicted this. "Only memory can answer your question, my son. For behind the Wall is the land in which we lived before our births."

Whom could he believe? The truth was that no one knew: if the knowledge had ever been possessed, it had been lost ages since.

Though this quest was unsuccessful, Shervane had learned many things in his year of study. With the returning spring he said farewell to Brayldon and the other friends he had known for such a little while, and set out along the ancient road that led him back to his own country. Once again he made the perilous journey through the great pass between the mountains, where walls of ice hung threatening against the sky. He came to the place where the road curved down once more toward the world of men, where there was warmth and running water and the breath no longer labored in the freezing air. Here, on the last rise of the road before it descended into the valley, one could see far out across the land to the distant gleam of the ocean. And there, almost lost in the mists of the edge of the world, Shervane could see the line of shadow that was his own country.

He went on down the great ribbon of stone until he came to the bridge that men had built across the cataract in the ancient days when the only other way had been destroyed by earthquake. But the bridge was gone: the storms and avalanches of early spring had swept away one of the mighty piers, and the beautiful metal rainbow lay a twisted ruin in the spray and foam a thousand feet below. The summer would have come and gone before the road could be opened once more: as Shervane sadly returned he knew that another year must pass ere he would see his home again.

He paused for many minutes on the last curve of the road, looking back toward the unattainable land that held all the things he loved. But the mists had closed over it, and he saw it no more. Resolutely he turned back along the road until the open lands had vanished and the mountains enfolded him again.

Brayldon was still in the city when Shervane returned. He was surprised and pleased to see his friend, and together they discussed what should be done in the year ahead. Shervane's cousins, who had grown fond of their guest, were not sorry to see him again, but their kindly suggestion that he should devote another year to study was not well received.

Shervane's plan matured slowly, in the face of considerable opposition. Even Brayldon was not enthusiastic at first, and much argument was needed before he would co-operate. Thereafter, the agreement of everyone else who mattered was only a question of time.

Summer was approaching when the two boys set out toward Brayldon's country. They rode swiftly, for the journey was a long one and must be completed before Trilorne began its winter fall. When they reached the lands that Brayldon knew, they made certain inquiries which caused much shaking of heads. But the answers they obtained were accurate, and soon the Shadow Land was all around them, and presently for the second time in his life Shervane saw the Wall.

It seemed not far away when they first came upon it, rising from a bleak and lonely plain. Yet they rode endlessly across that plain before the Wall grew any nearer—and then they had almost reached its base before they realized how close they were, for there was no way of judging its distance until one could reach out and touch it.

When Shervane gazed up at the monstrous ebony sheet that had so troubled his mind, it seemed to be overhanging and about to crush him beneath its falling weight. With difficulty, he tore his eyes away from the hypnotic sight, and went nearer to examine the material of which the Wall was built.

It was true, as Brayldon had told him, that it felt cold to the touch—colder than it had any right to be even in this sun-starved land. It felt neither hard nor soft, for its texture eluded the hand in a way that was difficult to analyze. Shervane had the impression that something was preventing him from actual contact with the surface, yet he could see no space between the Wall and his fingers when he forced them against it. Strangest of all was the uncanny silence of which Brayldon's uncle had spoken: every word was deadened and all sounds died away with unnatural swiftness.

Brayldon had unloaded some tools and instruments from the pack horses, and had begun to examine the Wall's surface. He found very quickly that no drills or cutters would mark it in any way, and presently he came to the conclusion Shervane had already reached. The Wall was not merely adamant: it was unapproachable.

At last, in disgust, he took a perfectly straight metal rule and pressed its edge against the wall. While Shervane held a mirror to reflect the feeble light of Trilorne along the line of contact, Brayldon peered at the rule from the other side. It was as he had thought: an infinitely narrow streak of light showed unbroken between the two surfaces.

Brayldon looked thoughtfully at his friend.

"Shervane," he said, "I don't believe the Wall is made of matter, as we know it."

"Then perhaps the legends were right that said it was never built at all, but created as we see it now."

"I think so too," said Brayldon. "The engineers of the First Dynasty had such powers. There are some very ancient buildings in my land that seem to have been made in a single operation from a substance that shows absolutely no sign of weathering. If it were black instead of colored, it would be very much like the material of the Wall."

He put away his useless tools and began to set up a simple portable theodolite.

"If I can do nothing else," he said with a wry smile, "at least I can find exactly how high it is!"

When they looked back for their last view of the Wall, Shervane wondered if he would ever see it again. There was nothing more he could learn: for the future, he must forget this foolish dream that he might one day master its secret. Perhaps there was no secret at all—perhaps beyond the wall the Shadow Land stretched round the curve of the world until it met that same barrier again. That, surely, seemed the likeliest thing. But if it were so, then why had the Wall been built, and by what race?

With an almost angry effort of will, he put these thoughts aside and rode forward into the light of Trilorne, thinking of a future in which the Wall would play no more part than it did in the lives of other men.

So two years had passed before Shervane could return to his home. In two years, especially when one is young, much can be forgotten and even the things nearest to the heart lose their distinctness, so that they can no longer be clearly recalled. When Shervane came through the last foot-hills of the mountains and was again in the country of his childhood, the joy of his home-coming was mingled with a strange sadness. So many things were forgotten that he had once thought his mind would hold forever.

The news of his return had gone before him, and soon he saw far ahead a line of horses galloping along the road. He pressed forward eagerly, wondering if Sherval would be there to greet him, and was a little disappointed when he saw that Grayle was leading the procession.

Shervane halted as the old man rode up to his horse. Then Grayle put his hand upon his shoulder, but for a while he turned away his head and could not speak.

And presently Shervane learned that the storms of the year before had destroyed more than the ancient bridge, for the lightning had brought his own home in ruins to the ground. Years before the appointed time, all the lands that Sherval had owned had passed into the possession of his son. Far more, indeed, than these, for the whole family had been assembled, according to its yearly custom, in the great house when the fire had come down upon it. In a single moment of time, everything between the mountains and the sea had passed into his keeping. He was the richest man his land had known for generations; and all these things he would have given to look again into the calm gray eyes of the father he would see no more.

Trilorne had risen and fallen in the sky many times since Shervane took leave of his childhood on the road before the mountains. The land had flourished in the passing years, and the possessions that had so suddenly become his had steadily increased their value. He had husbanded them well, and now he had time once more in which to dream. More than that—he had the wealth to make his dreams come true.

Often stories had come across the mountains of the work Brayldon was doing in the east, and although the two friends had never met since their youth they had exchanged messages regularly. Brayldon had achieved his ambitions: not only had he designed the two largest buildings erected since the ancient days, but a whole new city had been planned by him, though it would not be completed in his lifetime. Hearing of these things, Shervane remembered the aspirations of his own youth, and his mind went back across the years to the day when they had stood together beneath the majesty of the Wall. For a long time he wrestled with his thoughts, fearing to revive old longings that might not be assuaged. But at last he made his decision and wrote to Brayldon—for what was the use of wealth and power unless they could be used to shape one's dreams?

Then Shervane waited, wondering if Brayldon had forgotten the past in the years that had brought him fame. He had not long to wait: Brayldon could not come at once, for he had great works to carry to their completion, but when they were finished he would join his old friend. Shervane had thrown him a challenge that was worthy of his skill

—one which if he could meet would bring him more satisfaction than anything he had yet done.

Early the next summer he came, and Shervane met him on the road below the bridge. They had been boys when they last parted, and now they were nearing middle age, yet as they greeted one another the years seemed to fall away and each was secretly glad to see how lightly Time had touched the friend he remembered.

They spent many days in conference together, considering the plans that Brayldon had drawn up. The work was an immense one, and would take many years to complete, but it was possible to a man of Shervane's wealth. Before he gave his final assent, he took his friend to see Grayle.

The old man had been living for some years in the little house that Shervane had built him. For a long time he had played no active part in the life of the great estates, but his advice was always ready when it was needed, and it was invariably wise.

Grayle knew why Brayldon had come to this land, and he expressed no surprise when the architect unrolled his sketches. The largest drawing showed the elevation of the Wall, with a great stairway rising along its side from the plain beneath. At six equally spaced intervals the slowly ascending ramp leveled out into wide platforms, the last of which was only a short distance below the summit of the Wall. Springing from the stairway at a score of places along its length were flying buttresses which to Grayle's eye seemed very frail and slender for the work they had to do. Then he realized that the great ramp would be largely self-supporting, and on one side all the lateral thrust would be taken by the Wall itself.

He looked at the drawing in silence for a while, and then remarked quietly:

"You always managed to have your way, Shervane. I might have guessed that this would happen in the end."

"Then you think it a good idea?" Shervane asked. He had never gone against the old man's advice, and was anxious to have it now. As usual Grayle came straight to the point.

"How much will it cost?" he said.

Brayldon told him, and for a moment there was a shocked silence.

"That includes," the architect said hastily, "the building of a good road across the Shadow Land, and the construction of a small town for the workmen. The stairway itself is made from about a million identical blocks which can be dovetailed together to form a rigid structure. We shall make these, I hope, from the minerals we find in the Shadow Land."

He sighed a little.

"I should have liked to have built it from metal rods, jointed together, but that would have cost even more, for all the material would have to be brought over the mountains."

Grayle examined the drawing more closely.

"Why have you stopped short of the top?" he asked.

Brayldon looked at Shervane, who answered the question with a trace of embarrassment.

"I want to be the only one to make the final ascent," he replied. "The last stage will be by a lifting machine on the highest platform. There may be danger: that is why I am going alone."

That was not the only reason, but it was a good one. Behind the Wall, so Grayle had once said, lay madness. If that were true, no one else need face it.

Grayle was speaking once more in his quiet, dreamy voice.

"In that case," he said, "what you do is neither good nor bad, for it concerns you alone. If the Wall was built to keep something from our world, it will still be impassable from the other side."

Brayldon nodded.

"We had thought of that," he said with a touch of pride. "If the need should come, the ramp can be destroyed in a moment by explosives at selected spots."

"That is good," the old man replied. "Though I do not believe those stories, it is well to be prepared. When the work is finished, I hope I shall still be here. And now I shall try to remember what I heard of the Wall when I was as young as you were, Shervane, when you first questioned me about it."

Before the winter came, the road to the Wall had been marked out and the foundations of the temporary town had been laid. Most of the materials Brayldon needed were not hard to find, for the Shadow Land was rich in minerals. He had also surveyed the Wall itself and chosen the spot for the stairway. When Trilorne began to dip below the horizon, Brayldon was well content with the work that had been done.

By the next summer the first of the myriad concrete blocks had been made and tested to Brayldon's satisfaction, and before winter came again some thousands had been produced and part of the foundations laid. Leaving a trusted assistant in charge of the production, Brayldon could now return to his interrupted work. When enough of the blocks had been made, he would be back to supervise the building, but until then his guidance would not be needed.

Two or three times in the course of every year, Shervane rode out to the Wall to watch the stockpiles growing into great pyramids, and four years later Brayldon returned with him. Layer by layer the lines of stone started to creep up the flanks of the Wall, and the slim buttresses began to arch out into space. At first the stairway rose slowly, but as its summit narrowed the increase became more and more rapid. For a third of every year the work had to be abandoned, and there were anxious months in the long winter when Shervane stood on the borders of the Shadow Land, listening to the storms that thundered past him into the reverberating darkness. But Brayldon had built well, and every spring the work was standing unharmed as though it would outlive the Wall itself.

The last stones were laid seven years after the beginning of the work. Standing a mile away, so that he could see the structure in its entirety, Shervane remembered with wonder how all this had sprung from the few sketches Brayldon had shown him years ago, and he knew something of the emotion the artist must feel when his dreams become reality. And he remembered, too, the day when, as a boy by his father's side, he had first seen the Wall far off against the dusky sky of the Shadow Land.

There were guardrails around the upper platform, but Shervane did not care to go near its edge. The ground was at a dizzying distance, and he tried to forget his height by helping Brayldon and the workmen erect the simple hoist that would lift him the remaining twenty feet. When it was ready he stepped into the machine and turned to his friend with all the assurance he could muster.

"I shall be gone only a few minutes," he said with elaborate casualness. "Whatever I find, I'll return immediately."

He could hardly have guessed how small a choice was his.

Grayle was now almost blind and would not know another spring. But he recognized the approaching footsteps and greeted Brayldon by name before his visitor had time to speak.

"I am glad you came," he said. "I've been thinking of everything you told me, and I believe I know the truth at last. Perhaps you have guessed it already."

"No," said Brayldon. "I have been afraid to think of it."

The old man smiled a little.

"Why should one be afraid of something merely because it is strange? The Wall is wonderful, yes—but there's nothing terrible about it, to those who will face its secret without flinching.

"When I was a boy, Brayldon, my old master once said that time could never destroy the truth—it could only hide it among legends. He was right. From all the fables that have gathered around the Wall, I can now select the ones that are part of history.

"Long ago, Brayldon, when the First Dynasty was at its height, Trilorne was hotter than it is now and the Shadow Land was fertile and inhabited—as perhaps one day the Fire Lands may be when Trilorne is old and feeble. Men could go southward as they pleased, for there was no Wall to bar the way. Many must have done so, looking for new lands in which to settle. What happened to Shervane happened to them also, and it must have wrecked many minds—so many that the scientists of the First Dynasty built the Wall to prevent madness from spreading through the land. I cannot believe that this is true, but the legend says that it was made in a single day, with no labor, out of a cloud that encircled the world."

He fell into a reverie, and for a moment Brayldon did not disturb him. His mind was far in the past, picturing his world as a perfect globe floating in space while the Ancient Ones threw that band of darkness around the equator. False though that picture was in its most important detail, he could never wholly erase it from his mind.

As the last few feet of the Wall moved slowly past his eyes, Shervane needed all his courage lest he cry out to be lowered again. He remembered certain terrible stories he had once dismissed with laughter, for he came of a race that was singularly free from superstition. But what if, after all, those stories had been true, and the Wall had been built to keep some horror from the world?

He tried to forget these thoughts, and found it not hard to do so once he had passed the topmost level of the Wall. At first he could not interpret the picture his eyes brought him: then he saw that he was looking across an unbroken black sheet whose width he could not judge.

The little platform came to a stop, and he noted with half-conscious admiration how accurate Brayldon's calculations had been. Then, with a last word of assurance to the group below, he stepped onto the Wall and began to walk steadily forward.

At first it seemed as if the plain before him was infinite, for he could not even tell where it met the sky. But he walked on unfaltering, keeping his back to Trilorne. He wished he could have used his own shadow as a guide, but it was lost in the deeper darkness beneath his feet.

There was something wrong: it was growing darker with every footstep he took. Startled, he turned around and saw that the disk of Trilorne had now become pale and dusky, as if seen through a darkened glass. With mounting fear, he realized that this was by no means all that had happened—*Trilorne was smaller than the sun he had known all his life.*

He shook his head in an angry gesture of defiance. These things were fancies; he was imagining them. Indeed, they were so contrary to all experience that somehow he no longer felt frightened but strode resolutely forward with only a glance at the sun behind.

When Trilorne had dwindled to a point, and the darkness was all around him, it was time to abandon pretense. A wiser man would have turned back there and then, and Shervane had a sudden nightmare vision of himself lost in this eternal twilight between earth and sky, unable to retrace the path that led to safety. Then he remembered that as long as he could see Trilorne at all he could be in no real danger.

A little uncertainly now, he continued his way with many backward glances at the faint guiding light behind him. Trilorne itself had vanished, but there was still a dim glow in the sky to mark its place and presently he needed its aid no longer, for far ahead a second light was appearing in the heavens.

At first it seemed only the faintest of glimmers, and when he was sure of its existence he noticed that Trilorne had already disappeared. But he felt more confidence now, and as he moved onward, the returning light did something to subdue his fears.

When he saw that he was indeed approaching another sun, when he could tell beyond any doubt that it was expanding as a moment ago he had seen Trilorne contract, he forced all amazement down into the depths of his mind. He would only observe and record: later there would be time to understand these things. That his world might possess two suns, one shining upon it from either side, was not, after all, beyond imagination.

Now at last he could see, faintly through the darkness, the ebon line that marked the Wall's other rim. Soon he would be the first man in thousands of years, perhaps in eternity, to look upon the lands that it had sundered from his world. Would they be as fair as his own, and would there be people there whom he would be glad to greet?

But that they would be waiting, and in such a way, was more than he had dreamed.

Grayle stretched his hand out toward the cabinet beside him and fumbled for a large sheet of paper that was lying upon it. Brayldon watched him in silence, and the old man continued.

"How often we have all heard arguments about the size of the universe, and whether it has any boundaries! We can imagine no ending to space, yet our minds rebel at the idea of infinity. Some philosophers have imagined that space is limited by curvature in a higher dimension—

I suppose you know the theory. It may be true of other universes, if they exist, but for ours the answer is more subtle.

"Along the line of the Wall, Brayldon, our universe comes to an end —and yet does not. There was no boundary, nothing to stop one going onward before the Wall was built. The Wall itself is merely a man-made barrier, sharing the properties of the space in which it lies. Those properties were always there, and the Wall added nothing to them."

He held the sheet of paper toward Brayldon and slowly rotated it. "Here," he said, "is a plain sheet. It has, of course, two sides. *Can you imagine one that has not?"*

Brayldon stared at him in amazement.

"That's impossible—ridiculous!"

"But is it?" said Grayle softly. He reached toward the cabinet again and his fingers groped in its recesses. Then he drew out a long, flexible strip of paper and turned vacant eyes to the silently waiting Brayldon.

"We cannot match the intellects of the First Dynasty, but what their minds could grasp directly we can approach by analogy. This simple trick, which seems so trivial, may help you to glimpse the truth."

He ran his fingers along the paper strip, then joined the two ends together to make a circular loop.

"Here I have a shape which is perfectly familiar to you—the section of a cylinder. I run my finger around the inside, so—and now along the outside. The two surfaces are quite distinct: you can go from one to the other only by moving through the thickness of the strip. Do you agree?"

"Of course," said Brayldon, still puzzled. "But what does it prove?"

"Nothing," said Grayle. "But now watch—"

This sun, Shervane thought, was Trilorne's identical twin. The darkness had now lifted completely, and there was no longer the sensation, which he would not try to understand, of walking across an infinite plain.

He was moving slowly now, for he had no desire to come too suddenly upon that vertiginous precipice. In a little while he could see a distant horizon of low hills, as bare and lifeless as those he had left behind him. This did not disappoint him unduly, for the first glimpse of his own land would be no more attractive than this.

So he walked on: and when presently an icy hand fastened itself upon his heart, he did not pause as a man of lesser courage would have done. Without flinching, he watched that shockingly familiar landscape rise around him, until he could see the plain from which his journey had started, and the great stairway itself, and at last Brayldon's anxious, waiting face.

Again Grayle brought the two ends of the strip together, but now he had given it a half-twist so that the band was kinked. He held it out to Brayldon.

"Run your finger around it now," he said quietly.

Brayldon did not do so: he could see the old man's meaning.

"I understand," he said. "You no longer have two separate surfaces. It now forms a single continuous sheet—*a one-sided surface*—something that at first sight seems utterly impossible."

"Yes," replied Grayle very softly. "I thought you would understand. *A one-sided surface*. Perhaps you realize now why this symbol of the twisted loop is so common in the ancient religions, though its meaning has been completely lost. Of course, it is no more than a crude and simple analogy—an example in two dimensions of what must really occur in three. But it is as near as our minds can ever get to the truth."

There was a long, brooding silence. Then Grayle sighed deeply and turned to Brayldon as if he could still see his face.

"Why did you come back before Shervane?" he asked, though he knew the answer well enough.

"We had to do it," said Brayldon sadly, "but I did not wish to see my work destroyed."

Grayle nodded in sympathy.

"I understand," he said.

Shervane ran his eye up the long flight of steps on which no feet would ever tread again. He felt few regrets: he had striven, and no one could have done more. Such victory as was possible had been his.

Slowly he raised his hand and gave the signal. The Wall swallowed the explosion as it had absorbed all other sounds, but the unhurried grace with which the long tiers of masonry curtsied and fell was something he would remember all his life. For a moment he had a sudden, inexpressibly poignant vision of another stairway, watched by another Shervane, falling in identical ruins on the far side of the Wall.

But that, he realized, was a foolish thought: for none knew better than he that the Wall possessed no other side.

SECURITY CHECK

It is often said that in our age of assembly lines and mass production there's no room for the individual craftsman, the artist in wood or metal who made so many of the treasures of the past. Like most generalizations, this simply isn't true. He's rarer now, of course, but he's certainly not extinct. He has often had to change his vocation, but in his modest way he still flourishes. Even on the island of Manhattan he may be found, if you know where to look for him. Where rents are low and fire regulations unheard of, his minute, cluttered workshops may be discovered in the basements of apartment houses or in the upper stories of derelict shops. He may no longer make violins or cuckoo clocks or music boxes, but the skills he uses are the same as they always were, and no two objects he creates are ever identical. He is not contemptuous of mechanization: you will find several electric hand tools under the debris on his bench. He has moved with the times: he will always be around, the universal odd-job man who is never aware of it when he makes an immortal work of art.

Hans Muller's workshop consisted of a large room at the back of a deserted warehouse, no more than a vigorous stone's throw from the Queensborough Bridge. Most of the building had been boarded up awaiting demolition, and sooner or later Hans would have to move. The only entrance was across a weed-covered yard used as a parking place during the day, and much frequented by the local juvenile delinquents at night. They had never given Hans any trouble, for he knew better than to co-operate with the police when they made their periodic inquiries. The police fully appreciated his delicate position and did not press matters, so Hans was on good terms with everybody. Being a peaceable citizen, that suited him very well.

The work on which Hans was now engaged would have deeply puzzled his Bavarian ancestors. Indeed, ten years ago it would have puzzled

Hans himself. And it had all started because a bankrupt client had given him a TV set in payment for services rendered. . . .

Hans had accepted the offer reluctantly, not because he was old-fashioned and disapproved of TV, but simply because he couldn't imagine where he would find time to look at the darned thing. Still, he thought, at least I can always sell it for fifty dollars. But before I do that, let's see what the programs are like. . . .

His hand had gone out to the switch: the screen had filled with moving shapes—and, like millions of men before him, Hans was lost. He entered a world he had not known existed—a world of battling spaceships, of exotic planets and strange races—the world, in fact, of Captain Zipp, Commander of the Space Legion.

Only when the tedious recital of the virtues of Crunche, the Wonder Cereal, had given way to an almost equally tedious boxing match between two muscle-bound characters who seemed to have signed a non-aggression pact, did the magic fade. Hans was a simple man. He had always been fond of fairy tales—and *this* was the modern fairy tale, with trimmings of which the Grimm Brothers had never dreamed. So Hans did not sell his TV set.

It was some weeks before the initial naïve, uncritical enjoyment wore off. The first thing that began to annoy Hans was the furniture and general décor in the world of the future. He was, as has been indicated, an artist—and he refused to believe that in a hundred years taste would have deteriorated as badly as the Crunche sponsors seemed to imagine.

He also thought very little of the weapons that Captain Zipp and his opponents used. It was true that Hans did not pretend to understand the principles upon which the portable proton disintegrator was based, but however it worked, there was certainly no reason why it should be *that* clumsy. The clothes, the spaceship interiors—they just weren't convincing. How did he know? He had always possessed a highly developed sense of the fitness of things, and it could still operate even in this novel field.

We have said that Hans was a simple man. He was also a shrewd one, and he had heard that there was money in TV. So he sat down and began to draw.

Even if the producer of Captain Zipp had not lost patience with his set designer, Hans Muller's ideas would certainly have made him sit up and take notice. There was an authenticity and realism about them that made them quite outstanding. They were completely free from the element of phonyness that had begun to upset even Captain Zipp's most juvenile followers. Hans was hired on the spot.

He made his own conditions, however. What he was doing he did largely for love, notwithstanding the fact that it was earning him more money than anything he had ever done before in his life. He would take no assistants, and would remain in his little workshop. All that he wanted to do was to produce the prototypes, the basic designs. The mass production could be done somewhere else—he was a craftsman, not a factory.

The arrangement had worked well. Over the last six months Captain Zipp had been transformed and was now the despair of all the rival space operas. This, his viewers thought, was not just a serial about the future. It *was* the future—there was no argument about it. Even the actors seemed to have been inspired by their new surroundings: off the set, they sometimes behaved like twentieth-century time travelers stranded in the Victorian Age, indignant because they no longer had access to the gadgets that had always been part of their lives.

But Hans knew nothing about this. He toiled happily away, refusing to see anyone except the producer, doing all his business over the telephone—and watching the final result to ensure that his ideas had not been mutilated. The only sign of his connection with the slightly fantastic world of commercial TV was a crate of Crunche in one corner of the workshop. He had sampled one mouthful of this present from the grateful sponsor and had then remembered thankfully that, after all, he was not paid to eat the stuff.

He was working late one Sunday evening, putting the final touches to a new design for a space helmet, when he suddenly realized that he was no longer alone. Slowly he turned from the workbench and faced the door. It had been locked—how could it have been opened so silently? There were two men standing beside it, motionless, watching him. Hans felt his heart trying to climb into his gullet, and summoned up what courage he could to challenge them. At least, he felt thankfully, he had little money here. Then he wondered if, after all, this was a good thing. They might be annoyed. . . .

"Who are you?" he asked. "What are you doing here?"

One of the men moved toward him while the other remained watching alertly from the door. They were both wearing very new overcoats, with hats low down on their heads so that Hans could not see their faces. They were too well dressed, he decided, to be ordinary holdup men.

"There's no need to be alarmed, Mr. Muller," replied the nearer man, reading his thoughts without difficulty. "This isn't a holdup. It's official. We're from—Security."

"I don't understand."

The other reached into a portfolio he had been carrying beneath his coat, and pulled out a sheaf of photographs. He riffled through them until he had found the one he wanted.

"You've given us quite a headache, Mr. Muller. It's taken us two weeks to find you—your employers were so secretive. No doubt they were anxious to hide you from their rivals. However, here we are and I'd like you to answer some questions."

"I'm not a spy!" answered Hans indignantly as the meaning of the words penetrated. "You can't do this! I'm a loyal American citizen!"

The other ignored the outburst. He handed over the photograph.

"Do you recognize this?" he said.

"Yes. It's the inside of Captain Zipp's spaceship."

"And you designed it?"

"Yes."

Another photograph came out of the file.

"And what about this?"

"That's the Martian city of Paldar, as seen from the air."

"Your own idea?"

"Certainly," Hans replied, now too indignant to be cautious.

"And *this?"*

"Oh, the proton gun. I was quite proud of that."

"Tell me, Mr. Muller—are these all your own ideas?"

"Yes, *I* don't steal from other people."

His questioner turned to his companion and spoke for a few minutes in a voice too low for Hans to hear. They seemed to reach agreement on some point, and the conference was over before Hans could make his intended grab at the telephone.

"I'm sorry," continued the intruder. "But there has been a serious leak. It may be—uh—accidental, even unconscious, but that does not affect the issue. We will have to investigate you. Please come with us."

There was such power and authority in the stranger's voice that Hans began to climb into his overcoat without a murmur. Somehow, he no longer doubted his visitors' credentials and never thought of asking for any proof. He was worried, but not yet seriously alarmed. Of course, it was obvious what had happened. He remembered hearing about a science-fiction writer during the war who had described the atom bomb with disconcerting accuracy. When so much secret research was going on, such accidents were bound to occur. He wondered just what it was he had given away.

At the doorway, he looked back into his workshop and at the men who were following him.

"It's all a ridiculous mistake," he said. "If I *did* show anything secret in the program, it was just a coincidence. I've never done anything to annoy the FBI."

It was then that the second man spoke at last, in very bad English and with a most peculiar accent.

"What is the FBI?" he asked.

But Hans didn't hear him. He had just seen the spaceship.

✶ NO MORNING AFTER

But this is terrible!" said the Supreme Scientist. "Surely there is *something* we can do!"

"Yes, Your Cognizance, but it will be extremely difficult. The planet is more than five hundred light-years away, and it is very hard to maintain contact. However, we believe we can establish a bridgehead. Unfortunately, that is not the only problem. So far, we have been quite unable tc communicate with these beings. Their telepathic powers are exceedingl rudimentary—perhaps even nonexistent. And if we cannot talk to them there is no way in which we can help."

There was a long mental silence while the Supreme Scientist analyzec the situation and arrived, as he always did, at the correct answer.

"Any intelligent race must have *some* telepathic individuals," h mused. "We must send out hundreds of observers, tuned to catch the firs hint of stray thought. When you find a single responsive mind, concen trate all your efforts upon it. We *must* get our message through."

"Very good, Your Cognizance. It shall be done."

Across the abyss, across the gulf which light itself took half a thou sand years to span, the questing intellects of the planet Thaar sent out the tendrils of thought, searching desperately for a single human being who mind could perceive their presence. And as luck would have it, they e countered William Cross.

At least, they thought it was luck at the time, though later they we not so sure. In any case, they had little choice. The combination of ci cumstances that opened Bill's mind to them lasted only for seconds, a was not likely to occur again this side of eternity.

There were three ingredients in the miracle: it is hard to say if o was more important than another. The first was the accident of positic A flask of water, when sunlight falls upon it, can act as a crude le concentrating the light into a small area. On an immeasurably larg scale, the dense core of the Earth was converging the waves that came from Thaar. In the ordinary way, the radiations of thought are unaffected by matter—they pass through it as effortlessly as light through glass. But there is rather a lot of matter in a planet, and the whole Earth was acting as a gigantic lens. As it turned, it was carrying Bill through its focus, where the feeble thought impulses from Thaar were concentrated a hundredfold.

Yet millions of other men were equally well placed: they received no message. But they were not rocket engineers: they had not spent years thinking and dreaming of space until it had become part of their very being.

And they were not, as Bill was, blind drunk, teetering on the last knife-edge of consciousness, trying to escape from reality into the world of dreams, where there were no disappointments and setbacks.

Of course, he could see the Army's point of view. "You are paid, Dr. Cross," General Porter had pointed out with unnecessary emphasis, "to design missiles, *not*—ah—spaceships. What you do in your spare time is your own concern, but I must ask you not to use the facilities of the establishment for your hobby. From now on, all projects for the computing section will have to be cleared by me. That is all."

They couldn't sack him, of course: he was too important. But he was not sure that he wanted to stay. He was not really sure of anything except that the job had backfired on him, and that Brenda had finally gone off with Johnny Gardner—putting events in their order of importance.

Wavering slightly, Bill cupped his chin in his hands and stared at the whitewashed brick wall on the other side of the table. The only attempt at ornamentation was a calendar from Lockheed and a glossy six-by-eight from Aerojet showing L'il Abner Mark I making a boosted take-off. Bill gazed morosely at a spot midway between the two pictures, and emptied his mind of thought. The barriers went down. . . .

At that moment, the massed intellects of Thaar gave a soundless cry of triumph, and the wall in front of Bill slowly dissolved into a swirling mist. He appeared to be looking down a tunnel that stretched to infinity. As a matter of fact, he was.

Bill studied the phenomenon with mild interest. It had a certain novelty, but was not up to the standard of previous hallucinations. And when the voice started to speak in his mind, he let it ramble on for some time before he did anything about it. Even when drunk, he had an old-fashioned prejudice against starting conversations with himself.

"Bill," the voice began, "listen carefully. We have had great difficulty in contacting you, and this is extremely important."

Bill doubted this on general principles. *Nothing* was important any more.

"We are speaking to you from a very distant planet," continued the voice in a tone of urgent friendliness. "You are the only human being we have been able to contact, so you *must* understand what we are saying."

Bill felt mildly worried, though in an impersonal sort of way, since it was now rather hard to focus on his own problems. How serious was it, he wondered, when you started to hear voices? Well, it was best not to get excited. You can take it or leave it, Dr. Cross, he told himself. Let's take it until it gets to be a nuisance.

"O.K.," he answered with bored indifference. "Go right ahead and talk to me. I won't mind as long as it's interesting."

There was a pause. Then the voice continued, in a slightly worried fashion.

"We don't quite understand. Our message isn't merely *interesting.* It's vital to your entire race, and you must notify your government immediately."

"I'm waiting," said Bill. "It helps to pass the time."

Five hundred light-years away, the Thaarns conferred hastily among themselves. Something seemed to be wrong, but they could not decide precisely what. There was no doubt that they had established contact, yet this was not the sort of reaction they had expected. Well, they could only proceed and hope for the best.

"Listen, Bill," they continued. "Our scientists have just discovered that your sun is about to explode. It will happen three days from now—seventy-four hours, to be exact. Nothing can stop it. But there's no need to be alarmed. We can save you, if you'll do what we say."

"Go on," said Bill. This hallucination was ingenious.

"We can create what we call a bridge—it's a kind of tunnel through space, like the one you're looking into now. The theory is far too complicated to explain, even to one of your mathematicians."

"Hold on a minute!" protested Bill. "I am a mathematician, and a darn good one, even when I'm sober. And I've read all about this kind of thing in the science-fiction magazines. I presume you're talking about some kind of short cut through a higher dimension of space. That's old stuff—pre-Einstein."

A sensation of distinct surprise seeped into Bill's mind.

"We had no idea you were so advanced scientifically," said the Thaarns. "But we haven't time to talk about the theory. All that matters is this—if you were to step into that opening in front of you, you'd find yourself instantly on another planet. It's a short cut, as you said—in this case through the thirty-seventh dimension."

"And it leads to your world?"

"Oh no—you couldn't live here. But there are plenty of planets like Earth in the universe, and we've found one that will suit you. We'll establish bridgeheads like this all over Earth, so your people will only have to walk through them to be saved. Of course, they'll have to start building up civilization again when they reach their new homes, but it's their only hope. You have to pass on this message, and tell them what to do."

"I can just see them listening to me," said Bill. "Why don't you go and talk to the president?"

"Because yours was the only mind we were able to contact. Others seemed closed to us: we don't understand why."

"I could tell you," said Bill, looking at the nearly empty bottle in front of him. He was certainly getting his money's worth. What a remarkable thing the human mind was! Of course, there was nothing at all original in this dialogue: it was easy to see where the ideas came from. Only last week he'd been reading a story about the end of the world, and all this wishful thinking about bridges and tunnels through space was pretty obvious compensation for anyone who'd spent five years wrestling with recalcitrant rockets.

"If the sun does blow up," Bill asked abruptly—trying to catch his hallucination unawares—"what would happen?"

"Why, your planet would be melted instantly. All the planets, in fact, right out to Jupiter."

Bill had to admit that this was quite a grandiose conception. He let his mind play with the thought, and the more he considered it, the more he liked it.

"My dear hallucination," he remarked pityingly, "if I believed you, d'you know what I'd say?"

"But you *must* believe us!" came the despairing cry across the light-years.

Bill ignored it. He was warming to his theme.

"I'd tell you this. *It would be the best thing that could possibly happen.* Yes, it would save a whole lot of misery. No one would have to worry about the Russians and the atom bomb and the high cost of living. Oh, it would be wonderful! It's just what everybody really wants. Nice of you to come along and tell us, but just you go back home and pull your old bridge after you."

There was consternation on Thaar. The Supreme Scientist's brain, floating like a great mass of coral in its tank of nutrient solution, turned slightly yellow about the edges—something it had not done since the Xantil invasion, five thousand years ago. At least fifteen psychologists had nervous breakdowns and were never the same again. The main computer in the College of Cosmophysics started dividing every number in its memory circuits by zero, and promptly blew all its fuses.

And on Earth, Bill Cross was really hitting his stride.

"Look at *me,*" he said, pointing a wavering finger at his chest. "I've spent years trying to make rockets do something useful, and they tell me I'm only allowed to build guided missiles, so that we can all blow each other up. The sun will make a neater job of it, and if you did give us another planet we'd only start the whole damn thing all over again."

He paused sadly, marshaling his morbid thoughts.

"And now Brenda heads out of town without even leaving a note. So you'll pardon my lack of enthusiasm for your Boy Scout act."

He couldn't have said "enthusiasm" aloud, Bill realized. But he could still think it, which was an interesting scientific discovery. As he got drunker and drunker, would his cogitation—whoops, *that* nearly threw him!—finally drop down to words of one syllable?

In a final despairing exertion, the Thaarns sent their thoughts along the tunnel between the stars.

"You can't really mean it, Bill! Are *all* human beings like you?"

Now that was an interesting philosophical question! Bill considered it carefully—or as carefully as he could in view of the warm, rosy glow that was now beginning to envelop him. After all, things might be worse. He could get another job, if only for the pleasure of telling General Porter what he could do with his three stars. And as for Brenda—well, women were like streetcars: there'd always be another along in a minute.

Best of all, there was a second bottle of whisky in the Top Secret file. Oh, frabjous day! He rose unsteadily to his feet and wavered across the room.

For the last time, Thaar spoke to Earth.

"Bill!" it repeated desperately. "Surely all human beings can't be like you!"

Bill turned and looked into the swirling tunnel. Strange—it seemed to be lighted with flecks of starlight, and was really rather pretty. He felt proud of himself: not many people could imagine *that.*

"Like me?" he said. "No, they're not." He smiled smugly across the light-years, as the rising tide of euphoria lifted him out of his despondency. "Come to think of it," he added, "there are a lot of people much worse off than me. Yes, I guess I must be one of the lucky ones, after all."

He blinked in mild surprise, for the tunnel had suddenly collapsed upon itself and the whitewashed wall was there again, exactly as it had always been. Thaar knew when it was beaten.

"So much for *that* hallucination," thought Bill. "I was getting tired of it, anyway. Let's see what the next one's like."

As it happened, there wasn't a next one, for five seconds later he passed out cold, just as he was setting the combination of the file cabinet.

The next two days were rather vague and bloodshot, and he forgot all about the interview.

On the third day something was nagging at the back of his mind: he might have remembered if Brenda hadn't turned up again and kept him busy being forgiving.

And there wasn't a fourth day, of course.

✶ VENTURE TO THE MOON

THE STARTING LINE

The story of the first lunar expedition has been written so many times that some people will doubt if there is anything fresh to be said about it. Yet all the official reports and eyewitness accounts, the on-the-spot recordings and broadcasts never, in my opinion, gave the full picture. They said a great deal about the discoveries that were made—but very little about the men who made them.

As captain of the *Endeavour* and thus commander of the British party, I was able to observe a good many things you will not find in the history books, and some—though not all—of them can now be told. One day, I hope, my opposite numbers on the *Goddard* and the *Ziolkovski* will give their points of view. But as Commander Vandenburg is still on Mars and Commander Krasnin is somewhere inside the orbit of Venus, it looks as if we will have to wait a few more years for *their* memoirs.

Confession, it is said, is good for the soul. I shall certainly feel much happier when I have told the true story behind the timing of the first lunar flight, about which there has always been a good deal of mystery.

As everyone knows, the American, Russian, and British ships were assembled in the orbit of Space Station Three, five hundred miles above the Earth, from components flown up by relays of freight rockets. Though all the parts had been prefabricated, the assembly and testing of the ships took over two years, by which time a great many people—who did not realize the complexity of the task—were beginning to get slightly impatient. They had seen dozens of photos and telecasts of the three ships floating there in space beside Station Three, apparently quite complete and ready to pull away from Earth at a moment's notice. What the pictures didn't show was the careful and tedious work still in progress as thousands of pipes, wires, motors, and instruments were fitted and subjected to every conceivable test.

There was no definite target date for departure; since the moon is always at approximately the same distance, you can leave for it at almost any time you like—once you are ready. It makes practically no difference, from the point of view of fuel consumption, if you blast off at full moon or new moon or at any time in between. We were very careful to make no predictions about blast-off, though everyone was always trying to get us to fix the time. So many things can go wrong in a spaceship, and we were not going to say good-by to Earth until we were ready down to the last detail.

I shall always remember the last commanders' conference, aboard the space station, when we all announced that we were ready. Since it was a co-operative venture, each party specializing in some particular task, it had been agreed that we should all make our landings within the same twenty-four-hour period, on the preselected site in the Mare Imbrium. The details of the journey, however, had been left to the individual commanders, presumably in the hope that we would not copy each other's mistakes.

"I'll be ready," said Commander Vandenburg, "to make my first dummy take-off at 0900 tomorrow. What about you, gentlemen? Shall we ask Earth Control to stand by for all three of us?"

"That's O.K. by me," said Krasnin, who could never be convinced that his American slang was twenty years out of date.

I nodded my agreement. It was true that one bank of fuel gauges was still misbehaving, but that didn't really matter; they would be fixed by the time the tanks were filled.

The dummy run consisted of an exact replica of a real blast-off, with everyone carrying out the job he would do when the time came for the genuine thing. We had practiced, of course, in mock-ups down on Earth, but this was a perfect imitation of what would happen to us when we finally took off for the moon. All that was missing was the roar of the motors that would tell us that the voyage had begun.

We did six complete imitations of blast-off, took the ships to pieces to eliminate anything that hadn't behaved perfectly, then did six more. The *Endeavour,* the *Goddard,* and the *Ziolkovski* were all in the same state of serviceability. There now only remained the job of fueling up, and we would be ready to leave.

The suspense of those last few hours is not something I would care to go through again. The eyes of the world were upon us; departure time had now been set, with an uncertainty of only a few hours. All the final tests had been made, and we were convinced that our ships were as ready as humanly possible.

It was then that I had an urgent and secret personal radio call from a very high official indeed, and a suggestion was made which had so much authority behind it that there was little point in pretending that it wasn't an order. The first flight to the moon, I was reminded, was a co-operative venture—but think of the prestige if *we* got there first. It need only be by a couple of hours. . . .

I was shocked at the suggestion, and said so. By this time Vandenburg and Krasnin were good friends of mine, and we were all in this together. I made every excuse I could and said that since our flight paths had already been computed there wasn't anything that could be done about it. Each ship was making the journey by the most economical route, to conserve fuel. If we started together, we should arrive together—within seconds.

Unfortunately, someone had thought of the answer to that. Our three ships, fueled up and with their crews standing by, would be circling Earth in a state of complete readiness for several hours before they actually pulled away from their satellite orbits and headed out to the moon. At our five-hundred-mile altitude, we took ninety-five minutes to make one circuit of the Earth, and only once every revolution would the moment be ripe to begin the voyage. If we could jump the gun by one revolution, the others would have to wait that ninety-five minutes before they could follow. And so they would land on the moon ninety-five minutes behind us. . . .

I won't go into the arguments, and I'm still a little ashamed that I yielded and agreed to deceive my two colleagues. We were in the shadow of Earth, in momentary eclipse, when the carefully calculated moment came. Vandenburg and Krasnin, honest fellows, thought I was going to make one more round trip with them before we all set off together. I have seldom felt a bigger heel in my life than when I pressed the firing key and felt the sudden thrust of the motors as they swept me away from my mother world.

For the next ten minutes we had no time for anything but our instruments, as we checked to see that the *Endeavour* was forging ahead along her precomputed orbit. Almost at the moment that we finally escaped from Earth and could cut the motors, we burst out of shadow into the full blaze of the sun. There would be no more night until we reached the moon, after five days of effortless and silent coasting through space.

Already Space Station Three and the two other ships must be a thousand miles behind. In eighty-five more minutes Vandenburg and Krasnin would be back at the correct starting point and could take off after me, as we had all planned. But they could never overcome my lead, and I hoped they wouldn't be too mad at me when we met again on the moon.

I switched on the rear camera and looked back at the distant gleam of the space station, just emerging from the shadow of Earth. It was some moments before I realized that the *Goddard* and the *Ziolkovski* weren't still floating beside it where I'd left them. . . .

No; they were just half a mile away, neatly matching my velocity. I stared at them in utter disbelief for a second, before I realized that every one of us had had the same idea. "Why, you pair of double-crossers!" I gasped. Then I began to laugh so much that it was several minutes before I dared call up a very worried Earth Control and tell them that everything had gone according to plan—though in no case was it the plan that had been originally announced. . . .

We were all very sheepish when we radioed each other to exchange mutual congratulations. Yet at the same time, I think everyone was secretly pleased that it had turned out this way. For the rest of the trip, we were never more than a few miles apart, and the actual landing maneuvers were so well synchronized that our three braking jets hit the moon simultaneously.

Well, almost simultaneously. I might make something of the fact that the recorder tape shows I touched down two-fifths of a second ahead of Krasnin. But I'd better not, for Vandenburg was precisely the same amount ahead of me.

On a quarter-of-a-million-mile trip, I think you could call that a photo finish. . . .

ROBIN HOOD, F.R.S.

We had landed early in the dawn of the long lunar day, and the slanting shadows lay all around us, extending for miles across the plain. They would slowly shorten as the sun rose higher in the sky, until at noon they would almost vanish—but noon was still five days away, as we measured time on Earth, and nightfall was seven days later still. We had almost two weeks of daylight ahead of us before the sun set and the bluely gleaming Earth became the mistress of the sky.

There was little time for exploration during those first hectic days. We had to unload the ships, grow accustomed to the alien conditions surrounding us, learn to handle our electrically powered tractors and scooters, and erect the igloos that would serve as homes, offices, and labs until the time came to leave. At a pinch, we could live in the spaceships, but it would be excessively uncomfortable and cramped. The igloos were not exactly commodious, but they were luxury after five days in space. Made of tough, flexible plastic, they were blown up like balloons, and their interiors were then partitioned into separate rooms. Air locks allowed access to the outer world, and a good deal of plumbing linked to the ships' air-purification plants kept the atmosphere breathable. Needless to say, the American igloo was the biggest one, and had come complete with everything, *including* the kitchen sink—not to mention a washing machine, which we and the Russians were always borrowing.

It was late in the "afternoon"—about ten days after we had landed—before we were properly organized and could think about serious scientific work. The first parties made nervous little forays out into the wilderness around the base, familiarizing themselves with the territory. Of course, we already possessed minutely detailed maps and photographs of the region in which we had landed, but it was surprising how misleading they could sometimes be. What had been marked as a small hill on a chart often looked like a mountain to a man toiling along in a space suit, and apparently smooth plains were often covered knee-deep with dust, which made progress extremely slow and tedious.

These were minor difficulties, however, and the low gravity—which gave all objects only a sixth of their terrestrial weight—compensated for much. As the scientists began to accumulate their results and specimens, the radio and TV circuits with Earth became busier and busier, until they were in continuous operation. We were taking no chances; even if *we* didn't get home, the knowledge we were gathering would do so.

The first of the automatic supply rockets landed two days before sunset, precisely according to plan. We saw its braking jets flame briefly against the stars, then blast again a few seconds before touchdown. The actual landing was hidden from us, since for safety reasons the dropping ground was three miles from the base. And on the moon, three miles is well over the curve of the horizon.

When we got to the robot, it was standing slightly askew on its tripod shock absorbers, but in perfect condition. So was everything aboard it, from instruments to food. We carried the stores back to base in triumph, and had a celebration that was really rather overdue. The men had been working too hard, and could do with some relaxation.

It was quite a party; the high light, I think, was Commander Krasnin trying to do a Cossack dance in a space suit. Then we turned our minds to competitive sports, but found that, for obvious reasons, outdoor activities were somewhat restricted. Games like croquet or bowls would have been practical had we had the equipment; but cricket and football were definitely out. In that gravity, even a football would go half a mile if it were given a good kick—and a cricket ball would never be seen again.

Professor Trevor Williams was the first person to think of a practical lunar sport. He was our astronomer, and also one of the youngest men ever to be made a Fellow of the Royal Society, being only thirty when this ultimate accolade was conferred upon him. His work on methods of interplanetary navigation had made him world famous; less well known, however, was his skill as a toxophilite. For two years in succession he had been archery champion for Wales. I was not surprised, therefore, when I discovered him shooting at a target propped up on a pile of lunar slag.

The bow was a curious one, strung with steel control wire and shaped from a laminated plastic bar. I wondered where Trevor had got hold of it, then remembered that the robot freight rocket had now been cannibalized and bits of it were appearing in all sorts of unexpected places. The arrows, however, were the really interesting feature. To give them stability on the airless moon, where, of course, feathers would be useless, Trevor had managed to rifle them. There was a little gadget on the bow that set them spinning, like bullets, when they were fired, so that they kept on course when they left the bow.

Even with this rather makeshift equipment, it was possible to shoot a mile if one wished to. However, Trevor didn't want to waste arrows, which were not easy to make; he was more interested in seeing the sort of accuracy he could get. It was uncanny to watch the almost flat trajectory of the arrows: they seemed to be traveling parallel with the ground. If he wasn't careful, someone warned Trevor, his arrows might become lunar satellites and would hit him in the back when they completed their orbit.

The second supply rocket arrived the next day, but this time things didn't go according to plan. It made a perfect touchdown, but unfortunately the radar-controlled automatic pilot made one of those mistakes that such simple-minded machines delight in doing. It spotted the only really unclimbable hill in the neighborhood, locked its beam onto the summit of it, and settled down there like an eagle descending upon its mountain aerie.

Our badly needed supplies were five hundred feet above our heads, and in a few hours night would be falling. What was to be done?

About fifteen people made the same suggestion at once, and for the next few minutes there was a great scurrying about as we rounded up all the nylon line on the base. Soon there was more than a thousand yards of it coiled in neat loops at Trevor's feet while we all waited expectantly. He tied one end to his arrow, drew the bow, and aimed it experimentally straight toward the stars. The arrow rose a little more than half the height of the cliff; then the weight of the line pulled it back.

"Sorry," said Trevor. "I just can't make it. And don't forget—we'd have to send up some kind of grapnel as well, if we want the end to stay up there."

There was much gloom for the next few minutes, as we watched the coils of line fall slowly back from the sky. The situation was really somewhat absurd. In our ships we had enough energy to carry us a quarter of a million miles from the moon—yet we were baffled by a puny little cliff. If we had time, we could probably find a way up to the top from the other side of the hill, but that would mean traveling several miles. It would be dangerous, and might well be impossible, during the few hours of daylight that were left.

Scientists were never baffled for long, and too many ingenious (sometimes overingenious) minds were working on the problem for it to remain unresolved. But this time it was a little more difficult, and only three people got the answer simultaneously. Trevor thought it over, then said noncommittally, "Well, it's worth trying."

The preparations took a little while, and we were all watching anxiously as the rays of the sinking sun crept higher and higher up the sheer cliff looming above us. Even if Trevor could get a line and grapnel up there, I thought to myself, it would not be easy making the ascent while encumbered with a space suit. I have no head for heights, and was glad that several mountaineering enthusiasts had already volunteered for the job.

At last everything was ready. The line had been carefully arranged so that it would lift from the ground with the minimum of hindrance. A light grapnel had been attached to the line a few feet behind the arrow; we hoped that it would catch in the rocks up there and wouldn't let us down—all too literally—when we put our trust in it.

This time, however, Trevor was not using a single arrow. He attached four to the line, at two-hundred-yard intervals. And I shall never forget that incongruous spectacle of the space-suited figure, gleaming in the last rays of the setting sun, as it drew its bow against the sky.

The arrow sped toward the stars, and before it had lifted more than fifty feet Trevor was already fitting the second one to his improvised bow. It raced after its predecessor, carrying the other end of the long loop that was now being hoisted into space. Almost at once the third followed, lifting its section of line and I swear that the fourth arrow, with its section, was on the way before the first had noticeably slackened its momentum.

Now that there was no question of a single arrow lifting the entire length of line, it was not hard to reach the required altitude. The first two times the grapnel fell back; then it caught firmly somewhere up on the hidden plateau—and the first volunteer began to haul himself up the line. It was true that he weighed only about thirty pounds in this low gravity, but it was still a long way to fall.

He didn't. The stores in the freight rocket started coming down the cliff within the next hour, and everything essential had been lowered before nightfall. I must confess, however, that my satisfaction was considerably abated when one of the engineers proudly showed me the mouth organ he had had sent from Earth. Even then I felt certain that we would all be very tired of that instrument before the long lunar night had ended. . . .

But that, of course, was hardly Trevor's fault. As we walked back to the ship together, through the great pools of shadow that were flowing swiftly over the plain, he made a proposal that, I am sure, has puzzled thousands of people ever since the detailed maps of the first lunar expedition were published.

After all, it does seem a little odd that a flat and lifeless plain, broken by a single small mountain, should now be labeled on all the charts of the moon as Sherwood Forest.

GREEN FINGERS

I am very sorry, now that it's too late, that I never got to know Vladimir Surov. As I remember him, he was a quiet little man who could understand English but couldn't speak it well enough to make conversation. Even to his colleagues, I suspect he was a bit of an enigma. Whenever I went aboard the *Ziolkovski,* he would be sitting in a corner working on his notes or peering through a microscope, a man who clung to his privacy even in the tight and tiny world of a spaceship. The rest of the crew did not seem to mind his aloofness; when they spoke to him, it was clear that they regarded him with tolerant affection, as well as with respect. That was hardly surprising; the work he had done developing plants and trees that could flourish far inside the Arctic Circle had already made him the most famous botanist in Russia.

The fact that the Russian expedition had taken a botanist to the moon had caused a good deal of amusement, though it was really no odder than the fact that there were biologists on both the British and American ships. During the years before the first lunar landing, a good deal of evidence had accumulated hinting that some form of vegetation might exist on the moon, despite its airlessness and lack of water. The president of the U.S.S.R. Academy of Science was one of the leading proponents of this theory, and being too old to make the trip himself had done the next best thing by sending Surov.

The complete absence of any such vegetation, living or fossil, in the thousand or so square miles explored by our various parties was the first big disappointment the moon had reserved for us. Even those skeptics who were quite certain that no form of life could exist on the moon would have been very glad to have been proved wrong—as of course they were, five years later, when Richards and Shannon made their astonishing discovery inside the great walled plain of Eratosthenes. But *that* revelation still lay in the future; at the time of the first landing, it seemed that Surov had come to the moon in vain.

He did not appear unduly depressed, but kept himself as busy as the rest of the crew studying soil samples and looking after the little hydroponic farm whose pressurized, transparent tubes formed a gleaming network around the *Ziolkovski*. Neither we nor the Americans had gone in for this sort of thing, having calculated that it was better to ship food from Earth than to grow it on the spot—at least until the time came to set up a permanent base. We were right in terms of economics, but wrong in terms of morale. The tiny airtight greenhouses inside which Surov grew his vegetables and dwarf fruit trees were an oasis upon which we often feasted our eyes when we had grown tired of the immense desolation surrounding us.

One of the many disadvantages of being commander was that I seldom had much chance to do any active exploring; I was too busy preparing reports for Earth, checking stores, arranging programs and duty rosters, conferring with my opposite numbers in the American and Russian ships, and trying—not always successfully—to guess what would go wrong next. As a result, I sometimes did not go outside the base for two or three days at a time, and it was a standing joke that my space suit was a haven for moths.

Perhaps it is because of this that I can remember all my trips outside so vividly; certainly I can recall my only encounter with Surov. It was near noon, with the sun high above the southern mountains and the new Earth a barely visible thread of silver a few degrees away from it. Henderson, our geophysicist, wanted to take some magnetic readings at a series of check points a couple of miles to the east of the base. Everyone else was busy, and I was momentarily on top of my work, so we set off together on foot.

The journey was not long enough to merit taking one of the scooters, especially because the charges in the batteries were getting low. In any case, I always enjoyed walking out in the open on the moon. It was not merely the scenery, which even at its most awe-inspiring one can grow accustomed to after a while. No—what I never tired of was the effortless, slow-motion way in which every step took me bounding over the landscape, giving me the freedom that before the coming of space flight men only knew in dreams.

We had done the job and were halfway home when I noticed a figure moving across the plain about a mile to the south of us—not far, in fact, from the Russian base. I snapped my field glasses down inside my helmet and took a careful look at the other explorer. Even at close range, of course, you can't identify a man in a space suit, but because the suits are always coded by color and number that makes no practical difference.

"Who is it?" asked Henderson over the short-range radio channel to which we were both tuned.

"Blue suit, Number 3—that would be Surov. But I don't understand. *He's by himself.*"

It is one of the most fundamental rules of lunar exploration that no one goes anywhere alone on the surface of the moon. So many accidents can happen, which would be trivial if you were with a companion—but fatal if you were by yourself. How would you manage, for example, if your space suit developed a slow leak in the small of the back and you couldn't put on a repair patch? That may sound funny; but it's happened.

"Perhaps his buddy has had an accident and he's going to fetch help," suggested Henderson. "Maybe we had better call him."

I shook my head. Surov was obviously in no hurry. He had been out on a trip of his own, and was making his leisurely way back to the *Ziolkovski.* It was no concern of mine if Commander Krasnin let his people go out on solo trips, though it seemed a deplorable practice. And if Surov was breaking regulations, it was equally no concern of mine to report him.

During the next two months, my men often spotted Surov making his lone way over the landscape, but he always avoided them if they got too near. I made some discreet inquiries, and found that Commander Krasnin had been forced, owing to shortage of men, to relax some of his safety rules. But I couldn't find out what Surov was up to, though I never dreamed that his commander was equally in the dark.

It was with an "I told you so" feeling that I got Krasnin's emergency call. We had all had men in trouble before and had had to send out help, but this was the first time anyone had been lost and had not replied when his ship had sent out the recall signal. There was a hasty radio conference, a line of action was drawn up, and search parties fanned out from each of the three ships.

Once again I was with Henderson, and it was only common sense for us to backtrack along the route that we had seen Surov following. It was in what we regarded as "our" territory, quite some distance away from Surov's own ship, and as we scrambled up the low foothills it occurred to me for the first time that the Russian might have been doing something he wanted to keep from his colleagues. What it might be, I could not imagine.

Henderson found him, and yelled for help over his suit radio. But it was much too late; Surov was lying, face down, his deflated suit crumpled around him. He had been kneeling when something had smashed the plastic globe of his helmet; you could see how he had pitched forward and died instantaneously.

When Commander Krasnin reached us, we were still staring at the unbelievable object that Surov had been examining when he died. It was about three feet high, a leathery, greenish oval rooted to the rocks with a widespread network of tendrils. Yes—rooted; for it was a plant. A few yards away were two others, much smaller and apparently dead, since they were blackened and withered.

My first reaction was: "So there *is* life on the moon, after all!" It was not until Krasnin's voice spoke in my ears that I realized how much more marvelous was the truth.

"Poor Vladimir!" he said. "We knew he was a genius, yet we laughed at him when he told us of his dream. So he kept his greatest work a secret. He conquered the Arctic with his hybrid wheat, but *that* was only a beginning. He has brought life to the moon—and death as well."

As I stood there, in that first moment of astonished revelation, it still seemed a miracle. Today, all the world knows the history of "Surov's cactus," as it was inevitably if quite inaccurately christened, and it has lost much of its wonder. His notes have told the full story, and have described the years of experimentation that finally led him to a plant whose leathery skin would enable it to survive in vacuum, and whose far-ranging, acid-secreting roots would enable it to grow upon rocks where even lichens would be hard put to thrive. And we have seen the realization of the second stage of Surov's dream, for the cactus which will forever bear his name has already broken up vast areas of the lunar rock and so prepared a way for the more specialized plants that now feed every human being upon the moon.

Krasnin bent down beside the body of his colleague and lifted it effortlessly against the low gravity. He fingered the shattered fragments of the plastic helmet, and shook his head in perplexity.

"What could have happened to him?" he said. "It almost looks as if the plant did it, but that's ridiculous."

The green enigma stood there on the no-longer barren plain, tantalizing us with its promise and its mystery. Then Henderson said slowly, as if thinking aloud:

"I believe I've got the answer; I've just remembered some of the botany I did at school. If Surov designed this plant for lunar conditions, how would he arrange for it to propagate itself? The seeds would have to be scattered over a very wide area in the hope of finding a few suitable places to grow. There are no birds or animals here to carry them, in the way that happens on Earth. I can only think of one solution—and some of our terrestrial plants have already used it."

He was interrupted by my yell. Something had hit with a resounding clang against the metal waistband of my suit. It did no damage, but it was so sudden and unexpected that it took me utterly by surprise.

A seed lay at my feet, about the size and shape of a plum stone. A few yards away, we found the one that had shattered Surov's helmet as he bent down. He must have known that the plant was ripe, but in his eagerness to examine it he had forgotten what that implied. I have seen a cactus throw its seed a quarter of a mile under the low lunar gravity. Surov had been shot at point-blank range by his own creation.

ALL THAT GLITTERS

This is really Commander Vandenburg's story, but he is too many millions of miles away to tell it. It concerns his geophysicist, Dr. Paynter, who was generally believed to have gone to the moon to get away from his wife.

At one time or other, we were all supposed (often by our wives) to have done just that. However, in Paynter's case, there was just enough truth to make it stick.

It was not that he disliked his wife; one could almost say the contrary. He would do anything for her, but unfortunately the things that she wanted him to do cost rather too much. She was a lady of extravagant tastes, and such ladies are advised not to marry scientists—even scientists who go to the moon.

Mrs. Paynter's weakness was for jewelry, particularly diamonds. As might be expected, this was a weakness that caused her husband a good deal of worry. Being a conscientious as well as an affectionate husband, he did not merely worry about it—he did something about it. He became one of the world's leading experts on diamonds, from the scientific rather than the commercial point of view, and probably knew more about their composition, origin, and properties than any other man alive. Unfortunately, you may know a lot about diamonds without ever possessing any, and her husband's erudition was not something that Mrs. Paynter could wear around her neck when she went to a party.

Geophysics, as I have mentioned, was Dr. Paynter's real business; diamonds were merely a side line. He had developed many remarkable surveying instruments which could probe the interior of the Earth by means of electric impulses and magnetic waves, so giving a kind of X-ray picture of the hidden strata far below. It was hardly surprising, therefore, that he was one of the men chosen to pry into the mysterious interior of the moon.

He was quite eager to go, but it seemed to Commander Vandenburg that he was reluctant to leave Earth at this particular moment. A number of men had shown such symptoms; sometimes they were due to fears that could not be eradicated, and an otherwise promising man had to be left behind. In Paynter's case, however, the reluctance was quite impersonal. He was in the middle of a big experiment—something he had been working on all his life—and he didn't want to leave Earth until it was finished. However, the first lunar expedition could not wait for him, so he had to leave his project in the hands of his assistants. He was continually exchanging cryptic radio messages with them, to the great annoyance of the signals section of Space Station Three.

In the wonder of a new world waiting to be explored, Paynter soon forgot his earthly preoccupations. He would dash hither and yon over the lunar landscape on one of the neat little electric scooters the Americans had brought with them, carrying seismographs, magnetometers, gravity meters, and all the other esoteric tools of the geophysicist's trade. He was trying to learn, in a few weeks, what it had taken men hundreds of years to discover about their own planet. It was true that he had only a small sample of the moon's fourteen million square miles of territory to explore, but he intended to make a thorough job of it.

From time to time he continued to get messages from his colleagues back on Earth, as well as brief but affectionate signals from Mrs. P.

Neither seemed to interest him very much; even when you are not so busy that you hardly have time to sleep, a quarter of a million miles puts most of your personal affairs in a different perspective. I think that on the moon Dr. Paynter was really happy for the first time in his life; if so, he was not the only one.

Not far from our base there was a rather fine crater pit, a great blowhole in the lunar surface almost two miles from rim to rim. Though it was fairly close at hand, it was outside the normal area of our joint operations, and we had been on the moon for six weeks before Paynter led a party of three men off in one of the baby tractors to have a look at it. They disappeared from radio range over the edge of the moon, but we weren't worried about that because if they ran into trouble they could always call Earth and get any message relayed back to us.

Paynter and his men were gone forty-eight hours, which is about the maximum for continuous working on the moon, even with booster drugs. At first their little expedition was quite uneventful and therefore quite unexciting; everything went according to plan. They reached the crater, inflated their pressurized igloo and unpacked their stores, took their instrument readings, and then set up a portable drill to get core samples. It was while he was waiting for the drill to bring him up a nice section of the moon that Paynter made his second great discovery. He had made his first about ten hours before, but he didn't know it yet.

Around the lip of the crater, lying where they had been thrown up by the great explosions that had convulsed the lunar landscape three hundred million years before, were immense piles of rock which must have come from many miles down in the moon's interior. Anything he could do with his little drill, thought Paynter, could hardly compare with *this*. Unfortunately, the mountain-sized geological specimens that lay all around him were not neatly arranged in their correct order; they had been scattered over the landscape, much farther than the eye could see, according to the arbitrary violence of the eruptions that had blasted them into space.

Paynter climbed over these immense slag heaps, taking a swing at likely samples with his little hammer. Presently his colleagues heard him yell, and saw him come running back to them carrying what appeared to be a lump of rather poor quality glass. It was some time before he was sufficiently coherent to explain what all the fuss was about—and some time later still before the expedition remembered its real job and got back to work.

Vandenburg watched the returning party as it headed back to the ship. The four men didn't seem as tired as one would have expected, considering the fact that they had been on their feet for two days. Indeed, there was a certain jauntiness about their movements which even the space suits couldn't wholly conceal. You could see that the expedition had been a success. In that case, Paynter would have two causes for congratulation. The priority message that had just come from Earth was very cryptic, but it was clear that Paynter's work there—whatever it was—had finally reached a triumphant conclusion.

Commander Vandenburg almost forgot the message when he saw what Paynter was holding in his hand. He knew what a raw diamond looked like, and this was the second largest that anyone had ever seen. Only the Cullinan, tipping the scales at 3026 carats, beat it by a slender margin. "We ought to have expected it," he heard Paynter babble happily. "Diamonds are always found associated with volcanic vents. But somehow I never thought the analogy would hold here."

Vandenburg suddenly remembered the signal, and handed it over to Paynter. He read it quickly, and his jaw dropped. Never in his life, Vandenburg told me, had he seen a man so instantly deflated by a message of congratulation. The signal read: WE'VE DONE IT. TEST 541 WITH MODIFIED PRESSURE CONTAINER COMPLETE SUCCESS. NO PRACTICAL LIMIT TO SIZE. COSTS NEGLIGIBLE.

"What's the matter?" said Vandenburg, when he saw the stricken look on Paynter's face. "It doesn't seem bad news to me, whatever it means."

Paynter gulped two or three times like a stranded fish, then stared helplessly at the great crystal that almost filled the palm of his hand. He tossed it into the air, and it floated back in that slow-motion way everything has under lunar gravity.

Finally he found his voice.

"My lab's been working for years," he said, "trying to synthesize diamonds. Yesterday this thing was worth a million dollars. Today it's worth a couple of hundred. I'm not sure I'll bother to carry it back to Earth."

Well, he *did* carry it back; it seemed a pity not to. For about three months, Mrs. P. had the finest diamond necklace in the world, worth every bit of a thousand dollars—mostly the cost of cutting and polishing. Then the Paynter Process went into commercial production, and a month later she got her divorce. The grounds were extreme mental cruelty; and I suppose you could say it was justified.

WATCH THIS SPACE

It was quite a surprise to discover, when I looked it up, that the most famous experiment we carried out while we were on the moon had its beginnings way back in 1955. At that time, high-altitude rocket research had been going for only about ten years, mostly at White Sands, New Mexico. Nineteen fifty-five was the date of one of the most spectacular of those early experiments, one that involved the ejection of sodium onto the upper atmosphere.

On Earth, even on the clearest night, the sky between the stars isn't completely dark. There's a very faint background glow, and part of it is caused by the fluorescence of sodium atoms a hundred miles up. Since it would take the sodium in a good many cubic miles of the upper atmosphere to fill a single matchbox, it seemed to the early investigators that they could make quite a fireworks display if they used a rocket to dump a few pounds of the stuff into the ionosphere.

They were right. The sodium squirted out of a rocket above White Sands early in 1955 produced a great yellow glow in the sky which was visible, like a kind of artificial moonlight, for over an hour, before the atoms dispersed. This experiment wasn't done for fun (though it *was* fun) but for a serious scientific purpose. Instruments trained on this glow were able to gather new knowledge about the upper air—knowledge that went into the stockpile of information without which space flight would never have been possible.

When they got to the moon, the Americans decided that it would be a good idea to repeat the experiment there, on a much larger scale. A few hundred kilograms of sodium fired up from the surface would produce a display that would be visible from Earth, with a good pair of field glasses, as it fluoresced its way up through the lunar atmosphere.

(Some people, by the way, still don't realize that the moon *has* an atmosphere. It's about a million times too thin to be breathable, but if you have the right instruments you can detect it. As a meteor shield, it's first-rate, for though it may be tenuous it's hundreds of miles deep.)

Everyone had been talking about the experiment for days. The sodium bomb had arrived from Earth in the last supply rocket, and a very impressive piece of equipment it looked. Its operation was extremely simple; when ignited, an incendiary charge vaporized the sodium until a high pressure was built up, then a diaphragm burst and the stuff was squirted up into the sky through a specially shaped nozzle. It would be shot off soon after nightfall, and when the cloud of sodium rose out of the moon's shadow into direct sunlight it would start to glow with tremendous brilliance.

Nightfall, on the moon, is one of the most awe-inspiring sights in the whole of nature, made doubly so because as you watched the sun's flaming disk creep so slowly below the mountains you know that it will be fourteen days before you see it again. But it does not bring darkness—at least, not on this side of the moon. There is always the Earth, hanging motionless in the sky, the one heavenly body that neither rises nor sets. The light pouring back from her clouds and seas floods the lunar landscape with a soft, blue-green radiance, so that it is often easier to find your way around at night than under the fierce glare of the sun.

Even those who were not supposed to be on duty had come out to watch the experiment. The sodium bomb had been placed at the middle of the big triangle formed by the three ships, and stood upright with its nozzle pointing at the stars. Dr. Anderson, the astronomer of the American team, was testing the firing circuits, but everyone else was at a respectful distance. The bomb looked perfectly capable of living up to its name, though it was really about as dangerous as a soda-water siphon.

All the optical equipment of the three expeditions seemed to have been gathered together to record the performance. Telescopes, spectroscopes, motion-picture cameras, and everything else one could think of were lined up ready for action. And this, I knew, was nothing compared with the battery that must be zeroed on us from Earth. Every amateur astronomer who could see the moon tonight would be standing by in his back garden, listening to the radio commentary that told him of the progress of the experiment. I glanced up at the gleaming planet that dominated the sky above me; the land areas seemed to be fairly free from cloud, so the folks at home should have a good view. That seemed only fair; after all, they were footing the bill.

There were still fifteen minutes to go. Not for the first time, I wished there was a reliable way of smoking a cigarette inside a space suit without getting the helmet so badly fogged that you couldn't see. Our scientists had solved so many much more difficult problems; it seemed a pity that they couldn't do something about *that* one.

To pass the time—for this was an experiment where I had nothing to do—I switched on my suit radio and listened to Dave Bolton, who was making a very good job of the commentary. Dave was our chief navigator, and a brilliant mathematician. He also had a glib tongue and a picturesque turn of speech, and sometimes his recordings had to be censored by the B.B.C. There was nothing they could do about this one, however, for it was going out live from the relay stations on Earth.

Dave had finished a brief and lucid explanation of the purpose of the experiment, describing how the cloud of glowing sodium would enable us to analyze the lunar atmosphere as it rose through it at approximately a thousand miles an hour. "However," he went on to tell the waiting millions on Earth, "let's make one point clear. Even when the bomb has gone off, you won't see a darn thing for ten minutes—and neither will we. The sodium cloud will be completely invisible while it's rising up through the darkness of the moon's shadow. Then, quite suddenly, it will flash into brilliance as it enters the sun's rays, which are streaming past over our heads right now as we stare up into space. No one is quite sure how bright it will be, but it's a pretty safe guess that you'll be able to see it in any telescope bigger than a two-inch. So it should just be within the range of a good pair of binoculars."

He had to keep this sort of thing up for another ten minutes, and it was a marvel to me how he managed to do it. Then the great moment came, and Anderson closed the firing circuit. The bomb started to cook, building up pressure inside as the sodium volatilized. After thirty seconds, there was a sudden puff of smoke from the long, slender nozzle pointing up at the sky. And then we had to wait for another ten minutes while the invisible cloud rose to the stars. After all this build-up, I told myself, the result had better be good.

The seconds and minutes ebbed away. Then a sudden yellow glow began to spread across the sky, like a vast and unwavering aurora that became brighter even as we watched. It was as if an artist was sprawling strokes across the stars with a flame-filled brush. And as I stared at those strokes, I suddenly realized that someone had brought off the greatest advertising coup in history. For the strokes formed letters, and the letters formed two words—the name of a certain soft drink too well known to need any further publicity from me.

How had it been done? The first answer was obvious. Someone had placed a suitably cut stencil in the nozzle of the sodium bomb, so that the stream of escaping vapor had shaped itself to the words. Since there was nothing to distort it, the pattern had kept its shape during its invisible ascent to the stars. I had seen skywriting on Earth, but this was something on a far larger scale. Whatever I thought of them, I couldn't help admiring the ingenuity of the men who had perpetrated the scheme. The Os and As had given them a bit of trouble, but the Cs and Ls were perfect.

After the initial shock, I am glad to say that the scientific program proceeded as planned. I wish I could remember how Dave Bolton rose to the occasion in his commentary; it must have been a strain even for his quick wits. By this time, of course, half the Earth could see what he was describing. The next morning, every newspaper on the planet carried that famous photo of the crescent moon with the luminous slogan painted across its darkened sector.

The letters were visible, before they finally dispersed into space, for over an hour. By that time the words were almost a thousand miles long, and were beginning to get blurred. But they were still readable until they at last faded from sight in the ultimate vacuum between the planets.

Then the real fireworks began. Commander Vandenburg was absolutely furious, and promptly started to grill all his men. However, it was soon clear that the saboteur—if you could call him that—had been back on Earth. The bomb had been prepared there and shipped ready for immediate use. It did not take long to find, and fire, the engineer who had carried out the substitution. He couldn't have cared less, since his financial needs had been taken care of for a good many years to come.

As for the experiment itself, it was completely successful from the scientific point of view; all the recording instruments worked perfectly as they analyzed the light from the unexpectedly shaped cloud. But we never let the Americans live it down, and I am afraid poor Captain Vandenburg was the one who suffered most. Before he came to the moon he was a confirmed teetotaler, and much of his refreshment came from a certain wasp-waisted bottle. But now, as a matter of principle, he can only drink beer—and he hates the stuff.

A QUESTION OF RESIDENCE

I have already described the—shall we say—jockeying for position before take-off on the first flight to the moon. As it turned out, the American, Russian, and British ships landed just about simultaneously. No one has ever explained, however, why the British ship came back nearly two weeks after the others.

Oh, I know the official story; I ought to, for I helped to concoct it. It is true as far as it goes, but it scarcely goes far enough.

On all counts, the joint expedition had been a triumphant success There had been only one casualty, and in the manner of his death Vladimir Surov had made himself immortal. We had gathered knowledge that would keep the scientists of Earth busy for generations, and that would revolutionize almost all our ideas concerning the nature of the universe around us. Yes, our five months on the moon had been well spent, and we could go home to such welcomes as few heroes had ever had before.

However, there was still a good deal of tidying up to be done. The instruments that had been scattered all over the lunar landscape were still busily recording, and much of the information they gathered could not be automatically radioed back to Earth. There was no point in all three of the expeditions staying on the moon to the last minute; the personnel of one would be sufficient to finish the job. But who would volunteer to be caretaker while the others went back to gain the glory? It was a difficult problem, but one that would have to be solved very soon.

As far as supplies were concerned, we had little to worry about. The automatic freight rockets could keep us provided with air, food, and water for as long as we wished to stay on the moon. We were all in good health, though a little tired. None of the anticipated psychological troubles had cropped up, perhaps because we had all been so busy on tasks of absorbing interest that we had had no time to worry about going crazy. But, of course, we all looked forward to getting back to Earth and seeing our families again.

The first change of plan was forced upon us by the *Ziolkovski* being put out of commission when the ground beneath one of her landing legs suddenly gave way. The ship managed to stay upright, but the hull was badly twisted and the pressure cabin sprang dozens of leaks. There was much debate about on-the-spot repairs, but it was decided that it would be far too risky for her to take off in this condition. The Russians had no alternative but to thumb lifts back in the *Goddard* and the *Endeavour;* by using the *Ziolkovski's* unwanted fuel, our ships would be able to manage the extra load. However, the return flight would be extremely cramped and uncomfortable for all concerned because everyone would have to eat and sleep in shifts.

Either the American or the British ship, therefore, would be the first back to Earth. During those final weeks, as the work of the expedition was brought to its close, relations between Commander Vandenburg and myself were somewhat strained. I even wondered if we ought to settle the matter by tossing for it. . . .

Another problem was also engaging my attention—that of crew discipline. Perhaps this is too strong a phrase; I would not like it to be thought that a mutiny ever seemed probable. But all my men were now a little abstracted and liable to be found, if off duty, scribbling furiously in corners. I knew exactly what was going on, for I was involved in it myself. There wasn't a human being on the moon who had not sold exclusive rights to some newspaper or magazine, and we were all haunted by approaching deadlines. The radio-teletype to Earth was in continuous operation, sending tens of thousands of words a day, while even larger slabs of deathless prose were being dictated over the speech circuits.

It was Professor Williams, our very practical-minded astronomer, who came to me one day with the answer to my main problem.

"Skipper," he said, balancing himself precariously on the all-too-collapsible table I used as my working desk inside the igloo, "there's no technical reason, is there, why we should get back to Earth first?"

"No," I said, "merely a matter of fame, fortune, and seeing our families again. But I admit those aren't technical reasons. We could stay here another year if Earth kept sending supplies. If you want to suggest that, however, I shall take great pleasure in strangling you."

"It's not as bad as that. Once the main body has gone back, whichever party is left can follow in two or three weeks at the latest. They'll get a lot of credit, in fact, for self-sacrifice, modesty, and similar virtues."

"Which will be very poor compensation for being second home."

"Right—we need something else to make it worthwhile. Some more material reward."

"Agreed. What do you suggest?"

Williams pointed to the calendar hanging on the wall in front of me, between the two pin-ups we had stolen from the *Goddard*. The length of our stay was indicated by the days that had been crossed off in red ink; a big question mark in two weeks' time showed when the first ship would be heading back to Earth.

"There's your answer," he said. "If we go back then, do you realize what will happen? I'll tell you."

He did, and I kicked myself for not having thought of it first.

The next day, I explained my decision to Vandenburg and Krasnin.

"We'll stay behind and do the mopping up," I said. "It's a matter of common sense. The *Goddard's* a much bigger ship than ours and can carry an extra four people, while we can only manage two more, and even then it will be a squeeze. If you go first, Van, it will save a lot of people from eating their hearts out here for longer than necessary."

"That's very big of you," replied Vandenburg. "I won't hide the fact that we'll be happy to get home. And it's logical, I admit, now that the *Ziolkovski's* out of action. Still, it means quite a sacrifice on your part, and I don't really like to take advantage of it."

I gave an expansive wave.

"Think nothing of it," I answered. "As long as you boys don't grab all the credit, we'll take our turn. After all, we'll have the show here to ourselves when you've gone back to Earth."

Krasnin was looking at me with a rather calculating expression, and I found it singularly difficult to return his gaze.

"I hate to sound cynical," he said, "but I've learned to be a little suspicious when people start doing big favors without very good reasons. And frankly, I don't think the reason you've given is good enough. You wouldn't have anything else up your sleeve, would you?"

"Oh, very well," I sighed. "I'd hoped to get a *little* credit, but I see it's no use trying to convince anyone of the purity of my motives. I've got a reason, and you might as well know it. But please don't spread it around; I'd hate the folks back on Earth to be disillusioned. They still think of us as noble and heroic seekers after knowledge; let's keep it that way, for all our sakes."

Then I pulled out the calendar, and explained to Vandenburg and Krasnin what Williams had already explained to me. They listened with skepticism, then with growing sympathy.

"I had no idea it was *that* bad," said Vandenburg at last.

"Americans never have," I said sadly. "Anyway, that's the way it's been for half a century, and it doesn't seem to get any better. So you agree with my suggestion?"

"Of course. It suits us fine, anyhow. Until the next expedition's ready, the moon's all yours."

I remembered that phrase, two weeks later, as I watched the *Goddard* blast up into the sky toward the distant, beckoning Earth. It was lonely, then, when the Americans and all but two of the Russians had gone. We envied them the reception they got, and watched jealously on the TV screens their triumphant processions through Moscow and New York. Then we went back to work, and bided our time. Whenever we felt depressed, we would do little sums on bits of paper and would be instantly restored to cheerfulness.

The red crosses marched across the calendar as the short terrestrial days went by—days that seemed to have very little connection with the slow cycle of lunar time. At last we were ready; all the instrument readings were taken, all the specimens and samples safely packed away aboard the ship. The motors roared into life, giving us for a moment the weight we would feel again when we were back in Earth's gravity. Below us the rugged lunar landscape, which we had grown to know so well, fell swiftly away; within seconds we could see no sign at all of the buildings and instruments we had so laboriously erected and which future explorers would one day use.

The homeward voyage had begun. We returned to Earth in uneventful discomfort, joined the already half-dismantled *Goddard* beside Space

Station Three, and were quickly ferried down to the world we had left seven months before.

Seven months: that, as Williams had pointed out, was the all-important figure. We had been on the moon for more than half a financial year—and for all of us, it had been the most profitable year of our lives.

Sooner or later, I suppose, this interplanetary loophole will be plugged; the Department of Inland Revenue is still fighting a gallant rear-guard action, but we seem neatly covered under Section 57, paragraph 8 of the Capital Gains Act of 1972. We wrote our books and articles on the moon—and until there's a lunar government to impose income tax, we're hanging on to every penny.

And if the ruling finally goes against us—well, there's always Mars. . . .

✶ *PUBLICITY CAMPAIGN*

The concussion of the last atom bomb still seemed to linger as the lights came on again. For a long time, no one moved. Then the assistant producer said innocently: "Well, R.B., what do you think of it?"

R.B. heaved himself out of his seat while his acolytes waited to see which way the cat would jump. It was then that they noticed that R.B.'s cigar had gone out. Why, that hadn't happened even at the preview of "G.W.T.W.!"

"Boys," he said ecstatically, "we've got something here! How much did you say it cost, Mike?"

"Six and a half million, R.B."

"It was cheap at the price. Let me tell you, I'll eat every foot of it if the gross doesn't beat 'Quo Vadis.'" He wheeled, as swiftly as could be expected for one of his bulk, upon a small man still crouched in his seat at the back of the projection room. "Snap out of it, Joe! The Earth's saved! You've seen all these space films. How does this line up with the earlier ones?"

Joe came to with an obvious effort.

"There's no comparison," he said. "It's got all the suspense of 'The Thing,' without that awful letdown at the end when you saw the monster was human. The only picture that comes within miles of it is 'War of the Worlds.' Some of the effects in that were nearly as good as ours, but of course George Pal didn't have 3 D. And that sure makes a difference! When the Golden Gate Bridge went down, I thought that pier was going to hit me!"

"The bit I liked best," put in Tony Auerbach from Publicity, "was when the Empire State Building split right up the middle. You don't suppose the owners might sue us, though?"

"Of course not. No one expects *any* building to stand up to—what did the script call them?—city busters. And, after all, we wiped out the rest of New York as well. Ugh—that scene in the Holland Tunnel when the roof gave way! Next time, I'll take the ferry!"

"Yes, that was very well done—almost *too* well done. But what really got me was those creatures from space. The animation was perfect—how did you do it, Mike?"

"Trade secret," said the proud producer. "Still, I'll let you in on it. A lot of that stuff is genuine."

"What!"

"Oh, don't get me wrong! We haven't been on location to Sirius B. But they've developed a microcamera over at Cal Tech, and we used that to film spiders in action. We cut in the best shots, and I think you'd have a job telling which was micro and which was the full-sized studio stuff. Now you understand why I wanted the Aliens to be insects, and not octopuses, like the script said first."

"There's a good publicity angle here," said Tony. "One thing worries me, though. That scene where the monsters kidnap Gloria. Do you suppose the censor . . . I mean the way we've done it, it almost looks . . ."

"Aw, quit worrying! *That's* what people are supposed to think! Anyway, we make it clear in the next reel that they really want her for dissection, so that's all right."

"It'll be a riot!" gloated R.B., a faraway gleam in his eye as if he was already hearing the avalanche of dollars pouring into the box office. "Look—we'll put another million into publicity! I can just see the posters—get all this down, Tony. WATCH THE SKY! THE SIRIANS ARE COMING! And we'll make thousands of clockwork models—can't you imagine them scuttling around on their hairy legs! People love to be scared, and we'll scare them. By the time we've finished, no one will be able to look at the sky without getting the creeps! I leave it to you, boys—this picture is going to make *history!*"

He was right. "Monsters from Space" hit the public two months later. Within a week of the simultaneous London and New York *premières,* there could have been no one in the western world who had not seen the posters screaming EARTH BEWARE! or had not shuddered at the photographs of the hairy horrors stalking along deserted Fifth Avenue on their thin, many-jointed legs. Blimps cleverly disguised as spaceships cruised across the skies, to the vast confusion of pilots who encountered them, and clockwork models of the Alien invaders were everywhere, scaring old ladies out of their wits.

The publicity campaign was brilliant, and the picture would undoubtedly have run for months had it not been for a coincidence as disastrous as it was unforeseeable. While the number of people fainting at each performance was still news, the skies of Earth filled suddenly with long, lean shadows sliding swiftly through the clouds. . . .

Prince Zervashni was good-natured but inclined to be impetuous—a well-known failing of his race. There was no reason to suppose that his present mission, that of making peaceful contact with the planet Earth, would present any particular problems. The correct technique of approach had been thoroughly worked out over many thousands of years, as the Third Galactic Empire slowly expanded its frontiers, absorbing planet after planet, sun upon sun. There was seldom any trouble: really intelligent races can always co-operate, once they have got over the initial shock of learning that they are not alone in the universe.

It was true that humanity had emerged from its primitive, warlike stage only within the last generation. This, however, did not worry Prince Zervashni's chief adviser, Sigisnin II, Professor of Astropolitics.

"It's a perfectly typical Class E culture," said the professor. "Technically advanced, morally rather backward. However, they are already used to the conception of space flight, and will soon take us for granted. The normal precautions will be sufficient until we have won their confidence."

"Very well," said the prince. "Tell the envoys to leave at once."

It was unfortunate that the "normal precautions" did not allow for Tony Auerbach's publicity campaign, which had now reached new heights of interplanetary xenophobia. The ambassadors landed in New York's Central Park on the very day that a prominent astronomer, unusually hard up and therefore amenable to influence, announced in a widely reported interview that any visitors from space probably would be unfriendly.

The luckless ambassadors, heading for the United Nations Building, had got as far south as 60th Street when they met the mob. The encounter was very one-sided, and the scientists at the Museum of Natural History were most annoyed that there was so little left for them to examine.

Prince Zervashni tried once more, on the other side of the planet, but the news had got there first. This time the ambassadors were armed, and gave a good account of themselves before they were overwhelmed by sheer numbers. Even so, it was not until the rocket bombs started climbing up toward his fleet that the prince finally lost his temper and decided to take drastic action.

It was all over in twenty minutes, and was really quite painless. Then the prince turned to his adviser and said, with considerable understatement: "That appears to be that. And now—can you tell me exactly what went wrong?"

Sigisnin II knitted his dozen flexible fingers together in acute anguish. It was not only the spectacle of the neatly disinfected Earth that distressed him, though to a scientist the destruction of such a beautiful specimen is always a major tragedy. At least equally upsetting was the demolition of his theories and, with them, his reputation.

"I just don't understand it!" he lamented. "Of course, races at this level of culture are often suspicious and nervous when contact is first made. But they'd never had visitors before, so there was no reason for them to be hostile."

"Hostile! They were demons! I think they were all insane." The prince turned to his captain, a tripedal creature who looked rather like a ball of wool balanced on three knitting needles.

"Is the fleet reassembled?"

"Yes, Sire."

"Then we will return to Base at optimum speed. This planet depresses me."

On the dead and silent Earth, the posters still screamed their warnings from a thousand hoardings. The malevolent insectile shapes shown pouring from the skies bore no resemblance at all to Prince Zervashni, who apart from his four eyes might have been mistaken for a panda with purple fur—and who, moreover, had come from Rigel, not Sirius.

But, of course, it was now much too late to point this out.

ALL THE TIME IN THE WORLD

When the quiet knock came on the door, Robert Ashton surveyed the room in one swift, automatic movement. Its dull respectability satisfied him and should reassure any visitor. Not that he had any reason to expect the police, but there was no point in taking chances.

"Come in," he said, pausing only to grab Plato's *Dialogues* from the shelf beside him. Perhaps this gesture was a little too ostentatious, but it always impressed his clients.

The door opened slowly. At first, Ashton continued his intent reading, not bothering to glance up. There was the slightest acceleration of his heart, a mild and even exhilarating constriction of the chest. Of course, it couldn't possibly be a flatfoot: someone would have tipped him off. Still, any unheralded visitor was unusual and thus potentially dangerous.

Ashton laid down the book, glanced toward the door and remarked in a noncommittal voice: "What can I do for you?" He did not get up; such courtesies belonged to a past he had buried long ago. Besides, it was a woman. In the circles he now frequented, women were accustomed to receive jewels and clothes and money—but never respect.

Yet there was something about this visitor that drew him slowly to his feet. It was not merely that she was beautiful, but she had a poised and effortless authority that moved her into a different world from the flamboyant doxies he met in the normal course of business. There was a brain and a purpose behind those calm, appraising eyes—a brain, Ashton suspected, the equal of his own.

He did not know how grossly he had underestimated her.

"Mr. Ashton," she began, "let us not waste time. I know who you are and I have work for you. Here are my credentials."

She opened a large, stylish handbag and extracted a thick bundle of notes.

"You may regard this," she said, "as a sample."

Ashton caught the bundle as she tossed it carelessly toward him. It was the largest sum of money he had ever held in his life—at least a hundred fivers, all new and serially numbered. He felt them between his fingers. If they were not genuine, they were so good that the difference was of no practical importance.

He ran his thumb to and fro along the edge of the wad as if feeling a pack for a marked card, and said thoughtfully, "I'd like to know where you got these. If they aren't forgeries, they must be hot and will take some passing."

"They are genuine. A very short time ago they were in the Bank of England. But if they are of no use to you throw them in the fire. I merely let you have them to show that I mean business."

"Go on." He gestured to the only seat and balanced himself on the edge of the table.

She drew a sheaf of papers from the capacious handbag and handed it across to him.

"I am prepared to pay you any sum you wish if you will secure these items and bring them to me, at a time and place to be arranged. What is more, I will guarantee that you can make the thefts with no personal danger."

Ashton looked at the list, and sighed. The woman was mad. Still, she had better be humored. There might be more money where this came from.

"I notice," he said mildly, "that all these items are in the British Museum, and that most of them are, quite literally, priceless. By that I mean that you could neither buy nor sell them."

"I do not wish to sell them. I am a collector."

"So it seems. What are you prepared to pay for these acquisitions?"

"Name a figure."

There was a short silence. Ashton weighed the possibilities. He took a certain professional pride in his work, but there were some things that no amount of money could accomplish. Still, it would be amusing to see how high the bidding would go.

He looked at the list again.

"I think a round million would be a very reasonable figure for this lot," he said ironically.

"I fear you are not taking me very seriously. With your contacts, you should be able to dispose of these."

There was a flash of light and something sparkled through the air. Ashton caught the necklace before it hit the ground, and despite himself was unable to suppress a gasp of amazement. A fortune glittered through his fingers. The central diamond was the largest he had ever seen—it must be one of the world's most famous jewels.

His visitor seemed completely indifferent as he slipped the necklace into his pocket. Ashton was badly shaken; he knew she was not acting. To her, that fabulous gem was of no more value than a lump of sugar. This was madness on an unimaginable scale.

"Assuming that you can deliver the money," he said, "how do you imagine that it's physically possible to do what you ask? One might steal a single item from this list, but within a few hours the Museum would be solid with police."

With a fortune already in his pocket, he could afford to be frank. Besides, he was curious to learn more about his fantastic visitor.

She smiled, rather sadly, as if humoring a backward child.

"If I show you the way," she said softly, "will you do it?"

"Yes—for a million."

"Have you noticed anything strange since I came in? Is it not—very quiet?"

Ashton listened. My God, she was right! This room was never completely silent, even at night. There had been a wind blowing over the roof tops; where had it gone now? The distant rumble of traffic had ceased; five minutes ago he had been cursing the engines shunting in the marshaling yard at the end of the road. What had happened to them?

"Go to the window."

He obeyed the order and drew aside the grimy lace curtains with fingers that shook slightly despite all attempt at control. Then he relaxed. The street was quite empty, as it often was at this time in the midmorning. There was no traffic, and hence no reason for sound. Then he glanced down the row of dingy houses toward the shunting yard.

His visitor smiled as he stiffened with the shock.

"Tell me what you see, Mr. Ashton."

He turned slowly, face pale and throat muscles working.

"What are you?" he gasped. "A witch?"

"Don't be foolish. There is a simple explanation. It is not the world that has changed—but you."

Ashton stared again at that unbelievable shunting engine, the plume of steam frozen motionless above it as if made from cotton wool. He realized now that the clouds were equally immobile; they should have been scudding across the sky. All around him was the unnatural stillness of the high-speed photograph, the vivid unreality of a scene glimpsed in a flash of lightning.

"You are intelligent enough to realize what is happening, even if you cannot understand how it is done. Your time scale has been altered: a minute in the outer world would be a year in this room."

Again she opened the handbag, and this time brought forth what appeared to be a bracelet of some silvery metal, with a series of dials and switches molded into it.

"You can call this a personal generator," she said. "With it strapped about your arm, you are invincible. You can come and go without hindrance—you can steal everything on that list and bring it to me before one of the guards in the Museum has blinked an eyelid. When you have finished, you can be miles away before you switch off the field and step back into the normal world.

"Now listen carefully, and do exactly what I say. The field has a radius of about seven feet, so you must keep at least that distance from any other person. Secondly, you must not switch it off again until you have completed your task and I have given you your payment. *This is most important*. Now, the plan I have worked out is this. . . ."

No criminal in the history of the world had ever possessed such power. It was intoxicating—yet Ashton wondered if he would ever get used to it. He had ceased to worry about explanations, at least until the job was done and he had collected his reward. Then, perhaps, he would get away from England and enjoy a well-earned retirement.

His visitor had left a few minutes ahead of him, but when he stepped out into the street the scene was completely unchanged. Though he had prepared for it, the sensation was still unnerving. Ashton felt an impulse to hurry, as if this condition couldn't possibly last and he had to get the job done before the gadget ran out of juice. But that, he had been assured, was impossible.

In the High Street he slowed down to look at the frozen traffic, the paralyzed pedestrians. He was careful, as he had been warned, not to approach so close to anyone that they came within his field. How ridiculous people looked when one saw them like this, robbed of such grace as movement could give, their mouths half open in foolish grimaces!

Having to seek assistance went against the grain, but some parts of the job were too big for him to handle by himself. Besides, he could pay liberally and never notice it. The main difficulty, Ashton realized, would be to find someone who was intelligent enough not to be scared—or so stupid that he would take everything for granted. He decided to try the first possibility.

Tony Marchetti's place was down a side street so close to the police station that one felt it was really carrying camouflage too far. As he walked past the entrance, Ashton caught a glimpse of the duty sergeant at his desk and resisted a temptation to go inside to combine a little pleasure with business. But that sort of thing could wait until later.

The door of Tony's opened in his face as he approached. It was such a natural occurrence in a world where nothing was normal that it was a moment before Ashton realized its implications. Had his generator failed? He glanced hastily down the street and was reassured by the frozen tableau behind him.

"Well, if it isn't Bob Ashton!" said a familiar voice. "Fancy meeting you as early in the morning as this. That's an odd bracelet you're wearing. I thought I had the only one."

"Hello, Aram," replied Ashton. "It looks as if there's a lot going on that neither of us knows about. Have you signed up Tony, or is he still free?"

"Sorry. We've a little job which will keep him busy for a while."

"Don't tell me. It's at the National Gallery or the Tate."

Aram Albenkian fingered his neat goatee. "Who told you that?" he asked.

"No one. But, after all, you *are* the crookedest art dealer in the trade, and I'm beginning to guess what's going on. Did a tall, very good-looking brunette give you that bracelet and a shopping list?"

"I don't see why I should tell you, but the answer's no. It was a man."

Ashton felt a momentary surprise. Then he shrugged his shoulders. "I might have guessed that there would be more than one of them. I'd like to know who's behind it."

"Have you any theories?" said Albenkian guardedly.

Ashton decided that it would be worth risking some loss of information to test the other's reactions. "It's obvious they're not interested in money—they have all they want and can get more with this gadget. The woman who saw me said she was a collector. I took it as a joke, but I see now that she meant it seriously."

"Why do we come into the picture? What's to stop them doing the whole job themselves?" Albenkian asked.

"Maybe they're frightened. Or perhaps they want our—er—specialized knowledge. Some of the items on my list are rather well cased in. My theory is that they're agents for a mad millionaire."

It didn't hold water, and Ashton knew it. But he wanted to see which leaks Albenkian would try to plug.

"My dear Ashton," said the other impatiently, holding up his wrist. "How do you explain this little thing? I know nothing about science, but even I can tell that it's beyond the wildest dreams of our technologies. There's only one conclusion to be drawn from that."

"Go on."

"These people are from—somewhere else. Our world is being systematically looted of its treasures. You know all this stuff you read about rockets and spaceships? Well, someone else has done it first."

Ashton didn't laugh. The theory was no more fantastic than the facts.

"Whoever they are," he said, "they seem to know their way around pretty well. I wonder how many teams they've got? Perhaps the Louvre and the Prado are being reconnoitered at this very minute. The world is going to have a shock before the day's out."

They parted amicably enough, neither confiding any details of real importance about his business. For a fleeting moment Ashton thought of trying to buy over Tony, but there was no point in antagonizing Albenkian. Steve Regan would have to do. That meant walking about a mile, since of course any form of transport was impossible. He would die of old age before a bus completed the journey. Ashton was not clear what would happen if he attempted to drive a car when the field was operating, and he had been warned not to try any experiments.

It astonished Ashton that even such a nearly certified moron as Steve could take the accelerator so calmly; there was something to be said, after all, for the comic strips which were probably his only reading. After a few words of grossly simplified explanation, Steve buckled on the spare wristlet which, rather to Ashton's surprise, his visitor had handed over without comment. Then they set out on their long walk to the Museum.

Ashton, or his client, had thought of everything. They stopped once at a park bench to rest and enjoy some sandwiches and regain their breath. When at last they reached the Museum, neither felt any the worse for the unaccustomed exercise.

They walked together through the gates of the Museum—unable, despite logic, to avoid speaking in whispers—and up the wide stone steps into the entrance hall. Ashton knew his way perfectly. With whimsical humor he displayed his Reading Room ticket as they walked, at a respectful distance, past the statuesque attendants. It occurred to him that the occupants of the great chamber, for the most part, looked just the same as they normally did, even without the benefit of the acceleraor.

It was a straightforward but tedious job collecting the books that had been listed. They had been chosen, it seemed, for their beauty as works of art as much as for their literary content. The selection had been done by someone who knew his job. Had *they* done it themselves, Ashton wondered, or had they bribed other experts as they were bribing him? He wondered if he would ever glimpse the full ramifications of this plot.

There was a considerable amount of panel-smashing to be done, but Ashton was careful not to damage any books, even the unwanted ones. Whenever he had collected enough volumes to make a comfortable load, Steve carried them out into the courtyard and dumped them on the paving stones until a small pyramid had accumulated.

It would not matter if they were left for short periods outside the field of the accelerator. No one would notice their momentary flicker of existence in the normal world.

They were in the library for two hours of their time, and paused for another snack before passing to the next job. On the way Ashton stopped for a little private business. There was a tinkle of glass as the tiny case, standing in solitary splendor, yielded up its treasure: then the manuscript of *Alice* was safely tucked into Ashton's pocket.

Among the antiquities, he was not quite so much at home. There were a few examples to be taken from every gallery, and sometimes it was hard to see the reasons for the choice. It was as if—and again he remembered Albenkian's words—these works of art had been selected by someone with totally alien standards. This time, with a few exceptions, *they* had obviously not been guided by the experts.

For the second time in history the case of the Portland Vase was shattered. In five seconds, thought Ashton, the alarms would be going all over the Museum and the whole building would be in an uproar. And in five seconds he could be miles away. It was an intoxicating thought, and as he worked swiftly to complete his contract he began to regret the price he had asked. Even now, it was not too late.

He felt the quiet satisfaction of the good workman as he watched Steve carry the great silver tray of the Mildenhall Treasure out into the courtyard and place it beside the now impressive pile. "That's the lot," he said. "I'll settle up at my place this evening. Now let's get this gadget off you."

They walked out into High Holborn and chose a secluded side street that had no pedestrians near it. Ashton unfastened the peculiar buckle and stepped back from his cohort, watching him freeze into immobility as he did so. Steve was vulnerable again, moving once more with all other men in the stream of time. But before the alarm had gone out he would have lost himself in the London crowds.

When he re-entered the Museum yard, the treasure had already gone. Standing where it had been was his visitor of—how long ago? She was still poised and graceful, but, Ashton thought, looking a little tired. He approached until their fields merged and they were no longer separated by an impassable gulf of silence. "I hope you're satisfied," he said. "How did you move the stuff so quickly?"

She touched the bracelet around her own wrist and gave a wan smile. "We have many other powers besides this."

"Then why did you need my help?"

"There were technical reasons. It was necessary to remove the objects we required from the presence of other matter. In this way, we could gather only what we needed and not waste our limited—what shall I call them?—transporting facilities. Now may I have the bracelet back?"

Ashton slowly handed over the one he was carrying, but made no effort to unfasten his own. There might be danger in what he was doing, but he intended to retreat at the first sign of it.

"I'm prepared to reduce my fee," he said. "In fact I'll waive all payment—in exchange for this." He touched his wrist, where the intricate metal band gleamed in the sunlight.

She was watching him with an expression as fathomless as the Gioconda smile. (Had *that,* Ashton wondered, gone to join the treasure he had gathered? How much had they taken from the Louvre?)

"I would not call that reducing your fee. All the money in the world could not purchase one of those bracelets."

"Or the things I have given you."

"You are greedy, Mr. Ashton. You know that with an accelerator the entire world would be yours."

"What of that? Do you have any further interest in our planet, now you have taken what you need?"

There was a pause. Then, unexpectedly, she smiled. "So you have guessed I do not belong to your world."

"Yes. And I know that you have other agents besides myself. Do you come from Mars, or won't you tell me?"

"I am quite willing to tell you. But you may not thank me if I do."

Ashton looked at her warily. What did she mean by that? Unconscious of his action, he put his wrist behind his back, protecting the bracelet.

"Now, I am not from Mars, or any planet of which you have ever heard. You would not understand *what* I am. Yet I will tell you this. I am from the Future."

"The Future! That's ridiculous!"

"Indeed? I should be interested to know why."

"If that sort of thing were possible, our past history would be full of time travelers. Besides, it would involve a *reductio ad absurdum.* Going into the past could change the present and produce all sorts of paradoxes."

"Those are good points, though not perhaps as original as you suppose. But they only refute the possibility of time travel in general, not in the very special case which concerns us now."

"What is peculiar about it?" he asked.

"On very rare occasions, and by the release of an enormous amount of energy, it is possible to produce a—*singularity*—in time. During the fraction of a second when that singularity occurs, the past becomes accessible to the future, though only in a restricted way. We can send our minds back to you, but not our bodies."

"You mean," said Ashton, "that you are *borrowing* the body I see?"

"Oh, I have paid for it, as I am paying you. The owner has agreed to the terms. We are very conscientious in these matters."

Ashton was thinking swiftly. If this story was true, it gave him a definite advantage.

"You mean," he continued, "that you have no direct control over matter, and must work through human agents?"

"Yes. Even those bracelets were made here, under our mental control."

She was explaining too much too readily, revealing all her weaknesses. A warning signal was flashing in the back of Ashton's mind, but he had committed himself too deeply to retreat.

"Then it seems to me," he said slowly, "that you cannot force me to hand this bracelet back."

"That is perfectly true."

"That's all I want to know."

She was smiling at him now, and there was something in that smile that chilled him to the marrow.

"We are not vindictive or unkind, Mr. Ashton," she said quietly. "What I am going to do now appeals to my sense of justice. You have asked for that bracelet; you can keep it. Now I shall tell you just how useful it will be."

For a moment Ashton had a wild impulse to hand back the accelerator. She must have guessed his thoughts.

"No, it's too late. I insist that you keep it. And I can reassure you on one point. It won't wear out. It will last you"—again that enigmatic smile—"the rest of your life.

"Do you mind if we go for a walk, Mr. Ashton? I have done my work here, and would like to have a last glimpse of your world before I leave it forever."

She turned toward the iron gates, and did not wait for a reply. Consumed by curiosity, Ashton followed.

They walked in silence until they were standing among the frozen traffic of Tottenham Court Road. For a while she stood staring at the busy yet motionless crowds; then she sighed.

"I cannot help feeling sorry for them, and for you. I wonder what you would have made of yourselves."

"What do you mean by that?"

"Just now, Mr. Ashton, you implied that the future cannot reach back into the past, because that would alter history. A shrewd remark, but, I am afraid, irrelevant. You see, *your* world has no more history to alter."

She pointed across the road, and Ashton turned swiftly on his heels. There was nothing there except a newsboy crouching over his pile of papers. A placard formed an impossible curve in the breeze that was blowing through this motionless world. Ashton read the crudely lettered words with difficulty:

SUPER-BOMB TEST TODAY

The voice in his ears seemed to come from a very long way off.

"I told you that time travel, even in this restricted form, requires an enormous release of energy—far more than a single bomb can liberate, Mr. Ashton. But that bomb is only a trigger—"

She pointed to the solid ground beneath their feet. "Do you know anything about your own planet? Probably not; your race has learned so little. But even your scientists have discovered that, two thousand miles down, the Earth has a dense, liquid core. That core is made of compressed matter, and it can exist in either of two stable states. Given a certain stimulus, it can change from one of those states to another, just as a seesaw can tip over at the touch of a finger. But that change, Mr. Ashton, will liberate as much energy as all the earthquakes since the beginning of your world. The oceans and continents will fly into space; the sun will have a second asteroid belt.

"That cataclysm will send its echoes down the ages, and will open up to us a fraction of a second in your time. During that instant, we are trying to save what we can of your world's treasures. It is all that we can do; even if your motives were purely selfish and completely dishonest, you have done your race a service you never intended.

"And now I must return to our ship, where it waits by the ruins of Earth almost a hundred thousand years from now. You can keep the bracelet."

The withdrawal was instantaneous. The woman suddenly froze and became one with the other statues in the silent street. He was alone.

Alone! Ashton held the gleaming bracelet before his eyes, hypnotized by its intricate workmanship and by the powers it concealed. He had made a bargain, and he must keep it. He could live out the full span of his life—at the cost of an isolation no other man had ever known. If he switched off the field, the last seconds of history would tick inexorably away.

Seconds? Indeed, there was less time than that. For he knew that the bomb must already have exploded.

He sat down on the edge of the pavement and began to think. There was no need to panic; he must take things calmly, without hysteria. After all, he had plenty of time.

All the time in the world.

COSMIC CASANOVA

This time I was five weeks out from Base Planet before the symptoms became acute. On the last trip it had taken only a month; I was not certain whether the difference was due to advancing age or to something the dietitians had put into my food capsules. Or it could merely have been that I was busier; the arm of the galaxy I was scouting was heavily populated, with stars only a couple of light-years apart, so I had little time to brood over the girls I'd left behind me. As soon as one star had been classified, and the automatic search for planets had been completed, it was time to head for the next sun. And when, as happened in about one case out of ten, planets *did* turn up, I'd be furiously busy for several days seeing that Max, the ship's electronic computer, got all the information down on his tapes.

Now, however, I was through this densely packed region of space, and it sometimes took as much as three days to get from sun to sun. That was time enough for Sex to come tiptoeing aboard the ship, and for the memories of my last leave to make the months ahead look very empty indeed.

Perhaps I had overdone it, back on Diadne V, while my ship was being reprovisioned and I was supposed to be resting between missions. But a survey scout spends eighty per cent of his time alone in space, and human nature being what it is, he must be expected to make up for lost time. I had not merely done that; I'd built up considerable credit for the future—though not, it seemed, enough to last me through this trip.

First, I recalled wistfully, there had been Helene. She was blonde, cuddly, and compliant, though rather unimaginative. We had a fine time together until her husband came back from *his* mission; he was extremely decent about it but pointed out, reasonably enough, that Helene would now have very little time for other engagements. Fortunately, I had already made contact with Iris, so the hiatus was negligible.

Now Iris was really something. Even now, it makes me squirm to think of her. When that affair broke up—for the simple reason that a man has to get a little sleep sometime—I swore off women for a whole week. Then I came across a touching poem by an old Earth writer named John Donne—he's worth looking up, if you can read Primitive English—which reminded me that time lost could never be regained.

How true, I thought, so I put on my spaceman's uniform and wandered down to the beach of Diadne V's only sea. There was need to walk no more than a few hundred meters before I'd spotted a dozen possibilities, brushed off several volunteers, and signed up Natalie.

That worked out pretty well at first, until Natalie started objecting to Ruth (or was it Kay?). I can't *stand* girls who think they own a man, so I blasted off after a rather difficult scene that was quite expensive in crockery. This left me at loose ends for a couple of days; then Cynthia came to the rescue and—but by now you'll have gotten the general idea, so I won't bore you with details.

These, then, were the fond memories I started to work back through while one star dwindled behind me and the next flared up ahead. On this trip I'd deliberately left my pin-ups behind, having decided that they only made matters worse. This was a mistake; being quite a good artist in a rather specialized way, I started to draw my own, and it wasn't long before I had a collection it would be hard to match on any respectable planet.

I would hate you to think that this preoccupation affected my efficiency as a unit of the Galactic Survey. It was only on the long, dull runs between the stars, when I had no one to talk to but the computer, that I found my glands getting the better of me. Max, my electronic colleague, was good enough company in the ordinary course of events, but there are some things that a machine can't be expected to understand. I often hurt his feelings when I was in one of my irritable moods and lost my temper for no apparent reason. "What's the matter, Joe?" Max would say plaintively. "Surely you're not mad at me because I beat you at chess again? Remember, I warned you I would."

"Oh, go to hell!" I'd snarl back—and then I'd have an anxious five minutes while I straightened things out with the rather literal-minded Navigation Robot.

Two months out from Base, with thirty suns and four solar systems logged, something happened that wiped all my personal problems from my mind. The long-range monitor began to beep; a faint signal was coming from somewhere in the section of space ahead of me. I got the most accurate bearing that I could; the transmission was unmodulated, very narrow band—clearly a beacon of some kind. Yet no ship of ours, to the best of my knowledge, had ever entered this remote neck of the universe; I was supposed to be scouting completely unexplored territory.

This, I told myself, is IT—my big moment, the payoff for all the lonely years I'd spent in space. At some unknown distance ahead of me was another civilization—a race sufficiently advanced to possess hyper-radio.

I knew exactly what I had to do. As soon as Max had confirmed my readings and made his analysis, I launched a message carrier back to Base. If anything happened to me, the Survey would know where and could guess why. It was some consolation to think that if I didn't come home on schedule, my friends would be out here in force to pick up the pieces.

Soon there was no doubt where the signal was coming from, and I changed course for the small yellow star that was dead in line with the beacon. No one, I told myself, would put out a wave this strong unless they had space travel themselves; I might be running into a culture as advanced as my own—with all that implied.

I was still a long way off when I started calling, not very hopefully, with my own transmitter. To my surprise, there was a prompt reaction. The continuous wave immediately broke up into a string of pulses, repeated over and over again. Even Max couldn't make anything of the message; it probably meant "Who the heck are you?"—which was not a big enough sample for even the most intelligent of translating machines to get its teeth into.

Hour by hour the signal grew in strength; just to let them know I was still around and was reading them loud and clear, I occasionally shot the same message back along the way it had come. And then I had my second big surprise.

I had expected them—whoever or whatever they might be—to switch to speech transmission as soon as I was near enough for good reception. This was precisely what they did; what I had *not* expected was that their voices would be human, the language they spoke an unmistakable but to me unintelligible brand of English. I could identify about one word in ten; the others were either quite unknown or else distorted so badly that I could not recognize them.

When the first words came over the loud-speaker, I guessed the truth. This was no alien, nonhuman race, but something almost as exciting and perhaps a good deal safer as far as a solitary scout was concerned. I had established contact with one of the lost colonies of the First Empire—the pioneers who had set out from Earth in the early days of interstellar exploration, five thousand years ago. When the empire collapsed, most of these isolated groups had perished or had sunk back to barbarism. Here, it seemed, was one that had survived.

I talked back to them in the slowest and simplest English I could muster, but five thousand years is a long time in the life of any language and no real communication was possible. They were clearly excited at the contact—pleasurably, as far as I could judge. This is not always the case; some of the isolated cultures left over from the First Empire have become violently xenophobic and react almost with hysteria to the knowledge that they are not alone in space.

Our attempts to communicate were not making much progress, when a new factor appeared—one that changed my outlook abruptly. A woman's voice started to come from the speaker.

It was the most beautiful voice I'd ever heard, and even without the lonely weeks in space that lay behind me I think I would have fallen in love with it at once. Very deep, yet still completely feminine, it had a warm, caressing quality that seemed to ravish all my senses. I was so stunned, in fact, that it was several minutes before I realized that I could understand what my invisible enchantress was saying. She was speaking English that was almost fifty per cent comprehensible.

To cut a short story shorter, it did not take me very long to learn that her name was Liala, and that she was the only philologist on her planet to specialize in Primitive English. As soon as contact had been made with my ship, she had been called in to do the translating. Luck, it seemed, was very much on my side; the interpreter could so easily have been some ancient, white-bearded fossil.

As the hours ticked away and her sun grew ever larger in the sky ahead of me, Liala and I became the best of friends. Because time was short, I had to operate faster than I'd ever done before. The fact that no one else could understand exactly what we were saying to each other insured our privacy. Indeed, Liala's own knowledge of English was sufficiently imperfect for me to get away with some outrageous remarks; there's no danger of going too far with a girl who'll give you the benefit of the doubt by deciding you couldn't possibly have meant what she thought you said. . . .

Need I say that I felt very, very happy? It looked as if my official and personal interests were neatly coinciding. There was, however, just one slight worry. So far, I had not seen Liala. What if she turned out to be absolutely hideous?

My first chance of settling that important question came six hours from planet-fall. Now I was near enough to pick up video transmissions, and it took Max only a few seconds to analyze the incoming signals and adjust the ship's receiver accordingly. At last I could have my first close-ups of the approaching planet—and of Liala.

She was almost as beautiful as her voice. I stared at the screen, unable to speak, for timeless seconds. Presently she broke the silence. "What's the matter?" she asked. "Haven't you ever seen a girl before?"

I had to admit that I'd seen two or even three, but never one like her. It was a great relief to find that her reaction to me was quite favorable, so it seemed that nothing stood in the way of our future happiness—if we could evade the army of scientists and politicians who would surround me as soon as I landed. Our hopes of privacy were very slender; so much so, in fact, that I felt tempted to break one of my most ironclad rules. I'd even consider *marrying* Liala if that was the only way we could arrange matters. (Yes, that two months in space had really put a strain on my system. . . .)

Five thousand years of history—ten thousand, if you count mine as well—can't be condensed easily into a few hours. But with such a delightful tutor, I absorbed knowledge fast, and everything I missed, Max got down in his infallible memory circuits.

Arcady, as their planet was charmingly called, had been at the very frontier of interstellar colonization; when the tide of empire had retreated, it had been left high and dry. In the struggle to survive, the Arcadians had lost much of their original scientific knowledge, including the secret of the Star Drive. They could not escape from their own solar system, but they had little incentive to do so. Arcady was a fertile world and the low gravity—only a quarter of Earth's—had given the colonists the physical strength they needed to make it live up to its name. Even allowing for any natural bias on Liala's part, it sounded a very attractive place.

Arcady's little yellow sun was already showing a visible disk when I had my brilliant idea. That reception committee had been worrying me, and I suddenly realized how I could keep it at bay. The plan would need Liala's co-operation, but by this time that was assured. If I may say so without sounding too immodest, I have always had a way with women, and this was not my first courtship by TV.

So the Arcadians learned, about two hours before I was due to land, that survey scouts were very shy and suspicious creatures. Owing to previous sad experiences with unfriendly cultures, I politely refused to walk like a fly into their parlor. As there was only one of me, I preferred to meet only one of them, in some isolated spot to be mutually selected. If that meeting went well, I would then fly to the capital city; if not—I'd head back the way I came. I hoped that they would not think this behavior discourteous, but I was a lonely traveler a long way from home, and as reasonable people, I was sure they'd see my point of view. . . .

They did. The choice of the emissary was obvious, and Liala promptly became a world heroine by bravely volunteering to meet the monster from space. She'd radio back, she told her anxious friends, within an hour of coming aboard my ship. I tried to make it two hours, but she said that might be overdoing it, and nasty-minded people might start to talk.

The ship was coming down through the Arcadian atmosphere when I suddenly remembered my compromising pin-ups, and had to make a rapid spring-cleaning. (Even so, one rather explicit masterpiece slipped down behind a chart rack and caused me acute embarrassment when it was discovered by the maintenance crew months later.) When I got back to the control room, the vision screen showed the empty, open plain at the very center of which Liala was waiting for me; in two minutes, I would hold her in my arms, be able to drink the fragrance of her hair, feel her body yield in all the right places—

I didn't bother to watch the landing, for I could rely on Max to do his usual flawless job. Instead, I hurried down to the air lock and waited with what patience I could muster for the opening of the doors that barred me from Liala.

It seemed an age before Max completed the routine air check and gave the "Outer Door Opening" signal. I was through the exit before the metal disk had finished moving, and stood at last on the rich soil of Arcady.

I remembered that I weighed only forty pounds here, so I moved with caution despite my eagerness. Yet I'd forgotten, living in my fool's paradise, what a fractional gravity could do to the human body in the course of two hundred generations. On a small planet, evolution can do a lot in five thousand years.

Liala was waiting for me, and she was as lovely as her picture. There was, however, one trifling matter that the TV screen hadn't told me.

I've never liked big girls, and I like them even less now. If I'd still wanted to, I suppose I could have embraced Liala. But I'd have looked like such a fool, standing there on tiptoe with my arms wrapped around her knees.

✶ THE STAR

It is three thousand light-years to the Vatican. Once, I believed that space could have no power over faith, just as I believed that the heavens declared the glory of God's handiwork. Now I have seen that handiwork, and my faith is sorely troubled. I stare at the crucifix that hangs on the cabin wall above the Mark VI Computer, and for the first time in my life I wonder if it is no more than an empty symbol.

I have told no one yet, but the truth cannot be concealed. The facts are there for all to read, recorded on the countless miles of magnetic tape and the thousands of photographs we are carrying back to Earth. Other scientists can interpret them as easily as I can, and I am not one who would condone that tampering with the truth which often gave my order a bad name in the olden days.

The crew are already sufficiently depressed: I wonder how they will take this ultimate irony. Few of them have any religious faith, yet they will not relish using this final weapon in their campaign against me—that private, good-natured, but fundamentally serious, war which lasted all the way from Earth. It amused them to have a Jesuit as chief astrophysicist: Dr. Chandler, for instance, could never get over it (why are medical men such notorious atheists?). Sometimes he would meet me on the observation deck, where the lights are always low so that the stars shine with undiminished glory. He would come up to me in the gloom and stand staring out of the great oval port, while the heavens crawled slowly around us as the ship turned end over end with the residual spin we had never bothered to correct.

"Well, Father," he would say at last, "it goes on forever and forever, and perhaps *Something* made it. But how you can believe that Something has a special interest in us and our miserable little world—that just beats me." Then the argument would start, while the stars and nebulae would swing around us in silent, endless arcs beyond the flawlessly clear plastic of the observation port.

It was, I think, the apparent incongruity of my position that caused most amusement to the crew. In vain I would point to my three papers in the *Astrophysical Journal,* my five in the *Monthly Notices of the Royal Astronomical Society.* I would remind them that my order has long been famous for its scientific works. We may be few now, but ever since the eighteenth century we have made contributions to astronomy and geophysics out of all proportion to our numbers. Will my report on the Phoenix Nebula end our thousand years of history? It will end, I fear, much more than that.

I do not know who gave the nebula its name, which seems to me a very bad one. If it contains a prophecy, it is one that cannot be verified for several billion years. Even the word nebula is misleading: this is a far smaller object than those stupendous clouds of mist—the stuff of unborn stars—that are scattered throughout the length of the Milky Way. On the cosmic scale, indeed, the Phoenix Nebula is a tiny thing—a tenuous shell of gas surrounding a single star.

Or what is left of a star . . .

The Rubens engraving of Loyola seems to mock me as it hangs there above the spectrophotometer tracings. What would *you,* Father, have made of this knowledge that has come into my keeping, so far from the little world that was all the universe you knew? Would your faith have risen to the challenge, as mine has failed to do?

You gaze into the distance, Father, but I have traveled a distance beyond any that you could have imagined when you founded our order a thousand years ago. No other survey ship has been so far from Earth: we are at the very frontiers of the explored universe. We set out to reach the Phoenix Nebula, we succeeded, and we are homeward bound with our burden of knowledge. I wish I could lift that burden from my shoulders, but I call to you in vain across the centuries and the light-years that lie between us.

On the book you are holding the words are plain to read. AD MAIOREM DEI GLORIAM, the message runs, but it is a message I can no longer believe. Would you still believe it, if you could see what we have found?

We knew, of course, what the Phoenix Nebula was. Every year, in our galaxy alone, more than a hundred stars explode, blazing for a few hours or days with thousands of times their normal brilliance before they sink back into death and obscurity. Such are the ordinary novae—the commonplace disasters of the universe. I have recorded the spectrograms and light curves of dozens since I started working at the Lunar Observatory.

But three or four times in every thousand years occurs something beside which even a nova pales into total insignificance.

When a star becomes a *supernova,* it may for a little while outshine all the massed suns of the galaxy. The Chinese astronomers watched this happen in A.D. 1054, not knowing what it was they saw. Five centuries later, in 1572, a supernova blazed in Cassiopeia so brilliantly that it was visible in the daylight sky. There have been three more in the thousand years that have passed since then.

Our mission was to visit the remnants of such a catastrophe, to reconstruct the events that led up to it, and, if possible, to learn its cause. We came slowly in through the concentric shells of gas that had been blasted out six thousand years before, yet were expanding still. They were immensely hot, radiating even now with a fierce violet light, but were far too tenuous to do us any damage. When the star had exploded, its outer layers had been driven upward with such speed that they had escaped completely from its gravitational field. Now they formed a hollow shell large enough to engulf a thousand solar systems, and at its center burned the tiny, fantastic object which the star had now become—a White Dwarf, smaller than the Earth, yet weighing a million times as much.

The glowing gas shells were all around us, banishing the normal night of interstellar space. We were flying into the center of a cosmic bomb that had detonated millennia ago and whose incandescent fragments were still hurtling apart. The immense scale of the explosion, and the fact that the debris already covered a volume of space many billions of miles across, robbed the scene of any visible movement. It would take decades before the unaided eye could detect any motion in these tortured wisps and eddies of gas, yet the sense of turbulent expansion was overwhelming.

We had checked our primary drive hours before, and were drifting slowly toward the fierce little star ahead. Once it had been a sun like our own, but it had squandered in a few hours the energy that should have kept it shining for a million years. Now it was a shrunken miser, hoarding its resources as if trying to make amends for its prodigal youth.

No one seriously expected to find planets. If there had been any before the explosion, they would have been boiled into puffs of vapor, and their substance lost in the greater wreckage of the star itself. But we made the automatic search, as we always do when approaching an unknown sun, and presently we found a single small world circling the star at an immense distance. It must have been the Pluto of this vanished solar system, orbiting on the frontiers of the night. Too far from the central sun ever to have known life, its remoteness had saved it from the fate of all its lost companions.

The passing fires had seared its rocks and burned away the mantle of frozen gas that must have covered it in the days before the disaster. We landed, and we found the Vault.

Its builders had made sure that we should. The monolithic marker that stood above the entrance was now a fused stump, but even the first long-range photographs told us that here was the work of intelligence. A little later we detected the continent-wide pattern of radioactivity that had been buried in the rock. Even if the pylon above the Vault had been destroyed, this would have remained, an immovable and all but eternal beacon calling to the stars. Our ship fell toward this gigantic bull's-eye like an arrow into its target.

The pylon must have been a mile high when it was built, but now it looked like a candle that had melted down into a puddle of wax. It took us a week to drill through the fused rock, since we did not have the proper tools for a task like this. We were astronomers, not archaeologists, but we could improvise. Our original purpose was forgotten: this lonely monument, reared with such labor at the greatest possible distance from the doomed sun, could have only one meaning. A civilization that knew it was about to die had made its last bid for immortality.

It will take us generations to examine all the treasures that were placed in the Vault. They had plenty of time to prepare, for their sun must have given its first warnings many years before the final detonation. Everything that they wished to preserve, all the fruit of their genius, they brought here to this distant world in the days before the end, hoping that some other race would find it and that they would not be utterly forgotten. Would we have done as well, or would we have been too lost in our own misery to give thought to a future we could never see or share?

If only they had had a little more time! They could travel freely enough between the planets of their own sun, but they had not yet learned to cross the interstellar gulfs, and the nearest solar system was a hundred light-years away. Yet even had they possessed the secret of the Transfinite Drive, no more than a few millions could have been saved. Perhaps it was better thus.

Even if they had not been so disturbingly human as their sculpture shows, we could not have helped admiring them and grieving for their fate. They left thousands of visual records and the machines for projecting them, together with elaborate pictorial instructions from which it will not be difficult to learn their written language. We have examined many of these records, and brought to life for the first time in six thousand years the warmth and beauty of a civilization that in many ways must have been superior to our own. Perhaps they only showed us the best, and one can hardly blame them. But their worlds were very lovely, and their cities were built with a grace that matches anything of man's. We have watched them at work and play, and listened to their musical speech sounding across the centuries. One scene is still before my eyes—a group of children on a beach of strange blue sand, playing in the waves as children play on Earth. Curious whiplike trees line the shore, and some very large animal is wading in the shallows yet attracting no attention at all.

And sinking into the sea, still warm and friendly and life-giving, is the sun that will soon turn traitor and obliterate all this innocent happiness.

Perhaps if we had not been so far from home and so vulnerable to loneliness, we should not have been so deeply moved. Many of us had seen the ruins of ancient civilizations on other worlds, but they had never affected us so profoundly. This tragedy was unique. It is one thing for a race to fail and die, as nations and cultures have done on Earth. But to be destroyed so completely in the full flower of its achievement, leaving no survivors—how could that be reconciled with the mercy of God?

My colleagues have asked me that, and I have given what answers I can. Perhaps you could have done better, Father Loyola, but I have found nothing in the *Exercitia Spiritualia* that helps me here. They were not an evil people: I do not know what gods they worshiped, if indeed they worshiped any. But I have looked back at them across the centuries, and have watched while the loveliness they used their last strength to preserve was brought forth again into the light of their shrunken sun. They could have taught us much: why were they destroyed?

I know the answers that my colleagues will give when they get back to Earth. They will say that the universe has no purpose and no plan, that since a hundred suns explode every year in our galaxy, at this very moment some race is dying in the depths of space. Whether that race has done good or evil during its lifetime will make no difference in the end: there is no divine justice, for there is no God.

Yet, of course, what we have seen proves nothing of the sort. Anyone who argues thus is being swayed by emotion, not logic. God has no need to justify His actions to man. He who built the universe can destroy it when He chooses. It is arrogance—it is perilously near blasphemy—for us to say what He may or may not do.

This I could have accepted, hard though it is to look upon whole worlds and peoples thrown into the furnace. But there comes a point when even the deepest faith must falter, and now, as I look at the calculations lying before me, I know I have reached that point at last.

We could not tell, before we reached the nebula, how long ago the explosion took place. Now, from the astronomical evidence and the record in the rocks of that one surviving planet, I have been able to date it very exactly. I know in what year the light of this colossal conflagration reached our Earth. I know how brilliantly the supernova whose corpse now dwindles behind our speeding ship once shone in terrestrial skies. I know how it must have blazed low in the east before sunrise, like a beacon in that oriental dawn.

There can be no reasonable doubt: the ancient mystery is solved at last. Yet, oh God, there were so many stars you could have used. What was the need to give these people to the fire, that the symbol of their passing might shine above Bethlehem?

✶ OUT OF THE SUN

If you have only lived on Earth, you have never seen the sun. Of course, we could not look at it directly, but only through dense filters that cut its rays down to endurable brilliance. It hung there forever above the low, jagged hills to the west of the Observatory, neither rising nor setting, yet moving around a small circle in the sky during the eighty-eight-day year of our little world. For it is not quite true to say that Mercury keeps the same face always turned toward the sun; it wobbles slightly on its axis, and there is a narrow twilight belt which knows such terrestrial commonplaces as dawn and sunset.

We were on the edge of the twilight zone, so that we could take advantage of the cool shadows yet could keep the sun under continuous surveillance as it hovered there above the hills. It was a full-time job for fifty astronomers and other assorted scientists; when we've kept it up for a hundred years or so, we may know something about the small star that brought life to Earth.

There wasn't a single band of solar radiation that someone at the Observatory had not made a life's study and was watching like a hawk. From the far X rays to the longest of radio waves, we had set our traps and snares; as soon as the sun thought of something new, we were ready for it. So we imagined. . . .

The sun's flaming heart beats in a slow, eleven-year rhythm, and we were near the peak of the cycle. Two of the greatest spots ever recorded—each of them large enough to swallow a hundred Earths—had drifted across the disk like great black funnels piercing deeply into the turbulent outer layers of the sun. They were black, of course, only by contrast with the brilliance all around them; even their dark, cool cores were hotter and brighter than an electric arc. We had just watched the second of them disappear around the edge of the disk, wondering if it would survive to reappear two weeks later, when something blew up on the equator.

It was not too spectacular at first, partly because it was almost exactly beneath us—at the precise center of the sun's disk—and so was merged into all the activity around it. If it had been near the edge of the sun, and thus projected against the background of space, it would have been truly awe-inspiring.

Imagine the simultaneous explosion of a million H-bombs. You can't? Nor can anyone else—but that was the sort of thing we were watching climb up toward us at hundreds of miles a second, straight out of the sun's spinning equator. At first it formed a narrow jet, but it was quickly frayed around the edges by the magnetic and gravitational forces that were fighting against it. The central core kept right on, and it was soon obvious that it had escaped from the sun completely and was headed out into space—with us as its first target.

Though this had happened half a dozen times before, it was always exciting. It meant that we could capture some of the very substance of the sun as it went hurtling past in a great cloud of electrified gas. There was no danger; by the time it reached us it would be far too tenuous to do any damage, and, indeed, it would take sensitive instruments to detect it at all.

One of those instruments was the Observatory's radar, which was in continual use to map the invisible ionized layers that surround the sun for millions of miles. This was my department; as soon as there was any hope of picking up the oncoming cloud against the solar background, I aimed my giant radio mirror toward it.

It came in sharp and clear on the long-range screen—a vast, luminous island still moving outward from the sun at hundreds of miles a second. At this distance it was impossible to see its finer details, for my radar waves were taking minutes to make the round trip and to bring me back the information they were presenting on the screen. Even at its speed of not far short of a million miles an hour, it would be almost two days before the escaping prominence reached the orbit of Mercury and swept past us toward the outer planets. But neither Venus nor Earth would record its passing, for they were nowhere near its line of flight.

The hours drifted by; the sun had settled down after the immense convulsion that had shot so many millions of tons of its substance into space, never to return. The aftermath of that eruption was now a slowly twisting and turning cloud a hundred times the size of Earth, and soon it would be close enough for the short-range radar to reveal its finer structure.

Despite all the years I have been in the business, it still gives me a thrill to watch that line of light paint its picture on the screen as it spins in synchronism with the narrow beam of radio waves from the transmitter. I sometimes think of myself as a blind man exploring the space around him with a stick that may be a hundred million miles in length. For man is truly blind to the things I study; these great clouds of ionized gas moving far out from the sun are completely invisible to the eye and even to the most sensitive of photographic plates. They are ghosts that briefly haunt the solar system during the few hours of their existence; if they did not reflect our radar waves or disturb our magnetometers, we should never know that they were there.

The picture on the screen looked not unlike a photograph of a spiral nebula, for as the cloud slowly rotated it trailed ragged arms of gas for ten thousand miles around it. Or it might have been a terrestrial hurricane that I was watching from above as it spun through the atmosphere of Earth. The internal structure was extremely complicated, and was changing minute by minute beneath the action of forces which we have never fully understood. Rivers of fire were flowing in curious paths under what could only be the influence of electric fields; but why were they appearing from nowhere and disappearing again as if matter was being created and destroyed? And what were those gleaming nodules, larger than the moon, that were being swept along like boulders before a flood?

Now it was less than a million miles away; it would be upon us in little more than an hour. The automatic cameras were recording every complete sweep of the radar scan, storing up evidence which was to keep us arguing for years. The magnetic disturbance riding ahead of the cloud had already reached us; indeed, there was hardly an instrument in the Observatory that was not reacting in some way to the onrushing apparition.

I switched to the short-range scanner, and the image of the cloud expanded so enormously that only its central portion was on the screen. At the same time I began to change frequency, tuning across the spectrum to differentiate among the various levels. The shorter the wave length, the farther you can penetrate into a layer of ionized gas; by this technique I hoped to get a kind of X-ray picture of the cloud's interior.

It seemed to change before my eyes as I sliced down through the tenuous outer envelope with its trailing arms, and approached the denser core. "Denser," of course, was a purely relative word; by terrestrial standards even its most closely packed regions were still a fairly good vacuum. I had almost reached the limit of my frequency band, and could shorten the wave length no farther, when I noticed the curious, tight little echo not far from the center of the screen.

It was oval, and much more sharp-edged than the knots of gas we had watched adrift in the cloud's fiery streams. Even in that first glimpse, I knew that here was something very strange and outside all previous records of solar phenomena. I watched it for a dozen scans of the radar beam, then called my assistant away from the radio-spectrograph, with which he was analyzing the velocities of the swirling gas as it spun toward us.

"Look, Don," I asked him, "have you ever seen anything like that?"

"No," he answered after a careful examination. "What holds it together? It hasn't changed its shape for the last two minutes."

"That's what puzzles me. Whatever it is, it should have started to break up by now, with all that disturbance going on around it. But it seems as stable as ever."

"How big would you say it is?"

I switched on the calibration grid and took a quick reading.

"It's about five hundred miles long, and half that in width."

"Is this the largest picture you can get?"

"I'm afraid so. We'll have to wait until it's closer before we can see what makes it tick."

Don gave a nervous little laugh.

"This is crazy," he said, "but do you know something? I feel as if I'm looking at an amoeba under a microscope."

I did not answer; for, with what I can only describe as a sensation of intellectual vertigo, exactly the same thought had entered my mind.

We forgot about the rest of the cloud, but luckily the automatic cameras kept up their work and no important observations were lost. From now on we had eyes only for that sharp-edged lens of gas that was growing minute by minute as it raced toward us. When it was no farther away than is the moon from Earth, it began to show the first signs of its internal structure, revealing a curious mottled appearance that was never quite the same on two successive sweeps of the scanner.

By now, half the Observatory staff had joined us in the radar room, yet there was complete silence as the oncoming enigma grew swiftly across the screen. It was coming straight toward us; in a few minutes it would hit Mercury somewhere in the center of the daylight side, and that would be the end of it—whatever it was. From the moment we obtained our first really detailed view until the screen became blank again could not have been more than five minutes; for every one of us, that five minutes will haunt us all our lives.

We were looking at what seemed to be a translucent oval, its interior laced with a network of almost invisible lines. Where the lines crossed there appeared to be tiny, pulsing nodes of light; we could never be quite sure of their existence because the radar took almost a minute to paint the complete picture on the screen—and beween each sweep the object moved several thousand miles. There was no doubt, however, that the network itself existed; the cameras settled any arguments about that.

So strong was the impression that we were looking at a solid object that I took a few moments off from the radar screen and hastily focused one of the optical telescopes on the sky. Of course, there was nothing to be seen—no sign of anything silhouetted against the sun's pock-marked disk. This was a case where vision failed completely and only the electrical senses of the radar were of any use. The thing that was coming toward us out of the sun was as transparent as air—and far more tenuous.

As those last moments ebbed away, I am quite sure that every one of us had reached the same conclusion—and was waiting for someone to say it first. What we were seeing was impossible, yet the evidence was there before our eyes. We were looking at life, where no life could exist. . . .

The eruption had hurled the thing out of its normal environment, deep down in the flaming atmosphere of the sun. It was a miracle that it had survived its journey through space; already it must be dying, as the forces that controlled its huge, invisible body lost their hold over the electrified gas which was the only substance it possessed.

Today, now that I have run through those films a hundred times, the idea no longer seems so strange to me. For what is life but organized energy? Does it matter *what* form that energy takes—whether it is chemical, as we know it on Earth, or purely electrical, as it seemed to be here? Only the pattern is important; the substance itself is of no significance. But at the time I did not think of this; I was conscious only of a vast and overwhelming wonder as I watched this creature of the sun live out the final moments of its existence.

Was it intelligent? Could it understand the strange doom that had befallen it? There are a thousand such questions that may never be answered. It is hard to see how a creature born in the fires of the sun itself could know anything of the external universe, or could even sense the existence of something as unutterably cold as rigid nongaseous matter. The living island that was falling upon us from space could never have conceived, however intelligent it might be, of the world it was so swiftly approaching.

Now it filled our sky—and perhaps, in those last few seconds, it knew that something strange was ahead of it. It may have sensed the far-flung magnetic field of Mercury, or felt the tug of our little world's gravitational pull. For it had begun to change; the luminous lines that must have been what passed for its nervous system were clumping together in new patterns, and I would have given much to know their meaning. It may be that I was looking into the brain of a mindless beast in its last convulsion of fear—or of a godlike being making its peace with the universe.

Then the radar screen was empty, wiped clean during a single scan of the beam. The creature had fallen below our horizon, and was hidden from us now by the curve of the planet. Far out in the burning dayside of Mercury, in the inferno where only a dozen men have ever ventured and fewer still come back alive, it smashed silently and invisibly against the seas of molten metal, the hills of slowly moving lava. The mere impact could have meant nothing to such an entity; what it could not endure was its first contact with the inconceivable cold of solid matter.

Yes, *cold*. It had descended upon the hottest spot in the solar system, where the temperature never falls below seven hundred degrees Fahrenheit and sometimes approaches a thousand. And that was far, far colder to it than the antarctic winter would be to a naked man.

We did not see it die, out there in the freezing fire; it was beyond the reach of our instruments now, and none of them recorded its end. Yet every one of us knew when that moment came, and that is why we are not interested when those who have seen only the films and tapes tell us that we were watching some purely natural phenomenon.

How can one explain what we felt, in that last moment when half our little world was enmeshed in the dissolving tendrils of that huge but immaterial brain? I can only say that it was a soundless cry of anguish, a death pang that seeped into our minds without passing through the gateways of the senses. Not one of us doubted then, or has ever doubted since, that he had witnessed the passing of a giant.

We may have been both the first and the last of all men to see so mighty a fall. Whatever *they* may be, in their unimaginable world within the sun, our paths and theirs may never cross again. It is hard to see how we can ever make contact with them, even if their intelligence matches ours.

And does it? It may be well for us if we never know the answer. Perhaps they have been living there inside the sun since the universe was born, and have climbed to peaks of wisdom that we shall never scale. The future may be theirs, not ours; already they may be talking across the light-years to their cousins in other stars.

One day they may discover us, by whatever strange senses they possess, as we circle around their mighty, ancient home, proud of our knowledge and thinking ourselves lords of creation. They may not like what they find, for to them we should be no more than maggots, crawling upon the skins of worlds too cold to cleanse themselves from the corruption of organic life.

And then, if they have the power, they will do what they consider necessary. The sun will put forth its strength and lick the faces of its children; and thereafter the planets will go their way once more as they were in the beginning—clean and bright . . . and sterile.

✶ *TRANSIENCE*

The forest, which came almost to the edge of the beach, climbed away into the distance up the flanks of the low, misty hills. Underfoot, the sand was coarse and mixed with myriads of broken shells. Here and there the retreating tide had left long streamers of weed trailed across the beach. The rain, which seldom ceased, had for the moment passed inland, but ever and again large, angry drops would beat tiny craters in the sand.

It was hot and sultry, for the war between sun and rain was never-ending. Sometimes the mists would lift for a while and the hills would stand out clearly above the land they guarded. These hills arced in a semicircle along the bay, following the line of the beach, and beyond them could sometimes be seen, at an immense distance, a wall of mountains lying beneath perpetual clouds. The trees grew everywhere, softening the contours of the land so that the hills blended smoothly into each other. Only in one place could the bare, uncovered rock be seen, where long ago some fault had weakened the foundations of the hills, so that for a mile or more the sky line fell sharply away, drooping down to the sea like a broken wing.

Moving with the cautious alertness of a wild animal, the child came through the stunted trees at the forest's edge. For a moment he hesitated; then, since there seemed to be no danger, walked slowly out onto the beach.

He was naked, heavily built, and had coarse black hair tangled over his shoulders. His face, brutish though it was, might almost have passed in human society, but the eyes would have betrayed him. They were not the eyes of an animal, for there was something in their depths that no animal had ever known. But it was no more than a promise. For this child, as for all his race, the light of reason had yet to dawn. Only a hairsbreadth still separated him from the beasts among whom he dwelt.

The tribe had not long since come into this land, and he was the first ever to set foot upon that lonely beach. What had lured him from the known dangers of the forest into the unknown and therefore more terrible dangers of this new element, he could not have told even had he possessed the power of speech. Slowly he walked out to the water's edge, always with backward glances at the forest behind him; and as he did so, for the first time in all history, the level sand bore upon its face the footprints it would one day know so well.

He had met water before, but it had always been bounded and confined by land. Now it stretched endlessly before him, and the sound of its laboring beat ceaselessly upon his ears.

With the timeless patience of the savage, he stood on the moist sand that the water had just relinquished, and as the tide line moved out he followed it slowly, pace by pace. When the waves reached toward his feet with a sudden access of energy, he would retreat a little way toward the land. But something held him here at the water's edge, while his shadow lengthened along the sands and the cold evening wind began to rise around him.

Perhaps into his mind had come something of the wonder of the sea, and a hint of all that it would one day mean to man. Though the first gods of his people still lay far in the future, he felt a dim sense of worship stir within him. He knew that he was now in the presence of something greater than all the powers and forces he had ever met.

The tide was turning. Far away in the forest, a wolf howled once and was suddenly silent. The noises of the night were rising around him, and it was time to go.

Under the low moon, the two lines of footprints interlaced across the sand. Swiftly the oncoming tide was smoothing them away. But they would return in their thousands and millions, in the centuries yet to be.

The child playing among the rock pools knew nothing of the forest that had once ruled all the land around him. It had left no trace of its existence. As ephemeral as the mists that had so often rolled down from the hills, it, too, had veiled them for a little while and now was gone. In its place had come a checkerboard of fields, the legacy of a thousand years of patient toil. And so the illusion of permanence remained, though everything had altered save the line of the hills against the sky. On the beach, the sand was finer now, and the land had lifted so that the old tide line was far beyond the reach of the questing waves.

Beyond the sea wall and the promenade, the little town was sleeping through the golden summer day. Here and there along the beach, people lay at rest, drowsy with heat and lulled by the murmur of the waves.

Out across the bay, white and gold against the water, a great ship was moving slowly to sea. The boy could hear, faint and far away, the beat of its screws and could still see the tiny figures moving upon its decks and superstructure. To the child—and not to him alone—it was a thing of wonder and beauty. He knew its name and the land to which it was steaming; but he did not know that the splendid ship was both the last and greatest of its kind. He scarcely noticed, almost lost against the glare of the sun, the thin white vapor trails that spelled the doom of the proud and lovely giant.

Soon the great liner was no more than a dark smudge on the horizon, and the boy turned again to his interrupted play, to the tireless building of his battlements of sand. In the west the sun was beginning its long decline, but the evening was still far away.

Yet it came at last, when the tide was returning to the land. At his mother's words, the child gathered up his playthings and, wearily contented, began to follow his parents back to the shore. He glanced once only at the sand castles he had built with such labor and would not see again. Without regret he left them to the advancing waves, for tomorrow he would return and the future stretched endlessly before him.

That tomorrow would not always come, either for himself or for the world, he was still too young to know.

And now even the hills had changed, worn away by the weight of years. Not all the change was the work of nature, for one night in the long-forgotten past something had come sliding down from the stars, and the little town had vanished in a spinning tower of flame. But that was so long ago that it was beyond sorrow or regret. Like the fall of fabled Troy or the overwhelming of Pompeii, it was part of the irremediable past and could rouse no pity now.

On the broken sky line lay a long metal building supporting a maze of mirrors that turned and glittered in the sun. No one from an earlier age could have guessed its purpose. It was as meaningless as an observatory or a radio station would have been to ancient man. But it was neither of these things.

Since noon, Bran had been playing among the shallow pools left by the retreating tide. He was quite alone, though the machine that guarded him was watching unobtrusively from the shore. Only a few days ago, there had been other children playing beside the blue waters of this lovely bay. Bran sometimes wondered where they had vanished, but he was a solitary child and did not greatly care. Lost in his own dreams, he was content to be left alone.

In the last few hours he had linked the tiny pools with an intricate network of waterways. His thoughts were very far from Earth, both in space and time. Around him now were the dull, red sands of another world. He was Cardenis, prince of engineers, fighting to save his people from the encroaching deserts. For Bran had looked upon the ravaged face of Mars; he knew the story of its long tragedy and the help from Earth that had come too late.

Out to the horizon the sea was empty, untroubled by ships, as it had been for ages. For a little while, near the beginning of time, man had fought his brief war against the oceans of the world. Now it seemed that only a moment lay between the coming of the first canoes and the passing of the last great Megatheria of the seas.

Bran did not even glance at the sky when the monstrous shadow swept along the beach. For days past, those silver giants had been rising over the hills in an unending stream, and now he gave them little thought. All his life he had watched the great ships climbing through the skies of Earth on their way to distant worlds. Often he had seen them return from those long journeys, dropping down through the clouds with cargoes beyond imagination.

He wondered sometimes why they came no more, those returning voyagers. All the ships he saw now were outward bound; never one drove down from the skies to berth at the great port beyond the hills. Why this should be, no one would tell him. He had learned not to speak of it now, having seen the sadness that his questions brought.

Across the sands the robot was calling to him softly. "Bran," came the words, echoing the tones of his mother's voice, "Bran—it's time to go."

The child looked up, his face full of indignant denial. He could not believe it. The sun was still high and the tide was far away. Yet along the shore his mother and father were already coming toward him.

They walked swiftly, as though the time were short. Now and again his father would glance for an instant at the sky, then turn his head quickly away as if he knew well that there was nothing he could hope to see. But a moment later he would look again.

Stubborn and angry, Bran stood at bay among his canals and lakes. His mother was strangely silent, but presently his father took him by the hand and said quietly, "You must come with us, Bran. It's time we went."

The child pointed sullenly at the beach. "But it's too early. I haven't finished."

His father's reply held no trace of anger, only a great sadness. "There are many things, Bran, that will not be finished now."

Still uncomprehending, the boy turned to his mother.

"Then can I come again tomorrow?"

With a sense of desolating wonder, Bran saw his mother's eyes fill with sudden tears. And he knew at last that never again would he play upon the sands by the azure waters; never again would he feel the tug of the tiny waves about his feet. He had found the sea too late, and now must leave it forever. Out of the future, chilling his soul, came the first faint intimation of the long ages of exile that lay ahead.

He never looked back as they walked silently together across the clinging sand. This moment would be with him all his life, but he was still too stunned to do more than walk blindly into a future he could not understand.

The three figures dwindled into the distance and were gone. A long while later, a silver cloud seemed to lift above the hills and move slowly out to sea. In a shallow arc, as though reluctant to leave its world, the last of the great ships climbed toward the horizon and shrank to nothingness over the edge of the Earth.

The tide was returning with the dying day. As though its makers still walked within its walls, the low metal building upon the hills had begun to blaze with light. Near the zenith, one star had not waited for the sun to set, but already burned with a fierce white glare against the darkling sky. Soon its companions, no longer in the scant thousands that man had once known, began to fill the heavens. The Earth was now near the center of the universe, and whole areas of the sky were an unbroken blaze of light.

But rising beyond the sea in two long curving arms, something black and monstrous eclipsed the stars and seemed to cast its shadow over all the world. The tentacles of the Dark Nebula were already brushing against the frontiers of the solar system. . . .

In the east, a great yellow moon was climbing through the waves. Though man had torn down its mountains and brought it air and water, its face was the one that had looked upon Earth since history began, and it was still the ruler of the tides. Across the sand the line of foam moved steadily onward, overwhelming the little canals and planing down the tangled footprints.

On the sky line, the lights in the strange metal building suddenly died, and the spinning mirrors ceased their moonlight glittering. From far inland came the blinding flash of a great explosion, then another, and another fainter yet.

Presently the ground trembled a little, but no sound disturbed the solitude of the deserted shore.

Under the level light of the sagging moon, beneath the myriad stars, the beach lay waiting for the end. It was alone now, as it had been at the beginning. Only the waves would move, and but for a little while, upon its golden sands.

For Man had come and gone.

✶ THE SONGS OF DISTANT EARTH

Beneath the palm trees Lora waited, watching the sea. Clyde's boat was already visible as a tiny notch on the far horizon—the only flaw in the perfect mating of sea and sky. Minute by minute it grew in size, until it had detached itself from the featureless blue globe that encompassed the world. Now she could see Clyde standing at the prow, one hand twined around the rigging, statue-still as his eyes sought her among the shadows.

"Where are you, Lora?" his voice asked plaintively from the radio bracelet he had given her when they became engaged. "Come and help me—we've got a big catch to bring home."

So! Lora told herself; *that's* why you asked me to hurry down to the beach. Just to punish Clyde and to reduce him to the right state of anxiety, she ignored his call until he had repeated it half a dozen times. Even then she did not press the beautiful golden pearl set in the "Transmit" button, but slowly emerged from the shade of the great trees and walked down the sloping beach.

Clyde looked at her reproachfully, but gave her a satisfactory kiss as soon as he had bounded ashore and secured the boat. Then they started unloading the catch together, scooping fish large and small from both hulls of the catamaran. Lora screwed up her nose but assisted gamely, until the waiting sand sled was piled high with the victims of Clyde's skill.

It was a good catch; when she married Clyde, Lora told herself proudly, she'd never starve. The clumsy, armored creatures of this young planet's sea were not true fish; it would be a hundred million years before nature invented scales here. But they were good enough eating, and the first colonists had labeled them with names they had brought, with so many other traditions, from unforgotten Earth.

"That's the lot!" grunted Clyde, tossing a fair imitation of a salmon onto the glistening heap. "I'll fix the nets later—let's go!"

Finding a foothold with some difficulty, Lora jumped onto the sled behind him. The flexible rollers spun for a moment against the sand, then got a grip. Clyde, Lora, and a hundred pounds of assorted fish started racing up the wave-scalloped beach. They had made half the brief journey when the simple, carefree world they had known all their young lives came suddenly to its end.

The sign of its passing was written there upon the sky, as if a giant hand had drawn a piece of chalk across the blue vault of heaven. Even as Clyde and Lora watched, the gleaming vapor trail began to fray at its edges, breaking up into wisps of cloud.

And now they could hear, falling down through the miles above their heads, a sound their world had not known for generations. Instinctively they grasped each other's hands, as they stared at that snow-white furrow across the sky and listened to the thin scream from the borders of space. The descending ship had already vanished beyond the horizon before they turned to each other and breathed, almost with reverence, the same magic word: "Earth!"

After three hundred years of silence, the mother world had reached out once more to touch Thalassa. . . .

Why? Lora asked herself, when the long moment of revelation had passed and the scream of torn air ceased to echo from the sky. What had happened, after all these years, to bring a ship from mighty Earth to this quiet and contented world? There was no room for more colonists here on this one island in a watery planet, and Earth knew that well enough. Its robot survey ships had mapped and probed Thalassa from space five centuries ago, in the early days of interstellar exploration. Long before man himself had ventured out into the gulfs between the stars, his electronic servants had gone ahead of him, circling the worlds of alien suns and heading homeward with their store of knowledge, as bees bring honey back to the parent hive.

Such a scout had found Thalassa, a freak among worlds with its single large island in a shoreless sea. One day continents would be born here, but this was a new planet, its history still waiting to be written.

The robot had taken a hundred years to make its homeward journey, and for a hundred more its garnered knowledge had slept in the electronic memories of the great computers which stored the wisdom of Earth. The first waves of colonization had not touched Thalassa; there were more profitable worlds to be developed—worlds that were not nine-tenths water. Yet at last the pioneers had come; only a dozen miles from where she was standing now, Lora's ancestors had first set foot upon this planet and claimed it for mankind.

They had leveled hills, planted crops, moved rivers, built towns and factories, and multiplied until they reached the natural limits of their land. With its fertile soil, abundant seas, and mild, wholly predictable weather, Thalassa was not a world that demanded much of its adopted children. The pioneering spirit had lasted perhaps two generations; thereafter the colonists were content to work as much as necessary (but no more), to dream nostalgically of Earth, and to let the future look after itself.

The village was seething with speculation when Clyde and Lora arrived. News had already come from the northern end of the island that the ship had spent its furious speed and was heading back at a low altitude, obviously looking for a place to land. "They'll still have the old maps," someone said. "Ten to one they'll ground where the first expedition landed, up in the hills."

It was a shrewd guess, and within minutes all available transport was moving out of the village, along the seldom-used road to the west. As befitted the mayor of so important a cultural center as Palm Bay (population: 572; occupations: fishing, hydroponics; industries: none), Lora's father led the way in his official car. The fact that its annual coat of paint was just about due was perhaps a little unfortunate; one could only hope that the visitors would overlook the occasional patches of bare metal. After all, the car itself was quite new; Lora could distinctly remember the excitement its arrival had caused, only thirteen years ago.

The little caravan of assorted cars, trucks, and even a couple of straining sand sleds rolled over the crest of the hill and ground to a halt beside the weathered sign with its simple but impressive words:

LANDING SITE OF THE FIRST EXPEDITION TO THALASSA
1 JANUARY, YEAR ZERO
(28 May A.D. 2626)

The *first* expedition, Lora repeated silently. There had never been a second one—*but here it was. . . .*

The ship came in so low, and so silently, that it was almost upon them before they were aware of it. There was no sound of engines—only a brief rustling of leaves as the displaced air stirred among the trees. Then all was still once more, but it seemed to Lora that the shining ovoid resting on the turf was a great silver egg, waiting to hatch and to bring something new and strange into the peaceful world of Thalassa.

"It's so small," someone whispered behind her. "They couldn't have come from Earth in *that* thing!"

"Of course not," the inevitable self-appointed expert replied at once. "That's only a lifeboat—the real ship's up there in space. Don't you remember that the first expedition—"

"Sshh!" someone else remonstrated. "They're coming out!"

It happened in the space of a single heartbeat. One second the seamless hull was so smooth and unbroken that the eye looked in vain for any sign of an opening. And then, an instant later, there was an oval doorway with a short ramp leading to the ground. Nothing had moved, but something had *happened.* How it had been done, Lora could not imagine, but she accepted the miracle without surprise. Such things were only to be expected of a ship that came from Earth.

There were figures moving inside the shadowed entrance; not a sound came from the waiting crowd as the visitors slowly emerged and stood blinking in the fierce light of an unfamiliar sun. There were seven of them—all men—and they did not look in the least like the super-beings she had expected. It was true that they were all somewhat above the average in height and had thin, clear-cut features, but they were so pale that their skins were almost white. They seemed, moreover, worried and uncertain, which was something that puzzled Lora very much. For the first time it occurred to her that this landing on Thalassa might be unintentional, and that the visitors were as surprised to be here as the islanders were to greet them.

The mayor of Palm Bay, confronted with the supreme moment of his career, stepped forward to deliver the speech on which he had been frantically working ever since the car left the village. A second before he opened his mouth, a sudden doubt struck him and sponged his memory clean. Everyone had automatically assumed that this ship came from Earth—but that was pure guesswork. It might just as easily have been sent here from one of the other colonies, of which there were at least a dozen much closer than the parent world. In his panic over protocol, all that Lora's father could manage was: "We welcome you to Thalassa. You're from Earth—I presume?" That "I presume?" was to make Mayor Fordyce immortal; it would be a century before anyone discovered that the phrase was not quite original.

In all that waiting crowd, Lora was the only one who never heard the confirming answer, spoken in English that seemed to have speeded up a trifle during the centuries of separation. For in that moment, she saw Leon for the first time.

He came out of the ship, moving as unobtrusively as possible to join his companions at the foot of the ramp. Perhaps he had remained behind to make some adjustment to the controls; perhaps—and this seemed more likely—he had been reporting the progress of the meeting to the great mother ship, which must be hanging up there in space, far beyond the uttermost fringes of the atmosphere. Whatever the reason, from then onward Lora had eyes for no one else.

Even in that first instant, she knew that her life could never again be the same. This was something new and beyond all her experience, filling her at the same moment with wonder and fear. Her fear was for the love she felt for Clyde; her wonder for the new and unknown thing that had come into her life.

Leon was not as tall as his companions, but was much more stockily built, giving an impression of power and competence. His eyes, very dark and full of animation, were deep-set in rough-hewn features which no one could have called handsome, yet which Lora found disturbingly attractive. Here was a man who had looked upon sights she could not imagine—a man who, perhaps, had walked the streets of Earth and seen its fabled cities. What was he doing here on lonely Thalassa, and why were those lines of strain and worry about his ceaselessly searching eyes?

He had looked at her once already, but his gaze had swept on without faltering. Now it came back, as if prompted by memory, and for the first time he became conscious of Lora, as all along she had been aware of him. Their eyes locked, bridging gulfs of time and space and experience. The anxious furrows faded from Leon's brow, the tense lines slowly relaxed; and presently he smiled.

It was dusk when the speeches, the banquets, the receptions, the interviews were over. Leon was very tired, but his mind was far too active to allow him to sleep. After the strain of the last few weeks, when he had awakened to the shrill clamor of alarms and fought with his colleagues to save the wounded ship, it was hard to realize that they had reached safety at last. What incredible good fortune that this inhabited planet had been so close! Even if they could not repair the ship and complete the two centuries of flight that still lay before them, here at least they could remain among friends. No ship-wrecked mariners, of sea or space, could hope for more than that.

The night was cool and calm, and ablaze with unfamiliar stars. Yet there were still some old friends, even though the ancient patterns of the constellations were hopelessly lost. There was mighty Rigel, no fainter for all the added light-years that its rays must now cross before they reached his eyes. And that must be giant Canopus, almost in line with their destination, but so much more remote that even when they reached their new home, it would seem no brighter than in the skies of Earth.

Leon shook his head, as if to clear the stupefying, hypnotic image of immensity from his mind. Forget the stars, he told himself; you will face them again soon enough. Cling to this little world while you are upon it, even though it may be a grain of dust on the road between the Earth you will never see again and the goal that waits for you at journey's end, two hundred years from now.

His friends were already sleeping, tired and content, as they had a right to be. Soon he would join them—when his restless spirit would allow him to. But first he would see something of this world to which chance had brought him, this oasis peopled by his own kinsmen in the deserts of space.

He left the long, single-storied guesthouse that had been prepared for them in such obvious haste, and walked out into the single street of Palm Bay. There was no one about, though sleepy music came from a few houses. It seemed that the villagers believed in going to bed early—or perhaps they, too, were exhausted by the excitement and hospitality of the day. That suited Leon, who wanted only to be left alone until his racing thoughts had slowed to rest.

Out of the quiet night around him he became aware of the murmuring sea, and the sound drew his footsteps away from the empty street. It was dark among the palms, when the lights of the village had faded behind him, but the smaller of Thalassa's two moons was high in the south and its curious yellow glow gave him all the guidance he required. Presently he was through the narrow belt of trees, and there at the end of the steeply shelving beach lay the ocean that covered almost all of this world.

A line of fishing boats was drawn up at the water's edge, and Leon walked slowly toward them, curious to see how the craftsmen of Thalassa had solved one of man's oldest problems. He looked approvingly at the trim plastic hulls, the narrow outrigger float, the power-operated winch for raising the nets, the compact little motor, the radio with its direction-finding loop. This almost primitive, yet completely adequate, simplicity had a profound appeal to him; it was hard to think of a greater contrast with the labyrinthine complexities of the mighty ship hanging up there above his head. For a moment he amused himself with fantasy; how pleasant to jettison all his years of training and study, and to exchange the life of a starship propulsion engineer for the peaceful, undemanding existence of a fisherman! They must need someone to keep their boats in order, and perhaps he could think of a few improvements. . . .

He shrugged away the rosy dream, without bothering to marshal all its obvious fallacies, and began to walk along the shifting line of foam where the waves had spent their last strength against the land. Underfoot was the debris of this young ocean's newborn life—empty shells and carapaces that might have littered the coasts of Earth a billion years ago. Here, for instance, was a tightly wound spiral of limestone which he had surely seen before in some museum. It might well be; any design that had once served her purpose, Nature repeated endlessly on world after world.

A faint yellow glow was spreading swiftly across the eastern sky; even as Leon watched, Selene, the inner moon, edged itself above the horizon. With astonishing speed, the entire gibbous disk climbed out of the sea, flooding the beach with sudden light.

And in that burst of brilliance, Leon saw that he was not alone.

The girl was sitting on one of the boats, about fifty yards farther along the beach. Her back was turned toward him and she was staring out to sea, apparently unaware of his presence. Leon hesitated, not wishing to invade her solitude, and also being uncertain of the local mores in these matters. It seemed highly likely, at such a time and place, that she was waiting for someone; it might be safest, and most tactful, to turn quietly back to the village.

He had decided too late. As if startled by the flood of new light along the beach, the girl looked up and at once caught sight of him. She rose to her feet with an unhurried grace, showing no signs of alarm or annoyance. Indeed, if Leon could have seen her face clearly in the moonlight, he would have been surprised at the quiet satisfaction it expressed.

Only twelve hours ago, Lora would have been indignant had anyone suggested that she would meet a complete stranger here on this lonely beach when the rest of her world was slumbering. Even now, she might have tried to rationalize her behavior, to argue that she felt restless and could not sleep, and had therefore decided to go for a walk. But she knew in her heart that this was not the truth; all day long she had been haunted by the image of that young engineer, whose name and position she had managed to discover without, she hoped, arousing too much curiosity among her friends.

It was not even luck that she had seen him leave the guesthouse; she had been watching most of the evening from the porch of her father's residence, on the other side of the street. And it was certainly not luck, but deliberate and careful planning, that had taken her to this point on the beach as soon as she was sure of the direction Leon was heading.

He came to a halt a dozen feet away. (Did he recognize her? Did he guess that this was no accident? For a moment her courage almost failed her, but it was too late now to retreat.) Then he gave a curious, twisted smile that seemed to light up his whole face and made him look even younger than he was.

"Hello," he said. "I never expected to meet anyone at this time of night. I hope I haven't disturbed you."

"Of course not," Lora answered, trying to keep her voice as steady and emotionless as she could.

"I'm from the ship, you know. I thought I'd have a look at Thalassa while I'm here."

At those last words, a sudden change of expression crossed Lora's face; the sadness he saw there puzzled Leon, for it could have no cause. And then, with an instantaneous shock of recognition, he knew that he had seen this girl before, and understood what she was doing here. This was the girl who had smiled at him when he came out of the ship—no, that was not right; *he* had been the one who smiled. . . .

There seemed nothing to say. They stared at each other across the wrinkled sand, each wondering at the miracle that had brought them together out of the immensity of time and space. Then, as if in unconscious agreement, they sat facing each other on the gunwale of the boat, still without a word.

This is folly, Leon told himself. What am I doing here? What right have I, a wanderer passing through this world, to touch the lives of its people? I should make my apologies and leave this girl to the beach and the sea that are her birthright, not mine.

Yet he did not leave. The bright disk of Selene had risen a full hand's breadth above the sea when he said at last: "What's your name?"

"I'm Lora," she answered, in the soft, lilting accent of the islanders, which was so attractive, but not always easy to understand.

"And I'm Leon Carrell, Assistant Propulsion Engineer, Starship *Magellan*."

She gave a little smile as he introduced himself, and at that moment Leon was certain that she already knew his name. At the same time a completely irrelevant and whimsical thought struck him; until a few minutes ago he had been dead-tired, just about to turn back for his overdue sleep. Yet now he was fully awake and alert—poised, as it were, on the brink of a new and unpredictable adventure.

But Lora's next remark was predictable enough: "How do you like Thalassa?"

"Give me time," Leon countered. "I've only seen Palm Bay, and not much of that."

"Will you be here—very long?"

The pause was barely perceptible, but his ear detected it. *This* was the question that really mattered.

"I'm not sure," he replied, truthfully enough. "It depends on how long the repairs take."

"What went wrong?"

"Oh, we ran into something too big for our meteor screen to absorb. And—bang!—that was the end of the screen. So we've got to make a new one."

"And you think you can do that here?"

"We hope so. The main problem will be lifting about a million tons of water up to the *Magellan*. Luckily, I think Thalassa can spare it."

"Water? I don't understand."

"Well, you know that a starship travels at almost the speed of light; even then it takes years to get anywhere, so that we have to go into suspended animation and let the automatic controls run the ship."

Lora nodded. "Of course—that's how our ancestors got here."

"Well, the speed would be no problem if space was really empty—but it isn't. A starship sweeps up thousands of atoms of hydrogen, particles of dust, and sometimes larger fragments, every second of its flight. At nearly the speed of light, these bits of cosmic junk have enormous energy, and could soon burn up the ship. So we carry a shield about a mile ahead of us, and let *that* get burned up instead. Do you have umbrellas on this world?"

"Why—yes," Lora replied, obviously baffled by the incongruous question.

"Then you can compare a starship to a man moving head down through a rainstorm behind the cover of an umbrella. The rain is the cosmic dust between the stars, and our ship was unlucky enough to lose its umbrella."

"And you can make a new one of *water?*"

"Yes; it's the cheapest building material in the universe. We freeze it into an iceberg which travels ahead of us. What could be simpler than that?"

Lora did not answer; her thoughts seemed to have veered onto a new track. Presently she said, her voice so low and wistful that Leon had to bend forward to hear it against the rolling of the surf: "And you left Earth a hundred years ago."

"A hundred and four. Of course, it seems only a few weeks, since we were deep-sleeping until the autopilot revived us. All the colonists are still in suspended animation; they don't know that anything's happened."

"And presently you'll join them again, and sleep your way on to the stars."

Leon nodded, avoiding her eye. "That's right. Planet-fall will be a few months late, but what does that matter on a trip that takes three hundred years?"

Lora pointed to the island behind them, and then to the shoreless sea at whose edge they stood.

"It's strange to think that your sleeping friends up there will never know anything of all this. I feel sorry for them."

"Yes, only we fifty or so engineers will have any memories of Thalassa. To everyone else in the ship, our stop here will be nothing more than a hundred-year-old entry in the logbook."

He glanced at Lora's face, and saw again that sadness in her eyes.

"Why does that make you unhappy?"

She shook her head, unable to answer. How could one express the sense of loneliness that Leon's words had brought to her? The lives of men, and all their hopes and fears, were so little against the inconceivable immensities that they had dared to challenge. The thought of that three-hundred-year journey, not yet half completed, was something from which her mind recoiled in horror. And yet—in her own veins was the blood of those earlier pioneers who had followed the same path to Thalassa, centuries ago.

The night was no longer friendly; she felt a sudden longing for her home and family, for the little room that held everything she owned and that was all the world she knew or wanted. The cold of space was freezing her heart; she wished now that she had never come on this mad adventure. It was time—more than time—to leave.

As she rose to her feet, she noticed that they had been sitting on Clyde's boat, and wondered what unconscious prompting of her mind had brought her here to this one vessel out of all the little fleet lined up along the beach. At the thought of Clyde, a spasm of uncertainty, even of guilt, swept over her. Never in her life, except for the most fleeting moments, had she thought of any other man but him. Now she could no longer pretend that this was true.

"What's the matter?" asked Leon. "Are you cold?" He held out his hand to her, and for the first time their fingers touched as she automatically responded. But at the instant of contact, she shied like a startled animal and jerked away.

"I'm all right," she answered, almost angrily. "It's late—I must go home. Good-by."

Her reaction was so abrupt that it took Leon by surprise. Had he said anything to offend her? he wondered. She was already walking quickly away when he called after her: "Will I see you again?"

If she answered, the sound of the waves carried away her voice. He watched her go, puzzled and a little hurt, while not for the first time in his life he reflected how hard it was to understand the mind of a woman.

For a moment he thought of following her and repeating the question, but in his heart he knew there was no need. As surely as the sun would rise tomorrow, they would meet again.

And now the life of the island was dominated by the crippled giant a thousand miles out in space. Before dawn and after sunset, when the world was in darkness but the light of the sun still streamed overhead, the *Magellan* was visible as a brilliant star, the brightest object in all the sky except the two moons themselves. But even when it could not be seen—when it was lost in the glare of day or eclipsed by the shadow of Thalassa—it was never far from men's thoughts.

It was hard to believe that only fifty of the starship's crew had been awakened, and that not even half of those were on Thalassa at any one time. They seemed to be everywhere, usually in little groups of two or three, walking swiftly on mysterious errands or riding small anti-gravity scooters which floated a few feet from the ground and moved so silently that they made life in the village rather hazardous. Despite the most pressing invitations, the visitors had still taken no part in the cultural and social activities of the island. They had explained, politely but firmly, that until the safety of their ship was secured, they would have no time for any other interests. Later, certainly, but not now . . .

So Thalassa had to wait with what patience it could muster while the Earthmen set up their instruments, made their surveys, drilled deep into the rocks of the island, and carried out scores of experiments which seemed to have no possible connection with their problem. Sometimes they consulted briefly with Thalassa's own scientists, but on the whole they kept to themselves. It was not that they were unfriendly or aloof; they were working with such a fierce and dedicated intensity that they were scarcely aware of anyone around them.

After their first meeting, it was two days before Lora spoke to Leon again. She saw him from time to time as he hurried about the village, usually with a bulging brief case and an abstracted expression, but they were able to exchange only the briefest of smiles. Yet even this was enough to keep her emotions in turmoil, to banish her peace of mind, and to poison her relationship with Clyde.

As long as she could remember, he had been part of her life; they had had their quarrels and disagreements, but no one else had ever challenged his place in her heart. In a few months they would be married —yet now she was not even sure of that, or indeed of anything.

"Infatuation" was an ugly word, which one applied only to other people. But how else could she explain this yearning to be with a man who had come suddenly into her life from nowhere, and who must leave again in a few days or weeks? No doubt the glamour and romance of his origin was partly responsible, but that alone was not enough to account for it. There were other Earthmen better looking than Leon, yet she had eyes for him alone, and her life now was empty unless she was in his presence.

By the end of the first day, only her family knew about her feelings; by the end of the second, everyone she passed gave her a knowing smile. It was impossible to keep a secret in such a tight and talkative community as Palm Bay, and she knew better than to attempt it.

Her second meeting with Leon was accidental—as far as such things can ever be accidents. She was helping her father deal with some of the correspondence and inquiries that had flooded upon the village since the Earthmen's arrival, and was trying to make some sense out of her notes when the door of the office opened. It had opened so often in the last few days that she had ceased to look up; her younger sister was acting as receptionist and dealt with all the visitors. Then she heard Leon's voice; and the paper blurred before her eyes, the notes might have been in an unknown language.

"Can I see the mayor, please?"

"Of course, Mr.—?"

"Assistant Engineer Carrell."

"I'll go and fetch him. Won't you sit down?"

Leon slumped wearily on the ancient armchair that was the best the reception room could offer its infrequent visitors, and not until then did he notice that Lora was watching him silently from the other side of the room. At once he sloughed off his tiredness and shot to his feet.

"Hello—I didn't know you worked here."

"I live here; my father's the mayor."

This portentous news did not seem to impress Leon unduly. He walked over to the desk and picked up the fat volume through which Lora had been browsing between her secretarial duties.

"A Concise History of Earth," he read, *"from the Dawn of Civiliza-*

tion to the Beginning of Interstellar Flight. And all in a thousand pages! It's a pity it ends three hundred years ago."

"We hope that you'll soon bring us up to date. Has much happened since that was written?"

"Enough to fill about fifty libraries, I suppose. But before we go we'll leave you copies of all our records, so that your history books will only be a hundred years out of date."

They were circling around each other, avoiding the only thing that was important. When can we meet again? Lora's thoughts kept hammering silently, unable to break through the barrier of speech. And does he really like me or is he merely making polite conversation?

The inner door opened, and the mayor emerged apologetically from his office.

"Sorry to keep you waiting, Mr. Carrell, but the president was on the line—he's coming over this afternoon. And what can I do for you?"

Lora pretended to work, but she typed the same sentence eight times while Leon delivered his message from the captain of the *Magellan.* She was not a great deal wiser when he had finished; it seemed that the starship's engineers wished to build some equipment on a headland a mile from the village, and wanted to make sure there would be no objection.

"Of course!" said Mayor Fordyce expansively, in his nothing's-too-good-for-our-guests tone of voice. "Go right ahead—the land doesn't belong to anybody, and no one lives there. What do you want to do with it?"

"We're building a gravity inverter, and the generator has to be anchored in solid bedrock. It may be a little noisy when it starts to run, but I don't think it will disturb you here in the village. And of course we'll dismantle the equipment when we've finished."

Lora had to admire her father. She knew perfectly well that Leon's request was as meaningless to him as it was to her, but one would never have guessed it.

"That's perfectly all right—glad to be of any help we can. And will you tell Captain Gold that the president's coming at five this afternoon? I'll send my car to collect him; the reception's at five-thirty in the village hall."

When Leon had given his thanks and departed, Mayor Fordyce walked over to his daughter and picked up the slim pile of correspondence she had none-too-accurately typed.

"He seems a pleasant young man," he said, "but is it a good idea to get too fond of him?"

"I don't know what you mean."

"Now, Lora! After all, I *am* your father, and I'm not *completely* unobservant."

"He's not"—sniff—"a bit interested in me."

"Are you interested in him?"

"I don't know. Oh, Daddy, I'm so unhappy!"

Mayor Fordyce was not a brave man, so there was only one thing he could do. He donated his handkerchief, and fled back into his office.

It was the most difficult problem that Clyde had ever faced in his life, and there were no precedents that gave any help at all. Lora belonged to him—everyone knew that. If his rival had been another villager, or someone from any other part of Thalassa, he knew exactly what he would have done. But the laws of hospitality, and, above all, his natural awe for anything of Earth, prevented him from politely asking Leon to take his attentions elsewhere. It would not be the first time *that* had happened, and there had never been the slightest trouble on those earlier occasions. That could have been because Clyde was over six feet tall, proportionally broad, and had no excess fat on his one-hundred-and-ninety-pound frame.

During the long hours at sea, when he had nothing else to do but to brood, Clyde toyed with the idea of a short, sharp bout with Leon. It would be very short; though Leon was not as skinny as most of the Earthmen, he shared their pale, washed-out look and was obviously no match for anyone who led a life of physical activity. That was the trouble —it wouldn't be fair. Clyde knew that public opinion would be outraged if he had a fight with Leon, however justified he might be.

And how justified was he? That was the big problem that worried Clyde, as it had worried a good many billion men before him. It seemed that Leon was now practically one of the family; every time he called at the mayor's house, the Earthman seemed to be there on some pretext or other. Jealousy was an emotion that had never afflicted Clyde before, and he did not enjoy the symptoms.

He was still furious about the dance. It had been the biggest social event for years; indeed, it was not likely that Palm Bay would ever match it again in the whole of its history. To have the president of Thalassa, half the council, and fifty visitors from Earth in the village at the same moment was not something that could happen again this side of eternity.

For all his size and strength, Clyde was a good dancer—especially with Lora. But that night he had had little chance of proving it; Leon had been too busy demonstrating the latest steps from Earth (latest, that is, if you overlooked the fact that they must have passed out of fashion a hundred years ago—unless they had come back and were now the latest thing). In Clyde's opinion Leon's technique was very poor and the dances were ugly; the interest that Lora showed in them was perfectly ridiculous.

He had been foolish enough to tell her so when his opportunity came; and that had been the last dance he had had with Lora that evening. From then onward, he might not have been there, as far as she was concerned. Clyde had endured the boycott as long as he could, then had left for the bar with one objective in mind. He had quickly attained it, and not until he had come reluctantly to his senses the next morning did he discover what he had missed.

The dancing had ended early; there had been a short speech from the president—his third that evening—introducing the commander of the starship and promising a little surprise. Captain Gold had been equally brief; he was obviously a man more accustomed to orders than orations.

"Friends," he began, "you know why we're here, and I've no need to say how much we appreciate your hospitality and kindness. We shall never forget you, and we're only sorry that we have had so little time to see more of your beautiful island and its people. I hope you will forgive us for any seeming discourtesy, but the repair of our ship, and the safety of our companions, has had to take priority in our minds.

"In the long run, the accident that brought us here may be fortunate for us both. It has given us happy memories, and also inspiration. What we have seen here is a lesson to us. May we make the world that is waiting at the end of our journey as fair a home for mankind as you have made Thalassa.

"And before we resume our voyage, it is both a duty and a pleasure to leave with you all the records we can that will bridge the gap since you last had contact with Earth. Tomorrow we shall invite your scientists and historians up to our ship so that they can copy any of our information tapes they desire. Thus we hope to leave you a legacy which will enrich your world for generations to come. That is the very least we can do.

"But tonight, science and history can wait, for we have other treasures aboard. Earth has not been idle in the centuries since your forefathers left. Listen, now, to some of the heritage we share together, and which we will leave upon Thalassa before we go our way."

The lights had dimmed; the music had begun. No one who was present would ever forget that moment; in a trance of wonder, Lora had listened to what men had wrought in sound during the centuries of separation. Time had meant nothing; she had not even been conscious of Leon standing by her side, holding her hand, as the music ebbed and flowed around them.

These were the things that she had never known, the things that belonged to Earth, and to Earth alone. The slow beat of mighty bells, climbing like invisible smoke from old cathedral spires; the chant of patient boatmen, in a thousand tongues now lost forever, rowing home against the tide in the last light of day; the songs of armies marching into battles that time had robbed of all their pain and evil; the merged murmur of ten million voices as man's greatest cities woke to meet the dawn; the cold dance of the Aurora over endless seas of ice; the roar of mighty engines climbing upward on the highway to the stars. All these she had heard in the music and the songs that had come out of the night—the songs of distant Earth, carried to her across the light-years. . . .

A clear soprano voice, swooping and soaring like a bird at the very edge of hearing, sang a wordless lament that tore at the heart. It was a dirge for all loves lost in the loneliness of space, for friends and homes that could never again be seen and must fade at last from memory. It was a song for all exiles, and it spoke as clearly to those who were sundered from Earth by a dozen generations as to the voyagers to whom its fields and cities still seemed only weeks away.

The music had died into the darkness; misty-eyed, avoiding words, the people of Thalassa had gone slowly to their homes. But Lora had not gone to hers; against the loneliness that had pierced her very soul, there was only one defense. And presently she had found it, in the warm night of the forest, as Leon's arms tightened around her and their souls and bodies merged. Like wayfarers lost in a hostile wilderness, they had sought warmth and comfort beside the fire of love. While that fire burned, they were safe from the shadows that prowled in the night; and all the universe of stars and planets shrank to a toy that they could hold within their hands.

To Leon, it was never wholly real. Despite all the urgency and peril that had brought them here, he sometimes fancied that at journey's end it would be hard to convince himself that Thalassa was not a dream that had come in his long sleep. This fierce and foredoomed love, for example; he had not asked for it—it had been thrust upon him. Yet there were few men, he told himself, who would not have taken it, had they, too, landed, after weeks of grinding anxiety, on this peaceful, pleasant world.

When he could escape from work, he took long walks with Lora in the fields far from the village, where men seldom came and only the robot cultivators disturbed the solitude. For hours Lora would question him about Earth—but she would never speak of the planet that was the *Magellan's* goal. He understood her reasons well enough, and did his best to satisfy her endless curiosity about the world that was already "home" to more men than had ever seen it with their own eyes.

She was bitterly disappointed to hear that the age of cities had passed. Despite all that Leon could tell her about the completely decentralized culture that now covered the planet from pole to pole, she still thought of Earth in terms of such vanished giants as Chandrigar, London, Astrograd, New York, and it was hard for her to realize that they had gone forever, and with them the way of life they represented.

"When we left Earth," Leon explained, "the largest centers of population were university towns like Oxford or Ann Arbor or Canberra; some of them had fifty thousand students and professors. There are no other cities left of even half that size."

"But what happened to them?"

"Oh, there was no single cause, but the development of communications started it. As soon as anyone on Earth could see and talk to anyone else by pressing a button, most of the need for cities vanished. Then anti-gravity was invented, and you could move goods or houses or anything else through the sky without bothering about geography. *That* completed the job of wiping out distance, which the airplane had begun a couple of centuries earlier. After that, men started to live where they liked, and the cities dwindled away."

For a moment Lora did not answer; she was lying on a bank of grass, watching the behavior of a bee whose ancestors, like hers, had been citizens of Earth. It was trying vainly to extract nectar from one of Thalassa's native flowers; insect life had not yet arisen on this world, and the few indigenous flowers had not yet invented lures for air-borne visitors.

The frustrated bee gave up the hopeless task and buzzed angrily away; Lora hoped that it would have enough sense to head back to the orchards, where it would find more co-operative flowers. When she spoke again, it was to voice a dream that had now haunted mankind for almost a thousand years.

"Do you suppose," she said wistfully, "that we'll ever break through the speed of light?"

Leon smiled, knowing where her thoughts were leading. To travel faster than light—to go home to Earth, yet to return to your native world while your friends were still alive—every colonist must, at some time or other, have dreamed of this. There was no problem, in the whole history of the human race, that had called forth so much effort and that still remained so utterly intractable.

"I don't believe so," he said. "If it could be done, someone would have discovered how by this time. No—we have to do it the slow way, because there isn't any other. That's how the universe is built, and there's nothing we can do about it."

"But surely we could still keep in touch!"

Leon nodded. "That's true," he said, "and we try to. I don't know what's gone wrong, but you should have heard from Earth long before now. We've been sending out robot message carriers to all the colonies, carrying a full history of everything that's happened up to the time of departure, and asking for a report back. As the news returns to Earth, it's all transcribed and sent out again by the next messenger. So we have a kind of interstellar news service, with the Earth as the central clearing-house. It's slow, of course, but there's no other way of doing it. If the last messenger to Thalassa has been lost, there must be another on the way—maybe several, twenty or thirty years apart."

Lora tried to envisage the vast, star-spanning network of message carriers, shuttling back and forth between Earth and its scattered children, and wondered why Thalassa had been overlooked. But with Leon beside her, it did not seem important. He was here; Earth and the stars were very far away. And so also, with whatever unhappiness it might bring, was tomorrow. . . .

By the end of the week, the visitors had built a squat and heavily braced pyramid of metal girders, housing some obscure mechanism, on a rocky headland overlooking the sea. Lora, in common with the 571 other inhabitants of Palm Bay and the several thousand sight-seers who had descended upon the village, was watching when the first test was made. No one was allowed to go within a quarter of a mile of the machine—a precaution that aroused a good deal of alarm among the more nervous islanders. Did the Earthmen know what they were doing? Suppose that something went wrong. And *what* were they doing, anyway?

Leon was there with his friends inside that metal pyramid, making the final adjustments—the "coarse focusing," he had told Lora, leaving her none the wiser. She watched with the same anxious incomprehension as all her fellow islanders until the distant figures emerged from the machine and walked to the edge of the flat-topped rock on which it was built. There they stood, a tiny group of figures silhouetted against the ocean, staring out to sea.

A mile from the shore, something strange was happening to the water. It seemed that a storm was brewing—but a storm that kept within an area only a few hundred yards across. Mountainous waves were building up, smashing against each other and then swiftly subsiding again. Within a few minutes the ripples of the disturbance had reached the shore, but the center of the tiny storm showed no sign of movement. It was as if, Lora told herself, an invisible finger had reached down from the sky and was stirring the sea.

Quite abruptly, the entire pattern changed. Now the waves were no longer battering against each other; they were marching in step, moving more and more swiftly in a tight circle. A cone of water was rising from the sea, becoming taller and thinner with every second. Already it was a hundred feet high, and the sound of its birth was an angry roaring that filled the air and struck terror into the hearts of all who heard it. All, that is, except the little band of men who had summoned this monster from the deep, and who still stood watching it with calm assurance, ignoring the waves that were breaking almost against their feet.

Now the spinning tower of water was climbing swiftly up the sky, piercing the clouds like an arrow as it headed toward space. Its foam-capped summit was already lost beyond sight, and from the sky there began to fall a steady shower of rain, the drops abnormally large, like those which prelude a thunderstorm. Not all the water that was being lifted from Thalassa's single ocean was reaching its distant goal; some was escaping from the power that controlled it and was falling back from the edge of space.

Slowly the watching crowd drifted away, astonishment and fright already yielding to a calm acceptance. Man had been able to control gravity for half a thousand years, and this trick—spectacular though it was—could not be compared with the miracle of hurling a great starship from sun to sun at little short of the speed of light.

The Earthmen were now walking back toward their machine, clearly satisfied with what they had done. Even at this distance, one could see that they were happy and relaxed—perhaps for the first time since they had reached Thalassa. The water to rebuild the *Magellan's* shield was on its way out into space, to be shaped and frozen by the other strange forces that these men had made their servants. In a few days, they would be ready to leave, their great interstellar ark as good as new.

Even until this minute, Lora had hoped that they might fail. There was nothing left of that hope now, as she watched the man-made water-spout lift its burden from the sea. Sometimes it wavered slightly, its base shifting back and forth as if at the balance point between immense and invisible forces. But it was fully under control, and it would do the task that had been set for it. That meant only one thing to her; soon she must say good-by to Leon.

She walked slowly toward the distant group of Earthmen, marshaling her thoughts and trying to subdue her emotions. Presently Leon broke away from his friends and came to meet her; relief and happiness were written across his face, but they faded swiftly when he saw Lora's expression.

"Well," he said lamely, almost like a schoolboy caught in some crime, "we've done it."

"And now—how long will you be here?"

He scuffed nervously at the sand, unable to meet her eye.

"Oh, about three days—perhaps four."

She tried to assimilate the words calmly; after all, she had expected them—this was nothing new. But she failed completely, and it was as well that there was no one near them.

"You can't leave!" she cried desperately. "Stay here on Thalassa!"

Leon took her hands gently, then murmured: "No, Lora—this isn't my world; I would never fit into it. Half my life's been spent training for the work I'm doing now; I could never be happy here, where there aren't any more frontiers. In a month, I should die of boredom."

"Then take me with you!"

"You don't really mean that."

"But I do!"

"You only think so; you'd be more out of place in my world than I would be in yours."

"I could learn—there would be plenty of things I could do. As long as we could stay together!"

He held her at arm's length, looking into her eyes. They mirrored sorrow, and also sincerity. She really believed what she was saying, Leon told himself. For the first time, his conscience smote him. He had forgotten—or chosen not to remember—how much more serious these things could be to a woman than to a man.

He had never intended to hurt Lora; he was very fond of her, and would remember her with affection all his life. Now he was discovering, as so many men before him had done, that it was not always easy to say good-by.

There was only one thing to do. Better a short, sharp pain than a long bitterness.

"Come with me, Lora," he said. "I have something to show you."

They did not speak as Leon led the way to the clearing that the Earthmen used as a landing ground. It was littered with pieces of enigmatic equipment, some of them being repacked while others were being left behind for the islanders to use as they pleased. Several of the anti-gravity scooters were parked in the shade beneath the palms; even when not in use they spurned contact with the ground, and hovered a couple of feet above the grass.

But it was not these that Leon was interested in; he walked purposefully toward the gleaming oval that dominated the clearing, and spoke a few words to the engineer who was standing beside it. There was a short argument; then the other capitulated with fairly good grace.

"It's not fully loaded," Leon explained as he helped Lora up the ramp. "But we're going just the same. The other shuttle will be down in half an hour, anyway."

Already Lora was in a world she had never known before—a world of technology in which the most brilliant engineer or scientist of Thalassa would be lost. The island possessed all the machines it needed for its life and happiness; this was something utterly beyond its ken. Lora had once seen the great computer that was the virtual ruler of her people and with whose decisions they disagreed not once in a generation. That giant brain was huge and complex, but there was an awesome simplicity about this machine that impressed even her nontechnical mind. When Leon sat down at the absurdly small control board, his hands seemed to do nothing except rest lightly upon it.

Yet the walls were suddenly transparent—and there was Thalassa, already shrinking below them. There had been no sense of movement, no whisper of sound, yet the island was dwindling even as she watched. The misty edge of the world, a great bow dividing the blue of the sea from the velvet blackness of space, was becoming more curved with every passing second.

"Look," said Leon, pointing to the stars.

The ship was already visible, and Lora felt a sudden sense of disappointment that it was so small. She could see a cluster of portholes around the center section, but there appeared to be no other breaks anywhere on the vessel's squat and angular hull.

The illusion lasted only for a second. Then, with a shock of incredulity that made her senses reel and brought her to the edge of vertigo, she saw how hopelessly her eyes had been deceived. Those were not portholes; the ship was still miles away. What she was seeing were the gaping hatches through which the ferries could shuttle on their journeys between the starship and Thalassa.

There is no sense of perspective in space, where all objects are still clear and sharp whatever their distance. Even when the hull of the ship was looming up beside them, an endless curving wall of metal eclipsing the stars, there was still no real way of judging its size. She could only guess that it must be at least two miles in length.

The ferry berthed itself, as far as Lora could judge, without any intervention from Leon. She followed him out of the little control room, and when the air lock opened she was surprised to discover that they could step directly into one of the starship's passageways.

They were standing in a long tubular corridor that stretched in each direction as far as the eye could see. The floor was moving beneath their feet, carrying them along swiftly and effortlessly—yet strangely enough Lora had felt no sudden jerk as she stepped onto the conveyer that was now sweeping her through the ship. One more mystery she would never explain; there would be many others before Leon had finished showing her the *Magellan.*

It was an hour before they met another human being. In that time they must have traveled miles, sometimes being carried along by the moving corridors, sometimes being lifted up long tubes within which gravity had been abolished. It was obvious what Leon was trying to do; he was attempting to give her some faint impression of the size and complexity of this artificial world that had been built to carry the seeds of a new civilization to the stars.

The engine room alone, with its sleeping, shrouded monsters of metal and crystal, must have been half a mile in length. As they stood on the balcony high above that vast arena of latent power, Leon said proudly, and perhaps not altogether accurately: "These are mine." Lora looked down on the huge and meaningless shapes that had carried Leon to her across the light-years, and did not know whether to bless them for what they had brought or to curse them for what they might soon take away.

They sped swiftly through cavernous holds, packed with all the machines and instruments and stores needed to mold a virgin planet and to make it a fit home for humanity. There were miles upon miles of storage racks, holding in tape or microfilm or still more compact form the cultural heritage of mankind. Here they met a group of experts from Thalassa, looking rather dazed, trying to decide how much of all this wealth they could loot in the few hours left to them.

Had her own ancestors, Lora wondered, been so well equipped when they crossed space? She doubted it; their ship had been far smaller, and Earth must have learned much about the techniques of interstellar colonization in the centuries since Thalassa was opened up. When the *Magellan's* sleeping travelers reached their new home, their success was assured if their spirit matched their material resources.

Now they had come to a great white door which slid silently open as they approached, to reveal—of all incongruous things to find inside a spaceship—a cloakroom in which lines of heavy furs hung from pegs. Leon helped Lora to climb into one of these, then selected another for himself. She followed him uncomprehendingly as he walked toward a circle of frosted glass set in the floor; then he turned to her and said: "There's no gravity where we're going now, so keep close to me and do exactly as I say."

The crystal trap door swung upward like an opening watch glass, and out of the depths swirled a blast of cold such as Lora had never imagined, still less experienced. Thin wisps of moisture condensed in the freezing air, dancing around her like ghosts. She looked at Leon as if to say, "Surely you don't expect me to go down *there!*"

He took her arm reassuringly and said, "Don't worry—you won't notice the cold after a few minutes. I'll go first."

The trap door swallowed him; Lora hesitated for a moment, then lowered herself after him. *Lowered?* No; that was the wrong word; up and down no longer existed here. Gravity had been abolished—she was floating without weight in this frigid, snow-white universe. All around her were glittering honeycombs of glass, forming thousands and tens of thousands of hexagonal cells. They were laced together with clusters of pipes and bundles of wiring, and each cell was large enough to hold a human being.

And each cell did. There they were, sleeping all around her, the thousands of colonists to whom Earth was still, in literal truth, a memory of yesterday. What were they dreaming, less than halfway through their three-hundred-year sleep? Did the brain dream at all in this dim no man's land between life and death?

Narrow, endless belts, fitted with handholds every few feet, were strung across the face of the honeycomb. Leon grabbed one of these, and let it tow them swiftly past the great mosaic of hexagons. Twice they changed direction, switching from one belt to another, until at last they must have been a full quarter of a mile from the point where they had started.

Leon released his grip, and they drifted to rest beside one cell no different from all the myriads of others. But as Lora saw the expression on Leon's face, she knew why he had brought her here, and knew that her battle was already lost.

The girl floating in her crystal coffin had a face that was not beautiful, but was full of character and intelligence. Even in this centuries-long repose, it showed determination and resourcefulness. It was the face of a pioneer, of a frontierswoman who could stand beside her mate and help him wield whatever fabulous tools of science might be needed to build a new Earth beyond the stars.

For a long time, unconscious of the cold, Lora stared down at the sleeping rival who would never know of her existence. Had any love, she wondered, in the whole history of the world, ever ended in so strange a place?

At last she spoke, her voice hushed as if she feared to wake these slumbering legions.

"Is she your wife?"

Leon nodded.

"I'm sorry, Lora. I never intended to hurt you. . . ."

"It doesn't matter now. It was my fault, too." She paused, and looked more closely at the sleeping woman. "And your child as well?"

"Yes; it will be born three months after we land."

How strange to think of a gestation that would last nine months and three hundred years! Yet it was all part of the same pattern; and that, she knew now, was a pattern that had no place for her.

These patient multitudes would haunt her dreams for the rest of her life; as the crystal trap door closed behind her, and warmth crept back into her body, she wished that the cold that had entered her heart could be so easily dispelled. One day, perhaps, it would be; but many days and many lonely nights must pass ere that time came.

She remembered nothing of the journey back through the labyrinth of corridors and echoing chambers; it took her by surprise when she found herself once more in the cabin of the little ferry ship that had brought them up from Thalassa. Leon walked over to the controls, made a few adjustments, but did not sit down.

"Good-by, Lora," he said. "My work is done. It would be better if I stayed here." He took her hands in his; and now, in the last moment they would ever have together, there were no words that she could say. She could not even see his face for the tears that blurred her vision.

His hands tightened once, then relaxed. He gave a strangled sob, and when she could see clearly again, the cabin was empty.

A long time later a smooth, synthetic voice announced from the control board, "We have landed; please leave by the forward air lock." The pattern of opening doors guided her steps, and presently she was looking out into the busy clearing she had left a lifetime ago.

A small crowd was watching the ship with attentive interest, as if it had not landed a hundred times before. For a moment she did not understand the reason; then Clyde's voice roared, "Where is he? I've had enough of this!"

In a couple of bounds he was up the ramp and had gripped her roughly by the arm. "Tell him to come out like a man!"

Lora shook her head listlessly.

"He's not here," she answered. "I've said good-by to him. I'll never see him again."

Clyde stared at her disbelievingly, then saw that she spoke the truth. In the same moment she crumbled into his arms, sobbing as if her heart would break. As she collapsed, his anger, too, collapsed within him, and all that he had intended to say to her vanished from his mind. She belonged to him again; there was nothing else that mattered now.

For almost fifty hours the geyser roared off the coast of Thalassa, until its work was done. All the island watched, through the lenses of the television cameras, the shaping of the iceberg that would ride ahead of the *Magellan* on her way to the stars. May the new shield serve her better, prayed all who watched, than the one she had brought from Earth. The great cone of ice was itself protected, during these few hours while it was close to Thalassa's sun, by a paper-thin screen of polished metal that kept it always in shadow. The sunshade would be left behind as soon as the journey began; it would not be needed in the interstellar wastes.

The last day came and went; Lora's heart was not the only one to feel sadness now as the sun went down and the men from Earth made their final farewells to the world they would never forget—and which their sleeping friends would never remember. In the same swift silence with which it had first landed, the gleaming egg lifted from the clearing, dipped for a moment in salutation above the village, and climbed back into its natural element. Then Thalassa waited.

The night was shattered by a soundless detonation of light. A point of pulsing brilliance no larger than a single star had banished all the hosts of heaven and now dominated the sky, far outshining the pale disk of Selene and casting sharp-edged shadows on the ground—shadows that moved even as one watched. Up there on the borders of space the fires that powered the suns themselves were burning now, preparing to drive the starship out into immensity on the last leg of her interrupted journey.

Dry-eyed, Lora watched the silent glory on which half her heart was riding out toward the stars. She was drained of emotion now; if she had tears, they would come later.

Was Leon already sleeping or was he looking back upon Thalassa, thinking of what might have been? Asleep or waking, what did it matter now . . . ?

She felt Clyde's arms close around her, and welcomed their comfort against the loneliness of space. This was where she belonged; her heart would not stray again. *Good-by, Leon—may you be happy on that far world which you and your children will conquer for mankind. But think of me sometimes, two hundred years behind you on the road to Earth.*

She turned her back upon the blazing sky and buried her face in the shelter of Clyde's arms. He stroked her hair with clumsy gentleness, wishing that he had words to comfort her yet knowing that silence was best. He felt no sense of victory; though Lora was his once more, their old and innocent companionship was gone beyond recall. Leon's memory would fade, but it would never wholly die. All the days of his life, Clyde knew, the ghost of Leon would come between him and Lora—the ghost of a man who would be not one day older when they lay in their graves.

The light was fading from the sky as the fury of the star drive dwindled along its lonely and unreturning road. Only once did Lora turn away from Clyde to look again at the departing ship. Its journey had scarcely begun, yet already it was moving across the heavens more swiftly than any meteor; in a few moments it would have fallen below the edge of the horizon as it plunged past the orbit of Thalassa, beyond the barren outer planets, and on into the abyss.

She clung fiercely to the strong arms that enfolded her, and felt against her cheek the beating of Clyde's heart—the heart that belonged to her and which she would never spurn again. Out of the silence of the night there came a sudden, long-drawn sigh from the watching thousands, and she knew that the *Magellan* had sunk out of sight below the edge of the world. It was all over.

She looked up at the empty sky to which the stars were now returning—the stars which she could never see again without remembering Leon. But he had been right; that way was not for her. She knew now, with a wisdom beyond her years, that the starship *Magellan* was outward bound into history; and that was something of which Thalassa had no further part. Her world's story had begun and ended with the pioneers three hundred years ago, but the colonists of the *Magellan* would go on to victories and achievements as great as any yet written in the sagas of mankind. Leon and his companions would be moving seas, leveling mountains, and conquering unknown perils when her descendants eight generations hence would still be dreaming beneath the sun-soaked palms.

And which was better, who could say?

THE CITY AND THE STARS

Like a glowing jewel, the city lay upon the breast of the desert. Once it had known change and alteration, but now Time passed it by. Night and day fled across the desert's face, but in the streets of Diaspar it was always afternoon, and darkness never came. The long winter nights might dust the desert with frost, as the last moisture left in the thin air of Earth congealed—but the city knew neither heat nor cold. It had no contact with the outer world; it was a universe itself.

Men had built cities before, but never a city such as this. Some had lasted for centuries, some for millenniums, before Time had swept away even their names. Diaspar alone had challenged Eternity, defending itself and all it sheltered against the slow attrition of the ages, the ravages of decay, and the corruption of rust.

Since the city was built, the oceans of Earth had passed away and the desert had encompassed all the globe. The last mountains had been ground to dust by the winds and the rain, and the world was too weary to bring forth more. The city did not care; Earth itself could crumble and Diaspar would still protect the children of its makers, bearing them and their treasures safely down the stream of Time.

They had forgotten much, but they did not know it. They were as perfectly fitted to their environment as it was to them—for both had been designed together. What was beyond the walls of the city was no concern of theirs; it was something that had been shut out of their minds. Diaspar was all that existed, all that they needed, all that they could imagine. It mattered nothing to them that Man had once possessed the stars.

Yet sometimes the ancient myths rose up to haunt them, and they stirred uneasily as they remembered the legends of the Empire, when Diaspar was young and drew its lifeblood from the commerce of many suns. They did not wish to bring back the old days, for they were content in their eternal autumn. The glories of the Empire belonged to the past, and could remain there—for they remembered how the Empire had met its end, and at the thought of the Invaders the chill of space itself came seeping into their bones.

Then they would turn once more to the life and warmth of the city, to the long golden age whose beginning was already lost and whose end was yet more distant. Other men had dreamed of such an age, but they alone had achieved it.

They had lived in the same city, had walked the same miraculously unchanging streets, while more than a billion years had worn away.

CHAPTER ONE

It had taken them many hours to fight their way out of the Cave of the White Worms. Even now, they could not be sure that some of the pallid monsters were not pursuing them—and the power of their weapons was almost exhausted. Ahead, the floating arrow of light that had been their mysterious guide through the labyrinths of the Crystal Mountain still beckoned them on. They had no choice but to follow it, though as it had done so many times before it might lead them into yet more frightful dangers.

Alvin glanced back to see if all his companions were still with him. Alystra was close behind, carrying the sphere of cold but ever-burning light that had revealed such horrors and such beauty since their adventure had begun. The pale white radiance flooded the narrow corridor and splashed from the glittering walls; while its power lasted, they could see where they were going and could detect the presence of any visible dangers. But the greatest dangers in these caves, Alvin knew too well, were not the visible ones at all.

Behind Alystra, struggling with the weight of their projectors, came Narrillian and Floranus. Alvin wondered briefly why those projectors were so heavy, since it would have been such a simple matter to provide them with gravity neutralizers. He was always thinking of points like this, even in the midst of the most desperate adventures. When such thoughts crossed his mind, it seemed as if the structure of reality trembled for an instant, and that behind the world of the senses he caught a glimpse of another and totally different universe. . . .

The corridor ended in a blank wall. Had the arrow betrayed them again? No—even as they approached, the rock began to crumble into dust. Through the wall pierced a spinning metal spear, which broadened rapidly into a giant screw. Alvin and his friends moved back, waiting for the machine to force its way into the cave. With a deafening screech of metal upon rock—which surely must echo through all the recesses of the Mountain, and waken all its nightmare brood!—the subterrene smashed through the wall and came to rest beside them. A massive door opened, and Callistron appeared, shouting to them to hurry. ("Why Callistron?" wondered Alvin. "What's *he* doing here?") A moment later they were in safety, and the machine lurched forward as it began its journey through the depths of the earth.

The adventure was over. Soon, as always happened, they would be home, and all the wonder, the terror, and the excitement would be behind them. They were tired and content.

Alvin could tell from the tilt of the floor that the subterrene was heading down into the earth. Presumably Callistron knew what he was doing, and this was the way that led to home. Yet it seemed a pity. . . .

"Callistron," he said suddenly, "why don't we go upward? No one knows what the Crystal Mountain really looks like. How wonderful it would be to come out somewhere on its slopes, to see the sky and all the land around it. We've been underground long enough."

Even as he said these words, he somehow knew that they were wrong. Alystra gave a strangled scream, the interior of the subterrene wavered like an image seen through water, and behind and beyond the metal walls that surrounded him Alvin once more glimpsed that other universe. The two worlds seemed in conflict, first one and then the other predominating. Then, quite suddenly, it was all over. There was a snapping, rending sensation—and the dream had ended. Alvin was back in Diaspar, in his own familiar room, floating a foot or two above the floor as the gravity field protected him from the bruising contact of brute matter.

He was himself again. *This* was reality—and he knew exactly what would happen next.

Alystra was the first to appear. She was more upset than annoyed, for she was very much in love with Alvin.

"Oh, Alvin!" she lamented, as she looked down at him from the wall in which she had apparently materialized, "It was such an exciting adventure! Why did you have to spoil it?"

"I'm sorry. I didn't intend to—I just thought it would be a good idea . . ."

He was interrupted by the simultaneous arrival of Callistron and Floranus.

"Now listen, Alvin," began Callistron. "This is the *third* time you've interrupted a saga. You broke the sequence yesterday by wanting to climb out of the Valley of Rainbows. And the day before you upset everything by trying to get back to the Origin in that time track we were exploring. If you won't keep the rules, you'll have to go by yourself."

He vanished in high dudgeon, taking Floranus with him. Narillian never appeared at all; he was probably too fed up with the whole affair. Only the image of Alystra was left, looking sadly down at Alvin.

Alvin tilted the gravity field, rose to his feet, and walked toward the table he had materialized. A bowl of exotic fruit appeared upon it—not the food he had intended, for in his confusion his thoughts had wandered. Not wishing to reveal his error, he picked up the least dangerous-looking of the fruits and started to suck it cautiously.

"Well," said Alystra at last, "what are you going to do?"

"I can't help it," he said a little sulkily. "I think the rules are stupid. Besides, how can I remember them when I'm living a saga? I just behave in the way that seems natural. Didn't *you* want to look at the mountain?"

Alystra's eyes widened with horror.

"That would have meant going outside!" she gasped.

Alvin knew that it was useless to argue further. Here was the barrier that sundered him from all the people of his world, and which might doom him to a life of frustration. He was always wanting to go outside, both in reality and in dream. Yet to everyone in Diaspar, "outside" was a nightmare that they could not face. They would never talk about it if it could be avoided; it was something unclean and evil. Not even Jeserac, his tutor, would tell him why.

Alystra was still watching him with puzzled but tender eyes. "You're unhappy, Alvin," she said. "No one should be unhappy in Diaspar. Let me come over and talk to you."

Ungallantly, Alvin shook his head. He knew where *that* would lead, and at the moment he wanted to be alone. Doubly disappointed, Alystra faded from view.

In a city of ten million human beings, thought Alvin, there was no one to whom he could really talk. Eriston and Etania were fond of him in their way, but now that their term of guardianship was ending, they were happy enough to leave him to shape his own amusements and his own life. In the last few years, as his divergence from the standard pattern became more and more obvious, he had often felt his parents' resentment. Not with him—that, perhaps, was something he could have faced and fought—but with the sheer bad luck that had chosen them from all the city's millions, to meet him when he walked out of the Hall of Creation twenty years ago.

Twenty years. He could remember the first moment, and the first words he had ever heard: "Welcome, Alvin. I am Eriston, your appointed father. This is Etania, your mother." The words had meant nothing then, but his mind had recorded them with flawless accuracy. He remembered how he had looked down at his body; it was an inch or two taller now, but had scarcely altered since the moment of his birth. He had come almost fully grown into the world, and would have changed little save in height when it was time to leave it a thousand years hence.

Before that first memory, there was nothing. One day, perhaps, that nothingness would come again, but that was a thought too remote to touch his emotions in any way.

He turned his mind once more toward the mystery of his birth. It did not seem strange to Alvin that he might be created, in a single moment of time, by the powers and forces that materialized all the other objects of his everyday life. No; *that* was not the mystery. The enigma he had never been able to solve, and which no one would ever explain to him, was his uniqueness.

Unique. It was a strange, sad word—and a strange, sad thing to be. When it was applied to him—as he had often heard it done when no one thought he was listening—it seemed to possess ominous undertones that threatened more than his own happiness.

His parents, his tutor, everyone he knew, had tried to protect him from the truth, as if anxious to preserve the innocence of his long childhood. The pretense must soon be ended; in a few days he would be a full citizen of Diaspar, and nothing could be withheld from him that he wished to know.

Why, for example, did he not fit into the sagas? Of all the thousands of forms of recreation in the city, these were the most popular. When you entered a saga, you were not merely a passive observer, as in the crude entertainments of primitive times which Alvin had sometimes sampled. You were an active participant and possessed—or seemed to possess—free will. The events and scenes which were the raw material of your adventures might have been prepared beforehand by forgotten artists, but there was enough flexibility to allow for wide variation. You could go into these phantom worlds with your friends, seeking the excitement that did not exist in Diaspar—and as long as the dream lasted there was no way in which it could be distinguished from reality. Indeed, who could be certain that Diaspar itself was not the dream?

No one could ever exhaust all the sagas that had been conceived and recorded since the city began. They played upon all the emotions and were of infinitely varying subtlety. Some—those popular among the very young—were uncomplicated dramas of adventure and discovery. Others were purely explorations of psychological states, while others again were exercises in logic or mathematics which could provide the keenest of delights to more sophisticated minds.

Yet though the sagas seemed to satisfy his companions, they left Alvin with a feeling of incompleteness. For all their color and excitement, their varying locales and themes, there was something missing.

The sagas, he decided, never really got anywhere. They were always painted on such a narrow canvas. There were no great vistas, none of the rolling landscapes for which his soul craved. Above all, there was never a hint of the immensity in which the exploits of ancient man had really taken place—the luminous void between the stars and planets. The artists who had planned the sagas had been infected by the same strange phobia that ruled all the citizens of Diaspar. Even their vicarious adventures must take place cozily indoors, in subterranean caverns, or in neat little valleys surrounded by mountains that shut out all the rest of the world.

There was only one explanation. Far back in time, perhaps before Diaspar was founded, something had happened that had not only destroyed Man's curiosity and ambition, but had sent him homeward from the stars to cower for shelter in the tiny closed world of Earth's last city. He had renounced the Universe and returned to the artificial womb of Diaspar. The flaming, invincible urge that had once driven him over the Galaxy, and to the islands of mist beyond, had altogether died. No ships had entered the Solar System for countless aeons; out there among the stars the descendants of Man might still be building empires and wrecking suns—Earth neither knew nor cared.

Earth did not. But Alvin did.

CHAPTER TWO

The room was dark save for one glowing wall, upon which the tides of color ebbed and flowed as Alvin wrestled with his dreams. Part of the pattern satisfied him; he had fallen in love with the soaring lines of the mountains as they leaped out of the sea. There was a power and pride about those ascending curves; he had studied them for a long time, and then fed them into the memory unit of the visualizer, where they would be preserved while he experimented with the rest of the picture. Yet something was eluding him, though what it was he did not know. Again and again he had tried to fill in the blank spaces, while the instrument read the shifting patterns in his mind and materialized them upon the wall. It was no good. The lines were blurred and uncertain, the colors muddy and dull. If the artist did not know his goal, even the most miraculous of tools could not find it for him.

Alvin canceled his unsatisfactory scribblings and stared morosely at the three-quarters-empty rectangle he had been trying to fill with beauty. On a sudden impulse, he doubled the size of the existing design and shifted it to the center of the frame. No—that was a lazy way out, and the balance was all wrong. Worse still, the change of scale had revealed the defects in his construction, the lack of certainty in those at-first-sight confident lines. He would have to start all over again.

"Total erasure," he ordered the machine. The blue of the sea faded; the mountains dissolved like mist, until only the blank wall remained. They were as if they had never been—as if they were lost in the limbo that had taken all Earth's seas and mountains ages before Alvin was born.

The light came flooding back into the room and the luminous rectangle upon which Alvin had projected his dreams merged into its surroundings, to become one with the other walls. But were they walls? To anyone who had never seen such a place before, this was a very peculiar room indeed. It was utterly featureless and completely devoid of furniture, so that it seemed as if Alvin stood at the center of a sphere. No visible dividing lines separated walls from floor or ceiling. There was nothing on which the eye could focus; the space enclosing Alvin might have been ten feet or ten miles across, for all that the sense of vision could have told. It would have been hard to resist the temptation to walk forward, hands outstretched, to discover the physical limits of this extraordinary place.

Yet such rooms had been "home" to most of the human race for the greater part of its history. Alvin had only to frame the appropriate thought, and the walls would become windows opening upon any part of the city he chose. Another wish, and machines which he had never seen would fill the chamber with the projected images of any articles of furniture he might need. Whether they were "real" or not was a problem that had bothered few men for the last billion years. Certainly they were no less real than that other impostor, solid matter, and when they were no longer required they could be returned to the phantom world of the city's Memory Banks. Like everything else in Diaspar, they would never wear out—and they would never change, unless their stored patterns were canceled by a deliberate act of will.

Alvin had partly reconstructed his room when a persistent, bell-like chime sounded in his ear. He mentally framed the admission signal, and the wall upon which he had just been painting dissolved once more. As he had expected, there stood his parents, with Jeserac a little behind them. The presence of his tutor meant that this was no ordinary family reunion—but he knew that already.

The illusion was perfect, and it was not lost when Eriston spoke. In reality, as Alvin was well aware, Eriston, Etania, and Jeserac were all miles apart, for the builders of the city had conquered space as completely as they had subjugated time. Alvin was not even certain where his parents lived among the multitudinous spires and intricate labyrinths of Diaspar, for they had both moved since he had last been physically in their presence.

"Alvin," began Eriston, "it is just twenty years since your mother and I first met you. You know what that means. Our guardianship is now ended, and you are free to do as you please."

There was a trace—but merely a trace—of sadness in Eriston's voice. There was considerably more relief, as if Eriston was glad that a state of affairs that had existed for some time in fact now had legal recognition. Alvin had anticipated his freedom by a good many years.

"I understand," he answered. "I thank you for watching over me, and I will remember you in all my lives." That was the formal response; he had heard it so often that all meaning had been leached away from it—it was merely a pattern of sounds with no particular significance. Yet "all my lives" was a strange expression, when one stopped to consider it. He knew vaguely what it meant; now the time had come for him to know exactly. There were many things in Diaspar which he did not understand, and which he would have to learn in the centuries that lay ahead of him.

For a moment it seemed as if Etania wished to speak. She raised one hand, disturbing the iridescent gossamer of her gown, then let it fall back to her side. Then she turned helplessly to Jeserac, and for the first time Alvin realized that his parents were worried. His memory swiftly scanned the events of the past few weeks. No, there was nothing in his recent life that could have caused this faint uncertainty, this air of mild alarm that seemed to surround both Eriston and Etania.

Jeserac, however, appeared to be in command of the situation. He gave an inquiring look at Eriston and Etania, satisfied himself that they had nothing more to say, and launched forth on the dissertation he had waited many years to make.

"Alvin," he began, "for twenty years you have been my pupil, and I have done my best to teach you the ways of the city, and to lead you to the heritage which is yours. You have asked me many questions, and not all of them have I been able to answer. Some things you were not ready to learn, and some I did not know myself. Now your infancy is over, though your childhood is scarcely begun. It is still my duty to guide you, if you need my help. In two hundred years, Alvin, you may begin to know something of this city and a little of its history. Even I, who am nearing the end of this life, have seen less than a quarter of Diaspar, and perhaps less than a thousandth of its treasures."

There was nothing so far that Alvin did not know, but there was no way of hurrying Jeserac. The old man looked steadfastly at him across the gulf of centuries, his words weighed down with the uncomputable wisdom acquired during a long lifetime's contact with men and machines.

"Tell me, Alvin," he said, "have you ever asked yourself *where* you were before you were born—before you found yourself facing Etania and Eriston at the Hall of Creation?"

"I assumed I was nowhere—that I was nothing but a pattern in the mind of the city, waiting to be created—like this."

A low couch glimmered and thickened into reality beside Alvin. He sat down upon it and waited for Jeserac to continue.

"You are correct, of course," came the reply. "But that is merely part of the answer—and a very small part indeed. Until now, you have met only children of your own age, and they have been ignorant of the truth. Soon they will remember, but you will not, so we must prepare you to face the facts.

"For over a billion years, Alvin, the human race has lived in this city. Since the Galactic Empire fell, and the Invaders went back to the stars, this has been our world. Outside the walls of Diaspar, there is nothing except the desert of which our legends speak.

"We know little about our primitive ancestors, except that they were very short-lived beings and that, strange though it seems, they could reproduce themselves without the aid of memory units or matter organizers. In a complex and apparently uncontrollable process, the key patterns of each human being were preserved in microscopic cell structures actually created inside the body. If you are interested, the biologists can tell you more about it, but the method is of no great importance since it was abandoned at the dawn of history.

"A human being, like any other object, is defined by its structure—

its pattern. The pattern of a man, and still more the pattern which specifies a man's mind, is incredibly complex. Yet Nature was able to pack that pattern into a tiny cell, too small for the eye to see.

"What Nature can do, Man can do also, in his own way. We do not know how long the task took. A million years, perhaps—but what is that? In the end our ancestors learned how to analyze and store the information that would define any specific human being—and to use that information to re-create the original, as you have just created that couch.

"I know that such things interest you, Alvin, but I cannot tell you exactly how it is done. The way in which information is stored is of no importance; all that matters is the information itself. It may be in the form of written words on paper, of varying magnetic fields, or patterns of electric charge. Men have used all these methods of storage, and many others. Suffice to say that long ago they were able to store themselves—or, to be more precise, the disembodied patterns from which they could be called back into existence.

"So much, you already know. This is the way our ancestors gave us virtual immortality, yet avoided the problems raised by the abolition of death. A thousand years in one body is long enough for any man; at the end of that time, his mind is clogged with memories, and he asks only for rest—or a new beginning.

"In a little while, Alvin, I shall prepare to leave this life. I shall go back through my memories, editing them and canceling those I do not wish to keep. Then I shall walk into the Hall of Creation, but through a door which you have never seen. This old body will cease to exist, and so will consciousness itself. Nothing will be left of Jeserac but a galaxy of electrons frozen in the heart of a crystal.

"I shall sleep, Alvin, and without dreams. Then one day, perhaps a hundred thousand years from now, I shall find myself in a new body, meeting those who have been chosen to be my guardians. They will look after me as Eriston and Etania have guided you, for at first I will know nothing of Diaspar and will have no memories of what I was before. Those memories will slowly return, at the end of my infancy, and I will build upon them as I move forward into my new cycle of existence.

"That is the pattern of our lives, Alvin. We have all been here many, many times before, though as the intervals of nonexistence vary according to apparently random laws this present population will never repeat itself again. The new Jeserac will have new and different friends and interests, but the old Jeserac—as much of him as I wish to save—will still exist.

"That is not all. At any moment, Alvin, only a hundredth of the citizens of Diaspar live and walk its streets. The vast majority slumber in the Memory Banks, waiting for the signal that will call them forth onto the stage of existence once again. So we have continuity, yet change—immortality, but not stagnation.

"I know what you are wondering, Alvin. You want to know when you will recall the memories of your earlier lives, as your companions are already doing.

"There are no such memories, for you are unique. We have tried to keep this knowledge from you as long as we could, so that no shadow should lie across your childhood—though I think you must have guessed part of the truth already. We did not suspect it ourselves until five years ago, but now there is no doubt.

"You, Alvin, are something that has happened in Diaspar only a handful of times since the founding of the city. Perhaps you have been lying dormant in the Memory Banks through all the ages—or perhaps you were created only twenty years ago by some random permutation. You may have been planned in the beginning by the designers of the city, or you may be a purposeless accident of our own time.

"We do not know. All that we do know is this: You, Alvin, alone of the human race, have never lived before. In literal truth, you are the first child to be born on Earth for at least ten million years."

CHAPTER THREE

When Jeserac and his parents had faded from view, Alvin lay for a long time trying to hold his mind empty of thought. He closed his room around him, so that no one could interrupt his trance.

He was not sleeping; sleep was something he had never experienced, for that belonged to a world of night and day, and here there was only day. This was the nearest he could come to that forgotten state, and though it was not really essential to him he knew that it would help compose his mind.

He had learned little new; almost everything that Jeserac had told him he had already guessed. But it was one thing to have guessed it, another to have had that guess confirmed beyond possibility of refutation.

How would it affect his life, if at all? He could not be sure, and uncertainty was a novel sensation to Alvin. Perhaps it would make no difference whatsoever; if he did not adjust completely to Diaspar in this life, he would do so in the next—or the next.

Even as he framed the thought, Alvin's mind rejected it. Diaspar might be sufficient for the rest of humanity, but it was not enough for him. He did not doubt that one could spend a thousand lifetimes without exhausting all its wonders, or sampling all the permutations of experience it could provide. These things he could do—but if he could not do more, he would never be content.

There was only one problem to be faced. What more *was* there to do?

The unanswered question jolted him out of his reverie. He could not stay here while he was in this restless mood, and there was only one place in the city where he could find some peace of mind.

The wall flickered partially out of existence as he stepped through to the corridor, and its polarized molecules resisted his passage like a feeble wind blowing against his face. There were many ways in which he could be carried effortlessly to his goal, but he preferred to walk. His room was almost at the main city level, and a short passage brought him out onto a spiral ramp which led down to the street. He ignored the moving way, and kept to the narrow sidewalk—an eccentric thing to do, since he had several miles to travel. But Alvin liked the exercise, for it soothed his mind. Besides, there was so much to see that it seemed a pity to race past the latest marvels of Diaspar when you had eternity ahead of you.

It was the custom of the city's artists—and everyone in Diaspar was an artist at some time or another—to display their current productions along the side of the moving ways, so that the passers-by could admire their work. In this manner, it was usually only a few days before the entire population had critically examined any noteworthy creation, and also expressed its views upon it. The resulting verdict, recorded automatically by opinion-sampling devices which no one had ever been able to suborn or deceive—and there had been enough attempts—decided the fate of the masterpiece. If there was a sufficiently affirmative vote, its matrix would go into the memory of the city so that anyone who wished, at any future date, could possess a reproduction utterly indistinguishable from the original.

The less successful pieces went the way of all such works. They were either dissolved back into their original elements or ended in the homes of the artists' friends.

Alvin saw only one *objet d'art* on his journey that had any appeal to him. It was a creation of pure light, vaguely reminiscent of an unfolding flower. Slowly growing from a minute core of color, it would expand into complex spirals and curtains, then suddenly collapse and begin the cycle over again. Yet not precisely, for no two cycles were identical. Though Alvin watched through a score of pulsations, each time there were subtle and indefinable differences, even though the basic pattern remained the same.

He knew why he liked this piece of intangible sculpture. Its expanding rhythm gave an impression of space—even of escape. For that reason, it would probably not appeal to many of Alvin's compatriots. He made a note of the artist's name and decided to call him at the earliest opportunity.

All the roads, both moving and stationary, came to an end when they reached the park that was the green heart of the city. Here, in a circular space over three miles across, was a memory of what Earth had been in the days before the desert swallowed all but Diaspar. First there was a wide belt of grass, then low trees which grew thicker and thicker as one walked forward beneath their shade. At the same time the ground sloped gently downward, so that when at last one emerged from the narrow forest all sign of the city had vanished, hidden by the screen of trees.

The wide stream that lay ahead of Alvin was called, simply, the River. It possessed, and it needed, no other name. At intervals it was spanned by narrow bridges, and it flowed around the park in a complete, closed circle, broken by occasional lagoons. That a swiftly moving river could return upon itself after a course of less than six miles had never struck Alvin as at all unusual; indeed, he would not have thought twice about the matter if at some point in its circuit the River had flowed uphill. There were far stranger things than this in Diaspar.

A dozen young people were swimming in one of the little lagoons, and Alvin paused to watch them. He knew most of them by sight, if not by name, and for a moment was tempted to join in their play. Then the secret he was bearing decided him against it, and he contented himself with the role of spectator.

Physically, there was no way of telling which of these young citizens had walked out of the Hall of Creation this year and which had lived in Diaspar as long as Alvin. Though there were considerable variations in height and weight, they had no correlation with age. People were simply born that way, and although on the average the taller the person, the greater the age, this was not a reliable rule to apply unless one was dealing in centuries.

The face was a safer guide. Some of the newborn were taller than Alvin, but they had a look of immaturity, an expression of wondering surprise at the world in which they now found themselves that revealed them at once. It was strange to think that, slumbering untapped in their minds, were infinite vistas of lives that they would soon remember. Alvin envied them, yet he was not sure if he should. One's first existence was a precious gift which would never be repeated. It was wonderful to view life for the very first time, as in the freshness of the dawn. If only there were others like him, with whom he could share his thoughts and feelings!

Yet physically he was cast in precisely the same mold as those children playing in the water. The human body had changed not at all in the billion years since the building of Diaspar, since the basic design had been eternally frozen in the Memory Banks of the city. It had changed, however, a good deal from its original primitive form, though most of the alterations were internal and not visible to the eye. Man had rebuilt himself many times in his long history, in the effort to abolish those ills to which the flesh was once heir.

Such unnecessary appurtenances as nails and teeth had vanished. Hair was confined to the head; not a trace was left on the body. The feature that would most have surprised a man of the Dawn Ages was, perhaps, the disappearance of the navel. Its inexplicable absence would have given him much food for thought, and at first sight he would also have been baffled by the problem of distinguishing male from female. He might even have been tempted to assume that there was no longer any difference, which would have been a grave error. In the appropriate circumstances, there was no doubt about the masculinity of any male in Diaspar. It was merely that his equipment was now more neatly packaged when not required; internal stowage had vastly improved upon Nature's original inelegant and indeed downright hazardous arrangements.

It was true that reproduction was no longer the concern of the body, being far too important a matter to be left to games of chance played with chromosomes as dice. Yet, though conception and birth were not even memories, sex remained. Even in ancient times, not one-hundredth part of sexual activity had been concerned with reproduction. The disappearance of that mere one per cent had changed the pattern of human society and the meaning of such words as "father" and "mother"—but desire remained, though now its satisfaction had no profounder aim than that of any of the other pleasures of the senses.

Alvin left his playful contemporaries and continued on toward the center of the park. There were faintly marked paths here, crossing and crisscrossing through low shrubbery and occasionally diving into narrow ravines between great lichen-covered boulders. Once he came across a small polyhedral machine, no larger than a man's head, floating among the branches of a tree. No one knew how many varieties of robot there were in Diaspar; they kept out of the way and minded their business so effectively that it was quite unusual to see one.

Presently the ground began to rise again; Alvin was approaching the little hill that was at the exact center of the park, and therefore of the city itself. There were fewer obstacles and detours, and he had a clear view to the summit of the hill and the simple building that surmounted it. He was a little out of breath by the time he had reached his goal, and was glad to rest against one of the rose-pink columns and to look back over the way he had come.

There are some forms of architecture that can never change because they have reached perfection. The Tomb of Yarlan Zey might have been designed by the temple builders of the first civilizations man had ever known, though they would have found it impossible to imagine of what material it was made. The roof was open to the sky, and the single chamber was paved with great slabs which only at first sight resembled natural stone. For geological ages human feet had crossed and recrossed that floor and left no trace upon its inconceivably stubborn material.

The creator of the great park—the builder, some said, of Diaspar itself—sat with slightly downcast eyes, as if examining the plans spread across his knees. His face wore that curiously elusive expression that had baffled the world for so many generations. Some had dismissed it as no more than an idle whim of the artist's, but to others it seemed that Yarlan Zey was smiling at some secret jest.

The whole building was an enigma, for nothing concerning it could be traced in the historical records of the city. Alvin was not even sure what the word "Tomb" meant; Jeserac could probably tell him, because he was fond of collecting obsolete words and sprinkling his conversation with them, to the confusion of his listeners.

From this central vantage point, Alvin could look clear across the park, above the screening trees, and out to the city itself. The nearest buildings were almost two miles away, and formed a low belt completely surrounding the park. Beyond them, rank after rank in ascending height, were the towers and terraces that made up the main bulk of the city. They stretched for mile upon mile, slowly climbing up the sky, becoming ever more complex and monumentally impressive. Diaspar had been planned as an entity; it was a single mighty machine. Yet though its outward appearance was almost overwhelming in its complexity, it merely hinted at the hidden marvels of technology without which all these great buildings would be lifeless sepulchers.

Alvin stared out toward the limits of his world. Ten—twenty miles away, their details lost in distance, were the outer ramparts of the city, upon which seemed to rest the roof of the sky. There was nothing beyond them—nothing at all except the aching emptiness of the desert in which a man would soon go mad.

Then why did that emptiness call to him, as it called to no one else whom he had ever met? Alvin did not know. He stared out across the colored spires and battlements that now enclosed the whole dominion of mankind, as if seeking an answer to his question.

He did not find it. But at that moment, as his heart yearned for the unattainable, he made his decision.

He knew now what he was going do do with life.

CHAPTER FOUR

Jeserac was not very helpful, though he was not as un-co-operative as Alvin had half expected. He had been asked such questions before in his long career as mentor, and did not believe that even a Unique like Alvin could produce many surprises or set him problems which he could not solve.

It was true that Alvin was beginning to show certain minor eccentricities of behavior, which might eventually need correction. He did not join as fully as he should in the incredibly elaborate social life of the city or in the fantasy worlds of his companions. He showed no great interest in the higher realms of thought, though at his age that was hardly surprising. More remarkable was his erratic love life; he could not be expected to form any relatively stable partnerships for at least a century, yet the brevity of his affairs was already famous. They were intense while they lasted—but not one of them had lasted for more than a few weeks. Alvin, it seemed, could interest himself thoroughly only in one thing at a time. There were times when he would join wholeheartedly in the erotic games of his companions, or disappear with the partner of his choice for several days. But once the mood had passed, there would be long spells when he seemed totally uninterested in what should have been a major occupation at his age. This was probably bad for him, and it was certainly bad for his discarded lovers, who wandered despondently around the city and took an unusually long time to find consolation elsewhere. Alystra, Jeserac had noticed, had now arrived at this unhappy stage.

It was not that Alvin was heartless or inconsiderate. In love, as in everything else, it seemed that he was searching for a goal that Diaspar could not provide.

None of these characteristics worried Jeserac. A Unique might be expected to behave in such a manner, and in due course Alvin would conform to the general pattern of the city. No single individual, however eccentric or brilliant, could affect the enormous inertia of a society that had remained virtually unchanged for over a billion years. Jeserac did not merely believe in stability; he could conceive of nothing else.

"The problem that worries you is a very old one," he told Alvin, "but you will be surprised how many people take the world so much for granted that it never bothers them or even crosses their mind. It is true that the human race once occupied an infinitely greater space than this city. You have seen something of what Earth was like before the deserts came and the oceans vanished. Those records you are so fond of projecting are the earliest we possess; they are the only ones that show Earth as it was before the Invaders came. I do not imagine that many people have ever seen them; those limitless, open spaces are something we cannot bear to contemplate.

"And even Earth, of course, was only a grain of sand in the Galactic Empire. What the gulfs between the stars must have been like is a nightmare no sane man would try to imagine. Our ancestors crossed them at the dawn of history when they went out to build the Empire. They crossed them again for the last time when the Invaders drove them back to Earth.

"The legend is—and it is only a legend—that we made a pact with the Invaders. They could have the Universe if they needed it so badly, and we would be content with the world on which we were born.

"We have kept that pact and forgotten the vain dreams of our childhood, as you too will forget them, Alvin. The men who built this city, and designed the society that went with it, were lords of mind as well as matter. They put everything that the human race would ever need inside these walls—and then made sure that we would never leave them.

"Oh, the physical barriers are the least important ones. Perhaps there are routes that lead out of the city, but I do not think you would go along them for very far, even if you found them. And if you succeeded in the attempt, what good would it do? Your body would not last long in the desert, when the city could no longer protect or nourish it."

"If there is a route out of the city," said Alvin slowly, "then what is there to stop me from leaving?"

"That is a foolish question," answered Jeserac. "I think you already know the answer."

Jeserac was right, but not in the way he imagined. Alvin knew—or, rather, he had guessed. His companions had given him the answer, both in their waking life and in the dream adventures he had shared with them. They would never be able to leave Diaspar; what Jeserac did not know was that the compulsion which ruled their lives had no power over Alvin. Whether his uniqueness was due to accident or to an ancient design, he did not know, but this was one of its results. He wondered how many others he had yet to discover.

No one ever hurried in Diaspar, and this was a rule which even Alvin seldom broke. He considered the problem carefully for several weeks, and spent much time searching the earliest of the city's historical memories. For hours on end he would lie, supported by the impalpable arms of an antigravity field, while the hypnone projector opened his mind to the past. When the record was finished, the machine would blur and vanish—but still Alvin would lie staring into nothingness before he came back through the ages to meet reality again. He would see again the endless leagues of blue water, vaster than the land itself, rolling their waves against golden shores. His ears would ring with the boom of breakers stilled these billion years. He would remember the forests and the prairies, and the strange beasts that had once shared the world with Man.

Very few of these ancient records existed; it was generally accepted, though none knew the reason why, that somewhere between the coming of the Invaders and the building of Diaspar all memories of primitive times had been lost. So complete had been the obliteration that it was hard to believe it could have happened by accident alone. Mankind had lost its past, save for a few chronicles that might be wholly legendary. Before Diaspar there was simply the Dawn Ages. In that limbo were merged inextricably together the first men to tame fire and the first to release atomic energy—the first men to build a log canoe and the first to reach the stars. On the far side of this desert of time, they were all neighbors.

Alvin had intended to make this trip alone once more, but solitude was not always something that could be arranged in Diaspar. He had barely left his room when he encountered Alystra, who made no attempt to pretend that her presence was accidental.

It had never occurred to Alvin that Alystra was beautiful, for he had never seen human ugliness. When beauty is universal, it loses its power to move the heart, and only its absence can produce any emotional effect.

For a moment Alvin was annoyed by the meeting, with its reminder of passions that no longer moved him. He was still too young and self-reliant to feel the need for any lasting relationships, and when the time came he might find it hard to make them. Even in his most intimate moments, the barrier of his uniqueness came between him and his lovers. For all his fully formed body, he was still a child and would remain so for decades yet, while his companions one by one recalled the memories of their past lives and left him far behind. He had seen it happen before, and it made him wary of giving himself unreservedly to any other person. Even Alystra, who seemed so naïve and artless now, would soon become a complex of memories and talents beyond his imagination.

His mild annoyance vanished almost at once. There was no reason why Alystra should not come with him if she desired. He was not selfish and did not wish to clutch this new experience to his bosom like a miser. Indeed, he might be able to learn much from her reactions.

She asked no questions, which was unusual, as the express channel swept them out of the crowded heart of the city. Together they worked their way to the central high-speed section, never bothering to glance at the miracle beneath their feet. An engineer of the ancient world would have gone slowly mad trying to understand how an apparently solid roadway could be fixed at the sides while toward the center it moved at a steadily increasing velocity. But to Alvin and Alystra, it seemed perfectly natural that types of matter should exist that had the properties of solids in one direction and of liquids in another.

Around them the buildings rose higher and higher as if the city was strengthening its bulwarks against the outer world. How strange it would be, thought Alvin, if these towering walls became as transparent as glass, and one could watch the life within. Scattered throughout the space around him were friends he knew, friends he would one day know, and strangers he would never meet—though there could be very few of these, since in the course of his lifetime he would meet almost all the people in Diaspar. Most of them would be sitting in their separate rooms, but they would not be alone. They had only to form the wish and they could be, in all but physical fact, in the presence of any other person they chose. They were not bored, for they had access to everything that had happened in the realms of imagination or reality since the days when the city was built. To men whose minds were thus constituted, it was a completely satisfying existence. That it was also a wholly futile one, even Alvin did not yet comprehend.

As Alvin and Alystra moved outward from the city's heart, the number of people they saw in the streets slowly decreased, and there was no one in sight when they were brought to a smooth halt against a long platform of brightly colored marble. They stepped across the frozen whirlpool of matter where the substance of the moving way flowed back to its origin, and faced a wall pierced with brightly lighted tunnels. Alvin selected one without hesitation and stepped into it, with Alystra close behind. The peristaltic field seized them at once and propelled them forward as they lay back luxuriously, watching their surroundings.

It no longer seemed possible that they were in a tunnel far underground. The art that had used all of Diaspar for its canvas had been busy here, and above them the skies seemed open to the winds of heaven. All around were the spires of the city, gleaming in the sunlight. It was not the city that Alvin knew, but the Diaspar of a much earlier age. Although most of the great buildings were familiar, there were subtle differences that added to the interest of the scene. Alvin wished he could linger, but he had never found any way of retarding his progress through the tunnel.

All too soon they were set gently down in a large elliptical chamber, completely surrounded by windows. Through these they could catch tantalizing glimpses of gardens ablaze with brilliant flowers. There were gardens still in Diaspar, but these had existed only in the mind of the artist who conceived them. Certainly there were no such flowers as these in the world today.

Alystra was enchanted by their beauty, and was obviously under the impression that this was what Alvin had brought her to see. He watched her for a while as she ran gaily from scene to scene, enjoying her delight in each new discovery. There were hundreds of such places in the half-deserted buildings around the periphery of Diaspar, kept in perfect order by the hidden powers which watched over them. One day the tide of life might flow this way once more, but until then this ancient garden was a secret which they alone shared.

"We've further to go," said Alvin at last. "This is only the beginning." He stepped through one of the windows and the illusion was shattered. There was no garden behind the glass, but a circular passageway curving steeply upward. He could still see Alystra a few feet away, though he knew that she could not see him. But she did not hesitate, and a moment later was standing beside him in the passage.

Beneath their feet the floor began to creep slowly forward, as if eager to lead them to their goal. They walked along it for a few paces, until their speed was so great that further effort would be wasted.

The corridor still inclined upward, and in a hundred feet had curved through a complete right angle. But only logic knew this; to all the senses it was as if one was now being hurried along an absolutely level corridor. The fact that they were in reality moving straight up a vertical shaft thousands of feet deep gave them no sense of insecurity, for a failure of the polarizing field was unthinkable.

Presently the corridor began to slope "downward" again until once more it had turned through a right angle. The movement of the floor slowed imperceptibly until it came to rest at the end of a long hall lined with mirrors, and Alvin knew that there was no hope of hurrying Alystra here. It was not merely that some feminine characteristics had survived unchanged since Eve; no one could have resisted the fascination of this place. There was nothing like it, as far as Alvin knew, in the rest of Diaspar. Through some whim of the artist, only a few of the mirrors reflected the scene as it really was—and even those, Alvin was convinced, were constantly changing their position. The rest certainly reflected *something,* but it was faintly disconcerting to see oneself walking amid ever-changing and quite imaginary surroundings.

Sometimes there were people going to and fro in the world behind the mirror, and more than once Alvin had seen faces that he recognized. He realized well enough that he had not been looking at any friends he knew in this existence. Through the mind of the unknown artist he had been seeing into the past, watching the previous incarnations of people who walked the world today. It saddened him, by reminding him of his own uniqueness, to think that however long he waited before these changing scenes he would never meet any ancient echo of himself.

"Do you know where we are?" Alvin asked Alystra when they had completed the tour of the mirrors. Alystra shook her head. "Somewhere near the edge of the city, I suppose," she answered carelessly. "We seem to have gone a long way, but I've no idea how far."

"We're in the Tower of Loranne," replied Alvin. "This is one of the highest points in Diaspar. Come—I'll show you." He caught Alystra's hand and led her out of the hall. There were no exits visible to the eye, but at various points the pattern on the floor indicated side corridors. As one approached the mirrors at these points, the reflections seemed to fuse into an archway of light and one could step through into another passage. Alystra lost all conscious track of their twistings and turnings, and at last they emerged into a long, perfectly straight tunnel through which blew a cold and steady wind. It stretched horizontally for hundreds of feet in either direction, and its far ends were tiny circles of light.

"I don't like this place," Alystra complained. "It's cold." She had probably never before experienced real coldness in her life, and Alvin felt somewhat guilty. He should have warned her to bring a cloak—and a good one, for all clothes in Diaspar were purely ornamental and quite useless as a protection.

Since her discomfort was entirely his fault, he handed over his cloak without a word. There was no trace of gallantry in this; the equality of the sexes had been complete for far too long for such conventions to survive. Had matters been the other way around, Alystra would have given Alvin her cloak and he would have as automatically accepted.

It was not unpleasant walking with the wind behind them, and they soon reached the end of the tunnel. A wide-meshed filigree of stone prevented them from going any further, which was just as well, for they stood on the brink of nothingness. The great air duct opened on the sheer face of the tower, and below them was a vertical drop of at least a thousand feet. They were high upon the outer ramparts of the city, and Diaspar lay spread beneath them as few in their world could ever have seen it.

The view was the obverse of the one that Alvin had obtained from the center of the park. He could look down upon the concentric waves of stone and metal as they descended in mile-long sweeps toward the heart of the city. Far away, partly hidden by the intervening towers, he could glimpse the distant fields and trees and the eternally circling river. Further still, the remoter bastions of Diaspar climbed once more toward the sky.

Beside him, Alystra was sharing the view with pleasure but with no surprise. She had seen the city countless times before from other, almost equally well-placed vantage points—and in considerably more comfort.

"That's our world—all of it," said Alvin. "Now I want to show you something else." He turned away from the grating and began to walk toward the distant circle of light at the far end of the tunnel. The wind was cold against his lightly clad body, but he scarcely noticed the discomfort as he walked forward into the air stream.

He had gone only a little way when he realized that Alystra was making no attempt to follow. She stood watching, her borrowed cloak streaming down the wind, one hand half raised to her face. Alvin saw her lips move, but the words did not reach him. He looked back at her first with astonishment, then with an impatience that was not totally devoid of pity. What Jeserac had said was true. She could not follow him. She had realized the meaning of that remote circle of light from which the wind blew forever into Diaspar. Behind Alystra was the known world, full of wonder yet empty of surprise, drifting like a brilliant but tightly closed bubble down the river of time. Ahead, separated from her by no more than the span of a few footsteps, was the empty wilderness—the world of the desert—the world of the Invaders.

Alvin walked back to join her and was surprised to find that she was trembling. "Why are you frightened?" he asked. "We're still safely here in Diaspar. You've looked out of that window behind us—surely you can look out of this one as well!"

Alystra was staring at him as if he was some strange monster. By her standards, indeed, he was.

"I couldn't do it," she said at last. "Even thinking about it makes me feel colder than this wind. Don't go any farther, Alvin!"

"But there's no logic in it!" Alvin persisted remorselessly. "What possible harm would it do you to walk to the end of this corridor and look out? It's strange and lonely out there, but it isn't horrible. In fact, the longer I look the more beautiful I think—"

Alystra did not stay to hear him finish. She turned on her heels and fled back down the long ramp that had brought them up through the floor of this tunnel. Alvin made no attempt to stop her, since that would have involved the bad manners of imposing one's will upon another. Persuasion, he could see, would have been utterly useless. He knew that Alystra would not pause until she had returned to her companions. There was no danger that she would lose herself in the labyrinths of the city, for she would have no difficulty in retracing her footsteps. An instinctive ability to extricate himself from even the most complex of mazes had been merely one of the many accomplishments Man had learned since he started to live in cities. The long-extinct rat had been forced to acquire similar skills when he left the fields and threw in his lot with humanity.

Alvin waited for a moment, as if half-expecting Alystra to return. He was not surprised at her reaction—only at its violence and irrationality. Though he was sincerely sorry that she had gone, he could not help wishing that she had remembered to leave the cloak.

It was not only cold, but it was also hard work moving against the wind which sighed through the lungs of the city. Alvin was fighting both the air current and whatever force it was that kept it moving. Not until he had reached the stone grille, and could lock his arms around its bars, could he afford to relax. There was just sufficient room for him to force his head through the opening, and even so his view was slightly restricted, as the entrance to the duct was partly recessed into the city's wall.

Yet he could see enough. Thousands of feet below, the sunlight was taking leave of the desert. The almost horizontal rays struck through the grating and threw a weird pattern of gold and shadow far down the tunnel. Alvin shaded his eyes against the glare and peered down at the land upon which no man had walked for unknown ages.

He might have been looking at an eternally frozen sea. For mile after mile, the sand dunes undulated into the west, their contours grossly exaggerated by the slanting light. Here and there some caprice of the wind had carved curious whirlpools and gullies in the sand, so that it was sometimes hard to realize that none of this sculpture was the work of intelligence. At a very great distance, so far away indeed that he had no way of judging their remoteness, was a range of softly rounded hills. They had been a disappointment to Alvin; he would have given much to have seen in reality the soaring mountains of the ancient records and of his own dreams.

The sun lay upon the rim of the hills, its light tamed and reddened by the hundreds of miles of atmosphere it was traversing. There were two great black spots upon its disc; Alvin had learned from his studies that such things existed, but he was surprised that he could see them so easily. They seemed almost like a pair of eyes peering back at him as he crouched in his lonely spy hole with the wind whistling ceaselessly past his ears.

There was no twilight. With the going of the sun, the pools of shadow lying among the sand dunes flowed swiftly together into one vast lake of darkness. Color ebbed from the sky; the warm reds and golds drained away leaving an antarctic blue that deepened and deepened into night. Alvin waited for that breathless moment that he alone of all mankind had known—the moment when the first star shivers into life.

It had been many weeks since he had last come to this place, and he knew that the pattern of the night sky must have changed meanwhile. Even so, he was not prepared for his first glimpse of the Seven Suns.

They could have no other name; the phrase leaped unbidden to his lips. They formed a tiny, very compact and astonishingly symmetrical group against the afterglow of sunset. Six of them were arranged in a slightly flattened ellipse, which, Alvin was sure, was in reality a perfect circle, slightly tilted toward the line of vision. Each star was a different color; he could pick out red, blue, gold, and green, but the other tints eluded his eye. At the precise center of the formation was a single white giant—the brightest star in all the visible sky. The whole group looked exactly like a piece of jewelry; it seemed incredible, and beyond all stretching of the laws of chance, that Nature could ever have contrived so perfect a pattern.

As his eyes grew slowly accustomed to the darkness, Alvin could make out the great misty veil that had once been called the Milky Way. It stretched from the zenith down to the horizon, and the Seven Suns were entangled in its folds. The other stars had now emerged to challenge them, and their random groupings only emphasized the enigma of that perfect symmetry. It was almost as if some power had deliberately opposed the disorder of the natural Universe by setting its sign upon the stars.

Ten times, no more, the Galaxy had turned upon its axis since Man first walked on Earth. By its own standards, that was but a moment. Yet in that short period it had changed completely—changed far more than it had any right to do in the natural course of events. The great suns that had once burned so fiercely in the pride of youth were now guttering to their doom. But Alvin had never seen the heavens in their ancient glory, and so was unaware of all that had been lost.

The cold, seeping through into his bones, drove him back to the city. He extricated himself from the grating and rubbed the circulation back into his limbs. Ahead of him, down the tunnel, the light streaming out from Diaspar was so brilliant that for a moment he had to avert his eyes. Outside the city there were such things as day and night, but within it there was only eternal day. As the sun descended the sky above Diaspar would fill with light and no one would notice when the natural illumination vanished. Even before men had lost the need for sleep, they had driven darkness from their cities. The only night that ever came to Diaspar was a rare and unpredictable obscuration that sometimes visited the park and transformed it into a place of mystery.

Alvin came slowly back through the hall of mirrors, his mind still filled with night and stars. He felt inspired and yet depressed. There seemed no way in which he could ever escape out into that enormous emptiness—and no rational purpose in doing so. Jeserac had said that a man would soon die out in the desert, and Alvin could well believe him. Perhaps he might one day discover some way of leaving Diaspar, but if he did, he knew that he must soon return. To reach the desert would be an amusing game, no more. It was a game he could share with no one, and it would lead him nowhere. But at least it would be worth doing if it helped to quench the longing in his soul.

As if unwilling to return to the familiar world, Alvin lingered among the reflections from the past. He stood before one of the great mirrors and watched the scenes that came and went within its depths. Whatever mechanism produced these images was controlled by his presence, and to some extent by his thoughts. The mirrors were always blank when he first came into the room, but filled with action as soon as he moved among them.

He seemed to be standing in a large open courtyard which he had never seen in reality, but which probably still existed somewhere in Diaspar. It was unusually crowded, and some kind of public meeting seemed to be in progress. Two men were arguing politely on a raised platform while their supporters stood around and made interjections from time to time. The complete silence added to the charm of the scene, for imagination immediately went to work supplying the missing sounds. What were they debating? Alvin wondered. Perhaps it was not a real scene from the past, but a purely created episode. The careful balance of figures, the slightly formal movements, all made it seem a little too neat for life.

He studied the faces in the crowd, seeking for anyone he could recognize. There was no one here that he knew, but he might be looking at friends he would not meet for centuries to come. How many possible patterns of human physiognomy were there? The number was enormous, but it was still finite, especially when all the unesthetic variations had been eliminated.

The people in the mirror world continued their long-forgotten argument, ignoring the image of Alvin which stood motionless among them. Sometimes it was very hard to believe that he was not part of the scene himself, for the illusion was so flawless. When one of the phantoms in the mirror appeared to move behind Alvin, it vanished just as a real object would have done; and when one moved in front of him, he was the one who was eclipsed.

He was preparing to leave when he noticed an oddly dressed man standing a little apart from the main group. His movements, his clothes, everything about him, seemed slightly out of place in this assembly. He spoiled the pattern; like Alvin, he was an anachronism.

He was a good deal more than that. He was real, and he was looking at Alvin with a slightly quizzical smile.

CHAPTER FIVE

In his short lifetime, Alvin had met less than one-thousandth of the inhabitants of Diaspar. He was not surprised, therefore, that the man confronting him was a stranger. What did surprise him was to meet anyone at all here in this deserted tower, so near the frontier of the unknown.

He turned his back on the mirror world and faced the intruder. Before he could speak, the other had addressed him.

"You are Alvin, I believe. When I discovered that someone was coming here, I should have guessed it was you."

The remark was obviously not intended to give offense; it was a simple statement of fact, and Alvin accepted it as such. He was not surprised to be recognized; whether he liked it or not, the fact of his uniqueness, and its unrevealed potentialities, had made him known to everyone in the city.

"I am Khedron," continued the stranger, as if that explained everything. "They call me the Jester."

Alvin looked blank, and Khedron shrugged his shoulders in mock resignation.

"Ah, such is fame! Still, you are young and there have been no jests in your lifetime. Your ignorance is excused."

There was something refreshingly unusual about Khedron. Alvin searched his mind for the meaning of the strange word "Jester"; it evoked the faintest of memories, but he could not identify it. There were many such titles in the complex social structure of the city, and it took a lifetime to learn them all.

"Do you often come here?" Alvin asked, a little jealously. He had grown to regard the Tower of Loranne as his personal property and felt slightly annoyed that its marvels were known to anyone else. But had Khedron, he wondered, ever looked out across the desert or seen the stars sinking down into the west?

"No," said Khedron, almost as if answering his unspoken thoughts. "I have never been here before. But it is my pleasure to learn of unusual happenings in the city, and it is a very long time since anyone went to the Tower of Loranne."

Alvin wondered fleetingly how Khedron knew of his earlier visits, but quickly dismissed the matter from his mind. Diaspar was full of eyes and ears and other more subtle sense organs which kept the city aware of all that was happening within it. Anyone who was sufficiently interested could no doubt find a way of tapping these channels.

"Even if it is unusual for anyone to come here," said Alvin, still fencing verbally, "why should you be interested?"

"Because in Diaspar," replied Khedron, "the unusual is my prerogative. I had marked you down a long time ago; I knew we should meet some day. After my fashion, I too am unique. Oh, not in the way that you are: this is not my first life. I have walked a thousand times out of the Hall of Creation. But somewhere back at the beginning I was chosen to be Jester, and there is only one Jester at a time in Diaspar. Most people think that is one too many."

There was an irony about Khedron's speech that left Alvin still floundering. It was not the best of manners to ask direct personal questions, but after all Khedron had raised the subject.

"I'm sorry about my ignorance," said Alvin. "But what is a Jester, and what does he do?"

"You ask 'what,'" replied Khedron, "so I'll start by telling you 'why.' It's a long story, but I think you will be interested."

"I am interested in everything," said Alvin, truthfully enough.

"Very well. The men—if they were men, which I sometimes doubt

—who designed Diaspar had to solve an incredibly complex problem. Diaspar is not merely a machine, you know—it is a living organism, and an immortal one. We are so accustomed to our society that we can't appreciate how strange it would have seemed to our first ancestors. Here we have a tiny, closed world which never changes except in its minor details, and yet which is perfectly stable, age after age. It has probably lasted longer than the rest of human history—yet in *that* history there were, so it is believed, countless thousands of separate cultures and civilizations which endured for a little while and then perished. How did Diaspar achieve its extraordinary stability?"

Alvin was surprised that anyone should ask so elementary a question, and his hopes of learning something new began to wane.

"Through the Memory Banks, of course," he replied. "Diaspar is always composed of the same people, though their actual groupings change as their bodies are created or destroyed."

Khedron shook his head.

"That is only a very small part of the answer. With exactly the same people, you could build many different patterns of society. I can't prove that, and I've no direct evidence of it, but I believe it's true. The designers of the city did not merely fix its population; they fixed the laws governing its behavior. We're scarcely aware that those laws exist, but we obey them. Diaspar is a frozen culture, which cannot change outside of narrow limits. The Memory Banks store many other things outside the patterns of our bodies and personalities. They store the image of the city itself, holding its every atom rigid against all the changes that time can bring. Look at this pavement—it was laid down millions of years ago, and countless feet have walked upon it. Can you see any sign of wear? Unprotected matter, however adamant, would have been ground to dust ages ago. But as long as there is power to operate the Memory Banks, and as long as the matrices they contain can still control the patterns of the city, the physical structure of Diaspar will never change."

"But there have been *some* changes," protested Alvin. "Many buildings have been torn down since the city was built, and new ones erected."

"Of course—but only by discharging the information stored in the Memory Banks and then setting up new patterns. In any case, I was merely mentioning that as an example of the way the city preserves itself physically. The point I want to make is that in the same way there are machines in Diaspar that preserve our social structure. They watch for any changes, and correct them before they become too great. How do they do it? I don't know—perhaps by selecting those who emerge from the Hall of Creation. Perhaps by tampering with our personality atterns; we may think we have free will, but can we be certain of that?

"In any event, the problem was solved. Diaspar has survived and ome safely down the ages, like a great ship carrying as its cargo all that left of the human race. It is a tremendous achievement in social engi-eering, though whether it is worth doing is quite another matter.

"Stability, however, is not enough. It leads too easily to stagnation, nd thence to decadence. The designers of the city took elaborate steps avoid this, though these deserted buildings suggest that they did not ntirely succeed. I, Khedron the Jester, am part of that plan. A very mall part, perhaps. I like to think otherwise, but I can never be sure."

"And just what is that part?" asked Alvin, still very much in the dark, nd becoming a little exasperated.

"Let us say that I introduce calculated amounts of disorder into the ity. To explain my operations would be to destroy their effectiveness. udge me by my deeds, though they are few, rather than my words, ough they are many."

Alvin had never before met anyone quite like Khedron. The Jester as a real personality—a character who stood head and shoulders above e general level of uniformity which was typical of Diaspar. Though here seemed no hope of discovering precisely what his duties were and ow he carried them out, that was of minor importance. All that mat-ered, Alvin sensed, was that here was someone to whom he could talk—hen there was a gap in the monologue—and who might give him an-wers to many of the problems that had puzzled him for so long.

They went back together down through the corridors of the Tower f Loranne, and emerged beside the deserted moving way. Not until they ere once more in the streets did it occur to Alvin that Khedron had ever asked him what he had been doing out here at the edge of the nknown. He suspected that Khedron knew, and was interested but not urprised. Something told him that it would be very difficult to surprise hedron.

They exchanged index numbers, so that they could call each other henever they wished. Alvin was anxious to see more of the Jester, hough he fancied that his company might prove exhausting if it was oo prolonged. Before they met again, however, he wanted to find what is friends, and particularly Jeserac, could tell him about Khedron.

"Until our next meeting," said Khedron, and promptly vanished. lvin was somewhat annoyed. If you met anyone when you were merely rojecting yourself, and were not present in the flesh, it was good man-ers to make that clear from the beginning. It could sometimes put the arty who was ignorant of the facts at a considerable disadvantage.

Probably Khedron had been quietly at home all the time—wherever his home might be. The number that he had given Alvin would insure that any messages would reach him, but did not reveal where he lived. That at least was according to normal custom. You might be free enough with index numbers, but your actual address was something you disclosed only to your intimate friends.

As he made his way back into the city, Alvin pondered over all that Khedron had told him about Diaspar and its social organization. It was strange that he had met no one else who had ever seemed dissatisfied with their mode of life. Diaspar and its inhabitants had been designed as part of one master plan; they formed a perfect symbiosis. Throughout their long lives, the people of the city were never bored. Though their world might be a tiny one by the standard of earlier ages, its complexity was overwhelming, its wealth of wonder and treasure beyond calculation. Here Man had gathered all the fruits of his genius, everything that had been saved from the ruin of the past. All the cities that had ever been, so it was said, had given something to Diaspar; before the coming of the Invaders, its name had been known on all the worlds that Man had lost. Into the building of Diaspar had gone all the skill, all the artistry of the Empire. When the great days were coming to an end, men of genius had remolded the city and given it the machines that made it immortal. Whatever might be forgotten, Diaspar would live and bear the descendants of Man safely down the stream of time.

They had achieved nothing except survival, and were content with that. There were a million things to occupy their lives between the hour when they came, almost full-grown, from the Hall of Creation and the hour when, their bodies scarcely older, they returned to the Memory Banks of the city. In a world where all men and women possess an intelligence that would once have been the mark of genius, there can be no danger of boredom. The delights of conversation and argument, the intricate formalities of social intercourse—these alone were enough to occupy a goodly portion of a lifetime. Beyond those were the great formal debates, when the whole city would listen entranced while its keenest minds met in combat or strove to scale those mountain peaks of philosophy which are never conquered yet whose challenge never palls.

No man or woman was without some absorbing intellectual interest. Eriston, for example, spent much of his time in prolonged soliloquies with the Central Computer, which virtually ran the city, yet which had leisure for scores of simultaneous discussions with anyone who cared to match his wits against it. For three hundred years, Eriston had been trying to construct logical paradoxes which the machine could not resolve. He did not expect to make serious progress before he had used up several lifetimes.

Etania's interests were of a more esthetic nature. She designed and constructed, with the aid of the matter organizers, three-dimensional interlacing patterns of such beautiful complexity that they were really extremely advanced problems in topology. Her work could be seen all over Diaspar, and some of her patterns had been incorporated in the floors of the great halls of choreography, where they were used as the basis for evolving new ballet creations and dance motifs.

Such occupations might have seemed arid to those who did not possess the intellect to appreciate their subtleties. Yet there was no one in Diaspar who could not understand something of what Eriston and Etania were trying to do and did not have some equally consuming interest of his own.

Athletics and various sports, including many only rendered possible by the control of gravity, made pleasant the first few centuries of youth. For adventure and the exercise of the imagination, the sagas provided all that anyone could desire. They were the inevitable end product of that striving for realism which began when men started to reproduce moving images and to record sounds, and then to use these techniques to enact scenes from real or imaginary life. In the sagas, the illusion was perfect because all the sense impressions involved were fed directly into the mind and any conflicting sensations were diverted. The entranced spectator was cut off from reality as long as the adventure lasted; it was as if he lived a dream yet believed he was awake.

In a world of order and stability, which in its broad outlines had not changed for a billion years, it was perhaps not surprising to find an absorbing interest in games of chance. Humanity had always been fascinated by the mystery of the falling dice, the turn of a card, the spin of the pointer. At its lowest level, this interest was based on mere cupidity—and that was an emotion that could have no place in a world where everyone possessed all that they could reasonably need. Even when this motive was ruled out, however, the purely intellectual fascination of chance remained to seduce the most sophisticated minds. Machines that behaved in a purely random way—events whose outcome could never be predicted, no matter how much information one had—from these philosopher and gambler could derive equal enjoyment.

And there still remained, for all men to share, the linked worlds of love and art. Linked, because love without art is merely the slaking of desire, and art cannot be enjoyed unless it is approached with love.

Men had sought beauty in many forms—in sequences of sound, in lines upon paper, in surfaces of stone, in the movements of the human body, in colors ranged through space. All these media still survived in Diaspar, and down the ages others had been added to them. No one was yet certain if all the possibilities of art had been discovered; or if it had any meaning outside the mind of man.

And the same was true of love.

CHAPTER SIX

Jeserac sat motionless within a whirlpool of numbers. The first thousand primes, expressed in the binary scale that had been used for all arithmetical operations since electronic computers were invented, marched in order before him. Endless ranks of 1s and 0s paraded past, bringing before Jeserac's eyes the complete sequence of all those numbers that possessed no factors except themselves and unity. There was a mystery about the primes that had always fascinated Man, and they held his imagination still.

Jeserac was no mathematician, though sometimes he liked to believe he was. All he could do was to search among the infinite array of primes for special relationships and rules which more talented men might incorporate in general laws. He could find how numbers behaved, but he could not explain why. It was his pleasure to hack his way through the arithmetical jungle, and sometimes he discovered wonders that more skillful explorers had missed.

He set up the matrix of all possible integers, and started his computer stringing the primes across its surface as beads might be arranged at the intersections of a mesh. Jeserac had done this a hundred times before, and it had never taught him anything. But he was fascinated by the way in which the numbers he was studying were scattered, apparently according to no laws, across the spectrum of the integers. He knew the laws of distribution that had already been discovered, but always hoped to discover more.

He could scarcely complain about the interruption. If he had wished to remain undisturbed, he should have set his annunciator accordingly. As the gentle chime sounded in his ear, the wall of numbers shivered, the digits blurred together, and Jeserac returned to the world of mere reality.

He recognized Khedron at once, and was none too pleased. Jeserac did not care to be disturbed from his ordered way of life, and Khedron represented the unpredictable. However, he greeted his visitor politely enough and concealed all trace of his mild concern.

When two people met for the first time in Diaspar—or even for the hundredth—it was customary to spend an hour or so in an exchange of courtesies before getting down to business, if any. Khedron somewhat offended Jeserac by racing through these formalities in a mere fifteen minutes and then saying abruptly: "I'd like to talk to you about Alvin. You're his tutor, I believe."

"That is true," replied Jeserac. "I still see him several times a week—as often as he wishes."

"And would you say that he was an apt pupil?"

Jeserac thought that over; it was a difficult question to answer. The pupil-tutor relationship was extremely important and was, indeed, one of the foundations of life in Diaspar. On the average, ten thousand new minds came into the city every year. Their previous memories were still latent, and for the first twenty years of their existence everything around them was fresh and strange. They had to be taught to use the myriad machines and devices that were the background of everyday life, and they had to learn their way through the most complex society Man had ever built.

Part of this instruction came from the couples chosen to be the parents of the new citizens. The selection was by lot, and the duties were not onerous. Eriston and Etania had devoted no more than a third of their time to Alvin's upbringing, and they had done all that was expected of them.

Jeserac's duties were confined to the more formal aspects of Alvin's education; it was assumed that his parents would teach him how to behave in society and introduce him to an ever-widening circle of friends. They were responsible for Alvin's character, Jeserac for his mind.

"I find it rather hard to answer your question," Jeserac replied. "Certainly there is nothing wrong with Alvin's intelligence, but many of the things that should concern him seem to be a matter of complete indifference. On the other hand, he shows a morbid curiosity regarding subjects which we do not generally discuss."

"The world outside Diaspar, for example?"

"Yes—but how did you know?"

Khedron hesitated for a moment, wondering how far he should take Jeserac into his confidence. He knew that Jeserac was kindly and well-intentioned, but he knew also that he must be bound by the same taboos that controlled everyone in Diaspar—everyone except Alvin.

"I guessed it," he said at last.

Jeserac settled down more comfortably in the depths of the chair he had just materialized. This was an interesting situation, and he wanted to analyze it as fully as possible. There was not much he could learn, however, unless Khedron was willing to co-operate.

He should have anticipated that Alvin would one day meet the Jester, with unpredictable consequences. Khedron was the only other person in the city who could be called eccentric—and even his eccentricity had been planned by the designers of Diaspar. Long ago it had been discovered that without some crime or disorder, Utopia soon became unbearably dull. Crime, however, from the nature of things, could not be guaranteed to remain at the optimum level which the social equations demanded. If it was licensed and regulated, it ceased to be crime.

The office of Jester was the solution—at first sight naïve, yet actually profoundly subtle—which the city's designers had evolved. In all the history of Diaspar there were less than two hundred persons whose mental inheritance fitted them for this peculiar role. They had certain privileges that protected them from the consequences of their actions, though there had been Jesters who had overstepped the mark and paid the only penalty that Diaspar could impose—that of being banished into the future before their current incarnation had ended.

On rare and unforeseeable occasions, the Jester would turn the city upside-down by some prank which might be no more than an elaborate practical joke, or which might be a calculated assault on some currently cherished belief or way of life. All things considered, the name "Jester" was a highly appropriate one. There had once been men with very similar duties, operating with the same license, in the days when there were courts and kings.

"It will help," said Jeserac, "if we are frank with one another. We both know that Alvin is a Unique—that he has never experienced any earlier life in Diaspar. Perhaps you can guess, better than I can, the implications of that. I doubt if anything that happens in the city is totally unplanned, so there must be a purpose in his creation. Whether he will achieve that purpose—whatever it is—I do not know. Nor do I know whether it is good or bad. I cannot guess what it is."

"Suppose it concerns something external to the city?"

Jeserac smiled patiently; the Jester was having his little joke, as was only to be expected.

"I have told him what lies there; he knows that there is nothing outside Diaspar except the desert. Take him there if you can; perhaps *you* know a way. When he sees the reality, it may cure the strangeness in his mind."

"I think he has already seen it," said Khedron softly. But he said it to himself, and not to Jeserac.

"I do not believe that Alvin is happy," Jeserac continued. "He has formed no real attachments, and it is hard to see how he can while he still suffers from this obsession. But after all, he is very young. He may grow out of this phase, and become part of the pattern of the city."

Jeserac was talking to reassure himself; Khedron wondered if he really believed what he was saying.

"Tell me, Jeserac," asked Khedron abruptly, "does Alvin know that he is not the first Unique?"

Jeserac looked startled, then a little defiant.

"I might have guessed," he said ruefully, "that *you* would know that. How many Uniques have there been in the whole history of Diaspar? As many as ten?"

"Fourteen," answered Khedron without hesitation. "Not counting Alvin."

"You have better information than I can command," said Jeserac wryly. "Perhaps you can tell me what happened to those Uniques?"

"They disappeared."

"Thank you: I knew that already. That is why I have told Alvin as little as possible about his predecessors: it would hardly help him in his present mood. Can I rely on your co-operation?"

"For the moment—yes. I want to study him myself; mysteries have always intrigued me, and there are too few in Diaspar. Besides, I think that Fate may be arranging a jest beside which all my efforts will look very modest indeed. In that case, I want to make sure that I am present at its climax."

"You are rather too fond of talking in riddles," complained Jeserac. "Exactly what are you anticipating?"

"I doubt if my guesses will be any better than yours. But I believe this—neither you nor I nor anyone in Diaspar will be able to stop Alvin when he has decided what he wants to do. We have a very interesting few centuries ahead of us."

Jeserac sat motionless for a long time, his mathematics forgotten, after the image of Khedron had faded from sight. A sense of foreboding, the like of which he had never known before, hung heavily upon him. For a fleeting moment he wondered if he should request an audience with the Council—but would that not be making a ridiculous fuss about nothing? Perhaps the whole affair was some complicated and obscure jest of Khedron's, though he could not imagine why he had been chosen to be its butt.

He thought the matter over carefully, examining the problem from every angle. After little more than an hour, he made a characteristic decision.

He would wait and see.

Alvin wasted no time learning all that he could about Khedron. Jeserac, as usual, was his main source of information. The old tutor gave a carefully factual account of his meeting with the Jester, and added what little he knew about the other's mode of life. Insofar as such a thing was possible in Diaspar, Khedron was a recluse: no one knew where he lived or anything about his way of life. The last jest he had contrived had been a rather childish prank involving a general paralysis of the moving ways. That had been fifty years ago; a century earlier he had let loose a particularly revolting dragon which had wandered around the city eating every existing specimen of the works of the currently most popular sculptor. The artist himself, justifiably alarmed when the beast's single-minded diet became obvious, had gone into hiding and not emerged until the monster had vanished as mysteriously as it had appeared.

One thing was obvious from these accounts. Khedron must have a profound understanding of the machines and powers that ruled the city, and could make them obey his will in ways which no one else could do. Presumably there must be some overriding control which prevented any too-ambitious Jester from causing permanent and irreparable damage to the complex structure of Diaspar.

Alvin filed all this information away, but made no move to contact Khedron. Though he had many questions to ask the Jester, his stubborn streak of independence—perhaps the most truly unique of all his qualities—made him determined to discover all he could by his own unaided efforts. He had embarked on a project that might keep him busy for years, but as long as he felt that he was moving toward his goal he was happy.

Like some traveler of old mapping out an unknown land, he had begun the systematic exploration of Diaspar. He spent his weeks and days prowling through the lonely towers at the margin of the city, in the hope that somewhere he might discover a way out into the world beyond. During the course of his search he found a dozen of the great air vents opening high above the desert, but they were all barred—and even if the bars had not been there, the sheer drop of almost a mile was sufficient obstacle.

He found no other exits, though he explored a thousand corridors and ten thousand empty chambers. All these buildings were in that perfect and spotless condition which the people of Diaspar took for granted as part of the normal order of things. Sometimes Alvin would meet a wandering robot, obviously on a tour of inspection, and he never failed to question the machine. He learned nothing, because the machines he encountered were not keyed to respond to human speech or thoughts. Though they were aware of his presence, for they floated politely aside to let him pass, they refused to engage in conversation.

There were times when Alvin did not see another human being for days. When he felt hungry, he would go into one of the living apartments and order a meal. Miraculous machines of whose existence he seldom gave a thought would wake to life after aeons of slumber. The patterns they had stored in their memories would flicker on the edge of reality, organizing and directing the matter they controlled. And so a meal prepared by a master chef a hundred million years before would be called again into existence to delight the palate or merely to satisfy the appetite.

The loneliness of this deserted world—the empty shell surrounding the living heart of the city—did not depress Alvin. He was used to loneliness, even when he was among those he called his friends. This ardent exploration, absorbing all his energy and interest, made him forget for the moment the mystery of his heritage and the anomaly that cut him off from all his fellows.

He had explored less than one-hundredth of the city's rim when he decided that he was wasting his time. His decision was not the result of impatience, but of sheer common sense. If needs be, he was prepared to come back and finish the task, even if it took him the remainder of his life. He had seen enough, however, to convince him that if a way out of Diaspar did exist, it would not be found as easily as this. He might waste centuries in fruitless search unless he called upon the assistance of wiser men.

Jeserac had told him flatly that he knew no road out of Diaspar, and doubted if one existed. The information machines, when Alvin had questioned them, had searched their almost infinite memories in vain. They could tell him every detail of the city's history back to the beginning of recorded times—back to the barrier beyond which the Dawn Ages lay forever hidden. But they could not answer Alvin's simple question, or else some higher power had forbidden them to do so.

He would have to see Khedron again.

CHAPTER SEVEN

"You took your time," said Khedron, "but I knew you would call sooner or later."

This confidence annoyed Alvin; he did not like to think that his behavior could be predicted so accurately. He wondered if the Jester had watched all his fruitless searching and knew exactly what he had been doing.

"I am trying to find a way out of the city," he said bluntly. "There *must* be one, and I think you could help me find it."

Khedron was silent for a moment. There was still time, if he wished, to turn back from the road that stretched before him, and which led into a future beyond all his powers of prophecy. No one else would have hesitated; no other man in the city, even if he had the power, would have dared to disturb the ghosts of an age that had been dead for millions of centuries. Perhaps there was no danger, perhaps nothing could alter the perpetual changelessness of Diaspar. But if there was any risk of something strange and new coming into the world, this might be the last chance to ward it off.

Khedron was content with the order of things as it was. True, he might upset that order from time to time—but only by a little. He was a critic, not a revolutionary. On the placidly flowing river of time, he wished only to make a few ripples: he shrank from diverting its course. The desire for adventure, other than that of the mind, had been eliminated from him as carefully and thoroughly as from all the other citizens of Diaspar.

Yet he still possessed, though it was almost extinguished, that spark of curiosity that was once Man's greatest gift. He was still prepared to take a risk.

He looked at Alvin and tried to remember his own youth, his own dreams of half a thousand years before. Any moment of his past that he cared to choose was still clear and sharp when he turned his memory upon it. Like beads upon a string, this life and all the ones before it stretched back through the ages; he would seize and re-examine any one he wished. Most of those older Khedrons were strangers to him now; the basic patterns might be the same, but the weight of experience separated him from them forever. If he wished, he could wash his mind clear of all his earlier incarnations, when next he walked back into the

Hall of Creation to sleep until the city called him forth again. But that would be a kind of death, and he was not ready for that yet. He was still prepared to go on collecting all that life could offer, like a chambered nautilus patiently adding new cells to its slowly expanding spiral.

In his youth, he had been no different from his companions. It was not until he came of age and the latent memories of his earlier lives came flooding back that he had taken up the role for which he had been destined long ago. Sometimes he felt resentment that the intelligences which had contrived Diaspar with such infinite skill could even now, after all these ages, make him move like a puppet across their stage. Here, perhaps, was a chance of obtaining a long-delayed revenge. A new actor had appeared who might ring down the curtain for the last time on a play that already had seen far too many acts.

Sympathy, for one whose loneliness must be even greater than his own; an ennui produced by ages of repetition; and an impish sense of fun—these were the discordant factors that prompted Khedron to act.

"I may be able to help you," he told Alvin, "or I may not. I don't wish to raise any false hopes. Meet me in half an hour at the intersection of Radius 3 and Ring 2. If I cannot do anything else, at least I can promise you an interesting journey."

Alvin was at the rendezvous ten minutes ahead of time, though it was on the other side of the city. He waited impatiently as the moving ways swept eternally past him, bearing the placid and contented people of the city about their unimportant business. At last he saw the tall figure of Khedron appear in the distance, and a moment later he was for the first time in the physical presence of the Jester. This was no projected image; when they touched palms in the ancient greeting, Khedron was real enough.

The Jester sat down on one of the marble balustrades and regarded Alvin with a curious intentness.

"I wonder," he said, "if you know what you are asking. And I wonder what you would do if you obtained it. Do you *really* imagine that you could leave the city, even if you found a way?"

"I am sure of it," replied Alvin, bravely enough, though Khedron could sense the uncertainty in his voice.

"Then let me tell you something which you may not know. You see those towers there?" Khedron pointed to the twin peaks of Power Central and Council Hall, staring at each other across a canyon a mile deep. "Suppose I were to lay a perfectly firm plank between those two towers—a plank only six inches wide. Could you walk across it?"

Alvin hesitated.

"I don't know," he answered. "I wouldn't like to try."

"I'm quite sure you could never do it. You'd get giddy and fall off before you'd gone a dozen paces. Yet if that same plank was supported just clear of the ground, you'd be able to walk along it without difficulty."

"And what does that prove?"

"A simple point I'm trying to make. In the two experiments I've described, the plank would be exactly the same in both cases. One of those wheeled robots you sometimes meet could cross it just as easily if it was bridging those towers as if it was laid along the ground. *We* couldn't, because we have a fear of heights. It may be irrational, but it's too powerful to be ignored. It is built into us; we are born with it.

"In the same way, we have a fear of space. Show any man in Diaspar a road out of the city—a road that might be just like this road in front of us now—and he could not go far along it. He would have to turn back, as you would turn back if you started to cross a plank between those towers."

"But why?" asked Alvin. "There must have been a time—"

"I know, I know," said Khedron. "Men once went out over the whole world, and to the stars themselves. Something changed them and gave them this fear with which they are now born. You alone imagine that you do not possess it. Well, we shall see. I'm taking you to Council Hall."

The Hall was one of the largest buildings in the city, and was almost entirely given over to the machines that were the real administrators of Diaspar. Not far from its summit was the chamber where the Council met on those infrequent occasions when it had any business to discuss.

The wide entrance swallowed them up, and Khedron strode forward into the golden gloom. Alvin had never entered Council Hall before; there was no rule against it—there were few rules against anything in Diaspar—but like everyone else he had a certain half-religious awe of the place. In a world that had no gods, Council Hall was the nearest thing to a temple.

Khedron never hesitated as he led Alvin along corridors and down ramps that were obviously made for wheeled machines, not human traffic. Some of these ramps zigzagged down into the depths at such steep angles that it would have been impossible to keep a footing on them had not gravity been twisted to compensate for the slope.

They came at last to a closed door, which slid silently open as they approached, then barred their retreat. Ahead was another door, which did not open as they came up to it. Khedron made no move to touch the door, but stood motionless in front of it. After a short pause, a quiet voice said: "Please state your names."

"I am Khedron the Jester. My companion is Alvin."

"And your business?"

"Sheer curiosity."

Rather to Alvin's surprise, the door opened at once. In his experience, if one gave facetious replies to machines it always led to confusion and one had to go back to the beginning. The machine that had interrogated Khedron must have been a very sophisticated one—far up in the hierarchy of the Central Computer.

They met no more barriers, but Alvin suspected that they had passed many tests of which he had no knowledge. A short corridor brought them out abruptly into a huge circular chamber with a sunken floor, and set in that floor was something so astonishing that for a moment Alvin was overwhelmed with wonder. He was looking down upon the entire city of Diaspar, spread out before him with its tallest buildings barely reaching to his shoulder.

He spent so long picking out familiar places and observing unexpected vistas that it was some time before he paid any notice to the rest of the chamber. Its walls were covered with a microscopically detailed pattern of black and white squares; the pattern itself was completely irregular, and when he moved his eyes quickly he got the impression that it was flickering swiftly, though it never changed. At frequent intervals around the chamber were manually controlled machines of some type, each complete with a vision screen and a seat for the operator.

Khedron let Alvin look his fill. Then he pointed to the diminutive city and said: "Do you know what that is?"

Alvin was tempted to answer, "A model, I suppose," but that answer was so obvious that he was sure it must be wrong. So he shook his head and waited for Khedron to answer his own question.

"You remember," said the Jester, "that I once told you how the city was maintained—how the Memory Banks hold its pattern frozen forever. Those Banks are all around us, with all their immeasurable store of information, completely defining the city as it is today. Every atom of Diaspar is somehow keyed, by forces we have forgotten, to the matrices buried in these walls."

He waved toward the perfect, infinitely detailed simulacrum of Diaspar that lay below them.

"That is no model; it does not really exist. It is merely the projected image of the pattern held in the Memory Banks, and therefore it is absolutely identical with the city itself. These viewing machines here enable one to magnify any desired portion, to look at it life size or larger. They are used when it is necessary to make alterations in the design, though it is a very long time since that was done. If you want to know what Diaspar is like, this is the place to come. You can learn more here in a few days than you would in a lifetime of actual exploring."

"It's wonderful," said Alvin. "How many people know that it exists?"

"Oh, a good many, but it seldom concerns them. The Council comes down here from time to time; no alterations to the city can be made unless they are all here. And not even then, if the Central Computer doesn't approve of the proposed change. I doubt if this room is visited more than two or three times a year."

Alvin wanted to know how Khedron had access to it, and then remembered that many of his more elaborate jests must have involved a knowledge of the city's inner mechanisms that could have come only from very profound study. It must be one of the Jester's privileges to go anywhere and learn anything; he could have no better guide to the secrets of Diaspar.

"What you are looking for may not exist," said Khedron, "but if it does, this is where you will find it. Let me show you how to operate the monitors."

For the next hour Alvin sat before one of the vision screens, learning to use the controls. He could select at will any point in the city, and examine it with any degree of magnification. Streets and towers and walls and moving ways flashed across the screen as he changed the coordinates; it was as though he was an all-seeing, disembodied spirit that could move effortlessly over the whole of Diaspar, unhindered by any physical obstructions.

Yet it was not, in reality, Diaspar that he was examining. He was moving through the memory cells, looking at the dream image of the city—the dream that had had the power to hold the real Diaspar untouched by time for a billion years. He could see only that part of the city which was permanent; the people who walked its streets were no part of this frozen image. For his purpose, that did not matter. His concern now was purely with the creation of stone and metal in which he was imprisoned, and not those who shared—however willingly—his confinement.

He searched for and presently found the Tower of Loranne, and moved swiftly through the corridors and passageways which he had already explored in reality. As the image of the stone grille expanded before his eyes, he could almost feel the cold wind that had blown ceaselessly through it for perhaps half the entire history of mankind, and that was blowing now. He came up to the grille, looked out—and saw nothing. For a moment the shock was so great that he almost doubted his own memory; had his vision of the desert been nothing more than a dream?

Then he remembered the truth. The desert was no part of Diaspar, and therefore no image of it existed in the phantom world he was exploring. Anything might lie beyond that grille in reality; this monitor screen could never show it.

Yet it could show him something that no living man had ever seen. Alvin advanced his viewpoint through the grille, out into the nothingness beyond the city. He turned the control which altered the direction of vision, so that he looked backward along the way that he had come. And there behind him lay Diaspar—seen from the outside.

To the computers, the memory circuits, and all the multitudinous mechanisms that created the image at which Alvin was looking, it was merely a simple problem of perspective. They "knew" the form of the city; therefore they could show it as it would appear from the outside. Yet even though he could appreciate how the trick was done, the effect on Alvin was overwhelming. In spirit, if not in reality, he had escaped from the city. He appeared to be hanging in space, a few feet away from the sheer wall of the Tower of Loranne. For a moment he stared at the smooth gray surface before his eyes; then he touched the control and let his viewpoint drop toward the ground.

Now that he knew the possibilities of this wonderful instrument, his plan of action was clear. There was no need to spend months and years exploring Diaspar from the inside, room by room and corridor by corridor. From this new vantage point he could wing his way along the outside of the city, and could see at once any openings that might lead to the desert and the world beyond.

The sense of victory, of achievement, made him feel lightheaded and anxious to share his joy. He turned to Khedron, wishing to thank the Jester for having made this possible. But Khedron was gone, and it took only a moment's thought to realize why.

Alvin was perhaps the only man in Diaspar who could look unaffected upon the images that were now drifting across the screen. Khedron could help him in his search, but even the Jester shared the strange terror of the Universe which had pinned mankind for so long inside its little world. He had left Alvin to continue his quest alone.

The sense of loneliness, which for a little while had lifted from Alvin's soul, pressed down upon him once more. But this was no time for melancholy; there was too much to do. He turned back to the monitor screen, set the image of the city wall drifting slowly across it, and began his search.

Diaspar saw little of Alvin for the next few weeks, though only a few people noticed his absence. Jeserac, when he discovered that his erstwhile pupil was spending all his time at Council Hall instead of prowling around the frontier of the city, felt slightly relieved, imagining that Alvin could come to no trouble there. Eriston and Etania called his room once or twice, found that he was out and thought nothing of it. Alystra was a little more persistent.

For her own peace of mind, it was a pity that she had become infatuated with Alvin, when there were so many more suitable choices. Alystra had never had any difficulty in finding partners, but by comparison with Alvin all the other men she knew were nonentities, cast from the same featureless mold. She would not lose him without a struggle: his aloofness and indifference set a challenge which she could not resist.

Yet perhaps her motives were not entirely selfish, and were maternal rather than sexual. Though birth had been forgotten, the feminine instincts of protection and sympathy still remained. Alvin might appear to be stubborn and self-reliant and determined to have his own way, yet Alystra could sense his inner loneliness.

When she found that Alvin had disappeared, she promptly asked Jeserac what had happened to him. Jeserac, with only a momentary hesitation, told her. If Alvin did not want company, the answer was in his own hands. His tutor neither approved nor disapproved of this relationship. On the whole, he rather liked Alystra and hoped that her influence would help Alvin to adjust himself to life in Diaspar.

The fact that Alvin was spending his time at Council Hall could only mean that he was engaged on some research project, and this knowledge at least served to quell any suspicions Alystra might have concerning possible rivals. But though her jealousy was not aroused, her curiosity was. She sometimes reproached herself for abandoning Alvin in the Tower of Loranne, though she knew that if the circumstances were repeated she would do exactly the same thing again. There was no way of understanding Alvin's mind, she told herself, unless she could discover what he was trying to do.

She walked purposefully into the main hall, impressed but not overawed by the hush that fell as soon as she passed through the entrance.

The information machines were ranged side by side against the far wall, and she chose one at random.

As soon as the recognition signal lighted up, she said, "I am looking for Alvin; he is somewhere in this building. Where can I find him?"

Even after a lifetime, one never grew wholly accustomed to the complete absence of time lag when an information machine replied to an ordinary question. There were people who knew—or claimed to know—how it was done, and talked learnedly of "access time" and "storage space," but that made the final result none the less marvelous. Any question of a purely factual nature, within the city's truly enormous range of available information, could be answered immediately. Only if complex calculations were involved before a reply could be given would there be any appreciable delay.

"He is with the monitors," came the reply. It was not very helpful, since the name conveyed nothing to Alystra. No machine ever volunteered more information than it was asked for, and learning to frame questions properly was an art which often took a long time to acquire.

"How do I reach him?" asked Alystra. She would find what the monitors were when she got to them.

"I cannot tell you unless you have the permission of the Council."

This was a most unexpected, even a disconcerting, development. There were very few places in Diaspar that could not be visited by anyone who pleased. Alystra was quite certain that Alvin had *not* obtained Council permission, and this could only mean that a higher authority was helping him.

The Council ruled Diaspar, but the Council itself could be overridden by a superior power—the all-but-infinite intellect of the Central Computer. It was difficult not to think of the Central Computer as a living entity, localized in a single spot, though actually it was the sum total of all the machines in Diaspar. Even if it was not alive in the biological sense, it certainly possessed at least as much awareness and self-consciousness as a human being. It must know what Alvin was doing, and, therefore, it must approve, otherwise it would have stopped him or referred him to the Council, as the information machine had done to Alystra.

There was no point in staying here. Alystra knew that any attempt to find Alvin—even if she knew exactly where he was in this enormous building—would be doomed to failure. Doors would fail to open; slideways would reverse when she stood on them, carrying her backward instead of forward; elevator fields would be mysteriously inert, refusing to lift her from one floor to another. If she persisted, she would be gently conveyed out into the street by a polite but firm robot, or else shuttled round and round Council Hall until she grew fed up and left under her own volition.

She was in a bad temper as she walked out into the street. She was also more than a little puzzled, and for the first time felt that there was some mystery here which made her personal desires and interests seem very trivial indeed. That did not mean that they would be any the less important to her. She had no idea what she was going to do next, but she was sure of one thing. Alvin was not the only person in Diaspar who could be stubborn and persistent.

CHAPTER EIGHT

The image on the monitor screen faded as Alvin raised his hands from the control panel and cleared the circuits. For a moment he sat quite motionless, looking into the blank rectangle that had occupied all his conscious mind for so many weeks. He had circumnavigated his world; across that screen had passed every square foot of the outer wall of Diaspar. He knew the city better than any living man save perhaps Khedron; and he knew now that there was no way through the walls.

The feeling that possessed him was not mere despondency; he had never really expected that it would be as easy as this, that he would find what he sought at the first attempt. What was important was that he had eliminated one possibility. Now he must deal with the others.

He rose to his feet and walked over to the image of the city which almost filled the chamber. It was hard not to think of it as an actual model, though he knew that in reality it was no more than an optical projection of the pattern in the memory cells he had been exploring. When he altered the monitor controls and set his viewpoint moving through Diaspar, a spot of light would travel over the surface of this replica, so that he could see exactly where he was going. It had been a useful guide in the early days, but he soon had grown so skillful at setting the co-ordinates that he had not needed this aid.

The city lay spread out beneath him; he looked down upon it like a god. Yet he scarcely saw it as he considered, one by one, the steps he should now take.

If all else failed, there was one solution to the problem. Diaspar might be held in a perpetual stasis by its eternity circuits, frozen forever according to the pattern in the memory cells, but that pattern could itself be altered, and the city would then change with it. It would be possible to redesign a section of the outer wall so that it contained a doorway, feed this pattern into the monitors, and let the city reshape itself to the new conception.

Alvin suspected that the large areas of the monitor control board whose purpose Khedron had not explained to him were concerned with such alterations. It would be useless to experiment with them; controls that could alter the very structure of the city were firmly locked and could be operated only with the authority of the Council and the approval of the Central Computer. There was very little chance that the Council would grant him what he asked, even if he was prepared for decades or even centuries of patient pleading. That was not a prospect that appealed to him in the least.

He turned his thoughts toward the sky. Sometimes he had imagined, in fantasies which he was half-ashamed to recall, that he had regained the freedom of the air which man had renounced so long ago. Once, he knew, the skies of Earth had been filled with strange shapes. Out of space the great ships had come, bearing unknown treasures, to berth at the legendary Port of Diaspar. But the Port had been beyond the limits of the city; aeons ago it had been buried by the drifting sand. He could dream that somewhere in the mazes of Diaspar a flying machine might still be hidden, but he did not really believe it. Even in the days when small, personal flyers had been in common use, it was most unlikely that they had ever been allowed to operate inside the limits of the city.

For a moment he lost himself in the old, familiar dream. He imagined that he was master of the sky, that the world lay spread out beneath him, inviting him to travel where he willed. It was not the world of his own time that he saw, but the lost world of the dawn—a rich and living panorama of hills and lakes and forests. He felt a bitter envy of his unknown ancestors, who had flown with such freedom over all the earth and who had let its beauty die.

This mind-drugging reverie was useless; he tore himself back to the present and to the problem at hand. If the sky was unattainable and the way by land was barred, what remained?

Once again he had come to the point when he needed help, when he could make no further progress by his own efforts. He disliked admitting the fact, but was honest enough not to deny it. Inevitably, his thoughts turned to Khedron.

Alvin had never been able to decide whether he liked the Jester. He was very glad that they had met, and was grateful to Khedron for the assistance and implicit sympathy he had given him on his quest. There was no one else in Diaspar with whom he had so much in common, yet there was some element in the other's personality that jarred upon him. Perhaps it was Khedron's air of ironic detachment, which sometimes gave Alvin the impression that he was laughing secretly at all his efforts, even while he seemed to be doing his best to help. Because of this, as well as his own natural stubbornness and independence, Alvin hesitated to approach the Jester except as a last resort.

They arranged to meet in a small, circular court not far from Council Hall. There were many such secluded spots in the city, perhaps only a few yards from some busy thoroughfare, yet completely cut off from it. Usually they could be reached only on foot after a rather round-about walk; sometimes, indeed, they were at the center of skillfully contrived mazes which enhanced their isolation. It was rather typical of Khedron that he should have chosen such a place for a rendezvous.

The court was little more than fifty paces across, and was in reality located deep within the interior of some great building. Yet it appeared to have no definite physical limits, being bounded by a translucent blue-green material which glowed with a faint internal light. However, though there were no visible limits, the court had been so laid out that there was no danger of feeling lost in infinite space. Low walls, less than waist high and broken at intervals so that one could pass through them, managed to give the impression of safe confinement without which no one in Diaspar could ever feel entirely happy.

Khedron was examining one of these walls when Alvin arrived. It was covered with an intricate mosaic of colored tiles, so fantastically involved that Alvin did not even attempt to unravel it.

"Look at this mosaic, Alvin," said the Jester. "Do you notice anything strange about it?"

"No," confessed Alvin after a brief examination. "I don't care for it —but there's nothing strange about *that.*"

Khedron ran his fingers over the colored tiles. "You are not very observant," he said. "Look at these edges here—see how they have become rounded and softened. This is something that one very seldom sees in Diaspar, Alvin. It is wear—the crumbling away of matter under the assault of time. I can remember when this pattern was new, only eighty thousand years ago, in my last lifetime. If I come back to this spot a dozen lives from now, these tiles will have been worn completely away."

"I don't see anything very surprising about that," answered Alvin. "There are other works of art in the city not good enough to be preserved in the memory circuits, but not bad enough to be destroyed outright.

One day, I suppose, some other artist will come along and do a better job. And his work won't be allowed to wear out."

"I knew the man who designed this wall," said Khedron, his fingers still exploring the cracks in the mosaic. "Strange that I can remember that fact, when I don't recall the man himself. I could not have liked him, so I must have erased him from my mind." He gave a short laugh. "Perhaps I designed it myself, during one of my artistic phases, and was so annoyed when the city refused to make it eternal that I decided to forget the whole affair. There—I knew that piece was coming loose!"

He had managed to pull out a single flake of golden tile, and looked very pleased at this minor sabotage. He threw the fragment on the ground, adding, "Now the maintenance robots will have to do something about it!"

There was a lesson for him here, Alvin knew. That strange instinct known as intuition, which seemed to follow short cuts not accessible to mere logic, told him that. He looked at the golden shard lying at his feet, trying to link it somehow to the problem that now dominated his mind.

It was not hard to find the answer, once he realized that it existed.

"I see what you are trying to tell me," he said to Khedron. "There are objects in Diaspar that aren't preserved in the memory circuits, so I could never find them through the monitors at Council Hall. If I was to go there and focus on this court, there would be no sign of the wall we're sitting on."

"I think you might find the wall. But there would be no mosaic on it."

"Yes, I can see that," said Alvin, too impatient now to bother about such hairsplitting. "And in the same way, parts of the city might exist that had never been preserved in the eternity circuits, but which hadn't yet worn away. Still, I don't really see how that helps me. I *know* that the outer wall exists—and that it has no openings in it."

"Perhaps there is no way out," answered Khedron. "I can promise you nothing. But I think there is still a great deal that the monitors can teach us—if the Central Computer will let them. And it seems to have taken rather a liking to you."

Alvin pondered over this remark on their way to Council Hall. Until now, he had assumed that it was entirely through Khedron's influence that he had been able to gain access to the monitors. It had not occurred to him that it might be through some intrinsic quality of his own. Being a Unique had many disadvantages; it was only right that it should have some compensations.

The unchanging image of the city still dominated the chamber in which Alvin had spent so many hours. He looked at it now with a new understanding; all that he saw here existed—but all of Diaspar might not be mirrored here. Yet, surely, any discordances must be trivial, and, as far as he could see, undetectable.

"I attempted to do this many years ago," said Khedron, as he sat down at the monitor desk, "but the controls were locked against me. Perhaps they will obey me now."

Slowly, and then with mounting confidence as he regained access to long-forgotten skills, Khedron's fingertips moved over the control desk, resting for a moment at the nodal points in the sensitive grid buried in the panel before him.

"I think that's correct," he said at last. "Anyway we'll soon see."

The screen glowed into life, but instead of the picture that Alvin had expected, there appeared a somewhat baffling message:

REGRESSION WILL COMMENCE AS SOON AS YOU HAVE SET RATE CONTROL

"Foolish of me," muttered Khedron. "I got everything else right and forgot the most important thing of all." His fingers now moved with a confident assurance over the board, and as the message faded from the screen he swung around in his seat so that he could look at the replica of the city.

"Watch this, Alvin," he said. "I think we are both going to learn something new about Diaspar."

Alvin waited patiently, but nothing happened. The image of the city floated there before his eyes in all its familiar wonder and beauty—though he was conscious of neither now. He was about to ask Khedron what he should look for when a sudden movement caught his attention, and he turned his head quickly to follow it. It had been no more than a half-glimpsed flash or flicker, and he was too late to see what had made it. Nothing had altered; Diaspar was just as he had always known it. Then he saw that Khedron was watching him with a sardonic smile, so he looked again at the city. This time, the thing happened before his eyes.

One of the buildings at the edge of the park suddenly vanished, and was replaced instantly by another of quite different design. The transformation was so abrupt that had Alvin been blinking he would have missed it. He stared in amazement at the subtly altered city, but even during the first shock of astonishment his mind was seeking for the answer. He remembered the words that had appeared on the monitor screen —REGRESSION WILL COMMENCE—and he knew at once what was happening.

"That's the city as it was thousands of years ago," he said to Khedron. "We're going back in time."

"A picturesque but hardly accurate way of putting it," replied the Jester. "What is actually happening is that the monitor is remembering the earlier versions of the city. When any modifications were made, the memory circuits were not simply emptied; the information in them was taken to subsidiary storage units, so that it could be recalled whenever needed. I have set the monitor to regress through those units at the rate of a thousand years a second. Already, we're looking at the Diaspar of half a million years ago. We'll have to go much further back than that to see any real changes—I'll increase the rate."

He turned back to the control board, and even as he did so, not one building but a whole block whipped out of existence and was replaced by a large oval amphitheater.

"Ah, the Arena!" said Khedron. "I can remember the fuss when we decided to get rid of that. It was hardly ever used, but a great many people felt sentimental about it."

The monitor was now recalling its memories at a far higher rate; the image of Diaspar was receding into the past at millions of years a minute, and changes were occurring so rapidly that the eye could not keep up with them. Alvin noticed that the alterations to the city appeared to come in cycles; there would be a long period of stasis, then a whole rash of rebuilding would break out, followed by another pause. It was almost as if Diaspar were a living organism, which had to regain its strength after each explosion of growth.

Through all these changes, the basic design of the city had not altered. Buildings came and went, but the pattern of streets seemed eternal, and the park remained as the green heart of Diaspar. Alvin wondered how far back the monitor could go. Could it return to the founding of the city, and pass through the veil that sundered known history from the myths and legends of the Dawn?

Already they had gone five hundred million years into the past. Outside the walls of Diaspar, beyond the knowledge of the monitors, it would be a different Earth. Perhaps there might still be oceans and forests, even other cities which Man had not yet deserted in the long retreat to his final home.

The minutes drifted past, each minute an aeon in the little universe of the monitors. Soon, thought Alvin, the earliest of all these stored memories must be reached and the regression would end. But fascinating though this lesson was, he did not see how it could help him to escape from the city as it was here and now.

With a sudden, soundless implosion, Diaspar contracted to a fraction of its former size. The park vanished; the boundary wall of linked, titanic towers instantly evaporated. This city was open to the world, for the radial roads stretched out to the limits of the monitor image without obstruction. Here was Diaspar as it had been before the great change came upon mankind.

"We can go no further," said Khedron, pointing to the monitor screen. On it had appeared the words: REGRESSION CONCLUDED. "This must be the earliest version of the city that has been preserved in the memory cells. Before that, I doubt if the eternity circuits were used, and the buildings were allowed to wear out naturally."

For a long time, Alvin stared at this model of the ancient city. He thought of the traffic those roads had borne, as men came and went freely to all the corners of the world—and to other worlds as well. Those men were his ancestors; he felt a closer kinship to them than to the people who now shared his life. He wished that he could see them and share their thoughts, as they moved through the streets of that billion-year-remote Diaspar. Yet those thoughts could not have been happy ones, for they must have been living then beneath the shadow of the Invaders. In a few more centuries, they were to turn their faces from the glory they had won and build a wall against the Universe.

Khedron ran the monitor backward and forward a dozen times through the brief period of history that had wrought the transformation. The change from a small open city to a much larger closed one had taken little more than a thousand years. In that time, the machines that had served Diaspar so faithfully must have been designed and built, and the knowledge that would enable them to carry out their tasks had been fed into their memory circuits. Into the memory circuits, also, must have gone the essential patterns of all the men who were now alive, so that when the right impulse called them forth again they could be clothed in matter and would emerge reborn from the Hall of Creation. In some sense, Alvin realized, he must have existed in that ancient world. It was possible, of course, that he was completely synthetic—that his entire personality had been designed by artist-technicians who had worked with tools of inconceivable complexity toward some clearly envisaged goal. Yet he thought it more likely that he was a composite of men who had once lived and walked on Earth.

Very little of the old Diaspar had remained when the new city was created; the park had obliterated it almost completely. Even before the transformation, there had been a small, grass-covered clearing at the center of Diaspar, surrounding the junction of all the radial streets. Afterward it had expanded tenfold, wiping out streets and buildings alike. The Tomb of Yarlan Zey had been brought into existence at this time, replacing a very large circular structure which had previously stood at the meeting point of all the streets. Alvin had never really believed the legends of the Tomb's antiquity, but now it seemed that they were true.

"I suppose," said Alvin, struck by a sudden thought, "that we can explore this image, just as we explored the image of today's Diaspar?"

Khedron's fingers flickered over the monitor control board, and the screen answered Alvin's question. The long-vanished city began to expand before his eyes as his viewpoint moved along the curiously narrow streets. This memory of the Diaspar that once had been was still as sharp and clear as the image of the city he lived in today. For a billion years, the information circuits had held it in ghostly pseudo-existence, waiting for the moment when someone should call it forth again. And it was not, thought Alvin, merely a memory he was seeing now. It was something more complex than that—it was the memory of a memory.

He did not know what he could learn from it, and whether it could help him in his quest. No matter; it was fascinating to look into the past and to see a world that had existed in the days when men still roamed among the stars. He pointed to the low, circular building that stood at the city's heart.

"Let's start there," he told Khedron. "That seems as good a place as any to begin."

Perhaps it was sheer luck; perhaps it was some ancient memory; perhaps it was elementary logic. It made no difference, since he would have arrived at this spot sooner or later—this spot upon which all the radial streets of the city converged.

It took him ten minutes to discover that they did not meet here for reasons of symmetry alone—ten minutes to know that his long search had met its reward.

CHAPTER NINE

Alystra had found it very easy to follow Alvin and Khedron without their knowledge. They seemed in a great hurry—something which in itself was most unusual—and never looked back. It had been an amusing game to pursue them along the moving ways, hiding in the crowds yet always keeping them in sight. Toward the end their goal had been obvious; when they left the pattern of streets and went into the park, they could only be heading for the Tomb of Yarlan Zey. The park contained no other buildings, and people in such eager haste as Alvin and Khedron would not be interested merely in enjoying the scenery.

Because there was no way of concealing herself on the last few hundred yards to the Tomb, Alystra waited until Khedron and Alvin had disappeared into the marbled gloom. Then, as soon as they were out of sight, she hurried up the grass-covered slope. She felt fairly sure that she could hide behind one of the great pillars long enough to discover what Alvin and Khedron were doing; it did not matter if they detected her after that.

The Tomb consisted of two concentric rings of columns, enclosing a circular courtyard. Except in one sector, the columns screened off the interior completely, and Alystra avoided approaching through this opening, but entered the Tomb from the side. She cautiously negotiated the first ring of columns, saw that there was no one in sight, and tiptoed across to the second. Through the gaps, she could see Yarlan Zey looking out through the entrance, across the park he had built, and beyond that to the city over which he had watched for so many ages.

And there was no one else in all this marble solitude. The Tomb was empty.

At that moment, Alvin and Khedron were a hundred feet underground, in a small, boxlike room whose walls seemed to be flowing steadily upward. That was the only indication of movement; there was no trace of vibration to show that they were sinking swiftly into the earth, descending toward a goal that even now neither of them fully understood.

It had been absurdly easy, for the way had been prepared for them. (By whom? wondered Alvin. By the Central Computer? Or by Yarlan Zey himself, when he transformed the city?) The monitor screen had shown them the long, vertical shaft plunging into the depths, but they had followed its course only a little way when the image had blanked out. That meant, Alvin knew, that they were asking for information that the monitor did not possess, and perhaps never had possessed.

He had scarcely framed this thought when the screen came to life once more. On it appeared a brief message, printed in the simplified script that machines had used to communicate with men ever since they had achieved intellectual equality:

STAND WHERE THE STATUE GAZES—AND REMEMBER:
DIASPAR WAS NOT ALWAYS THUS

The last five words were in larger type, and the meaning of the entire message was obvious to Alvin at once. Mentally framed code messages had been used for ages to unlock doors or set machines in action. As for "Stand where the statue gazes"—that was really *too* simple.

"I wonder how many people have read this message?" said Alvin thoughtfully.

"Fourteen, to my knowledge," replied Khedron. "And there may have been others." He did not amplify this rather cryptic remark, and Alvin was in too great a hurry to reach the park to question him further.

They could not be certain that the mechanisms would still respond to the triggering impulse. When they reached the Tomb, it had taken them only a moment to locate the single slab, among all those paving the floor, upon which the gaze of Yarlan Zey was fixed. It was only at first sight that the statue seemed to be looking out across the city; if one stood directly in front of it, one could see that the eyes were downcast and that the elusive smile was directed toward a spot just inside the entrance to the Tomb. Once the secret was realized, there could be no doubt about it. Alvin moved to the next slab, and found that Yarlan Zey was no longer looking toward him.

He rejoined Khedron, and mentally echoed the words that the Jester spoke aloud: "Diaspar was not always thus." Instantly, as if the millions of years that had lapsed since their last operation had never existed, the waiting machines responded. The great slab of stone on which they were standing began to carry them smoothly into the depths.

Overhead, the patch of blue suddenly flickered out of existence. The shaft was no longer open; there was no danger that anyone should accidentally stumble into it. Alvin wondered fleetingly if another slab of stone had somehow been materialized to replace the one now supporting him and Khedron, then decided against it. The original slab probably still paved the Tomb; the one upon which they were standing might only exist for infinitesimal fractions of a second, being continuously re-created at greater and greater depths in the earth to give the illusion of steady downward movement.

Neither Alvin nor Khedron spoke as the walls flowed silently past them. Khedron was once again wrestling with his conscience, wondering if this time he had gone too far. He could not imagine where this route might lead, if indeed it led anywhere. For the first time in his life, he began to understand the real meaning of fear.

Alvin was not afraid; he was too excited. This was the sensation he had known in the Tower of Loranne, when he had looked out across the untrodden desert and seen the stars conquering the night sky. He had merely gazed at the unknown then; he was being carried toward it now.

The walls ceased to flow past them. A patch of light appeared at one side of their mysteriously moving room, grew brighter and brighter, and was suddenly a door. They stepped through it, took a few paces along the short corridor beyond—and then were standing in a great, circular cavern whose walls came together in a sweeping curve three hundred feet above their heads.

The column down whose interior they had descended seemed far too slim to support the millions of tons of rock above it; indeed, it did not seem to be an integral part of the chamber at all, but gave the impression of being an afterthought. Khedron, following Alvin's gaze, arrived at the same conclusion.

"This column," he said, speaking rather jerkily, as if anxious to find something to say, "was built simply to house the shaft down which we came. It could never have carried the traffic that must have passed through here when Diaspar was still open to the world. *That* came through those tunnels over there; I suppose you recognize what they are?"

Alvin looked toward the walls of the chamber, more than a hundred yards away. Piercing them at regular intervals were large tunnels, twelve of them, radiating in all directions exactly as the moving ways still did today. He could see that they sloped gently upward, and now he recognized the familiar gray surface of the moving ways. These were only the severed stumps of the great roads; the strange material that gave them life was now frozen into immobility. When the park had been built, the hub of the moving way system had been buried. But it had never been destroyed.

Alvin began to walk toward the nearest of the tunnels. He had gone only a few paces when he realized that something was happening to the ground beneath his feet. *It was becoming transparent*. A few more yards, and he seemed to be standing in midair without visible support. He stopped and stared down into the void beneath him.

"Khedron!" he called. "Come and look at this!"

The other joined him, and together they gazed at the marvel beneath their feet. Faintly visible, at an indefinite depth, lay an enormous map—a great network of lines converging toward a spot beneath the central shaft. They stared at it in silence for a moment; then Khedron said quietly: "You realize what this is?"

"I think so," replied Alvin. "It's a map of the entire transport system, and those little circles must be the other cities of Earth. I can just see names beside them, but they're too faint to read."

"There must have been some form of internal illumination once," said Khedron absently. He was tracing the lines beneath his feet, following them with his eyes out toward the walls of the chamber.

"I thought so!" he exclaimed suddenly. "Do you see how all these radiating lines lead toward the small tunnels?"

Alvin had noticed that besides the great arches of the moving ways there were innumerable smaller tunnels leading out of the chamber—tunnels that sloped *downward* instead of up.

Khedron continued without waiting for a reply.

"It would be hard to think of a simpler system. People would come down the moving ways, select the place they wished to visit, and then follow the appropriate line on the map."

"And what happened to them after that?" asked Alvin. Khedron was silent, his eyes searching out the mystery of those descending tunnels. There were thirty or forty of them, all looking exactly the same. Only the names on the map would have enabled one to distinguish between them, and those names were indecipherable now.

Alvin had wandered away and was circumnavigating the central pillar. Presently his voice came to Khedron, slightly muffled and overlaid with echoes from the walls of the chamber.

"What is it?" called Khedron, not wishing to move, because he had nearly succeeded in reading one of the dimly visible groups of characters. But Alvin's voice was insistent, so he went to join him.

Far beneath was the other half of the great map, its faint webwork radiating to the points of the compass. This time, however, not all of it was too dim to be clearly seen, for one of the lines—and only one—was brilliantly illuminated. It seemed to have no connection with the rest of the system, and pointed like a gleaming arrow to one of the downward-sloping tunnels. Near its end the line transfixed a circle of golden light, and against that circle was the single word LYS. That was all.

For a long time Alvin and Khedron stood gazing down at that silent symbol. To Khedron it was a challenge he knew he could never accept—and which, indeed, he would rather did not exist. But to Alvin it hinted at the fulfillment of all his dreams; though the word Lys meant nothing to him, he let it roll around his mouth, tasting its sibilance like some exotic flavor. The blood was pounding in his veins, and his cheeks were flushed as by a fever. He stared around this great concourse, trying to imagine it as it had been in the ancient days, when air transport had come to an end but the cities of Earth still had contact with one another. He thought of the countless millions of years that had passed with the traffic steadily dwindling and the lights on the great map dying one by one, until at last only this single line remained. How long, he wondered, had it gleamed there among its darkened companions, waiting to guide the steps that never came, until Yarlan Zey had sealed the moving ways and closed Diaspar against the world?

And that had been a billion years ago. Even then, Lys must have lost touch with Diaspar. It seemed impossible that it could have survived; perhaps, after all, the map meant nothing now.

Khedron broke into his reverie at last. He seemed nervous and ill at ease, not at all like the confident and self-assured person that he had always been in the city above.

"I do not think that we should go any further now," he said. "It may not be safe until—until we are more prepared."

There was wisdom in this, but Alvin recognized the underlying note of fear in Khedron's voice. Had it not been for that, he might have been sensible, but a too-acute awareness of his own valor, combined with a contempt for Khedron's timidity, drove Alvin onward. It seemed foolish to have come so far, only to turn back when the goal might be in sight.

"I'm going down that tunnel," he said stubbornly, as if challenging Khedron to stop him. "I want to see where it leads." He set off resolutely, and after a moment's hesitation the Jester followed him along the arrow of light that burned beneath their feet.

As they stepped into the tunnel, they felt the familiar tug of the peristaltic field, and in a moment were being swept effortlessly into the depths. The journey lasted scarcely a minute; when the field released them they were standing at one end of a long narrow chamber in the form of a half-cylinder. At its distant end, two dimly lit tunnels stretched away toward infinity.

Men of almost every civilization that had existed since the Dawn would have found their surroundings completely familiar, yet to Alvin and Khedron this was a glimpse of another world. The purpose of the long, streamlined machine that lay aimed like a projectile at the far tunnel was obvious, but that made it none the less novel. Its upper portion was transparent, and looking through the walls Alvin could see rows of luxuriously appointed seats. There was no sign of any entrance, and the entire machine was floating about a foot above a single metal rod that stretched away into the distance, disappearing in one of the tunnels. A few yards away another rod led to the second tunnel, but no machine floated above it. Alvin knew, as surely as if he had been told, that somewhere beneath unknown, far-off Lys, that second machine was waiting in another such chamber as this.

Khedron began to talk, a little too swiftly.

"What a peculiar transport system! It could only handle a hundred people at a time, so they could not have expected much traffic. And why did they go to all this trouble to bury themselves in the Earth if the skies were still open? Perhaps the Invaders would not even permit them to fly, though I find that hard to believe. Or was this built during the transition period, while men still traveled but did not wish to be reminded of space? They could go from city to city, and never see the sky and the stars." He gave a nervous laugh. "I feel sure of one thing, Alvin. When Lys existed, it was much like Diaspar. All cities must be essentially the same. No wonder that they were all abandoned in the end, and merged into Diaspar. What was the point of having more than one?"

Alvin scarcely heard him. He was busy examining the long projectile, trying to find the entrance. If the machine was controlled by some mental or verbal code order, he might never be able to make it obey him, and it would remain a maddening enigma for the rest of his life.

The silently opening door took him completely unawares. There was no sound, no warning when a section of the wall simply faded from sight and the beautifully designed interior lay open before his eyes.

This was the moment of choice. Until this instant, he had always been able to turn back if he wished. But if he stepped inside that welcoming door, he knew what would happen, though not where it would lead. He would no longer be in control of his own destiny, but would have placed himself in the keeping of unknown forces.

He scarcely hesitated. He was afraid to hold back, being fearful that if he waited too long this moment might never come again—or that if it did, his courage might not match his desire for knowledge. Khedron opened his mouth in anxious protest, but before he could speak, Alvin had stepped through the entrance. He turned to face Khedron, who was standing framed in the barely visible rectangle of the doorway, and for a moment there was a strained silence while each waited for the other to speak.

The decision was made for them. There was a faint flicker of translucence, and the wall of the machine had closed again. Even as Alvin raised his hand in farewell, the long cylinder started to ease itself forward. Before it had entered the tunnel, it was already moving faster than a man could run.

There had been a time when, every day, millions of men made such journeys, in machines basically the same as this, as they shuttled between their homes and their humdrum jobs. Since that far-off day, Man had explored the Universe and returned again to Earth—had won an empire, and had it wrestled from his grasp. Now such a journey was being made again, in a machine wherein legions of forgotten and unadventurous men would have felt completely at home.

And it was to be the most momentous journey any human being had undertaken for a billion years.

Alystra had searched the Tomb a dozen times, though once was quite sufficient, for there was nowhere anyone could hide. After the first shock of surprise, she had wondered if what she had followed across the park had not been Alvin and Khedron at all, but only their projections. But that made no sense; projections were materialized at any spot one wished to visit, without the trouble of going there in person. No sane person would "walk" his projected image a couple of miles, taking half an hour to reach his destination, when he could be there instantly. No; it was the real Alvin and the real Khedron that she had followed into the Tomb.

Somewhere, then, there must be a secret entrance. She might as well look for it while she was waiting for them to come back.

As luck would have it, she missed Khedron's reappearance, for she was examining a column behind the statue when he emerged on the other side of it. She heard his footsteps, turned toward him, and saw at once that he was alone.

"Where is Alvin?" she cried.

It was some time before the Jester answered. He looked distraught and irresolute, and Alystra had to repeat her question before he took any notice of her. He did not seem in the least surprised to find her there.

"I do not know where he is," he answered at last. "I can only tell you that he is on his way to Lys. Now you know as much as I do."

It was never wise to take Khedron's words at their face value. But Alystra needed no further assurance that the Jester was not playing his role today. He was telling her the truth—whatever it might mean.

CHAPTER TEN

When the door closed behind him, Alvin slumped into the nearest seat. All strength seemed suddenly to have been drained from his legs: at last he knew, as he had never known before, that fear of the unknown that haunted all his fellow men. He felt himself trembling in every limb, and his sight became misty and uncertain. Could he have escaped from this speeding machine he would willingly have done so, even at the price of abandoning all his dreams.

It was not fear alone that overwhelmed him, but a sense of unutterable loneliness. All that he knew and loved was in Diaspar; even if he was going into no danger, he might never see his world again. He knew, as no man had known for ages, what it meant to leave one's home forever. In this moment of desolation, it seemed to him of no importance whether the path he was following led to peril or to safety; all that mattered to him now was that it led away from home.

The mood slowly passed; the dark shadows lifted from his mind. He began to pay attention to his surroundings, and to see what he could learn from the unbelievably ancient vehicle in which he was traveling. It did not strike Alvin as particularly strange or marvelous that this buried transport system should still function perfectly after such aeons of time. It was not preserved in the eternity circuits of the city's own monitors, but there must be similar circuits elsewhere guarding it from change or decay.

For the first time he noticed the indicator board that formed part of the forward wall. It carried a brief but reassuring message:

LYS
35 MINUTES

Even as he watched, the number changed to "34." That at least was useful information, though since he had no idea of the machine's speed it told him nothing about the length of the journey. The walls of the tunnel were one continual blur of gray, and the only sensation of movement was a very slight vibration he would never have noticed had he not looked for it.

Diaspar must be many miles away by now, and above him would be the desert with its shifting sand dunes. Perhaps at this very moment he was racing below the broken hills he had watched so often from the Tower of Loranne.

His imagination sped onward to Lys, as if impatient to arrive ahead of his body. What sort of a city would it be? No matter how hard he tried, he could only picture another and smaller version of Diaspar. He wondered if it still existed, then assured himself that not otherwise would this machine be carrying him swiftly through the Earth.

Suddenly there was a distinct change in the vibration underfoot.

The vehicle was slowing down—there was no question of that. The time must have passed more swiftly than he had thought; somewhat surprised, Alvin glanced at the indicator.

LYS
23 MINUTES

Feeling puzzled, and a little worried, he pressed his face against the side of the machine. His speed was still blurring the walls of the tunnel into a featureless gray, yet now from time to time he could catch a glimpse of markings that disappeared almost as quickly as they came. And at each disappearance, they seemed to remain in his field of vision for a little longer.

Then, without any warning, the walls of the tunnel were snatched away on either side. The machine was passing, still at a very great speed, through an enormous empty space, far larger even than the chamber of the moving ways.

Peering in wonder through the transparent walls, Alvin could glimpse beneath him an intricate network of guiding rods, rods that crossed and crisscrossed to disappear into a maze of tunnels on either side. A flood of bluish light poured down from the arched dome of the ceiling, and silhouetted against the glare he could just make out the frameworks of great machines. The light was so brilliant that it pained the eyes, and Alvin knew that this place had not been intended for man. A moment later, his vehicle flashed past row after row of cylinders, lying motionless above their guide rails. They were much larger than the one in which he was traveling, and Alvin guessed that they must have been used for transporting freight. Around them were grouped incomprehensible, many-jointed mechanisms, all silent and stilled.

Almost as quickly as it had appeared, the vast and lonely chamber vanished behind him. Its passing left a feeling of awe in Alvin's mind; for the first time he really understood the meaning of that great, darkened map below Diaspar. The world was more full of wonder than he had ever dreamed.

Alvin glanced again at the indicator. It had not changed; he had taken less than a minute to flash through the great cavern. The machine was accelerating again; though there was little sense of motion, the tunnel walls were flowing past on either side at a speed he could not even guess.

It seemed an age before that indefinable change of vibration occurred again. Now the indicator was reading:

LYS
1 MINUTE

That minute was the longest that Alvin had ever known. More and more slowly moved the machine; this was no mere slackening of its speed. It was coming at last to rest.

Smoothly and silently the long cylinder slid out of the tunnel into a cavern that might have been the twin of the one below Diaspar. For a moment Alvin was too excited to see anything clearly; the door had been open for a considerable time before he realized that he could leave the vehicle. As he hurried out of the machine, he caught a last glimpse of the indicator. Its wording had now changed and its message was infinitely reassuring:

DIASPAR
35 MINUTES

As he began to search for a way out of the chamber, Alvin found the first hint that he might be in a civilization different from his own. The way to the surface clearly lay through a low, wide tunnel at one end of the cavern—and leading up through the tunnel was a flight of steps. Such a thing was extremely rare in Diaspar; the architects of the city had built ramps or sloping corridors whenever there was a change of level. This was a survival from the days when most robots had moved on wheels, and so found steps an impassable barrier.

The stairway was very short, and ended against doors that opened automatically at Alvin's approach. He walked into a small room like that which had carried him down the shaft under the Tomb of Yarlan Zey, and was not surprised when a few minutes later the doors opened again to reveal a vaulted corridor rising slowly to an archway that framed a semicircle of sky. There had been no sensation of movement, but Alvin knew that he must have risen many hundreds of feet. He hurried forward up the slope to the sunlit opening, all fear forgotten in his eagerness to see what lay before him.

He was standing at the brow of a low hill, and for an instant it seemed as if he were once again in the central park of Diaspar. Yet if this were indeed a park, it was too enormous for his mind to grasp. The city he had expected to see was nowhere visible. As far as the eye could reach there was nothing but forest and grass-covered plains.

Then Alvin lifted his eyes to the horizon, and there above the trees, sweeping from right to left in a great arc that encircled the world, was a line of stone which would have dwarfed the mightiest giants of Diaspar. It was so far away that its details were blurred by sheer distance, but there was something about its outlines that Alvin found puzzling. Then his eyes became at last accustomed to the scale of that colossal landscape, and he knew that those far-off walls had not been built by man.

Time had not conquered everything; Earth still possessed mountains of which she could be proud.

For a long time Alvin stood at the mouth of the tunnel, slowly growing accustomed to the strange world in which he had found himself. He was half stunned by the impact of sheer size and space; that ring of misty mountains could have enclosed a dozen cities as large as Diaspar. Search as he might, however, Alvin could see no trace of human life. Yet the road that led down the hillside seemed well-kept; he could do no better than accept its guidance.

At the foot of the hill, the road disappeared between great trees that almost hid the sun. As Alvin walked into their shadow, a strange medley of scents and sounds greeted him. The rustle of the wind among the leaves he had known before, but underlying that were a thousand vague noises that conveyed nothing to his mind. Unknown odors assailed him, smells that had been lost even to the memory of his race. The warmth, the profusion of scent and color, and the unseen presences of a million living things, smote him with almost physical violence.

He came upon the lake without any warning. The trees to the right suddenly ended, and before him was a great expanse of water, dotted with tiny islands. Never in his life had Alvin seen so much water; by comparison, the largest pools in Diaspar were scarcely more than puddles. He walked slowly down to the edge of the lake and cupped the warm water in his hands, letting it trickle through his fingers.

The great silver fish that suddenly forced its way through the underwater reeds was the first nonhuman creature that Alvin had ever seen. It should have been utterly strange to him, yet its shape teased his mind with a haunting familiarity. As it hung there in the pale green void, its fins a faint blur of motion, it seemed the very embodiment of power and speed. Here, incorporated in living flesh, were the graceful lines of the great ships that had once ruled the skies of Earth. Evolution and science had come to the same answers; and the work of Nature had lasted longer.

At last Alvin broke the lake's enchantment, and continued along the winding road. The forest closed around him once more, but only for a little while. Presently the road ended, in a great clearing half a mile wide and twice as long—and Alvin understood why he had seen no trace of Man before.

The clearing was full of low, two-storied buildings, colored in soft shades that rested the eye even in the full glare of the sun. Most were of clean, straightforward design, but several were built in a complex architectural style involving the use of fluted columns and gracefully fretted stone. In these buildings, which seemed of great age, the immeasurably ancient device of the pointed arch was used.

As he walked slowly toward the village, Alvin was still struggling to grasp his new surroundings. Nothing was familiar; even the air had changed, with its hint of throbbing, unknown life. And the tall, golden-haired people going among the buildings with such unconscious grace were obviously of a different stock from the men of Diaspar.

They took no notice of Alvin, and that was strange, for his clothing was totally different from theirs. Since the temperature never changed in Diaspar, dress there was purely ornamental and often extremely elaborate. Here it seemed mainly functional, designed for use rather than display, and frequently consisted of a single sheet draped around the body.

It was not until Alvin was well inside the village that the people of Lys reacted to his presence, and then their response took a somewhat unexpected form. A group of five men emerged from one of the houses and began to walk purposefully toward him—almost as if, indeed, they had been expecting his arrival. Alvin felt a sudden, heady excitement, and the blood pounded in his veins. He thought of all the fateful meetings men must have had with other races on far-off worlds. Those he was meeting now were of his own species—but how far had they diverged in the aeons that had sundered them from Diaspar?

The delegation came to a halt a few feet away from Alvin. Its leader smiled, holding out his hand in the ancient gesture of friendship.

"We thought it best to meet you here," he said. "Our home is very different from Diaspar, and the walk from the terminus gives visitors a chance to become—acclimatized."

Alvin accepted the outstretched hand, but for a moment was too surprised to reply. Now he understood why all the other villagers had ignored him so completely.

"You knew I was coming?" he said at length.

"Of course. We always know when the carriers start to move. Tell me—how did you discover the way? It has been such a long time since the last visit that we feared the secret had been lost."

The speaker was interrupted by one of his companions.

"I think we'd better restrain our curiosity, Gerane. Seranis is waiting."

The name "Seranis" was preceded by a word unfamiliar to Alvin, and he assumed that it was a title of some kind. He had no difficulty in understanding the others, and it never occurred to him that there was anything surprising about this. Diaspar and Lys shared the same linguistic heritage, and the ancient invention of sound recording had long ago frozen speech in an unbreakable mold.

Gerane gave a shrug of mock resignation. "Very well," he smiled. "Seranis has few privileges—I should not rob her of this one."

As they walked deeper into the village, Alvin studied the men around him. They appeared kindly and intelligent, but these were virtues he had taken for granted all his life, and he was looking for ways in which they differed from a similar group in Diaspar. There were differences, but it was hard to define them. They were all somewhat taller than Alvin, and two of them showed the unmistakable marks of physical age. Their skins were very brown, and in all their movements they seemed to radiate a vigor and zest which Alvin found refreshing, though at the same time a little bewildering. He smiled as he remembered Khedron's prophecy that, if he ever reached Lys, he would find it exactly the same as Diaspar.

The people of the village now watched with frank curiosity as Alvin followed his guides; there was no longer any pretense that they took him for granted. Suddenly there were shrill, high-pitched shouts from the trees on the right, and a group of small, excited creatures burst out of the woods and crowded around Alvin. He stopped in utter amazement, unable to believe his eyes. Here was something that his world had lost so long ago that it lay in the realms of mythology. This was the way that life had once begun; these noisy, fascinating creatures were human children.

Alvin watched them with wondering disbelief—and with another sensation which tugged at his heart but which he could not yet identify. No other sight could have brought home to him so vividly his remoteness from the world he knew. Diaspar had paid, and paid in full, the price of immortality.

The party halted before the largest building Alvin had yet seen. It stood in the center of the village and from a flagpole on its small circular tower a green pennant floated along the breeze.

All but Gerane dropped behind as he entered the building. Inside it was quiet and cool; sunlight filtering through the translucent walls lit up everything with a soft, restful glow. The floor was smooth and resilient, inlaid with fine mosaics. On the walls, an artist of great ability and power had depicted a set of forest scenes. Mingled with these paintings were other murals which conveyed nothing to Alvin's mind, yet which were attractive and pleasant to look upon. Let into one wall was a rectangular screen filled with a shifting maze of colors—presumably a visiphone receiver, though a rather small one.

They walked together up a short circular stairway that led them out onto the flat roof of the building. From this point, the entire village was visible, and Alvin could see that it consisted of about a hundred buildings. In the distance the trees opened out to enclose wide meadows, where animals of several different types were grazing. Alvin could not imagine what these were; most of them were quadrupeds, but some seemed to have six or even eight legs.

Seranis was waiting for him in the shadow of the tower. Alvin wondered how old she was; her long, golden hair was touched with gray, which he guessed must be some indication of age. The presence of children, with all the consequences that implied, had left him very confused. Where there was birth, then surely there must also be death, and the life span here in Lys might be very different from that in Diaspar. He could not tell whether Seranis was fifty, five hundred, or five thousand years old, but looking into her eyes he could sense that wisdom and depth of experience he sometimes felt when he was with Jeserac.

She pointed to a small seat, but though her eyes smiled a welcome she said nothing until Alvin had made himself comfortable—or as comfortable as he could be under that intense though friendly scrutiny. Then she sighed, and addressed Alvin in a low, gentle voice.

"This is an occasion which does not often arise, so you will excuse me if I do not know the correct behavior. But there are certain rights due to a guest, even if an unexpected one. Before we talk, there is something about which I should warn you. I can read your mind."

She smiled at Alvin's obvious consternation, and added quickly: "There is no need to let that worry you. No right is respected more strongly than that of mental privacy. I will enter your mind only if you invite me to. But it would not be fair to hide this fact from you, and it will explain why we find speech somewhat slow and difficult. It is not often used here."

This revelation, though slightly alarming, did not surprise Alvin. Once both men and machines had possessed this power, and the unchanging machines could still read their masters' orders. But in Diaspar, man himself had lost the gift he had once shared with his slaves.

"I do not know what brought you from your world to ours," continued Seranis, "but if you are looking for life, your search has ended. Apart from Diaspar, there is only desert beyond our mountains."

It was strange that Alvin, who had questioned accepted beliefs so often before, did not doubt the words of Seranis. His only reaction was one of sadness that all his teaching had been so nearly true.

"Tell me about Lys," he begged. "Why have you been cut off from Diaspar for so long, when you seem to know so much about us?"

Seranis smiled at his eagerness.

"Presently," she said. "But first I would like to know something about you. Tell me how you found the way here, and why you came."

Haltingly at first, and then with growing confidence, Alvin told his story. He had never spoken with such freedom before; here at last was someone who would not laugh at his dreams, because they knew those dreams were true. Once or twice Seranis interrupted him with swift questions, when he mentioned some aspect of Diaspar that was unfamiliar to her. It was hard for Alvin to realize that things which were part of his everyday life would be meaningless to someone who had never lived in the city and knew nothing of its complex culture and social organization. Seranis listened with such understanding that he took her comprehension for granted; not until much later did he realize that many other minds besides hers were listening to his words.

When he had finished, there was silence for a while. Then Seranis looked at him and said quietly: "Why did you come to Lys?"

Alvin glanced at her in surprise.

"I've told you," he said. "I wanted to explore the world. Everyone told me that there was only desert beyond the city, but I had to see for myself."

"And was that the only reason?"

Alvin hesitated. When at last he answered, it was not the indomitable explorer who spoke, but the lost child who had been born into an alien world.

"No," he said slowly, "that wasn't the only reason—though I did not know it until now. I was lonely."

"Lonely? In Diaspar?" There was a smile on the lips of Seranis, but sympathy in her eyes, and Alvin knew that she expected no further answer.

Now that he had told his story, he waited for her to keep her share of the bargain. Presently Seranis rose to her feet and began to pace to and fro on the roof.

"I know the questions you wish to ask," she said. "Some of them I can answer, but it would be wearisome to do it in words. If you will open your mind to me, I will tell you what you need to know. You can trust me: I will take nothing from you without your permission."

"What do you want me to do?" said Alvin cautiously.

"Will yourself to accept my help—look at my eyes—and forget everything," commanded Seranis.

Alvin was never sure what happened then. There was a total eclipse of all his senses, and though he could never remember acquiring it, when he looked into his mind the knowledge was there.

He saw back into the past, not clearly, but as a man on some high mountain might look out across a misty plain. He understood that Man had not always been a city dweller, and that since the machines gave him freedom from toil there had always been a rivalry between two different types of civilization. In the Dawn Ages there had been thousands of cities, but a large part of mankind had preferred to live in relatively small communities. Universal transport and instantaneous communication had given them all the contact they required with the rest of the world, and they felt no need to live huddled together with millions of their fellows.

Lys had been little different, in the early days, from hundreds of other communities. But gradually, over the ages, it developed an independent culture which was one of the highest that mankind had ever known. It was a culture based largely upon the direct use of mental power, and this set it apart from the rest of human society, which came to rely more and more upon machines.

Through the aeons, as they advanced along their different roads, the gulf between Lys and the cities widened. It was bridged only in times of great crisis; when the Moon was falling, its destruction was carried out by the scientists of Lys. So also was the defense of Earth against the Invaders, who were held at bay in the final Battle of Shalmirane.

That great ordeal exhausted mankind; one by one the cities died and the desert rolled over them. As the population fell, humanity began the migration that was to make Diaspar the last and greatest of all cities.

Most of these changes did not affect Lys, but it had its own battle to fight—the battle against the desert. The natural barrier of the mountains was not enough, and many ages passed before the great oasis was made secure. The picture was blurred here, perhaps deliberately. Alvin could not see what had been done to give Lys the virtual eternity that Diaspar had achieved.

The voice of Seranis seemed to come to him from a great distance—yet it was not her voice alone, for it was merged into a symphony of words, as though many other tongues were chanting in unison with hers.

"That, very briefly, is our history. You will see that even in the Dawn Ages we had little to do with the cities, though their people often came into our land. We never hindered them, for many of our greatest men came from outside, but when the cities were dying we did not wish to be involved in their downfall. With the ending of air transport there was only one way into Lys—the carrier system from Diaspar. It was closed at your end, when the park was built—and you forgot us, though we have never forgotten you.

"Diaspar has surprised us. We expected it to go the way of all other cities, but instead it has achieved a stable culture that may last as long as Earth. It is not a culture that we admire, yet we are glad that those who wish to escape have been able to do so. More than you might think have made the journey, and they have almost always been outstanding men who brought something of value with them when they came to Lys."

The voice faded; the paralysis of Alvin's senses ebbed away and he was himself again. He saw with astonishment that the sun had fallen far below the trees and that the eastern sky already held a hint of night. Somewhere a great bell vibrated with a throbbing boom that pulsed slowly into silence, leaving the air tense with mystery and premonition. Alvin found himself trembling slightly, not with the first touch of the evening's chill, but through sheer awe and wonder at all that he had learned. It was very late, and he was far from home. He had a sudden need to see his friends again, and to be among the familiar sights and scenes of Diaspar.

"I must return," he said. "Khedron—my parents—they will be expecting me."

That was not wholly true; Khedron would certainly be wondering what had happened to him, but as far as Alvin was aware no one else knew that he had left Diaspar. He could not have explained the reason for this mild deceit, and was slightly ashamed of himself as soon as he had uttered the words.

Seranis looked at him thoughtfully.

"I am afraid it is not as easy as that," she said.

"What do you mean?" asked Alvin. "Won't the carrier that brought me here take me back again?" He still refused to face the fact that he might be held in Lys against his will, though the idea had briefly crossed his mind.

For the first time, Seranis seemed slightly ill at ease.

"We have been talking about you," she said—not explaining who the "we" might be, nor exactly how they had consulted together. "If you return to Diaspar, the whole city will know about us. Even if you promised to say nothing, you would find it impossible to keep our secret."

"Why should you wish it kept?" asked Alvin. "Surely it would be a good thing for both our peoples if they could meet again."

Seranis looked displeased.

"We do not think so," she said. "If the gates were opened, our land would be flooded with the idly curious and the sensation seekers. As it is now, only the best of your people have ever reached us."

This reply radiated so much unconscious superiority, yet was based on such false assumptions, that Alvin felt his annoyance quite eclipse his alarm.

"That isn't true," he said flatly. "I do not believe you would find another person in Diaspar who could leave the city, even if he wanted to —even if he knew that there was somewhere to go. If you let me return, it would make no difference to Lys."

"It is not my decision," explained Seranis, "and you underestimate the powers of the mind if you think that the barriers that keep your people inside their city can never be broken. However, we do not wish to hold you here against your will, but if you return to Diaspar we must erase all memories of Lys from your mind." She hesitated for a moment. "This has never risen before; all your predecessors came here to stay."

Here was a choice that Alvin refused to accept. He wanted to explore Lys, to learn all its secrets, to discover the ways in which it differed from his own home, but equally he was determined to return to Diaspar, so that he could prove to his friends that he had been no idle dreamer. He could not understand the reasons prompting this desire for secrecy; even if he had, it would not have made any difference in his behavior.

He realized that he must play for time or else convince Seranis that what she asked of him was impossible.

"Khedron knows where I am," he said. "You cannot erase *his* memories."

Seranis smiled. It was a pleasant smile, and one that in any other circumstances would have been friendly enough. But behind it Alvin glimpsed, for the first time, the presence of overwhelming and implacable power.

"You underestimate us, Alvin," she replied. "That would be very easy. I can reach Diaspar more quickly than I can cross Lys. Other men have come here before, and some of them told their friends where they were going. Yet those friends forgot them, and they vanished from the history of Diaspar."

Alvin had been foolish to ignore this possibility, though it was obvious, now that Seranis had pointed it out. He wondered how many times, in the millions of years since the two cultures were separated, men from

Lys had gone into Diaspar in order to preserve their jealously guarded secret. And he wondered just how extensive were the mental powers which these strange people possessed and did not hesitate to use.

Was it safe to make any plans at all? Seranis had promised that she would not read his mind without his consent, but he wondered if there might be circumstances in which that promise would not be kept.

"Surely," he said, "you don't expect me to make the decision at once. Cannot I see something of your country before I make my choice?"

"Of course," replied Seranis. "You can stay here as long as you wish, and still return to Diaspar eventually if you change your mind. But if you can decide within the next few days, it will be very much easier. You do not want your friends to be worried, and the longer you are missing the harder it will be for us to make the necessary adjustments."

Alvin could appreciate that; he would like to know just what those "adjustments" were. Presumably someone from Lys would contact Khedron—without the Jester ever being aware of it—and tamper with his mind. The fact of Alvin's disappearance could not be concealed, but the information that he and Khedron had discovered could be obliterated. As the ages passed, Alvin's name would join those of the other Uniques who had mysteriously vanished without trace and had then been forgotten.

There were many mysteries here, and he seemed no closer to solving any of them. Was there any purpose behind the curious, one-sided relationship between Lys and Diaspar, or was it merely a historical accident? Who and what were the Uniques, and if the people from Lys could enter Diaspar, why had they not canceled the memory circuits that held the clue to their existence? Perhaps that was the only question to which Alvin could give a plausible answer. The Central Computer might be too stubborn an opponent to tackle, and would hardly be affected by even the most advanced of mental techniques.

He put these problems aside; one day, when he had learned a great deal more, he might have some chance of answering them. It was idle to speculate, to build pyramids of surmise on a foundation of ignorance.

"Very well," he said, though not too graciously, for he was still annoyed that this unexpected obstacle had been placed in his path. "I'll give you my answer as soon as I can, if you will show me what your land is like."

"Good," said Seranis, and this time her smile held no hidden threat. "We are proud of Lys, and it will be a pleasure to show you how men can live without the aid of cities. Meanwhile, there is no need for you to worry—your friends will not be alarmed by your absence. We shall see to that, if only for our own protection."

It was the first time Seranis had ever made a promise that she could not keep.

CHAPTER ELEVEN

Try as she would, Alystra could extract no further information from Khedron. The Jester had recovered quickly from his initial shock, and from the panic that had sent him flying back to the surface when he found himself alone in the depths beneath the Tomb. He also felt ashamed of his cowardly behavior, and wondered if he would ever have the courage to return to the chamber of the moving ways and the network of world-ranging tunnels that radiated from it. Although he felt that Alvin had been impatient, if not indeed foolhardy, he did not really believe that he would run into any danger. He would return in his own good time, Khedron was certain of that. Well, almost certain; there was just enough doubt to make him feel the need for caution. It would be wise, he decided, to say as little as possible for the time being, and to pass the whole thing off as another joke.

Unfortunately for this plan, he had not been able to mask his emotions when Alystra encountered him on his return to the surface. She had seen the fear written so unmistakably in his eyes, and had at once interpreted it as meaning that Alvin was in danger. All Khedron's reassurances were in vain, and she became more and more angry with him as they walked together back through the park. At first Alystra had wanted to remain at the Tomb, waiting for Alvin to return in whatever mysterious manner he had vanished. Khedron had managed to convince her that this would be a waste of time, and was relieved when she followed him back to the city. There was a chance that Alvin might return almost at once, and he did not wish anyone else to discover the secret of Yarlan Zey.

By the time they had reached the city, it was obvious to Khedron that his evasive tactics had failed completely and that the situation was seriously out of hand. It was the first time in his life that he had ever been at a loss and had not felt himself capable of dealing with any problem that arose. His immediate and irrational fear was being slowly replaced by a profounder and more firmly based alarm. Until now, Khedron had given little thought to the consequences of his actions. His own interests, and a mild but genuine sympathy toward Alvin, had been sufficient motive for all that he had done. Though he had given encouragement and assistance to Alvin, he had never believed that anything like this could ever really happen.

Despite the gulf of years and experience between them, Alvin's will had always been more powerful than his own. It was too late to do anything about it now; Khedron felt that events were sweeping him along toward a climax utterly beyond his control.

In view of this, it was a little unfair that Alystra obviously regarded him as Alvin's evil genius and showed an inclination to blame him for all that had happened. Alystra was not really vindictive, but she was annoyed, and part of her annoyance focused on Khedron. If any action of hers caused him trouble, she would be the last person to be sorry.

They parted in stony silence when they had reached the great circular way that surrounded the park. Khedron watched Alystra disappear into the distance and wondered wearily what plans were brewing in her mind.

There was only one thing of which he could be certain now. Boredom would not be a serious problem for a considerable time to come.

Alystra acted swiftly and with intelligence. She did not bother to contact Eriston and Etania; Alvin's parents were pleasant nonentities for whom she felt some affection but no respect. They would only waste time in futile arguments and would then do exactly as Alystra was doing now.

Jeserac listened to her story without apparent emotion. If he was alarmed or surprised, he concealed it well—so well that Alystra was somewhat disappointed. It seemed to her that nothing so extraordinary and important as this had ever happened before, and Jeserac's matter-of-fact behavior made her feel deflated. When she had finished, he questioned her at some length, and hinted, without actually saying so, that she might have made a mistake. What reason was there for supposing that Alvin had really left the city? Perhaps it had all been a trick at her expense; the fact that Khedron was involved made this seem highly probable. Alvin might be laughing at her, concealed somewhere in Diaspar, at this very moment.

The only positive reaction she got out of Jeserac was a promise to make inquiries and to contact her again within a day. In the meantime she was not to worry, and it would also be best if she said nothing to anyone else about the whole affair. There was no need to spread alarm over an incident that would probably be cleared up in a few hours.

Alystra left Jeserac in a mood of mild frustration. She would have been more satisfied could she have seen his behavior immediately after she had left.

Jeserac had friends on the Council; he had been a member himself in his long life, and might be again if he was unlucky. He called three of his most influential colleagues and cautiously aroused their interest. As Alvin's tutor, he was well aware of his own delicate position and was anxious to safeguard himself. For the present, the fewer who knew what had happened, the better.

It was immediately agreed that the first thing to do was to contact Khedron and ask him for an explanation. There was only one defect in this excellent plan. Khedron had anticipated it and was nowhere to be found.

If there was any ambiguity about Alvin's position, his hosts were very careful not to remind him of it. He was free to go anywhere he wished in Airlee, the little village over which Seranis ruled—though that was too strong a word to describe her position. Sometimes it seemed to Alvin that she was a benevolent dictator, but at others it appeared that she had no powers at all. So far he had failed completely to understand the social system of Lys, either because it was too simple or else so complex that its ramifications eluded him. All he had discovered for certain was that Lys was divided into innumerable villages, of which Airlee was a quite typical example. Yet in a sense there were no typical examples, for Alvin had been assured that every village tried to be as unlike its neighbors as possible. It was all extremely confusing.

Though it was very small, and contained less than a thousand people, Airlee was full of surprises. There was hardly a single aspect of life that did not differ from its counterpart in Diaspar. The differences extended even to such fundamentals as speech. Only the children used their voices for normal communication; the adults scarcely ever spoke, and after a while Alvin decided that they did so only out of politeness to him. It was a curiously frustrating experience to feel oneself enmeshed in a great net of soundless and undetectable words, but after a while Alvin grew accustomed to it. It seemed surprising that vocal speech had survived at all since there was no longer any use for it, but Alvin later discovered that the people of Lys were very fond of singing, and indeed of all forms of music. Without this incentive, it was very likely that they would long ago have become completely mute.

They were always busy, engaged on tasks or problems which were usually incomprehensible to Alvin. When he could understand what they were doing, much of their work seemed quite unnecessary. A considerable part of their food, for example, was actually grown, and not synthesized in accordance with patterns worked out ages ago. When Alvin commented on this, it was patiently explained to him that the people of Lys liked to watch things grow, to carry out complicated genetic experiments and to evolve ever more subtle tastes and flavors. Airlee was famous for its fruit, but when Alvin ate some choice samples they seemed to him no better than those he could have conjured up in Diaspar by no more effort than raising a finger.

At first he wondered if the people of Lys had forgotten, or had never possessed, the powers and machines that he took for granted and upon which all life in Diaspar was based. He soon found that this was not the case. The tools and the knowledge were there, but they were used only when it was essential. The most striking example of this was provided by the transport system, if it could be dignified by such a name. For short distances, people walked, and seemed to enjoy it. If they were in a hurry, or had small loads to move, they used animals which had obviously been developed for the purpose. The freight-carrying species was a low, six-legged beast, very docile and strong but of poor intelligence. The racing animals were of a different breed altogether, normally walking on four legs but using only their heavily muscled hind limbs when they really got up speed. They could cross the entire width of Lys in a few hours, and the passenger rode in a pivoted seat strapped on the creature's back. Nothing in the world would have induced Alvin to risk such a ride, though it was a very popular sport among the younger men. Their finely bred steeds were the aristocrats of the animal world, and were well aware of it. They had fairly large vocabularies, and Alvin often overheard them talking boastfully among themselves about past and future victories. When he tried to be friendly and attempted to join in the conversation, they pretended that they could not understand him, and if he persisted would go bounding off in outraged dignity.

These two varieties of animal sufficed for all ordinary needs, and gave their owners a great deal of pleasure which no mechanical contrivances could have done. But when extreme speed was required or vast loads had to be moved, the machines were there, and were used without hesitation.

Though the animal life of Lys presented Alvin with a whole world of new interests and surprises, it was the two extremes of the human population range that fascinated him most of all. The very young and the very old—both were equally strange to him and equally amazing. Airlee's most senior inhabitant had barely attained his second century, and had only a few more years of life before him. When *he* had reached that age, lvin reminded himself, his body would scarcely have altered, whereas his old man, who had no chain of future existences to look forward to s compensation, had almost exhausted his physical powers. His hair vas completely white, and his face an unbelievably intricate mass of rinkles. He seemed to spend most of his time sitting in the sun or valking slowly around the village exchanging soundless greetings with veryone he met. As far as Alvin could tell he was completely contented, sking no more of life, and was not distressed by its approaching end.

Here was a philosophy so much at variance with that of Diaspar as o be completely beyond Alvin's comprehension. Why should anyone ccept death when it was so unnecessary, when you had the choice of iving for a thousand years and then leaping forward through the millenniums to make a new start in a world that you have helped to shape? This vas one mystery he was determined to solve as soon as he had the chance f discussing it frankly. It was very hard for him to believe that Lys had nade this choice of its own free will, if it knew the alternative that existed.

He found part of his answer among the children, those little creatures vho were as strange to him as any of the animals of Lys. He spent much f his time among them, watching them at their play and eventually being ccepted by them as a friend. Sometimes it seemed to him that they were iot human at all, their motives, their logic, and even their language were o alien. He would look unbelievingly at the adults and ask himself how t was possible that they could have evolved from these extraordinary reatures who seemed to spend most of their lives in a private world of heir own.

And yet, even while they baffled him, they aroused within his heart feeling he had never known before. When—which was not often, but ometimes happened—they burst into tears of utter frustration or depair, their tiny disappointments seemed to him more tragic than Man's ong retreat after the loss of his Galactic Empire. That was something too iuge and remote for comprehension, but the weeping of a child could ierce one to the heart.

Alvin had met love in Diaspar, but now he was learning something qually precious, and without which love itself could never reach its iighest fulfillment but must remain forever incomplete. He was learning enderness.

f Alvin was studying Lys, Lys was also studying him, and was not lissatisfied with what it had found. He had been in Airlee for three days vhen Seranis suggested that he might like to go further afield and see omething more of her country. It was a proposal he accepted at once—

on condition that he was not expected to ride one of the village's prize racing beasts.

"I can assure you," said Seranis, with a rare flash of humor, "that no one here would dream of risking one of their precious animals. Since this is an exceptional case, I will arrange transport in which you will feel more at home. Hilvar will act as your guide, but of course you can go wherever you please."

Alvin wondered if that was strictly true. He imagined that there would be some objection if he tried to return to the little hill from whose summit he had first emerged into Lys. However, that did not worry him for the moment since he was in no hurry to go back to Diaspar, and indeed had given little thought to the problem after his initial meeting with Seranis. Life here was still so interesting and so novel that he was still quite content to live in the present.

He appreciated Seranis's gesture in offering her son as his guide, though doubtless Hilvar had been given careful instructions to see that he did not get into mischief. It had taken Alvin some time to get accustomed to Hilvar, for a reason which he could not very well explain to him without hurting his feelings. Physical perfection was so universal in Diaspar that personal beauty had been completely devalued; men noticed it no more than the air they breathed. This was not the case in Lys, and the most flattering adjective that could be applied to Hilvar was "homely." By Alvin's standards, he was downright ugly, and for a while he had deliberately avoided him. If Hilvar was aware of this, he showed no sign of it, and it was not long before his good-natured friendliness had broken through the barrier between them. The time was to come when Alvin would be so accustomed to Hilvar's broad, twisted smile, his strength, and his gentleness that he could scarcely believe he had ever found him unattractive, and would not have had him changed for any consideration in the world.

They left Airlee soon after dawn in a small vehicle which Hilvar called a ground-car, and which apparently worked on the same principle as the machine that had brought Alvin from Diaspar. It floated in the air a few inches above the turf, and although there was no sign of any guide rail, Hilvar told him that the cars could run only on predetermined routes. All the centers of population were linked together in this fashion, but during his entire stay in Lys Alvin never saw another ground-car in use.

Hilvar had put a great deal of effort into organizing this expedition, and was obviously looking forward to it quite as much as Alvin. He had planned the route with his own interests in mind, for natural history was his consuming passion and he hoped to find new types of insect life in the relatively uninhabited regions of Lys which they would be visiting. He intended to travel as far south as the machine could take them, and the rest of the way they would have to go on foot. Not realizing the full implications of this, Alvin made no objections.

They had a companion with them on the journey—Krif, the most spectacular of Hilvar's many pets. When Krif was resting, his six gauzy wings lay folded along his body, which glittered through them like a jeweled scepter. If something disturbed him, he would rise into the air with a flicker of iridescence and a faint whirring of invisible wings. Though the great insect would come when called and would—sometimes—obey simple orders, it was almost wholly mindless. Yet it had a definite personality of its own, and for some reason was suspicious of Alvin, whose sporadic attempts to gain its confidence always ended in failure.

To Alvin, the journey across Lys had a dreamlike unreality. Silent as a ghost, the machine slid across rolling plains and wound its way through forests, never deviating from its invisible track. It traveled perhaps ten times as fast as a man could comfortably walk; seldom indeed was any inhabitant of Lys in a greater hurry than that.

They passed through many villages, some larger than Airlee but most of them built along very smiliar lines. Alvin was interested to notice the subtle but significant differences in clothing and even physical appearance that occurred as they moved from one community to the next. The civilization of Lys was composed of hundreds of distinct cultures, each contributing some special talent toward the whole. The ground-car was well stocked with Airlee's most famous product, a small, yellow peach which was gratefully received whenever Hilvar gave away some samples. He often stopped to talk to friends and to introduce Alvin, who never ceased to be impressed by the simple courtesy with which everyone used vocal speech as soon as they knew who he was. It must often have been very tedious to them, but as far as he could judge they always resisted the temptation to lapse into telepathy and he never felt excluded from their conversation.

They made their longest pause at a tiny village almost hidden in a sea of tall golden grass, which soared high above their heads and which undulated in the gentle wind as if it was endowed with life. As they moved through it, they were continually overtaken by rolling waves as the countless blades bowed in unison above them. At first it was faintly disturbing, for Alvin had a foolish fancy that the grass was bending down to look at him, but after a while he found the continual motion quite restful.

Alvin soon discovered why they had made this stop. Among the little crowd that had already gathered before the car came gliding into the village was a shy, dark girl whom Hilvar introduced as Nyara. They were obviously very pleased to see one another again, and Alvin felt envious of their patent happiness at this brief reunion. Hilvar was clearly torn between his duties as a guide and his desire to have no other company but Nyara, and Alvin soon rescued him from his quandary by setting off on a tour of exploration by himself. There was not much to see in the little village, but he took his time.

When they started on their way again, there were many questions he was anxious to ask Hilvar. He could not imagine what love must be like in a telepathic society, and after a discreet interval he broached the subject. Hilvar was willing enough to explain, even though Alvin suspected that he had made his friend interrupt a prolonged and tender mental leave-taking.

In Lys, it seemed, all love began with mental contact, and it might be months or years before a couple actually met. In this way, Hilvar explained, there could be no false impressions, no deceptions on either side. Two people whose minds were open to one another could hide no secrets. If either attempted it, the other partner would know at once that something was being concealed.

Only very mature and well-balanced minds could afford such honesty; only love based upon absolute unselfishness could survive it. Alvin could well understand that such a love would be deeper and richer than anything his people could know; it could be so perfect, in fact, that he found it hard to believe that it could ever occur at all.

Yet Hilvar assured him that it did, and became starry-eyed and lost in his own reveries when Alvin pressed him to be more explicit. There were some things that could not be communicated; one either knew them or one did not. Alvin decided sadly that he could never attain the kind of mutual understanding which these fortunate people had made the very basis of their lives.

When the ground-car emerged from the savanna, which ended abruptly as though a frontier had been drawn beyond which the grass was not permitted to grow, there was a range of low, heavily wooded hills ahead of them. This was an outpost, Hilvar explained, of the main rampart guarding Lys. The real mountains lay beyond, but to Alvin even these small hills were an impressive and awe-inspiring sight.

The car came to a halt in a narrow, sheltered valley which was still flooded by the warmth and light of the descending sun. Hilvar looked at Alvin with a kind of wide-eyed candor which, one could have sworn, was totally innocent of any guile.

"This is where we start to walk," he said cheerfully, beginning to throw equipment out of the vehicle. "We can't ride any farther."

Alvin looked at the hills surrounding them, then at the comfortable seat in which he had been riding.

"Isn't there a way around?" he asked, not very hopefully.

"Of course," replied Hilvar. "But we're not going around. We're going to the top, which is much more interesting. I'll put the car on automatic so that it will be waiting for us when we get down the other side."

Determined not to give in without a struggle, Alvin made one last effort.

"It will soon be dark," he protested. "We'll never be able to go all that way before sunset."

"Exactly," said Hilvar, sorting packages and equipment with incredible speed. "We'll spend the night on the summit, and finish the journey in the morning."

For once, Alvin knew when he was beaten.

The gear that they were carrying looked very formidable, but though it was bulky it weighed practically nothing. It was all packed in gravity-polarizing containers that neutralized its weight, leaving only inertia to be contended with. As long as Alvin moved in a straight line, he was not conscious that he was carrying any load. Dealing with these containers required a little practice, for if he attempted to make a sudden change of direction his pack seemed to develop a stubborn personality and did its best to keep him on his original course, until he had overcome its momentum.

When Hilvar had adjusted all the straps and satisfied himself that everything was in order, they began to walk slowly up the valley. Alvin looked back wistfully as the ground-car retraced its track and disappeared from sight; he wondered how many hours would elapse before he could again relax in its comfort.

Nevertheless, it was very pleasant climbing upward with the mild sun beating on their backs, and seeing ever-new vistas unfold around them. There was a partly obliterated path which disappeared from time to time but which Hilvar seemed able to follow even when Alvin could see no trace of it. He asked Hilvar what had made the path, and was told that there were many small animals in these hills—some solitary, and some living in primitive communities which echoed many of the features of human civilization. A few had even discovered, or been taught, the use of tools and fire. It never occurred to Alvin that such creatures might be other than friendly; both he and Hilvar took this for granted, for it had been so many ages since anything on Earth had challenged the supremacy of Man.

They had been climbing for half an hour when Alvin first noticed the faint, reverberating murmur in the air around him. He could not detect its source, for it seemed to come from no particular direction. It never ceased, and it grew steadily louder as the landscape widened around them. He would have asked Hilvar what it was, but it had become necessary to save his breath for more essential purposes.

Alvin was in perfect health; indeed, he had never had an hour's illness in his life. But physical well-being, however important and necessary it might be, was not sufficient for the task he was facing now. He had the body, but he did not possess the skill. Hilvar's easy strides, the effortless surge of power which took him up every slope, filled Alvin with envy—and a determination not to give in while he could still place one foot in front of the other. He knew perfectly well that Hilvar was testing him, and did not resent the fact. It was a good-natured game, and he entered into the spirit of it even while the fatigue spread slowly through his legs.

Hilvar took pity on him when they had completed two-thirds of the ascent, and they rested for a while propped up against a westward-facing bank, letting the mellow sunlight drench their bodies. The throbbing thunder was very strong now, and although Alvin questioned him Hilvar refused to explain it. It would, he said, spoil the surprise if Alvin knew what to expect at the end of the climb.

They were now racing against the sun, but fortunately the final ascent was smooth and gentle. The trees that had covered the lower part of the hill had now thinned out, as if they too were tired of the fight against gravity, and for the last few hundred yards the ground was carpeted with short, wiry grass on which it was very pleasant to walk. As the summit came in sight, Hilvar put forth a sudden burst of energy and went racing up the slope. Alvin decided to ignore the challenge; indeed, he had no choice. He was quite content to plod steadily onward, and when he had caught up with Hilvar to collapse in contented exhaustion by his side.

Not until he had regained his breath was he able to appreciate the view spread out beneath him, and to see the origin of the endless thunder which now filled the air. The ground ahead fell away steeply from the crest of the hill—so steeply, indeed, that it soon became an almost vertical cliff. And leaping far out from the face of the cliff was a mighty ribbon of water, which curved out through space to crash into the rocks a thousand feet below. There it was lost in a shimmering mist of spray, while up from the depths rose that ceaseless, drumming thunder that reverberated in hollow echoes from the hills on either side.

Most of the waterfall was now in shadow, but the sunlight streaming past the mountain still illuminated the land beneath, adding the final touch of magic to the scene. For quivering in evanescent beauty above the base of the fall was the last rainbow left on Earth.

Hilvar waved his arm in a sweep which embraced the whole horizon.

"From here," he said, raising his voice so that it could be heard above the thunder of the waterfall, "you can see right across Lys."

Alvin could well believe him. To the north lay mile upon mile of forest, broken here and there by clearings and fields and the wandering threads of a hundred rivers. Hidden somewhere in that vast panorama was the village of Airlee, but it was hopeless to try to find it. Alvin fancied that he could catch a glimpse of the lake past which the path led to the entrance into Lys, but decided that his eyes had tricked him. Still further north, trees and clearings alike were lost in a mottled carpet of green, rucked here and there by lines of hills. And beyond that, at the very edge of vision, the mountains that hemmed Lys from the desert lay like a bank of distant clouds.

East and west the view was little different, but to the south the mountains seemed only a few miles away. Alvin could see them very clearly, and he realized that they were far higher than the little peak on which he was standing. They were separated from him by country that was much wilder than the land through which he had just passed. In some indefinable way it seemed deserted and empty, as if Man had not lived here for many, many years.

Hilvar answered Alvin's unspoken question.

"Once that part of Lys was inhabited," he said. "I don't know why it was abandoned, and perhaps one day we shall move into it again. Only the animals live there now."

Indeed, there was nowhere any sign of human life—none of the clearings or well-disciplined rivers that spoke of Man's presence. Only in one spot was there any indication that he had ever lived here, for many miles away a solitary white ruin jutted above the forest roof like a broken fang. Elsewhere, the jungle had returned to its own.

The sun was sinking below the western walls of Lys. For a breathless moment, the distant mountains seemed to burn with golden flames; then the land they guarded was swiftly drowned with shadow and the night had come.

"We should have done this before," said Hilvar, practical as ever, as he started to unload their equipment. "It'll be pitch dark in five minutes—and cold, too."

Curious pieces of apparatus began to cover the grass. A slim tripod extended a vertical rod carrying a pear-shaped bulge at its upper end. Hilvar raised this until the pear was just clear of their heads, and gave some mental signal which Alvin could not intercept. At once their little encampment was flooded with light, and the darkness retreated. The pear gave not only light but also heat, for Alvin could feel a gentle, caressing glow that seemed to sink into his very bones.

Carrying the tripod in one hand and his pack in the other, Hilvar walked down the slope while Alvin hurried behind, doing his best to keep in the circle of light. He finally pitched camp in a small depression a few hundred yards below the crest of the hill, and started to put the rest of his equipment into operation.

First came a large hemisphere of some rigid and almost invisible material which englobed them completely and protected them from the cool breeze which had now begun to blow up the face of the hill. The dome appeared to be generated by a small rectangular box which Hilvar placed on the ground and then ignored completely, even to the extent of burying it beneath the rest of his paraphernalia. Perhaps this also projected the comfortable, semitransparent couches on which Alvin was so glad to relax. It was the first time he had seen furniture materialized in Lys, where it seemed to him that the houses were terribly cluttered up with permanent artifacts which would be much better kept safely out of the way in Memory Banks.

The meal which Hilvar produced from yet another of his receptacles was also the first purely synthetic one that Alvin had eaten since reaching Lys. There was a steady blast of air, sucked through some orifice in the dome overhead, as the matter-converter seized its raw material and performed its everyday miracle. On the whole, Alvin was much happier with purely synthetic food. The way in which the other kind was prepared struck him as being appallingly unhygienic, and at least with the matter-converters you knew exactly what you were eating.

They settled down for their evening meal as the night deepened around them and the stars came out. When they had finished, it was completely dark beyond their circle of light, and at the edge of that circle Alvin could see dim shapes moving as the creatures of the forest crept out of their hiding places. From time to time he caught the glint of reflected light as pale eyes stared back at him, but whatever beasts were waching out there would come no closer, so he could see nothing more of them.

It was very peaceful, and Alvin felt utterly content. For a while they lay on their couches and talked about the things that they had seen, the mystery that enmeshed them both, and the many ways in which their two cultures differed. Hilvar was fascinated by the miracle of the Eternity Circuits which had put Diaspar beyond the reach of time, and Alvin found some of his questions very hard to answer.

"What I don't understand," said Hilvar, "is how the designers of Diaspar made certain that nothing would ever go wrong with the memory circuits. You tell me that the information defining the city, and all the people who live in it, is stored as patterns of electric charge inside crystals. Well, crystals will last forever—but what about all the circuits associated with them? Aren't there ever any failures of *any* kind?"

"I asked Khedron that same question, and he told me that the Memory Banks are virtually triplicated. Any one of the three banks can maintain the city, and if anything goes wrong with one of them, the other two automatically correct it. Only if the same failure occurred simultaneously in two of the banks would any permanent damage be done—and the chances of that are infinitesimal."

"And how is the relation maintained between the pattern stored in the memory units and the actual structure of the city? Between the plan, as it were, and the thing it describes?"

Alvin was now completely out of his depth. He knew that the answer involved technologies that relied on the manipulation of space itself—but how one could lock an atom rigidly in the position defined by data stored elsewhere was something he could not begin to explain.

On a sudden inspiration, he pointed to the invisible dome protecting them from the night.

"Tell me how this roof above our heads is created by that box you're sitting on," he answered, "and then I'll explain how the Eternity Circuits work."

Hilvar laughed.

"I suppose it's a fair comparison. You'd have to ask one of our field theory experts if you wanted to know that. I certainly couldn't tell you."

This reply made Alvin very thoughtful. So there were still men in Lys who understood how their machines worked; that was more than could be said of Diaspar.

Thus they talked and argued, until presently Hilvar said: "I'm tired. What about you—are you going to sleep?"

Alvin rubbed his still-weary limbs.

"I'd like to," he confessed, "but I'm not sure I can. It still seems a strange custom to me."

"It is a good deal more than a custom," smiled Hilvar. "I have been told that it was once a necessity to every human being. We still like to sleep at least once a day, even if only for a few hours. During that time the body refreshes itself, and the mind as well. Does no one in Diaspar *ever* sleep?"

"Only on very rare occasions," said Alvin. "Jeserac, my tutor, has done it once or twice, after he had made some exceptional mental effort. A well-designed body should have no need for such rest periods; we did away with them millions of years ago."

Even as he spoke these rather boastful words, his actions belied them. He felt a weariness such as he had never before known; it seemed to spread from his calves and thighs until it flowed through all his body. There was nothing unpleasant about the sensation—rather the reverse. Hilvar was watching him with an amused smile, and Alvin had enough faculties left to wonder if his companion was exercising any of his mental powers upon him. If so, he did not object in the least.

The light flooding down from the metal pear overhead sank to a faint glow, but the warmth it was radiating continued unabated. By the last flicker of light, Alvin's drowsy mind registered a curious fact which he would have to inquire about in the morning.

Hilvar had stripped off his clothes, and for the first time Alvin saw how much the two branches of the human race had diverged. Some of the changes were merely ones of emphasis or proportion, but others, such as the external genitals and the presence of teeth, nails, and definite body hair, were more fundamental. What puzzled him most of all, however, was the curious small hollow in the pit of Hilvar's stomach.

When, some days later, he suddenly remembered the subject, it took a good deal of explaining. By the time that Hilvar had made the functions of the navel quite clear, he had uttered many thousands of words and drawn half a dozen diagrams.

And both he and Alvin had made a great step forward in understanding the basis of each other's cultures.

CHAPTER TWELVE

The night was at its deepest when Alvin woke. Something had disturbed him, some whisper of sound that had crept into his mind despite the endless thunder of the falls. He sat up in the darkness, straining his eyes across the hidden land, while with indrawn breath he listened to the drumming roar of the water and the softer, more fugitive sounds of the creatures of the night.

Nothing was visible. The starlight was too dim to reveal the miles of country that lay hundreds of feet below; only a jagged line of darker night eclipsing the stars told of the mountains on the southern horizon. In the darkness beside him Alvin heard his companion roll over and sit up.

"What is it?" came a whispered voice.

"I thought I heard a noise."

"What sort of noise?"

"I don't know: perhaps it was just imagination."

There was a silence while two pairs of eyes peered out into the mystery of the night. Then, suddenly, Hilvar caught Alvin's arm.

"Look!" he whispered.

Far to the south glowed a solitary point of light, too low in the heavens to be a star. It was a brilliant white, tinged with violet, and even as they watched it began to climb the spectrum of intensity, until the eye could no longer bear to look upon it. Then it exploded—and it seemed as if lightning had struck below the rim of the world. For a brief instant the mountains, and the land they encircled, were etched with fire against the darkness of the night. Ages later came the ghost of a far-off explosion, and in the woods below a sudden wind stirred among the trees. It died away swiftly, and one by one the routed stars crept back into the sky.

For the second time in his life, Alvin knew fear. It was not as personal and imminent as it had been in the chamber of the moving ways, when he had made the decision that took him to Lys. Perhaps it was awe rather than fear; he was looking into the face of the unknown, and it was as if he had already sensed that out there beyond the mountains was something he must go to meet.

"What was that?" he whispered at length.

There was a pause so long that he repeated the question.

"I am trying to find out," said Hilvar, and was silent again. Alvin guessed what he was doing and did not interrupt his friend's silent quest.

Presently Hilvar gave a little sigh of disappointment. "Everyone is asleep," he said. "There was no one who could tell me. We must wait until morning, unless I wake one of my friends. And I would not like to do that unless it is really important."

Alvin wondered what Hilvar would consider a matter of real importance. He was just going to suggest, a little sarcastically, that this might well merit interrupting someone's sleep. Before he could make the proposal, Hilvar spoke again.

"I've just remembered," he said, rather apologetically, "it's a long time since I came here, and I'm not quite certain about my bearings. But that must be Shalmirane."

"Shalmirane! Does it still exist?"

"Yes; I'd almost forgotten. Seranis once told me that the fortress lies in those mountains. Of course, it's been in ruins for ages, but perhaps someone still lives there."

Shalmirane! To these children of two races, so widely differing in culture and history, this was indeed a name of magic. In all the long story of Earth, there had been no greater epic than the defense of Shalmirane against an invader who had conquered all the Universe. Though the true facts were utterly lost in the mists which had gathered so thickly around the Dawn Ages, the legends had never been forgotten and would last as long as man endured.

Presently Hilvar's voice came again out of the darkness.

"The people of the south could tell us more. I have some friends there; I will call them in the morning."

Alvin scarcely heard him; he was deep in his own thoughts, trying to remember all that he had ever heard of Shalmirane. It was little enough; after this immense lapse of time, no one could tell the truth from the legend. All that was certain was that the Battle of Shalmirane marked the end of Man's conquests and the beginning of his long decline.

Among those mountains, thought Alvin, might lie the answers to all the problems that had tormented him for so many years.

"How long," he said to Hilvar, "would it take us to reach the fortress?"

"I've never been there, but it's much farther than I intended to go. I doubt if we can do it in a day."

"Can't we use the ground-car?"

"No; the way lies through the mountains and no cars can go there."

Alvin thought it over. He was tired, his feet were sore, and the muscles of his thighs were still aching from the unaccustomed effort. It was very tempting to leave it for another time. Yet there might be no other time.

Beneath the dim light of the failing stars, not a few of which had died since Shalmirane was built, Alvin wrestled with his thoughts and presently made his decision. Nothing had changed; the mountains resumed their watch over the sleeping land. But a turning point in history had come and gone, and the human race was moving toward a strange new future.

Alvin and Hilvar slept no more that night, but broke camp with the first glow of dawn. The hill was drenched with dew, and Alvin marveled at the sparkling jewelry which weighed down each blade and leaf. The "swish" of the wet grass fascinated him as he plowed through it, and looking back up the hill he could see his path stretching behind him like a dark band across the shining ground.

The sun had just lifted above the eastern wall of Lys when they reached the outskirts of the forest. Here, Nature had returned to her own. Even Hilvar seemed somewhat lost among the gigantic trees that blocked the sunlight and cast pools of shadow on the jungle floor. Fortunately the river from the fall flowed south in a line too straight to be altogether natural, and by keeping to its edge they could avoid the denser undergrowth. A good deal of Hilvar's time was spent in controlling Krif, who disappeared occasionally into the jungle or went skimming wildly across the water. Even Alvin, to whom everything was still so new, could feel that the forest had a fascination not possessed by the smaller, more cultivated woods of northern Lys. Few trees were alike; most of them were in various stages of devolution and some had reverted through the ages almost to their original, natural forms. Many were obviously not of Earth at all—probably not even of the Solar System. Watching like sentinels over the lesser trees were giant sequoias, three or four hundred feet high. Once they had been called the oldest things on Earth; they were still a little older than Man.

The river was widening now; ever and again it opened into small lakes, upon which tiny islands lay at anchor. There were insects here, brilliantly colored creatures swinging to and fro over the surface of the water. Once, despite Hilvar's commands, Krif darted away to join his distant cousins. He disappeared instantly in a cloud of glittering wings, and the sound of angry buzzing floated toward them. A moment later the cloud erupted and Krif came back across the water, almost too quickly for the eye to follow. Thereafter he kept very close to Hilvar and did not stray again.

Toward evening they caught occasional glimpses of the mountains ahead. The river that had been so faithful a guide was flowing sluggishly now, as if it too were nearing the end of its journey. But it was clear that they could not reach the mountains by nightfall; well before sunset the forest had become so dark that further progress was impossible. The great trees lay in pools of shadow, and a cold wind was sweeping through the leaves. Alvin and Hilvar settled down for the night beside a giant redwood whose topmost branches were still ablaze with sunlight.

When at last the hidden sun went down, the light still lingered on the dancing waters. The two explorers—for such they now considered themselves, and such indeed they were—lay in the gathering gloom, watching the river and thinking of all that they had seen. Presently Alvin felt once again steal over him that sense of delicious drowsiness he had known for the first time on the previous night, and he gladly resigned himself to sleep. It might not be needed in the effortless life of Diaspar, but he welcomed it here. In the final moment before unconsciousness overcame him, he found himself wondering who last had come this way, and how long since.

The sun was high when they left the forest and stood at last before the mountain walls of Lys. Ahead of them the ground rose steeply to the sky in waves of barren rock. Here the river came to an end as spectacular as its beginning, for the ground opened in its path and it sank roaring from sight. Alvin wondered what happened to it, and through what subterranean caves it traveled before it emerged again into the light of day. Perhaps the lost oceans of Earth still existed, far down in the eternal darkness, and his ancient river still felt the call that drew it to the sea.

For a moment Hilvar stood looking at the whirlpool and the broken land beyond. Then he pointed to a gap in the hills.

"Shalmirane lies in that direction," he said confidently. Alvin did not ask how he knew; he assumed that Hilvar's mind had made brief contact with that of a friend many miles away, and the information he needed had been silently passed to him.

It did not take long to reach the gap, and when they had passed through it they found themselves facing a curious plateau with gently sloping sides. Alvin felt no tiredness now, and no fear—only a taut expectancy and a sense of approaching adventure. What he would discover, he had no conception. That he would discover something he did not doubt at all.

As they approached the summit, the nature of the ground altered abruptly. The lower slopes had consisted of porous, volcanic stone, piled here and there in great mounds of slag. Now the surface turned suddenly to hard, glassy sheets, smooth and treacherous, as if the rock had once run in molten rivers down the mountain.

The rim of the plateau was almost at their feet. Hilvar reached it first, and a few seconds later Alvin overtook him and stood speechless at his side. For they stood on the edge, not of the plateau they had expected, but of a giant bowl half a mile deep and three miles in diameter. Ahead of them the ground plunged steeply downward, slowly leveling out at the bottom of the valley and rising again, more and more steeply, to the opposite rim. The lowest part of the bowl was occupied by a circular lake, the surface of which trembled continually, as if agitated by incessant waves.

Although it lay in the full glare of the sun, the whole of that great depression was ebon black. What material formed the crater, Alvin and Hilvar could not even guess, but it was black as the rock of a world that had never known a sun. Nor was that all, for lying beneath their feet and ringing the entire crater was a seamless band of metal, some hundred feet wide, tarnished by immeasurable age but still showing no slightest sign of corrosion.

As their eyes grew accustomed to the unearthly scene, Alvin and Hilvar realized that the blackness of the bowl was not as absolute as they had thought. Here and there, so fugitive that they could only see them indirectly, tiny explosions of light were flickering in the ebon walls. They came at random, vanishing as soon as they were born, like the reflections of stars on a broken sea.

"It's wonderful!" gasped Alvin. "But what *is* it?"

"It looks like a reflector of some kind."

"But it's so black!"

"Only to our eyes, remember. We do not know what radiations they used."

"But surely there must be more than this! Where *is* the fortress?"

Hilvar pointed to the lake.

"Look carefully," he said.

Alvin stared through the quivering roof of the lake, trying to plumb the secrets it concealed within its depths. At first he could see nothing; then, in the shallows near its edge, he made out a faint reticulation of light and shade. He was able to trace the pattern out toward the center of the lake until the deepening water hid all further details.

The dark lake had engulfed the fortress. Down there lay the ruins of once mighty buildings, overthrown by time. Yet not all of them had been submerged, for on the far side of the crater Alvin now noticed piles of jumbled stones, and great blocks that must once have formed part of massive walls. The waters lapped around them, but had not yet risen far enough to complete their victory.

"We'll go around the lake," said Hilvar, speaking softly as if the majestic desolation had struck awe into his soul. "Perhaps we may find something in those ruins over there."

For the first few hundred yards the crater walls were so steep and smooth that it was difficult to stand upright, but after a while they reached the gentler slopes and could walk without difficulty. Near the border of the lake the smooth ebony of the surface was concealed by a thin layer of soil, which the winds of Lys must have brought here through the ages.

A quarter of a mile away, titanic blocks of stone were piled one upon the other, like the discarded toys of an infant giant. Here, a section of a massive wall was still recognizable; there, two carven obelisks marked what had once been a mighty entrance. Everywhere grew mosses and creeping plants, and tiny stunted trees. Even the wind was hushed.

So Alvin and Hilvar came to the ruins of Shalmirane. Against those walls, and against the energies they had housed, forces that could shatter a world to dust had flamed and thundered and been utterly defeated. Once these peaceful skies had blazed with fires torn from the hearts of suns, and the mountains of Lys must have quailed like living things beneath the fury of their masters.

No one had ever captured Shalmirane. But now the fortress, the impregnable fortress, had fallen at last—captured and destroyed by the patient tendrils of the ivy, the generations of blindly burrowing worms, and the slowly rising waters of the lake.

Overawed by its majesty, Alvin and Hilvar walked in silence toward the colossal wreck. They passed into the shadow of a broken wall, and entered a canyon where the mountains of stone had split asunder. Before them lay the lake, and presently they stood with the dark water lapping at their feet. Tiny waves, no more than a few inches high, broke endlessly upon the narrow shore.

Hilvar was the first to speak, and his voice held a hint of uncertainty which made Alvin glance at him in sudden surprise.

"There's something here I don't understand," he said slowly. "There's no wind, so what causes these ripples? The water should be perfectly still."

Before Alvin could think of any reply, Hilvar dropped to the ground, turned his head on one side, and immersed his right ear in the water. Alvin wondered what he hoped to discover in such a ludicrous position; then he realized that he was listening. With some repugnance—for the rayless waters looked singularly uninviting—he followed Hilvar's example.

The first shock of coldness lasted only for a second; when it passed he could hear, faint but distinct, a steady, rhythmic throbbing. It was as if he could hear, from far down in the depths of the lake, the beating of a giant heart.

They shook the water from their hair and stared at each other with silent surmise. Neither liked to say what he thought—that the lake was alive.

"It would be best," said Hilvar presently, "if we searched among these ruins and kept away from the lake."

"Do you think there's something down there?" asked Alvin, pointing to the enigmatic ripples that were still breaking against his feet. "Could it be dangerous?"

"Nothing that possesses a mind is dangerous," Hilvar replied. (Is that true? thought Alvin. What of the Invaders?) "I can detect no thoughts of any kind here, but I do not believe we are alone. It is very strange."

They walked slowly back toward the ruins of the fortress, each carrying in his mind the sound of that steady, muffled pulsing. It seemed to Alvin that mystery was piling upon mystery, and that for all his efforts he was getting further and further from any understanding of the truths he sought.

It did not seem that the ruins could teach them anything, but they searched carefully among the piles of rubble and the great mounds of stone. Here, perhaps, lay the graves of buried machines—the machines that had done their work so long ago. They would be useless now, thought Alvin, if the Invaders returned. Why had they never come back? But that was yet another mystery: he had enough enigmas to deal with—there was no need to seek for any more.

A few yards from the lake they found a small clearing among the rubble. It had been covered with weeds, but they were now blackened and charred by tremendous heat, so that they crumbled to ashes as Alvin and Hilvar approached, smearing their legs with streaks of charcoal. At the center of the clearing stood a metal tripod, firmly anchored to the ground, and supporting a circular ring which was tilted on its axis so that it pointed to a spot halfway up the sky. At first sight it seemed that the ring enclosed nothing; then, as Alvin looked more carefully, he saw that it was filled with a faint haze that tormented the eye by lurking at the edge of the visible spectrum. It was the glow of power, and from this mechanism, he did not doubt, had come the explosion of light that had lured them to Shalmirane.

They did not venture any closer, but stood looking at the machine from a safe distance. They were on the right track, thought Alvin; now it only remained to discover who, or what, had set this apparatus here, and what their purpose might be. That tilted ring—it was clearly aimed out into space. Had the flash they had observed been some kind of signal? That was a thought which had breath-taking implications.

"Alvin," said Hilvar suddenly, his voice quiet but urgent, "we have visitors."

Alvin spun on his heels and found himself staring at a triangle of lidless eyes. That, at least, was his first impression; then behind the staring eyes he saw the outlines of a small but complex machine. It was hanging in the air a few feet above the ground, and it was like no robot he had ever before seen.

Once the initial surprise had worn off, he felt himself the complete master of the situation. All his life he had given orders to machines, and the fact that this one was unfamiliar was of no importance. For that matter, he had never seen more than a few per cent of the robots that provided his daily needs in Diaspar.

"Can you speak?" he asked.

There was silence.

"Is anyone controlling you?"

Still silence.

"Go away. Come here. Rise. Fall."

None of the conventional control thoughts produced any effect. The machine remained contemptuously inactive. That suggested two possibilities. It was either too unintelligent to understand him or it was very intelligent indeed, with its own powers of choice and volition. In that case, he must treat it as an equal. Even then he might underestimate it, but it would bear him no resentment, for conceit was not a vice from which robots often suffered.

Hilvar could not help laughing at Alvin's obvious discomfiture. He was just about to suggest that he should take over the task of communicating, when the words died on his lips. The stillness of Shalmirane was shattered by an ominous and utterly unmistakable sound—the gurgling splash of a very large body emerging from water.

It was the second time since he had left Diaspar that Alvin wished he were at home. Then he remembered that this was not the spirit in which to meet adventure, and he began to walk slowly but deliberately toward the lake.

The creature now emerging from the dark water seemed a monstrous parody, in living matter, of the robot that was still subjecting them to its silent scrutiny. That same equilateral arrangement of eyes could be no coincidence; even the pattern of tentacles and little jointed limbs had been roughly reproduced. Beyond that, however, the resemblance ceased. The robot did not possess—it obviously did not require—the fringe of delicate, feathery palps which beat the water with a steady rhythm, the stubby multiple legs on which the beast was humping itself ashore, or the ventilating inlets, if that was what they were, which now wheezed fitfully in the thin air.

Most of the creature's body remained in the water; only the first ten feet reared itself into what was clearly an alien element. The entire beast was about fifty feet long, and even anyone with no knowledge of biology would have realized that there was something altogether wrong about it. It had an extraordinary air of improvisation and careless design, as if its components had been manufactured without much forethought and thrown roughly together when the need arose.

Despite its size and their initial doubts, neither Alvin nor Hilvar felt the slightest nervousness once they had had a clear look at the dweller in the lake. There was an engaging clumsiness about the creature which made it quite impossible to regard it as a serious menace, even if there was any reason to suppose it might be dangerous. The human race had long ago overcome its childhood terror of the merely alien in appearance. That was a fear which could no longer survive after the first contact with friendly extraterrestrial races.

"Let me deal with this," said Hilvar quietly. "I'm used to handling animals."

"But this isn't an animal," whispered Alvin in return. "I'm sure it's intelligent, and owns that robot."

"The robot may own *it*. In any case, its mentality must be very strange. I can still detect no sign of thought. Hello—what's happening?"

The monster had not moved from its half-raised position at the water's edge, which it seemed to be maintaining with considerable effort. But a semitransparent membrane had begun to form at the center of the triangle of eyes—a membrane that pulsed and quivered and presently started to emit audible sounds. They were low-pitched, resonant boomings which created no intelligible words, though it was obvious that the creature was trying to speak to them.

It was painful to watch this desperate attempt at communication. For several minutes the creature struggled in vain; then, quite suddenly, it seemed to realize that it had made a mistake. The throbbing membrane contracted in size, and the sounds it emitted rose several octaves in frequency until they entered the spectrum of normal speech. Recognizable words began to form, though they were still interspersed with gibberish. It was as if the creature was remembering a vocabulary it had known long ago but had had no occasion to use for many years.

Hilvar tried to give what assistance he could.

"We can understand you now," he said, speaking slowly and distinctly. "Can we help you? We saw the light you made. It brought us here from Lys."

At the word "Lys" the creature seemed to drop as if it had suffered some bitter disappointment.

"Lys," it repeated; it could not manage the "s" very well, so that the word sounded like "Lyd." "Always from Lys. No one else ever comes. We call the Great Ones, but they do not hear."

"Who are the Great Ones?" asked Alvin, leaning forward eagerly. The delicate, ever-moving palps waved briefly toward the sky.

"The Great Ones," it said. "From the planets of eternal day. They will come. The Master promised us."

This did not seem to make matters any clearer. Before Alvin could continue his cross-examination, Hilvar intervened again. His questioning was so patient, so sympathetic, and yet so penetrating that Alvin knew better than to interrupt, despite his eagerness. He did not like to admit that Hilvar was his superior in intelligence, but there was no doubt that his flair for handling animals extended even to this fantastic being. What was more, it seemed to respond to him. Its speech became more distinct as the conversation proceeded, and where at first it had been brusque to the point of rudeness, it presently elaborated its answers and volunteered information on its own.

Alvin lost all consciousness of the passage of time as Hilvar pieced together the incredible story. They could not discover the whole truth; there was endless room for conjecture and debate. As the creature answered Hilvar's questions ever more and more willingly, its appearance began to change. It slumped back into the lake, and the stubby legs that had been supporting it seemed to dissolve into the rest of its body. Presently a still more extraordinary change occurred; the three huge eyes slowly closed, shrank to pinpoints, and vanished completely. It was as if the creature had seen all that it wished to for the moment, and therefore had no further use for eyes.

Other and more subtle alterations were continually taking place, and eventually almost all that remained above the surface of the water was the vibrating diaphragm through which the creature spoke. Doubtless this too would be dissolved back into the original amorphous mass of protoplasm when it was no longer required.

Alvin found it hard to believe that intelligence could reside in so unstable a form—and his biggest surprise was yet to come. Though it seemed obvious that the creature was not of terrestrial origin, it was some time before even Hilvar, despite his greater knowledge of biology, realized the type of organism they were dealing with. It was not a single entity; in all their conversations with it, it always referred to itself as "we." In fact, it was nothing less than a colony of independent creatures, organized and controlled by unknown forces.

Animals of a remotely similar type—the medusae, for example—had once flourished in the ancient oceans of Earth. Some of them had been of great size, trailing their translucent bodies and forests of stinging tentacles over fifty or a hundred feet of water. But none of them had attained even the faintest flicker of intelligence, beyond the power to react to simple stimuli.

There was certainly intelligence here, though it was a failing, degenerating intelligence. Never was Alvin to forget this unearthly meeting, as Hilvar slowly pieced together the story of the Master, while the protean polyp groped for unfamiliar words, the dark lake lapped at the ruins of Shalmirane, and the trioptic robot watched them with unwavering eyes.

CHAPTER THIRTEEN

The Master had come to Earth amid the chaos of the Transition Centuries, when the Galactic Empire was crumbling but the lines of communication among the stars had not yet completely broken. He had been of human origin, though his home was a planet circling one of the Seven Suns. While still a young man, he had been forced to leave his native world, and its memory had haunted him all his life. His expulsion he blamed on vindictive enemies, but the fact was that he suffered from an incurable malady which, it seemed, attacked only Homo sapiens among all the intelligent races of the Universe. That disease was religious mania.

Throughout the earlier part of its history, the human race had brought forth an endless succession of prophets, seers, messiahs, and evangelists who convinced themselves and their followers that to them alone were the secrets of the Universe revealed. Some of them succeeded in establishing religions that survived for many generations and influenced billions of men; others were forgotten even before their deaths.

The rise of science, which with monotonous regularity refuted the cosmologies of the prophets and produced miracles which they could never match, eventually destroyed all these faiths. It did not destroy the awe, nor the reverence and humility, which all intelligent beings felt as they contemplated the stupendous Universe in which they found themselves. What it did weaken, and finally obliterate, were the countless religions, each of which claimed, with unbelievable arrogance, that it was the sole repository of the truth and that its millions of rivals and predecessors were all mistaken.

Yet, though they never possessed any real power once humanity had reached a very elementary level of civilization, all down the ages isolated cults had continued to appear, and however fantastic their creeds they had always managed to attract some disciples. They thrived with particular strength during periods of confusion and disorder, and it was not surprising that the Transition Centuries had seen a great outburst of irrationality. When reality was depressing, men tried to console themselves with myths.

The Master, even if he was expelled from his own world, did not leave it unprovided. The Seven Suns had been the center of galactic power and science, and he must have possessed influential friends. He had made his hegira in a small but speedy ship, reputed to be one of the fastest ever built. With him into exile he had taken another of the ultimate products of galactic science—the robot that was looking at Alvin and Hilvar even now.

No one had ever known the full talents and functions of this machine. To some extent, indeed, it had become the Master's alter ego; without it, the religion of the Great Ones would probably have collapsed after the Master's death. Together they had roved among the star clouds on a zigzag trail which led at last, certainly not by accident, back to the world from which the Master's ancestors had sprung.

Entire libraries had been written about that saga, each work therein inspiring a host of commentaries until, by a kind of chain reaction, the original volumes were lost beneath mountains of exegesis and annotation. The Master had stopped at many worlds, and made disciples among many races. His personality must have been an immensely powerful one for it to have inspired humans and nonhumans alike, and there was no doubt that a religion of such wide appeal must have contained much that was fine and noble. Probably the Master was the most successful—as he was also the last—of all mankind's messiahs. None of his predecessors could have won so many converts or had their teachings carried across such gulfs of time and space.

What those teachings were neither Alvin nor Hilvar could ever discover with any accuracy. The great polyp did its desperate best to convey them, but many of the words it used were meaningless and it had a habit of repeating sentences or whole speeches with a kind of swift mechanical delivery that made them very hard to follow. After a while Hilvar did his best to steer the conversation away from these meaningless morasses of theology in order to concentrate on ascertainable facts.

The Master and a band of his most faithful followers had arrived on Earth in the days before the cities had passed away, and while the Port of Diaspar was still open to the stars. They must have come in ships of many kinds; the polyps, for example, in one filled with the waters of the sea which was their natural home. Whether the movement was well received on Earth was not certain; but at least it met no violent opposition, and after further wanderings it set up its final retreat among the forests and mountains of Lys.

At the close of his long life, the Master's thoughts had turned once more toward the home from which he had been exiled, and he had asked his friends to carry him out into the open so that he could watch the stars. He had waited, his strength waning, until the culmination of the Seven Suns, and toward the end he babbled many things which were to inspire yet more libraries of interpretation in future ages. Again and again he spoke of the "Great Ones" who had now left this universe of space and matter but who would surely one day return, and he charged his followers to remain to greet them when they came. Those were his last rational words. He was never again conscious of his surroundings, but just before the end he uttered one phrase that had come down the ages to haunt the minds of all who heard it: *"It is lovely to watch the colored shadows on the planets of eternal light."* Then he died.

At the Master's death, many of his followers broke away, but others remained faithful to his teachings, which they slowly elaborated through the ages. At first they believed that the Great Ones, whoever they were, would soon return, but that hope faded with the passing centuries. The story here grew very confused, and it seemed that truth and legend were inextricably intertwined. Alvin had only a vague picture of generations of fanatics, waiting for some great event which they did not understand to take place at some unknown future date.

The Great Ones never returned. Slowly the power of the movement failed as death and disillusion robbed it of its disciples. The short-lived human followers were the first to go, and there was something supremely ironic in the fact that the very last adherent of a human prophet was a creature utterly unlike Man.

The great polyp had become the Master's last disciple for a very simple reason. It was immortal. The billions of individual cells from which its body was built would die, but before that happened they would have reproduced themselves. At long intervals the monster would disintegrate into its myriad separate cells, which would go their own way and multiply by fission if their environment was suitable. During this phase the polyp did not exist as a self-conscious, intelligent entity—and here Alvin was irresistibly reminded of the manner in which the inhabitants of Diaspar spent their quiescent millenniums in the city's Memory Banks.

In due time some mysterious biological force brought the scattered components together again, and the polyp began a new cycle of existence. It returned to awareness and recollected its earlier lives, though often imperfectly since accident sometimes damaged the cells that carried the delicate patterns of memory.

Perhaps no other form of life could have kept faith so long to a creed otherwise forgotten for a billion years. In a sense, the great polyp was a helpless victim of its biological nature. Because of its immortality, it could not change, but was forced to repeat eternally the same invariant pattern.

The religion of the Great Ones, in its later stages, had become identified with a veneration of the Seven Suns. When the Great Ones stubbornly refused to appear, attempts were made to signal their distant home. Long ago the signaling had become no more than a meaningless ritual, now maintained by an animal that had forgotten how to learn and a robot that had never known how to forget.

As the immeasurably ancient voice died away into the still air, Alvin found himself overwhelmed by a surge of pity. The misplaced devotion, the loyalty that had held to its futile course while suns and planets passed away—he could never have believed such a tale had he not seen the evidence before his eyes. More than ever before the extent of his ignorance saddened him. A tiny fragment of the past had been illuminated for a little while, but now the darkness had closed over it again.

The history of the Universe must be a mass of such disconnected threads, and no one could say which were important and which were trivial. This fantastic tale of the Master and the Great Ones seemed like another of the countless legends that had somehow survived from the civilizations of the Dawn. Yet the very existence of the huge polyp, and of the silently watching robot, made it impossible for Alvin to dismiss the whole story as a fable built of self-delusion upon a foundation of madness.

What was the relationship, he wondered, between these two entities, which though so different in every possible way had maintained their extraordinary partnership over such aeons of time? He was somehow certain that the robot was much the more important of the two. It had been the confidant of the Master and must still know all his secrets.

Alvin looked at the enigmatic machine that still regarded him so steadily. Why would it not speak? What thoughts were passing through its complicated and perhaps alien mind? Yet, surely, if it had been designed to serve the Master, its mind would not be altogether alien, and it should respond to human orders.

As he thought of all the secrets which that stubbornly mute machine must possess, Alvin felt a curiosity so great that it verged upon greed. It seemed unfair that such knowledge should be wasted and hidden from the world; here must lie wonders beyond even the ken of the Central Computer in Diaspar.

"Why won't your robot speak to us?" he asked the polyp, when Hilvar had momentarily run out of questions. The answer was one he had half expected.

"It was against the Master's wishes for it to speak with any voice but his, and his voice is silent now."

"But it will obey you?"

"Yes; the Master placed it in our charge. We can see through its eyes, wherever it goes. It watches over the machines that preserve this lake and keep its water pure. Yet it would be truer to call it our partner than our servant."

Alvin thought this over. An idea, still vague and half-formed, was beginning to take shape in his mind. Perhaps it was inspired by pure lust for knowledge and power; when he looked back on this moment he could never be certain just what his motives were. They might be largely selfish, but they also contained some element of compassion. If he could do so, he would like to break this futile sequence and release these creatures from their fantastic fate. He was not sure what could be done about the polyp, but it might be possible to cure the robot of its insanity and at the same time to release its priceless, pent-up memories.

"Are you certain," he said slowly, talking to the polyp but aiming his words at the robot, "that you are really carrying out the Master's wishes by remaining here? He desired the world to know of his teachings, but they have been lost while you hide here in Shalmirane. It was only by chance that we discovered you, and there may be many others who would like to hear the doctrine of the Great Ones."

Hilvar glanced at him sharply, obviously uncertain of his intentions. The polyp seemed agitated, and the steady beating of its respiratory equipment faltered for a few seconds. Then it replied, in a voice not altogether under control: "We have discussed this problem for many years. But we cannot leave Shalmirane, so the world must come to us, no matter how long it takes."

"I have a better idea," said Alvin eagerly. "It is true that *you* may have to stay here in the lake, but there is no reason why your companion should not come with us. He can return whenever he wishes or whenever you need him. Many things have changed since the Master died—things which you should know about, but which you can never understand if you stay here."

The robot never moved, but in its agony of indecision the polyp sank completely below the surface of the lake and remained there for several minutes. Perhaps it was having a soundless argument with its colleague; several times it began to re-emerge, thought better of it, and sank into the water again. Hilvar took this opportunity to exchange a few words with Alvin.

"I'd like to know what you are trying to do," he said softly, his voice half-bantering and half-serious. "Or don't you know yourself?"

"Surely," replied Alvin, "you feel sorry for these poor creatures? Don't you think it would be a kindness to rescue them?"

"I do, but I've learned enough about you to be fairly certain that altruism isn't one of your dominant emotions. You must have some other motive."

Alvin smiled ruefully. Even if Hilvar did not read his mind—and he had no reason to suppose that he did—he could undoubtedly read his character.

"Your people have remarkable mental powers," he replied, trying to divert the conversation from dangerous ground. "I think they might be able to do something for the robot, if not for this animal." He spoke very softly, lest he be overheard. The precaution might have been a useless one, but if the robot did intercept his remarks it gave no sign of it.

Fortunately, before Hilvar could press the inquiry any further, the polyp emerged once more from the lake. In the last few minutes it had become a good deal smaller and its movements were more disorganized. Even as Alvin watched, a segment of its complex, translucent body broke away from the main bulk and then disintegrated into multitudes of smaller sections, which swiftly dispersed. The creature was beginning to break up before their eyes.

Its voice, when it spoke again, was very erratic and hard to understand.

"Next cycle starting," it jerked out in a kind of fluctuating whisper. "Did not expect it so soon—only few minutes left—stimulation too great—cannot hold together much longer."

Alvin and Hilvar stared at the creature in horrified fascination. Even though the process they were watching was a natural one, it was not pleasant to watch an intelligent creature apparently in its death throes. They also felt an obscure sense of guilt; it was irrational to have the feeling, since it was of no great importance *when* the polyp began another cycle, but they realized that the unusual effort and excitement caused by their presence was responsibile for this premature metamorphosis.

Alvin realized that he would have to act quickly or his opportunity would be gone—perhaps only for a few years, perhaps for centuries.

"What have you decided?" he said eagerly. "Is the robot coming with us?"

There was an agonizing pause while the polyp tried to force its dissolving body to obey its will. The speech diaphragm fluttered, but no audible sound came from it. Then, as if in a despairing gesture of farewell, it waved its delicate palps feebly and let them fall back into the water, where they promptly broke adrift and went floating out into the lake. In a matter of minutes, the transformation was over. Nothing of the creature larger than an inch across remained. The water was full of tiny, greenish specks, which seemed to have a life and mobility of their own and which rapidly disappeared into the vastness of the lake.

The ripples on the surface had now altogether died away, and Alvin knew that the steady pulse beat that had sounded in the depths would now be stilled. The lake was dead again—or so it seemed. But that was an illusion; one day the unknown forces that had never failed to do their duty in the past would exert themselves again, and the polyp would be reborn. It was a strange and wonderful phenomenon, yet was it so much stranger than the organization of the human body, itself a vast colony of separate, living cells?

Alvin wasted little effort on such speculations. He was oppressed by his sense of failure, even though he had never clearly conceived the goal he was aiming for. A dazzling opportunity had been missed and might never again return. He stared sadly out across the lake, and it was some time before his mind registered the message which Hilvar was speaking quietly in his ear.

"Alvin," his friend said softly. "I think you have won your point."

He spun swiftly on his heels. The robot, which until now had been floating aloofly in the distance, never approaching within twenty feet of them, had moved up in silence and was now poised a yard above his head. Its unmoving eyes, with their wide angles of vision, gave no indication of its direction of interest. Probably it saw the entire hemisphere in front of it with equal clarity, but Alvin had little doubt that its attention was now focused upon him.

It was waiting for his next move. To some extent, at least, it was now under his control. It might follow him to Lys, perhaps even to Diaspar—unless it changed its mind. Until then, he was its probationary master.

CHAPTER FOURTEEN

The journey back to Airlee lasted almost three days—partly because Alvin, for his own reasons, was in no hurry to return. The physical exploration of Lys had now taken second place to a more important and exciting project; he was slowly making contact with the strange, obsessed intelligence which had now become his companion.

He suspected that the robot was trying to use him for its own purposes, which would be no more than poetic justice. What its motives were he could never be quite certain, since it still stubbornly refused to speak to him. For some reason of his own—perhaps fear that it might reveal too many of his secrets—the Master must have placed very efficient blocks upon its speech circuits, and Alvin's attempts to clear them were completely unsuccessful. Even indirect questioning of the "If you say nothing I shall assume you mean 'Yes'" type failed; the robot was much too intelligent to be taken in by such simple tricks.

In other respects, however, it was more co-operative. It would obey any orders that did not require it to speak or reveal information. After a while Alvin found that he could control it, as he could direct the robots in Diaspar, by thought alone. This was a great step forward, and a little later the creature—it was hard to think of it as a mere machine—relaxed its guard still further and allowed him to see through its eyes. It did not object, it seemed, to such passive forms of communication, but it blocked all attempts at closer intimacy.

Hilvar's existence it ignored completely; it would obey none of his commands, and its mind was closed to all his probing. At first this was something of a disappointment to Alvin, who had hoped that Hilvar's greater mental powers would enable him to force open this treasure chest of hidden memories. It was not until later that he realized the advantage of possessing a servant who would obey no one else in all the world.

The member of the expedition who strongly objected to the robot was Krif. Perhaps he imagined that he now had a rival, or perhaps he disapproved, on general principles, of anything that flew without wings. When no one was looking, he had made several direct assaults on the robot, which had infuriated him still further by taking not the slightest notice of his attacks. Eventually Hilvar had been able to calm him down, and on the homeward journey in the ground-car he seemed to have resigned himself to the situation. Robot and insect escorted the vehicle as it glided silently through forest and field—each keeping to the side of its respective master and pretending that its rival was not there.

Seranis was already waiting for them as the car floated into Airlee. It was impossible, Alvin thought, to surprise these people. Their interlinked minds kept them in touch with everything that was happening in their land. He wondered how they had reacted to his adventures in Shalmirane, which presumably everyone in Lys now knew about.

Seranis seemed to be worried and more uncertain than he had ever seen her before, and Alvin remembered the choice that now lay before him. In the excitement of the last few days he had almost forgotten it; he did not like to spend energy worrying about problems that still lay in the future. But the future was now upon him; he must decide in which of these two worlds he wished to live.

The voice of Seranis was troubled when she began to speak, and Alvin had the sudden impression that something had gone awry with the plans that Lys had been making for him. What had been happening during his absence? Had emissaries gone into Diaspar to tamper with Khedron's mind—and had they failed in their duty?

"Alvin," began Seranis, "there are many things I did not tell you before, but which you must now learn if you are to understand our actions.

"You know one of the reasons for the isolation of our two races. The fear of the Invaders, that dark shadow in the depths of every human mind, turned your people against the world and made them lose themselves in their own dreams. Here in Lys that fear has never been so great, though we bore the burden of the final attack. We had a better reason for our actions, and what we did, we did with open eyes.

"Long ago, Alvin, men sought immortality and at last achieved it. They forgot that a world which had banished death must also banish life. The power to extend his life indefinitely might bring contentment to the individual, but brought stagnation to the race. Ages ago we sacrificed our immortality, but Diaspar still follows the false dream. That is why our ways parted—*and why they must never meet again.*"

Although the words had been more than half expected, the blow seemed none the less for its anticipation. Yet Alvin refused to admit the failure of all his plans—half-formed though they were—and only part of his brain was listening to Seranis now. He understood and noted all her words, but the conscious portion of his mind was retracing the road to Diaspar, trying to imagine every obstacle that could be placed in his way.

Seranis was clearly unhappy. Her voice was almost pleading as it spoke, and Alvin knew that she was talking not only to him but to her son. She must be aware of the understanding and affection that had grown up between them during the days they had spent together. Hilvar was watching his mother intently as she spoke, and it seemed to Alvin that his gaze held not merely concern but also more than a trace of censure.

"We do not wish to make you do anything against your will, but you must surely realize what it would mean if our people met again. Between our culture and yours is a gulf as great as any that ever separated Earth from its ancient colonies. Think of this one fact, Alvin. You and Hilvar are now of nearly the same age—*but both he and I will have been dead for centuries while you are still a youth.* And this is only your first in an infinite series of lives."

The room was very quiet, so quiet that Alvin could hear the strange, plaintive cries of unknown beasts in the fields beyond the village. Presently he said, almost in a whisper: "What do you want me to do?"

"We hoped that we could give you the choice of staying here or returning to Diaspar, but now that is impossible. Too much has happened for us to leave the decision in your hands. Even in the short time you have been here, your influence has been highly disturbing. No, I am not reproving you; I am sure you intended no harm. But it would have been best to leave the creatures you met in Shalmirane to their own destiny.

"And as for Diaspar—" Seranis gave a gesture of annoyance. "Too many people know where you have gone; we did not act in time. What is most serious, the man who helped you discover Lys has vanished; neither your Council nor our agents can discover him, so he remains a potential danger to our security. Perhaps you are surprised that I am telling you all this, but it is quite safe for me to do so. I am afraid we have only one choice before us; we must send you back to Diaspar with a false set of memories. Those memories have been constructed with great care, and when you return home you will know nothing of us. You will believe that you have had rather dull and dangerous adventures in gloomy underground caverns, where the roofs continually collapsed behind you and you kept alive only through eating unappetizing weeds and drinking from occasional springs. For the rest of your life you will believe this to be the truth, and everyone in Diaspar will accept your story. There will be no mystery, then, to lure any future explorers; they will think they know all there is to be known about Lys."

Seranis paused and looked at Alvin with anxious eyes. "We are very sorry that this is necessary and ask your forgiveness while you still remember us. You may not accept our verdict, but we know many facts that are hidden from you. At least you will have no regrets, for you will believe that you have discovered all that there is to be found."

Alvin wondered if that was true. He was not sure that he would ever settle down to the routine of life in Diaspar, even when he had convinced himself that nothing worthwhile existed beyond its walls. What was more, he had no intention of putting the matter to the test.

"When do you wish me to undergo this—treatment?" Alvin asked.

"Immediately. We are ready now. Open your mind to me, as you did before, and you will know nothing until you find yourself back in Diaspar."

Alvin was silent for a while. Then he said quietly: "I would like to say good-by to Hilvar."

Seranis nodded.

"I understand. I will leave you here for a while and return when you are ready." She walked over to the stairs that led down to the interior of the house, and left them alone on the roof.

It was some time before Alvin spoke to his friend; he felt a great sadness, yet also an unbroken determination not to permit the wreck of all his hopes. He looked once more down upon the village where he had found a measure of happiness and which he might never see again if those who were ranged behind Seranis had their way. The ground-car was still standing beneath one of the wide-branching trees, with the patient robot hanging in the air above it. A few children had gathered around to examine this strange newcomer, but none of the adults seemed in the least interested.

"Hilvar," said Alvin abruptly, "I'm very sorry about this."

"So am I," Hilvar answered, his voice unstable with emotion. "I had hoped that you could have remained here."

"Do you think that what Seranis wants to do is right?"

"Do not blame my mother. She is only doing as she is asked," replied Hilvar. Though he had not answered his question, Alvin had not the heart to ask it again. It was unfair to put such a strain on his friend's loyalty.

"Then tell me this," asked Alvin, "how could your people stop me if I tried to leave with my memories untouched?"

"It would be easy. If you tried to escape, we would take control of your mind and force you to come back."

Alvin had expected as much and was not discouraged. He wished that he could confide in Hilvar, who was obviously upset by their impending separation, but he dared not risk the failure of his plans. Very carefully, checking every detail, he traced out the only road that could lead him back to Diaspar on the terms he wished.

There was one risk which he had to face, and against which he could do nothing to protect himself. If Seranis broke her promise and dipped into his mind, all his careful preparations might be in vain.

He held out his hand to Hilvar, who grasped it firmly but seemed unable to speak.

"Let's go downstairs to meet Seranis," said Alvin. "I'd like to see some of the people in the village before I go."

Hilvar followed him silently into the peaceful coolness of the house and then out through the hallway and onto the ring of colored grass that surrounded the building. Seranis was waiting for them there, looking calm and resolute. She knew that Alvin was trying to hide something from her, and thought again of the precautions she had taken. As a man may flex his muscles before some great effort, she ran through the compulsion patterns she might have to use.

"Are you ready, Alvin?" she asked.

"Quite ready," replied Alvin, and there was a tone in his voice that made her look at him sharply.

"Then it will be best if you make your mind a blank, as you did before. You will feel and know nothing after that, until you find yourself back in Diaspar."

Alvin turned to Hilvar and said in a quick whisper that Seranis could not hear: "Good-by, Hilvar. Don't worry—*I'll be back.*" Then he faced Seranis again.

"I don't resent what you are trying to do," he said. "No doubt you believe it is for the best, but I think you are wrong. Diaspar and Lys should not remain apart forever; one day they may need each other desperately. So I am going home with all that I have learned—*and I do not think that you can stop me.*"

He waited no longer, and it was just as well. Seranis never moved, but instantly he felt his body slipping from his control. The power that had brushed aside his own will was even greater than he had expected, and he realized that many hidden minds must be aiding Seranis. Helplessly he began to walk back into the house, and for an awful moment he thought his plan had failed.

Then there came a flash of steel and crystal, and metal arms closed swiftly around him. His body fought against them, as he had known that it must do, but his struggles were useless. The ground fell away beneath him and he caught a glimpse of Hilvar, frozen by surprise, with a foolish smile upon his face.

The robot was carrying him a dozen feet above the ground, much faster than a man could run. It took Seranis only a moment to understand his ruse, and his struggles died away as she relaxed her control. But she was not defeated yet, and presently there happened that which Alvin had feared and done his best to counteract.

There were now two separate entities fighting inside his mind, and one of them was pleading with the robot, begging it to set him down. The real Alvin waited, breathlessly, resisting only a little against forces he knew he could not hope to fight. He had gambled; there was no way of telling beforehand if his uncertain ally would obey orders as complex as those that he had given it. Under no circumstances, he had told the robot, must it obey any further commands of his until he was safely inside Diaspar. Those were the orders. If they were obeyed, Alvin had placed his fate beyond the reach of human interference.

Never hesitating, the machine raced on along the path he had so carefully mapped out for it. A part of him was still pleading angrily to be released, but he knew now that he was safe. And presently Seranis understood that too, for the forces inside his brain ceased to war with one another. Once more he was at peace, as ages ago an earlier wanderer had been when, lashed to the mast of his ship, he had heard the song of the Sirens die away across the wine-dark sea.

CHAPTER FIFTEEN

Alvin did not relax until the chamber of the moving ways was around him once more. There had still been the danger that the people of Lys might be able to stop, or even to reverse, the vehicle in which he was traveling, and bring him back helplessly to his starting point. But his return was an uneventful repetition of the outward trip; forty minutes after he had left Lys he was in the Tomb of Yarlan Zey.

The servants of the Council were waiting for him, dressed in the formal black robes which they had not worn for centuries. Alvin felt no surprise, and little alarm, at the presence of this reception committee. He had now overcome so many obstacles that one more made little difference. He had learned a great deal since leaving Diaspar, and with that knowledge had come a confidence verging upon arrogance. Moreover, he now had a powerful, if erratic, ally. The best minds of Lys had been unable to interfere with his plans; somehow, he believed that Diaspar could do no better.

There were rational grounds for this belief, but it was based partly upon something beyond reason—a faith in his destiny which had slowly been growing in Alvin's mind. The mystery of his origin, his success in doing what no earlier man had ever done, the way in which new vistas had opened up before him, and the manner in which obstacles had failed to halt him—all these things added to his self-confidence. Faith in one's own destiny was among the most valuable of the gifts which the gods could bestow upon a man, but Alvin did not know how many it had led to utter disaster.

"Alvin," said the leader of the city's proctors, "we have orders to accompany you wherever you go, until the Council has heard your case and rendered its verdict."

"With what offense am I charged?" asked Alvin. He was still exhilarated by the excitement and elation of his escape from Lys and could not yet take this new development very seriously. Presumably Khedron had talked; he felt a brief annoyance at the Jester for betraying his secret.

"No charge has been made," came the reply. "If necessary, one will be framed after you have been heard."

"And when will that be?"

"Very soon, I imagine." The proctor was obviously ill at ease and was not sure how to handle his unwelcome assignment. At one moment he would treat Alvin as a fellow citizen, and then he would remember his duties as a custodian and would adopt an attitude of exaggerated aloofness.

"This robot," he said abruptly, pointing to Alvin's companion, "where did it come from? Is it one of ours?"

"No," replied Alvin. "I found it in Lys, the country I have been to. I have brought it here to meet the Central Computer."

This calm statement produced a considerable commotion. The fact that there was something outside Diaspar was hard enough to accept, but that Alvin should have brought back one of its inhabitants and proposed to introduce it to the brain of the city was even worse. The proctors looked at each other with such helpless alarm that Alvin could hardly refrain from laughing at them.

As they walked back through the park, his escort keeping discreetly at the rear and talking among itself in agitated whispers, Alvin considered his next move. The first thing he must do was to discover exactly what had happened during his absence. Khedron, Seranis had told him, had vanished. There were countless places where a man could hide in Diaspar, and since the Jester's knowledge of the city was unsurpassed it was not likely that he would be found until he chose to reappear. Perhaps, thought Alvin, he could leave a message where Khedron would be bound to see it, and arrange a rendezvous. However, the presence of his guard might make that impossible.

He had to admit that the surveillance was very discreet. By the time he had reached his apartment, he had almost forgotten the existence of the proctors. He imagined that they would not interfere with his movements unless he attempted to leave Diaspar, and for the time being he had no intention of doing that. Indeed, he was fairly certain that it would be impossible to return to Lys by his original route. By this time, surely, the underground carrier system would have been put out of action by Seranis and her colleagues.

The proctors did not follow him into his room; they knew that there was only the one exit, and stationed themselves outside that. Having had no instructions regarding the robot, they let it accompany Alvin. It was not a machine which they had any desire to interfere with, since its alien construction was obvious. From its behavior they could not tell whether it was a passive servant of Alvin's or whether it was operating under its own volition. In view of this uncertainty, they were quite content to leave it severely alone.

Once the wall had sealed itself behind him, Alvin materialized his favorite divan and threw himself down upon it. Luxuriating in his familiar surroundings, he called out of the memory units his last efforts in painting and sculpture, and examined them with a critical eye. If they had failed to satisfy him before, they were doubly displeasing now, and he could take no further pride in them. The person who had created them no longer existed; into the few days he had been away from Diaspar, it seemed to Alvin that he had crowded the experience of a lifetime.

He canceled all these products of his adolescence, erasing them forever and not merely returning them to the Memory Banks. The room was empty again, apart from the couch on which he was reclining, and the robot that still watched with wide, unfathomable eyes. What did the robot think of Diaspar? wondered Alvin. Then he remembered that it was no stranger here, for it had known the city in the last days of its contact with the stars.

Not until he felt thoroughly at home once more did Alvin begin to call his friends. He began with Eriston and Etania, though out of a sense of duty rather than any real desire to see and speak to them again. He was not sorry when their communicators informed him that they were unavailable, but he left them both a brief message announcing his return.

This was quite unnecessary, since by now the whole city would know that he was back. However, he hoped that they would appreciate his thoughtfulness; he was beginning to learn consideration, though he had not yet realized that, like most virtues, it had little merit unless it was spontaneous and unself-conscious.

Then, acting on a sudden impulse, he called the number that Khedron had given him so long ago in the Tower of Loranne. He did not, of course, expect an answer, but there was always the possibility that Khedron had left a message.

His guess was correct; but the message itself was shatteringly unexpected.

The wall dissolved, and Khedron was standing before him. The Jester looked tired and nervous, no longer the confident, slightly cynical person who had set Alvin on the path that led to Lys. There was a haunted look in his eyes, and he spoke as though he had very little time.

"Alvin," he began, "this is a recording. Only you can receive it, but you can make what use of it you wish. It will not matter to me.

"When I got back to the Tomb of Yarlan Zey, I found that Alystra had been following us. She must have told the Council that you had left Diaspar, and that I had helped you. Very soon the proctors were looking for me, and I decided to go into hiding. I am used to that—I have done it before when some of my jests failed to be appreciated." (There, thought Alvin, was a flash of the old Khedron.) "They could not have found me in a thousand years—but someone else nearly did. There are strangers in Diaspar, Alvin; they could only have come from Lys, and they are looking for me. I do not know what this means, and I do not like it. The fact that they nearly caught me, though they are in a city that must be strange to them, suggests that they possess telepathic powers. I could fight the Council, but this is an unknown peril which I do not care to face.

"I am therefore anticipating a step which I think the Council might well force upon me, since it has been threatened before. I am going where no one can follow, and where I shall escape whatever changes are now about to happen to Diaspar. Perhaps I am foolish to do this; that is something which only time can prove. I shall know the answer one day.

"By now you will have guessed that I have gone back into the Hall of Creation, into the safety of the Memory Banks. Whatever happens, I put my trust in the Central Computer, and the forces it controls for the benefit of Diaspar. If anything tampers with the Central Computer, we are all lost. If not, I have nothing to fear.

"To me, only a moment will seem to pass before I walk forth into Diaspar again, fifty or a hundred thousand years from now. I wonder what sort of city I shall find? It will be strange if you are there; some day, I suppose, we will meet again. I cannot say whether I look forward to that meeting, or fear it.

"I have never understood you, Alvin, though there was a time when I was vain enough to think I did. Only the Central Computer knows the truth, as it knows the truth about those other Uniques who have appeared from time to time down the ages and then were seen no more. Have you discovered what happened to them?

"One reason, I suppose, why I am escaping into the future is because I am impatient. I want to see the results of what you have started, but I am anxious to miss the intermediate stages—which I suspect may be unpleasant. It will be interesting to see, in that world which will be around me in only a few minutes of apparent time from now, whether you are remembered as a creator or as a destroyer—or whether you are remembered at all.

"Good-by, Alvin. I had thought of giving you some advice, but I do not suppose you would take it. You will go your own way, as you always have, and your friends will be tools to use or discard as occasion suits.

"That is all. I can think of nothing more to say."

For a moment Khedron—the Khedron who no longer existed save as a pattern of electric charges in the memory cells of the city—looked at Alvin with resignation and, it seemed, with sadness. Then the screen was blank again.

Alvin remained motionless for a long time after the image of Khedron had faded. He was searching his soul as he had seldom done before in all his life, for he could not deny the truth of much that Khedron had said. When had he paused, in all his schemes and adventures, to consider the effect of what he was doing upon any of his friends? He had brought anxiety to them and might soon bring worse—all because of his insatiable curiosity and the urge to discover what should not be known.

He had never been fond of Khedron; the Jester's astringent personality prevented any close relationship, even if Alvin had desired it. Yet now, as he thought of Khedron's parting words, he was shaken with remorse. Because of his actions, the Jester had fled from this age into the unknown future.

But surely, thought Alvin, he had no need to blame himself for that. It proved only what he had already known—that Khedron was a coward. Perhaps he was no more of a coward than anyone else in Diaspar; he had the additional misfortune of possessing a powerful imagination. Alvin could accept some responsibility for his fate, but by no means all.

Who else in Diaspar had he harmed or distressed? He thought of

Jeserac, his tutor, who had been patient with what must have been his most difficult pupil. He remembered all the little kindnesses that his parents had shown him over the years; now that he looked back upon them, there were more than he had imagined.

And he thought of Alystra. She had loved him, and he had taken that love or ignored it as he chose. Yet what else was he to have done? Would she have been any happier had he spurned her completely?

He understood now why he had never loved Alystra, or any of the women he had known in Diaspar. That was another lesson that Lys had taught him. Diaspar had forgotten many things, and among them was the true meaning of love. In Airlee he had watched the mothers dandling their children on their knees, and had himself felt that protective tenderness for all small and helpless creatures that is love's unselfish twin. Yet now there was no woman in Diaspar who knew or cared for what had once been the final aim of love.

There were no real emotions, no deep passions, in the immortal city. Perhaps such things only thrived because of their very transience, because they could not last forever and lay always under the shadow which Diaspar had banished.

That was the moment, if such a moment ever existed, when Alvin realized what his destiny must be. Until now he had been the unconscious agent of his own impulses. If he could have known so archaic an analogy, he might have compared himself to a rider on a runaway horse. It had taken him to many strange places, and might do so again, but in its wild galloping it had shown him its powers and taught him where he really wished to go.

Alvin's reverie was rudely interrupted by the chimes of the wall screen. The timbre of the sound told him at once that this was no incoming call, but that someone had arrived to see him. He gave the admission signal, and a moment later was facing Jeserac.

His tutor looked grave, but not unfriendly.

"I have been asked to take you to the Council, Alvin," he said. "It is waiting to hear you." Then Jeserac saw the robot and examined it curiously. "So this is the companion you have brought back from your travels. I think it had better come with us."

This suited Alvin very well. The robot had already extricated him from one dangerous situation, and he might have to call upon it again. He wondered what the machine had thought about the adventures and vicissitudes in which he had involved it, and wished for the thousandth time that he could understand what was going on inside its closely shuttered mind. Alvin had the impression that for the moment it had decided to watch, analyze, and draw its own conclusion, doing nothing of its own volition until it had judged the time was ripe. Then, perhaps quite suddenly, it might decide to act; and what it chose to do might not suit Alvin's plans. The only ally he possessed was bound to him by the most tenuous ties of self-interest and might desert him at any moment.

Alystra was waiting for them on the ramp that led out into the street. Even if Alvin had wished to blame her for whatever part she had played in revealing his secret, he did not have the heart to do so. Her distress was too obvious, and her eyes brimmed with tears as she ran up to greet him.

"Oh, Alvin!" she cried. "What are they going to do with you?"

Alvin took her hands in his with a tenderness that surprised them both. "Don't worry, Alystra," he said. "Everything is going to be all right. After all, at the very worst the Council can only send me back to the Memory Banks—and somehow I don't think that will happen."

Her beauty and her unhappiness were so appealing that, even now, Alvin felt his body responding to her presence after its old fashion. But it was the lure of the body alone; he did not disdain it, but it was no longer enough. Gently he disengaged his hands and turned to follow Jeserac toward the Council Chamber.

Alystra's heart was lonely, but no longer bitter, as she watched him go. She knew now that she had not lost him, for he had never belonged to her. And with the acceptance of that knowledge, she had begun to put herself beyond the power of vain regrets.

Alvin scarcely noticed the curious or horrified glances of his fellow citizens as he and his retinue made their way through the familiar streets. He was marshaling the arguments he might have to use, and arranging his story in the form most favorable to himself. From time to time he assured himself that he was not in the least alarmed and that he was still master of the situation.

They waited only a few minutes in the anteroom, but it was long enough for Alvin to wonder why, if he was unafraid, his legs felt so curiously weak. He had known this sensation before when he had forced himself up the last slopes of that distant hill in Lys, where Hilvar had shown him the waterfall from whose summit they had seen the explosion of light that had drawn them to Shalmirane. He wondered what Hilvar was doing now, and if they would ever meet again. It was suddenly very important to him that they should.

The great doors dilated, and he followed Jeserac into the Council Chamber. The twenty members were already seated around their crescent-shaped table, and Alvin felt flattered as he noticed that there were no empty places. This must be the first time for many centuries that the entire Council had been gathered together without a single abstention. Its rare meetings were usually a complete formality, all ordinary business being dealt with by a few visiphone calls and, if necessary, an interview between the President and the Central Computer.

Alvin knew by sight most of the members of the Council, and felt reassured by the presence of so many familiar faces. Like Jeserac, they did not seem unfriendly—merely anxious and puzzled. They were, after all, reasonable men. They might be annoyed that someone had proved them wrong, but Alvin did not believe that they would bear him any resentment. Once this would have been a very rash assumption, but human nature had improved in some respects.

They would give him a fair hearing, but what they thought was not all-important. His judge now would not be the Council. It would be the Central Computer.

CHAPTER SIXTEEN

There were no formalities. The President declared the meeting open and then turned to Alvin.

"Alvin," he said, kindly enough, "we would like you to tell us what has happened to you since you disappeared ten days ago."

The use of the word "disappeared," thought Alvin, was highly significant. Even now, the Council was reluctant to admit that he had really gone outside Diaspar. He wondered if they knew that there had been strangers in the city, and rather doubted it. In that event, they would have shown considerably more alarm.

He told his story clearly and without any dramatics. It was strange and unbelievable enough to their ears, and needed no embellishment. Only at one place did he depart from strict accuracy, for he said nothing about the manner of his escape from Lys. It seemed more than likely that he might want to use the same method again.

It was fascinating to watch the way in which the attitude of the Council members altered during the course of his narrative. At first they were skeptical, refusing to accept the denial of all that they had believed, the violation of their deepest prejudices. When Alvin told them of his passionate desire to explore the world beyond the city, and his irrational conviction that such a world did exist, they stared at him as if he was some strange and incomprehensible animal. To their minds, indeed, he was. But finally they were compelled to admit that he had been right, and that they had been mistaken. As Alvin's story unfolded, any doubts they may have had slowly dissolved. They might not like what he had told them, but they could no longer deny its truth. If they felt tempted to do so, they had only to look at Alvin's silent companion.

There was only one aspect of his tale that roused their indignation—and then it was not directed toward him. A buzz of annoyance went around the chamber as Alvin explained the anxiety of Lys to avoid contamination with Diaspar, and the steps that Seranis had taken to prevent such a catastrophe. The city was proud of its culture, and with good reason. That anyone should regard them as inferiors was more than the Council members could tolerate.

Alvin was very careful not to give offense in anything he said; he wanted, as far as possible, to win the Council to his side. Throughout, he tried to give the impression that he had seen nothing wrong in what he had done, and that he expected praise rather than censure for his discoveries. It was the best policy he could have adopted, for it disarmed most of his would-be critics in advance. It also had the effect—though he had not intended this—of transferring any blame to the vanished Khedron. Alvin himself, it was clear to his listeners, was too young to see any danger in what he was doing. The Jester, however, should certainly have known better and had acted in a thoroughly irresponsible fashion. They did not yet know how fully Khedron himself had agreed with them.

Jeserac, as Alvin's tutor, was also deserving of some censure, and from time to time several of the councilors gave him thoughtful glances. He did not seem to mind, though he was perfectly well aware of what they were thinking. There was a certain honor in having instructed the most original mind that had come into Diaspar since the Dawn Ages, and nothing could rob Jeserac of that.

Not until Alvin had finished the factual account of his adventures did he attempt a little persuasion. Somehow, he would have to convince these men of the truths that he had learned in Lys, but how could he make them really understand something that they had never seen and could hardly imagine?

"It seems a great tragedy," he said, "that the two surviving branches of the human race should have become separated for such an enormous period of time. One day, perhaps, we may know how it happened, but it is more important now to repair the break—to prevent it happening again. When I was in Lys I protested against their view that they were superior to us; they may have much to teach us, but we also have much to teach them. If we both believe that we have nothing to learn from the other, is it not obvious that we will *both* be wrong?"

He looked expectantly along the line of faces, and was encouraged to go on.

"Our ancestors," he continued, "built an empire that reached to the stars. Men came and went at will among all those worlds—and now their descendants are afraid to stir beyond the walls of their city. *Shall I tell you why?"* He paused; there was no movement at all in the great, bare room.

"It is because we are afraid—afraid of something that happened at the beginning of history. I was told the truth in Lys, though I guessed it long ago. Must we always hide like cowards in Diaspar, pretending that nothing else exists—because a billion years ago the Invaders drove us back to Earth?"

He had put his finger on their secret fear—the fear that he had never shared and whose power he could therefore never fully understand. Now let them do what they pleased; he had spoken the truth as he saw it.

The President looked at him gravely.

"Have you anything more to say," he asked, "before we consider what is to be done?"

"Only one thing. I would like to take this robot to the Central Computer."

"But why? You know that the Computer is already aware of everything that has happened in this room."

"I still wish to go," replied Alvin politely but stubbornly. "I ask permission both of the Council and the Computer."

Before the President could reply, a clear, calm voice sounded through the chamber. Alvin had never heard it before in his life, but he knew what it was that spoke. The information machines, which were no more than outlying fragments of this great intelligence, could speak to men—but they did not possess this unmistakable accent of wisdom and authority.

"Let him come to me," said the Central Computer.

Alvin looked at the President. It was to his credit that he did not attempt to exploit his victory. He merely asked, "Have I your permission to leave?"

The President looked around the Council Chamber, saw no disagreement there, and replied a little helplessly: "Very well. The proctors will accompany you, and will bring you back here when we have finished our discussion."

Alvin gave a slight bow of thanks, the great doors expanded before him, and he walked slowly out of the chamber. Jeserac had accompanied him, and when the doors had closed once more, he turned to face his tutor.

"What do you think the Council will do now?" he asked anxiously. Jeserac smiled.

"Impatient as ever, aren't you?" he said. "I do not know what my guess is worth, but I imagine that they will decide to seal the Tomb of Yarlan Zey so that no one can ever again make your journey. Then Diaspar can continue as before, undisturbed by the outside world."

"That is what I am afraid of," said Alvin bitterly.

"And you still hope to prevent it?"

Alvin did not at once reply; he knew that Jeserac had read his intentions, but at least his tutor could not foresee his plans, for he had none. He had come to the stage when he could only improvise and meet each new situation as it arose.

"Do you blame me?" he said presently, and Jeserac was surprised by the new note in his voice. It was a hint of humility, the barest suggestion that for the first time Alvin sought the approval of his fellow men. Jeserac was touched by it, but he was too wise to take it very seriously. Alvin was under a considerable strain, and it would be unsafe to assume that any improvement in his character was permanent.

"That is a very hard question to answer," said Jeserac slowly. "I am tempted to say that all knowledge is valuable, and it cannot be denied that you have added much to our knowledge. But you have also added to our dangers, and in the long run which will be more important? How often have you stopped to consider that?"

For a moment master and pupil regarded each other pensively, each perhaps seeing the other's point of view more clearly than ever before in his life. Then, with one impulse, they turned together down the long passage from the Council Chamber, with their escort still following patiently in the rear.

This world, Alvin knew, had not been made for Man. Under the glare of the fierce blue lights—so dazzling that they pained the eyes—the long, broad corridors seemed to stretch to infinity. Down these great passageways the robots of Diaspar must come and go throughout their endless lives, yet not once in centuries did they echo to the sound of human feet.

Here was the underground city, the city of machines without which Diaspar could not exist. A few hundred yards ahead, the corridor would open into a circular chamber more than a mile across, its roof supported by great columns that must also bear the unimaginable weight of Power

Center. Here, according to the maps, the Central Computer brooded eternally over the fate of Diaspar.

The chamber was there, and it was even vaster than Alvin had dared imagine—but where was the Computer? Somehow he had expected to meet a single huge machine, naïve though he knew that this conception was. The tremendous but meaningless panorama beneath him made him pause in wonder and uncertainty.

The corridor along which they had come ended high in the wall of the chamber—surely the largest cavity ever built by Man—and on either side long ramps swept down to the distant floor. Covering the whole of that brilliantly lit expanse were hundreds of great white structures, so unexpected that for a moment Alvin thought he must be looking down upon a subterranean city. The impression was startlingly vivid, and it was one that he never wholly lost. Nowhere at all was the sight he had expected—the familiar gleam of metal which since the beginning of time Man had learned to associate with his servants.

Here was the end of an evolution almost as long as Man's. Its beginnings were lost in the mists of the Dawn Ages, when humanity had first learned the use of power and sent its noisy engines clanking about the world. Steam, water, wind—all had been harnessed for a little while and then abandoned. For centuries the energy of matter had run the world until it too had been superseded, and with each change the old machines were forgotten and new ones took their place. Very slowly, over thousands of years, the ideal of the perfect machine was approached—that ideal which had once been a dream, then a distant prospect, and at last reality:

No machine may contain any moving parts.

Here was the ultimate expression of that ideal. Its achievement had taken Man perhaps a hundred million years, and in the moment of his triumph he had turned his back upon the machine forever. It had reached finality, and thenceforth could sustain itself eternally while serving him.

Alvin no longer asked himself which of these silent white presences was the Central Computer. He knew that it comprised them all—and that it extended far beyond this chamber, including within its being all the countless other machines in Diaspar, whether they were mobile or motionless. As his own brain was the sum of many billion separate cells, arrayed throughout a volume of space a few inches across, so the physical elements of the Central Computer were scattered throughout the length and breadth of Diaspar. This chamber might hold no more than the switching system whereby all these dispersed units kept in touch with one another.

Uncertain where to go next, Alvin stared down the great sweeping ramps and across the silent arena. The Central Computer must know that he was here, as it knew everything that was happening in Diaspar. He could only wait for its instructions.

The now-familiar yet still awe-inspiring voice was so quiet and so close to him that he did not believe that his escort could also hear it. "Go down the left-hand ramp," it said. "I will direct you from there."

He walked slowly down the slope, the robot floating above him. Neither Jeserac nor the proctors followed; he wondered if they had received orders to remain here, or whether they had decided that they could supervise him just as well from their vantage point without the bother of making his long descent. Or perhaps they had come as close to the central shrine of Diaspar as they cared to approach.

At the foot of the ramp, the quiet voice redirected Alvin, and he walked between an avenue of sleeping titan shapes. Three times the voice spoke to him again, until presently he knew that he had reached his goal.

The machine before which he was standing was smaller than most of its companions, but he felt dwarfed as he stood beneath it. The five tiers with their sweeping horizontal lines gave the impression of some crouching beast, and looking from it to his own robot Alvin found it hard to believe that both were products of the same evolution, and both described by the same word.

About three feet from the ground a wide transparent panel ran the whole length of the structure. Alvin pressed his forehead against the smooth, curiously warm material and peered into the machine. At first he saw nothing; then, by shielding his eyes, he could distinguish thousands of faint points of light hanging in nothingness. They were ranged one beyond the other in a three-dimensional lattice, as strange and as meaningless to him as the stars must have been to ancient man. Though he watched for many minutes, forgetful of the passage of time, the colored lights never moved from their places and their brilliance never changed.

If he could look into his own brain, Alvin realized, it would mean as little to him. The machine seemed inert and motionless because he could not see its thoughts.

For the first time, he began to have some dim understanding of the powers and forces that sustained the city. All his life he had accepted without question the miracle of the synthesizers, which age after age provided in an unending stream all the needs of Diaspar. Thousands of times he had watched that act of creation, seldom remembering that somewhere must exist the prototype of that which he had seen come into the world.

As a human mind may dwell for a little while upon a single thought, so the infinitely greater brains which were but a portion of the Central Computer could grasp and hold forever the most intricate ideas. The patterns of all created things were frozen in these eternal minds, needing only the touch of a human will to make them reality.

The world had indeed gone far since, hour upon hour, the first cavemen had patiently chipped their arrowheads and knives from the stubborn stone.

Alvin waited, not caring to speak until he had received some further sign of recognition. He wondered how the Central Computer was aware of his presence, and could see him and hear his voice. Nowhere were there any signs of sense organs—none of the grilles or screens or emotionless crystal eyes through which robots normally had knowledge of the world around them.

"State your problem," said the quiet voice in his ear. It seemed strange that this overwhelming expanse of machinery should sum up its thoughts so softly. Then Alvin realized that he was flattering himself; perhaps not even a millionth part of the Central Computer's brain was dealing with him. He was just one of the innumerable incidents that came to its simultaneous attention as it watched over Diaspar.

It was hard to talk to a presence who filled the whole of the space around you. Alvin's words seemed to die in the empty air as soon as he had uttered them.

"What am I?" he asked.

If he had put that question to one of the information machines in the city, he knew what the reply would have been. Indeed, he had often done so, and they had always answered, "You are a Man." But now he was dealing with an intelligence of an altogether different order, and there was no need for painstaking semantic accuracy. The Central Computer would know what he meant, but that did not mean that it would answer him.

Indeed, the reply was exactly what Alvin had feared.

"I cannot answer that question. To do so would be to reveal the purpose of my builders, and hence to nullify it."

"Then my role was planned when the city was laid down?"

"That can be said of all men."

This reply made Alvin pause. It was true enough; the human inhabitants of Diaspar had been designed as carefully as its machines. The fact that he was a Unique gave Alvin rarity, but there was no necessary virtue in that.

He knew that he could learn nothing further here regarding the mystery of his origin. It was useless to try to trick this vast intelligence, or to hope that it would disclose information it had been ordered to conceal. Alvin was not unduly disappointed; he felt that he had already begun to glimpse the truth, and in any case this was not the main purpose of his visit.

He looked at the robot he had brought from Lys, and wondered how to make his next step. It might react violently if it knew what he was planning, so it was essential that it should not overhear what he intended to say to the Central Computer.

"Can you arrange a zone of silence?" he asked.

Instantly, he sensed the unmistakable "dead" feeling, the total blanketing of all sounds, which descended when one was inside such a zone. The voice of the Computer, now curiously flat and sinister, spoke to him: "No one can hear us now. Say what you wish."

Alvin glanced at the robot; it had not moved from its position. Perhaps it suspected nothing, and he had been quite wrong in ever imagining that it had plans of its own. It might have followed him into Diaspar like a faithful, trusting servant, in which case what he was planning now seemed a particularly churlish trick.

"You have heard how I met this robot," Alvin began. "It must possess priceless knowledge about the past, going back to the days before the city as we know it existed. It may even be able to tell us about other worlds than Earth, since it followed the Master on his travels. Unfortunately, its speech circuits are blocked. I do not know how effective that block is, but I am asking you to clear it."

His voice sounded dead and hollow as the zone of silence absorbed every word before it could form an echo. He waited, within that invisible and unreverberant void, for his request to be obeyed or rejected.

"Your order involves two problems," replied the Computer. "One is moral, one technical. This robot was designed to obey the orders of a certain man. What right have I to override them, even if I can?"

It was a question which Alvin had anticipated and for which he had prepared several answers.

"We do not know what exact form the Master's prohibition took," he replied. "If you can talk to the robot, you may be able to persuade it that the circumstances in which the block was imposed have now changed."

It was, of course, the obvious approach. Alvin had attempted it himself, without success, but he hoped that the Central Computer, with its infinitely greater mental resources, might accomplish what he had failed to do.

"That depends entirely upon the nature of the block," came the reply. "It is possible to set up a block which, if tampered with, will cause the contents of the memory cells to be erased. However, I think it unlikely that the Master possessed sufficient skill to do that; it requires somewhat specialized techniques. I will ask your machine if an erasing circuit has been set up in its memory units."

"But suppose," said Alvin in sudden alarm, "it causes erasure of memory merely to *ask* if an erasing circuit exists?"

"There is a standard procedure for such cases, which I shall follow. I shall set up secondary instructions, telling the machine to ignore my question if such a situation exists. It is then simple to insure that it will become involved in a logical paradox, so that whether it answers me or whether it says nothing it will be forced to disobey its instructions. In such an event all robots act in the same manner, for their own protection. They clear their input circuits and act as if no question has been asked."

Alvin felt rather sorry that he had raised the point, and after a moment's mental struggle decided that he too would adopt the same tactics and pretend that he had never asked the question. At least he was reassured on one point—the Central Computer was fully prepared to deal with any booby traps that might exist in the robot's memory units. Alvin had no wish to see the machine reduced to a pile of junk; rather than that, he would willingly return it to Shalmirane with its secrets still intact.

He waited with what patience he could while the silent, impalpable meeting of intellects took place. Here was an encounter between two minds, both of them created by human genius in the long-lost golden age of its greatest achievement. And now both were beyond the full understanding of any living man.

Many minutes later, the hollow, anechoic voice of the Central Computer spoke again.

"I have established partial contact," it said. "At least I know the nature of the block, and I think I know why it was imposed. There is only one way in which it can be broken. Not until the Great Ones come to Earth will this robot speak again."

"But that is nonsense!" protested Alvin. "The Master's other disciple believed in them, too, and tried to explain what they were like to us. Most of the time it was talking gibberish. The Great Ones never existed, and never will exist."

It seemed a complete impasse, and Alvin felt a sense of bitter, helpless disappointment. He was barred from the truth by the wishes of a man who had been insane, and who had died a billion years ago.

"You may be correct," said the Central Computer, "in saying that the Great Ones never existed. But that does not mean that they never will exist."

There was another long silence while Alvin considered the meaning of this remark, and while the minds of the two robots made their delicate contact again. And then, without any warning, he was in Shalmirane.

CHAPTER SEVENTEEN

It was just as he had last seen it, the great ebon bowl drinking the sunlight and reflecting none back to the eye. He stood among the ruins of the fortress, looking out across the lake, whose motionless waters showed that the giant polyp was now a dispersed cloud of animalcules and no longer an organized, sentient being.

The robot was still beside him, but of Hilvar there was no sign. He had no time to wonder what that meant, or to worry about his friend's absence, for almost at once there occurred something so fantastic that all other thoughts were banished from his mind.

The sky began to crack in two. A thin wedge of darkness reached from horizon to zenith, and slowly widened as if night and chaos were breaking in upon the Universe. Inexorably the wedge expanded until it embraced a quarter of the sky. For all his knowledge of the real facts of astronomy, Alvin could not fight against the overwhelming impression that he and his world lay beneath a great blue dome—and that *something* was now breaking through that dome from outside.

The wedge of night had ceased to grow. The powers that had made it were peering down into the toy universe they had discovered, perhaps conferring among themselves as to whether it was worth their attention. Underneath that cosmic scrutiny, Alvin felt no alarm, no terror. He knew that he was face to face with power and wisdom, before which a man might feel awe but never fear.

And now they had decided—they would waste some fragments of Eternity upon Earth and its peoples. They were coming through the window they had broken in the sky.

Like sparks from some celestial forge, they drifted down to Earth.

Thicker and thicker they came, until a waterfall of fire was streaming down from heaven and splashing in pools of liquid light as it reached the ground. Alvin did not need the words that sounded in his ears like a benediction:

"The Great Ones have come."

The fire reached him, and it did not burn. It was everywhere, filling the great bowl of Shalmirane with its golden glow. As he watched in wonder, Alvin saw that it was not a featureless flood of light, but that it had form and structure. It began to resolve itself into distinct shapes, to gather into separate fiery whirlpools. The whirlpools spun more and more swiftly on their axes, their centers rising to form columns within which Alvin could glimpse mysterious evanescent shapes. From these glowing totem poles came a faint musical note, infinitely distant and hauntingly sweet.

"The Great Ones have come."

This time there was a reply. As Alvin heard the words: "The servants of the Master greet you. We have been waiting for your coming," he knew that the barriers were down. And in that moment, Shalmirane and its strange visitors were gone, and he was standing once more before the Central Computer in the depths of Diaspar.

It had all been illusion, no more real than the fantasy world of the sagas in which he had spent so many of the hours of his youth. But how had it been created; whence had come the strange images he had seen?

"It was an unusual problem," said the quiet voice of the Central Computer. "I knew that the robot must have some visual conception of the Great Ones in its mind. If I could convince it that the sense impressions it received coincided with that image, the rest would be simple."

"And how did you do that?"

"Basically, by asking the robot what the Great Ones were like, and then seizing the pattern it formed in its thoughts. The pattern was very incomplete, and I had to improvise a good deal. Once or twice the picture I created began to depart badly from the robot's conception, but when that happened I could sense the machine's growing perplexity and modify the image before it became suspicious. You will appreciate that I could employ hundreds of circuits where it could employ only one, and switch from one image to the other so quickly that the change could not be perceived. It was a kind of conjuring trick; I was able to saturate the robot's sensory circuits and also to overwhelm its critical faculties. What you saw was only the final, corrected image—the one which best fitted the Master's revelation. It was crude, but it sufficed. The robot was convinced of its genuineness long enough for the block to be lifted, and in that moment I was able to make complete contact with its mind. It is no longer insane; it will answer any questions you wish."

Alvin was still in a daze; the afterglow of that spurious apocalypse still burned in his mind, and he did not pretend fully to understand the Central Computer's explanation. No matter; a miracle of therapy had been accomplished, and the doors of knowledge had been flung open for him to enter.

Then he remembered the warning that the Central Computer had given him, and asked anxiously: "What about the moral objections you had to overriding the Master's orders?"

"I have discovered why they were imposed. When you examine his life story in detail, as you can now do, you will see that he claimed to have produced many miracles. His disciples believed him, and their conviction added to his power. But, of course, all those miracles had some simple explanation—when indeed they occurred at all. I find it surprising that otherwise intelligent men should have let themselves be deceived in such a manner."

"So the Master was a fraud?"

"No; it is not as simple as that. If he had been a mere impostor, he would never have achieved such success, and his movement would not have lasted so long. He was a good man, and much of what he taught was true and wise. In the end, he believed in his own miracles, but he knew that there was one witness who could refute them. The robot knew all his secrets; it was his mouthpiece and his colleague, yet if it was ever questioned too closely it could destroy the foundations of his power. So he ordered it never to reveal its memories until the last day of the Universe, when the Great Ones would come. It is hard to believe that such a mixture of deception and sincerity could exist in the same man, but such was the case."

Alvin wondered what the robot felt about this escape from its ancient bondage. It was, surely, a sufficiently complex machine to understand such emotions as resentment. It might be angry with the Master for having enslaved it—and equally angry with Alvin and the Central Computer for having tricked it back into sanity.

The zone of silence had been lifted; there was no further need for secrecy. The moment for which Alvin had been waiting had come at last. He turned to the robot, and asked it the question that had haunted him ever since he had heard the story of the Master's saga.

And the robot replied.

Jeserac and the proctors were still waiting patiently when he rejoined them. At the top of the ramp, before they entered the corridor, Alvin looked back across the cave, and the illusion was stronger than ever. Lying beneath him was a dead city of strange white buildings, a city bleached by a fierce light not meant for human eyes. Dead it might be, for it had never lived, but it pulsed with energies more potent than any that had ever quickened organic matter. While the world endured, these silent machines would still be here, never turning their minds from the thoughts that men of genius had given them long ago.

Though Jeserac tried to question Alvin on the way back to the Council Chamber, he learned nothing of his talk with the Central Computer. This was not merely discretion on Alvin's part; he was still too much lost in the wonder of what he had seen, too intoxicated with success, for any coherent conversation. Jeserac had to muster what patience he could, and hope that presently Alvin would emerge from his trance.

The streets of Diaspar were bathed with a light that seemed pale and wan after the glare of the machine city. But Alvin scarcely saw them; he had no regard for the familiar beauty of the great towers drifting past him, or the curious glances of his fellow citizens. It was strange, he thought, how everything that had happened to him led up to this moment. Since he had met Khedron, events seemed to have moved automatically toward a predetermined goal. The monitors—Lys—Shalmirane—at every stage he might have turned aside with unseeing eyes, but something had led him on. Was he the maker of his own destiny, or was he especially favored by Fate? Perhaps it was merely a matter of probabilities, of the operation of the laws of chance. Any man might have found the path his footsteps had traced, and countless times in the past ages others must have gone almost as far. Those earlier Uniques, for example—what had happened to them? Perhaps he was merely the first to be lucky.

All the way back through the streets, Alvin was establishing closer and closer rapport with the machine he had released from its age-long thralldom. It had always been able to receive his thoughts, but previously he had never known whether it would obey any orders he gave it. Now that uncertainty was gone; he could talk to it as he would to another human being, though since he was not alone he directed it not to use verbal speech but such simple thought images as he could understand. He sometimes resented the fact that robots could talk freely to one another on the telepathic level, whereas Man could not—except in Lys. Here was another power that Diaspar had lost or deliberately set aside.

He continued the silent but somewhat one-sided conversation while they were waiting in the anteroom of the Council Chamber. It was impossible not to compare his present situation with that in Lys, when Seranis and her colleagues had tried to bend him to their wills. He hoped that there would be no need for another conflict, but if one should arise he was now far better prepared for it.

His first glance at the faces of the Council members told Alvin what their decision had been. He was neither surprised nor particularly disappointed, and he showed none of the emotion the Councilors might have expected as he listened to the President's summing-up.

"Alvin," began the President, "we have considered with great care the situation which your discovery has brought about, and we have reached this unanimous decision. Because no one wishes any change in our way of life, and because only once in many millions of years is anyone born who is capable of leaving Diaspar even if the means exists, the tunnel system to Lys is unnecessary and may well be a danger. The entrance to the chamber of the moving ways has therefore been sealed.

"Moreover, since it is possible that there may be other ways of leaving the city, a search will be made of the monitor memory units. That search has already begun.

"We have also considered what action, if any, need be taken with regard to you. In view of your youth, and the peculiar circumstances of your origin, it is felt that you cannot be censured for what you have done. Indeed, by disclosing a potential danger to our way of life, you have done the city a service, and we record our appreciation of that fact."

There was a murmur of applause, and expressions of satisfaction spread across the faces of the Councilors. A difficult situation had been speedily dealt with, they had avoided the necessity of reprimanding Alvin, and now they could go their ways again feeling that they, the chief citizens of Diaspar, had done their duty. With reasonably good fortune, it might be centuries before the need arose again.

The President looked expectantly at Alvin; perhaps he hoped that Alvin would reciprocate and express his appreciation of the Council for letting him off so lightly. He was disappointed.

"May I ask one question?" said Alvin politely.

"Of course."

"The Central Computer, I take it, approved of your action?"

In the ordinary way, this would have been an impertinent question to ask. The Council was not supposed to justify its decisions or explain how it had arrived at them. But Alvin himself had been taken into the confidence of the Central Computer, for some strange reason of its own. He was in a privileged position.

The question clearly caused some embarrassment, and the reply came rather reluctantly.

"Naturally we consulted with the Central Computer. It told us to use our own judgment."

Alvin had expected as much. The Central Computer would have been conferring with the Council at the same moment as it was talking to him—at the same moment, in fact, as it was attending to a million other tasks in Diaspar. It knew, as did Alvin, that any decision the Council now made was of no importance. The future had passed utterly beyond its control at the very moment when, in happy ignorance, it had decided that the crisis had been safely dealt with.

Alvin felt no sense of superiority, none of the sweet anticipation of impending triumph, as he looked at these foolish old men who thought themselves the rulers of Diaspar. He had seen the real ruler of the city, and had spoken to it in the grave silence of its brilliant, buried world. That was an encounter which had burned most of the arrogance out of his soul, but enough was left for a final venture that would surpass all that had gone before.

As he took leave of the Council, he wondered if they were surprised at his quiet acquiescence, his lack of indignation at the closing of the path to Lys. The proctors did not accompany him; he was no longer under observation, at least in so open a manner. Only Jeserac followed him out of the Council Chamber and into the colored, crowded streets.

"Well, Alvin," he said. "You were on your best behavior, but you cannot deceive me. What are you planning?"

Alvin smiled.

"I knew that you would suspect something; if you will come with me, I will show you why the subway to Lys is no longer important. And there is another experiment I want to try; it will not harm you, but you may not like it."

"Very well, I am still supposed to be your tutor, but it seems that the roles are now reversed. Where are you taking me?"

"We are going to the Tower of Loranne, and I am going to show you the world outside Diaspar."

Jeserac paled, but he stood his ground. Then, as if not trusting himself with words, he gave a stiff little nod and followed Alvin out onto the smoothly gliding surface of the moving way.

Jeserac showed no fear as they walked along the tunnel through which that cold wind blew forever into Diaspar. The tunnel had changed now; the stone grille that had blocked access to the outer world was gone. It served no structural purpose, and the Central Computer had removed it without comment at Alvin's request. Later, it might instruct the monitors to remember the grille again and bring it back into existence. But for the moment the tunnel gaped unfenced and unguarded in the sheer outer wall of the city.

Not until Jeserac had almost reached the end of the air shaft did he realize that the outer world was now upon him. He looked at the widening circle of sky, and his steps became more and more uncertain until they finally slowed to a halt. Alvin remembered how Alystra had turned and fled from this same spot, and he wondered if he could induce Jeserac to go any further.

"I am only asking you to *look,*" he begged, "not to leave the city. Surely you can manage to do that!"

In Airlee, during his brief stay, Alvin had seen a mother teaching her child to walk. He was irresistibly reminded of this as he coaxed Jeserac along the corridor, making encouraging remarks as his tutor advanced foot by reluctant foot. Jeserac, unlike Khedron, was no coward. He was prepared to fight against his compulsion, but it was a desperate struggle. Alvin was almost as exhausted as the older man by the time he had succeeded in getting Jeserac to a point where he could see the whole, uninterrupted sweep of the desert.

Once there, the interest and strange beauty of the scene, so alien to all that Jeserac had ever known in this or any previous existence, seemed to overcome his fears. He was clearly fascinated by the immense vista of the rolling sand dunes and the far-off, ancient hills. It was late afternoon, and in a little while all this land would be visited by the night that never came to Diaspar.

"I asked you to come here," said Alvin, speaking quickly as if he could hardly control his impatience, "because I realize that you have earned more right than anyone to see where my travels have led me. I wanted you to see the desert, and I also want you to be a witness, so that the Council will know what I have done.

"As I told the Council, I brought this robot home from Lys in the hope that the Central Computer would be able to break the block that had been imposed on its memories by the man known as the Master. By a trick which I still don't fully understand, the Computer did that. Now I have access to all the memories of this machine, as well as to the special skills that had been designed into it. I'm going to use one of those skills now. Watch."

On a soundless order which Jeserac could only guess, the robot floated out of the tunnel entrance, picked up speed, and within seconds was no more than a distant metallic gleam in the sunlight. It was flying low over the desert, across the sand dunes that lay crisscrossed like frozen waves. Jeserac had the unmistakable impression that it was searching—though for what, he could not imagine.

Then, abruptly, the glittering speck soared away from the desert and came to rest a thousand feet above the ground. At the same moment, Alvin gave an explosive sigh of satisfaction and relief. He glanced quickly at Jeserac, as if to say: "This is it!"

At first, not knowing what to expect, Jeserac could see no change. Then, scarcely believing his eyes, he saw that a cloud of dust was slowly rising from the desert.

Nothing is more terrible than movement where no movement should ever be again, but Jeserac was beyond surprise or fear as the sand dunes began to slide apart. Beneath the desert something was stirring like a giant awakening from its sleep, and presently there came to Jeserac's ears the rumble of falling earth and the shriek of rock split asunder by irresistible force. Then, suddenly, a great geyser of sand erupted hundreds of feet into the air and the ground was hidden from sight.

Slowly the dust began to settle back into a jagged wound torn across the face of the desert. But Jeserac and Alvin still kept their eyes fixed steadfastly upon the open sky, which a little while ago had held only the waiting robot. Now at last Jeserac knew why Alvin had seemed so indifferent to the decision of the Council, why he had shown no emotion when he was told that the subway to Lys had been closed.

The covering of earth and rock could blur but could not conceal the proud lines of the ship still ascending from the riven desert. As Jeserac watched, it slowly turned toward them until it had foreshortened to a circle. Then, very leisurely, the circle started to expand.

Alvin began to speak, rather quickly, as if the time were short.

"This robot was designed to be the Master's companion and servant —and, above all, the pilot of his ship. Before he came to Lys, he landed at the Port of Diaspar, which now lies out there beneath those sands. Even in his day, it must have been largely deserted; I think that the Master's ship was one of the last ever to reach Earth. He lived for a while in Diaspar before he went to Shalmirane; the way must still have been open in those days. But he never needed the ship again, and all these ages it has been waiting out there beneath the sands. Like Diaspar itself, like this robot—like everything that the builders of the past considered really important—it was preserved by its own eternity circuits. As long as it had a source of power, it could never wear out or be destroyed; the image carried in its memory cells would never fade, and that image controlled its physical structure."

The ship was now very close, as the controlling robot guided it toward the tower. Jeserac could see that it was about a hundred feet long and sharply pointed at both ends. There appeared to be no windows or other openings, though the thick layer of earth made it impossible to be certain of this.

Suddenly they were spattered with dirt as a section of the hull opened outward, and Jeserac caught a glimpse of a small, bare room with a second door at its far end. The ship was hanging only a foot away from the mouth of the air vent, which it had approached very cautiously like a sensitive, living thing.

"Good-by, Jeserac," said Alvin. "I cannot go back into Diaspar to say farewell to my friends: please do that for me. Tell Eriston and Etania that I hope to return soon; if I do not, I am grateful for all that they did. And I am grateful to you, even though you may not approve of the way I have applied your lessons.

"And as for the Council—tell it that a road that has once been opened cannot be closed again merely by passing a resolution."

The ship was now only a dark stain against the sky, and of a sudden Jeserac lost it altogether. He never saw its going, but presently there echoed down from the heavens the most awe-inspiring of all the sounds that Man had ever made—the long-drawn thunder of air falling, mile after mile, into a tunnel of vacuum drilled suddenly across the sky.

Even when the last echoes had died away into the desert, Jeserac never moved. He was thinking of the boy who had gone—for to Jeserac, Alvin would always be a child, the only one to come into Diaspar since the cycle of birth and death had been broken, so long ago. Alvin would never grow up; to him the whole Universe was a plaything, a puzzle to be unraveled for his own amusement. In his play he had now found the ultimate, deadly toy which might wreck what was left of human civilization—but whatever the outcome, to him it would still be a game.

The sun was now low on the horizon, and a chill wind was blowing from the desert. But Jeserac still waited, conquering his fears; and presently for the first time in his life he saw the stars.

CHAPTER EIGHTEEN

Even in Diaspar, Alvin had seldom seen such luxury as that which lay before him when the inner door of the air lock slid aside. Whatever else he had been, at least the Master was no ascetic. Not until some time later did it occur to Alvin that all this comfort might be no vain extravagance; this little world must have been the Master's only home on many long journeys among the stars.

There were no visible controls of any kind, but the large, oval screen which completely covered the far wall showed that this was no ordinary room. Ranged in a half circle before it were three low couches; the rest of the cabin was occupied by two small tables and a number of padded chairs—some of them obviously not designed for human occupants.

When he had made himself comfortable in front of the screen, Alvin looked around for the robot. To his surprise, it had disappeared; then he located it, neatly stowed away in a recess beneath the curved ceiling. It had brought the Master across space to Earth and then, as his servant, followed him into Lys. Now it was ready, as if the intervening aeons had never been, to carry out its old duties once again.

Alvin threw it an experimental command, and the great screen shivered into life. Before him was the Tower of Loranne, curiously foreshortened and apparently lying on its side. Further trials gave him views of the sky, of the city, and of great expanses of desert. The definition was brilliantly, almost unnaturally, clear, although there seemed to be no actual magnification. Alvin experimented for a little while until he could obtain any view he wished; then he was ready to start.

"Take me to Lys." The command was a simple one, but how could the ship obey it when he himself had no idea of the direction? Alvin had not considered this, and when it did occur to him the machine was already moving across the desert at a tremendous speed. He shrugged his shoulders, accepting thankfully the fact that he now had servants wiser than himself.

It was difficult to judge the scale of the picture racing up the screen, but many miles must be passing every minute. Not far from the city the color of the ground had changed abruptly to a dull gray, and Alvin knew that he was now passing over the bed of one of the lost oceans. Once Diaspar must have been very near the sea, though there had never been any hint of this even in the most ancient records. Old though the city was, the oceans must have passed away long before its founding.

Hundreds of miles later, the ground rose sharply and the desert returned. Once Alvin halted his ship above a curious pattern of intersecting lines, showing faintly through the blanket of sand. For a moment it puzzled him; then he realized that he was looking down upon the ruins of some forgotten city. He did not stay for long; it was heartbreaking to think that billions of men had left no other trace of their existence save these furrows in the sand.

The smooth curve of the horizon was breaking up at last, crinkling into mountains that were beneath him almost as soon as they were glimpsed. The machine was slowing now, slowing and falling to earth in a great arc a hundred miles in length. And then below him was Lys, its forests and endless rivers forming a scene of such incomparable beauty that for a while he could go no further. To the east, the land was shadowed and the great lakes floated upon it like pools of darker night. But toward the sunset, the waters danced and sparkled with light, throwing back toward him such colors as he had never imagined.

It was not difficult to locate Airlee—which was fortunate, for the robot could guide him no further. Alvin had expected this, and felt a little glad to have discovered some limits to its powers. It was unlikely that it would ever have heard of Airlee, so the position of the village would never have been stored in its memory cells.

After a little experimenting, Alvin brought his ship to rest on the hillside that had given him his first glimpse of Lys. It was quite easy to control the machine; he had only to indicate his general desires and the robot attended to the details. It would, he imagined, ignore dangerous or impossible orders, though he had no intention of giving any if he could avoid it. Alvin was fairly certain that no one could have seen his arrival. He thought this rather important, for he had no desire to engage in mental combat with Seranis again. His plans were still somewhat vague, but he was running no risks until he had established friendly relations. The robot could act as his ambassador, while he remained safely in the ship.

He met no one on the road to Airlee. It was strange to sit in the spaceship while his field of vision moved effortlessly along the familiar path, and the whispering of the forest sounded in his ears. As yet he was unable to identify himself fully with the robot, and the strain of controlling it was still considerable.

It was nearly dark when he reached Airlee, and the little houses were floating in pools of light. Alvin kept to the shadows and had almost reached Seranis's home before he was discovered. Suddenly there was an angry, high-pitched buzzing and his view was blocked by a flurry of wings. He recoiled involuntarily before the onslaught; then he realized what had happened. Krif was once again expressing his resentment of anything that flew without wings.

Not wishing to hurt the beautiful but stupid creature, Alvin brought the robot to a halt and endured as best he could the blows that seemed to be raining upon him. Though he was sitting in comfort a mile away, he could not avoid flinching and was glad when Hilvar came out to investigate.

At his master's approach Krif departed, still buzzing balefully. In the silence that followed, Hilvar stood looking at the robot for a while. Then he smiled.

"Hello, Alvin," he said. "I'm glad you've come back. Or are you still in Diaspar?"

Not for the first time, Alvin felt an envious admiration for the speed and precision of Hilvar's mind.

"No," he said, wondering as he did so how clearly the robot echoed his voice. "I'm in Airlee, not very far away. But I'm staying here for the present."

Hilvar laughed.

"I think that's just as well. Seranis has forgiven you, but as for the Assembly—well, that is another matter. There is a conference going on here at the moment—the first we have ever had in Airlee."

"Do you mean," asked Alvin, "that your councilors have actually come here? With your telepathic powers, I should have thought that meetings weren't necessary."

"They are rare, but there are times when they are felt desirable. I don't know the exact nature of the crisis, but three Senators are already here and the rest are expected soon."

Alvin could not help smiling at the way in which events in Diaspar had been mirrored here. Wherever he went, he now seemed to be leaving a trail of consternation and alarm behind him.

"I think it would be a good idea," he said, "if I could talk to this Assembly of yours—as long as I can do so in safety."

"It would be safe for you to come here yourself," said Hilvar, "if the Assembly promises not to try and take over your mind again. Otherwise, I should stay where you are. I'll lead your robot to the Senators—they'll be rather upset to see it."

Alvin felt again that keen but treacherous sense of enjoyment and exhilaration as he followed Hilvar into the house. He was meeting the rulers of Lys on more equal terms now; though he felt no rancor against them, it was very pleasant to know that he was now master of the situation, and in command of powers which even yet he had not fully turned to account.

The door of the conference room was locked, and it was some time before Hilvar could attract attention. The minds of the Senators, it seemed, were so completely engaged that it was difficult to break into their deliberations. Then the walls slid reluctantly aside, and Alvin moved his robot swiftly forward into the chamber.

The three Senators froze in their seats as he floated toward them, but only the slightest flicker of surprise crossed Seranis's face. Perhaps Hilvar had already sent a warning, or perhaps she had expected that, sooner or later, Alvin would return.

"Good evening," he said politely, as if this vicarious entry were the most natural thing in the world. "I've decided to come back."

Their surprise certainly exceeded his expectations. One of the Senators, a young man with graying hair, was the first to recover.

"How did you get here?" he gasped.

The reason for his astonishment was obvious. Just as Diaspar had done, so Lys must also have put the subway out of action.

"Why, I came here just as I did last time," said Alvin, unable to resist amusing himself at their expense.

Two of the Senators looked fixedly at the third, who spread his hands in a gesture of baffled resignation. Then the young man who had addressed him before spoke again.

"Didn't you have any—difficulty?" he asked.

"None at all," said Alvin, determined to increase their confusion. He saw that he had succeeded.

"I've come back," he continued, "under my own free will, and because I have some important news for you. However, in view of our previous disagreement I'm remaining out of sight for the moment. If I appear personally, will you promise not to try to restrict my movements again?"

No one said anything for a while, and Alvin wondered what thoughts were being silently interchanged. Then Seranis spoke for them all.

"We won't attempt to control you again—though I don't think we were very successful before."

"Very well," replied Alvin. "I will come to Airlee as quickly as I can."

He waited until the robot had returned; then, very carefully, he gave the machine its instructions and made it repeat them back to him. Seranis, he was quite sure, would not break her word; nevertheless he preferred to safeguard his line of retreat.

The air lock closed silently behind him as he left the ship. A moment later there was a whispering "hiss . . ." like a long-drawn gasp of surprise, as the air made way for the rising ship. For an instant a dark shadow blotted out the stars; then the ship was gone.

Not until it had vanished did Alvin realize that he had made a slight but annoying miscalculation of the kind that could bring the best-laid plans to disaster. He had forgotten that the robot's senses were more acute than his own, and the night was far darker than he had expected. More than once he lost the path completely, and several times he barely avoided colliding with trees. It was almost pitch-black in the forest, and once something quite large came toward him through the undergrowth. There was the faintest crackling of twigs, and two emerald eyes were looking steadfastly at him from the level of his waist. He called softly, and an incredibly long tongue rasped across his hand. A moment later a powerful body rubbed affectionately against him and departed without a sound. He had no idea what it could be.

Presently the lights of the village were shining through the trees ahead, but he no longer needed their guidance for the path beneath his feet had now become a river of dim blue fire. The moss upon which he was walking was luminous, and his footprints left dark patches which slowly disappeared behind him. It was a beautiful and entrancing sight, and when Alvin stooped to pluck some of the strange moss it glowed for minutes in his cupped hands before its radiance died.

Hilvar met him for the second time outside the house, and for the second time introduced him to Seranis and the Senators. They greeted him with a kind of wary and reluctant respect; if they wondered where the robot had gone, they made no comment.

"I'm very sorry," Alvin began, "that I had to leave your country in such an undignified fashion. It may interest you to know that it was nearly as difficult to escape from Diaspar." He let that remark sink in, then added quickly, "I have told my people all about Lys, and I did my best to give a favorable impression. But Diaspar will have nothing to do with you. In spite of all I could say, it wishes to avoid contamination with an inferior culture."

It was most satisfying to watch the Senators' reactions, and even the urbane Seranis colored slightly at his words. If he could make Lys and Diaspar sufficiently annoyed with each other, thought Alvin, his problem would be more than half solved. Each would be so anxious to prove the superiority of its way of life that the barriers between them would soon go down.

"Why have you come back to Lys?" asked Seranis.

"Because I want to convince you, as well as Diaspar, that you have made a mistake." He did not add his other reason—that in Lys was the only friend of whom he could be certain and whose help he now needed.

The Senators were still silent, waiting for him to continue, and he knew that looking through their eyes and listening through their ears were many other unseen intelligences. He was the representative of Diaspar, and the whole of Lys was judging him by what he might say. It was a great responsibility, and he felt humbled before it. He marshaled his thoughts and then began to speak.

His theme was Diaspar. He painted the city as he had last seen it, dreaming on the breast of the desert, its towers glowing like captive rainbows against the sky. From the treasure house of memory he recalled the songs that the poets of old had written in praise of Diaspar, and he spoke of the countless men who had spent their lives to increase its beauty. No one, he told them, could ever exhaust the city's treasures, however long they lived; always there would be something new. For a while he described some of the wonders which the men of Diaspar had wrought; he tried to make them catch a glimpse at least of the loveliness that the artists of the past had created for men's eternal admiration. And he wondered a little wistfully if it were indeed true that the music of Diaspar was the last sound that Earth had ever broadcast to the stars.

They heard him to the end without interruption or questioning. When he had finished it was very late, and Alvin felt more tired than he could ever before remember. The strain and excitement of the long day had told on him at last, and quite suddenly he was asleep.

When he awoke, he was in an unfamiliar room and it was some moments before he remembered that he was no longer in Diaspar. As consciousness returned, so the light grew around him, until presently he was bathed in the soft, cool radiance of the morning sun, streaming through the now transparent walls. He lay in drowsy half-awareness, recalling the events of the previous day and wondering what forces he had now set in motion.

With a soft, musical sound, one of the walls began to pleat itself up in a manner so complicated that it eluded the eye. Hilvar stepped through the opening that had been formed and looked at Alvin with an expression half of amusement, half of serious concern.

"Now that you're awake, Alvin," he said, "perhaps you'll at least tell me what your next move is, and how you managed to return here. The Senators are just leaving to look at the subway; they can't understand how you managed to come back through it. Did you?"

Alvin jumped out of bed and stretched himself mightily.

"Perhaps we'd better overtake them," he said. "I don't want to make them waste their time. As for the question you asked me—in a little while I'll show you the answer to that."

They had almost reached the lake before they overtook the three Senators, and both parties exchanged slightly self-conscious greetings. The Committee of Investigation could see that Alvin knew where it was going, and the unexpected encounter had clearly put it somewhat at a loss.

"I'm afraid I misled you last night," said Alvin cheerfully. "I didn't come to Lys by the old route, so your attempt to close it was quite unnecessary. As a matter of fact, the Council of Diaspar also closed it at their end, with equal lack of success."

The Senators' faces were a study in perplexity as one solution after another chased through their brains.

"Then how *did* you get here?" said the leader. There was a sudden, dawning comprehension in his eyes, and Alvin could tell that he had begun to guess the truth. He wondered if he had intercepted the command his mind had just sent winging across the mountains. But he said nothing, and merely pointed in silence to the northern sky.

Too swiftly for the eye to follow, a needle of silver light arced across the mountains, leaving a mile-long trail of incandescence. Twenty thousand feet above Lys, it stopped. There was no deceleration, no slow braking of its colossal speed. It came to a halt instantly, so that the eye that had been following it moved on across a quarter of the heavens before the brain could arrest its motion. Down from the skies crashed a mighty peal of thunder, the sound of air battered and smashed by the violence of the ship's passage. A little later the ship itself, gleaming splendidly in the sunlight, came to rest upon the hillside a hundred yards away.

It was difficult to say who was the most surprised, but Alvin was the first to recover. As they walked—very nearly running—toward the spaceship, he wondered if it normally traveled in this meteoric fashion. The thought was disconcerting, although there had been no sensation of movement on his first voyage. Considerably more puzzling, however, was the fact that a day ago this resplendent creature had been hidden beneath a thick layer of iron-hard rock—the coating it had still retained when it had torn itself loose from the desert. Not until Alvin had reached the ship, and burned his fingers by incautiously resting them on the hull, did he understand what had happened. Near the stern there were still traces of earth, but it had been fused into lava. All the rest had been swept away, leaving uncovered the stubborn shell which neither time nor any natural force could ever touch.

With Hilvar by his side, Alvin stood in the open door and looked back at the silent Senators. He wondered what they were thinking—what, indeed, the whole of Lys was thinking. From their expressions, it almost seemed as if they were beyond thought.

"I am going to Shalmirane," said Alvin, "and I will be back in Airlee within an hour or so. But that is only a beginning, and while I am away, there is a thought I would leave with you.

"This is no ordinary flyer of the kind in which men traveled over the Earth. It is a spaceship, one of the fastest ever built. If you want to know where I found it, you will find the answer in Diaspar. But you will have to go there, for Diaspar will never come to you."

He turned to Hilvar, and gestured to the door. Hilvar hesitated for a moment only, looking back once at the familiar scenes around him. Then he stepped forward into the air lock.

The Senators watched until the ship, now moving quite slowly—for it had only a little way to go—had disappeared into the south. Then the gray-haired young man who led the group shrugged his shoulders philosophically and turned to one of his colleagues.

"You've always opposed us for wanting change," he said, "and so far you have won. But I don't think the future lies with either of our groups now. Lys and Diaspar have both come to the end of an era, and we must make the best of it."

"I am afraid you are right," came the gloomy reply. "This is a crisis, and Alvin knew what he was saying when he told us to go to Diaspar. They know about us now, so there is no further purpose in concealment. I think we had better get in touch with our cousins—we may find them more anxious to co-operate now."

"But the subway is closed at both ends!"

"We can open ours; it will not be long before Diaspar does the same."

The minds of the Senators, those in Airlee and those scattered over the whole width of Lys, considered the proposal and disliked it heartily. But they saw no alternative.

Sooner than he had any right to expect, the seed that Alvin had planted was beginning to flower.

The mountains were still swimming in shadow when they reached Shalmirane. From their height the great bowl of the fortress looked very small; it seemed impossible that the fate of Earth had once depended on that tiny ebon circle.

When Alvin brought the ship to rest among the ruins by the lakeside, the desolation crowded in upon him, chilling his soul. He opened the air lock, and the stillness of the place crept into the ship. Hilvar, who had scarcely spoken during the entire flight, asked quietly: "Why have you come here again?"

Alvin did not answer until they had almost reached the edge of the lake. Then he said: "I wanted to show you what this ship was like. And

I also hoped that the polyp might be in existence once more; I feel I owe it a debt, and I want to tell it what I've discovered."

"In that case," replied Hilvar, "you will have to wait. You have come back much too soon."

Alvin had expected that; it had been a remote chance and he was not disappointed that it had failed. The waters of the lake were perfectly still, no longer beating with that steady rhythm that had so puzzled them on their first visit. He knelt down at the water's edge and peered into the cold, dark depths.

Tiny translucent bells, trailing almost invisible tentacles, were drifting to and fro beneath the surface. Alvin plunged in his hand and scooped one up. He dropped it at once, with a slight exclamation of annoyance. It had stung him.

Some day—perhaps years, perhaps centuries in the future—these mindless jellies would reassemble and the great polyp would be reborn as its memories linked together and its consciousness flashed into existence once again. Alvin wondered how it would receive the discoveries he had made; it might not be pleased to learn the truth about the Master. Indeed, it might refuse to admit that all its ages of patient waiting had been in vain.

Yet had they? Deluded though these creatures might have been, their long vigil had at last brought its reward. As if by a miracle, they had saved from the past knowledge that else might have been lost forever. Now they could rest at last, and their creed could go the way of a million other faiths that had once thought themselves eternal.

CHAPTER NINETEEN

Hilvar and Alvin walked in reflective silence back to the waiting ship, and presently the fortress was once more a dark shadow among the hills. It dwindled swiftly until it became a black and lidless eye, staring up forever into space, and soon they lost it in the great panorama of Lys.

Alvin did nothing to check the machine; still they rose until the whole of Lys lay spread beneath them, a green island in an ocher sea. Never before had Alvin been so high; when finally they came to rest the whole crescent of the Earth was visible below. Lys was very small now, only an emerald stain against the rusty desert—but far around the curve of the globe something was glittering like a many-colored jewel. And so for the first time, Hilvar saw the city of Diaspar.

They sat for a long while watching the Earth turn beneath them. Of all Man's ancient powers, this surely was the one he could least afford to lose. Alvin wished he could show the world as he saw it now to the rulers of Lys and Diaspar.

"Hilvar," he said at last, "do you think that what I'm doing is right?"

The question surprised Hilvar, who did not suspect the sudden doubts that sometimes overwhelmed his friend, and still knew nothing of Alvin's meeting with the Central Computer and the impact which that had had upon his mind. It was not an easy question to answer dispassionately; like Khedron, though with less cause, Hilvar felt that his own character was becoming submerged. He was being sucked helplessly into the vortex which Alvin left behind him on his way through life.

"I believe you are right," Hilvar answered slowly. "Our two peoples have been separated for long enough." That, he thought, was true, though he knew that his own feelings must bias his reply. But Alvin was still worried.

"There's one problem that bothers me," he said in a troubled voice, "and that's the difference in our life spans." He said no more, but each knew what the other was thinking.

"I've been worried about that as well," Hilvar admitted, "but I think the problem will solve itself in time when our people get to know each other again. We can't *both* be right—our lives may be too short, and yours are certainly far too long. Eventually there will be a compromise."

Alvin wondered. That way, it was true, lay the only hope, but the ages of transition would be hard indeed. He remembered again those bitter words of Seranis: *"Both he and I will have been dead for centuries while you are still a young man."* Very well; he would accept the conditions. Even in Diaspar all friendships lay under the same shadow; whether it was a hundred or a million years away made little difference at the end.

Alvin knew, with a certainty that passed all logic, that the welfare of the race demanded the mingling of these two cultures; in such a cause individual happiness was unimportant. For a moment Alvin saw humanity as something more than the living background of his own life, and he accepted without flinching the unhappiness his choice must one day bring.

Beneath them the world continued on its endless turning. Sensing his friend's mood, Hilvar said nothing, until presently Alvin broke the silence.

"When I first left Diaspar," he said, "I did not know what I hoped to find. Lys would have satisfied me once—more than satisfied me—yet now everything on Earth seems so small and unimportant. Each discovery I've made has raised bigger questions, and opened up wider horizons. I wonder where it will end. . . ."

Hilvar had never seen Alvin in so thoughtful a mood, and did not wish to interrupt his soliloquy. He had learned a great deal about his friend in the last few minutes.

"The robot told me," Alvin continued, "that this ship can reach the Seven Suns in less than a day. Do you think I should go?"

"Do you think I could stop you?" Hilvar replied quietly.

Alvin smiled.

"That's no answer," he said. "Who knows what lies out there in space? The Invaders may have left the Universe, but there may be other intelligences unfriendly to Man."

"Why should there be?" Hilvar asked. "That's one of the questions our philosophers have been debating for ages. A truly intelligent race is not likely to be unfriendly."

"But the Invaders—?"

"They are an enigma, I admit. If they were really vicious, they must have destroyed themselves by now. And even if they have not—" Hilvar pointed to the unending deserts below. "Once we had an Empire. What have we now that they would covet?"

Alvin was a little surprised that anyone else shared this point of view, so closely allied to his own.

"Do all your people think this way?" he asked.

"Only a minority. The average person doesn't worry about it, but would probably say that if the Invaders really wanted to destroy Earth, they'd have done it ages ago. I don't suppose anyone is actually afraid of them."

"Things are very different in Diaspar," said Alvin. "My people are great cowards. They are terrified of leaving their city, and I don't know what will happen when they hear that I've located a spaceship. Jeserac will have told the Council by now, and I would like to know what it is doing."

"I can tell you that. It is preparing to receive its first delegation from Lys. Seranis has just told me."

Alvin looked again at the screen. He could span the distance between Lys and Diaspar in a single glance; though one of his aims had been achieved, that seemed a small matter now. Yet he was very glad; now, surely, the long ages of sterile isolation would be ending.

The knowledge that he had succeeded in what had once been his main mission cleared away the last doubts from Alvin's mind. He had fulfilled his purpose here on Earth, more swiftly and more thoroughly than he had dared to hope. The way lay clear ahead for what might be his last, and would certainly be his greatest, adventure.

"Will you come with me, Hilvar?" he said, all too conscious of what he was asking.

Hilvar looked at him steadfastly.

"There was no need to ask that, Alvin," he said. "I told Seranis and all my friends that I was leaving with you—a good hour ago."

They were very high when Alvin gave the robot its final instructions. The ship had come almost to rest and the Earth was perhaps a thousand miles below, nearly filling the sky. It looked very uninviting; Alvin wondered how many ships in the past had hovered here for a little while and then continued on their way.

There was an appreciable pause, as if the robot was checking controls and circuits that had not been used for geological ages. Then came a very faint sound, the first that Alvin had ever heard from a machine. It was a tiny humming, which soared swiftly octave by octave until it was lost at the edge of hearing. There was no sense of change or motion, but suddenly he noticed that the stars were drifting across the screen. The Earth reappeared, and rolled past—then appeared again, in a slightly different position. The ship was "hunting," swinging in space like a compass needle seeking the north. For minutes the skies turned and twisted around them, until at last the ship came to rest, a giant projectile aimed at the stars.

Centered in the screen the great ring of the Seven Suns lay in its rainbow-hued beauty. A little of Earth was still visible as a dark crescent edged with the gold and crimson of the sunset. Something was happening now, Alvin knew, beyond all his experience. He waited, gripping his seat, while the seconds drifted by and the Seven Suns glittered on the screen.

There was no sound, only a sudden wrench that seemed to blur the vision—but Earth had vanished as if a giant hand had whipped it away. They were alone in space, alone with the stars and a strangely shrunken sun. Earth was gone as though it had never been.

Again came that wrench, and with it now the faintest murmur of sound, as if for the first time the generators were exerting some appreciable fraction of their power. Yet for a moment it seemed that nothing had happened; then Alvin realized that the sun itself was gone and that the stars were creeping slowly past the ship. He looked back for an instant and saw—nothing. All the heavens behind had vanished utterly, obliterated by a hemisphere of night. Even as he watched, he could see the stars plunge into it, to disappear like sparks falling upon water. The ship was traveling far faster than light, and Alvin knew that the familiar space of Earth and sun held him no more.

When that sudden, vertiginous wrench came for the third time, his heart almost stopped beating. The strange blurring of vision was unmistakable now: for a moment his surroundings seemed distorted out of recognition. The meaning of that distortion came to him in a flash of insight he could not explain. *It was real, and no delusion of his eyes.* Somehow he was catching, as he passed through the thin film of the Present, a glimpse of the changes that were occurring in the space around him.

At the same instant the murmur of the generators rose to a roar that shook the ship—a sound doubly impressive for it was the first cry of protest that Alvin had ever heard from a machine. Then it was all over, and the sudden silence seemed to ring in his ears. The great generators had done their work; they would not be needed again until the end of the voyage. The stars ahead flared blue-white and vanished into the ultraviolet. Yet by some magic of Science or Nature the Seven Suns were still visible, though now their positions and colors were subtly changed. The ship was hurtling toward them along a tunnel of darkness, beyond the boundaries of space and time, at a velocity too enormous for the mind to contemplate.

It was hard to believe that they had now been flung out of the Solar System at a speed which unless it were checked would soon take them through the heart of the Galaxy and into the greater emptiness beyond. Neither Alvin nor Hilvar could conceive the real immensity of their journey; the great sagas of exploration had completely changed Man's outlook toward the Universe and even now, millions of centuries later, the ancient traditions had not wholly died. There had once been a ship, legend whispered, that had circumnavigated the Cosmos between the rising and the setting of the sun. The billions of miles between the stars meant nothing before such speeds. To Alvin this voyage was very little greater, and perhaps less dangerous, than his first journey to Lys.

It was Hilvar who voiced both their thoughts as the Seven Suns slowly brightened ahead.

"Alvin," he remarked, "that formation can't possibly be natural."

The other nodded.

"I've thought that for years, but it still seems fantastic."

"The system may not have been built by Man," agreed Hilvar, "but intelligence must have created it. Nature could never have formed that perfect circle of stars, all equally brilliant. And there's nothing else in the visible Universe like the Central Sun."

"Why should such a thing have been made, then?"

"Oh, I can think of many reasons. Perhaps it's a signal, so that any strange ship entering our Universe will know where to look for life. Perhaps it marks the center of galactic administration. Or perhaps—and somehow I feel that this is the real explanation—it's simply the greatest of all works of art. But it's foolish to speculate now. In a few hours we shall know the truth."

"We shall know the truth." Perhaps, thought Alvin—but how much of it shall we ever know? It seemed strange that now, while he was leaving Diaspar, and indeed Earth itself, at a speed beyond all comprehension, his mind should turn once more to the mystery of his origin. Yet perhaps it was not so surprising; he had learned many things since he had first arrived in Lys, but until now he had had not a single moment for quiet reflection.

There was nothing he could do now but sit and wait; his immediate future was controlled by the wonderful machine—surely one of the supreme engineering achievements of all time—that was now carrying him into the heart of the Universe. Now was the moment for thought and reflection, whether he wished it or not. But first he would tell Hilvar all that had happened to him since their hasty parting only two days before.

Hilvar absorbed the tale without comment and without asking for any explanations; he seemed to understand at once everything that Alvin described, and showed no signs of surprise even when he heard of the meeting with the Central Computer and the operation it had performed upon the robot's mind. It was not that he was incapable of wonder, but that the history of the past was full of marvels that could match anything in Alvin's story.

"It's obvious," he said, when Alvin had finished talking, "that the Central Computer must have received special instructions regarding you when it was built. By now, you must have guessed why."

"I think so. Khedron gave me part of the answer when he explained how the men who designed Diaspar had taken steps to prevent it becoming decadent."

"Do you think you—and the other Uniques before you—are part of the social mechanism which prevents complete stagnation? So that whereas the Jesters are short-term correcting factors, you and your kind are long-term ones?"

Hilvar had expressed the idea better than Alvin could, yet this was not exactly what he had in mind.

"I believe the truth is more complicated than that. It almost looks as if there was a conflict of opinion when the city was built, between those who wanted to shut it off completely from the outside world, and those who wanted to maintain some contacts. The first faction won, but the others did not admit defeat. I think Yarlan Zey must have been one of their leaders, but he was not powerful enough to act openly. He did his best, by leaving the subway in existence and by insuring that at long intervals someone would come out of the Hall of Creation who did not share the fears of all his fellow men. In fact, I wonder—" Alvin paused, and his eyes veiled with thought so that for a moment he seemed oblivious of his surroundings.

"What are you thinking now?" asked Hilvar.

"It's just occurred to me—perhaps *I* am Yarlan Zey. It's perfectly possible. He may have fed his personality into the Memory Banks, relying on it to break the mold of Diaspar before it was too firmly established. One day I must discover what happened to those earlier Uniques; that may help to fill in the gaps in the picture."

"And Yarlan Zey—or whoever it was—also instructed the Central Computer to give special assistance to the Uniques, whenever they were created," mused Hilvar, following this line of logic.

"That's right. The ironic thing is that I could have got all the information I needed direct from the Central Computer, without any assistance from poor Khedron. It would have told me more than it ever told him. But there's no doubt that he saved me a good deal of time, and taught me much that I could never have learned by myself."

"I think your theory covers all the known facts," said Hilvar cautiously. "Unfortunately, it still leaves wide open the biggest problem of all—the original purpose of Diaspar. Why did your people try to pretend that the outer world didn't exist? *That's* a question I'd like to see answered."

"It's a question I intend to answer," replied Alvin. "But I don't know when—or how."

So they argued and dreamed, while hour by hour the Seven Suns drifted apart until they had filled that strange tunnel of night in which the ship was riding. Then, one by one, the six outer stars vanished at the brink of darkness and at last only the Central Sun was left. Though it could no longer be fully in their space, it still shone with the pearly light that marked it out from all other stars. Minute by minute its brilliance increased, until presently it was no longer a point but a tiny disc. And now the disc was beginning to expand before them.

There was the briefest of warnings: for a moment a deep, bell-like note vibrated through the room. Alvin clenched the arms of his chair, though it was a futile enough gesture.

Once again the great generators exploded into life, and with an abruptness that was almost blinding, the stars reappeared. The ship had dropped back into space, back into the Universe of suns and planets, the natural world where nothing could move more swiftly than light.

They were already within the system of the Seven Suns, for the great ring of colored globes now dominated the sky. And what a sky it was! All the stars they had known, all the familiar constellations, had gone. The Milky Way was no longer a faint band of mist far to one side of the heavens; they were now at the center of creation, and its great circle divided the Universe in twain.

The ship was still moving very swiftly toward the Central Sun, and the six remaining stars of the system were colored beacons ranged around the sky. Not far from the nearest of them were the tiny sparks of circling planets, worlds that must have been of enormous size to be visible over such a distance.

The cause of the Central Sun's nacreous light was now clearly visible. The great star was shrouded in an envelope of gas which softened its radiation and gave it its characteristic color. The surrounding nebula could only be seen indirectly, and it was twisted into strange shapes that eluded the eye. But it was there, and the longer one stared the more extensive it seemed to be.

"Well, Alvin," said Hilvar, "we have a good many worlds to take our choice from. Or do you hope to explore them all?"

"It's lucky that won't be necessary," admitted Alvin. "If we can make contact anywhere, we'll get the information we need. The logical thing would be to head for the largest planet of the Central Sun."

"Unless it's too large. Some planets, I've heard, were so big that human life could not exist on them—men would be crushed under their own weight."

"I doubt if that will be true here, since I'm sure this system is entirely artificial. In any case, we'll be able to see from space whether there are any cities and buildings."

Hilvar pointed to the robot.

"Our problem has been solved for us. Don't forget—our guide has been here before. He is taking us home—and I wonder what he thinks about it?"

That was something that Alvin had also wondered. But was it accurate—did it make any sense at all—to imagine that the robot felt anything resembling human emotions now that it was returning to the ancient home of the Master, after so many aeons?

In all his dealings with it, since the Central Computer had released the blocks that made it mute, the robot had never shown any sign of feelings or emotion. It had answered his questions and obeyed his commands, but its real personality had proved utterly inaccessible to him. That it had a personality Alvin was sure; otherwise he would not have felt that obscure sense of guilt which afflicted him when he recalled the trick he had played upon it—and upon its now dormant companion.

It still believed in everything that the Master had taught it; though it had seen him fake his miracles and tell lies to his followers, these inconvenient facts did not affect its loyalty. It was able, as had many humans before it, to reconcile two conflicting sets of data.

Now it was following its immemorial memories back to their origin. Almost lost in the glare of the Central Sun was a pale spark of light, with around it the fainter gleams of yet smaller worlds. Their enormous journey was coming to its end; in a little while they would know if it had been in vain.

CHAPTER TWENTY

The planet they were approaching was now only a few million miles away, a beautiful sphere of multicolored light. There could be no darkness anywhere upon its surface, for as it turned beneath the Central Sun, the other stars would march one by one across its skies. Alvin now saw very clearly the meaning of the Master's dying words: *"It is lovely to watch the colored shadows on the planets of eternal light."*

Now they were so close that they could see continents and oceans and a faint haze of atmosphere. Yet there was something puzzling about its markings, and presently they realized that the divisions between land and water were curiously regular. This planet's continents were not as Nature had left them—but how small a task the shaping of a world must have been to those who built its suns!

"Those aren't oceans at all!" Hilvar exclaimed suddenly. "Look—you can see markings in them!"

Not until the planet was nearer could Alvin see clearly what his friend meant. Then he noticed faint bands and lines along the continental borders, well inside what he had taken to be the limits of the sea. The sight filled him with a sudden doubt, for he knew too well the meaning of those lines. He had seen them once before in the desert beyond Diaspar, and they told him that his journey had been in vain.

"This planet is as dry as Earth," he said dully. "Its water has all gone—those markings are the salt beds where the seas have evaporated."

"They would never have let that happen," replied Hilvar. "I think that, after all, we are too late."

His disappointment was so bitter that Alvin did not trust himself to speak again but stared silently at the great world ahead. With impressive slowness the planet turned beneath the ship, and its surface rose majestically to meet them. Now they could see buildings—minute white incrustations everywhere save on the ocean beds themselves.

Once this world had been the center of the Universe. Now it was still, the air was empty and on the ground were none of the scurrying dots that spoke of life. Yet the ship was still sliding purposefully over the frozen sea of stone—a sea which here and there had gathered itself into great waves that challenged the sky.

Presently the ship came to rest, as if the robot had at last traced its memories to their source. Below them was a column of snow-white stone springing from the center of an immense marble amphitheater. Alvin waited for a little while; then, as the machine remained motionless, he directed it to land at the foot of the pillar.

Even until now, Alvin had half hoped to find life on this planet. That hope vanished instantly as the air lock opened. Never before in his life, even in the desolation of Shalmirane, had he been in utter silence. On Earth there was always the murmur of voices, the stir of living creatures, or the sighing of the wind. Here were none of these, nor ever would be again.

"Why did you bring us to this spot?" asked Alvin. He felt little interest in the answer, but the momentum of his quest still carried him on even when he had lost all heart to pursue it further.

"The Master left from here," replied the robot.

"I thought that would be the explanation," said Hilvar. "Don't you see the irony of all this? He fled from this world in disgrace—now look at the memorial they built for him!"

The great column of stone was perhaps a hundred times the height of a man, and was set in a circle of metal slightly raised above the level of the plain. It was featureless and bore no inscription. For how many thousands or millions of years, wondered Alvin, had the Master's disciples gathered here to do him honor? And had they ever known that he died in exile on distant Earth?

It made no difference now. The Master and his disciples alike were buried in oblivion.

"Come outside," urged Hilvar, trying to jolt Alvin out of his mood of depression. "We have traveled halfway across the Universe to see this place. At least you can make the effort to step outdoors."

Despite himself, Alvin smiled and followed Hilvar through the air lock. Once outside, his spirits began to revive a little. Even if this world was dead, it must contain much of interest, much that would help him to solve some of the mysteries of the past.

The air was musty, but breathable. Despite the many suns in the sky, the temperature was low. Only the white disc of the Central Sun provided any real heat, and that seemed to have lost its strength in its passage through the nebulous haze around the star. The other suns gave their quota of color, but no warmth.

It took only a few minutes to make sure that the obelisk could tell them nothing. The stubborn material of which it was made showed definite signs of age; its edges were rounded, and the metal on which it was standing had been worn away by the feet of generations of disciples and visitors. It was strange to think that they might be the last of many billions of human beings ever to stand upon this spot.

Hilvar was about to suggest that they should return to the ship and fly across to the nearest of the surrounding buildings when Alvin noticed a long, narrow crack in the marble floor of the amphitheater. They walked along it for a considerable distance, the crack widening all the time until presently it was too broad for a man's legs to straddle.

A moment later they stood beside its origin. The surface of the arena had been crushed and splintered into an enormous shallow depression, more than a mile long. No intelligence, no imagination was needed to picture its cause. Ages ago—though certainly long after this world had been deserted—an immense cylindrical shape had rested here, then lifted once more into space and left the planet to its memories.

Who had they been? Where had they come from? Alvin could only stare and wonder. He would never know if he had missed these earlier visitors by a thousand or a million years.

They walked in silence back to their own ship (how tiny that would have looked beside the monster which once had rested here!) and flew slowly across the arena until they came to the most impressive of the buildings flanking it. As they landed in front of the ornate entrance, Hilvar pointed out something that Alvin had noticed at the same moment.

"These buildings don't look safe. See all that fallen stone over there —it's a miracle they're still standing. If there were any storms on this planet, they would have been flattened ages ago. I don't think it would be wise to go inside any of them."

"I'm not going to; I'll send the robot—it can travel far faster than we can, and it won't make any disturbance which might bring the roof crashing down on top of it."

Hilvar approved of this precaution, but he also insisted on one which Alvin had overlooked. Before the robot left on its reconnaissance, Alvin made it pass on a set of instructions to the almost equally intelligent brain of the ship, so that whatever happened to their pilot they could at least return safely to Earth.

It took little time to convince both of them that this world had nothing to offer. Together they watched miles of empty, dust-carpeted corridors and passageways drift across the screen as the robot explored these empty labyrinths. All buildings designed by intelligent beings, whatever form their bodies may take, must comply with certain basic laws, and after a while even the most alien forms of architecture or design fail to evoke surprise, and the mind becomes hypnotized by sheer repetition, incapable of absorbing any more impressions. These buildings, it seemed, had been purely residential, and the beings who had lived in them had been approximately human in size. They might well have been men; it was true that there were a surprising number of rooms and enclosures that could be entered only by flying creatures, but that did not mean that the builders of this city were winged. They could have used the personal antigravity devices that had once been in common use but of which there was now no trace in Diaspar.

"Alvin," said Hilvar at last, "we could spend a million years exploring these buildings. It's obvious that they've not merely been abandoned —they were carefully stripped of everything valuable that they possessed. We are wasting our time."

"Then what do you suggest?" asked Alvin.

"We should look at two or three other areas of this planet and see if they are the same—as I expect they are. Then we should make an equally quick survey of the other planets, and only land if they seem fundamentally different or we notice something unusual. That's all we can hope to do unless we are going to stay here for the rest of our lives."

It was true enough; they were trying to contact intelligence, not to carry out archaeological research. The former task could be achieved in a few days, if it could be achieved at all. The latter would take centuries of labor by armies of men and robots.

They left the planet two hours later, and were thankful enough to go. Even when it had been bustling with life, Alvin decided, this world of endless buildings would have been very depressing. There were no signs of any parks, any open spaces where there could have been vegetation. It had been an utterly sterile world, and it was hard to imagine the psychology of the beings who had lived here. If the next planet was identical with this, Alvin decided, he would probably abandon the search there and then.

It was not; indeed, a greater contrast would have been impossible to imagine.

This planet was nearer the sun, and even from space it looked hot. It was partly covered with low clouds, indicating that water was plentiful, but there were no signs of any oceans. Nor was there any sign of intelligence; they circled the planet twice without glimpsing a single artifact of any kind. The entire globe, from poles down to the equator, was clothed with a blanket of virulent green.

"I think we should be very careful here," said Hilvar. "This world is alive—and I don't like the color of that vegetation. It would be best to stay in the ship, and not to open the air lock at all."

"Not even to send out the robot?"

"No, not even that. You have forgotten what disease is, and though my people know how to deal with it, we are a long way from home and there may be dangers here which we cannot see. I think this is a world that has run amok. Once it may have been all one great garden or park, but when it was abandoned Nature took over again. It could never have been like this while the system was inhabited."

Alvin did not doubt that Hilvar was right. There was something evil, something hostile to all the order and regularity on which both Lys and Diaspar were based, in the biological anarchy below. Here a ceaseless battle had raged for a billion years; it would be well to be wary of the survivors.

They came cautiously down over a great level plain, so uniform that its flatness posed an immediate problem. The plain was bordered by higher ground, completely covered with trees whose height could only be guessed—they were so tightly packed, and so enmeshed with undergrowth, that their trunks were virtually buried. There were many winged creatures flying among their upper branches, though they moved so swiftly that it was impossible to tell whether they were birds or insects—or neither.

Here and there a forest giant had managed to climb a few scores of feet above its battling neighbors, who had formed a brief alliance to tear it down and destroy the advantage it had won. Despite the fact that this was a silent war, fought too slowly for the eye to see, the impression of merciless, implacable conflict was overwhelming.

The plain, by comparison, appeared placid and uneventful. It was flat, to within a few inches, right out to the horizon, and seemed to be covered with a thin, wiry grass. Though they descended to within fifty feet of it, there was no sign of any animal life, which Hilvar found somewhat surprising. Perhaps, he decided, it had been scared underground by their approach.

They hovered just above the plain while Alvin tried to convince Hilvar that it would be safe to open the air lock, and Hilvar patiently explained such conceptions as bacteria, fungi, viruses, and microbes—ideas which Alvin found hard to visualize, and harder still to apply to himself. The argument had been in progress for some minutes before they noticed a peculiar fact. The vision screen, which a moment ago had been showing the forest ahead of them, had now become blank.

"Did you turn that off?" said Hilvar, his mind, as usual, just one jump ahead of Alvin's.

"No," replied Alvin, a cold shiver running down his spine as he thought of the only other explanation. "Did *you* turn it off?" he asked the robot.

"No," came the reply, echoing his own.

With a sigh of relief, Alvin dismissed the idea that the robot might have started to act on its own volition—that he might have a mechanical mutiny on his hands.

"Then why is the screen blank?" he asked.

"The image receptors have been covered."

"I don't understand," said Alvin, forgetting for a moment that the robot would only act on definite orders or questions. He recovered himself quickly and asked: "What's covered the receptors?"

"I do not know."

The literal-mindedness of robots could sometimes be as exasperating as the discursiveness of humans. Before Alvin could continue the interrogation, Hilvar interrupted.

"Tell it to lift the ship—slowly," he said, and there was a note of urgency in his voice.

Alvin repeated the command. There was no sense of motion; there never was. Then, slowly, the image re-formed on the vision screen, though for a moment it was blurred and distorted. But it showed enough to end the argument about landing.

The level plain was level no longer. A great bulge had formed immediately below them—a bulge which was ripped open at the top where the ship had torn free. Huge pseudopods were waving sluggishly across the gap, as if trying to recapture the prey that had just escaped from their clutches. As he stared in horrified fascination, Alvin caught a glimpse of a pulsing scarlet orifice, fringed with whiplike tentacles which were beating in unison, driving anything that came into their reach down into that gaping maw.

Foiled of its intended victim, the creature sank slowly into the ground—and it was then that Alvin realized that the plain below was merely the thin scum on the surface of a stagnant sea.

"What was that—*thing?*" he gasped.

"I'd have to go down and study it before I could tell you that," Hilvar replied matter-of-factly. "It may have been some form of primitive animal—perhaps even a relative of our friend in Shalmirane. Certainly it was not intelligent, or it would have known better than to try to eat a spaceship."

Alvin felt shaken, though he knew that they had been in no possible danger. He wondered what else lived down there beneath that innocent sward, which seemed to positively invite him to come out and run upon its springy surface.

"I could spend a lot of time here," said Hilvar, obviously fascinated by what he had just seen. "Evolution must have produced some very interesting results under these conditions. Not only evolution, but *devolution* as well, as higher forms of life regressed when the planet was deserted. By now equilibrium must have been reached and—you're not leaving already?" His voice sounded quite plaintive as the landscape receded below them.

"I am," said Alvin. "I've seen a world with no life, and a world with too much, and I don't know which I dislike more."

Five thousand feet above the plain, the planet gave them one final surprise. They encountered a flotilla of huge, flabby balloons drifting down the wind. From each semitransparent envelope, clusters of tendrils dangled to form what was virtually an inverted forest. Some plants, it seemed, in the effort to escape from the ferocious conflict on the surface had learned to conquer the air. By a miracle of adaptation, they had managed to prepare hydrogen and store it in bladders, so that they could lift themselves into the comparative peace of the lower atmosphere.

Yet it was not certain that even here they had found security. Their downward-hanging stems and leaves were infested with an entire fauna of spidery animals, which must spend their lives floating far above the surface of the globe, continuing the universal battle for existence on their lonely aerial islands. Presumably they must from time to time have some contact with the ground; Alvin saw one of the great balloons suddenly collapse and fall out of the sky, its broken envelope acting as a crude parachute. He wondered if this was an accident, or part of the life cycle of these strange entities.

Hilvar slept while they waited for the next planet to approach. For some reason which the robot could not explain to them, the ship traveled slowly—at least by comparison with its Universe-spanning haste—now that it was within a Solar System. It took almost two hours to reach the world that Alvin had chosen for his third stop, and he was a little surprised that any mere interplanetary journey should last so long.

He woke Hilvar as they dropped down into the atmosphere.

"What do you make of *that?"* he asked, pointing to the vision screen.

Below them was a bleak landscape of blacks and grays, showing no sign of vegetation or any other direct evidence of life. But there was indirect evidence; the low hills and shallow valleys were dotted with perfectly formed hemispheres, some of them arranged in complex, symmetrical patterns.

They had learned caution on the last planet, and after carefully considering all the possibilities remained poised high in the atmosphere while they sent the robot down to investigate. Through its eyes, they saw one of the hemispheres approach until the robot was floating only a few feet away from the completely smooth, featureless surface.

There was no sign of any entrance, nor any hint of the purpose which the structure served. It was quite large—over a hundred feet high; some of the other hemispheres were larger still. If it was a building, there appeared to be no way in or out.

After some hesitation, Alvin ordered the robot to move forward and touch the dome. To his utter astonishment, it refused to obey him. This indeed was mutiny—or so at first sight it seemed.

"Why won't you do what I tell you?" asked Alvin, when he had recovered from his astonishment.

"It is forbidden," came the reply.

"Forbidden by whom?"

"I do not know."

"Then how—no, cancel that. Was the order built into you?"

"No."

That seemed to eliminate one possibility. The builders of these domes might well have been the race who made the robot, and might have included this taboo in the machine's original instructions.

"When did you receive the order?" asked Alvin.

"I received it when I landed."

Alvin turned to Hilvar, the light of a new hope burning in his eyes. "There's intelligence here! Can you sense it?"

"No," Hilvar replied. "This place seems as dead to me as the first world we visited."

"I'm going outside to join the robot. Whatever spoke to it may speak to me."

Hilvar did not argue the point, though he looked none too happy. They brought the ship to earth a hundred feet away from the dome, not far from the waiting robot, and opened the air lock.

Alvin knew that the lock could not be opened unless the ship's brain had already satisfied itself that the atmosphere was breathable. For a moment he thought it had made a mistake—the air was so thin and gave such little sustenance to his lungs. Then, by inhaling deeply, he found that he could grasp enough oxygen to survive, thought he felt that a few minutes here would be all that he could endure.

Panting hard, they walked up to the robot and to the curving wall of the enigmatic dome. They took one more step—then stopped in unison as if hit by the same sudden blow. In their minds, like the tolling of a mighty gong, had boomed a single message:

DANGER. COME NO CLOSER.

That was all. It was a message not in words, but in pure thought. Alvin was certain that any creature, whatever its level of intelligence, would receive the same warning, in the same utterly unmistakable fashion—deep within its mind.

It was a warning, not a threat. Somehow they knew that it was not directed *against* them; it was for their protection. Here, it seemed to say, is something intrinsically dangerous, and we, its makers, are anxious that no one shall be hurt through blundering ignorantly into it.

Alvin and Hilvar stepped back several paces, and looked at each other, each waiting for the other to say what was in his mind. Hilvar was the first to sum up the position.

"I was right, Alvin," he said. "There is no intelligence here. That warning is automatic—triggered by our presence when we get too close."

Alvin nodded in agreement.

"I wonder what they were trying to protect," he said. "There could be buildings—anything—under these domes."

"There's no way we can find out, if all the domes warn us off. It's interesting—the difference between the three planets we've visited. They took everything away from the first—they abandoned the second without bothering about it—but they went to a lot of trouble here. Perhaps they expected to come back some day, and wanted everything to be ready for them when they returned."

"But they never did—and that was a long time ago."

"They may have changed their minds."

It was curious, Alvin thought, how both he and Hilvar had unconsciously started using the word "they." Whoever or whatever "they" had been, their presence had been strong on that first planet—and was even stronger here. This was a world that had been carefully wrapped up, and put away until it might be needed again.

"Let's go back to the ship," panted Alvin. "I can't breathe properly here."

As soon as the air lock had closed behind them, and they were at ease once more, they discussed their next move. To make a thorough investigation, they should sample a large number of domes, in the hope that they might find one that had no warning and which could be entered. If that failed—but Alvin would not face that possibility until he had to.

He faced it less than an hour later, and in a far more dramatic form than he would have dreamed. They had sent the robot down to half a dozen domes, always with the same result, when they came across a scene that was badly out of place on this tidy, neatly packaged world.

Below them was a broad valley, sparsely sprinkled with the tantalizing, impenetrable domes. At its center was the unmistakable scar of a great explosion—an explosion that had thrown debris for miles in all directions and burned a shallow crater in the ground.

And beside the crater was the wreckage of a spaceship.

CHAPTER TWENTY-ONE

They landed close to the scene of this ancient tragedy, and walked slowly, conserving their breath, toward the immense, broken hull towering above them. Only a short section—either the prow or the stern—of the ship remained; presumably the rest had been destroyed in the explosion. As they approached the wreck, a thought slowly dawned in Alvin's mind, becoming stronger and stronger until it attained the status of certainty.

"Hilvar," he said, finding it hard to talk and walk at the same time,

"I believe this is the ship that landed on the first planet we visited."

Hilvar nodded, preferring not to waste air. The same idea had already occurred to him. It was a good object lesson, he thought, for incautious visitors. He hoped it would not be lost on Alvin.

They reached the hull and stared up into the exposed interior of the ship. It was like looking into a huge building that had been roughly sliced in two; floors and walls and ceilings, broken at the point of the explosion, gave a distorted chart of the ship's cross section. What strange beings, wondered Alvin, still lay where they had died in the wreckage of their vessel?

"I don't understand this," said Hilvar suddenly. "This portion of the ship is badly damaged, but it's still fairly intact. Where's the rest of it? Did it break in two out in space, and this part crash here?"

Not until they had sent the robot exploring again, and had themselves examined the area around the wreckage, did they learn the answer. There was no shadow of doubt; any reservations they might have had were banished when Alvin found the line of low mounds, each ten feet long, on the little hill beside the ship.

"So they landed here," mused Hilvar, "and ignored the warning. They were inquisitive, just as you are. They tried to open that dome."

He pointed to the other side of the crater, to the smooth, still unmarked shell within which the departed rulers of this world had sealed their treasures. But it was no longer a dome: it was now an almost complete sphere, for the ground in which it had been set had been blasted away.

"They wrecked their ship, and many of them were killed. Yet despite that, they managed to make repairs and leave again, cutting off this section and stripping out everything of value. What a task that must have been!"

Alvin scarcely heard him. He was looking at the curious marker that had first drawn him to this spot—the slim shaft ringed by a horizontal circle a third of the way down from its tip. Alien and unfamiliar though it was, he could respond to the mute message it had carried down the ages.

Underneath those stones, if he cared to disturb them, was the answer to one question at least. It could remain unanswered; whatever these creatures might have been, they had earned their right to rest.

Hilvar scarcely heard the words Alvin whispered as they walked slowly back to the ship.

"I hope they got home," he said.

"And where now?" asked Hilvar, when they were once more out in space.

Alvin stared thoughtfully at the screen before replying.

"Do you think I should go back?" he said.

"It would be the sensible thing to do. Our luck may not hold out much longer, and who knows what other surprises these planets may have waiting for us?"

It was the voice of sanity and caution, and Alvin was now prepared to give it greater heed than he would have done a few days before. But he had come a long way, and waited all his life, for this moment; he would not turn back while there was still so much to see.

"We'll stay in the ship from now on," he said, "and we won't touch surface anywhere. That should be safe enough, surely."

Hilvar shrugged his shoulders, as if refusing to accept any responsibility for what might happen next. Now that Alvin was showing a certain amount of caution, he thought it unwise to admit that he was equally anxious to continue their exploring, though he had long ago abandoned all hope of meeting intelligent life upon any of these planets.

A double world lay ahead of them, a great planet with a smaller satellite beside it. The primary might have been the twin of the second world they had visited; it was clothed in that same blanket of livid green. There would be no point in landing here; this was a story they already knew.

Alvin brought the ship low over the surface of the satellite; he needed no warning from the complex mechanisms which protected him to know that there was no atmosphere here. All shadows had a sharp, clean edge, and there were no gradations between night and day. It was the first world on which he had seen something approaching night, for only one of the more distant suns was above the horizon in the area where they made first contact. The landscape was bathed in a dull red light, as though it had been dipped in blood.

For many miles they flew low above mountains that were still as jagged and sharp as in the distant ages of their birth. This was a world that had never known change or decay, had never been scoured by winds and rains. No eternity circuits were needed here to preserve objects in their pristine freshness.

But if there was no air, then there could have been no life—or could there have been?

"Of course," said Hilvar, when Alvin put the question to him, "there's nothing biologically absurd in the idea. Life can't originate in airless space—but it can evolve forms that will survive in it. It must have happened millions of times, whenever an inhabited planet lost its atmosphere."

"But would you expect *intelligent* life forms to exist in a vacuum? Wouldn't they have protected themselves against the loss of their air?"

"Probably, if it occurred *after* they achieved enough intelligence to stop it happening. But if the atmosphere went while they were still in the primitive state, they would have to adapt or perish. After they had adapted, they might then develop a very high intelligence. In fact, they probably would—the incentive would be so great."

The argument, decided Alvin, was a purely theoretical one, as far as this planet was concerned. Nowhere was there any sign that it had ever borne life, intelligent or otherwise. But in that case, what was the purpose of this world? The entire multiple system of the Seven Suns, he was now certain, was artificial, and this world must be part of its grand design.

It could, conceivably, be intended purely for ornament—to provide a moon in the sky of its giant companion. Even in that case, however, it seemed likely that it would be put to *some* use.

"Look," said Hilvar, pointing to the screen. "Over there, on the right."

Alvin changed the ship's course, and the landscape tilted around them. The red-lit rocks blurred with the speed of their motion; then the image stabilized, and sweeping below was the unmistakable evidence of life.

Unmistakable—yet also baffling. It took the form of a wide-spaced row of slender columns, each a hundred feet from its neighbor and twice as high. They stretched into the distance, dwindling in hypnotic perspective, until the far horizon swallowed them up.

Alvin swung the ship to the right, and began to race along the line of columns, wondering as he did so what purpose they could ever have served. They were absolutely uniform, marching in an unbroken file over hills and down into valleys. There was no sign that they had ever supported anything; they were smooth and featureless, tapering very slightly toward the top.

Quite abruptly, the line changed its course, turning sharply through a right angle. Alvin overshot by several miles before he reacted and was able to swing the ship around in the new direction.

The columns continued with the same unbroken stride across the landscape, their spacing perfectly regular. Then, fifty miles from the last change of course, they turned abruptly through another right angle. At this rate, thought Alvin, we will soon be back where we started.

The endless sequence of columns had so mesmerized them that when it was broken they were miles past the discontinuity before Hilvar cried out and made Alvin, who had noticed nothing, turn the ship back. They descended slowly, and as they circled above what Hilvar had found, a fantastic suspicion began to dawn in their minds—though at first neither dared mention it to the other.

Two of the columns had been broken off near their bases, and lay stretched out upon the rocks where they had fallen. Nor was that all; the two columns adjoining the gap had been bent outward by some irresistible force.

There was no escape from the awesome conclusion. Now Alvin knew what they had been flying over; it was something he had seen often enough in Lys, but until this moment the shocking change of scale had prevented recognition.

"Hilvar," he said, still hardly daring to put his thoughts into words, "do you know what this is?"

"It seems hard to believe, but we've been flying around the edge of a corral. This thing is a fence—a fence that hasn't been strong enough."

"People who keep pets," said Alvin, with the nervous laugh men sometimes use to conceal their awe, "should make sure they know how to keep them under control."

Hilvar did not react to his forced levity; he was staring at the broken barricade, his brow furrowed with thought.

"I don't understand it," he said at last. "Where could it have got food on a planet like this? And why did it break out of its pen? I'd give a lot to know what kind of animal it was."

"Perhaps it was left here, and broke out because it was hungry," Alvin surmised. "Or something may have made it annoyed."

"Let's go lower," said Hilvar. "I want to have a look at the ground."

They descended until the ship was almost touching the barren rock, and it was then that they noticed that the plain was pitted with innumerable small holes, no more than an inch or two wide. Outside the stockade, however, the ground was free from these mysterious pockmarks; they stopped abruptly at the line of the fence.

"You are right," said Hilvar. "It was hungry. But it wasn't an animal: it would be more accurate to call it a plant. It had exhausted the soil inside its pen, and had to find fresh food elsewhere. It probably moved quite slowly; perhaps it took years to break down those posts."

Alvin's imagination swiftly filled in the details he could never know with certainty. He did not doubt that Hilvar's analysis was basically correct, and that some botanical monster, perhaps moving too slowly for the eye to see, had fought a sluggish but relentless battle against the barriers that hemmed it in.

It might still be alive, even after all these ages, roving at will over the face of this planet. To look for it, however, would be a hopeless task, since it would mean quartering the surface of an entire globe. They made a desultory search in the few square miles around the gap, and located one great circular patch of pockmarks, almost five hundred feet across, where the creature had obviously stopped to feed—if one could apply that word to an organism that somehow drew its nourishment from solid rock.

As they lifted once more into space, Alvin felt a strange weariness come over him. He had seen so much, yet learned so little. There were many wonders on all these planets, but what he sought had fled them long ago. It would be useless, he knew, to visit the other worlds of the Seven Suns. Even if there was still intelligence in the Universe, where could he seek it now? He looked at the stars scattered like dust across the vision screen, and knew that what was left of time was not enough to explore them all.

A feeling of loneliness and oppression such as he had never before experienced seemed to overwhelm him. He could understand now the fear of Diaspar for the great spaces of the Universe, the terror that had made his people gather in the little microcosm of their city. It was hard to believe that, after all, they had been right.

He turned to Hilvar for support. But Hilvar was standing, fists tightly clenched and with a glazed look in his eyes. His head was tilted on one side; he seemed to be listening, straining every sense into the emptiness around them.

"What is it?" said Alvin urgently. He had to repeat the question before Hilvar showed any sign of hearing it. He was still staring into nothingness when he finally replied.

"There's something coming," he said slowly. "Something that I don't understand."

It seemed to Alvin that the cabin had suddenly become very cold, and the racial nightmare of the Invaders reared up to confront him in all its terror. With an effort of will that sapped his strength, he forced his mind away from panic.

"Is it friendly?" he asked. "Shall I run for Earth?"

Hilvar did not answer the first question—only the second. His voice was very faint, but showed no sign of alarm or fear. It held rather a vast astonishment and curiosity, as if he had encountered something so surprising that he could not be bothered to deal with Alvin's anxious query.

"You're too late," he said. "It's already here."

The Galaxy had turned many times on its axis since consciousness first came to Vanamonde. He could recall little of those first aeons and the creatures who had tended him then—but he could remember still his desolation when they had gone and left him alone among the stars. Down the ages since, he had wandered from sun to sun, slowly evolving and increasing his powers. Once he had dreamed of finding again those who had attended his birth, and though the dream had faded now, it had never wholly died.

On countless worlds he had found the wreckage that life had left behind, but intelligence he had discovered only once—and from the Black Sun he had fled in terror. Yet the Universe was very large, and the search had scarcely begun.

Far away though it was in space and time, the great burst of power from the heart of the Galaxy beckoned to Vanamonde across the light-years. It was utterly unlike the radiation of the stars, and it had appeared in his field of consciousness as suddenly as a meteor trail across a cloudless sky. He moved through space and time toward it, to the latest moment of its existence, sloughing from him in the way he knew the dead, unchanging pattern of the past.

The long metal shape, with its infinite complexities of structure, he could not understand, for it was as strange to him as almost all the things of the physical world. Around it still clung the aura of power that had drawn him across the Universe, but that was of no interest to him now. Carefully, with the delicate nervousness of a wild beast half poised for flight, he reached out toward the two minds he had discovered.

And then he knew that his long search was ended.

Alvin grasped Hilvar by the shoulders and shook him violently, trying to drag him back to a greater awareness of reality.

"Tell me what's happening!" he begged. "What do you want me to do?"

The remote, abstracted look slowly faded from Hilvar's eyes.

"I still don't understand," he said, "but there's no need to be frightened—I'm sure of that. Whatever it is, it won't harm us. It seems simply—interested."

Alvin was about to reply when he was suddenly overwhelmed by a sensation unlike any he had ever known before. A warm, tingling glow seemed to spread through his body; it lasted only a few seconds, but when it was gone he was no longer merely Alvin. Something was sharing his brain, overlapping it as one circle may partly cover another. He was conscious, also, of Hilvar's mind close at hand, equally entangled in whatever creature had descended upon them. The sensation was strange rather than unpleasant, and it gave Alvin his first glimpse of true telepathy—the power which in his people had so degenerated that it could now be used only to control machines.

Alvin had rebelled at once when Seranis had tried to dominate his mind, but he did not struggle against this intrusion. It would have been useless, and he knew that this creature, whatever it might be, was not unfriendly. He let himself relax, accepting without resistance the fact that an infinitely greater intelligence than his own was exploring his mind. But in that belief, he was not wholly right.

One of these minds, Vanamonde saw at once, was more sympathetic and accessible than the other. He could tell that both were filled with wonder at his presence, and that surprised him greatly. It was hard to believe that they could have forgotten; forgetfulness, like mortality, was beyond the comprehension of Vanamonde.

Communication was very difficult; many of the thought-images in their minds were so strange that he could hardly recognize them. He was puzzled and a little frightened by the recurrent fear pattern of the Invaders; it reminded him of his own emotions when the Black Sun first came into his field of knowledge.

But they knew nothing of the Black Sun, and now their own questions were beginning to form in his mind.

"What are you?"

He gave the only reply he could.

"I am Vanamonde."

There came a pause (how long the pattern of their thoughts took to form!) and then the question was repeated. They had not understood; that was strange, for surely their kind had given him his name for it to be among the memories of his birth. Those memories were very few, and they began strangely at a single point in time, but they were crystal clear.

Again their tiny thoughts struggled up into his consciousness.

"Where are the people who built the Seven Suns? What happened to them?"

He did not know; they could scarcely believe him, and their disappointment came sharp and clear across the abyss separating their minds from his. But they were patient and he was glad to help them, for their quest was the same as his and they gave him the first companionship he had ever known.

As long as he lived, Alvin did not believe he would ever again undergo so strange an experience as this soundless conversation. It was hard to believe that he could be little more than a spectator, for he did not care to admit, even to himself, that Hilvar's mind was in some ways so much more capable than his own. He could only wait and wonder, half dazed by the torrent of thought just beyond the limits of his understanding.

Presently Hilvar, rather pale and strained, broke off the contact and turned to his friend.

"Alvin," he said, his voice very tired. "There's something strange here. I don't understand it at all."

The news did a little to restore Alvin's self-esteem, and his face must have shown his feelings for Hilvar gave a sudden, sympathetic smile.

"I can't discover what this—Vanamonde—is," he continued. "It's a creature of tremendous knowledge, but it seems to have very little intelligence. Of course," he added, "its mind may be of such a different order that we can't understand it—yet somehow I don't believe that is the right explanation."

"Well, what *have* you learned?" asked Alvin with some impatience. "Does it know anything about the Seven Suns?"

Hilvar's mind still seemed very far away.

"They were built by many races, including our own," he said absently. "It can give me facts like that, but it doesn't seem to understand their meaning. I believe it's conscious of the past, without being able to interpret it. Everything that's ever happened seems jumbled together in its mind."

He paused thoughtfully for a moment; then his face lightened.

"There's only one thing to do; somehow or other, we must get Vanamonde to Earth so that our philosophers can study him."

"Would that be safe?" asked Alvin.

"Yes," answered Hilvar, thinking how uncharacteristic his friend's remark was. "Vanamonde is friendly. More than that, in fact, he seems almost affectionate."

And quite suddenly the thought that all the while had been hovering at the edge of Alvin's consciousness came clearly into view. He remembered Krif and all the small animals that were constantly escaping, to the annoyance or alarm of Hilvar's friends. And he recalled—how long ago that seemed!—the zoological purpose behind their expedition to Shalmirane.

Hilvar had found a new pet.

CHAPTER TWENTY-TWO

How completely unthinkable, Jeserac mused, this conference would have seemed only a few short days ago. The six visitors from Lys sat facing the Council, along a table placed across the open end of the horseshoe. It was ironic to remember that not long ago Alvin had stood at that same spot and heard the Council rule that Diaspar must be closed again from the world. Now the world had broken in upon it with a vengeance—and not only the world, but the Universe.

The Council itself had already changed. No less than five of its members were missing. They had been unable to face the responsibilities and problems now confronting them, and had followed the path that Khedron had already taken. It was, thought Jeserac, proof that Diaspar had failed if so many of its citizens were unable to face their first real challenge in millions of years. Many thousands of them had already fled into the brief oblivion of the Memory Banks, hoping that when they awoke the crisis would be past and Diaspar would be its familiar self again. They would be disappointed.

Jeserac had been co-opted to fill one of the vacant places on the Council. Though he was under something of a cloud, owing to his position as Alvin's tutor, his presence was so obviously essential that no one had suggested excluding him. He sat at one end of the horseshoe-shaped table—a position which gave him several advantages. Not only could he study the profiles of the visitors, but he could also see the faces of his fellow Councilors—and their expressions were sufficiently instructive.

There was no doubt that Alvin had been right, and the Council was slowly realizing the unpalatable truth. The delegates from Lys could think far more swiftly than the finest minds in Diaspar. Nor was that their only advantage, for they also showed an extraordinary degree of coordination which Jeserac guessed must be due to their telepathic powers. He wondered if they were reading the Councilors' thoughts, but decided that they would not have broken the solemn assurance without which this meeting would have been impossible.

Jeserac did not think that much progress had been made; for that matter, he did not see how it could have been made. The Council, which had barely accepted the existence of Lys, still seemed incapable of realizing what had happened. But it was clearly frightened—and so, he guessed, were the visitors, though they managed to conceal the fact better.

Jeserac himself was not as terrified as he had expected; his fears were still there, but he had faced them at last. Something of Alvin's own recklessness—or was it courage?—had begun to change his outlook and give him new horizons. He did not believe he would ever be able to set foot beyond the walls of Diaspar, but now he understood the impulse that had driven Alvin to do so.

The President's question caught him unawares, but he recovered himself quickly.

"I think," he said, "that it was sheer chance that this situation never arose before. We know that there were fourteen earlier Uniques, and there must have been some definite plan behind their creation. That plan, I believe, was to insure that Lys and Diaspar would not remain apart forever. Alvin has seen to that, but he has also done something which I do not imagine was ever in the original scheme. Could the Central Computer confirm that?"

The impersonal voice replied at once.

"The Councilor knows that I cannot comment on the instructions given to me by my designers."

Jeserac accepted the mild reproof.

"Whatever the cause, we cannot dispute the facts. Alvin has gone out into space. When he returns, you may prevent him leaving again—though I doubt if you will succeed, for he may have learned a great deal by then. And if what you fear has happened, there is nothing any of us can do about it. Earth is utterly helpless—as she has been for millions of centuries."

Jeserac paused and glanced along the tables. His words had pleased no one, nor had he expected them to do so.

"Yet I don't see why we should be alarmed. Earth is in no greater danger now than she has always been. Why should two men in a single small ship bring the wrath of the Invaders down upon us again? If we'll be honest with ourselves, we must admit that the Invaders could have destroyed our world ages ago."

There was a disapproving silence. This was heresy—and once Jeserac himself would have condemned it as such.

The President interrupted, frowning heavily.

"Is there not a legend that the Invaders spared Earth itself only on condition that Man never went into space again? And have we not now broken those conditions?"

"A legend, yes," said Jeserac. "We accept many things without question, and this is one of them. However, there is no proof of it. I find it hard to believe that anything of such importance would not be recorded in the memories of the Central Computer, yet it knows nothing of this pact. I have asked it, though only through the information machines. The Council may care to ask the question directly."

Jeserac saw no reason why he should risk a second admonishment by trespassing on forbidden territory, and waited for the President's reply.

It never came, for in that moment the visitors from Lys suddenly started in their seats, while their faces froze in simultaneous expressions of incredulity and alarm. They seemed to be listening while some faraway voice poured its message into their ears.

The Councilors waited, their own apprehension growing minute by minute as the soundless conversation proceeded. Then the leader of the delegation shook himself free from his trance, and turned apologetically to the President.

"We have just had some very strange and disturbing news from Lys," he said.

"Has Alvin returned to Earth?" asked the President.

"No—not Alvin. Something else."

As he brought his faithful ship down in the glade of Airlee, Alvin wondered if ever in human history any ship had brought such a cargo to Earth—if indeed, Vanamonde was located in the physical space of the machine. There had been no sign of him on the voyage; Hilvar believed, and his knowledge was more direct, that only Vanamonde's sphere of attention could be said to have any position in space. Vanamonde himself was not located anywhere—perhaps not even *anywhen.*

Seranis and five Senators were waiting for them as they emerged from the ship. One of the Senators Alvin had already met on his last visit; the other two from that previous meeting were, he gathered, now in Diaspar. He wondered how the delegation was faring, and how the city had reacted to the presence of the first intruders from outside in so many millions of years.

"It seems, Alvin," said Seranis drily, after she had greeted her son, "that you have a genius for discovering remarkable entities. Still, I think it will be some time before you can surpass your present achievement."

For once, it was Alvin's turn to be surprised.

"Then Vanamonde's arrived?"

"Yes, hours ago. Somehow he managed to trace the path your ship made on its outward journey—a staggering feat in itself, and one which raises interesting philosophical problems. There is some evidence that he reached Lys at the moment you discovered him, so that he is capable of infinite speeds. And that is not all. In the last few hours he has taught us more of history than we thought existed."

Alvin looked at her in amazement. Then he understood; it was not hard to imagine what the impact of Vanamonde must have been upon this people, with their keen perceptions and their wonderfully interlocking minds. They had reacted with surprising speed, and he had a sudden incongruous picture of Vanamonde, perhaps a little frightened, surrounded by the eager intellects of Lys.

"Have you discovered what he is?" Alvin asked.

"Yes. That was simple, though we still don't know his origin. He's a pure mentality and his knowledge seems to be unlimited. But he's childish, and I mean that quite literally."

"Of course!" cried Hilvar. "I should have guessed!"

Alvin looked puzzled, and Seranis took pity on him.

"I mean that although Vanamonde has a colossal, perhaps an infinite mind, he's immature and undeveloped. His actual intelligence is less than that of a human being"—she smiled a little wryly—"though his thought processes are much faster and he learns very quickly. He also has some powers we do not yet understand. The whole of the past seems open to his mind, in a way that's difficult to describe. He may have used that ability to follow your path back to Earth."

Alvin stood in silence, for once somewhat overcome. He realized how right Hilvar had been to bring Vanamonde to Lys. And he knew how lucky he had been ever to outwit Seranis; that was not something he would do twice in a lifetime.

"Do you mean," he asked, "that Vanamonde has only just been born?"

"By his standards, yes. His actual age is very great, though apparently less than Man's. The extraordinary thing is that he insists that *we* created him, and there's no doubt that his origin is bound up with all the great mysteries of the past."

"What's happening to Vanamonde now?" asked Hilvar in a slightly possessive voice.

"The historians of Grevarn are questioning him. They are trying to map out the main outlines of the past, but the work will take years. Vanamonde can describe the past in perfect detail, but as he doesn't understand what he sees it's very difficult to work with him."

Alvin wondered how Seranis knew all this; then he realized that probably every waking mind in Lys was watching the progress of the great research. He felt a sense of pride in the knowledge that he had now made as great a mark on Lys as on Diaspar, yet with that pride was mingled frustration. Here was something that he could never fully share nor understand: the direct contact even between human minds was as great a mystery to him as music must be to a deaf man or color to a blind one. Yet the people of Lys were now exchanging thoughts with this unimaginably alien being, whom he had led to Earth but whom he could never detect with any sense that he possessed.

There was no place for him here; when the inquiry was finished, he would be told the answers. He had opened the gates of infinity, and now felt awe—even fear—for all that he had done. For his own peace of mind, he must return to the tiny, familiar world of Diaspar, seeking its shelter while he came to grips with his dreams and his ambition. There was irony here; the one who had spurned the city to venture out among the stars was coming home as a frightened child runs back to its mother.

CHAPTER TWENTY-THREE

Diaspar was none too pleased to see Alvin again. The city was still in a ferment, like a giant beehive that had been violently stirred with a stick. It was still reluctant to face reality, but those who refused to admit the existence of Lys and the outside world no longer had a place to hide. The Memory Banks had ceased to accept them; those who tried to cling to their dreams, and to seek refuge in the future, now walked in vain into the Hall of Creation. The dissolving, heatless flame refused to greet them; they no longer awoke, their minds washed clean, a hundred thousand years further down the river of time. No appeal to the Central Computer was of any avail, nor would it explain the reason for its actions. The intended refugees had to turn sadly back into the city, to face the problems of their age.

Alvin and Hilvar had landed at the periphery of the park, not far from Council Hall. Until the last moment, Alvin was not certain that he could bring the ship into the city, through whatever screens fenced its sky from the outer world. The firmament of Diaspar, like all else about it, was artificial, or at least partly so. Night, with its starry reminder of all that man had lost, was never allowed to intrude upon the city; it was protected also from the storms that sometimes raged across the desert and filled the sky with moving walls of sand.

The invisible guardians let Alvin pass, and as Diaspar lay spread out beneath him, he knew that he had come home. However much the Universe and its mysteries might call him, this was where he was born and where he belonged. It would never satisfy him, yet always he would return. He had gone halfway across the Galaxy to learn this simple truth.

The crowds had gathered even before the ship landed, and Alvin wondered how his fellow citizens would receive him now that he had returned. He could read their faces easily enough, as he watched them through the viewing screen before he opened the air lock. The dominant emotion seemed to be curiosity—in itself something new in Diaspar. Mingled with that was apprehension, while here and there were unmistakable signs of fear. No one, Alvin thought a little wistfully, seemed glad to see him back.

The Council, on the other hand, positively welcomed him—though not out of pure friendship. Though he had caused this crisis, he alone could give the facts on which future policy must be based. He was listened to with deep attention as he described his flight to the Seven Suns and his meeting with Vanamonde. Then he answered innumerable questions, with a patience which probably surprised his interrogators. Uppermost in their minds, he quickly discovered, was the fear of the Invaders, though they never mentioned the name and were clearly unhappy when he broached the subject directly.

"If the Invaders are still in this Universe," Alvin told the Council, "then surely I should have met them at its very center. But there is no intelligent life among the Seven Suns; we had already guessed that before Vanamonde confirmed it. I believe that the Invaders departed ages ago; certainly Vanamonde, who appears to be at least as old as Diaspar, knows nothing of them."

"I have a suggestion," said one of the Councilors suddenly. "Vanamonde may be a descendant of the Invaders, in some way beyond our present understanding. He has forgotten his origin, but that does not mean that one day he may not be dangerous again."

Hilvar, who was present merely as a spectator, did not wait for permission to speak. It was the first time that Alvin had ever seen him angry.

"Vanamonde has looked into my mind," he said, "and I have glimpsed something of his. My people have already learned much about him, though they have not yet discovered what he is. But one thing is certain—he is friendly, and was glad to find us. We have nothing to fear from him."

There was a brief silence after this outburst, and Hilvar relaxed with a somewhat embarrassed expression. It was noticeable that the tension in the Council Chamber lessened from then on, as if a cloud had lifted from the spirits of those present. Certainly the President made no attempt, as he was supposed to do, to censure Hilvar for his interruption.

It was clear to Alvin, as he listened to the debate, that three schools of thought were represented on the Council. The conservatives, who were in a minority, still hoped that the clock could be turned back and that the old order could somehow be restored. Against all reason, they clung to the hope that Diaspar and Lys could be persuaded to forget each other again.

The progressives were an equally small minority; the fact that there were any on the Council at all pleased and surprised Alvin. They did not exactly welcome this invasion of the outer world, but they were determined to make the best of it. Some of them went so far as to suggest that there might be a way of breaking through the psychological barriers which for so long had sealed Diaspar even more effectively than the physical ones.

Most of the Council, accurately reflecting the mood of the city, had adopted an attitude of watchful caution, while they waited for the pattern of the future to emerge. They realized that they could make no general plans, nor try to carry out any definite policy, until the storm had passed.

Jeserac joined Alvin and Hilvar when the session was over. He seemed to have changed since they had last met—and last parted—in the Tower of Loranne, with the desert spread out beneath them. The change was not one that Alvin had expected, though it was one that he was to encounter more and more often in the days to come.

Jeserac seemed younger, as if the fires of life had found fresh fuel and were burning more brightly in his veins. Despite his age, he was one of those who could accept the challenge that Alvin had thrown to Diaspar.

"I have some news for you, Alvin," he said. "I think you know Senator Gerane."

Alvin was puzzled for a moment; then he remembered.

"Of course—he was one of the first men I met in Lys. Isn't he a member of their delegation?"

"Yes; we have grown to know each other quite well. He is a brilliant man, and understands more about the human mind than I would have believed possible—though he tells me that by the standards of Lys he is only a beginner. While he is here, he is starting a project which will be very close to your heart. He is hoping to analyze the compulsion which keeps us in the city, and he believes that once he has discovered how it was imposed, he will be able to remove it. About twenty of us are already co-operating with him."

"And you are one of them?"

"Yes," replied Jeserac, showing the nearest approach to bashfulness that Alvin had ever seen or ever would see. "It is not easy, and certainly not pleasant—but it is stimulating."

"How does Gerane work?"

"He is operating through the sagas. He has had a whole series of them constructed, and studies our reactions when we are experiencing them. I never thought, at my age, that I should go back to my childhood recreations again!"

"What are the sagas?" asked Hilvar.

"Imaginary dream worlds," explained Alvin. "At least, most of them are imaginary, though some are probably based on historical facts. There are millions of them recorded in the memory cells of the city; you can take your choice of any kind of adventure or experience you wish, and it will seem utterly real to you while the impulses are being fed into your mind." He turned to Jeserac.

"What kind of sagas does Gerane take you into?"

"Most of them are concerned, as you might expect, with leaving Diaspar. Some have taken us back to our very earliest lives, to as near to the founding of the city as we can get. Gerane believes that the closer he can get to the origin of this compulsion, the more easily he will be able to undermine it."

Alvin felt very encouraged by this news. His work would be merely half accomplished if he had opened the gates of Diaspar—only to find that no one would pass through them.

"Do you *really* want to be able to leave Diaspar?" asked Hilvar shrewdly.

"No," replied Jeserac, without hesitation. "I am terrified of the idea. But I realize that we were completely wrong in thinking that Diaspar was all the world that mattered, and logic tells me that something has to be done to rectify the mistake. Emotionally, I am still quite incapable of leaving the city; perhaps I always shall be. Gerane thinks he can get some of us to come to Lys, and I am willing to help him with the experiment—even though half the time I hope that it will fail."

Alvin looked at his old tutor with a new respect. He no longer discounted the power of suggestion, nor underestimated the forces which could compel a man to act in defiance of logic. He could not help comparing Jeserac's calm courage with Khedron's panic flight into the future—though with his new understanding of human nature he no longer cared to condemn the Jester for what he had done.

Gerane, he was certain, would accomplish what he had set out to do.

Jeserac might be too old to break the pattern of a lifetime, however willing he might be to start afresh. That did not matter, for others would succeed, with the skilled guidance of the psychologists of Lys. And once a few had escaped from their billion-year-old mold, it would only be a question of time before the remainder could follow.

He wondered what would happen to Diaspar—and to Lys—when the barriers were fully down. Somehow, the best elements of both must be saved, and welded into a new and healthier culture. It was a terrifying task, and would need all the wisdom and all the patience that each could bring to bear.

Some of the difficulties of the forthcoming adjustments had already been encountered. The visitors from Lys had, politely enough, refused to live in the homes provided for them in the city. They had set up their own temporary accommodation in the park, among surroundings which reminded them of Lys. Hilvar was the only exception; though he disliked living in a house with indeterminate walls and ephemeral furniture, he bravely accepted Alvin's hospitality, reassured by the promise that they would not stay here for long.

Hilvar had never felt lonely in his life, but he knew loneliness in Diaspar. The city was stranger to him than Lys had been to Alvin, and he was oppressed and overwhelmed by its infinite complexity and by the myriads of strangers who seemed to crowd every inch of space around him. He knew, if only in a tenuous manner, everyone in Lys, whether he had met them or not. In a thousand lifetimes he could never know everyone in Diaspar, and though he realized that this was an irrational feeling, it left him vaguely depressed. Only his loyalty to Alvin held him here in a world that had nothing in common with his own.

He had often tried to analyze his feelings toward Alvin. His friendship sprang, he knew, from the same source that inspired his sympathy for all small and struggling creatures. This would have astonished those who thought of Alvin as willful, stubborn, and self-centered, needing no affection from anyone and incapable of returning it even if it was offered.

Hilvar knew better than this; he had sensed it instinctively even from the first. Alvin was an explorer, and all explorers are seeking something they have lost. It is seldom that they find it, and more seldom still that the attainment brings them greater happiness than the quest.

What Alvin was seeking, Hilvar did not know. He was driven by forces that had been set in motion ages before, by the men of genius who planned Diaspar with such perverse skill—or by the men of even greater genius who had opposed them. Like every human being, Alvin was in some measure a machine, his actions predetermined by his inheritance. That did not alter his need for understanding and sympathy, nor did it render him immune to loneliness or frustration. To his own people, he was so unaccountable a creature that they sometimes forgot that he still shared their emotions. It needed a stranger from a totally different environment to see him as another human being.

Within a few days of arriving in Diaspar, Hilvar had met more people than in his entire life. Met them—and had grown to know practically none. Because they were so crowded together, the inhabitants of the city maintained a reserve that was hard to penetrate. The only privacy they knew was that of the mind, and they still clung to this even as they made their way through the endless social activities of Diaspar. Hilvar felt sorry for them, though he knew that they felt no need for his sympathy. They did not realize what they were missing—they could not understand the warm sense of community, the feeling of *belonging,* which linked everyone together in the telepathic society of Lys. Indeed, though they were polite enough to try to conceal it, it was obvious that most of the people he spoke to looked upon him pityingly as leading an incredibly dull and drab existence.

Eriston and Etania, Alvin's guardians, Hilvar quickly dismissed as kindly but totally baffled nonentities. He found it very confusing to hear Alvin refer to them as his father and mother—words which in Lys still retained their ancient biological meaning. It required a continual effort of imagination to remember that the laws of life and death had been repealed by the makers of Diaspar, and there were times when it seemed to Hilvar that despite all the activity around him, the city was half empty because it had no children.

He wondered what would happen to Diaspar now that its long isolation was over. The best thing the city could do, he decided, was to destroy the Memory Banks which had held it entranced for so many ages. Miraculous though they were—perhaps the supreme triumph of the science that had produced them—they were the creations of a sick culture, a culture that had been afraid of many things. Some of those fears had been based on reality, but others, it now seemed, lay only in the imagination. Hilvar knew a little of the pattern that was beginning to emerge from the exploration of Vanamonde's mind. In a few days, Diaspar would know it too—and would discover how much of its past had been a myth.

Yet if the Memory Banks were destroyed, within a thousand years the city would be dead, since its people had lost the power to reproduce themselves. That was the dilemma that had to be faced, but already Hilvar had glimpsed one possible solution. There was always an answer to any technical problem, and his people were masters of the biological sciences. What had been done could be undone, if Diaspar so wished.

First, however, the city would have to learn what it had lost. Its education would take many years—perhaps many centuries. But it was beginning; very soon the impact of the first lesson would shake Diaspar as profoundly as had contact with Lys itself.

It would shake Lys too. For all the difference between the two cultures, they had sprung from the same roots—and they had shared the same illusions. They would both be healthier when they looked once more, with a calm and steadfast gaze, into the past which they had lost.

CHAPTER TWENTY-FOUR

The amphitheater had been designed to hold the entire waking population of Diaspar, and scarcely one of its ten million places was empty. As he looked down the great curving sweep from his vantage point high up the slope, Alvin was irresistibly reminded of Shalmirane. The two craters were of the same shape, and almost the same size. If one packed the crater of Shalmirane with humanity, it would look very much like this.

There was, however, one fundamental difference between the two. The great bowl of Shalmirane existed; this amphitheater did not. Nor had it ever done so; it was merely a phantom, a pattern of electronic charges, slumbering in the memory of the Central Computer until the need came to call it forth. Alvin knew that in reality he was still in his room, and that all the myriads of people who appeared to surround him were equally in their own homes. As long as he made no attempt to move from this spot, the illusion was perfect. He could believe that Diaspar had been abolished and that all its citizens had been assembled here in this enormous concavity.

Not once in a thousand years did the life of the city stop so that all its people could meet in Grand Assembly. In Lys also, Alvin knew, the equivalent of this gathering was taking place. There it would be a meeting of minds, but perhaps associated with it would be an apparent meeting of bodies, as imaginary yet as seemingly real as this.

He could recognize most of the faces around him, out to the limits of unaided vision. More than a mile away, and a thousand feet below, was the little circular stage upon which the attention of the entire world was now fixed. It was hard to believe that he could see anything from such a distance, but Alvin knew that when the address began, he would hear and observe everything that happened as clearly as anyone else in Diaspar.

The stage filled with mist; the mist became Callitrax, leader of the group whose task it had been to reconstruct the past from the information which Vanamonde had brought to Earth. It had been a stupendous, almost an impossible undertaking, and not merely because of the spans of time involved. Only once, with the mental help of Hilvar, had Alvin been given a brief glimpse into the mind of the strange being they had discovered—or who had discovered them. To Alvin, the thoughts of Vanamonde were as meaningless as a thousand voices shouting together in some vast, echoing cave. Yet the men of Lys could disentangle them, could record them to be analyzed at leisure. Already, so it was rumored—though Hilvar would neither deny nor confirm this—what they had discovered was so strange that it bore scarcely any resemblance to the history which all the human race had accepted for a billion years.

Callitrax began to speak. To Alvin, as to everyone else in Diaspar, the clear, precise voice seemed to come from a point only a few inches away. Then, in a manner that was hard to define, just as the geometry of a dream defies logic yet rouses no surprise in the mind of the dreamer, Alvin was standing beside Callitrax while at the same time he retained his position high up on the slope of the amphitheater. The paradox did not puzzle him; he simply accepted it without question, like all the other masteries over time and space which science had given him.

Very briefly, Callitrax ran through the accepted history of the race. He spoke of the unknown peoples of the Dawn Civilizations, who had left behind them nothing but a handful of great names and the fading legends of the Empire. Even at the beginning, so the story went, Man had desired the stars—and had at last attained them. For millions of years he had expanded across the Galaxy, gathering system after system beneath his sway. Then, out of the darkness beyond the rim of the Universe, the Invaders had struck and wrenched from him all that he had won.

The retreat to the Solar System had been bitter and must have lasted many ages. Earth itself was barely saved by the fabulous battles that raged around Shalmirane. When all was over, Man was left with only his memories and the world on which he had been born.

Since then, all else had been long-drawn anticlimax. As an ultimate irony, the race that had hoped to rule the Universe had abandoned most of its own tiny world, and had split into the two isolated cultures of Lys and Diaspar—oases of life in a desert that sundered them as effectively as the gulfs between the stars.

Callitrax paused; to Alvin, as to everyone in the great assembly, it seemed that the historian was looking directly at him with eyes that had witnessed things which even now they could not wholly credit.

"So much," said Callitrax, "for the tales we have believed since our records began. I must tell you now that they are false—false in every detail—*so false that even now we have not wholly reconciled them with the truth.*"

He waited for the full meaning of his words to strike home. Then, speaking slowly and carefully, he gave to both Lys and Diaspar the knowledge that had been won from the mind of Vanamonde.

It was not even true that Man had reached the Stars. The whole of his little empire was bounded by the orbits of Pluto and Persephone, for interstellar space proved a barrier beyond his power to cross. His entire civilization was huddled around the sun, and was still very young when—the stars reached him.

The impact must have been shattering. Despite his failures, Man had never doubted that one day he would conquer the depths of space. He believed too that if the Universe held his equals, it did not hold his superiors. Now he knew that both beliefs were wrong, and that out among the stars were minds far greater than his own. For many centuries, first in the ships of other races and later in machines built with borrowed knowledge, Man had explored the Galaxy. Everywhere he found cultures he could understand but could not match, and here and there he encountered minds which would soon have passed altogether beyond his comprehension.

The shock was tremendous, but it proved the making of the race. Sadder and infinitely wiser, Man had returned to the Solar System to brood upon the knowledge he had gained. He would accept the challenge, and slowly he evolved a plan which gave hope for the future.

Once the physical sciences had been Man's greatest interest. Now he turned even more fiercely to genetics and the study of the mind. Whatever the cost, he would drive himself to the limits of his evolution.

The great experiment had consumed the entire energies of the race for millions of years. All that striving, all that sacrifice and toil, became only a handful of words in Callitrax's narrative. It had brought Man his greatest victories. He had banished disease; he could live forever if he wished, and in mastering telepathy he had bent the most subtle of all powers to his will.

He was ready to go out again, relying upon his own resources, into the great spaces of the Galaxy. He would meet as an equal the races of the worlds from which he had once turned aside. And he would play his full part in the story of the Universe.

These things he did. From this age, perhaps the most spacious of all history, came the legends of the Empire. It had been an Empire of many races, but this had been forgotten in the drama, too tremendous for tragedy, in which it had come to its end.

The Empire had lasted for at least a million years. It must have known many crises, perhaps even wars, but all these were lost in the sweep of great races moving together toward maturity.

"We can be proud," continued Callitrax, "of the part our ancestors played in this story. Even when they had reached their cultural plateau, they lost none of their initiative. We deal now with conjecture rather than proved fact, but it seems certain that the experiments which were at once the Empire's downfall and its crowning glory were inspired and directed by Man.

"The philosophy underlying these experiments appears to have been this. Contact with other species had shown Man how profoundly a race's world-picture depended upon its physical body and the sense organs with which it was equipped. It was argued that a true picture of the Universe could be attained, if at all, only by a mind that was free from such physical limitations—a pure mentality, in fact. This was a conception common among many of Earth's ancient religious faiths, and it seems strange that an idea which had no rational origin should finally become one of the greatest goals of science.

"No disembodied intelligence had ever been encountered in the natural Universe; the Empire set out to create one. We have forgotten, with so much else, the skills and knowledge that made this possible. The scientists of the Empire had mastered all the forces of Nature, all the secrets of time and space. As our minds are the by-product of an immensely intricate arrangement of brain cells, linked together by the network of the nervous system, so they strove to create a brain whose components were not material, but patterns embossed upon space itself. Such a brain, if one can call it that, would use electrical or yet higher forces for its operation, and would be completely free from the tyranny of matter. It could function with far greater speed than any organic intelligence; it could endure as long as there was an erg of free energy left in the Universe, and no limit could be seen for its powers. Once created, it would develop potentialities which even its makers could not foresee.

"Largely as a result of the experience gained in his own regeneration, Man suggested that the creation of such beings should be attempted. It was the greatest challenge ever thrown out to intelligence in the Universe, and after centuries of debate it was accepted. All the races of the Galaxy joined together in its fulfillment.

"More than a million years were to separate the dream from the reality. Civilizations were to rise and fall, again and yet again the age-long toil of worlds was to be lost, but the goal was never forgotten. One day we may know the full story of this, the greatest sustained effort in all history. Today we only know that its ending was a disaster that almost wrecked the Galaxy.

"Into this period Vanamonde's mind refuses to go. There is a narrow region of time which is blocked to him; but only, we believe, by his own fears. At its beginning we can see the Empire at the summit of its glory, taut with the expectation of coming success. At its end, only a few thousand years later, the Empire is shattered and the stars themselves are dimmed as though drained of their power. Over the Galaxy hangs a pall of fear, a fear with which is linked the name: 'The Mad Mind.'

"What must have happened in that short period is not hard to guess. The pure mentality had been created, but it was either insane or, as seems more likely from other sources, was implacably hostile to matter. For centuries it ravaged the Universe until brought under control by forces at which we cannot guess. Whatever weapon the Empire used in its extremity squandered the resources of the stars; from the memories of that conflict spring some, though not all, of the legends of the Invaders. But of this I shall presently say more.

"The Mad Mind could not be destroyed, for it was immortal. It was driven to the edge of the Galaxy and there imprisoned in a way we do not understand. Its prison was a strange artificial star known as the Black Sun, and there it remains to this day. When the Black Sun dies, it will be free again. How far in the future that day lies there is no way of telling."

Callitrax became silent, as if lost in his own thoughts, utterly unconscious of the fact that the eyes of all the world were upon him. In the long silence, Alvin glanced over the packed multitude around him, seeking to read their minds as they faced this revelation—and this unknown threat which must now replace the myth of the Invaders. For the most part, the faces of his fellow citizens were frozen in disbelief; they were still struggling to reject their false past, and could not yet accept the yet stranger reality that had superseded it.

Callitrax began to speak again in a quiet, more subdued voice as he described the last days of the Empire. This was the age, Alvin realized as the picture unfolded before him, in which he would have liked to have lived. There had been adventure then, and a superb and dauntless courage—the courage that could snatch victory from the teeth of disaster.

"Though the Galaxy had been laid waste by the Mad Mind, the resources of the Empire were still enormous, and its spirit was unbroken. With a courage at which we can only marvel, the great experiment was resumed and a search made for the flaw that had caused the catastrophe. There were now, of course, many who opposed the work and predicted further disasters, but they were overruled. The project went ahead and, with the knowledge so bitterly gained, this time it succeeded.

"The new race that was born had a potential intellect that could not even be measured. But it was completely infantile; we do not know if this was expected by its creators, but it seems likely that they knew it to be inevitable. Millions of years would be needed before it reached maturity, and nothing could be done to hasten the process. Vanamonde was the first of these minds; there must be others elsewhere in the Galaxy, but we believe that only a very few were created, for Vanamonde has never encountered any of his fellows.

"The creation of the pure mentalities was the greatest achievement of Galactic civilization; in it Man played a major and perhaps a dominant part. I have made no reference to Earth itself, for its story is merely a tiny thread in an enormous tapestry. Since it had always been drained of its most adventurous spirits, our planet had inevitably become highly conservative, and in the end it opposed the scientists who created Vanamonde. Certainly it played no part at all in the final act.

"The work of the Empire was now finished; the men of that age looked around at the stars they had ravaged in their desperate peril, and they made their decision. They would leave the Universe to Vanamonde.

"There is a mystery here—a mystery we may never solve, for Vanamonde cannot help us. All we know is that the Empire made contact with—something—very strange and very great, far away around the curve of the Cosmos, at the other extremity of space itself. What it was we can only guess, but its call must have been of immense urgency, and immense promise. Within a very short period of time our ancestors and their fellow races have gone upon a journey which we cannot follow. Vanamonde's thoughts seem to be bounded by the confines of the Galaxy, but through his mind we have watched the beginnings of this great and mysterious adventure. Here is the image that we have reconstructed; now you are going to look more than a billion years into the past—"

A pale wraith of its former glory, the slowly turning wheel of the Galaxy hung in nothingness. Throughout its length were the great empty rents which the Mad Mind had torn—wounds that in ages to come the drifting stars would fill. But they would never replace the splendor that had gone.

Man was about to leave his Universe, as long ago he had left his world. And not only Man, but the thousand other races that had worked with him to make the Empire. They were gathered together, here at the edge of the Galaxy, with its whole thickness between them and the goal they would not reach for ages.

They had assembled a fleet before which imagination quailed. Its flagships were suns, its smallest vessels, planets. An entire globular cluster, with all its solar systems and all their teeming worlds, was about to be launched across infinity.

The long line of fire smashed through the heart of the Universe, leaping from star to star. In a moment of time a thousand suns had died, feeding their energies to the monstrous shape that had torn along the aix of the Galaxy, and was now receding into the abyss. . . .

"So the Empire left our Universe, to meet its destiny elsewhere. When its heirs, the pure mentalities, have reached their full stature, it may return again. But that day must still lie far ahead.

"This, in its briefest and most superficial outlines, is the story of Galactic civilization. Our own history, which to us seems so important, is no more than a belated and trivial epilogue, though one so complex that we have not been able to unravel all its details. It seems that many of the older, less adventurous races refused to leave their homes; our direct ancestors were among them. Most of these races fell into decadence and are now extinct, though some may still survive. Our own world barely escaped the same fate. During the Transition Centuries—which actually lasted for millions of years—the knowledge of the past was lost or else deliberately destroyed. The latter, hard though it is to believe, seems more probable. For ages, Man sank into a superstitious yet still scientific barbarism during which he distorted history to remove his sense of impotence and failure. The legends of the Invader are completely false, although the desperate struggle against the Mad Mind undoubtedly contributed something to them. Nothing drove our ancestors back to Earth except the sickness in their souls.

"When we made this discovery, one problem in particular puzzled us in Lys. The Battle of Shalmirane never occurred—yet Shalmirane existed, and exists to this day. What is more, it was one of the greatest weapons of destruction ever built.

"It took us some time to resolve this puzzle, but the answer, once it was found, was very simple. Long ago our Earth had a single giant satellite, the Moon. When, in the tug of war between the tides and gravity, the Moon at last began to fall, it became necessary to destroy it. Shalmirane was built for that purpose, and around its use were woven the legends you all know."

Callitrax smiled a little ruefully at his immense audience.

"There are many such legends, partly true and partly false, and other paradoxes in our past which have not yet been resolved. That problem, though, is one for the psychologist rather than the historian. Even the records of the Central Computer cannot be wholly trusted, and bear clear evidence of tampering in the very remote past.

"On Earth, only Diaspar and Lys survived the period of decadence —Diaspar thanks to the perfection of its machines, Lys owing to its partial isolation and the unusual intellectual powers of its people. But both cultures, even when they had struggled back to their former level, were distorted by the fears and myths they had inherited.

"These fears need haunt us no longer. It is not my duty as a historian to predict the future, only to observe and interpret the past. But its lesson is clear enough; we have lived too long out of contact with reality, and now the time has come to rebuild our lives."

CHAPTER TWENTY-FIVE

Jeserac walked in silent wonder through the streets of a Diaspar he had never seen. So different was it, indeed, from the city in which he had passed all his lives that he would never have recognized it. Yet he knew that it was Diaspar, though *how* he knew, he did not pause to ask.

The streets were narrow, the buildings lower—and the park was gone. Or, rather, it did not yet exist. This was the Diaspar before the change, the Diaspar that had been open to the world and to the Universe. The sky above the city was pale blue and flecked with raveled wisps of cloud, slowly twisting and turning in the winds that blew across the face of this younger Earth.

Passing through and beyond the clouds were more substantial voyagers of the sky. Miles above the city, lacing the heavens with their silent tracery, the ships that linked Diaspar with the outer world came and went upon their business. Jeserac stared for a long time at the mystery and wonder of the open sky, and for a moment fear brushed against his soul. He felt naked and unprotected, conscious that this peaceful, blue dome above his head was no more than the thinnest of shells—that beyond it lay space, with all its mystery and menace.

The fear was not strong enough to paralyze his will. In part of his mind Jeserac knew that this whole experience was a dream, and a dream could not harm him. He would drift through it, savoring all that it brought to him, until he woke once more in the city that he knew.

He was walking into the heart of Diaspar, toward the point where in his own age stood the Tomb of Yarlan Zey. There was no tomb here, in this ancient city—only a low, circular building with many arched doorways leading into it. By one of those doorways a man was waiting for him.

Jeserac should have been overcome with astonishment, but nothing could surprise him now. Somehow it seemed right and natural that he should now be face to face with the man who had built Diaspar.

"You recognize me, I imagine," said Yarlan Zey.

"Of course; I have seen your statue a thousand times. You are Yarlan Zey, and this is Diaspar as it was a billion years ago. I know I am dreaming, and that neither of us is really here."

"Then you need not be alarmed at anything that happens. So follow me, and remember that nothing can harm you, since whenever you wish you can wake up in Diaspar—in your own age."

Obediently, Jeserac followed Yarlan Zey into the building, his mind a receptive, uncritical sponge. Some memory, or echo of a memory, warned him of what was going to happen next, and he knew that once he would have shrunk from it in horror. Now, however, he felt no fear. Not only did he feel protected by the knowledge that this experience was not real, but the presence of Yarlan Zey seemed a talisman against any dangers that might confront him.

There were few people drifting down the glideways that led into the depths of the building, and they had no other company when presently they stood in silence beside the long, streamlined cylinder which, Jeserac knew, could carry him out of the city on a journey that would once have shattered his mind. When his guide pointed to the open door, he paused for no more than a moment on the threshold, and then was through.

"You see?" said Yarlan Zey with a smile. "Now relax, and remember that you are safe—that nothing can touch you."

Jeserac believed him. He felt only the faintest tremor of apprehension as the tunnel entrance slid silently toward him, and the machine in which he was traveling began to gain speed as it hurtled through the depths of the earth. Whatever fears he might have had were forgotten in his eagerness to talk with this almost mythical figure from the past.

"Does it not seem strange to you," began Yarlan Zey, "that though the skies are open to us, we have tried to bury ourselves in the Earth? It is the beginning of the sickness whose ending you have seen in your age. Humanity is trying to hide; it is frightened of what lies out there in space, and soon it will have closed all the doors that lead into the Universe."

"But I saw spaceships in the sky above Diaspar," said Jeserac.

"You will not see them much longer. We have lost contact with the stars, and soon even the planets will be deserted. It took us millions of years to make the outward journey—but only centuries to come home again. And in a little while we will have abandoned almost all of Earth itself."

"Why did you do it?" asked Jeserac. He knew the answer, yet somehow felt impelled to ask the question.

"We needed a shelter to protect us from two fears—fear of death, and fear of space. We were a sick people, and wanted no further part in the Universe—so we pretended that it did not exist. We had seen chaos raging through the stars, and yearned for peace and stability. Therefore Diaspar had to be closed, so that nothing new could ever enter it.

"We designed the city that you know, and invented a false past to conceal our cowardice. Oh, we were not the first to do that—but we were the first to do it so thoroughly. And we redesigned the human spirit, robbing it of ambition and the fiercer passions, so that it would be contented with the world it now possessed.

"It took a thousand years to build the city and all its machines. As each of us completed his task, his mind was washed clean of its memories, the carefully planned pattern of false ones was implanted, and his identity was stored in the city's circuits until the time came to call it forth again.

"So at last there came a day when there was not a single man alive in Diaspar; there was only the Central Computer, obeying the orders which we had fed into it, and controlling the Memory Banks in which we were sleeping. There was no one who had any contact with the past—and so at this point, history began.

"Then, one by one, in a predetermined sequence, we were called out of the memory circuits and given flesh again. Like a machine that had just been built and was now set operating for the first time, Diaspar began to carry out the duties for which it had been designed.

"Yet some of us had had doubts even from the beginning. Eternity was a long time; we recognized the risks involved in leaving no outlet, and trying to seal ourselves completely from the Universe. We could not defy the wishes of our culture, so we worked in secret, making the modifications we thought necessary.

"The Uniques were our invention. They would appear at long intervals and would, if circumstances allowed them, discover if there was anything beyond Diaspar that was worth the effort of contacting. We never imagined that it would take so long for one of them to succeed—nor did we imagine that his success would be so great."

Despite that suspension of the critical faculties which is the very essence of a dream, Jeserac wondered fleetingly how Yarlan Zey could speak with such knowledge of things that had happened a billion years after his time. It was very confusing . . . he did not know where in time or space he was.

The journey was coming to an end; the walls of the tunnel no longer flashed past him at such breakneck speed. Yarlan Zey began to speak with an urgency, and an authority, which he had not shown before.

"The past is over; we did our work, for better or for ill, and that is finished with. When you were created, Jeserac, you were given that fear of the outer world, and that compulsion to stay within the city, that you share with everyone else in Diaspar. You know now that that fear was groundless, that it was artificially imposed on you. I, Yarlan Zey, who gave it to you, now release you from its bondage. Do you understand?"

With those last words, the voice of Yarlan Zey became louder and louder, until it seemed to reverberate through all of space. The subterranean carrier in which he was speeding blurred and trembled around Jeserac as if his dream was coming to an end. Yet as the vision faded, he could still hear that imperious voice thundering into his brain: "You are no longer afraid, Jeserac. *You are no longer afraid.*"

He struggled up toward wakefulness, as a diver climbs from the ocean depths back to the surface of the sea. Yarlan Zey had vanished, but there was a strange interregnum when voices which he knew but could not recognize talked to him encouragingly, and he felt himself supported by friendly hands. Then like a swift dawn reality came flooding back.

He opened his eyes, and saw Alvin and Hilvar and Gerane standing anxiously beside him. But he paid no heed to them; his mind was too filled with the wonder that now lay spread before him—the panorama of forests and rivers, and the blue vault of the open sky.

He was in Lys; and he was not afraid.

No one disturbed him as the timeless moment imprinted itself forever on his mind. At last, when he had satisfied himself that this indeed was real, he turned to his companions.

"Thank you, Gerane," he said. "I never believed you would succeed."

The psychologist, looking very pleased with himself, was making delicate adjustments to a small machine that hung in the air beside him.

"You gave us some anxious moments," he admitted. "Once or twice you started to ask questions that couldn't be answered logically, and I was afraid I would have to break the sequence."

"Suppose Yarlan Zey had not convinced me—what would you have done then?"

"We would have kept you unconscious, and taken you back to Diaspar where you could have waked up naturally, without ever knowing that you'd been to Lys."

"And that image of Yarlan Zey you fed into my mind—how much of what he said was the truth?"

"Most of it, I believe. I was much more anxious that my little saga should be convincing rather than historically accurate, but Callitrax has examined it and can find no errors. It is certainly consistent with all that we know about Yarlan Zey and the origins of Diaspar."

"So now we can really open the city," said Alvin. "It may take a long time, but eventually we'll be able to neutralize this fear so that everyone who wishes can leave Diaspar."

"It *will* take a long time," replied Gerane dryly. "And don't forget that Lys is hardly large enough to hold several hundred million extra people, if all your people decide to come here. I don't think that's likely, but it's possible."

"That problem will solve itself," answered Alvin. "Lys may be tiny, but the world is wide. Why should we let the desert keep it all?"

"So you are still dreaming, Alvin," said Jeserac with a smile. "I was wondering what there was left for you to do."

Alvin did not answer; that was a question which had become more and more insistent in his own mind during the past few weeks. He remained lost in thought, falling behind the others, as they walked down the hill toward Airlee. Would the centuries that lay ahead of him be one long anticlimax?

The answer lay in his own hands. He had discharged his destiny; now, perhaps, he could begin to live.

CHAPTER TWENTY-SIX

There is a special sadness in achievement, in the knowledge that a long-desired goal has been attained at last, and that life must now be shaped toward new ends. Alvin knew that sadness as he wandered alone through the forests and fields of Lys. Not even Hilvar accompanied him, for there are times when a man must be apart even from his closest friends.

He did not wander aimlessly, though he never knew which village would be his next port of call. He was seeking no particular place, but a mood, an influence—indeed, a way of life. Diaspar had no need of him now; the ferments he had introduced into the city were working swiftly, and nothing he could do would accelerate or retard the changes that were happening there.

This peaceful land would also change. Often he wondered if he had done wrong, in the ruthless drive to satisfy his own curiosity, by opening up the ancient way between the two cultures. Yet surely it was better that Lys should know the truth—that it also, like Diaspar, had been partly founded upon fears and falsehoods.

Sometimes he wondered what shape the new society would take. He believed that Diaspar must escape from the prison of the Memory Banks, and restore again the cycle of life and death. Hilvar, he knew, was sure that this could be done, though his proposals were too technical for Alvin to follow. Perhaps the time would come again when love in Diaspar was no longer completely barren.

Was *this,* Alvin wondered, what he had always lacked in Diaspar—what he had really been seeking? He knew now that when power and ambition and curiosity were satisfied, there still were left the longings of the heart. No one had really lived until they had achieved that synthesis of love and desire which he had never dreamed existed until he came to Lys.

He had walked upon the planets of the Seven Suns—the first man to do so in a billion years. Yet that meant little to him now; sometimes he thought he would give all his achievements if he could hear the cry of a newborn child, and know that it was his own.

In Lys, he might one day find what he wanted; there was a warmth and understanding about its people, which, he now realized, was lacking in Diaspar. But before he could rest, before he could find peace, there was one decision yet to be made.

Into his hands had come power; that power he still possessed. It was a responsibility he had once sought and accepted with eagerness, but now he knew that he could have no peace while it was still his. Yet to throw it away would be the betrayal of a trust.

He was in a village of tiny canals, at the edge of a wide lake, when he made his decision. The colored houses, which seemed to float at anchor upon the gentle waves, formed a scene of almost unreal beauty.

There was life and warmth and comfort here—everything he had missed among the desolate grandeur of the Seven Suns.

One day humanity would once more be ready for space. What new chapter Man would write among the stars, Alvin did not know. That would be no concern of his; his future lay here on Earth.

But he would make one more flight before he turned his back upon the stars.

When Alvin checked the upward rush of the ascending ship, the city was too distant to be recognized as the work of Man, and the curve of the planet was already visible. Presently they could see the line of twilight, thousands of miles away on its unending march across the desert. Above and around were the stars, still brilliant for all the glory they had lost.

Hilvar and Jeserac were silent, guessing but not knowing with certainty why Alvin was making this flight, and why he had asked them to come with him. Neither felt like speech, as the desolate panorama unfolded below them. Its emptiness oppressed them both, and Jeserac felt a sudden contemptuous anger for the men of the past who had let Earth's beauty die through their own neglect.

He hoped that Alvin was right in dreaming that all this could be changed. The power and the knowledge still existed—it needed only the will to turn back the centuries and make the oceans roll again. The water was still there, deep down in the hidden places of the Earth; or if necessary, transmutation plants could be built to make it.

There was so much to do in the years that lay ahead. Jeserac knew that he stood between two ages; around him he could feel the pulse of mankind beginning to quicken again. There were great problems to be faced—but Diaspar would face them. The recharting of the past would take centuries, but when it was finished Man would have recovered almost all that he had lost.

Yet could he regain it all? Jeserac wondered. It was hard to believe that the Galaxy would be reconquered, and even if that were achieved, what purpose would it serve?

Alvin broke into his reverie, and Jeserac turned from the screen.

"I wanted you to see this," said Alvin quietly. "You may never have another chance."

"You're not leaving Earth?"

"No; I want nothing more of space. Even if any other civilizations still survive in this Galaxy, I doubt if they will be worth the effort of finding. There is so much to do here; I know now that this is my home, and I am not going to leave it again."

He looked down at the great deserts, but his eyes saw instead the waters that would be sweeping over them a thousand years from now. Man had rediscovered his world, and he would make it beautiful while he remained upon it. And after that—

"We aren't ready to go out to the stars, and it will be a long time before we can face their challenge again. I have been wondering what I should do with this ship; if it stays here on Earth, I shall always be tempted to use it, and will never have any peace of mind. Yet I cannot waste it; I feel that it has been given into my trust, and I must use it for the benefit of the world.

"So this is what I have decided to do. I'm going to send it out of the Galaxy, with the robot in control, to discover what happened to our ancestors—and, if possible, *what* it was they left our Universe to find. It must have been something wonderful for them to have abandoned so much to go in search of it.

"The robot will never tire, however long the journey takes. One day our cousins will receive my message, and they'll know that we are waiting for them here on Earth. They will return, and I hope that by then we will be worthy of them, however great they have become."

Alvin fell silent, staring into a future he had shaped but which he might never see. While Man was rebuilding his world, this ship would be crossing the darkness between the galaxies, and in thousands of years to come it would return. Perhaps he would still be here to meet it, but if not, he was well content.

"I think you are wise," said Jeserac. Then, for the last time, the echo of an ancient fear rose up to plague him. "But suppose," he added, "the ship makes contact with something we do not wish to meet. . . ." His voice faded away as he recognized the source of his anxiety and he gave a wry, self-deprecatory smile that banished the last ghost of the Invaders.

"You forget," said Alvin, taking him more seriously than he expected, "that we will soon have Vanamonde to help us. We don't know what powers he possesses, but everyone in Lys seems to think they are potentially unlimited. Isn't that so, Hilvar?"

Hilvar did not reply at once. It was true that Vanamonde was the other great enigma, the question mark that would always lie across the future of humanity while it remained on Earth. Already, it seemed certain, Vanamonde's evolution toward self-consciousness had been accelerated by his contact with the philosophers of Lys. They had great hopes of future co-operation with the childlike supermind, believing that they could foreshorten the aeons which his natural development would require.

"I am not sure," confessed Hilvar. "Somehow, I don't think that we should expect too much from Vanamonde. We can help him now, but we will be only a brief incident in his total life span. I don't think that his ultimate destiny has anything to do with ours."

Alvin looked at him in surprise.

"Why do you feel that?" he asked.

"I can't explain it," said Hilvar. "It's just an intuition." He could have added more, but he kept his silence. These matters were not capable of communication, and though Alvin would not laugh at his dream, he did not care to discuss it even with his friend.

It was more than a dream, he was sure of that, and it would haunt him forever. Somehow it had leaked into his mind, during that indescribable and unsharable contact he had had with Vanamonde. Did Vanamonde himself know what his lonely destiny must be?

One day the energies of the Black Sun would fail and it would release its prisoner. And then, at the end of the Universe, as time itself was faltering to a stop, Vanamonde and the Mad Mind must meet each other among the corpses of the stars.

That conflict might ring down the curtain on Creation itself. Yet it was a conflict that had nothing to do with Man, and whose outcome he would never know. . . .

"Look!" said Alvin suddenly. "This is what I wanted to show you. Do you understand what it means?"

The ship was now above the Pole, and the planet beneath them was a perfect hemisphere. Looking down upon the belt of twilight, Jeserac and Hilvar could see at one instant both sunrise and sunset on opposite sides of the world. The symbolism was so perfect, and so striking, that they were to remember this moment all their lives.

In this Universe the night was falling; the shadows were lengthening toward an east that would not know another dawn. But elsewhere the stars were still young and the light of morning lingered; and along the path he once had followed, Man would one day go again.